golden daughter

Tales of Goldstone Wood

Heartless

Veiled Rose

Moonblood

Starflower

Dragonwitch

Shadow Hand

Novellas of Goldstone Wood

Goddess Tithe

golden daughter

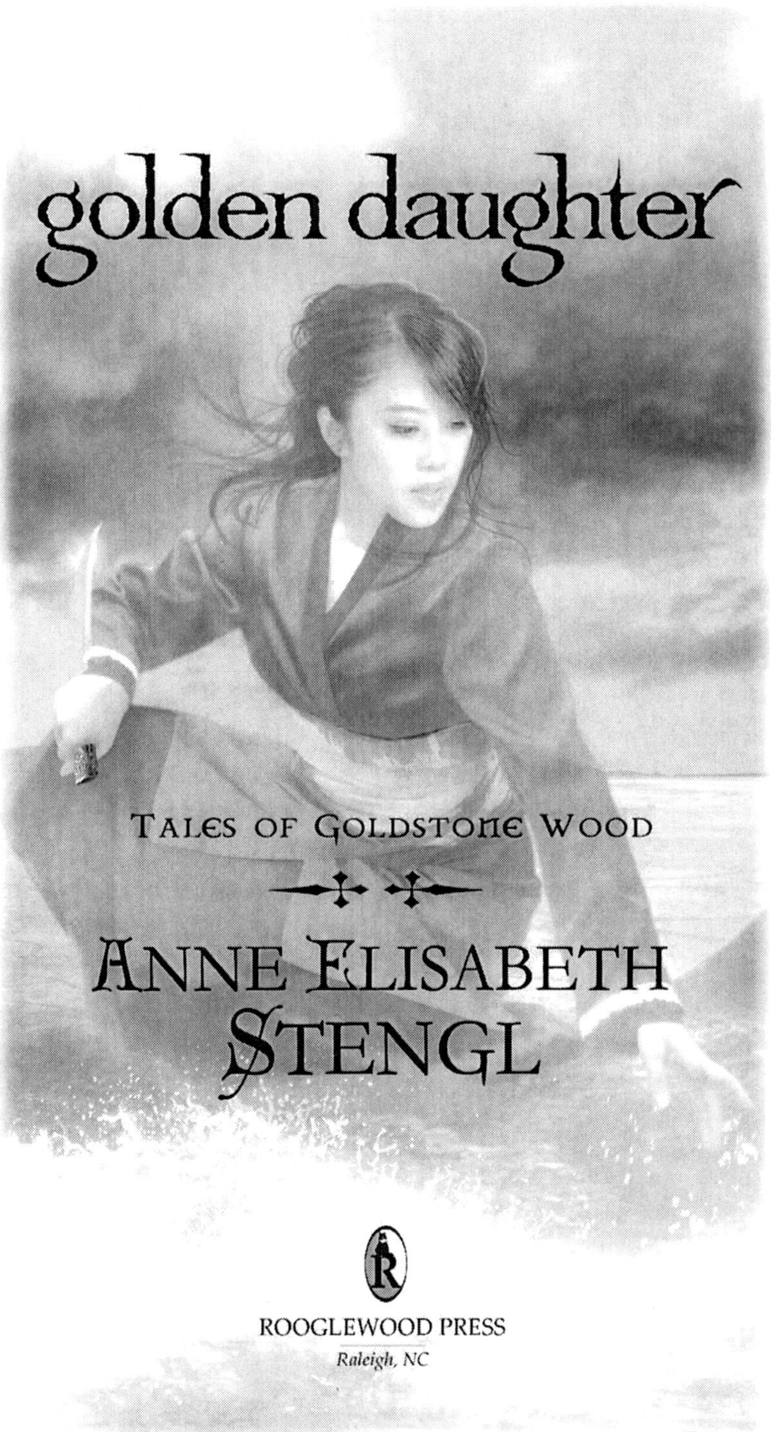

TALES OF GOLDSTONE WOOD

ANNE ELISABETH STENGL

ROOGLEWOOD PRESS
Raleigh, NC

Published by Rooglewood Press
www.RooglewoodPress.com

Printed in the United States of America

ISBN-13: 978-0-9894478-5-0

Book design by A.E. de Silva
Cover art by Julia Popova
Stock image "Constellation of Time" by FractalAngel

For your creativity and for all the many ways
in which you challenge and inspire me,
I dedicate this story to you, my writing students:

Rebecca Fox

Hannah Williams

Camryn Lockhart

Savannah Jezowski

Rebeka Borshevsky

Clara Diane Thompson

Allison Ruvidich

A Note to the Reader

I WAS NOT PRESENT for the events I have recorded within this volume, and it was with great difficulty that I compiled the story I now share with you. Bear in mind, my primary source of information has the unfortunate tendency of dramatizing the truth for the sake of poetic impact, therefore, I cannot vouch for the veracity of this document. But through a certain amount of interpretation and speculation, I believe this is the truest account to be had of that dreadful Night we all remember and the months and years (as mortals count them) leading up to that event.

To those who are reading the Tales of Goldstone Wood in chronological order, be it known that this particular tale takes place but a single mortal year after the defeat of Cren Cru and the liberation of his captives. Scarcely more than twenty years have transpired since the final death of the Dragonwitch.

For those of you new to these tales, have no fear! You need no knowledge of previous stories in the history of these worlds to understand the adventures herein recounted.

If you are curious to know more about the people and places of ancient Noorhitam and the surrounding nations, see the glossary in the back of this volume for further details.

May Lumé shine bright upon your path.

Dame Imraldera of the Haven

PROLOGUE

THE SKY DRIPPED STARS, like diamonds turned liquid and running in shimmering streams to pool beyond the horizon.

But not really.

In truth, there was not a star in sight and wouldn't be for many miles yet. If one could bear to think in terms of miles or distances of mortal measurement here. The young woman did not. Nor did she consider words like *stars*, *diamonds*, or *horizon*. These were nothing more than barriers a weaker mind would attempt to inflict upon the incomprehensible, a futile bastion against the oncoming sweep of madness.

Madness, the young woman knew, was inescapable here. But it could be borne if accepted as naturally as a body accepts the necessity of air and breathes in and out without thinking.

This was the secret, she considered, as she stood upon the edge of the formless wasteland that forever shifted before her gaze, presenting her with visions fantastic, grotesque, and beautiful by turns. This was the secret, ultimately, to the skill she practiced: No thinking. Merely being. Merely floating, experiencing the madness without thought.

She watched the glow of the melted stars rising above the distant horizon, spilling over in a winding ribbon that twisted over inexplicable landscapes to run at last in a thin, fluid trickle of light beneath her bare feet. And she did not think "I am standing on starlight." She did not think "This is impossible."

Instead she felt without thought: *Beautiful.*

A presence loomed behind her. A vast, unknowable presence, an entity that may or may not be living. She wanted to turn, to look at it. To see again the unknowable, unreachable Wood. But that road led only to frustration. No matter how many times she pursued the Wood, seeking to walk in its green-gold shadows—no matter how persistently she chased it, exerting all her will and power—always it eluded her. Perhaps she simply was not yet strong enough.

So she refused to turn but gazed out instead upon the formless hinterland beyond the Wood. Shifting visions presented themselves before her eyes, and she felt the beauty of the star-trail under her feet. She began to walk. The hem of her robe was soon stained with light. Above her, the stars ceased to melt but broke into blossoms of many-colored brilliance, like a rose window come suddenly to life. They whirled and gyrated and cast weird patterns upon the ground. Still the young woman only felt: *Beautiful, beautiful, beautiful . . .*

And the thought that was scarcely a thought: *The others do not know. They cannot do this. Poor fools.*

The blossoms in the sky vanished. They were not, after all, not real stars. All was dark now save for the thin silver trail and the continued glow beyond the horizon. The young woman made for that glow with more intensity than she should have permitted herself to feel. Unlike the Wood, the horizon sometimes seemed to draw a little closer. She believed she might, with enough exertion, reach it one day. So far, however, she had not succeeded.

None of them have penetrated this deep into the Dream, she thought. *But what does it matter if I cannot go all the way?*

She smelled harimau spice. The scent was real, too real, and she knew that she smelled it with her own mortal body, somewhere far from where she now walked. The knowledge brought her up short, and she stood still, draining herself of all thoughts, all anxieties.

The scent faded away then vanished. That had been close. She had almost awakened. She was not ready to wake yet.

Beautiful, beautiful, she felt. Her feet moved, splashing the starlight, and she continued down this strange path once more.

Perhaps tonight. Perhaps tonight . . .

She could hear the chanting. Always, when she came this far, she heard it. If she turned her head to the right or the left, she discerned flickering shadows of movement in the deeper whorls of darkness. Sometimes she even believed she could discern individual voices. But she smiled a little and continued on her way. If the old men knew how close she came to the chanting phantoms, they would never permit her to undergo the Sleep, would never permit her to step outside her body and wander these strange, otherworldly roads.

As if they could stop her. Poor fools. Poor fools.

"Allow me to wake her, Besur. She is troubled. She has ventured too far tonight."

"Stay your hand, Brother Yaru! No one touches her."

At the word of the High Priest of the Crown of the Moon, the men gathered in the room trembled and withdrew, hiding behind the fans they quietly waved to clear their faces of smoke and incense. The Besur stood above the young woman lying in quiet repose upon low cushions. He scattered another handful of harimau spice into a golden bowl of burning coals, his face shielded by a mask to keep out as much of the scent as possible. Always his eyes studied the girl's face, watching for any sign she might give of her progress, of the sights she even now beheld.

The only indication of trouble was a slight knot that formed ever so briefly between her delicate brows. Enough to worry Brother Yaru. The meddler, the boot-scraper! He did not believe what was plain to the eyes of all other men in the Crown of the Moon. He did not believe because he was so old, and age had addled the little sense with which he had been born.

Brother Yaru did not believe that any woman—particularly a maiden so young, so fresh, so unspoiled as the girl who lay before them—could do what he, in all the decades of his life, had not achieved.

But she would do it. The High Priest gazed upon the girl with solemn pride and not a little fear. She would do what generations of Dream Walkers had never managed to achieve.

She would find the gate to Hulan's Garden. And she would walk among the true stars.

The young woman progressed beyond the chanting now, and the phantom chanters, foiled yet again in their attempts to follow her, faded into nothing. The silver trail beneath her feet trickled away, and she walked on darkness swirling like mist. Still the glow on the horizon, the elusive glow, guided her footsteps. Even in darkness she would pursue it. Soon enough the strange sights of the Dream would present themselves again to her mind's eye. She would deal with them then. For now, she merely walked.

My dear. My own. My beauty.

She continued walking. It was best while under the Sleep to ignore all voices calling, however intriguing. This one whispered to her from what seemed a great distance, and something about it made her recall the depths of a summer sky at midnight, the depths beyond the stars.

My sweet. My love. Will you hear me?

The young woman's feet faltered. She cursed herself, but the voice had been close this time, as though it had leapt across a thousand miles in an instant and even now spoke just behind her left ear.

"I've come so far. I've come so far," she told herself.

But the horizon's glow was as distant as ever, and the voice was so very near.

So young. So fresh. So lovely. Let me hear your voice.

"Who are you?" the young woman asked, and it was the first she had spoken aloud this Sleep.

I am near. I am far. I am imprisoned.

"Who has imprisoned you?" the young woman asked. It was safest, if one chose to interact with a Dream, to ask only questions and give no answers.

It would be difficult to understand in mortal words. Let us say only that my brother imprisons me. He fears me. Do you fear me?

No answers. Only questions. "Should I fear you?" the young woman said.

Never. Always. Sometimes.

But the young woman was not afraid. Not here. Not even the phantom chanters could frighten her. In the Realm of the Dream, she was most powerful. She walked with ease that left the priests of the Crown of the Moon trembling and making signs of reverence and awe whenever she crossed their paths.

She was Lady Hariawan, Dream Walker, and she laughed.

"Do you have a name?" she asked through that laugh, smiling even as she continued to face the horizon, her goal.

The voice at her ear said, *I do. If you would know it, you must turn and look at me.*

"Why would I want to do that?" And still the young woman laughed. Her laughter brought small red and blue flowers bursting into life around her, flowing through the darkness and up over distant hills. Though, of course, there were no flowers or hills, and the young woman would not think of them as such. "Why would I want to look at you?" she asked.

Because I know what you truly desire. I know what you seek. And I can give it to you.

"I seek the gate to Hulan's Garden."

And there she made her mistake, the first ever she had made since undergoing the Sleep. She knew it as soon as she'd spoken. She had not asked a question.

Now the Dream, whatever it might be, had power over her.

That is not what you seek, said the voice in her ear. *There is no good to come of trying to deceive me, for I cannot be deceived.*

The flowers at her feet withered, rotted, fell from their stems, and lay dead upon the ground. She began to tremble. She half expected to smell harimau, but she did not. She was still deep in the Sleep, deeper perhaps than ever before.

Turn and look at me, Umeer Melati.

"How . . . how do you know my name?"

Turn and look at me, Umeer Melati.

"What will I see if I do?"

Turn and look at me, Umeer Melati.

The young woman drew a long breath, though she did not truly breathe here. She drew a breath, hoping to still the racing of her heart, though she had no heart here. And the dead flowers upon the ground became spiders and ran in all directions, away, hissing as they went.

Turn and look at me, Umeer Melati.

She turned.

She saw an uncut pillar of stone. It rose above her head, three times her own height and taller, and it was blacker than night itself. And yet, deep inside, beneath the rough surface, the young woman believed she saw something white. Something that moved. Overhead, dark clouds churned. Beneath them, more clouds, these shot with lightning. The stone, more solid than anything else in this realm, stood suspended on air.

The young woman took a step. Then a second. She leaned forward, peering into the depths of the stone at that which moved in its center. She lifted a hand to touch it.

"*Hag! Crone! Withered mortal!*"

The voice like fire roared through the young woman's mind, and a harsh, searing wind blew against her shoulders and the back of her head so that her hair singed. She felt it with a physical force that was startling here in the Dream. She struggled to turn around, but the power of that wind was too great. It blasted her against the stone, and then the stone was gone and she was on her knees in the darkness. No clouds, no wasteland, only the ongoing roar. She felt herself burning when she should have felt nothing at all, for she had no corporeal substance here, merely imagined form. But the burning was as real as flesh, as real as blood, and she screamed.

Movement agitated the darkness on either side of her peripheral vision. She had an impression of enormous, pounding wings. She fell forward, turning so as to land on one shoulder. Gathering all the strength she possessed—which was considerable here, in the Dream, where her powers were unparalleled among her kind—she looked up.

Eyes set in deep, dark hollows blazed with raging fire. There was a rush, a bellow, and then a crack like the breaking of worlds.

The scream filled the small chamber, and all the priests gathered screamed as well, dropped their fans, and covered their ears in terror. The Besur's mouth fell open, but his own cry died in his throat as he leaped forward and grabbed the young woman. Her body convulsed upon the cushions. She struck at him, but her limbs were delicate, and she could make no impression upon his sturdy frame.

He saw that she still slept even though she screamed. He should never have allowed her to dream-walk so far, so long!

Still holding the girl, the High Priest reached out and overturned the golden bowls, scattering coals across the floor. Even as he did so, he felt a last shudder pass through the girl, and then she lay still in his arms.

"Lady Hariawan?" he asked, his voice drowned out in the continued screams of his brethren. He rose up, clutching the girl to his breast, and shouted at the lot of them, "Silence! Silence, you dogs!"

The shock of their Besur's bellowed curses was enough to bring most of them, even Brother Yaru, back to reason. They clustered together at the door, ready to bolt, their gazes fixed upon the young woman limp in the Besur's grasp.

Her eyelids fluttered, delicate as butterfly wings. Then she looked up, looked around, and they saw no fear in her empty gaze.

Instead they saw the burn, shaped like a hand, spreading in ugly stain across her face, like a pool of spilled blood.

"Lady Hariawan!" gasped the Besur, holding her gently. "My child, what did you see?"

The young woman said nothing. She did not speak for three days.

PART ONE

Anwar

1

OFFICIALLY THE EMPEROR'S Golden Daughters did not exist, which made them more desirable to the right sort of buyer. And only the right sort of buyer knew of their existence, which made Princess Safiya's task significantly easier.

What did not make her task easier was the fact that the right sort of buyer tended to be a stuffy, self-centered, completely piggish sort, reminding her of nothing so much as the empress's pet monkey: hideously assured of its own useless but prominent place in the world, with absolutely no one to tell it otherwise.

The right sort of buyer made her skin crawl.

Not that anyone would guess as much upon meeting Princess Safiya. She sat serenely in her open pavilion surrounded by jasmine and honeysuckle, her face a lake of calm mirroring the outer world and revealing none of the thoughts lurking beneath. As a girl, Princess Safiya had hated the face paint women of her status were obliged to wear daily. As an older, wiser woman, she appreciated it for the mask it was, particularly when meeting silk-robed monkey-men such as the one bowing before her now.

"Welcome, Ambassador Ratnavira," the princess said, allowing her face paint to do the smiling for her. "I trust the Lordly Sun shone bright upon your road and the Lady Moon gazed gently upon your rests."

Ambassador Ratnavira, trembling with excitement, beat his forehead against the lowest step of her pavilion. Princess Safiya could see the red mark on his brow when he straightened and stood once more, grinning just like the empress's monkey.

But he was the right sort of buyer. And ultimately, this could be the only good end to all her efforts.

"Revered Mother of Golden Worth," the ambassador said, his voice bowing and scraping even as he himself stood upright, "all the wearisome leagues of my travels melt away as I find myself at last before the gracious luminance of your face . . ."

He continued in this vein for some while, and the princess occupied herself by reading his secrets. These were not particularly interesting secrets. Before her stood a man who had risen to power via the ladder of flattery and well-timed bribes rather than aptitude; this much he told her by his voice inflection. He was the younger son of a minor lord, possibly a tribal chieftain; his ugly, raw features bespoke a rural heritage rather than the delicate inbreeding one expected of the Aja elite. His blackened fingernails and the lines about his mouth indicated his addiction to the Red Flower, but he sought to disguise the addiction via enormous jeweled rings and layers of inexpertly applied face paint. He was also a patron of cheap operas and all the lewd life surrounding cheap operas; the signs of oncoming disease were unmistakable.

In short, he was just the sort of person to represent a rich, powerful, and much-hated Prince of Aja. Just the sort of client Princess Safiya had come to expect and despise.

"So my honored Prince Amithnal bids me hasten back with a bride worthy of the very gods themselves, as promised in the agreement you, Revered Mother, signed upon receipt of the advanced half-sum."

Princess Safiya said nothing as the ambassador's voice trailed off awkwardly at the end of his rehearsed speech. She allowed the silence to linger longer than was absolutely necessary and watched the monkey-man's eyes shift nervously. She could see him trying to recall everything he had just said, wondering if he'd made a mistake somewhere, wondering if he'd somehow managed, despite all his careful rehearsal, to offend the Revered Mother.

But she couldn't let him writhe for long. It wouldn't be fair to her girls.

She stood, and the ambassador took an involuntary step back, which he then tried to cover with a nervous bow.

"The test is prepared," Princess Safiya said. "Prince Amithnal will have his bride based upon the results. Walk with me now, Ambassador, and listen carefully to what I say."

She stepped down from her pavilion, and serving children scrambled behind her to carry the train of her golden robe, while others angled oil-paper umbrellas to prevent any sunlight from touching her face and possibly melting the paint she wore. Ambassador Ratnavira fell into obsequious step beside her, his stained fingers twisting his too-tight rings in unsuppressed eagerness. What did he expect this test to be? Some variation on one of his cheap operas?

Princess Safiya made doubly certain that her voice betrayed none of her thoughts. "It is important, Ambassador, that you speak as little as possible while seated at the banquet. The Golden Daughters will read your voice and learn more than they should before completing the test. You must also understand that *this is no test* to the Crouching Shadow I have hired."

The ambassador stumbled, taken by a sudden fit of nervous coughing. Princess Safiya paused, the shadows of the two umbrellas settling around her, and watched fear shake the little Aja man to his core.

"You hired a Crouching Shadow?" he cried. "But they—they do not exist!"

"Neither do the Golden Daughters," Princess Safiya replied calmly. "Shall we continue?" Without waiting for the ambassador, she proceeded, obliging him to trot to catch up.

"But surely it is too dangerous!" the ambassador protested.

Princess Safiya did not reply.

"Who is the target?" the ambassador demanded, and his shaking voice told her he had already guessed the answer.

"Why, the honored Aja ambassador, of course," Princess Safiya said, turning her painted smile upon the little monkey-man. For a moment she almost hoped he would faint, so ashen was his face.

But Ambassador Ratnavira pulled himself together and said bravely, "Prince Amithnal will not suffer his representative to be so treated. Should I die at your table, the reputation of the Golden Daughters will be forever impugned. You will be dishonored throughout the Continent and throughout the island nations!"

A hint of a real smile twitched at the corners of Princess Safiya's painted mouth. "So little faith you show in the legend you have come far to purchase! Do you not believe the Golden Daughters will be everything I have promised?"

The ambassador licked his thin lips and continued twisting his rings. "A Crouching Shadow is—"

"The greatest threat a man such as Prince Amithnal may hope to face in his lifetime," Princess Safiya supplied. "An assassin of unprecedented cunning and ability. You recall the story of Lord Dae-Ho of Dong Min and his ten thousand warriors?"

The ambassador had seen enough cheap opera to know the story well. His lips murmured a silent prayer. But Safiya continued mercilessly: "When sought by his twin brother, Dae-Ko the Usurper, Lord Dae-Ho entombed himself alive in a secret underground palace and placed a guard of ten thousand warriors throughout his subterranean labyrinth extending twenty miles on each side. But his brother hired one Crouching Shadow. Only one. Within a week, all ten thousand warriors and Lord Dae-Ho himself lay dead in a grave of their own making."

"Light of the Lordly Sun!" the ambassador whispered. He wiped his sweating brow, smearing paint. "And you have summoned one of those devils here?"

"Indeed," said Princess Safiya. "To exact excruciating vengeance upon my faithless lover. At the banquet, within an hour, this Crouching Shadow will place gold leaf into your tea. You will be expected to suffer mightily of inexplicable stomach pains, expiring at last by the week's end, thus restoring my honor and ensuring the Crouching Shadow's completed payment. Unless, of course, the stories you have heard of the Golden Daughters prove true."

Princess Safiya continued down the walkway from her pavilion, enjoying both the scents of the sumptuous garden around her and the muttered curses of her companion. This was the one part of the entire process she always found enjoyable: watching the groveling monkey-men squirm.

"But the girls . . . the esteemed Daughters," the ambassador said, nearly forgetting his fawning language in the midst of near-panic. "They know, do they not? They know to watch for the Crouching Shadow?"

"Certainly not!" Princess Safiya replied, feigning surprise. "What would that prove to your honored Prince Amithnal? That I can provide him with a bride who, so long as she is told everything in advance, might save him from assassination? Do you think such a bride would be worth the price Prince Amithnal has committed to pay?"

"So you mean—"

"Yes, I do mean exactly that, Ambassador," Princess Safiya said. "To the principal players, this little theater to which we even now wend our way is no act, but real to the very direst extreme. And you will see how the Golden Daughters perform their parts. When the curtain falls, you yourself will choose the bride of your prince, and you will know that in the choice, you may well be saving his life."

Here Princess Safiya turned and fixed the little man with a stare of surprising intensity from behind the elegant blue and red paint rimming her eyes. "My Daughters do not fail."

With those words, she withdrew from the depths of her voluminous sleeve a certain document written in red characters to look like blood. She held it up for the ambassador's inspection. "We can take no chances. Sign here, if you please, indicating that you have heard and understood the parameters of the test in which you are about to take part."

The ambassador swore again. But he had come too far to back out now. Besides, if he returned to his master with neither the bride-price nor the bride, his head would be forfeit. Prince Amithnal was not a forgiving patron.

"Gold leaf, you say?" the ambassador whispered as he signed his name and watched Princess Safiya tuck the document back into her sleeve. "Is that not . . . is that not a painful way to go?"

"Have no fear," Princess Safiya said, continuing along the path. The rooftops of the eastern quarter of Manusbau Palace came into sight, and she spied the silk-covered litters borne by strong slaves coming up the path toward them. It would be unseemly, after all, for her or the ambassador to arrive at the banquet on foot. "Have no fear. The poison will never cross your lips."

Little lion dogs—probably no more than half a dozen but making themselves seem like a hundred strong—ran barking underfoot as slaves carried honored guests into the Butterfly Hall where the banquet was laid. Every new guest was considered an intruder and possible threat, and the lion dogs protested in high yips and low snorts as the slaves stepped carefully around them.

The Radiant Reflection of Hulan's Countenance, Empress Timiran, royal mother of all Noorhitam, sat in serene boredom at a separate table set above the others, fanned with peacock feathers and feeding her fat monkey delicacies off gold platters. The monkey always got his first pick of any fare served at the empress's table, and he had the pot belly to show for it.

At a lower table, three of the emperor's lesser wives sat in gaudy glory only slightly less magnificent than that of the empress. Princess Safiya, the emperor's favored sister, took her place among these, nodding kindly to the pretty queens, who were sweet, if rather simple.

Lower still were the tables of the banquet guests, various visitors to Manusbau Palace from all reaches of the Continent. None of these were important enough for the emperor himself to bother with, but were just important enough that the empress must be brought out and put on display. They were all men: aspiring politicians, stuffy princes of lesser kingdoms, and even a warlord or two of distant provinces come to negotiate terms of peace with the Emperor of Noorhitam. These last looked particularly out of place in the Butterfly Hall and handled with great trepidation the porcelain teacups served to them.

Serving girls with flowers in their hair fluttered about as they tended to the needs of the guests. Their faces were painted moon-white with bright orange sun-spots on each cheek. Ten of these girls wore red chrysanthemums in their hair. Otherwise they were indistinguishable as they rushed about with cups and trays and platters.

Prince Amithnal's sweating ambassador sat between a warlord and a Dong Min councilor, saying little and eating less. Every time a serving girl offered him food or drink, he winced and his eyes lifted nervously to Princess Safiya, who ignored him. He had been instructed to eat and drink as though nothing were afoot. Despite his fondness for cheap opera, the ambassador had the acting ability of the monkey he so resembled.

Princess Safiya sighed and looked around for her assassin. He appeared presently.

The lion dogs started their thunderous barking again and ran skittering across the hall even as the door opened and a court herald stepped through. The dogs rushed at his feet, snarling and making all sorts of vicious threats which none of them had the courage to carry out. The herald aimed a kick at one of the dogs, which dodged him easily, then cleared his throat and announced in a loud voice that filled the hall, "Lord Dok-Kasemsan, head of the House of Dok, beloved brother of the Fan Clan."

Another colorful litter was borne into the hall, and when it was lowered and the curtains drawn back, Lord Dok-Kasemsan, a Pen-Chan of remarkable poise and beauty, stepped forth.

Princess Safiya smiled inwardly at the sight of him. He was everything an assassin ought to be: striking, colorful, dignified, and important. The sort of man no one would expect to indulge in the lethal arts.

He was his own best disguise.

The herald led him across the room to genuflect before the bored empress. Then he was seated at a table across the hall from Ambassador Ratnavira. Not once did Kasemsan look the ambassador's way. Not a glance, not a gesture betrayed the predatory focus on which Princess Safiya knew all his being centered.

What mastery! What genius! His very spirit was a poison-tipped knife. Were she the sentimental sort, she would be half-inclined to love him.

But he was doomed. And there was no point in becoming sentimental over a doomed man.

Princess Safiya kept her head bowed, her expression as bored as that of the empress. But from beneath her long, false lashes, she watched the ten girls with the chrysanthemums in their hair. How frail they looked! How delicate and unthreatening. Yet with their black eyes they each perceived more than any five ordinary persons combined. And behind their painted smiles, their mouths were fixed in concentration that never, never relaxed.

Except . . .

Except what in Hulan's name was Sairu grinning about?

"Princess? May I beg a word?"

Safiya frowned and turned abruptly to the voice speaking at her elbow. "Ah. Brother Yaru," she said, trying to disguise her impatience behind cool regality.

The old priest bowed and grinned at her. He alone of all the men in that room dared approach the upraised tables of the queens and the empress without an escort. Despite their rough-woven robes and lives of restraint, priests enjoyed a number of privileges lesser men did not.

This was more than slightly annoying. Especially now.

"May I surmise from your presence here, Princess Safiya, that one of your legendary tests is even now underway?"

Princess Safiya hid her face behind a fan. "Esteemed brother, I would beg you to lower your voice," she said.

"Oh, of course! Of course!" Brother Yaru said, glancing about, his wrinkled face alight with boyish eagerness. He knew all the stories surrounding the Golden Daughters, but not even he could spot them in a crowd. He searched the faces of those present like a child searching for pixies under toadstools. "Forgive me, Princess, but I find this most fortuitous. You see, I come on behalf of a new client."

Princess Safiya fluttered her fan coldly. "I never discuss business with more than one client at a time. And certainly not with—"

She stopped. She had not risen to her position as Golden Mother without reason. She read the secrets in Brother Yaru's face. She could not understand them all, but she read them even so.

"Who sent you, brother?" she asked, lowering her voice still further so that the priest was obliged to lean in behind her fan.

"The Besur himself," Brother Yaru whispered. "It is a matter of utmost urgency. I am not at liberty to divulge the High Priest's secrets. But he would be most grateful if Princess Safiya would send one of her own to the Crown of the Moon tonight."

With this, Brother Yaru slipped away, losing himself in the crowded hall as he went from table to table, stealing dainties and muttering blessings to all who would listen.

Princess Safiya sat in stunned silence, still hiding behind her fan. The High Priest? But he could not desire a bride! That went against everything the priests of the Crown of the Moon stood for. And yet she could not doubt the truth of Brother Yaru's words. He was far too simple a man to take part in duplicity. No, it must be true. But why?

Again one of the girls caught her eye. Sairu, standing along the wall with a platter in each hand, looked right at her and smiled.

What had gotten into that girl? Did she think this one great joke? Did she—

A sudden commotion exploded a few tables down. Princess Safiya lowered her fan and turned, as did everyone else in the hall, to where Lord Dok-Kasemsan stood. He had leaped to his feet with a shouted curse, knocking over the low table and scattering dishes in broken shards across the floor. At first no one could understand what he said. But Princess Safiya knew right away.

"How did you do it? *How?*" And then, "I am dead! I'm a dead man! How did you do it?"

He turned suddenly, fire in his gaze, and stared at Princess Safiya. "You witch!" he shouted. "You fire-kissed witch!" Then he choked and spat as the gold-leaf poison—his own poison—took effect on his body. His entire frame, so beautiful, so poised, shuddered.

Then he charged straight at Princess Safiya, a knife in his hand.

He never reached her. One of the serving girls knelt and sent her silver platter sliding across the polished floor. His foot landed on it, and he fell with a crash, striking his head. The next moment, guards leaped upon him and dragged him from the room, unconscious.

The Butterfly Hall lay in stunned silence.

Then the empress said, “How amusing. Monkey wants sugared dates. Will someone bring him sugared dates?”

The spell was broken. The room erupted in voices, all talking at once. Princess Safiya rose quietly and, with children trailing behind to carry her train, exited the Butterfly Hall. Over the course of the next half hour, one by one, the ten serving girls with chrysanthemums in their hair slipped unnoticed after her.

2

IN A MUCH COLDER part of the world, a different test commenced.

Sunan had arrived at the gates of the Suthinnakor Center of Learning at three o'clock that morning. He had thought to arrive before the other Tribute Scholars and therefore enjoy the advantage of beginning his test early.

He had thought wrong.

Every Tribute Scholar from every province in the Nua-Pratut Kingdom had the exact same idea. Some had arrived at the gates of the Center of Learning at three o'clock *the morning before*. Indeed, Sunan realized with glum ire, he would have needed to set up a tent and camp in the street for a good week in advance to have had any hope of being the first Tribute Scholar admitted on the day of the Gruung Exams.

Three hours later, the bellowing horn sounded and (Sunan surmised from the stir in the crowd of scholars surrounding him) the gates were opened. His heart rose one moment . . . and plummeted the next. Guards at the gate must search each scholar from head to toe before permitting him to pass through. The Gruung Exams were too important, and cheating too rampant, to allow anyone into the Center without a full body search.

Which meant another two hours passed before Sunan himself was led into a pavilion just outside the gates and made to strip. He was even obliged to remove his undergarments. Too many past scholars had been caught with illegal notes and intricately written texts painted on the insides of their linens.

The Gruung Exams were that significant. And that hard.

Upon completing this most undignified search, the guards gave Sunan a loose garment of outrageously itchy wool. The itch would help him to focus, or so Sunan's uncle had told him in advance. Somehow, as he grimaced his way into the garment, Sunan didn't believe his uncle and silently cursed him with fire boils.

Walking stiffly to avoid letting his body touch any more of the wool robe than absolutely necessary, Sunan was marched through the doors of the Center of Learning. For an all-too-brief moment, his heart thrilled. At last! Here he was. A Tribute Scholar about to take his Gruung, standing upon the very threshold of his future. A future none would have believed possible for the son of a buffalo-dung warlord. A future none would have dreamed—

"There," grunted a guard, pointing to a large pile of ill-wrapped sacks just within the door. "Take one."

Sunan bowed and did as he was told. He heard a clink inside the sack, and knew it for the sound of a pitcher and a chamber pot knocking against each other. Also in the sack would be simple bedding, a little food, an ink stone, ink, and brushes: all that he would be permitted to have for the next seventy-two hours.

Sunan, flanked by guards, was led now into the outer court of the Center. He tried to drink in what he could of the moment, the long-dreamed-of moment. He tried to admire the gilded walls, the tapestries, the swirling pattern on the floor beneath his feet.

But it was too much, too terrible, and the wretched wool seam was digging into the back of his neck.

The outer court displayed hundreds of tiny windowless chambers, each lit by a single lantern. Sunan was ushered into one of these, and a slave boy scurried in with a water skin and looked at Sunan expectantly. Realizing what was required, Sunan unwrapped the sack he'd been issued and pulled out the water pitcher. The slave boy filled it and backed from the room.

The guard outside shut the door. Sunan heard the sound of a bolt falling into place.

"Light of the Lordly Sun!" Sunan prayed, then kicked himself for this superstitious display. He sounded like a Chhayan urchin, not the Tribute Scholar he was. His hands shaking, he hastily unpacked the rest of his sack, arranging the bedroll in one corner, the chamber pot in another, and the scholarly tools in a third.

And now . . .

Now he must write.

The time passed quickly. Sunan had mentally rehearsed his essays a thousand times, and he fell to them now with a will. He had only seventy-two hours to write eight distinct essays with eight distinct parts to each. He must prove the breadth of his knowledge in arithmetic, music, writing, rituals, public and private ceremonies, and poetry, not to mention the militaristic arts of strategy and subterfuge. To prove his knowledge, he must quote extensively from the classics. A single misquote—even one character out of place or one word substituted for another—and he would be disqualified.

His brain churned out words at a fevered pace, but he must control his hand, he must control his brush and ink. Haste was the sign of a weak mind. Everything must be deliberate, every movement, every thought. As he finished each essay, he dropped it into a certain slot in the door, there to be retrieved, read, and judged by the Masters. This accomplished, he immediately turned to the next one.

At last, after five hours of work, he realized he must stop and eat at least a bite, and probably drink some water. He set aside his brush and, with no little irritation, took time to nurture his feeble mortal body. Why must scholars be limited by such needs? It was somehow unjust.

But it was still necessary. He remembered Uncle Kasemsan telling him about his own Gruung Exam, many years ago:

"Four students died during those three days. Their bodies were wrapped in their own straw mats and tossed over the Center walls. Their families never came to retrieve them."

Sunan could not afford so dishonorable a death. He had worked too hard.

So he ate, drank, and even permitted carefully timed sleeps. He had been practicing controlled sleep for the last few years in preparation for his Gruung. Too much sleep, and he would not have time to finish; too little, and he'd end up wrapped in a straw mat.

His whole life came down to the balance of drive and restraint.

But one thing he could not restrain. Ten hours into his exam, he removed the wool garment and worked naked. He was cold, to be sure, but the relief from the itch was worth any risk of a chill.

So the seventy-two hours passed. When the room went suddenly dark, Sunan knew that the time was up, for the oil of the single lantern was carefully measured. He set aside his brush, relieved that he had finished his final sentence and reasonably confident the sentence had finished his final thought. Stubble lined his cheek, ink stained his fingers, and his whole body shivered with exhaustion and cold. But he'd not died! There was a grace.

And he knew with a deep inner confidence that he had done well. Well enough to merit top marks.

So he dropped his final scroll through the slot and slithered back into the horrible wool garment. He knelt to wait in the center of the room. In due time, guards came and he was escorted to the outer court, where hundreds of other students, hollow-eyed, trembling, but triumphant, waited. Sunan's gaze ran over them dully, and he wondered if anyone had died.

They shuffled around, ringing the wide stone steps that led up to the Middle Court. Drifts of snow lined the wall, carefully swept aside by slaves. The stone beneath the scholars' bare feet was like ice. But no one cared, no one complained.

Those who had passed would be called up those stairs and into their new life within the Center of Learning. Those who had not passed would crawl, disgraced, back out the gate through which they had come, doomed to face the disappointed stares of their families and friends.

Sunan shifted in the wool garment, trying to move the itchy seams to less-sensitive portions of his body. Unable and unwilling to meet the gazes of his fellow students, he instead studied the two stone statues at the base of the staircase. These were interesting enough, worthy of a second or third glance. They were recognizably Anwar and Hulan, the Lordly Sun and his Lady Moon, carved in jade, with faces more real than life. Each held a scepter, the one topped with a many-rayed sun, the other with a crescent moon. Snow dusted their heads and shoulders.

Sunan frowned suddenly as his eye lit upon an anomaly: Perched upon the right shoulder of each of these familiar figures was a tall songbird, its wings outspread. No snow shrouded its form, which shone bright and clear.

This was not the classical depiction. While Anwar and Hulan were common enough figures throughout the known eastern world, he had never before seen them portrayed thus. Not once in all the pored-over scrolls and documents had Sunan encountered a single reference to a songbird in the legends of the Sun and the Moon.

So what in Anwar's name was it doing on the shoulders of those statues?

"Tribute Scholar Number One."

The voice boomed from the top of the stairs, shattering all murky musing in Sunan's head. He and all the gathered scholars stood upright and gazed toward the top of the stair where stood Overseer Rangsun, the great leader of the Center of Learning. The mere sight of him raised the spirits and hopes of all those gathered.

The overseer read out each Tribute Scholar's number and, following that, one of two words: pass or fail. Scholars scrambled in their sleeves to find their numbers then listened breathlessly as the results were read. No one spoke a word of jubilation or defeat. Those who passed proceeded without further ceremony—for what further ceremony was needed?—up the staircase to the Middle Court. They were now Presented Scholars.

And those who failed vanished without a word.

Sunan found his number sewn into the hem of his sleeve. One hundred two. So he must wait and wait and wait. His whole life, his whole being, his whole future rested on the words of Overseer Rangsun. But he must wait.

Finally, Tribute Scholar Ninety-nine. A pass.

Tribute Scholar One Hundred. A fail.

Tribute Scholar One Hundred One. A fail.

Now. Now, now, now! Sunan felt his heart plummet and soar and plummet again. Now! Read it now!

"Tribute Scholar One Hundred Three," read the overseer.

Four more numbers were read before Sunan found his breath again. Blood rushed to his ears, and for a terrible moment he thought he would faint. Where was his number? The overseer had skipped his number! Could Sunan have let his mind drift, even for a moment, and missed it? Could the overseer have made a mistake?

"Tribute Scholar One Hundred Ten," read the overseer, and on down the list.

Sunan stood alone in the crowd, his heart hammering, his head spinning. Scholars passed up the stairs; scholars retreated through the gate. What must he do? Where must he go?

Where was his number?

Another hour passed, and the Lordly Sun rose high above and beat down upon the yard, unable to melt the snow or ease the cold. But Sunan sweated inside his woolen robe.

At last the courtyard was empty. He stood alone at the base of the stairs, gazing up into the face of the overseer.

Overseer Rangsun rolled up his long scroll, passed it to a near attendant, and then dismissed him with a flick of his wrist. Lifting the edge of his embroidered robes, he began to descend the stair. Sunan trembled. Should he flee? Should he assume that his name had not been called because he had failed and hasten away through the gate? But Overseer Rangsun was now at the bottom step. He stood with his hands folded inside his deep sleeves and lifted heavy-lidded eyes to study Sunan.

"Sunan, son of Juong-Khla," the overseer said.

"Honored Overseer!" Sunan gasped and bowed low. His ears burned at the sound of his father's name spoken here in the Center of Learning. It was as evil as a curse.

"You will be pleased to know," Overseer Rangsun said, his voice mild as a spring breeze, "that you far exceeded all expectations and achieved the top score of this year's Gruung."

For a moment the world went black, and Sunan suspected that he fainted. Somehow he managed to stay on his feet until his eyes were able to refocus and blood flowed back to his brain. With sparks exploding on the edge of his vision, he bowed again, deeper than before. He opened his mouth to speak, but words would not come.

It didn't matter. Overseer Rangsun continued: "Unfortunately, due to the circumstances of your birth and less-than-desirable parentage, the Center of Learning does not feel that it can accept you into the Middle Court."

Once more the world went black. Once more Sunan managed to stay on his feet. When he opened his mouth again, only one word emerged.

"Spitfire."

It was a vile curse. Not something he should have dared even think in the presence of Overseer Rangsun. He deserved to be flogged. For one wild instant, he hoped he would be flogged. Anything to distract his mind from the roaring flames that even now consumed him.

But the overseer merely nodded in mild understanding. "Indeed. Spitfire," he said. "It does seem unfair that the sins of your father should cast such a pall upon your own life. This is the world in which we live, Juong-Khla Sunan. You will never be a Presented Scholar."

Please kill me now, Sunan wanted to say. Instead, he clamped his teeth down upon his tongue.

"However," Overseer Rangsun continued, "you will remain a Tribute Scholar, which is perhaps honor enough for a half-Chhayan. You will find work, respectable work. You will never achieve your potential, but you will not die in a ditch."

"Yes, Honored Overseer," Sunan whispered.

The overseer smiled then. It wasn't a smile that reached his eyes, merely a twist of his thin lips and white mustache. "All is not lost," he said. "You see, while I know the unfortunate facts surrounding your parentage, I know the fortunate facts as well. Your mother was a daughter of the Fan Clan, sister to Lord Dok-Kasemsan. I knew your uncle Kasemsan rather well.

He was a Presented Scholar here himself, back in his day."

Sunan nodded.

"Your uncle was many things in his life."

At first Sunan said nothing. Then he blinked as some of the overseer's words found their way through the roar of fire in his brain to a place of comprehension. "Was? Honored Overseer, my uncle is—Are you saying he's—"

"Dead?" The overseer's cold smile grew. "Oh, yes. Or as good as. My sources can tell me only so much on such short notice. But we will assume death. Word will not reach his household for many weeks, and you must take care that you say nothing of the matter to his wife or family."

"But—But how? How can he—" Sunan put a hand to his throbbing temple, shaking his head. This must all be part of some horrible dream. He must have allowed himself to oversleep. Time to wake up! Time to wake up now and finish his test, or he'd never be a Presented Scholar!

Mastering himself with an effort, he managed to say, "My uncle left only three months ago to meet a friend in Lunthea Maly. He cannot be dead."

"*Should not* be dead, perhaps," the overseer agreed. "But you, as a student of the classics, must know that anything *can* happen. The death of your uncle was both more unlikely and more likely than you yet realize."

With those strange words, the overseer reached further up his sleeve and withdrew a tiny scroll sealed in melted gold. He handed this to Sunan.

"You have gifts, son of Juong-Khla. Gifts that will be of keen interest to others. You will never be a Presented Scholar. But you may realize your true value if you wish." He tucked his hands away again, and his eyes disappeared almost entirely beneath his heavy lids. "You must choose whether or not to read the document I have just given you. If you choose not to read it, you will remain a Tribute Scholar and achieve what sort of life you may. Should you choose to read it, you will face another choice: a choice of life or instant death." He shrugged. "It's up to you. May Anwar shine upon your decision."

With that, the overseer turned and ascended the stair to the Middle Court, leaving Sunan barefoot on the stones below.

3

DESPITE ANYTHING OVERSEER Rangsun's sources might say, Lord Dok-Kasemsan wasn't dead. Not yet. And if he did die, it would not be of gold-leaf poisoning.

"Indeed, Honored Mother, while he will know some discomfort for months to come, the dosage I gave him is not lethal."

Princess Safiya smiled at Jen-ling, the oldest of the Golden Daughters and the winner of today's test. The girls stood in a line across from their mistress, each maid painted to look exactly like her sister, all individuality imperceptible save to the trained eye. Even the number of flowers in their hair was the same.

But Jen-ling stood a step forward from the others and gave her report. The unconscious body of Lord Dok-Kasemsan lay on the floor between her and Princess Safiya.

"And tell me, Jen-ling," said the princess, "how did you discern both assassin and target in the crowded Butterfly Hall?" She already knew how Jen-ling had done it. But she asked the question for the benefit of Ambassador Ratnavira, who stood behind a painted screen nearby, listening eagerly.

Princess Safiya could almost hear him twisting his too-tight rings.

"Lord Dok-Kasemsan asked for a second pot of tea," Jen-ling said, "though I knew he had drunk but a single cup from the pot he was served upon his arrival."

The girls were trained to watch for any such small incongruities. Their perception for detail seemed as natural to them as basic sight or smell. Furthermore, they not only picked up on variances, but also kept any number of them listed in their heads. Jen-ling could easily have had her eye on twelve or twenty suspects at a time.

And the Golden Daughters knew to treat everyone as a suspect. There needn't be an apparent crime for them to spot an apparent criminal.

Jen-ling went on to explain how Lord Dok-Kasemsan had slipped poison into his teapot under the pretense of stirring the brewing leaves inside. The gold flakes had been up his sleeve in a pouch, and he had shaken them out delicately as he stirred. Only someone who knew what to look for could possibly have seen it.

Jen-ling had. She also saw him exchange the pot for another on its way to Ambassador Ratnavira's table. He had calculated brilliantly, Jen-ling admitted, waiting to send it until exactly when the Ambassador's cup was near-empty. Indeed, the girl's voice was full of admiration for the foe lying unconscious at her feet.

It had been but the work of a moment to switch teapots and send a measured portion of Lord Dok-Kasemsan's own poison his way.

Princess Safiya felt the excitement emanating from behind the screen. Ambassador Ratnavira stood to gain many great rewards from his prince for bringing home so worthy a bride.

"As you have already surmised," Princess Safiya said, "this was a test of your skills. You, Jen-ling, have passed. Your reward is a contracted marriage to Prince Amithnal of Aja. Your training is complete, my child. Your life's work as a protector of your master will now commence."

Jen-ling bowed, and not even Princess Safiya could read the expression behind her painted mask. This was, after all, the whole purpose of the Golden Daughters: Marriage that was no true marriage; a life of service; secret honor, the more valuable for its secrecy.

"You may go and prepare yourself for your upcoming journey to Aja," Princess Safiya said. She rose from her seat and stepped around the prone body of Kasemsan to kiss Jen-ling solemnly upon the brow. "You have satisfied my every wish for you, child. And you have brought still greater honor to the name of your mighty father. May Anwar and Hulan shine bright upon your path."

So Jen-ling retreated, and eight of the other girls followed. Only Sairu remained, her hands folded within her sleeves, her head bowed. And that same smile upon her face. As though she laughed at some joke no one else could see.

Princess Safiya frowned, a small crease forming in the white paint between her brows. But she turned to the screen and called to the ambassador, "Are you satisfied?"

The little man came wheezing into view, bowing and scraping and twisting his rings. "Oh, Revered Mother!" he exclaimed. "Such a jewel, such a prize has never graced the household of an Aja prince! My master will be delighted beyond measure!"

Delighted, yes. And secure in the knowledge that he would live to a ripe old age of manipulation and wickedness, ever protected by his pretty new bride.

"I will see you this evening," Princess Safiya said, indicating the door with a sweep of her arm. "We will sign the final charter approving Jen-ling's selection. Until then, Ambassador."

What a relief to be free of the odious man's presence!

Even as Ratnavira vanished through the doorway, Princess Safiya turned to inspect Kasemsan again. Pretending to ignore Sairu—though she knew the girl wasn't fooled in the least—she knelt beside the Pen-Chan lord's still body, studying his face. The face of a Crouching Shadow. She had known neither his name nor any personal information about him when she contracted him for this role. The Crouching Shadows were almost as secretive as the Golden Daughters. Almost.

She had not been surprised in the least to discover her assassin's identity. As soon as word reached her that a Pen-Chan lord from the Nua-Pratut Kingdom had come to Lunthea Maly, she had said to herself, "Ah!

That will be he." When her sources brought her more details, such as timing, travel plans, and his pretenses for being within the city, she had felt her initial suspicions confirmed.

And when he'd entered the Butterfly Hall today, he might as well have announced his intentions with drums and fanfare. He was much too obviously *not* the sort of person one would expect to take money for committing murder.

She studied his handsome face and form, noting that he was a scholar, probably a Gruung Presented Scholar with a position of some honor within Suthinnakor City. A family man, generally faithful to his wife if not loving. Keenly intelligent but quick to wrath, as his display in the Butterfly Hall had proven. An *interesting* man. A man with secrets.

A shame that he would now be left to rot in the dungeons of Manusbau Palace and . . .

Why was that girl smiling?

"Very well, Sairu." Princess Safiya stood and only just managed to suppress the frown trying to force its way onto her face. "I see that you're near bursting. What is the joke? What have the rest of us missed?"

Sairu raised her face, the sun spots on her cheeks rising with her grin. She was a little smaller than her sisters; indeed, were it not for the bulk of her serving-girl robes, she would run the risk of disappearing if she turned sideways. And she never could manage the required solemnity of a proper Golden Daughter. A mistress of less discernment than Princess Safiya would have dismissed her long ago. But Princess Safiya was no fool.

"I should like to accept Brother Yaru's assignment, Honored Mother," Sairu said.

For a moment Princess Safiya's face did not move a muscle. But indeed, she reasoned with herself, it could not be too difficult for Sairu to guess at least some of Brother Yaru's whisperings in the Butterfly Hall. She could not have heard a word, but she may have read his face and even perhaps glimpsed some of Princess Safiya's own expression behind her fan.

Princess Safiya lowered her lids briefly, indicating Kasemsan with a glance. "You did not pass today's test. What makes you think you are worthy of any assignment?"

Still that smile. Sairu's eyes sparkled. "The ambassador was in no danger."

"Oh? And how did you come to that conclusion?"

"Because you would not have allowed anything to happen to him."

Princess Safiya narrowed her eyes. "So you recognized the test?"

"Ambassador Ratnavira gave it away the moment he entered the hall," the girl replied. "He kept looking at you. And sweating like a pig."

"And the assassin? When did you spot him?"

"The same moment you did, Honored Mother. You were so pleased when he was presented. Your face gave it away."

Anwar blight it! She must start wearing heavier paint around her eyes.

"So why did you not step forward, Sairu? Why did you allow Jen-ling to win the test?"

Here the girl had the grace at least to look ashamed. "I did not like the look of the ambassador. If he is the representative of his master, I do not think I would like his master either."

Princess Safiya considered what she knew of Prince Amithnal and could make no argument. "We do not get to select our own patrons," she said sternly.

Sairu only smiled. After all, she had chosen this time.

Feeling as though she had lost an argument, Princess Safiya returned to her chair, sitting carefully so as not to crush the folds of her silken robe more than necessary. She took time to arrange her sleeves, composing herself before addressing the girl again. "So you will pick and choose your assignments, is that it? You will decline marriage to a prince and enter service to the priesthood? Without knowing even what that service might entail?"

Sairu tilted her head to one side. "They require a bodyguard for one of their Dream Walkers."

Princess Safiya nearly stood upright, so startled was she by this statement. How in Hulan's name had the girl arrived at such a conclusion? No one spoke of the Dream Walkers outside the temple grounds. If any doings in the world were more secret than those of the Golden Daughters, they would be those of the priests within the Crown of the Moon. Light of the Lordly Sun, Sairu should not even know the Dream Walkers existed!

"And why," Princess Safiya said quietly, hoping her voice betrayed none of her surprise but knowing that it must, "do you speak such wild fancy?"

"Because nothing less would induce the temple orders to seek help from the outside," Sairu replied with infuriating calm and logic. "Officially speaking, they care nothing for their own lives, given over as they are in service to Anwar and Hulan. But the Dream Walkers are different. They are sacred and valuable and rare. And they have enemies."

"How would you know that?"

"All who are sacred, valuable, and rare have enemies, Honored Mother."

Princess Safiya stood unspeaking before the girl. Kasemsan groaned in agonized sleep. Soon he would open his eyes to a whole new world of pain and shame, and she regretted it for his sake, particularly since she would be the primary source.

"Sairu," she said at last, "Brother Yaru and the Besur may not wish it known, even by you, that they seek protection for a Dream Walker. They will believe all was done with utmost secrecy."

Sairu's smile glowed. She knew now that she had won. She had done what the Golden Daughters never did: She had chosen her own patron.

"I am as adept at playing ignorant as I am at playing sweet," she said. "I will reveal nothing."

And she would. That smile of hers was more deceptive by far than the expressionless stares of her sisters.

"You realize this means no marriage for you, child," Princess Safiya said.

"I prefer it so."

Kasemsan groaned again, and his eyelids fluttered. Princess Safiya wanted to smack him for forcing her decision by this early stirring. But she blinked slowly to disguise the emotion and said only, "Very well. You have your wish. You will go to the Crown of the Moon tonight and present yourself to the Besur. And may Hulan shine upon your decision."

Sairu bowed. Her pitying gaze lingered for a moment on the stricken

Nua-Pratut lord. Then she withdrew, drifting as softly from the room as a blossom blown upon a spring wind.

Princess Safiya sat quietly, gazing down upon her prey without seeing him. Her mind was busy with small connections, details, threads weaving through time and space to form patterns invisible to other eyes.

And she thought: *It all comes together somehow. The assassin, the ambassador, the Besur, Sairu, and the Dream Walkers. They weave together, though they may not know it, and they form a picture I cannot yet see.*

But I will see it.

Kasemsan's eyes fluttered open, and his mouth twisted in a silent expression of agony. Poison burned in his gut; but more painful still was the burn of failure. He had never known failure before, not once in his life.

Princess Safiya's face appeared before his eyes, and for a moment he thought she must be an angel come to fetch him from this world, so beautiful was her countenance bending over him in his torment.

But then she spoke, and he knew she was no angel.

"Tell me, Crouching Shadow," she said, "for what purpose you have come to Lunthea Maly."

"I . . . I came to fulfill the assassination of Ambassador Ratnavira," he gasped, the words like fire in his throat.

"No," she replied, shaking her head gently. She placed a hand upon his forehead, and he cried out, for her skin was cold. "No, do not think you will fool me." She stared deep into his eyes. For a moment, the briefest possible moment, she believed she saw something stirring in the darkness of his left pupil. A living something existing in a realm beyond mortality. A tiny, angry parasite.

She blinked. When she looked again, Kasemsan's eyes were empty of all save his fear. She blinked once more; now even the memory of what she had glimpsed vanished from her mind, as though carefully removed by some unseen hand.

It did not matter. Princess Safiya bent over her prisoner like a tiger crouched above its still-living prey. "I saw that you lay awake as I spoke to the girl. I saw you listening," she said. "Now tell me, my lord, and keep nothing back. What is your true purpose in Lunthea Maly? What does your order want of the Dream Walkers?"

Sairu made her way from Princess Safiya's chambers out to the walkways of the encircling gardens. The Masayi, abode of the Golden Daughters, was an intricate complex of buildings linked by blossom-shrouded walkways, calm with fountains and clear, lotus-filled pools where herons strutted and spotted fish swam.

Here she had lived all the life she could remember.

The Masayi was but a small part of Manusbau Palace, which comprised the whole of Sairu's existence. She had never stepped beyond the palace walls. To do so would be to pass into a world of corruption, corruption to which a Golden Daughter would not be impervious until she was safely chartered to a master and her life's purpose was affixed in her heart and mind. Meanwhile, she must live securely embalmed in this tomb, waiting for life to begin.

Sairu's mouth curved gently at the corners, and she took small steps as she had been trained—slow, dainty steps that disguised the swiftness with which she could move at need. Even in private she must maintain the illusion, even here within the Masayi.

A cat sat on the doorstep of the Chrysanthemum House, grooming itself in the sunlight. She stepped around it and proceeded into the red-hung halls of the Daughters' quarters and on to her private chambers. There she must gather what few things she would take with her—fewer things even than Jen-ling would take on her journey to Aja. For Jen-ling would be the wife of a prince and must give every impression of a bride on her wedding journey.

I wonder who my master will be? Sairu thought as she slid back the rattan door to her chamber and entered the quiet simplicity within. She removed her elaborate costume and exchanged it for a robe of plain red without embellishments. She washed the serving-girl cosmetics from her face and painted on the daily mask she and her sisters wore—white with black spots beneath each eye and a red stripe down her chin. It was elegant and effortless, and to the common eye it made her indistinguishable from her sisters.

The curtain moved behind her. Calmly she turned to see the same cat slip into her room. Cats abounded throughout Manusbau Palace, kept on purpose near the storehouses to manage the vermin. But they seldom entered private chambers.

Sairu, kneeling near her window with her paint pots around her, watched the cat as it moved silkily across the room, stepped onto her sleeping cushions, and began kneading the soft fabric, purring all the while. Its claws snagged the delicate threads. But it was a cat. As far as it was concerned, it had every right to enjoy or destroy what it willed.

At last it seemed to notice Sairu. It turned sleepy eyes to her and blinked.

Sairu smiled. In a voice as sweet as honey, she asked, "Who are you?"

The cat twitched its tail softly and went on purring.

The next moment, Sairu was across the room, her hand latched onto the cat's scruff. She pushed it down into the cushions and held it there as it yowled and snarled, trying to catch at her with its claws.

"Who are you?" she demanded, her voice fierce this time. "*What* are you? Are you an evil spirit sent to haunt me?"

"No, dragons eat it! I mean, *rrrraww! Mreeeow! Yeeeowrl!*"

The cat twisted and managed to lash out at her with its back feet, its claws catching in the fabric of her sleeve. One claw scratched her wrist, startling her just enough that she loosened her hold. The cat took advantage of the opportunity and, hissing like a fire demon, leapt free. It sprang across the room, knocking over several of her paint pots, and spun about, back-arched and snarling. Every hair stood on end, and its ears lay flat to its skull.

Sairu drew a dagger from her sleeve and crouched, prepared for anything. The smile lingered on her mouth, but her eyes flashed. "Who sent you?" she demanded. "Why have you come to me now? You must know of my assignment."

"*Meeeeowrl*," the cat said stubbornly and showed its fangs in another hiss.

"I see it in your face," Sairu said, moving carefully to shift her weight and prepare to spring. "You are no animal. Who is your master, devil?"

The cat dodged her spring easily enough, which surprised her. Sairu was quick and rarely missed a target. Her knife sank into the floor and stuck there, but she released it and whipped another from the opposite sleeve even as she whirled about.

Any self-respecting cat would have made for the window or the door. This one sprang back onto the cushions and crouched there, tail lashing. Its eyes were all too sentient, but it said only "*Meeeeow*," as though trying to convince itself.

Sairu chewed the inside of her cheek. Then, in a soft, smooth voice, she said, "We have ways of dealing with devils in this country. Do you know what they are, demon-cat?"

The cat's ears came up. "*Prreeowl*?" it said.

"Allow me to enlighten you." And Sairu put her free hand to her mouth and produced a long, piercing whistle. The household erupted with the voices of a dozen and more lion dogs.

The little beasts, slipping and sliding and crashing into walls, their claws clicking and clattering on the tiles, careened down the corridor and poured into Sairu's room. Fluffy tails wagging, pushed-in noses twitching, they roared like the lions they believed themselves to be and fell upon the cat with rapacious joy.

The cat uttered one long wail and vanished out the window. Sairu, dogs milling at her feet, leapt up and hurried to look out after it, expecting to see a tawny tail slipping from sight. But she saw nothing.

The devil was gone. For the moment at least.

Sairu sank down on her cushions, and her lap was soon filled with wriggling, snuffling hunters eager for praise. She petted them absently, but her mind was awhirl. She had heard of devils taking the form of animals and speaking with the tongues of men. But she had never before seen it. She couldn't honestly say she'd even believed it.

"What danger is my new master in?" she wondered. "From what must I protect him?"

4

EVER AFTER THAT FATEFUL day, the smell of crushed ginger would fill Sunan's memory with overwhelming sensations of shame.

He would not have guessed it at the time. But when he passed through the gates of the Center of Learning into the streets of Suthinnakor City, the first thing Sunan encountered was a street vendor plying his wares of cabbage dumplings to hungry students. The dumplings were seasoned with ginger, and the smell wafted over Sunan even as he stumbled blindly past, oblivious to the hopeful cries of the vendor. His stomach churned at the very idea of food, and he hastened on to the end of the street and there paused a moment, expecting to be sick.

It might have been wise, he realized upon reflection, to have stopped and retrieved his own clothing. Or at least his shoes. Snow fell in noncommittal gusts, just enough to dust the streets and turn to oozing mud. Sunan's bare feet froze, so he started walking again with the faint hope of warming them. The sensation of mud churning between his toes was a welcome distraction; and he focused on the revulsion of it, shuddering and cursing at each step.

Anything was better than facing the explosion of thoughts inside his brain.

He had made no plans for a return journey, arranged no litter or conveyance. He was supposed to mount the stairs to the Middle Court and enter his new life as a Presented Scholar. He wasn't supposed to slink back to his uncle's house in disgrace.

His uncle, who was dead.

No, no, he wouldn't think about that. It was nonsense anyway. Uncle Kasemsan had been far too much alive the last time Sunan saw him to possibly be dead now. It just couldn't be. And Sunan had bigger problems to consider.

The snow dusted his shoulders with a white mantle. Though it was very light, any observer would have thought it weighed him down like lead, so heavily did he slump and droop and finally collapse again against a wall. He tried to warm his feet with his hands, rubbing the toes to make the blood move. Vaguely he was aware of the bustle in the street, the lives of thousands going on around him just as though the world hadn't shattered. He heard merchants shouting, tradesmen arguing, babies squalling, young men calling lewd remarks to housemaids running errands. Donkeys brayed, dogs barked, geese honked, cart wheels squelched in mud, and no one cared about one barefoot young man who stood vigorously massaging his feet. As though he could massage hope back into his dreams.

In the street a beast of burden lowed deep in its belly. The sound plucked at Sunan's ears, and he frowned, though he did not know why.

Then as he drew a breath, he inhaled a certain unforgettable smell. Just as, in the future, the scent of ginger would recall memories of this one horrible day, so this smell—one he had not encountered for the last eight years—swept over his brain like a deadly wave, destroying all in its path. It was a musty, dung-laden smell layered with a scent of broad spaces, keen winds, wildflowers, and blood. The heavy odor permeated every layer of clothing, every pore of the skin, and congealed there in an infesting funk that only years of washing in aromatic soaps might someday erase.

Only one creature in the world could produce such a stench: a Chhayan buffalo.

Sunan's head shot up, and he stared out into the crowded street. Once more he heard the deep-bellied low, and this time he spotted the beast, nearly swallowed in the crowds of Suthinnakor. But nothing, nothing in all the known world, could swallow that smell.

Suddenly Sunan no longer stood half-frozen in the streets of a Pen-Chan city. He was on the wide plains of the Noorhitam hinterlands, his body dripping with sweat, his shirt open from throat to navel, a cloth tied about his forehead to keep more sweat from dripping into his eyes. And he rode astride a Chhayan buffalo, swatting it with a thorny stick every few paces to keep it moving, his body aching with every lurch of the great beast's spine. Five more buffalo were yoked around him, pulling a great covered gurta, a moveable dwelling upon wheels, its walls made of buffalo hides that stank nearly as bad as the living beasts.

For that moment he was back in the life he had labored so hard these eight years to leave behind. That life which even now reached out from the past and marred him, as though he still reeked of buffalo.

The moment passed. He returned to the cold city. The beast moved on its way, leaving its smell in its wake, its protesting bellows echoing. Chhayan buffalo never approved of cramped cities, used as they were to the open hinterlands.

Sunan stood, one foot still clutched in his hands, scarcely daring to breathe. Then he cursed, "Anwar's elbow!" and started running.

Chhayans rarely if ever came this far north. They were far too busy wreaking havoc upon their conquerors down south. Not since Sunan's father led a raid into Nua-Pratut and stole Sunan's mother away as a victory bride some twenty-five years ago had Chhayans bothered with any of the small northern kingdoms.

So Sunan knew, even before he turned at last up the incline leading to his uncle's city home, what he would find when he reached it. He knew, even before he entered the heavy wooden gates, what he would see in the courtyard of his uncle's house, standing there in all the audacity of its existence, stinking up this fine site as though it hadn't a care in the world.

Sure enough, there stood the same Chhayan buffalo harnessed to a miniature of the very gurta in which Sunan had spent his boyhood years. Its side was even emblazoned with the same brilliant tiger in orange and black pigments.

"No," Sunan whispered. "No, no, no. Not today. Not now."

But the flap on the back of the gurta flew open, and a face, familiar even though it had aged from boyhood to manhood, gazed out at Sunan and burst into a wide grin.

"Sunan! I've come at last!"

And, just as Sunan knew must happen, out leaped his half-brother. Eight years ago, Jovann had been a scrawny lad, all bone and sinew and that same enormous grin. Now a young man grown, he was still little more than bone, sinew, and grin, but enlarged and toughened by years on the wild hinterlands.

Sunan, numb and frozen, found himself caught in a long-limbed embrace, and his nose was assaulted almost past bearing by the stink of buffalo. He tried to speak, to make some protest, but the smell seemed to have tangled up his vocal cords. He could only grunt as Jovann pounded his back with both hands then clutched him by the shoulders and stepped back to grin at him from arm's length.

"You look a fright!" Jovann said. "Not what I expected of my wealthy, learned, Pen-Chan brother. Hulan's heel, you haven't even got a pair of shoes! What are you, Sunan, a slave?"

The one thing in all the worlds that could overwhelm the overwhelming stench of buffalo took hold of Sunan with a grip he had nearly forgotten to be possible. He shouldn't have forgotten; after all, this had been as much a part of his life as his own beating heart since that day, all those years ago, when his mother had held him close in the darkness of their own small gurta and whispered: *"You have a brother now, Sunan. Your father's new bride gave birth this morning, and you have a brother. Try not to hate him. Though he takes everything from you, try not to hate him."*

But of course Sunan hated him. For his mother's sake. For his own.

The flame of renewed hatred loosened his tongue, and he found himself suddenly both very warm and very controlled. He spoke in a measured voice and even forced a smile onto his lips.

"Jovann. You surprise me with this unexpected honor. What brings you to the house of my uncle this spring?"

Jovann blinked, perhaps taken aback at his brother's formal tone. He released Sunan's shoulders and stepped back, still grinning, but also bowing respectfully as a younger brother should to his elder. "I've come to see you, of course," he said. "Father sent me at my request. It's netherworld-cold out here, Sunan! Would your uncle let your poor relative inside, do you think?"

"Uncle Kasemsan is not home at present," Sunan said, the overseer's dark words flashing once more through his mind. He stifled these quickly, unable to face them just now. "And my aunt and cousins are at their winter house on the coast. You find me alone here in Suthinnakor."

"All the better!" Jovann replied. "I didn't relish the notion of bowing and scraping to a houseful of Pen-Chans, my Chhayan manners offending at every turn. This is much more to my liking. Will you have me inside?" This last was spoken with a slight hesitancy. Jovann was a dense one, Sunan always thought, but even he was not entirely unaware of his half-brother's feelings toward him, no matter how he pretended otherwise.

Sunan inclined his head and swept an arm with great dignity, as though he were clothed in his regular robes and not the dreadful woolen garment of the Gruung. He led his brother to the front door. Other men climbed out of the gurta and swarmed around the buffalo's head. Jovann called to them cheerfully, bidding them find shelter for the beast then join him inside. A whole host of stinky Chhayans ensconced in his uncle's house. Thank Anwar the family was not in residence!

Jovann at least had the awareness to remove his boots at the threshold before stepping through. Old Kiut, Uncle Kasemsan's servant, came rushing to the door, his mouth open to make loud protests. But one glimpse of Sunan—Sunan, who should not be there but should instead be in the Middle Court of the Center of Learning—and he shut his mouth. He bowed, saying nothing of either the Gruung or Sunan's strange guest but instead merely asking, "Shall I have food laid out in the lower room, master?"

Sunan nodded. "And bring hot drinks," he said. Nothing more. They would not speak of his failure. To speak of it would do it too much honor.

He shuddered inside but fixed his attention on his brother, thankful in that moment for a distraction, however hateful.

Jovann was grinning again. "He calls you 'master,' but you're the barefoot one! Really, Sunan, what is this rig of yours? I expected to meet you in silks and satins, but you're dressed worse than any Chhayan dog-boy I ever saw. Is this some part of your great studies of which I've heard rumor? Some practice of self-discipline necessary to sharpen the mind?"

Sunan refused to grace this with an answer. He nodded coldly and indicated for Jovann to follow him down the passage. As he led the way, he could almost feel Jovann's eyes bugging as he took in the wealth and elegance of Lord Dok-Kasemsan's dwelling, which far out-matched anything to be found among the nomadic Chhayan warlords. Nua-Pratut, though a small kingdom, led the world in arts, music, and refinements. Masterpieces of paint or silk adorned the walls, and stunning works of pottery—shaped, glazed, and fired in extraordinary designs—stood upon carved pedestals in various corners and under windows. Jovann would only ever have seen their like amid the loot his father had stolen from Nua-Pratut more than twenty years ago, and all of that was long since damaged beyond any real value.

Sunan escorted his half-brother to the lower chamber where Old Kiut would soon lay out a meal. There Sunan excused himself and hurried to his own chambers to change out of the Gruung robe. Strange . . . he had somehow grown accustomed to its wretched itch in the last few hours, and it was with a sense of loss, not relief, that he removed it. Perhaps he had come to believe he and the robe deserved each other. Perhaps he merely hated to part with that last link to what he had believed his future would be.

Either way, he flung it aside and carefully washed and scented himself, knowing it would be many months before he would rid his body of the buffalo stink. But spicy perfumes helped, and his body shivered with chilled delight as he slid into a silk robe and secured it at his waist. He added a fur cloak and thick slippers, and slicked his hair into a tight braid down his back.

There was nothing for it then. He must return to his brother and find out what evil inspiration had led their father to send Jovann across many miles and mountains to plague Sunan just now, at his lowest ebb.

Sunan met Old Kiut on his way and ordered him to see to it that the other Chhayans in Jovann's company were housed, fed, and not permitted to disturb him and his brother. Old Kiut nodded and bowed himself away, and Sunan continued to the lower chamber alone. He found Jovann reclining at the table, one elbow propped upon a cushion, the other hand scooping up herbed rice with a fold of flat bread. Jovann sat upright when Sunan entered.

"No, don't stand," Sunan said, taking a seat opposite his brother. He could not find the stomach for food, but he took up a steaming mug of honey-tea and held it, grateful for the warmth in his hands and the steam in his nostrils.

"It's fine fare," Jovann said between mouthfuls. "Better than what I've been eating these last five months! There's little good hunting over the mountains, and I do get sick of dried buffalo jerk and withered dates."

Sunan's stomach churned again. He could still taste the dung-tang of buffalo jerk on his tongue. He took a gulp of the honey-tea, glad when it scalded his mouth. Maybe it would scald away the memory.

He set down his mug then and said, "Why are you here, Jovann?"

"To see you," Jovann replied.

"Yes. But why? Father wouldn't send his heir over treacherous mountain passes in the middle of winter without some cause."

"Can't a man be allowed to visit his brother, especially after eight years of separation?" Jovann asked, grinning again. Then his grin faded and his young face, reddened and toughened by sun and wind, became serious. "In truth, I wanted to come; and when Father first said he was going to send someone to you, I begged him for days to let it be me. I don't think I would have persuaded him, but Mother took my side, and your mother too. He said he couldn't fight the three of us and relented at last."

Sunan's cheek twitched at the mention of his mother. His mother who should be here in Suthinnakor with him but whom his father would not set free. He took another sip of tea and allowed it to burn away the sharp words he initially wished to speak. Instead he said, "Tell me first why Father wished to send someone at all. Then, if you must, tell me why it had to be you."

Jovann looked embarrassed and dug around in his bowl of rice, stirring the vegetables and spices with his finger. Realizing what he was doing, he dipped his finger in a nearby cleanser bowl and wiped it on a soft towel. "Father is . . . He is himself, as you know he must be."

"By that you mean he is still obsessed with driving the Kitar people from Noorhitam?" Sunan supplied.

Jovann nodded. "He carries the grudge of two hundred years heavily in his heart. And he still believes it possible for the Chhayans to reclaim their land. To reclaim the city of Lunthea Maly from the usurpers."

Sunan smiled grimly and said in a voice laced with venom, "May Hulan shine upon his endeavors."

"I don't think Father looks to Hulan for aid anymore." Jovann leaned across the table, his eyes suddenly alight and eager. "He says Hulan forsook us in favor of the Kitar. He speaks instead of new allegiances, powerful allies such as we Chhayans have never before known."

"*We* Chhayans?"

"Oh come, Sunan. Don't pretend your blood doesn't flow with as much Chhayan pride as ever it did. I know they've dressed you up and filled your head with all sorts of northern notions, poetry and the like. But you didn't grow up on the plains only to forget the world of sky and earth and long horizons!"

That was the strange thing about Jovann, Sunan remembered now with a sudden lurch. Illiterate little scrap of Chhayan dog-boy that he was, Jovann was full of passion, full of spirit! With a few words he could inspire a snake to give up its poison in favor of pious living. With a few more, he could almost make Sunan forget his Pen-Chan heritage and all the culture and learning and history, all the merit and prestige with which it shielded him, in favor of the wildness of the Chhayans. The Chhayans who claimed half his very soul, half his spirit.

For a moment the stench of buffalo gave way before the gusts of a rushing plains wind carrying rain and storm and violence on its shoulders. And Sunan's ears rang with the throaty battle cries of his father's warriors, the Tiger Men of Juong-Khla; men who had never heard of the arithmetic, music, rituals, ceremonies, and poetry of Nua-Pratut. And the wish of his childhood—of earning the impossible, the favor of his mighty father—struck him full in the heart.

Hated desire. He despised himself for ever cherishing it, and despised Jovann still more for recalling the wish to his mind.

"Who are these new allies?" Sunan asked, sipping again at his tea, which had cooled considerably and was now drinkable.

Jovann shrugged. "I've not met them myself. Father says I'm not yet ready. But I've seen the light of hope ignite once more in the eyes of our people. They know. They know the time is near. And you can help us, Sunan."

"I? How can I help in this fool enterprise of our father? Does he seek a clan poet, or does he somehow believe Pen-Chan rituals will bring him that extra level of polished cunning he lacks?"

"I know your studies have not been confined to poetry," Jovann persisted. "We hear rumors and tales, even out in the wilds. And remember, it's not so long since our father made war on Nua-Pratut."

Sunan smiled a grim smile that made Jovann blush, realizing his error. The lad bowed his head, saying nothing, his silence offering a swift apology. After all, even he had seen the tears of his father's first wife, which she silently wept on a certain day every summer, though she never spoke of her sorrow.

But Jovann had traveled too far to forsake his purpose now. He sat back from the table, allowing his face to be hidden from the lantern light. But his eyes still shone with the passion of his words.

"Father needs the secret of the Long Fire," he said.

Sunan did not speak for some time. He sipped his tea and regarded his brother and allowed the words to ring in their ears.

Jovann could not long bear it. "He needs it, Sunan," he urged. "He needs it for this final great push. His allies have promised him victory, but to have this victory, he must fight with fire. With the Long Fire such as he witnessed all those years ago. Surely you have learned the secret of it by now?"

"Black powder," Sunan whispered.

"If you know it, you must give it to us!" Jovann urged. "And if you don't, you must find it. And you will write it out, and I will carry it back."

"Write it out?" Sunan scoffed. "And what good would that do you? Neither you, nor my father, nor any man in the Khla tribe could read it. Or," he added bitterly, "do you depend on the talents of my disfavored mother to fulfill your dreams?"

"Our new allies can interpret any writing. And they will teach us to control the Long Fire. Lunthea Maly does not hold the secret, and they will not be able to defend themselves against us."

"And so you, a rabble of Chhayan nomads, will run the Emperor of Noorhitam from his own city. You will drive your conquerors out of the land, using . . ." Sunan shook his head, ready to laugh at the absurdity of it all. "Using *explosions*."

Jovann studied him across the table. So intense. So confident. So assured of his place in the world. His father's heir, his father's favorite, the bright son of the Khla tribe. Even now Sunan could see the gleam of desired mastery in his eyes. The young man thought it possible, in his youthful madness, that he might someday rule his people from the Emperor of Noorhitam's own throne.

"It is within our grasp," Jovann insisted.

"And why do you say this, brother?" Sunan said, snarling through his smile. "Did you see it in one of your dreams?"

Jovann visibly paled, his reddened skin turning white under the lantern's glow. But his eyes remained fervent, and his face took on the hard lines of his father's. A warrior's face, a master's. His voice was deep when he spoke:

"I saw it all. I entered the Wood even as I have done before, and I received the vision. I saw myself standing before the Emperor of Noorhitam, and I knew it was he, though I have never seen his face. He sat weak before me, pleading. Begging me for something I could not hear. But I was strong, and I stood before him, ragged Chhayan that I am. I saw it, Sunan, as clearly as I see you now. More clearly even! And I know it will come to pass."

"Have you told our father of this?" Sunan asked wryly, for he knew how their father felt about Jovann's dreams. The weak wanderings of the mind were not fitting for a warlord's son and heir. Juong-Khla had long ago forbidden Jovann from speaking of such things.

Jovann shook his head, frustrated but earnest. "You know I haven't. But it doesn't matter. It will be true even so."

"And did you see yourself wielding the 'Long Fire,' as you call it, in this dream?"

Again Jovann shook his head.

"Then what makes you so certain I will give over the secret of black powder to you?"

"You won't give it to me," Jovann replied. "You will give it to our father. And you will hope that, in the giving, he will welcome you home."

Sunan rose so swiftly that Jovann drew himself halfway up, his fists clenched, his shoulders tensed. But Sunan took a deep breath and adjusted the cloak over his shoulders. His belly burned like a raging furnace, but he swallowed and suppressed the rising heat. "Eat well, brother," he said. "Tomorrow you will be back to buffalo jerk and withered dates."

He turned to the door, and his hand was already at the panel when Jovann's voice arrested him with a word:

"Wait."

Sunan didn't turn, but he did pause. He could hear his brother gathering himself to speak something he did not wish to say.

"I saw a vision about you as well, Sunan. I've had it many times in the last year, and I came to tell you."

Sunan did not reply. But his stillness betrayed his curiosity.

"In my vision," Jovann persisted, "I saw you kneeling before a powerful shadow. And then it touched you, and you rose up. You rose up in the form of a dragon. A great fire-filled dragon, Sunan, such as the legends speak of! And you were mighty, and you were beautiful, and all who saw you trembled, even our father. You were terrible in the eyes of the Khla warriors, and you led them into battle."

Sunan felt his heart racing as his brother's words washed over him. He did not understand them, but they thrilled him. Thrilled him deeply, even enough to shroud the shame of that day and fill him with a brief, painful hope once more. He leaned against the door, suddenly weak with longing.

"But there was more." Jovann hesitated, and it was with difficulty he continued. "I saw you fight. I saw you face a warrior armed only with a small knife. Beware this warrior, Sunan! Beware her, for she will be your undoing."

"She?"

Sunan turned then and fixed his brother with a stare full of such hatred, it might have struck him dead upon the spot. But Jovann knelt with his eyes closed, his palms flat on the table before him, and sweat beaded his brow as he recalled his dream.

A shudder passed through Sunan. "So this is why you begged our father to let you come. Did you travel so far to insult me to my face?"

Jovann's eyes flew wide. "No!" he cried. "No, to give you warning! It will come to pass, and I fear—"

But Sunan heard no more. He was out through the door and into the passage already. He knew if he remained even a moment longer he would surely murder his brother, there at his uncle's table.

5

THE OLD GATEKEEPER of the temple hated his job. He hated the tedium of it, hated the poor working conditions, hated that other gatekeepers of finer gates surrounding the Crown of the Moon looked down on him. He hated that his club foot prevented him from being a soldier, hated that his ugly face prevented him from being a lover. He hated the priests he served, hated the food he ate, hated the hours he kept. He was so deeply embedded in his hatred that he could never imagine leaving it for a different, less hateful life.

His one joy came every sunset in the form of the coal-children scuttling up the road from the mines to deliver their wares to the temple. The coal-children, ragged and huddled and wheezing with sickness, were all smaller than he. And they squeaked when kicked.

"You're late," the gatekeeper growled when, in response to a timid knock, he slid back the lookout hatch and gazed out on the little coal-girl weighed down by her burden. The sun had already set and the moon was not yet up, leaving only the small light of the outer lantern to illuminate her general outline. By this light alone the gatekeeper could make out no details beyond her fearful trembling.

But the trembling brought a grin to his lips, and he opened the gate, which groaned on its hinges as he drew it back. "Hurry up with you," he said, beckoning. His smile grew as he watched the little girl make her way heavily through the entrance, her feet shuffling with each step. "Your fellows have been'n gone hours ago. What kept you, lazy scum?" And he put out a hand to seize the girl's thin shoulder.

His cry was thin and high, and abruptly shut off. But the pain in his hand, where his index finger was twisted and drawn back at an angle that did not quite allow for a break—though a break would almost be welcome relief—did not cease, even as the grip pinching his throat in just the right place prevented his voice from escaping. He stared up into the shadowed face of the coal-girl who had suddenly grown, looming over him as he knelt cringing at her feet.

"I know all about you," she said. He could not discern her expression for the shadows, but he could hear the smile behind her words. "I see your life in your eyes, though we have never met. One of a too-large family, given less to eat than your brothers because of your deformity. Ran away to join the army, which would not have you, so you threw yourself upon the mercy of the priests. And mercy they granted you, but not too much, for one such as you can bear only so much of mercy. So here you sit, day in and day out, and you have coal enough to warm your feet, food enough to fill your belly, strong drink enough to poison your soul, and yet you will never, never breathe a word of thanks. Not to the priests, not to the goddess they serve. I know all about you, predator of the night, stalking the weak simply because they are weaker than you."

She twisted his finger just a fraction more, and the gatekeeper choked with his need to scream. With just a little more pressure the girl brought him flat on his back and placed a foot on his throat.

"Leave the children alone," she said.

And then she was gone, vanished into the darkness within the gate. The gatekeeper crawled away, murmuring prayers he'd heard the priests utter over the years and making signs to ward off evil spirits.

These signs did not work, however, for the next moment he looked into the glowing eyes of what must be a demon. It couldn't be a cat, after all, for no cat would stare at him so intently before opening its mouth to say: "Lumé love me, but your breath does stink!"

Then the demon was gone after the girl, and the gatekeeper was left to pick up the remnants of his sanity.

For the most part the priests of the Crown of the Moon made a point to forget that the foundations of the holy temple of their goddess—the center of their religion—were laid by Chhayan hands many centuries ago. In fact, the worship of Anwar and Hulan was an inherited Chhayan practice, stolen and tweaked over two hundred years to suit Kitar sensibilities, but ultimately, at its roots, nothing more than the faith of nomadic barbarians.

It seemed fair enough to everyone concerned: conquer the country, conquer the religion. Make use of the best parts of both. And no one could argue that the priests of the Kitar—who didn't have a national religion of their own beyond a vague ancestor-worship that was greatly out of fashion—had significantly *improved* their new faith with their own holy writs, ceremonies, sacrifices, and sacred days. Indeed, it had grown into such a popular religion that other surrounding nations, including Dong Min, Aja, and more, had taken it up and built temples of their own. Even the king of Nua-Pratut, a nation famed across the eastern Continent for its severe intellectualism, had ordered a few small shrines in honor of the Lordly Sun and Lady Moon put up in various cities . . . a concession the priests of the Crown of the Moon wore as a badge of pride.

It was all silly nonsense. Or almost all.

Sairu made her way through the twisting gardens and passages of the temple as confidently as though she had walked them dozens of times before. As confidently as though this were not the first time in all her life she had stepped beyond the boundaries of Manusbau Palace; as though her heart didn't pound with a wild fury of liberation she tried her utmost to suppress because, really, she wasn't free but about to enter a lifetime of servitude.

It didn't matter. Not even her encounter with that wretched gatekeeper could dampen her spirits, because she had known all along that wickedness prowled beyond the sanctity of Manusbau, and she was prepared to deal harshly with wickedness as necessary. She felt like a goshawk freed for the first time from the falconer's wrist. And although she knew she would return immediately at first summoning, for the moment she could soar high and pretend she would fly on forever and never return.

She wore a simple brown robe and, depending on whom she passed, she assumed a different form within it. When she passed priests, she became a huddled coal-girl once more. When she passed servants, she drew herself up, puffed herself out, and became a slow, sedate, muttering priest of a low order. Thus no one stopped her, no one gave her a second glance, and she progressed deep into the Crown of the Moon.

She had studied maps of its layout earlier that same evening and committed them to memory according to the techniques Princess Safiya had ingrained in her since she first joined the Golden Daughters. The central building of the sprawling temple was the magnificent Hulan's Throne, which towered above the rest and rivaled even the Emperor's own abode in Manusbau for glory. The thin moon rising in the deepening sky looked sallow as she gleamed down upon the marvelous edifice built in her honor. It was a bit sad, Sairu thought as she hurried along her way, climbing the garden paths up to Hulan's Throne.

Something on wings fluttered before her face, startling her as it darted on down the hill. Surprised, Sairu turned to look after it and found her attention suddenly arrested by something she should have passed by without a glance. It seemed to her that the wan moon shone suddenly a little brighter and struck a stone so that it must catch her eye. She looked down into a small garden valley set apart from the rest of the gardens by its unkempt appearance. Weeds grew thick, and trees spread untamed limbs crawling with parasitic vines. No reflecting pool lay in sight to catch the moon's smile as she passed overhead.

Instead, all that lay in the midst of this wreckage were large white stones. Foundation stones, Sairu thought, thickly crusted with black fungus so that she would have missed them had not the moon shone upon them just so and made them shine.

In the shadows of the vine-draped trees, a bird sang suddenly. Its silver voice rose, the sound of moonlight itself.

Sairu was transfixed like a spotted fawn caught suddenly in the hunter's torchlight. She stood thus for no more than a moment, but in that moment felt a sudden rush of timelessness stretching out from those stones below, reaching up to touch her face. She thought she saw a tall building, of humble work compared to the temple yet boasting two great sets of doors swung open, one facing east, the other west. Between them, high in the rafters, hung a lantern filled with light more brilliant than the sun and the moon combined.

For that moment, as the beauty of the songbird's voice washed over her, Sairu thought she heard the glory of eternal music.

Then it was gone.

She stood on the darkened path, breathing in the perfume of the priests' fine garden, black-cherry and golden-pear blossoms in full bloom. Below her lay only an untidy patch of earth and ruts and weeds with a few half-buried stones jutting up from forgotten darkness.

Sairu had been prepared all her life to encounter wickedness. But no one had prepared her for what she had just witnessed, and she could not make it fit within her realm of understanding or expectation. Her brow creasing in a small frown even as her mouth forced a smile, she hastened on her way, determined . . . well, not to forget what she had glimpsed, but merely to think upon it later.

Now she must hurry on and meet her new master.

The Besur, High Priest of the Crown of the Moon, sat in an inner chamber within Hulan's Throne and waited. Patience was, after all, one of the Twelve Mighty Virtues. And should not a high priest be well versed in all virtues, mighty or otherwise?

One nervous finger tapped out the passage of time on the arm of his chair as he tried to remember Brother Yaru's exact words. Did the old fool receive an approval from the Golden Mother? He had implied as much, but Brother Yaru was not as sharp as he had once been. The Besur's finger increased its tempo, and he cursed himself for not sending a younger priest. But then, whom could he trust more than Brother Yaru, simple though the man might be?

"I should have gone myself," he muttered.

His voice caused a slight stirring across the room. The Besur raised his gaze quickly, startled by the movement. She had been so still. So very still. Three days now, and she scarcely did more than breathe on her own. She moved when they moved her, sat where they placed her, ate what they put in her mouth; otherwise she might have been no more alive than a wooden puppet.

But when he spoke, he thought she tilted her head to one side. The jeweled pendants on her headdress swung slightly even now. But her eyes remained closed, her hands quiet in her lap.

It was no use, the Besur thought. They could not wait, not with her in this state. Rumor would spread, if not from the priests themselves then from the temple slaves. And the Besur hated to order deaths, especially when the crime was no greater than a little gossip. No, they must make arrangements quickly, with or without—

A soft knock at the door. It must be Brother Yaru come to explain himself. The Besur glanced again at the still form across the room then hurried to answer the door. Not a task he was used to doing for himself, surrounded as he always was by slaves. But no slave could be permitted this far into Hulan's Throne.

The door whispered in its grooves as he slid it back. The passage beyond the chamber was lit by a single lantern, light enough to tell him that the figure he now faced was not Brother Yaru.

"Who are you?" the Besur demanded. "Do I know you?"

"We haven't met, Honored Besur, no fear," said a bright young voice. The next moment the low hood was thrown back, and the Besur drew himself up in surprise.

"What are you doing here?" he growled. "Women are not permitted within the sanctity of Hulan's Throne!"

"Which seems odd when one recalls that Hulan herself is thought to be female," said the girl with a cheerful grin. Then she looked around the

Besur's ample girth, spied the quiet one seated across the room, and raised a wry eyebrow. "No women at all, Honored Besur?"

"Get out! Get out at once, before I summon the guards!"

"I'll go if you wish it," said she. "But will you look at this first?" With that, she raised her arm and drew back the long sleeve of her garment, revealing her left wrist for the Besur's inspection. He saw, scarred there, the contours of a small carnation.

Sairu had been branded thus the day she entered the Masayi. Her agonized cries at the pain of it had been nothing to her irritation when, days later, she had noticed that the applied burn was crooked. She'd marched straight away to Princess Safiya and demanded it be done over again.

"*A brand cannot be undone,*" Princess Safiya had replied. "*Besides, it is your own fault for flinching from the iron.*"

Shamed, Sairu then looked upon her crooked mark as a badge of weakness rather than the honor it was meant to be. But it had motivated her to excel. To never flinch again.

Crooked or not, the mark was recognized by the Besur. His eyes rounded and filled suddenly with respect as he looked anew at the young woman before him. "Golden Daughter!" he exclaimed and, rather to Sairu's surprise, made a sign of reverence. "I had given up hope of your coming."

"Of course I came, Honored Besur," Sairu replied, grinning still and enjoying herself perhaps more than she ought. She had studied the Besur many times over the years, a man of great dignity bordering on pomposity, who believed in the sacredness of his traditions, if not in his religion. From the time she was a child attending ceremonies and observing fasts, Sairu wondered what use there was in clinging to a faith that even the High Priest himself did not believe.

Thus Sairu had lost her faith. And been left a little hollow without it.

But this did not mean she must lose the purpose for which she'd been trained, honed, and sharpened throughout the years. So she made a returning sign of reverence, adding a deep bow. "May I meet my new master?" she asked.

As soon as she spoke, she realized her error. Rising from her bow, she looked, not at the Besur, but across the room at the young woman sitting so quietly. And she knew immediately that this was to be her charge, her assignment.

A *mistress*, not a master at all! Such a thing was unheard of among the Golden Daughters.

"Allow me to present the lady Hariawan," said the Besur, leading her across the room to stand before the low cushioned chair upon which the young woman sat. A brazier of coal—no doubt hauled up from the mines by little coal-children—burned near her left elbow, casting her face half in warm light, half in deep shadow. Even in that strange glow, Sairu could see that the lady was very beautiful, like a painted statue or one of Empress Timiran's hand-crafted dolls.

Hariawan, Sairu knew, was not the lady's name, not her birth name anyway. It was merely an indication of her heritage. She was from the Hari Tribe of the Awan Clan, selected from among the other girls of her tribe to be the clan's temple tribute. Sairu inwardly shuddered at this. Everyone knew what sort of opulent yet simultaneously wretched lives temple-tribute girls lived. The world beyond Manusbau and the Masayi was full of wickedness, even within the temple walls.

Why then was she called *lady*? And why would she require a Golden Daughter's services?

She's a Dream Walker, Sairu thought, and her heart raced in her breast. She had not realized women were capable of such power.

The Besur bowed before the motionless young woman and spoke to her in a voice of surprising gentleness. "My lady?" he said. "My lady, do you hear me? This is . . . forgive me, Revered Daughter, what is your name?"

Sairu smiled and, rather than answering, stepped before Lady Hariawan herself and went down upon her knees. She took the lady's hands in hers, startled at how cold they were, and gazed up into that immobile face, her eyes narrowing as she studied what she could see of it beneath the heavy shadow.

She saw a burn. A red, ugly mark across Lady Hariawan's right cheek. A burn shaped like a hand.

Would the priests brand a Dream Walker? No, certainly not. Who then?

Who would dare? And, more to the point, who would come close enough to have the opportunity?

The burn looked new, and though it had been treated, must still cause a great deal of pain. Sairu's heart began to race, and her wrist throbbed suddenly with the memory of her own branding. But that had been nothing in comparison: a momentary bite of heat leaving a minute scar. Lady Hariawan's beauty, however incomparable, would be marred forever by that enormous mark.

For the first time in her life, Sairu knew rage. Whoever had dared to harm Lady Hariawan would never have a second chance! She would see to that. She would make him pay.

"My lady," she said, her voice slightly thick in her throat. "My lady, I am Masayi Sairu, Golden Daughter of the Anuk Anwar. If you will have me, I pledge my life to your service and protection. I will guard you with all that is in my being. I will care for your needs, tend your hurts, punish your enemies. If you will have me, I will be more than a slave, better than a sister to you. This I pledge upon my father's name and the name of the Golden Mother."

It was a simple speech, rather different from the one she had been trained to give. For that speech was intended for a husband, to be spoken at the commencement of the false marriage into which every Golden Daughter entered, and was more formal, grand, and full of promises. But it could not be more sincere.

The lady remained still as stone, and the light moved softly across her frozen face.

The Besur cleared his throat. "Lady Hariawan is sick and, for the sake of her health, is to travel from Lunthea Maly. She will go north to Daramuti Temple in the Khir Mountains, to the care of Brother Tenuk, the abbot there. You will accompany her and watch over her in her convalescence."

"I will watch over her for the rest of her life," Sairu said, rising slowly, folding her hands, and addressing herself to the Besur. She was quite short, but Princess Safiya had taught her how to face a man as though she towered over him. "Tell me, Honored Besur, the real reason for her journey to Daramuti."

The Besur did not move or blink for a long, silent moment. At last he said, “I will not. And you will ask no questions. Not of me. Not of Lady Hariawan.”

So that’s how it would be. Well, Sairu did not need to ask questions in order to learn answers. She smiled demurely and inclined her head. “Very well, Honored Besur. But if I may, I do have one unrelated question, if you would be so good as to answer.”

“And that would be?”

“How many of my dogs may I bring with me on this journey?”

The Besur’s well-plucked brows slid down into a puzzled frown. “Dogs? I—I don’t think—”

“As many as you like.”

The jeweled pendants on Lady Hariawan’s headdress caught the brazier’s light and refracted it against the walls in little star-like pinpoints as she raised her burned face, her eyes still closed. “I had dogs as a child. I shall be glad of them.”

“Lady Hariawan!” exclaimed the Besur, flinging himself at her feet. “My lady, you are awake! You are present with us once more?”

But Lady Hariawan did not acknowledge him. Instead, she opened her eyes, which were startlingly deep, dark, and full of secrets. She met Sairu’s curious gaze. “Bring as many dogs as you like,” she said.

“Thank you, my lady,” Sairu replied.

6

SOME HATREDS BURN BRIGHT and hot, flaring up in sudden passion then sinking back like a banked bed of coals to smolder, sometimes for years. It is too easy to forget such hatreds, to believe even that they've gone for good and are no longer a controlling influence.

But no more than a few stokes are needed to send these hatreds raging into full, all-consuming life, taking a heart by surprise. And it is in surprise that sudden decisions are made, changing the course of life and death forever.

Sunan, caught in the grip of surging hate he had believed long dead, moved like the shadow of a storm through the halls of his uncle's house, outwardly silent, even benign, but dragging thunder in his wake. How could it be that all these years later—years of refinement, of learning, of fine-tuned restraint in the pursuit of true high-mindedness—one evening could dash his stoicism to pieces and leave him a callow boy once more, unprepared to combat these emotions?

When he shut his eyes he sat beside his mother at the secondary fire, eating leftovers from Jovann's pot. The night was dark and hot, full of stinging insects, the deep-bellied grumbles of the buffalo, and the murmured conversations of Juong-Khla's tribe, the Tiger People, at their own fires surrounding. Little worlds of light in the darkness of eternity.

But Sunan's world was set apart, if only in his mind. And he watched his brother, Jovann, the second son, born of the second wife, sit at Juong-Khla's right hand, eating the choice cuts of the day's hunt.

"It will destroy you, my son," his mother warned him. "If you do not confront and defeat this hate, it will first transform and then destroy you."

And she would take him by the hand and speak to him of the Pen-Chan practices of meditation and the emptying of emotions to the attainment of harmony. But though her words were fair and wise, Sunan, even now in his memory, could see his own hatred reflected in her eyes.

He slid the door of his private chamber shut behind him and stood rigid in the half-light. The day was nearly done, the day that marked the apex of his shame. And when it ended, what then? What purpose might he strive after now to prove himself, to prove his worth, to create meaning for his life? The stoicism with which he shielded himself shuddered, and he could almost feel the cracks running up and down his spirit, ready to shatter and leave him exposed to all torment.

He took a step into the room. Something crunched beneath his foot. He looked down.

It was the overseer's scroll. The little scroll sealed in gold which had been handed him at the base of the stairs to the Middle Court. How it had come to be on the floor by his door was a mystery swiftly solved. Sunan glanced to his bed where he had tossed the Gruung robe, but it was no longer there. Old Kiut must have spirited it away to be washed or burned; it hardly mattered which.

But the scroll had fallen from the sleeve to wait here for him. He picked it up, turning it between his fingers, mildly curious and glad of a distraction. What was it the Honored Overseer had said?

"Should you choose to read it, you will face another choice: a choice of life or instant death."

Would the overseer be true to his word?

A bitter line marred Sunan's brow, the only outward sign of the loathing within. Oddly enough, not loathing of his brother, though he may not have recognized as much at the time. No, he hated not Jovann but Sunan, his own wretched self. The blood polluting his veins. He had done everything right. Everything. He had fulfilled every task, honored every test, worked himself to the bone. And for what?

"Life or instant death," Sunan whispered, and the gold on the seal seemed to flash with its own inner light before his eyes. "Is there a difference?"

With a reckless sneer, he broke the seal, unrolled the scroll, and read.

His eyes widened.

For a heartbeat he could not move.

Then he whirled around and stared into the face of his death in the form of a man standing behind him, sword upraised.

Sunan didn't scream. He recalled enough of his highly tuned restraint to smother any sound before it burst from his open mouth. But he fell back, tripped over his own feet, and landed flat. He smashed the open scroll in his fist, his other hand upraised, a feeble shield against the weapon suspended in the darkness above his head.

The man spoke. "What is your choice, Kasemsan's kin?"

"D—don't! Don't kill me!" Sunan gasped. If his father could have heard him then, he would have disowned his son for a coward upon the spot. But then, his father had never lain at the feet of a Crouching Shadow.

The ghastly image above him was more real than real, and not until many hours later did Sunan realize that the face he had gazed upon in such terror was an elaborate mask. It was a mask reminiscent of those worn on feast days, depicting the visage of Anwar; save where the masks of Anwar seemed to smile, this was a death's rictus painted black as night. In that moment Sunan could have believed the figure before him was no man at all, but the very incarnation of death.

Although the Mask lowered his sword, something about his stance, the turn of his head, bespoke his eagerness to slay. "So you accept," he said.

"Who are you?"

"I have no time for foolish questions," said the Mask without raising the sword. But he took another step into the room. Sunan tried to scramble back, but his feet caught on the edge of his robe, pinning him in place. "Do you accept the terms, Kasemsan's kin, or would you prefer to die now?"

"I accept!" Sunan cried.

The Mask's sword lashed out. Quick as a darting swallow it struck Sunan upon his upraised hand, neatly slicing one finger. A thin ribbon of red beaded and spilled long before Sunan felt any pain. He stared at the wound as though it were fatal.

"Say it again," said the Mask. "Say it again with blood."

"I—I accept the terms of your proposal," Sunan whispered. "I am—I am at your service."

"Excellent."

With that, the sword vanished and the stranger in the mask crossed his arms, still standing above Sunan. Sunan made no move to rise, though he felt the disgrace of cowering before his enemy. Chhayans did not cower. They died before they bowed their heads. But, with the warmth of his own blood spilling swiftly now down his hand, palm, and wrist, soaking into the sleeve of his robe, Sunan knew that, despite the shame, he was not ready to die.

"Until further command arrives from our Master," the Mask said, "you will remain in this city. Should you attempt to leave, it will be seen as a breaking of your blood oath, and your life is forfeit. To me."

Sunan nodded. "My uncle?" he managed to ask.

"Presumed dead. You must honor his name. You must finish what he began."

"But—but what did he begin?"

The Mask did not respond.

Sunan persisted. "The stories are true? You are an assassin?"

If a mask could sneer without moving a carved muscle, this one became suddenly disdainful. "A mystery such as the Crouching Shadows is not so easily explained."

"Not an assassin then?"

The Mask's clothing was dark and blended into the very air, leaving only the mask itself to catch small highlights. Thus it looked like a disembodied head as it lowered, and Sunan found himself staring through the eyeholes, desperate to catch some glimpse of the wearer beyond, but failing.

"Make no mistake, Kasemsan's kin," said the voice behind the cage of carved teeth, "assassin or not, I will kill you if you betray your oath."

"I won't betray my oath," Sunan said, though the words could scarcely squeeze through the tightness of his throat.

"Excellent," said the Mask again. "And to prove that we are a fair order, I am commanded by our Master to grant you a wish. Tonight I will fulfill the dearest dream of your heart. Tomorrow you will thank me. And you will be glad that the Crouching Shadows have chosen to call you *friend*."

"What wish?" Sunan asked. His finger was beginning to throb. The slice of the sword was so thin and precise, he suspected it had gone to the bone. He felt light-headed, as though he'd taken too much fine wine.

Now the rictus seemed to smile. It was not at all a pleasant smile. "The wish that even now galls your spirit with longing." The Mask bowed gracefully, darkness bending darkness. "Tomorrow you will thank me."

And then Sunan was alone. He sat staring at the place where the Mask had been. Slowly his eyes turned to look at the seeping blood of his wound.

He realized slowly, almost painfully, what the Mask had said.

Suddenly he was on his feet and crying out, "Don't kill him! I beg of you!"

He could not say why, either then or later. After all, he hated Jovann. But he stood now in trembling darkness, his voice fading to nothing. He whispered one last time, "Please. Don't kill him."

He did not know whether or not the Crouching Shadow heard.

7

DAWN HAD NOT YET taken hold of the new day, but the innermost courtyard of the Crown of the Moon was crowded with servants and donkeys and supplies and priests (these last, out of a desperate need to feel important, issuing cross-purposed commands). Lady Hariawan, wrapped in elegant fur-lined robes against the early chill, was seated in an alcove to watch and wait until they were ready to mount her up and send her into exile. Despite the fine cut and cloth, her garments were far humbler than those Sairu had seen her in the night before, and a flat hat with a thickly veiled brim covered her head after the fashion of a pilgrimess.

Sairu, standing beside her chair, sensed a nearly palpable shield hammered out of the silence surrounding her new mistress.

Someone touched her arm. Sairu turned without surprise and smiled at the Besur. She could see by the expression on his face exactly what sort of conversation they were about to have, and she sighed, though the sigh did nothing to taint her smile. Long ago Princess Safiya had warned her and her sisters of the likelihood of these sorts of conversations.

"Dangers abound beyond Lunthea Maly," the Besur said, his voice a whispered hiss.

Sairu fluttered her lashes. "Really?"

She watched the muscles of his throat constrict, watched the twitch of his lower left lid. "Lady Hariawan *must* be protected at all costs," the Besur said, as though she couldn't discern as much for herself. "I wish to the Lordly Sun this journey were not necessary, and only the gravest need would push me to such an extreme. But between Hulan's Throne and Daramuti Temple, any number of perils might set upon you."

"Perils?" Sairu said. "Highway robbers? Hustlers? Cads, perhaps? Pickpockets? Pestilence?" Her brows lifted, her eyes widened. "Toll gates?"

The Besur paled. She could see him churning through a number of calculations, and half expected him to call off the entire journey there and then. No concern of hers if he did! She could protect her lady equally well from within the Crown of the Moon.

But the Besur did not seem to think this a worthy option. He grimaced as though in pain and spoke through his teeth. "I wish you would allow me to send an armed escort. It would be better—"

"If you wanted an armed escort," Sairu interrupted, her voice dripping honey, her face full of simple innocence, "you should have hired a pack of mercenaries rather than a Golden Daughter." Her smile grew. "Reverend Besur, do you not trust me?"

He opened his mouth but had the good sense to close it again.

"An armed escort would draw undue attention to Lady Hariawan's departure. If you want a covert removal to Daramuti, then covert you must be. I will see my mistress safe far better than any number of ruffians you might barter a little coin for. You have my word and the word of the Masayi."

The Besur was silent. Then, in a voice near a snarl, he said, "You have never been outside Manusbau's walls."

It was an accusation, or as close to one as the High Priest dared deliver. And, though she hated to admit it even to herself, Sairu's stomach dropped. Doubt and fear were not permitted into the thoughts of the Golden Daughters, and Sairu could not honestly recall the last time she had doubted herself in any given context. But then, those contexts had all been orchestrated and arranged by Princess Safiya who—no matter how heartless she might seem to an outsider—ultimately desired only the best for the girls in her charge. Thus, no matter what test Sairu had faced, it was always with the knowledge that one who cared for her had arranged it.

But this was no test. Princess Safiya was no longer in charge.

Sairu dropped her gaze demurely, her head bowed, as subservient as any handmaiden of Manusbau. Then her eyes flashed up to meet the Besur's, and he drew back from her renewed smile.

"Reverend Besur," she said, "have you ever found a snake in your bed?"

"What?"

"Found a snake in your bed," she repeated. "Have you ever entered the safety of your chamber, undressed yourself, and slipped beneath your blankets only to feel the brush of dry scales? Then pain. Fire. And, worse than fire, terror rising up inside you, from the pit of you, drowning and choking. And as the pain increases, so does the terror."

"I—Honored Daughter, I don't—"

"And you know it's a test, because everything is a test, and if you fail the test, you die. But this doesn't decrease the terror or the pain, which is now, mere seconds later, so overwhelming that you are certain it cannot get worse. But it can.

"Have you ever thrown back your coverlet and seen the face of evil flicking its tongue at you? The face of your death?"

"Please," the Besur murmured, glancing at Lady Hariawan as though concerned she might overhear, "I would prefer—"

"And though, a moment before, you had thought yourself afraid, suddenly you know that you never knew the meaning of fear until *this* moment. Have you experienced this, Reverend Besur?" She took a step toward him and watched him back away. "Have you taken that snake by the back of its head and crushed its skull on the stones of your floor, beaten it until it went limp in your grasp? Then taken your knife and skinned it then and there, though your hands are shaking and your vision is blurring and each breath is like knives in your lungs? And have you then wrapped the skin of that snake—that very same snake—around your thigh and pressed and pressed and pressed, Reverend Besur, until you see that skin turn green with its own poison drawn from your wound?"

He looked sick now, as green as the poison she described.

Sairu blinked slowly, her eyes twinkling. "I have never stepped beyond Manusbau's walls. But I know how to deal with snakes of all kinds."

Once more the Besur glanced toward Lady Hariawan. When Sairu followed his gaze, she could mark no change in her lady's expression. Why then did she feel as though she could . . . smell? Taste? *Hear* a smile?

Just then a slave from the Masayi entered the courtyard, dragged behind three small lion dogs straining at their leashes. At sight of Sairu—who was their very light, center, and purpose for being—the trio exploded into yipping chorus, nearly pulling the poor slave off his feet. Sairu smiled again, a smile she saved for her little pack, far lovelier than the smiles she turned upon the rest of the world. She knelt to receive kisses and excited paws clawing at her clothes.

That was when Lady Hariawan spoke: "What are their names, please?"

It was the first sound her mistress had made since the night before, when Sairu met her in the inner chamber of Hulan's Throne. Sairu looked up, surprised, but could discern no sign of interest or curiosity. Lady Hariawan's face was as beautiful and tranquil as ever behind its protective veils.

Still, a question was as good as a command. So Sairu, ignoring the Besur (who was expressing in sneers everything he dared not say aloud at the dogs' arrival), presented her pets to her mistress. She bowed and picked up each one in turn, giving its name.

"This is Dumpling. He is pack-alpha. This is Rice Cake, his wife, and this is Sticky Bun, who is not to be trusted."

She didn't know quite what she expected in response. Princess Safiya had taught her early on that even no response is a response. No face is ever truly blank. Except . . .

Except Lady Hariawan's, Anwar blight it!

"I thought there would be more," Lady Hariawan said. "I told you to bring as many as you liked."

"I like to bring no more than these," Sairu replied. "A journey to the mountains is too great for little paws. They must be carried. We could not comfortably accommodate more."

Lady Hariawan made no reply. Nor did she reach out to pet any of the fluffy heads offered her. But when, half an hour later, she was assisted onto the back of a tall, handsome mule, she motioned to the slave holding the dogs' leashes.

"I will carry one," she said.

There was no good in protesting, and Sairu did not bother to try. With reluctance, she took Sticky Bun from the slave and handed him into her mistress's arms. The little dog scrambled and nearly got himself dropped before he finally settled into place. Sairu loaded Dumpling and Rice Cake into baskets hung for that purpose on either side of her own donkey's saddle. But Lady Hariawan did not wish for a basket. She would carry the dog on her own.

So they began their journey, passing first through the long grounds of the Crown of the Moon itself. And before they had even reached the northernmost gate, Sticky Bun, catching a certain scent, let loose a fit of barking. Dumpling and Rice Cake raised an echoing chorus, but they were held in place by the basket lids and could only get their faces out. Sticky Bun, however, leapt from Lady Hariawan's grasp. He landed with a jarring thud all too near the mule's hooves, and Sairu, riding just behind, thought her heart would surely stop.

But Sticky Bun shook himself out and, shattering the morning stillness with his yips, waddled at high speed off into the temple gardens. Sairu slid off her donkey and gave pursuit, shouting, "*Sticky Bun!*" Which is not a good name for shouting if one hopes to maintain any sense of dignity.

She found the dog beneath a spreading cherry tree, leaping and scraping his frantic paws on the trunk. She scooped him up and tucked him under one arm, then peered into the blossom-thick branches above.

A flash of orange slipped out of her vision. Branches stirred and were still. Petals dropped like soft snow upon her face.

"Hush, Sticky Bun!" Sairu snapped, and clamped the yapping dog's muzzle shut with one hand. He continued to squirm in her arms, but she held him tightly pressed to her side and stared up into the shadows of the cherry tree's branches, willing her eyes to see what they could not.

It was no use. The cat was gone. But she knew what she had glimpsed. She knew to be on her guard.

Irked but still smiling, Sairu turned from the tree and hastened back to her waiting donkey and the traveling party. Lady Hariawan watched her approach and, when she was near, held out her arms.

"He's a wicked one, my mistress," Sairu warned. "He will leap again, I fear."

Lady Hariawan said nothing but continued to reach for the dog. Sairu had no choice but to obey and hand Sticky Bun over.

Many pilgrims were to be seen in the crowded streets of Lunthea Maly, all wearing garb similar to Lady Hariawan's, though perhaps not so finely made: a fur-trimmed cloak of black or brown, and the veil-trimmed hat worn by both men and women seeking the holy places of Anwar and Hulan. Most of these pilgrims were not permitted within the grounds of the Crown of the Moon, but numerous shrines surrounded the outer walls, and people would travel many leagues to knock their foreheads against smooth stones and offer prayers to silent figures carved in ivory and jade.

"One million," Sairu whispered, her voice lost in the noise of the street traffic. "One million worshippers." That was the number recorded of those who traveled to Lunthea Maly each year from across the Noorhitam Empire. Some even journeyed from the Outer Islands, many days beyond sight of the Continent, sailing through all weather just to make their reverence outside the walls of the magnificent temple.

It was a good plan, Sairu decided as she turned her head this way and that, counting the number of pilgrims' hats she spied even now. There must be some twenty readily visible, and this was but one street. No one would notice their small company making its way through the twisting crush of city life. They were, to all apparent purposes, but one more pilgrimage returning to faraway lands after a few moments of sacred worship.

Thus Sairu smiled despite the cat, despite the Besur's disbelief, despite her own heart ramming in her throat at the sights, sounds, and smells that beat upon her senses. Sights, sounds, and smells for which she had studied and prepared all her life, but which she had never encountered until now. Look! Was that a merchant of Ipoa Province peddling fine clothes? And there! Was that a blind widow begging alms from those hastening by? And here a thief picking a pocket, and there a lady of fly-by-night virtue wafting her fan, and here an onion merchant, and there a group of scuttling coal children, and there a pompous city chancellor, and there, and there . . .

So much *life!*

Sairu shook herself and focused her gaze upon the figure before her, riding straight and poised on the back of the tall mule. On her right rode a temple slave who had been introduced to Sairu as Tu Syed. On her left rode a much older slave named Tu Domchu. Tu Syed was the leader, Tu Domchu his second, and four more slaves—two riding before Lady Hariawan, two riding behind Sairu—accompanied them as well. Six slaves in total, and no more. Sairu would not hear of a greater company.

She narrowed her eyes, studying what she could of each slave in turn. Tu Syed was a middle-aged man of expensive tastes, considered a figure of some elite status among his brethren. She saw in a glance that he had been born enslaved, but into a good house with all the right advantages. Thus he carried himself with a snobbish air that Sairu did not quite like. By contrast, Tu Domchu slouched in his saddle, spitting between gaps in his teeth and scratching himself vigorously from time to time. He was much older than the other slaves, and Sairu wondered why he should be included in their company at all. He would not have been her first choice.

The other four were less interesting. Loyal, she decided, but not to Lady Hariawan. No, their loyalty was to the temple and to the Besur. Not to their mistress. Certainly not to Sairu. This meant they could be trusted only as far as they could be seen, and no farther.

They'd probably made journeys rather like this in the past. Escorting a temple girl hastened off to the country because of "ill-health." And they would return the girl a year later, all better again, and some family in the country had a new baby to feed, a new pair of hands to raise for work on the farm. This was not a new business to the slaves of the Crown of the Moon.

Sairu shuddered, and her smile slipped for the first time that day. She did not like the slaves thinking such thoughts about her mistress. Whatever else went on within the Crown of the Moon, Lady Hariawan herself was sacred, was pure. One had only to look at her to see as much! She was above such baseness, and no one would dare touch her.

Yet she did bear a hand-shaped burn hidden behind the veils of her pilgrim's hat. It was a great puzzle. But, as with all puzzles, there was a key. And Sairu would work it out in the end.

They journeyed through the city most of that day, their mounts' hooves clopping on stone streets or kicking up dust and debris on unpaved surfaces. The crush of people was immense, and Sairu often found mounted strangers so close to her that she could feel the warmth of their bodies. The sun was setting by the time they reached the outer walls, but the city went on for some while beyond that, stretching out into the surrounding landscape. It was dusk by the time they came to a road that could truly be considered *beyond* the boundaries of Lunthea Maly. And even here small encampments, some grand, some humble, lined the road for miles. Merchant caravans, traveling nobles, country folk seeking a new life in the big city. And everywhere, absolutely everywhere, more pilgrims.

They all had stories. They all had missions. They were all so interesting, and Sairu's heart burst with the wish to know them, to study them, to read their souls in their faces as the Golden Mother had taught her. But no. She was commissioned now. She had but one goal, the all-consuming goal of her life: She must care for her mistress.

Then they came to a place that Sairu had never felt any desire to see, and all other thoughts were driven from her mind.

She felt it long before she saw it—a low cloud of misery spread across the landscape, reaching out as though to catch in its irresistible grasp those who passed by. Of course she had known all along that, taking the northern road out of the city, they must necessarily ride near this place. But somehow she had managed to make herself forget until they were nearly upon it.

Lembu Rana. The Valley of Suffering.

The nearer they came, the more little figures they passed on the road. Little figures wrapped in heavy bandages and rags, supporting themselves on canes or crude crutches made of fallen tree limbs. Many were missing their feet or hands, or even whole arms. They moved with their heads bowed and, at the first sign of someone coming, would dive off the road and crouch trembling in a ditch.

The road wound on, and soon Sairu found that if she looked to her right she could see into a valley with high, naturally hewn walls on all sides, lined with stones to hold back erosion. She stared down at the village huddled below, where the living dead gathered in their misery to eke out a sort of life for themselves. Until their bodies at last betrayed them and they succumbed to their sickness.

Succumbed to leprosy.

Sairu shivered. She felt the unease in Tu Syed, Tu Domchu, and the others as well. One of the young slaves even cursed several times, loud enough that Tu Syed scolded him, and he apologized to the ladies present. Sairu, however, did not blame him. She felt like cursing, herself.

Only Lady Hariawan did not react. Indeed, to all appearances she was entirely unaware of the horror near which they passed.

And soon they passed beyond Lembu Rana and into the farther roads, both the great city and the lepers' village well at their backs. They proceeded at the plodding pace set by Lady Hariawan's mule, their only light the glow of the Lady Moon and her children above. The donkeys began to pull at their bits and reach for scrub to chew, and even the mule put back its ears and began to drag its feet. Still Lady Hariawan did not call a halt.

"She's not going to," Sairu whispered suddenly. She twisted her neck, which crackled with soreness, for she had never ridden so long in one stretch before. But Lady Hariawan would keep on riding, riding, riding until her mule dropped dead . . . or she herself did.

She could not be trusted with any decision-making.

"We'll make camp here," Sairu declared in a loud voice, and the slaves, all of whom had fallen into an uneasy stupor, startled and looked around at her. Who was she, after all, to speak for the mistress? Nothing but a handmaiden!

But Sairu urged her donkey up beside Lady Hariawan's mule. She found Sticky Bun, held gently, fast asleep in the lady's arms. Lady Hariawan herself stared into the space between her mule's ears and did not seem to hear Sairu when she spoke.

"My mistress, you are tired," Sairu insisted, and reached out to touch her arm. "We must rest now."

Sairu's fingers scarcely brushed the heavy wool of the cloak, but Lady Hariawan startled and turned to her with wide, staring eyes, nearly dropping Sticky Bun, who growled and wriggled in protest. Lady Hariawan gazed unseeing at Sairu.

"Please, my mistress," Sairu urged gently, saying again, "you are tired. Let us stop."

Recognition slowly crept into Lady Hariawan's eyes. She nodded slowly but said nothing even as Sairu issued commands to the slaves. Tu Domchu and a younger slave helped their mistress down from the mule and placed her upon some blankets out of the way; she might have been nothing more than a porcelain doll to be dressed, propped up, and ignored. Tu Syed ordered his brethren to build one fire for her and another for themselves a little ways off. Slaves though they were, they were not about to share their meal or fire with a woman, much less with a temple girl and her handmaiden.

Sairu unpacked a large purple eggplant from among their supplies and placed it near the fire to roast. Then she set about erecting a tent and making other small preparations while her dogs milled about her feet and whined piteously for their own supper. All this time, Lady Hariawan sat still as stone and scarcely seemed to see the flames of the campfire under her fixed gaze.

The cloak slipped from her shoulders. Though the evening was cold, she made no move to draw it back into place.

"What a baby you are!" Sairu exclaimed when she found her mistress sitting so exposed, nothing but her light gown to protect her from the night air. "A helpless baby! Did no one teach you even to keep yourself warm?" She wrapped the cloak back in place and, when Lady Hariawan made no move, picked up one of her mistress's hands and made her clutch it at the throat.

"There," Sairu said, and cast an irritable eye over her shoulder at Tu Syed and the others, none of whom had noticed Lady Hariawan's state. A useless lot they were, they and their condescending noses!

Frowning, which felt uncomfortable on her characteristically cheerful face, Sairu pulled the roasted eggplant away from the fire and dug her knife into the top of it, loosening the skin. She worked efficiently, burning her fingers only slightly in the eggplant's hot juices. And she watched her lady across the flames.

Sticky Bun lay at Lady Hariawan's side, hoping for pettings and signs of affection that never came. Yet he remained beside her, though Dumpling and Rice Cake took up their usual positions on either side of Sairu, watching her work with intent eyes, in case the strips of eggplant skin might miraculously transform into beef jerk.

Suddenly Dumpling growled. Sairu glanced at him and saw his head come up, his pushed-in nose begin to twitch. Rice Cake echoed him a moment later, and then Sticky Bun, still pressed to Lady Hariawan's side, followed suit.

It was that cat.

Sairu, her eggplant peeled, sliced it in half and, using the tip of her knife, began to flick the little seeds out of the fleshy center. All the while, her eyes scanned the darkness beyond the firelight. That cat was near, she was certain of it. Whatever and whoever it was, it had followed them from the city, stalking them out here into the night.

The dogs' growling continued. They never forgot a scent. Then they silenced as swiftly as they'd begun, their heads settling down upon their outstretched paws, their plumy tails thumping the ground expectantly.

Sairu pulled a small pot of oil from her supplies and splashed a drop or two over the eggplant pulp. Using a stone, she began grinding and twisting, making a mash that she seasoned with a little salt and other assorted spices. As she ground, her mind worked swiftly, turning over what she knew and what she had yet to find out. None of the dangers the Besur spoke of had given Sairu a moment of concern.

But this cat . . . this cat was a different story.

"Did you really kill the snake?"

Sairu startled, almost failing to recognize the sound of her mistress's voice. "I'm sorry, what did you say?"

"Did you really kill the snake?"

Lady Hariawan's gaze fixed on Sairu's hands as they mashed the eggplant. Sairu did not answer at first, trying to discern what the question might mean. Then she laughed, recalling the story she had told the Besur that morning. "Oh!" she said. "You mean that tale of the snake in my bed? Dear Anwar, no. I'm not so stupid as to get myself bitten, and I have no interest in killing without need."

Lady Hariawan continued to watch the grinding stone, saying nothing. How did she feel, knowing Sairu had intentionally deceived the High Priest? Was she shocked? Angry? Appalled?

Did she feel anything?

The mash complete, Sairu scooped the eggplant into a wooden bowl, sprinkled it with more herbs, added two pieces of flatbread, and handed it to her mistress. Lady Hariawan accepted it but did not eat. She stared at it. As though she stared at the stone-crushed skull of a serpent.

Sticky Bun, sensing an opportunity, put his flat nose up to the bowl, determining whether or not he dared to help himself. Sairu spoke his name sharply, and he backed down, pink tongue lolling, bright gaze fixed. Sairu served her own meal and was well into it before Lady Hariawan spoke again.

"But you do kill?"

Sairu swallowed her mouthful slowly, considering her words. "I can," she said at last. "I have."

"Have you ever killed a man?"

Something in Sairu's gut churned, and she suddenly hadn't much appetite. She lowered her bowl, trusting Dumpling and Rice Cake not to take advantage, and studied her mistress across the fire. Lady Hariawan was still staring unseeing into her own bowl.

"I have never killed a man," Sairu said, a knot forming between her brows. "We make a point not to, generally speaking. We are protectors, not killers."

"But you could kill." Lady Hariawan's face was empty, faraway.

"You needn't worry about that, my mistress," Sairu said. "You needn't worry about anything. I am here, and I will protect you, and no one and nothing will harm you."

"I do not worry," said Lady Hariawan. But she put up a hand to her cheek. One long finger lightly traced the shape of the burn.

Suddenly Lady Hariawan put her bowl down before Sticky Bun and said, "Eat, dog."

Sticky Bun did not wait for a second invitation. He fell to with a will and was soon joined by both Dumpling and Rice Cake, eager to share in such bounty. Sairu stared, surprised. She never spoiled her dogs, never slipped them tidbits, but obliged them to wait until after she had eaten before receiving their own meals. She opened her mouth, wishing to protest but unable to. A lifetime of careful training killed the words on her lips. A Golden Daughter did not contradict her master. Or mistress.

"What a thing it is, this loyalty of theirs. This love," said Lady Hariawan, watching the dogs as they ate. "They would die for you. In time, perhaps they would die for me. We are like gods to them. We control their lives, their deaths. What a thing it is."

Sairu's mouth went dry.

"Would you teach me how to kill?" Lady Hariawan asked suddenly, looking up from the dogs and fixing Sairu with her inscrutable eyes. "I should like to know."

Sairu did not wait to consider her answer. "No, my mistress," she said.

"I thought not." Lady Hariawan shrugged and sank into herself. Her gaze remained upon Sairu for some moments but at last slid back to study the flames. "So I walk helpless among my enemies. But they will fear me in the other place, so long as they do not find me in this."

"*Study each face*," Princess Safiya had told Sairu long ago. "*Read each soul within the eyes, read each heart. People will always tell you something about themselves, some truth behind the words they speak.*"

What was Lady Hariawan saying behind her words?

"You speak of another place, my mistress," Sairu said, her voice gentle, soothing, as though she spoke to a frightened animal. "Do you mean . . . do you mean the Realm of Dreams?"

But it was no use. Lady Hariawan sank back into silence which she did not break for many days.

The cat watched the little campsite, sitting upwind where the dogs could not catch his scent. His ears cupped to catch every word exchanged, then flattened with consternation at what he heard.

Somewhere in the darkness, a day bird sang a song incongruous in the night. The cat turned toward that song, gazing up into the branches of a young pistache tree. He saw the bird alight upon a lower branch, its white breast illuminated by the glow of the moon above.

"She didn't like me," the cat said, speaking in the language of his race. "I thought she'd say, 'Oh, look at the fluffy sweetness!' and fold me into her arms. Instead, she drew a knife on me."

The bird ruffled its wings and tilted its head to one side. A bright eye gazed down at the cat.

"I know, I know," said the cat with an irritable sniff. "I'll do my part; that I promise you. I'll make certain they meet, just so long as you get him well on his way. Can't be two places at once, now can I?"

The bird chirped. Its song held something of a question.

"Of course I trust you," said the cat. With those words, he bowed his head, his chin sinking into the white ruff around his neck. "I trust you, and I will obey. But she might be a little more obliging when all's said and done!"

The bird hopped along the branch of the pistache tree, which swayed delicately, wafting tremulous leaves. Then, with a sudden spreading of its wings, the bird took flight and vanished into the night, following the blue glow of the North Star.

8

HOW SWIFTLY DID THE songbird fly across that night-bound land? It would be impossible to say. No mortal eye could follow its flight. It crossed over farm country, wild country, cities, plains, rivers, and forests in the twinkling of an eye, and not even the Lady Moon in her heavens above could keep her great white gaze fixed upon it. It soared over mountains ancient and asleep, their highest peaks shrouded in snow, their deepest crevices lost in shadows. It followed no road, no guide-posts, no signs, but the shimmering radiance of the North Star seemed to create a path before it, and it flew straight and true, faster than a streak of lightning.

And then a gateway opened in the sky, and it crossed from this world into the Between where the silent Wood stands tall.

The Wood is bigger by far than any mortal mind can comprehend. It is not a world in itself but rather the seat of worlds, containing within its vastness doorways into every realm and demesne, mortal and immortal alike. One would think, upon stepping into the green shadows of its by-ways, that there could be nothing more than the Wood, nothing beyond. Yet this is not true, for beyond its endless borders is an endlessness greater still. Beyond the Wood lies the Dream. And beyond the Dream lies . . .

But these thoughts are not meant for mortal minds to fathom. And even Faerie kings and queens, immortal and beautiful, standing upon the threshold of understanding, turn away at the last for fear of losing their sanity in the burning enormity of all that lies beyond Time, beyond Space. Perhaps not even the Wood itself fully comprehends the great Secrets hinted at in the songs of the Sun, the Moon, and their children.

The Wood is a living presence. But it does not live as a mortal lives, nor does it perceive life as a mortal perceives life. Indeed, were the Wood to turn its enormous collective consciousness (if consciousness it may be called) to consider the plight of mortals, it would scarcely believe such creatures to *live* at all. How could anything so small, so isolated, so trapped in a single, linear stream of Time be said to be alive?

And how could anyone ever care for such a sad collection of beings?

This thought is as incomprehensible to the Wood as, to a Faerie king or queen, is the thought of All That Is Beyond All That Is. So the Wood (if it can be said to think) turns away from such wonderings and, on the whole, ignores mortals unless forced to do otherwise.

Since mortals remain, for the most part, unaware of the Wood's existence, they are never particularly hurt by the snub.

The songbird passed into the Wood, and the Wood trembled at its coming, a tremble not of dread but of pure delight. The Wood knew this bird and what that small, brown, winged body contained within its delicate frame. So the trees themselves bowed and waved and even laughed together as the bird—a thrush, and a handsome representative of its kind—flitted past, darting from shadow to light as quickly as light itself. The thrush sang as it flew, and its voice, like a silver bell, chased darkness into hiding. A path opened up before the thrush's song, leading to a tall, solemn grove that stood rather close to the edge of the Wood, though no end could be seen to the forest green.

A certain tree stood in the center of this grove, a gnarled grandmother of an oak with a twisted base so broad it would take four grown men standing with their arms wrapped around it, fingertip to fingertip, to span its girth. The soft grass growing at its base swelled with the spread of its mighty roots. The Grandmother was too old and too mighty for other, younger trees to dare approach, so the shadowing spread of her branches marked a clear circle all around her. And still, her boughs were too thick to allow so much as a glimpse of sky or sun, so that one standing beneath her must wonder if there were indeed any sky above.

The thrush alighted in the branches of the Grandmother, which spoke a greeting in the language of trees. This language is impossible to translate, but the thrush understood, and it sang an answer which pleased the Grandmother from her leafy crown to the very deepest reaches of her roots. Though there was no wind, her branches moved, groaned, and swayed in a solemn tree-dance, and her leaves whispered a song in response to the thrush's own music.

Their song, combined, reached out from the Between into the mortal world to touch the ears of a young man who sat alone and frustrated in a dark bedchamber.

Jovann sat quite still upon the bed the old servant had made up for him in the guest quarters of Dok-Kasemsan's house. These were fine quarters indeed, hung with elegant wall-hangings, carpeted in woolen hook-rugs dyed in fantastic patterns. The bed itself was a massive structure, larger than the average Khla gurta. Carved posts, painted scarlet, rose up from all four corners, and three sides were closed in with scroll-work screens shaped in a variety of Pen-Chan figures. These figures indicated pleasant dreams, good luck, longevity, and happiness, though Jovann could read none of them. To him they looked strange and possibly unfriendly. The bedding itself was, he suspected, silk. He couldn't say for certain, having never encountered silk before.

He did not like it.

How could a man be expected to sleep in a room so large? Any number of enemies might hide in the shadows beyond the small circle of his lamplight. And yet if an attack were made, there would be little room for maneuvering. No exit either, save through the one door, for there were no windows, only painted hangings made to look like windows, depicting fantastic landscapes from Pen-Chan epics.

A Khla man would never submit to closing his eyes in such a chamber. He would sleep in his own small, secure gurta, his face to the opening, a hidden escape hatch at his back, and his weapon by his hand. That, or he would sleep under the sky with all the world in which to maneuver should need arise.

Jovann considered his Chhayan comrades, all of whom had opted to sleep outside with their buffalo and gurta. The cold did not bother them, nor the hard stones of the courtyard, so unlike the warm, grassy plains of their homelands. Better cold and stones than confinement! How tempted Jovann had been to join them.

But he had seen the sneer on the old servant's face, and his pride had urged him to accept hospitality he did not crave.

After all, if the Chhayan people were to take back their stolen land, they would have to learn to live in houses and palaces. They would have to learn to trade with people whom they had only ever plundered. They would have to learn the arts of politics and subtlety in place of heaving axes and throwing spears. They could not expect to establish a credible hold in this modern world if they clung to their traditional ways.

If they were to succeed in their re-establishment, they would have to lose their hearts.

Jovann frowned, a deep line marring his brow. He sat cross-legged in the center of the bed, facing the opening, a knife across his knee. He had left his bow and sword with his comrades, of course, for it would be the very end of all rudeness to bring such weapons into his host's house, even with the master away. But he did not trust the winding passages of this great structure, which seemed to him like an evil labyrinth. So he had kept his knife hidden in his boot. He held it now like a child clutching at its mother's hand, seeking comfort.

There could be no comfort, ultimately.

My people will never give up the plains, he thought. *So why not let the*

Kitars keep their cursed cities?

This was treasonous thinking. If his father, mighty Juong-Khla, ever knew that his son entertained such thoughts, he would cut him off without hesitation and name some more promising warrior his heir. The Kitars were dogs—No, worse than dogs! They deserved to be run from every shelter across the whole Noorhitam Empire! Better to see their cities burned and the ground on which they stood sown with salt than to let Kitars live on what should be Chhayan land!

The line on Jovann's brow deepened, and he bowed his chin to his chest, closing his eyes. He must not forget to hate his people's enemies. He must not forget the thirst for vengeance that had driven the Chhayan people for the last two hundred years. He must not forget. He must not forgive. He must not . . .

A voice called to him from across leagues unimaginable:

Will you follow me, Jovann?

Suddenly Jovann no longer sat on that barge of a bed in that stifling chamber. His body remained where it sat, cross-legged, a knife on its knee. But his mind soared quite suddenly out of the lamp-lit chamber and into a pure white light. He felt his heart ease, as though he had been liberated from a cage. For he knew where he was bound. He had made this journey many times before.

Will you follow me? the voice called, and it was the voice of silver.

At first, all was white and empty around him. Then Jovann saw two trees standing tall with their branches and roots entwined, forming a gateway. He moved toward this gateway, his mind assuming a shape with which he was familiar: his own body, his own limbs. In this realm he could take any shape or no shape, he knew, for he was outside his body and not limited by its restraints. But he felt more comfortable in a familiar form.

The nearer he drew to the two trees, the more trees he perceived around him. Indeed, he looked ahead into the great Wood, though behind him he still felt only white emptiness. He moved toward the Wood with confidence and stood beneath the two trees, gazing into a clearing in the center of which stood the enormous Grandmother Tree. Beyond the clearing, the Wood went on and on forever, Jovann believed. Forever and forever . . .

Jovann's earliest memory was of the Wood. From the time he was a small boy, scarcely able to walk on his own two legs without the support of his mother's hand, he would hear the voice calling to him from far away. The silver voice that spoke always in song. And he would follow that voice through the white, through the gate, and into this clearing before the Grandmother Tree.

It was all as familiar to him as his mother's face, as his father's gurta, as his own hunting bow.

The Grandmother Tree spoke a greeting in the language of trees, which Jovann did not understand. But Jovann bowed respectfully as he approached, walking in the deep green shadows of her branches. On a high branch sat the songbird, and it too spoke in a language Jovann did not know. But its words, when they struck his ears, shifted and changed and became something he could understand.

"Greetings, Jovann," said the bird.

"Greetings, my Lord," said Jovann. He did not know if the bird was indeed a lord, but it had always seemed to him wisest to address with respect a creature so obviously unlike any he encountered in his own world.

As Jovann drew nearer, the bird fluttered to a lower branch until they could look one another in the eye. "Will you see the future?" the bird asked.

"I will, my Lord," Jovann replied, even as he always did when he came to this place. He stood quite near to the Grandmother now and could count every speckle on the songbird's breast. "I will see what you will show me."

"If you see," sang the bird, "you will become caught up in the course of events. You will not be able to hide."

"I do not wish to hide," Jovann said. "Let me see."

"Look then," said the bird.

And the Grandmother's branches shook as though in a tremendous gale, and gold and green leaves fell down upon Jovann and continued falling in torrent, but never piling up about him, always vanishing before they touched the ground. Jovann stared into the whirl of light and shadow, and he saw . . .

He sees his father, Juong-Khla, and there is fire at his head and he cradles fire in his arms. He rides on a beast that Jovann first takes for a horse but then realizes is the Tiger. Juong-Khla rides this beast, driving it with spurs that bloody its flanks, driving it down a dark, shadow-strewn path, and the only light is the fire he carries.

Before him suddenly appears a man upon a throne, a man Jovann has never before met but whom he recognizes immediately: the Emperor of Noorhitam. The Kitar monster, the Chhayan's great enemy.

And Jovann, in the dream, sees his father hurl the fire in his arms at the Emperor, who screams and bursts into flame.

The leaves ceased to fall. Jovann stood with his shoulders back and his head upraised, gazing into the branches. The songbird, perched upon its branch, sang down to him:

"Did you see, Jovann?"

"I saw," Jovann replied. "But you have shown me this vision before, my Lord, and still it does not take place."

"It is the future sung by the stars according to the Song I have given them," said the bird. "But the Song may yet be sung anew."

Jovann shook his head. "No. No, that cannot be. This future must take place! And I know how it will happen. The fire I see my father bearing is the Long Fire of the Pen-Chans. My brother will give me the secret, and we will use it to kill the emperor."

"The Song," said the songbird, tilting its head to one side and studying Jovann with a single bright eye, "may yet be sung anew."

There was a whir of wings, and Jovann had but one more fleeting glimpse before the humble brown bird vanished, disappearing into the vastness of the Wood. He stood alone with the Grandmother Tree.

"I have seen the future," Jovann said, glaring at the tree. "I have seen it, and it must be as I have seen. It must!"

The Grandmother offered no comment. Her silence struck Jovann as disapproving.

"Anwar blight it," Jovann cursed and turned away from the tree, proceeding back the way he had come, to the twined tree-gate. Beyond the gate he could see more Wood. But once he passed through, the Wood was gone, replaced by the white light. Through this he hastened.

And then he was opening his eyes, seated once more upon the enormous bed in the dark bedchamber of Dok-Kasemsan's house.

Juong-Khla had long ago forbidden Jovann to speak of the Wood and these strange out-of-body experiences. For a time Jovann had wondered if perhaps it were all nothing more than an invention of his imagination, and he even doubted his own sanity. But he did not doubt anymore. He knew the Wood, he knew the songbird, and he knew the Grandmother Tree. He knew the visions he received, and he believed in them as he had never believed in Anwar or Hulan.

He rolled his head from side to side, his body having grown stiff as it sat rigidly awaiting his spirit's return. He wondered how long he had been away. It could have been moments or hours. Time did not seem to matter in the Wood as it did here in his own world.

Something moved.

Jovann raised his head like a wolf on alert, and his grip on his knife tightened. Something had moved in the corner, beyond the lamp. Something large.

Sliding carefully, each movement under his control, Jovann unfolded his body until he stood upon the bed, balanced on the soft cushions. He stepped across to the edge and sprang down to the floor, landing in a crouch. His eyes fixed upon that darkened corner hung with a heavy painted banner of woven bamboo depicting some Pen-Chan artist's idea of heaven, complete with ugly angels. Could it have been the banner itself he had seen wafting in some breeze? But how could there be a breeze in this room without windows?

Jovann crept toward the corner, his teeth bared, his knife at the ready. If anyone stood in that corner, they would find they did not like meeting a Chhayan prince at such close quarters! They would find—

The room went dark.

Jovann inhaled the stink of some fetid sack as it went over his head. He felt it pull tight about his throat, and he tried to cry out but could not. One hand flew up to tear at the sack, the other lashing out with the knife at the coward who stood behind him, the coward who had taken him by surprise! He twisted violently.

Something struck him hard across the temple, and he knew no more.

9

THE DARKNESS WAS ALMOST HEAVY enough to smother the pain of his bleeding wound. But that pain pulsed with a rhythmic promise to continue for hours, even days to come, and could not be long ignored.

Sunan stood, breathing lightly and feeling the warmth of blood trickling down his hand and into his sleeve. His own voice, crying out after the assassin, still rang in his ears. How long he stood there, frozen in place, he could not guess.

Then suddenly he was in motion. He hardly knew what he did, for there was no time to stop and think and reason. All his Pen-Chan training fell away, giving place to Chhayan instinct, and he leapt across his room, flung back the door, and darted into the passage beyond. It was empty. Of course it was. Did he really expect to find the Crouching Shadow simply standing there? The man—if it was a man—had not even exited the room by the door as far as Sunan knew. Perhaps he had simply evaporated into thin air by some unholy means or magic.

It did not matter. Sunan stumbled the first few steps, and then he was running through his uncle's house, down a narrow flight of stairs, and into the guest wing where, he believed, Jovann would have been given a room. Surely he had not gone to bed yet. Surely he had not even left the dining table. Surely the Crouching Shadow had not yet had a chance to fulfill his promise.

But somehow he knew that the mere minutes he had felt passing by since his angry conversation with his brother had turned into hours while he stood frozen in the dark. Time itself had escaped him. He would be too late.

"No!" Sunan growled between his teeth. "It will not be so!" He flung open the door of each room as he came to it. There were three fine chambers reserved for guests of Lord Dok-Kasemsan. The first two were empty. The third, however, Sunan could see had been made up, with a lamp on a carved stand burning low and bedding already disarrayed. But it too was empty.

Sunan stood in the doorway, leaning heavily on the frame, his chest heaving with more fear than exertion. His eyes scanned what could be seen of the room by lamplight.

They lit upon a Chhayan knife lying in the middle of the room. Jovann's knife. Carved with the head of a tiger on its hilt.

"He's dead, then," Sunan whispered. And he believed that his heart stopped.

Was he sad? Did he mourn his brother's end? Was he ashamed? Did he regret the part he had played in this evil event by the secret wishes of his spirit?

No. He was none of those things: not sad, not sorry, not shamed.

With a rush and a roar, mad terror swept over him. He turned and fled the chamber.

Old Kiut stood outside his master's study, wringing his hands and wishing to Anwar's vaulting heavens that Lord Dok-Kasemsan were home. He would never stand for letting his halls be overrun with stinking Chhayan filth. He would never stand for his shifty-eyed, half-Chhayan nephew to go rooting through his documents, his secrets, his labored-after studies.

Were he home, he would order ten lashes for any servant who permitted such atrocities to be perpetrated upon this fine Pen-Chan household.

At this thought Old Kiut wrung his hands again, offering yet another pleading bleat. "Please, please, Master Sunan! Please come out of there and leave your uncle's—Oh! Oh!"

This unhappy moan followed a resounding thud which could only be Kasemsan's massive chest tumbling from its place above the old inlaid armoire and landing with a crack upon the floor. Kasemsan's massive chest which Old Kiut was under strict orders *never* to disturb, not even at the height of spring cleaning. "Oh, great Anwar's chin-hair!"

"Go away, Kiut."

Young Sunan did not sound at all the reserved student Kiut had become grudgingly accustomed to seeing about his master's house. Indeed, he sounded as rough and uncouth as those dreadful Chhayans Kiut had been forced to serve earlier that evening. Kiut saw the lantern light shift beyond the wicker woven wall as Sunan knelt to inspect the chest's overturned contents.

"No, Master Sunan," Kiut persisted. "I cannot sanction you to desecrate your uncle's property! When my Lord Dok-Kasemsan returns—"

"*If* he returns," the voice within snarled. "*If* he returns, I will answer for the consequences." The lantern light flickered, and for a brief, hopeful moment, Kiut thought the lord's young nephew was indeed ready to exit the chamber. But instead the door was drawn aside, and the face that looked out at the old servant was so twisted with sick fear that Kiut could have believed he gazed upon a nightmare and not upon a person at all.

"Go away," Sunan said.

"But Master Sunan—"

"Do I look as though I joke?"

He didn't. Not at all. He looked a man on the verge of breaking something, possibly a neck if it fell under his hand at an untimely moment.

"Um . . . " Kiut bowed and backed away. "May Anwar shine on all your endeavors."

It was a prayer with a double meaning. While on one hand a blessing, it could also mean "Don't you dare get caught in shady business!" Wrapping himself in that prayer, Kiut made his escape, leaving his master's secrets to be rooted through, and may Anwar spare them all!

Sunan drew the door shut again and turned to the tipped-over chest. Documents littered the floor, documents and other small boxes and parcels that contained who-knew-what secrets. He didn't know quite what he was looking for, but he knelt in the mess and dug through, his heart beating in time with his frantically shaking hands. One of his hands moved more stiffly than the other, hastily wrapped up in a thin scarf as it was, to stop the flow of blood.

He came upon a scroll with a broken seal still attached. The seal was melted gold.

The Crouching Shadows. His uncle was one of the Crouching Shadows. The words of the overseer's message burned like fire in Sunan's brain. And it was impossible and horrible, and suddenly made far too much sense to be denied. Uncle Kasemsan, always so dignified, always so refined, always so tranquil. A beautiful man with a melodic voice that chanted the family's evening prayers with a serene rhythm one might expect to hear among the stars themselves.

The last man in the world one would expect to turn a knife upon another living soul, especially not for pay.

Sunan closed his eyes even as his hand closed upon the gold-sealed scroll. He saw the Mask again and heard the voice behind it saying, *"A mystery such as the Crouching Shadows is not so easily explained."*

Maybe his uncle wasn't an assassin. Maybe he was something much worse.

Sunan opened the scroll. A beautiful calligraphy unrolled before his eyes, and he read in the language and letters of the Pen-Chan:

I feel that life is long,
Sorrowful and unbearable
But
I cannot flee away
Since I am not a bird
And I have not the wings

To fly.

A chill like the breath of a dead child ran up his spine. He read the words again, and a third time.

"It's a code," he whispered.

Had he not that very morning finished his final Gruung essay on subterfuge? And one entire section had been devoted to his study of code-writing, both classic examples and modern ideas, mixed with his own faltering theories. He recognized a code when he saw one, and he saw one now, written in his uncle's own hand under the guise of fatalist poetry.

The oil in his lamp sank lower and lower as he sat in the middle of his uncle's chamber floor, studying that document. And while he turned the full force of his mind upon those secretive words and phrases—those cryptic brushstrokes, lines, blots, and sweeps of finest Aja ink—his heart beat faster and faster.

Sunan was a Pen-Chan scholar. He knew how to subvert the weakness of his emotions beneath the iron strength of his intellect. But even so he could feel fear and urgency scraping at the back of his conscience, crying out, *Hurry! Hurry! Hurry before it's too late!*

The night wore on. Sweat dripped the seconds down his forehead with the precision of a water-clock. He blinked now and then, but otherwise might have been a statue, captured in stone forever, studying those lines.

Then, just as the rim of the far horizon beyond Suthinnakor glowed bright with the coming of Anwar and the new day, Sunan drew a long breath and all but collapsed. His hand shook so hard that he nearly dropped the scroll. But it didn't matter.

His uncle's poem had given over its secrets.

Sulfur.

Charcoal.

Saltpeter.

Still shaking, Sunan climbed to his feet and nearly fell again, for his legs were numb. Soon he was grimacing with the pain of returning blood-flow, but he didn't have time for pain. Half-dragging himself across the room, slinking his dead feet behind him, he pulled his uncle's calligraphy box from the armoire and withdrew brushes and parchment. He wrote swiftly, wondering if his mother would even recognize his hand, so furious were the strokes, lacking their usual beauty and precision. He would never have dared write with such ferocity for his Gruung! His sliced finger throbbed beneath its bindings, but he hardly felt it.

At last he sat back and read over what he had put to paper.

Honored Father,

I place in your hands the secret of the Long Fire or, as it is called by my mother's people, "black powder." I would remind you that the Pen-Chans created this blend for medicinal purposes, not for war, and it is said that those who use it to bring death will bring Death upon themselves. But this, you will claim, is naught but Pen-Chan superstition. So I give you warning of my own: Be certain your fuse is long, and shoot your arrow soon upon lighting, or you will lose your face and hands.

I remain respectfully your son,

Juong-Khla Sunan

He could not say why, when he wrote, he referred to "death" the second time as though by name. For some reason, as he formed the letters, his hand seemed to move of its own accord and add the dash that changed the word and altered the meaning, however slightly.

He would have been marked down in his Gruung for such an error. But he would not bother to rewrite the letter now.

Instead, below the rest, he wrote the secret recipe of the black powder. The secret recipe held only by Pen-Chans, discovered by alchemists seeking the secret to eternal life, who instead discovered the secret to new, sudden, and fantastically destructive death.

But the restrained Pen-Chans knew how to hold onto such a secret. How to use it only in greatest need, to inspire fear and protect their small nation. Thus they had rebuffed the forces of Noorhitam and earned the isolated privacy of Nua-Pratut where they could safely pursue their studies and build their brilliant culture. The Pen-Chans knew how to handle a beast such as the black powder. How to use it. How to guard it.

Chhayans, on the other hand . . .

"You are releasing the beast, Sunan," he whispered to himself even as he blew the scroll dry and sealed it with his uncle's stamp.

But perhaps his father would accept this gift in exchange for his own life.

The night had left a new film of undisturbed snow upon the whole of the city, but already the Chhayan buffalo, nervous in their harnesses, had stamped it all into brown muck. The Chhayans stood nervously at the heads of their animals or worked to secure the gurta flaps and test the wheels. But the moment Sunan appeared in the doorway, every one of them turned dark eyes upon him, questions and threats in every face.

Their leader, a large man named Vibul whom Sunan remembered as a lieutenant of sorts in the Khla clan, strode forward to face Sunan. It was strange to gaze upon Vibul's face once more, recalling the old scars, noticing the new. It was an ugly face, full of the Tiger that raged within every Chhayan man, woman, and child.

"Where is Jovann?" Vibul said with no other greeting, not even the salute due the son of his master. His small eyes flashed. "Where is Juong-Khla's heir?"

The words were intended to wound, this naming of the second son as heir. They cut into Sunan's gut, into that place he had long thought suppressed and surmounted. But he would not allow himself to react, no matter how deep the wound.

He held up the scroll he had written. "You will take this to my father," Sunan said, and his voice was deep, his throat thick. "You have journeyed far for this purpose, and I give it to you now."

"Where is Jovann?" Vibul repeated, and took a threatening step closer, his hand moving to a large knife at his side. "He has not been seen since he dined with you. What have you done to him?"

"I have done nothing," Sunan said, still holding out the scroll. "Jovann is where he is. I know nothing more. If you have lost him, then—"

"Lost him?" The knife was out now, held in Vibul's great scarred fist.

The clansman took another threatening step, but Sunan dared not recoil. He quietly reached back to grasp the doorframe, as though to hold himself in place, to face whatever came—even a deathblow—with honor and not the shame of retreat.

"Lost him?" Vibul repeated, bearing down upon him. "We have not lost him! What have you done with him? Where is our young master? Have you dishonored yourself still deeper, Pen-Chan scum? Does the blood of your own brother stain your hands?"

The knife was up now, flashing in Anwar's early light. Sunan paled but refused to break Vibul's gaze. In a voice as calm as he had ever heard Uncle Kasemsan use, he said, "Your accusations are unjust. You dishonor your tongue."

"You? Speak to *me* of dishonor?" Vibul roared like a bull and took one more step.

One last step.

For, the next moment, even as his arm flexed for a killing stroke, he fell flat on his back, thudding thickly into the mud-churned snow. A bright silver dart tipped in black feathers was embedded in his throat.

Vibul gurgled. He tried to speak. One hand, fluttering like a butterfly over a blossom, moved to his neck and touched the black feathers, delicately, making no effort to withdraw the dart. His eyes bulged, and he sought Sunan's face but could not find it in the darkness, the velvety shadow crouching above him, reaching down, overwhelming.

In ten seconds he was dead.

All eyes in the courtyard stared in horror, Sunan's included. But Sunan rallied himself first and called out to another of the Chhayan men. "Come here!" he cried. "Come and take this message."

The Chhayan, his gaze flickering to the still form of Vibul, hastened to Sunan, bowed, and took the scroll. "See that you place it in my father's hands," Sunan said. "See that you do so, or you . . ."

He faltered. After all, what did he know of these new, terrible friends he had somehow made? The Crouching Shadows, men or monsters, who had taken him on his blood oath and now guarded him from unseen places? What did he know of their plans or their purposes?

But he had come too far to back down now.

". . . or you will suffer the same fate as Vibul."

"Yes, Juong-Khla Sunan!" the poor Chhayan stuttered, bowing again and again as he clutched the scroll and backed away. Then he fled back to the gurta and safety among his brethren. Only then did he turn back and cry out in a desperate voice, "What of Jovann? What of the master's son?"

Sunan felt the blood draining from his face, as though the last of his courage drained from his spirit. But he steadied his voice and replied, "He may . . . He may yet join you on the road. Watch for him. But if not, you must bear word of his death to Juong-Khla. That is . . . all."

With those words he fell back into his uncle's house and drew the door shut, dropping the bolt. Jovann was dead. He must be! The Mask had promised him his dearest wish, had it not? And what had he ever wished for more than the death of his father's favorite? The favorite who stole all his hopes, all his chances, stole the love and respect that should have been his! Who wouldn't wish as much? Who wouldn't welcome the fulfillment of a lifetime's desire?

Sunan stood in the darkness of the passage, filled with the sickness of a dream come true.

PART TWO

Hulan

1

THE MONKS OF DARAMUTI assumed that their abbot, Brother Tenuk, was old. Seventy, possibly even eighty years, a venerable age worthy of honor and reverence. His hair was silver, his face lined, his skin white and paper thin. His hands, as they turned to their work of prayer, or blessing, or even the task of weeding the kitchen garden (a task the abbot of Daramuti traditionally took upon himself to prove his great humility among the brethren), shivered like little flowers in a summer gale. Every vein stood out thick and blue. His lips were thin, and his teeth, though all accounted for, were yellow, set in pale, bruise-colored gums.

In truth, he was no more than forty-five.

But he kept this knowledge to himself. If word were to get out that he was half the age expected, he would lose the loyalty of the temple. Abbot or not, they would call him cursed and turn from him in fear.

They would be right to turn away. For he was cursed. And he fully intended to betray them all.

Brother Tenuk walked with a cane, his abbot's hood pulled low over his forehead. This time of year, with the warmth of the summer rising even into these high, cold reaches of the Khir Mountains, Anwar would deign to turn his face and shine on the white stone pathways of Daramuti.

The warmth was welcome. The glare, however, was not, and the abbot gripped his hood with one hand to make certain it shaded his eyes. And he muttered to himself words that none hearing would have expected from a holy servant of Anwar and Hulan.

"Blast you, Lordly Sun, even as you blast us."

No one did hear him, of course. Brother Tenuk was careful to keep his blasphemy to himself. Besides, his voice was so thin and quivery that it took some effort on the part of the temple monks to understand him even when he stood shouting within inches of their faces.

Monks and acolytes bowed and made reverence as their abbot passed. There were no servants or slaves at Daramuti, for each man there considered himself too meek and humble to be served by another. They all worked the grounds; they all maintained the house. They traded a little with the lower villages of the Khir mountains, their gift of writing their most valuable commodity. So they got by. Once in a while the great priests of Lunthea Maly would remember to send a small something to help maintain a remote mountain shrine, but this happened too infrequently to be counted. Some of the young monks grumbled about this forgetfulness on the part of their richer brethren. Brother Tenuk, however, never did.

Sometimes it is good to be forgotten.

Up the stone path Brother Tenuk climbed at his achingly slow pace. It was a long walk to his destination, and some had urged him to make the journey no more, to send others in his place. But years of mountain living had made him much tougher than he looked, and Brother Tenuk was not a man to be swayed from any determined course. Otherwise, he would never have become abbot of Daramuti.

What a relief it was to escape the main hall and some of the more obsequious acolytes now and then. Up here by the dovecote, one mostly dealt with doves. Brother Tenuk liked doves. They were loyal. Furthermore, they were *uncomplicated* in their loyalty. A complicated loyalty, such as that which he commanded at Daramuti, was tenuous. But the doves could always be trusted.

They were rock doves, bred carefully for their pure white plumage. They soothed the nerves with their gentle cooing chorus, and Brother Tenuk liked to think they sounded pleased to see him when he drew near.

"Good morning, my beauties," he said as he approached. He did not open the door to enter the cote itself, for he did not feel it right to invade the doves' privacy unless absolutely necessary. They must raise their young and live their lives free of interference. But he peered into the empty crannies of those doves long gone: the messenger birds with whom he hated to part, but which he was obliged to send every year to Lunthea Maly and the Crown of the Moon. Not that he was given any of their doves in return! Oh, no. The Besur had no interest in *receiving* messages from Daramuti, only in sending them as he saw fit. *If* he saw fit.

Most of the Lunthea Maly doves were never seen again. And the loss of each one left a hole in Brother Tenuk's rather battered heart.

But today, to his surprise, when he peered into what should have been an empty crevice, he saw a bundle of white feathers and a bright, blinking eye.

"Nejla!" he cried, for he knew the names of all his birds, though the other monks couldn't tell them apart. He dropped his cane, dropped his hood, and put both trembling hands in to cup the bird and pull her out. He inspected her little body, checking for signs of harm. Other than travel-wear, however, she was well and whole and beautiful. He clucked and cooed at her. The youngest acolyte of Daramuti—who had received a caning from his abbot just that morning—would not have believed Brother Tenuk capable of such tender sounds.

The abbot's shivering fingers felt the dove's leg. Sure enough, he found wrapped there a small cylinder of parchment tied with string. "What do they want now, Nejla?" Brother Tenuk said, his tone still soft though his brow darkened. He removed the message and, still holding the bird gently in one hand, unrolled the slip of parchment with the other and read:

Envoy coming. Send guide for Khir Road. Three months.

That was all.

"Envoy? Guide?" Brother Tenuk muttered. Disgusted, he dropped the missive, letting it fall to the stones. Why would an envoy journey from Lunthea Maly? Daramuti sent people *to* the great city; they never received people *from* it. It simply wasn't done. And three months? What was that supposed to mean? Send a guide three months from now? Expect a three-month visit?

"And what happened to my other birds?" Brother Tenuk growled. He began stroking Nejla with one quivering finger. And as he stroked her, he thought of her two sisters. He knew that, just to be certain, the Besur would have sent all three birds, hoping one would get through to Daramuti. But where were the other two? Still holding Nejla, still stroking her with his finger, he peered into her sisters' boxes, gently calling their names. They were not to be found.

They had not survived the journey.

Darkness fell upon the abbot's heart. A darkness that had less to do with the birds than he might have realized.

"If you stroke that bird any harder, you risk crushing its skull."

A rush of fear spread from the back of Brother Tenuk's brain, flowing through his spirit and body alike. His hands clenched, and the poor dove struggled and flapped to escape his clutches. To escape him! Her master! Her master who loved her more than anyone else ever could love such a humble creature! How could she betray him with such distrust? For a moment he hated her.

But he knew from whence that hatred came. He knew that if he acted on it—even as his whole heart willed him to—he would regret it in another minute. So he forced himself, by superhuman effort, to let the bird go. She fluttered away into the cote and out of sight.

Brother Tenuk rubbed his hands slowly together, as though he could somehow rub away both the fear and the loathing. Gathering himself with as much dignity as his ravaged body would permit, he turned to face the one who had spoken.

The Dragon smiled at him.

It was not a pleasant smile as smiles go. One cannot expect a dragon to smile pleasantly, even one wearing a form very like a man's, as this

Dragon did. But it was only *like* a man's form, and not a very good likeness at that. He was seven feet tall and more, and frightfully emaciated, skeletal even. Indeed, at first glance one might believe one looked into the face of a living skeleton, so white and thin and strangely elongated was this fantastic figure. On second glance, however, keen eyes would see that the skin was pure white, translucent, and so tightly stretched that the black bone beneath could be seen. As though this form of flesh and blood only just contained the true form, striving to keep the sinister reality from bursting forth.

Yet none of this gave away the Dragon's true nature. He might be merely some ghoul or specter risen up from the grave. No, the truth of his spirit was revealed in the deep sockets of his eyes.

For there burned a fire that could not be suppressed.

When he smiled, he revealed a mouth full of black, sharp teeth, rather too long to fit properly into that jaw. The Dragon, when assuming a guise, couldn't be bothered to concern himself with correct proportions and such nonsense.

"Greetings, Tenuk," he said, and the air shimmered around his mouth.

"Master," said Tenuk. With a sigh and many creakings, he lowered himself to the ground, knocking his forehead against the guano-spattered paving stones. "How may I serve you?"

"Oh please," said the Dragon. "How many times have I told you to call me Brother?"

Many times, Tenuk was sure. But he thought he would rather die than obey. So he merely repeated, "How may I serve you?"

The Dragon moved around Tenuk's prone body, his black cloak sweeping the stones. That cloak shrouded him, from the high collar about his shoulders all the way down to his feet. He kept his arms tucked away inside, and the effect was such that the first time a young Tenuk met the Dragon he had believed a disembodied head floated toward him out of the darkness. He'd been so frightened, he'd aged a good ten years in the space of a single scream.

Now he knew better. And he thought a disembodied head rather less frightening than the reality looming above him.

The Dragon looked over the dovecote, inspecting it with a curious eye.

The doves had gone silent, frozen on their perches as though caught in the sights of a great, wicked hawk. The Dragon sniffed, unimpressed. He turned to look down once more on Brother Tenuk, who was still kneeling, still pressing his forehead to the ground.

"I need you to do something for me. And you must be very cautious how you go about it. You have enjoyed anonymity for years, able to pursue your work unobserved. But now"—and here the Dragon grimaced, showing his fangs—"now one of those thrice-cursed Knights of the Farthest Shore is on his way up to this temple. He'll be watching for any sign of treachery, of that you may be certain."

Was the Dragon afraid? Brother Tenuk lifted his head just enough that he could turn and glimpse the gruesome figure from the tail of his eye. No, he wasn't afraid. Disgusted, perhaps. Or nervous.

"I hate them," said the Dragon, meeting Tenuk's gaze. He smiled again, and his voice was unsettlingly calm. But both venom and flame scored every word. "I hate them so much, those pathetic knights. I wish I could burn them all to little piles of ash. But *He* would notice. And I do not want to draw *His* attention. Not just yet. Soon. Soon . . ."

Brother Tenuk sighed and, after a considering moment, straightened upright. His back protested with sharp cracks, and he could not find the strength to stand. So he remained kneeling, his hands folded in his lap, servile as any new acolyte. "How may I serve you, Master?" he asked again, hoping the Dragon would come to the point and be on his way. It was an unlikely wish. The Dragon had a fondness for talk, particularly if it made those around him uncomfortable.

The Dragon turned from Tenuk and peered into one of the little alcoves where a mother dove sat on her nest. He licked his pale lips slowly with a long red tongue. Then he said, "The company coming from Lunthea Maly brings the Dream Walker. The one we seek."

"Do they?" said Tenuk, suddenly interested despite his fear and revulsion. "The one of whom we've heard tell? The one who can—"

"Yes. The very one." The Dragon put out a hand, reaching into the alcove, but his knuckles were too large to fit. So he stretched out one long, searching finger.

Tenuk struggled up to his feet against all the pains of his aged body. "That's good!" he cried, hoping to distract the Dragon, to draw his attention away from the dove on her nest. "That's very good. At long last, eh? And will you be taking the Dream Walker back with you to Lunthea Maly? Back to my good lord?"

"No," said the Dragon. "I dare not get caught within sniffing distance of this place. Not with that knight on the loose. I've encountered him in the past, and I'm not eager to renew the acquaintance." His tongue flicked out again like a snake's testing the air. "Indeed, you will not see me again for some time. You must discover the identity of the Dream Walker yourself. And when you do, you must invent some pretense to send him on to Lunthea Maly."

"How will I recognize him?"

"That I cannot tell you. But my sources say that your so-called high priest hired a person of some legendary prominence—a Golden Daughter, I believe it is called? Funny title. Have you heard of them?"

"No," Brother Tenuk admitted. "I have not."

"I would imagine they're female. Beyond that, your guess is as good as mine. But this Golden Daughter has been hired by your high priest to protect the Dream Walker. She is coming along with the envoy, and you will, I'm certain, be able to discover her identity. Then it's merely a matter of extrapolation. Whomever she is guarding must be the Dream Walker. Find a good excuse—a careful excuse, for we do not want to draw the attention of your superiors—pack him up, and send him back to Lunthea Maly. Do you understand?"

Brother Tenuk did not answer. He had heard the Dragon's words, but all in a distant, foggy drone. His attention was fixed on the Dragon's hand, slowly sliding out from the dove nest, its long index finger extended.

From the tip of his talon hung the dead body of the little white dove. Her breast was bright crimson with her blood.

Kulap. That was her name. Kulap, who sat upon her first nest. Kulap, whose eggs would now rot away, forgotten and cold.

As he spoke, the Dragon idly twirled the limp form like a child's toy, then lifted it to his face for disinterested inspection. His mouth opened like a cat's as he sniffed, as though to better inhale the scent of death. He repeated his question, "Do you understand?" and turned to Tenuk for an answer. As he did so, he bit off the dove's head.

Tenuk stared, all the color draining from his face. For a long moment he could not speak. Then he said, "You didn't have to kill her."

"What? Oh, this?" The Dragon flicked the headless form from his talon into the grass lining the path. "Well. You didn't have to love her." He wiped his hand on his cloak and fixed Tenuk with one bright red eye. "Do you understand what is required of you, Brother Tenuk? Answer me."

Tenuk nodded. Then, his eyes still fixed on the place where the thick grass bent, he whispered, "Yes, Master. I will find the Dream Walker. I will send him back to Lunthea Maly."

"And you will take care," said the Dragon. "You will not draw the attention of the knight. And you will send a message in advance to your clan lord, alerting him of your success and informing him where he may find the Dream Walker."

Tenuk said nothing.

"Aren't you curious to know how you will send this message to your clan lord?"

"How," said Tenuk in a thin thread of a voice, "will I send this message to my clan lord?"

"Ah! I wondered if you would ask." With that, the Dragon threw his cloak back over his shoulder, revealing his other arm, which had remained hidden until now. And there on his arm, clutching with reptilian claws, was a raven. Its eyes were as red as Kulap's blood, and its feathers might have been dipped in the Midnight of the Black Dogs. It was large even for its kind, and something about it, something about the way it clung to the Dragon's arm, made a man feel that if he closed one eye and squinted, he would look upon a small winged reptile and not a bird at all.

It turned its head to study Tenuk, and its bright eye was intelligent. Sentient, even. It was no mortal bird.

"My servant here will carry your message. When you have sent away the Dream Walker, you may speak your message to him. No need to tie a missive to his leg. Speak your message and turn him loose after sunset. In the meanwhile . . ." The Dragon turned once more to the little nest where Kulap had rested. He bent, sniffing at the opening.

Then he put up his arm and seemed somehow to push the enormous raven inside. The space was much too small and the bird far too big. But sizes did not matter to the Dragon. He simply ignored such mortal laws and so bent them to his will. The bird vanished inside the nest.

"He'll be comfortable," said the Dragon, turning his blackened smile upon Tenuk once more. "Don't bother feeding him. He'll look after himself. There is plenty of good hunting around here." This with a sweep of his arm that indicated the whole of the dovecote.

Tenuk stared at the monster. In his mind's eye he saw the bloodied stump where Kulap's head had been. He bowed. "Very good, Master."

The Dragon folded himself back into his cloak so that only his white face was visible. "Do not fail me, brother," he said. "Do not bring my wrath down upon you."

Suddenly the Dragon was leaning over Tenuk, his burning eyes so close that the abbot could feel blisters forming on his forehead, on his mouth, across his cheeks. But this was nothing to the heat of the Dragon's breath when he spoke, which seared the very hair from Tenuk's head.

"The time is upon us. The Gold Gong is even now prepared. All is made ready! Do not fail me."

The voices of cooing doves fell softly upon Brother Tenuk's ears. He cracked open his eyelids and found that he lay prone upon the white-spattered stones, flat on his face before the dovecote. Had he fainted from the heat of Anwar blazing down upon his head? Had he dreamed that dreadful encounter?

Groaning, Tenuk pulled himself up and slowly, ever so slowly got to his feet. How old he had become! Older even than he had been that morning. He put up a quivering hand and touched his head. All his silvery white hair was gone, leaving him bald save for glaring liver-spots.

Muttering unintelligible curses, he crept to the cote and peered into a certain nest hole. He should see Kulap in there, warming her eggs. Soft little

Kulap, only hatched herself last spring. Gentle little Kulap, cooing her lullabies to her growing young.

Instead, Tenuk saw a red, scale-rimmed eye surrounded by dense black feathers.

"Curse you," Tenuk whispered. But not to the raven, nor even to the Dragon. His hatred had run far too deep to curse either of them. "Curse you for driving me to this!" he snarled.

And, shading his eyes, he glared up into the sky where Anwar and Hulan danced their celestial paces in time to the Song they sang.

2

TU SYED CONSIDERED himself a gentleman. A slave, yes, but a gentleman slave with a certain degree of elegance, a taste for the finer things, and an unswerving devotion to his own dignity.

Which is why he and Tu Domchu huddled close together with their fellow slaves, wide eyes staring at the terrible sight unfolding before them, dreading that they might become the next victims. They watched a man of impressive height and breadth being torn apart, piece by piece, by a slip of a handmaiden.

Tu Syed, as commanded by the Besur, had hired one Master Pirwura to guide them across the treacherous terrain between the rural town of Lestari and the beginning of the road into the Khir Mountains. The wretched handmaiden had been against it from the start.

"It can't be that hard," she'd said. "A few days, and we'll see the mountains for ourselves! We don't need a guide to get there."

Tu Syed had given her his most condescending sneer, not a sneer to be taken lightly. She'd smiled back. How he'd come to *hate* that smile in the last two-and-a-half months! "The Besur wishes us to take no chances. This

Master Pirwura is the most highly recommended guide in the territory. And he says that Chhayan bandits abound in the countryside around here, bandits who, unholy dogs that they are, wouldn't think twice before setting upon a band of Kitar pilgrims. He will give us protection as well as leadership."

Her smile had only grown. "*I'll* protect you, Tu Syed. Don't you trust me?"

But of course he didn't. She couldn't weigh more than six stone dripping wet! What good was she save for feeding and clothing Lady Hariawan and smiling at people in that unsettling manner?

So he'd hired Master Pirwura, and they'd set out across the wide plains country toward the Khir Mountains. Lestari was considered the last mark of civilization in this part of the nation, and Tu Syed didn't wonder. No one but peasant shepherds and cattle-herders lived out here, and it was all too easy to imagine Chhayan nomads shrieking their heathen battle cries and falling with dreadful bloodlust upon a gentleman (a slave, yes, but a *gentleman* slave) such as Tu Syed. It was a good thing they had a hero-adventurer type on hand to keep them safe.

So Tu Syed thought with a certain smug satisfaction when, near the end of their journey, even as the Khir Mountains loomed large above them, and nothing but empty wild land stretched as far as the eye could see on all other sides, they heard the first yodeling shriek. The Chhayan bandits! They were come at last! And sure enough, they appeared the next moment, rising up out of the ground like undead spirits, their horses shaking free the debris of their camouflage, their weapons held high above their heads as they set upon their prey!

And did that tiny little nothing of a handmaiden do *anything?* She just sat there on her donkey, smiling away. Her mistress was no better. Lady Hariawan didn't bother to look up from the pommel of her saddle. At least the dogs had the good grace to bark their heads off, useless creatures though they were.

But Master Pirwura, like a true hero, had shouted orders to the slaves, told them to circle their donkeys and form a wall around their mistress. Then he had set to with a will, his hewing blade flying, his voice bellowing.

How those Chhayans fled at the very sight of him, knowing his reputation as they must! They hardly put up a fight at all! Cowardly, weak-livered dog men.

So Tu Syed had tried a smile of his own the handmaiden's way. But it had clashed against hers, and he looked away again quickly, wondering why he suddenly felt so stupid. After all, hadn't he just been proven right?

Master Pirwura returned from routing the bandits, wiping sweat from his brow and a drop of red blood from his lip. "They'll not trouble innocents in these parts again!" he'd declared. And then he'd said, "I will, of course, require my ten percent extra for defense."

"Naturally, naturally!" Tu Syed had said, bobbing and grinning his gratitude.

They'd continued on their way until, that evening, they'd reached the foothills of the Khir Mountains and the beginning of the long, winding, upward road.

"This is as far as I go," Master Pirwura had said, and asked for his payment. But before Tu Syed could so much as reach for his purse, that sun-blighted handmaiden had urged her donkey forward between the hero and the slave. She dismounted and tilted her head prettily.

"We don't pay cheats," she said. "Certainly not extra."

That's when it began, the exchange that left Tu Syed and his brethren all but clinging to each other in terror as they watched the battle raging between mighty Pirwura and the girl.

A battle that was frighteningly one-sided.

"What a nice-looking son you have," Sairu said in a voice of syrup. "A bit pimply, to be sure, but most boys will grow out of that in time. Not much of a horseman, but he did make a great noise. I'm sure he does you proud."

"What do you mean?" Master Pirwura cried. "I have no son!"

"Nephew then?" the girl suggested. But she shook her head. "No. No, he's your son. The other one was your nephew, and the third and fourth are friends, I would imagine. What percentage do they get of your earnings for these little escapades? Or do they do it just for fun? It must be exciting to play Chhayan bandit and to see all our frightened faces!"

Master Pirwura protested. He blustered. He roared. He threatened.

And then the handmaiden's weapons really came out.

"So your wife left you for another man, did she?"

The look upon the mighty Pirwura's face could have turned the stomach of the most stoic Pen-Chan. He went a shade of green Tu Syed would not have believed humanly possible. His mouth opened, and he seemed to sway where he stood. Then he growled, but with a quaver in his voice: "Where did you hear that?"

"I didn't," Sairu replied. "I read it."

"Read it?"

"In your face, Master Pirwura. Or is that even your name? It means 'The Honored Warrior,' which does seem rather presumptuous for a pig-keeper. Don't try to protest! I figured out your true profession long ago. Pig-keeping has a way of staining the soul, though I mean no insult when I say it. I've met pigs I quite liked. But pig-keeping isn't particularly heroic, and your wife was always ashamed, wasn't she?"

"I—you—Who told you? Who knows?" Pirwura gasped.

"Oh, that's right. You're not from Lestari or this region, are you? No one here knows the truth, because you came from down south, by your accent, possibly as far as Tumbam, though I think I detect a trace of western influence as well, which implies possibly a little Chhayan in your heritage? Oh, those dastardly Chhayans! You know how they wriggle their way into things."

"No!" Pirwura shouted. "I'm not! I'm not anything like that! I am Kitar, full-blooded!"

"I see." Sairu blinked slowly. "It was your wife who was Chhayan. That makes sense, that does. A Chhayan woman wants her man to fight. She wants her man to be a hero. Not a pig-keeper. So you couldn't keep her, not for long. Only long enough to give you that boy of yours.

"But you'll show her. You'll show them all! You'll make a hero of yourself, one way or another, and earn some coin while you're at it. Hahaha!" Here she laughed, but her laugh was far more pitying than her smile, and almost sounded sad. "Poor man! Even *I* know you can never purchase the respect of a Chhayan. You might as well try to catch the wind in a net."

The big man's nostrils flared as he drew a deep breath. His chest, already broad, expanded, and Tu Syed watched his hands clench into massive fists. Oh, Anwar's light! Oh, Hulan's mercy! He'd smash the girl flat as a rice cake!

But in that moment, her three stupid dogs set up their barking. And, though Tu Syed could have sworn they'd been secure in their carrier baskets, they leapt forth suddenly and swarmed Pirwura, biting at his ankles, tearing at his calves. The big man screamed and tried to kick, but the lion dogs were used to dodging kicks from irked Masayi slaves, and they avoided his feet with ease and dove in again with their vicious sharp teeth. At least one landed a solid bite and, though Pirwura was huge and the dog no bigger than a sack of sugar, the man doubled over with pain.

The girl caught him by the arm. She twisted, and he gasped and fell to his knees. "We don't pay cheats," she said again. "Not extra. You take your earned pay and be on your way, pig-keeper."

With a final wrench, she flattened him. Then she let go and backed away carefully, avoiding his grabbing arms with the neatness of a dancer. And then she smiled at him.

That was the end. The final blow. Pale and shaking, Master Pirwura turned to Tu Syed and held out his hand. Afraid to go anywhere near him, Tu Syed tossed him three bright coins as originally agreed upon. No one spoke a word, not until their guide was mounted on his own shaggy pony and well on his way back down the narrow road they had followed.

"Give my best to your son!" Sairu called out to his back.

He made a rude gesture. Then he was gone.

Sairu turned to the servants. They cringed. Every one of them had secrets he did not wish read from his face, certainly not out loud! Though they knew they could gain no help from that quarter, they all lifted pleading eyes to Lady Hariawan, who sat upon her mule, unaware of all that went on around her. Her gaze was fixed upon the dogs milling at Sairu's feet.

Sairu, sensing some distress in her mistress's placid face, picked up Sticky Bun and hastened to the side of the tall mule. "Here, my mistress," she said, holding up the dog.

Lady Hariawan received him into her arms, and he settled down, panting and licking his chops with pleasure at a rending well done. Lady Hariawan remained silent, but she stroked the dog's head with one long finger.

Sairu took hold of the mule's reins and rubbed its broad brown cheek. "Shall we continue?"

The road up into the Khir Mountains was clear this time of year and would be for a few more months. The winter snows were melted, and rushing spring torrents had passed on their way, dragging chunks of the road along with them. It was not a safe way to travel without a guide. The Besur had done everything in his power to impress this truth upon Sairu. "*I will send messages to Daramuti,*" he had promised. "*A guide will come for you. You must await him.*"

But though they made camp and waited that night and well into the next day, no guide appeared.

"We must continue to wait," Tu Syed insisted, nervously watching how the handmaiden's gaze kept turning to the road and following it into the thick trees, then on up to the lofty mountain heights. He half expected her to go plunging in at any moment, and he dreaded what he would have to do then. Because he couldn't, as a gentleman, let a maiden like her go traipsing off into the wild on her own. Or could he?

He twisted his fingers together. "Please, my dear young woman," he said, which was condescending to the extreme, and earned him another of Sairu's smiles. But he soldiered on bravely. "The Besur assures me that slavers use this road to transport their wares across the mountains into Nua-Pratut. Is this not true, Tu Domchu?" He turned to his second for support.

Tu Domchu spat a thin stream from between two teeth. Then he twisted his lips as though limbering them up for better expulsion. Feeling Tu Syed's gaze upon him, he lifted one grey eyebrow and glanced his way. "Yup," he said, and no one could say whether or not he'd heard the question.

With a sigh, Tu Syed addressed himself to Sairu. "You see? The Besur does not want us to risk Lady Hariawan's safety among slavers."

"Just as he did not want us to risk her safety among the Chhayan bandits who abound in the plains behind us?" Sairu said. "How thrilling."

"We daren't make that climb without assistance," Tu Syed insisted, though his voice dropped to a hesitant whisper now. After all, he didn't want to risk the girl suddenly proclaiming all his closest secrets to the company present. Perish the thought! "It would—it would be hazardous to the wellbeing of Lady Hariawan."

This, Tu Syed knew, was his only weapon. But it was a sharp one. In the last months, he had seen how Sairu cared for her mistress with a consideration and concern far beyond that of a normal handmaiden. Which was quite nonsensical, really! Who took *that* much care for a temple girl?

The argument worked, however. Sairu's smile faded, and she turned her attention to Lady Hariawan, who sat by the campfire, staring into it without seeing. Sticky Bun lay belly-up beside her, snoring as he slept, his little paws twitching now and then as he chased invisible prey. Dumpling and Rice Cake piled atop each other nearby, their tawny coats indistinguishable from one another so that they looked like one lumpy, two-headed dog.

Sairu drew a long breath, making certain she inhaled silently so that Tu Syed would not hear and guess at her frustration. After all, they did not know if the messages had gotten through. How many carrier doves could the Besur have from Daramuti, a remote mountain temple? Two, maybe three at most? And what was the likelihood that any had survived the return journey?

She did a quick calculation and frowned at the conclusion she reached. But at the same time, while the "Chhayan bandits" had proved fanciful enough, she knew for certain that slavers did, in fact, use this mountain trail and use it often. She had already spotted signs the others had not even thought to look for. Not least of which was a pair of manacles lying in the brush where they had been tossed from the road. Manacles still wrapped around boney wrists from a pair of severed hands. The flesh on those hands had long since rotted away, leaving only bare bone that stood out to Sairu like a beacon.

Only slavers could be so cruel to their property. She wondered momentarily what had happened to the poor mutilated slave. Had they bound up his wounds and sold him to the mills, where he could pull a chain attached to his waist and shoulders and still earn back whatever the price paid for him? Or did the rest of his remains lie somewhere alongside the road through the Khir Mountains?

She shuddered. So much life, beautiful life, teemed beyond Manusbau's walls. But where there was life, there was death as well.

"We will wait," she said, "We will wait until dawn the day after tomorrow. Then, if no one comes, we will continue."

Tu Syed frowned at her tone of command. After all, who had put her in charge of the decision-making? Nevertheless he bowed, murmured thanks, and backed away, temporarily relieved.

Sairu remained where she stood, hands folded demurely, head tilted, gazing up the road into the forest, into the mountains. Somewhere in those heights nestled Daramuti, the site of Lady Hariawan's rest. If Lady Hariawan could ever truly rest.

Suddenly she saw movement in the brush. Another might have mistaken the flash of red for the coat of a fox gone a-hunting, but Sairu knew better. She had seen that same flash, caught glimpses of that same shadow far too many times in the last few months to doubt what she saw now.

"Dumpling!" she cried.

Instantly her pack alpha was on his feet, disentangling himself from Rice Cake, and running with all the speed of his stubby legs to her side. Rice Cake and Sticky Bun righted themselves with snorts and growls and followed their intrepid leader. All three caught the scent, and Sairu did not need to issue a command. The lion dogs threw themselves into the brush in swift pursuit, following the trail of the cat. Sairu hastened after.

"Where are you going?" Tu Syed called desperately behind her, but she ignored him, disappearing into the thick green of the foothills, climbing and stumbling and hastening as fast as she could, following the barks of her dogs, who followed their enemy.

This time, she told herself, this time they would succeed! Many times in the last few months they had repeated this same chase, but always the demon somehow, even when cornered beyond all hope of escape, disappeared. Once, right before her very eyes. One moment she had looked into that wicked face and those bright golden eyes . . . the next, it was gone.

Devil's work, she knew. Devil's work and devil's luck! But not this time. This time she would catch him.

She was gaining on the dogs now and knew they must have their quarry cornered, possibly treed. With renewed vigor she pushed forward, tripping over low brambles, ignoring how branches cut at her face and arms. One hand plunged into the thick folds of her sleeve and withdrew grasping a bright knife. She was close now. The barks were an uproar of viciousness.

Then suddenly a man's deep voice barked in answer: "Away, you craven, hasty-witted hedge-pigs! Ger-off me, you pribbling, motley-minded wag-tails!"

The lion dogs' barks changed to squeals of dismay.

Sairu felt her heart stop. For a moment she froze where she was. But the next, all three furry bodies barreled past her, tuck-tailed and terrified, but apparently unscathed. Relieved, Sairu's heart thudded back into motion. Then she ground her teeth and hurried on, determined not to lose her prey. For half a second she thought she saw the form and shadow of a man through a curtain of green boughs.

Then she pushed through, stumbled, and found herself looking down into the smug face of an orange cat.

"You!" she cried.

"Hullo," said the cat. "Took you long enough."

3

THE DEMON SAT BENEATH a wild Katuru tree, its heart-shaped leaves casting delicate shadows across his face and body. Little one-winged seed pods fell in twirls from the high branches, and for a moment he looked quite magical and solemn and beautiful.

He purred like the cat who had not only got the cream but also knocked the creamer over, destroying a silk tablecloth in the process.

Sairu took a threatening step but paused even as she adjusted her grip on her dagger. She knew how quickly he could move, how in an instant he could disappear as though he stepped from this world into another in the blink of an eye. But she was done being stalked, and she was determined not to lose him this time. So while longing to lunge at him and stick that fluffy tail on the end of her blade, she kept herself in check.

And she smiled. "Have I kept you waiting?"

"Absolutely," the demon replied. "I've been skulking about, trying to catch your attention for *hours* now, but you were so caught up in your mortal business, you didn't notice." He stood, his tail lashing the air irritably, and took a pace toward her. "But really, setting your dogs on me? Again? After all we've been through?"

"What exactly have we been through?"

"Um, I don't know about you, but I'd count nearly three months of hard travel across wide and wild mortal countryside as rather much."

"We are not traveling companions," said Sairu.

"Speak for yourself."

"One of these days, my dogs will catch you."

"I'd like to see them tr—no. No, I take that back. I've seen them try plenty, thank you, and would prefer if you called them off entirely. Before I'm obliged to do something *drastic*."

Sairu narrowed her eyes. "I've never seen them in such a state. I've never seen them afraid. What did you do to them just now?"

"Wouldn't you like to know?" purred the cat.

"I would," said she, carefully lifting and placing another foot. He was watching her too closely, however, and moved along with every move of hers so that they circled each other at achingly slow speed. The Katuru tree watched and rustled its leaves and dropped more seed pods.

"You'll just have to wonder then," said the devil-cat. "We have more pressing matters to attend to at this moment. For instance, that guide you're waiting for? He's not coming."

Gently Sairu slipped her free hand up into the opposite sleeve, withdrawing another knife from hiding. "Oh, isn't he? How sad. I suppose we'll have to continue on our way without him."

"If you do that, you're sure to make a swift and sorry end," said the devil-cat, his gaze flicking from one knife to the other.

"I know how to handle myself," Sairu said.

The devil-cat laid his ears back, disgusted. "Arrogant miss, aren't you? Don't you hear what I'm telling you? Your guide isn't coming because he *didn't make it*. Your guide who knows this road better than you ever will—though I won't say he knows it well, because no one seems altogether at ease in these mountains. They aren't friendly mountains. Were I in the Between, I wouldn't go anywhere *near* them, and they're bad enough on *this* side, even mostly asleep. You'll need a guide to make it through, but you'll not have this fellow because he was taken by slavers.

Not five miles up the road, in fact."

While the cat talked, Sairu had brought herself very slowly into a partial crouch, preparing for a spring. But she stopped now, and her smile slipped lopsided. "Slavers?"

"Indeed. As nasty a collection of brutes as you ever did see. On their return journey from Nua-Pratut with a couple of leftovers who didn't make the sales. And now they've taken your guide and will try their luck in rural Noorhitam and on to Aja."

The devil-cat sat then and began to groom one white paw as though he hadn't a care in the world, much less an armed threat crouching but a few feet away, ready to attack. He licked five times then chewed at his toes, purring as he did so. When quite through, he placed that paw neatly beside its mate and blinked up at Sairu.

It was like having her own smile turned back upon her. Sairu shuddered and, for the first time in her life, felt sympathy for all those upon whom she'd inflicted that very look.

"Well," said she, "we'll have to rescue him, I suppose."

Much to her surprise, the cat stood up, one forepaw neatly curled in mid-step. "I was hoping you'd say that! Shall we be on our way then?"

Tu Syed's heart leapt with terror at the sudden crashing in the woods off the road. He sprang to his feet, swearing by Anwar and as many of the starry host as he could name.

But it was just the girl returning from her ramble.

"By all the holy lights above us!" Tu Syed exclaimed as she burst into their encampment, her three dogs at her heels. "Where the devil have you been? Lady Hariawan was . . . was . . ."

Tu Syed was a truthful man at heart. He couldn't bring himself to say that Lady Hariawan had been worried. Indeed, Lady Hariawan had been nothing of the sort. She had been practically comatose as always: upright, cross-legged, head bent, and breathing deep the whole time Sairu was gone. Tu Syed and his cohorts had been the worriers. And it was they who felt waves of relief at the handmaiden's return, like a nest full of starlings lifting their beaks to the return of their mother. Tu Syed covered his relief with scowls and bluster. "You have no right to simply—"

"No time! No time!" Sairu gasped as she neared the camp. She scooped up Dumpling and dumped him unceremoniously in the slave's startled arms. "Hold him. Don't let him follow me. The others will obey him, but you've got to keep him with you."

"What?" Tu Syed stammered, his stomach jumping inside with renewed terror. "You can't leave us! The sun will soon set, and then—"

"I'll be back before dawn," Sairu said, casting a quick glance Lady Hariawan's way. But Lady Hariawan still had not moved and made no indication that she would move for many hours yet. Sairu fixed Tu Syed with a stern eye. "Make certain she does not get cold."

Then she ran back toward the forest of the lower foot-hills, her pilgrim's robes flying behind her. Dumpling yipped and wriggled in Tu Syed's arms, but he held the beast tight, and the other two sat whining at his feet. "Where are you going?" he shouted after her retreating back.

Over her shoulder she called, "To find our guide!" and vanished into the greenery.

Sairu pushed her way quickly down the trail she had made for herself, following the broken branches and undergrowth she had bent her first time coming this way. She nearly ran over the demon-cat, who appeared suddenly in her path.

"Are we well rid of the hedge-pigs?" the demon-cat asked, springing out of her way and crouching low, tail lashing.

Sairu did not bother to answer what the cat could clearly see and smell for himself. "Lead on, demon," she said. "But remember, I am not one to be easily fooled, and if this proves a trap, you will regret it."

"Haven't I heard rumor that the young ladies of your order read faces?" said the cat, turning and leading the way into the forest. "Can you not read trustworthiness in my face?"

"I've never before tried to read the face of a cat," Sairu replied.

"A pity. Once you learn to read a cat, no face will be closed to you. Not even the face of that stone-cold mistress you serve."

Sairu, her smiles long gone behind lines of concentration, glared at the furry ear-tufts below her but did not bother to answer. She believed the creature was telling the truth, though she did not believe him trustworthy. But she kept her thoughts to herself and was nearly as silent as the cat himself as she followed him up into the hills. They did not use the road, but she glimpsed it now and then. When she asked the cat why he did not take that way, as it would be easier than navigating the thick forest itself, his hide shivered.

"I don't trust that road," he said. "I don't know it, and I don't like it. Should we succeed in rescuing your guide, I'll walk it then, but not before."

Sairu did not question this. She did not understand it but felt that further questions would only confuse the matter. Better to contemplate the issue at a later, more leisurely moment.

Although cold breezes blew down from the mountain, summer was hot in the plains country, and the heat rose up to follow Sairu even as she followed the cat. She was soon sweating with exertion and even began to miss her grouchy old donkey. Yet a small part of her heart—a part she tried to calm like a silly, giddy child—kept squealing and jumping with joy.

This was *such* a world! Such a wild, wonderful, weird world, so far from all the cultured gardens of Manusbau and the Masayi! Yes, there had been untamed portions within the walls of the Emperor's great palace, places where deer, boar, and even spotted panthers were permitted to wander freely, where the Golden Daughters often met to practice the woodcraft Sairu employed even now, moving through rugged terrain with the same silence as the panthers. But these were all, ultimately, so tended, so nurtured, so cared for, both the grounds and the animals therein, that they could hardly be called *wild* anymore. Not truly wild like this land.

It began to grow dark, darker still because they walked beneath the trees, which effectively blocked out any lingering daylight. The cat progressed at the same pace, but Sairu was obliged to slow and choose her steps carefully. Soon the cat was out of sight.

Sairu stopped. She wasn't afraid, not even while this far out in a territory not her own, filled with threats she could not see. She did not need to see threats to sense them, and she felt herself a match for any one of them. In the first few miles of this venture, she had avoided five poisonous snakes, innumerable poisonous spiders, at least one pitfall, and spotted signs of wildcats and even mountain dogs along the way. As long as she knew what to expect, she did not fear.

She did not fear even when she *didn't* know what to expect. This was the whole purpose of a Golden Daughter.

Still, she was not one for recklessness, so she stopped when the cat disappeared, drew one of her knives, and sniffed the air, seeking a certain scent. If slavers did indeed reside nearby, they would have built a campfire by now. She should smell smoke.

"One thing I've never liked about humans is your tendency to lag behind."

Sairu smiled down at the cat. His eyes shone with unnatural light, like two bright lanterns, and reflected off his white chest and tufty paws. But his orange coat looked blue in the gloom.

"One thing I've never liked about cats is your tendency to look down on everyone." She wrinkled her nose at him. "But then, you're no cat, are you?"

"Why would you say that?"

"I don't believe cats speak in the tongues of men."

"Good," said the cat. "Neither do I."

"Thus I surmise that you're no cat."

"Oh, I'm a cat all right. But who says I'm speaking your tongue?"

"It is a logical assumption. After all, I do not speak cat, and yet I understand you."

At this, the cat twitched an ear, and it struck Sairu as a patronizing sort of ear twitch, which she did not appreciate. "Keep up," he said, and turned once more into the forest, moving slower now so that Sairu had time to feel out her way as she followed him. They had progressed in near-silence for a few minutes when finally Sairu caught the scent of smoke.

Another minute more and they crested the hill and gazed down into a rock-strewn valley through which a stream ran. On the far side of the stream was the campfire surrounded by four, five—no, six figures. And a single sentry on that boulder up above, sitting cross-legged with his head bent. Hardly a worthy lookout. Seven then. Seven total.

And the slaves lay in a pile of limbs, sickness, and despair just beyond the firelight. Sairu couldn't be certain from this distance, but she believed there were five of them.

"Which one is our guide?" she asked the cat.

"How should I know?" the cat replied.

"Because you told me he was captured. You must know which one he is."

"Well, I don't," said the cat. "I never set eyes on the man."

"How did you—"

"I have my sources, all right? Nagging wench!" With this he sat down and set to grooming again, washing his face with delicate care. "You'd best rescue them all. Just to be certain."

"And what will you do?"

He gave her a sideways look. "Probably work on my tail. It's collected a number of burs."

"You're not going to help me?"

Here he smiled his cattish smile at her again, so smug in the glow of his own eyes that it took every ounce of self-control Sairu possessed not to smack him on his pink nose. "Do you *need* my help?"

Sairu vowed to herself then and there that one day she would get the best of this demon. She would turn his own words back on him and leave him speechless even as she now was. One day she would serve him what he served her, and she would enjoy watching him eat it!

But . . . not today.

The slopes down into the rocky valley were scrub-covered, but no trees grew upon them, so cover was sparse. The sun had dropped behind the horizon, leaving only a purple haze low in the sky. Up above, clouds scuttled across the face of Hulan, blocking out the stars for long intervals. Occasionally the blue North Star—*Chiev*, as he was named by the priests—would peer through, as though curious to see what went on in the world of mortals. But his light was not strong enough to reveal Sairu to those below.

Princess Safiya always counseled her girls to act at once when they saw the need, not to plan. "*Begin to act,*" she always said, "*and the plan will come. Wait to act, and the plan will wait as well.*"

It wasn't a mantra suited to every aspect of life, but it suited Sairu rather well, for she hated sitting still. Leaving the cat to his ablutions, she slid carefully down the steep incline, feeling out where she placed her feet so as to make the least noise possible. At first her heart leapt about in her breast with the thrill of danger.

And then, as she drew near and began to read the slavers below her, her heart calmed to a slow, steady pulse. This was her element, and everything inside her went quiet, analytical, precise. No room for fear. No room for anxiety. Room enough for the right amount of nerves to keep her senses keen, but no more.

She read the slavers by the light of their own fire. It was difficult to discern much from their faces, cast into flickering red and black contrasts as they were. But she read enough. She saw how they sat near to each other but not too near, with weapons lying across their knees or beside their legs. They ate simple travelers' fare, watching each other even as they tore into the tough beef jerk and stale flatbread. Each face was uglier than the last, not in feature but in expression. Their eyes were dead inside, but their mouths were alive with malice.

She turned from them to read their slaves and learned more about the slavers in the process. The five wretches sat together in a lump, underfed, hopeless, and weak. And yet they were bound to an unnecessary extreme, heads attached by chains to their wrists, wrists attached by more chains to their ankles. In addition, ropes secured cruel wooden bars behind their backs, over which their elbows were hooked, rendering it impossible to sit comfortably or to sleep.

One more lay facedown, hooked elbows pointed at the sky, trembling with a ravaging fever. Helpless as a sickly lamb, and yet they hobbled him like that!

The sight of that one slave alone told Sairu everything she needed to know about the slavers. They were cowards. She could make use of cowards.

Keeping well out the firelight, she crept along the bank of the stream and crossed over. She considered using stones to avoid wetting her feet, but the chance of slipping in the dark was too great. So she walked in the water, slowly dipping each toe and sinking it beneath the running gurgle until it found secure ground. Not a sound she made could be heard over the voice of the stream itself, but she could hear the slavers' voices as they talked amongst themselves, and she even picked up a few of their names.

Soon, her shoes filled and dripping, she climbed out on the far side. Here she faced a rocky slope so steep that she was obliged to catch hold of the stout-growing scrub to pull herself up. She could not take the easiest route, for that would bring her too close to the sentry's line of vision, which she dared not risk even in the dark. But she was in no hurry, so she climbed slowly, testing her weight on branches and uncertain footholds as she went.

At last she was level with the top of the boulder upon which the sentry sat above his fellows. Scarcely daring to breathe, she navigated a narrow path and, like the shadow of a passing owl, slid onto the boulder and crept across, stepping on the balls of her feet, crouching to support herself with her fingers.

The sentry, oblivious, nodded at his post. But he had not survived all these years in his hateful profession by being stupid. Possessed of a certain animal cunning, he sat upright suddenly, sniffing the air. Something was wrong. Very wrong. Something was—

One knifepoint pressed deep into the flesh of his thick throat, and another touched between his ribs. He gasped, but his survival instinct kicked in, and he made no other sound. If he wasn't dead yet, then whoever was behind him wanted something. He waited.

A voice, so soft it might almost have been a woman's, whispered in his ear. "Call your friend Guntur's name. Call it once. If you say one word more, I will kill you."

For a moment the sentry could not breathe enough to make a sound. Then he called out in a loud but trembling voice, "*Guntur!*" And that was the last he knew until the following morning when he woke with a horrendous headache.

Sairu backed away from the unconscious sentry into the shadows on the far side of the boulder, pressing herself against the steep slope wall. She heard a voice below, "Eh? What's that? Bouru, did you call me?"

When no answer came, there was a murmured conference below. Then Sairu heard the heavy sound of a man climbing the easier trail up to the boulder. Hulan peered out from behind a cloud to reveal Guntur's large shape as he found his balance and made his way across to the sentry's form, which still sat cross-legged in place. "Bouru? What is—"

Then he too went deathly still as he felt the knife at his throat and the other at his rib. Big man that he was, his innards turned to curdled milk, and he whimpered softly then swallowed his voice when the knife pressed deeper.

"Call your friend Kechik. Just the name," hissed a voice in the darkness. "One word more and you die."

"Kechik!" Guntur cried, his voice a thin wail, which was not what Sairu had in mind. Irked, she struck the slaver in that tender place behind the ear, and the bruise stayed with him as a reminder of that night for weeks to come. But he knew no more until late the next day. He sank to his knees and then on to his side.

Sairu peered over the edge of the boulder, using the propped-up form of Bouru as a shield. She saw the next slaver get to his feet, heard him calling, "Guntur? What is it? Bouru?"

It wouldn't work much longer. Possibly this once more, then she'd have to move into the second stage of her plan. As Kechik started toward the wall, Sairu swiftly stripped the first two slavers of their weapons, her mind calmly running through her next three, four, five steps.

But none of them came to pass. For down below, several voices cried out at once: "Great Hulan's eye!"

Sairu felt her heart stop then start again. Afraid of what she might see, she peered around Bouru into the camp below. "Oh, great Hulan's eye!" she breathed in echo of the slavers.

For Lady Hariawan stood just within the circle of firelight.

4

SHE WASN'T WEARING HER cloak, and this little fact filled Sairu with such an unprecedented burst of rage toward Tu Syed that it was just as well the poor man was wringing his hands a good five miles distant, unaware how dearly Sairu wished to throttle him.

The night blew a cold wind through the forest of the foothills, and the rocky valley seemed to gather it up and freeze it cooler still. Lady Hariawan shivered, blinking in the firelight like a new lamb just come into the world. She was very frail and very beautiful to look upon, and not a single man there was unaffected.

This did not stop them from scrambling for their weapons. Once armed, however, they stood staring at the lovely apparition, as mute as she and far more uncertain.

She took a step. They all backed away. Then someone said, "Is it a ghost?"

All of them feared ghosts. All of them had left men and women dead or dying on this same trail. If the dead ever returned for vengeance, none of the slavers would dare beg for mercy.

But another man scoffed at this suggestion. "She's no ghost!" he snarled. Then his voice softened strangely, an appalling sound from his cruel mouth. "She's an angel."

And Sairu knew by the tone of his voice that this man truly believed in angels. That he needed them somehow, as a man needs to know that dawn will follow the desolation of midnight. He needed them to exist so that one such as he, a man as far from an angel as any could become, wouldn't ultimately *matter* that much. He could commit his sins—such minor sins in the grand scheme of the universe—and they didn't really hurt anything, because the angels would work their greater good, and everything would be all right in the end. And they'd forgive him. Of course they'd forgive him. That's what angels were for.

"She's a Dara come down from the heavens," said the slaver whose name was Idrus, the leader of this band.

Sairu clung to the lookout boulder, and her mind screamed at her, *Go! Go! Go! Get down there!* But she couldn't make herself move.

One of the slavers, a thin man with a scar down his face and neck, stepped forward suddenly, nocked an arrow to his bow, and pointed it mere inches from Lady Hariawan's breastbone. Her pilgrim hat was gone, and only her long black hair—caught and snarled during her passage through the forest—veiled her face as she looked down at the bright tip of the arrow.

"Who are you, girl?" the thin slaver demanded. "Who sent you? Was it Nhean the Butcher sent you to spy? To count our numbers?"

"Back away from her, Eyso," Idrus growled. "She isn't the Butcher's pawn. Look at her! She isn't of this world."

Even as he spoke, Lady Hariawan lifted her face. Her hair parted, revealing her lovely features, her liquid eyes, her gentle mouth, her thin brows lightly puckered. She did, indeed, appear angelic.

Save for the red burn across her face, which seemed to writhe in the firelight.

The thin slaver gasped. "She's no angel!" he declared, his hands trembling even as he drew back his arm. "She's a demon sent from hell to—"

He never finished. His scream cut off whatever else he might have said as Idrus's cleaver struck him a death blow from behind. The arrow fell unused at Lady Hariawan's feet.

That scream awoke Sairu, and suddenly she was flinging herself over the edge of the boulder, scrambling for handholds and footholds she did not know were there, falling when she found none, catching herself when possible. She was down to the stream's level in ten beats of her heart, and already another man was dead. Three of the remaining four fixed fury-filled gazes upon Idrus, Lady Hariawan's defender.

"Murderer!" one shouted, nocking his own arrow to the ready. Idrus roared and raised his cleaver, then roared again in agony as the arrow planted in his chest. He fell over backwards, convulsed, and was still.

But Sairu saw none of this. Before the archer could ready a second arrow, she flung herself into him, knocking him over against his two fellows. They turned upon him, terror leaping in their eyes, and one, a little younger than the others, swung the weapon in his hand. He did not kill, but his blow struck home, and the archer fell to his knees, screaming and clutching his shoulder and useless arm.

By then Sairu was across the stream and grabbing Lady Hariawan by her wrist. "Come away! Come away!" she urged breathlessly and tugged her mistress toward the incline and the trees.

But Lady Hariawan seemed to slip like smoke from her grasp. Before Sairu could catch her again, she was kneeling, she was reaching out.

Then she stood, poised, the dead Eyso's bow in her hands, her arm drawing back the string. The bow should have been far, far too heavy for her thin arms to draw, but she bent it with apparent ease.

Sairu, staring at her, thought suddenly, *The Hari Tribe of the Awan Clan. The Emperor's foremost artillery brigade.*

She learned more about her mistress in that moment than she had learned in all the previous weeks.

"I have never killed a man," Lady Hariawan said. Her soft voice filled the whole of the valley, and even the wounded archer swallowed the curses he'd been spitting at the younger slaver and turned to stare at the pale lady. She pointed the arrow-tip first at him, then at the other two, thoughtfully. "I should like to know how," she said.

Something moved inside Sairu. *Don't let her kill. Don't let her!*

With a gasp she threw herself in front of her mistress, her arms wide, her chest open to the arrow. "Please," she gasped, truly frightened for perhaps the first time in her life. "Please, you cannot do this. Put it down. Put it down, my mistress."

"My father slew fifty men in a single day. He was honored among the people."

"But you don't need to kill. You don't have to," Sairu pleaded. She sensed the slavers gathering themselves behind her. She half expected to feel their weapons in her exposed back, but she dared not turn from Lady Hariawan and face them. Her own death was preferable to her mistress's spilling their blood.

"Put it down, I beg of you," she said. Trying to catch Lady Hariawan's gaze was like trying to catch starlight and hold it in her hand. Her mistress's eyes wandered here and there, up to the sky, down to the stream, around in a world no one else saw.

The hand holding the string began to quiver.

Then, with a shudder and a deep, deep sigh, Lady Hariawan lowered her weapon and stood still, her head bent so that her black hair covered her face.

Sairu whirled about in time to see the three slavers tripping and falling over themselves to escape, leaving behind their supplies, leaving behind their bound wares, fleeing into the darkness of the mountain forests.

Trying not to think about what she did, Sairu knelt beside the dead body of Lady Hariawan's erstwhile protector and found on his person a set of keys. Then, hardly knowing how she got there, so steady and dreadful was the pound of blood throbbing in her head, she was kneeling before the five bound slaves, undoing their chains, and sliding the poles out from behind their backs and arms. She only paused when she reached the chains of the largest slave, a huge brute of a man with murder in his eyes. She stared into his face and saw death there. But not her own death.

She saw the death of a wife and of a child. She saw the burning of a village, of lands and of crops. She saw the death of dreams, simple dreams, dreams of life and love and growth, all vanished in fire and hatred.

And she saw the death of the slavers as clear as a bloody dawn.

Sairu undid his bindings and stood back as he shook his wrists and ankles free of the manacles and broke the wood pole. "Your captors flee into the dark," she said. "If you hurry, you will catch them."

The slave said nothing. He brushed past her, knelt at the body of one of the dead, took up a sword with a hewing blade, then vanished. Three more slaves followed after, and Sairu never saw any of them again.

She turned to the last two slaves and focused on the one wearing very tattered and dirty monk's robes. She smiled at him and for once did not receive a cringing response.

"O great daughter of all goodness and grace!" said the monk, whose eyes were so wrinkled as to have almost disappeared, but whose cheeks were as smooth as a child's. "I thought I was bound for the Aja slave markets and a most unholy end! You and your great lady are indeed angels, even as that wicked Idrus declared. You are—"

"We are come from Lunthea Maly, my mistress and I," Sairu said, gently removing the manacles from around his hands. His wrists were raw where the chains had chafed, and one showed signs of a nasty infection developing under the skin. "Are you the guide sent from Daramuti?"

"I am!" he gasped. "How did you know? How did you learn of my unlucky fate? Where—where is the rest of your company? Surely you are not . . ."

But though the monk continued talking at a great rate, Sairu heard no more. For Lady Hariawan approached, moving unsteadily, her hands extended and shaking. Her gaze, more bright and aware than Sairu had ever before seen it, fixed upon the slave lying in the dirt, the one wracked with fever.

"Don't touch him," Sairu warned, but too late. Lady Hariawan knelt and caught the slave by the back of his shoulders. Tatters of what might have been a shirt were mostly torn away, revealing welts and bloody flesh beneath. Whoever this man was, he'd been a nuisance to his masters, an unwilling product in their line. And he bore the many marks of his opposition. Some of the places where the slavers' whips had lashed showed signs of infection far more advanced than the tender places on the monk's bony wrists.

Sairu shuddered at the sight. "Please, my mistress," she pleaded. "Don't touch him. You may do him more harm."

"Unbind him," Lady Hariawan said, not letting go. Sairu obeyed, sliding the pole out from behind his arms so that he might collapse more completely upon the ground. She thought by the sound of his breath that he might be awake, and she pitied him. In that state of agony, he had probably not slept for some while.

The chains fell away with thick-sounding clinks. Lady Hariawan touched the back of the slave's head, putting her fingers into the mats of dirt and blood. Sairu winced again and wished she could draw her mistress away.

Suddenly Lady Hariawan turned the slave over, rolling him so that he rested in her lap. Sairu's eyes widened in surprise. She hadn't expected the fevered slave to be quite so well-made and fine-featured.

"All right, put him down," Sairu said sternly. "He's getting blood on your garments. Please put him down, and I'll see what I can do for him."

Lady Hariawan cradled him like a baby, one arm supporting his neck and shoulders, the other wrapped along his body and arm. He was heavy, but she held firm and rocked to and fro, gazing into his face.

"I heard you," she said. "I heard you calling. I came as fast as I could."

"I didn't call you," Sairu said, then frowned. Lady Hariawan had not been speaking to her.

The slave groaned and his eyelids fluttered. Slowly, as though it pained him, he opened his eyes and gazed up into Lady Hariawan's beautiful, serene face. He opened his mouth. His throat constricted in an effort to speak, and one hand even lifted, hesitantly, as though he sought to touch her cheek.

Then, with a deep sigh, he sank back into the fevered stupor that was not sleep, that was nothing like sleep, but that was hardly wakeful either.

Lady Hariawan's eyes flashed suddenly to Sairu's face. In that moment she looked almost . . . normal. Like a lovely palace princess giving orders to her slaves and expecting immediate gratification of every whim.

"You will take him," she said to Sairu. "You will heal him. And he will come with us."

"Yes, my mistress," Sairu whispered.

5

SAIRU TOOK THE ROAD back to where Tu Syed and the others waited. Had she tried to return through the forest in the dark, she was fairly certain she would have lost herself rather miserably. How had Lady Hariawan managed it, following without Sairu's knowledge, without a guide? It made no sense from any angle she viewed it. This was another puzzle she would understand in time, but for now she must focus on the road, avoid the pitfalls she could just discern by Chiev's blue light, and move as fast as possible.

Of the cat she saw no sign.

She shivered as she ran, despite the sweat gathering on her brow and the pound of her heart. Deep inside, beneath the action and the need for decision-making, a small, central piece of Sairu was very quiet and very still.

She was no more than a mile from where she'd left Tu Syed and the others when she heard herself whispering, "It leaves a stain."

The Golden Mother had not warned her. Not of this feeling, not of this sensation. Perhaps she did not know it herself, though Sairu doubted as much. Princess Safiya knew everything, or as close to everything as a mortal under Hulan's eye could know. If she had not experienced something for herself, she would have read the experience in another's face, studied it, pulled it to pieces, and understood it with all the acumen of a Pen-Chan man of science dissecting a dog to understand its inner workings.

But knowing the layout of organs and the function of circulatory systems is not the same as truly *knowing* a dog. No more, Sairu suspected, did Princess Safiya truly *know* this feeling.

"It leaves a stain," Sairu repeated. "One cannot encounter death and walk away unstained."

She found herself thinking suddenly of the first death she had caused. Of the young panther that—all according to a pre-arranged plan, no doubt—set upon her in the overgrown grounds of Manusbau. She had fended it off and successfully brought it to ground. In the end it lay broken at her feet.

But in her memory it was not the panther lying before her, nor was it panther blood on her hands. It was the blood of Idrus the slaver and his men.

Princess Safiya had never warned her. For the first time in her life Sairu resented the Golden Mother.

She found Tu Syed and his brethren where she had left them, sitting in a huddled circle, their eyes wide with terror of the night around them. They startled and a few screamed when the three dogs abruptly started barking and raced into the night beyond the firelight. Sairu called out, "Dumpling! Rice Cake! Sticky Bun!" and the slaves, hearing her voice, relaxed into quivering puddles of nerves.

"Lady Hariawan! Lady Hariawan!" Tu Syed exclaimed, blindly stumbling toward Sairu in the dark. He couldn't find the breath to say more and was probably just as happy not to see the smile Sairu fixed upon him.

"My mistress is safe," Sairu assured him, which wasn't exactly a lie, at least, not so far as she knew. She had last seen Lady Hariawan sitting with the injured slave in her arms while the monk guide bowed repeatedly and assured Sairu that he would protect them all until her return.

There was no other choice. Lady Hariawan would not leave the valley without the strange slave, and he was too heavy to be carried by even the three of them combined, should such a thing be possible. The only way was to bring the donkeys and the big, stolid mule.

"Pack up," Sairu commanded Tu Syed; and none of the slaves, however much they might resent being ordered about by a girl, dared question or complain. "We must hurry."

She found sturdy branches, wrapped them in oiled cloth, and lit a few torches at the fire before kicking dirt over the embers and spreading the coals. Three of the slaves carried the torches, which made some of the donkeys nervous. But the end of the world itself could not perturb Lady Hariawan's mule, and the donkeys all looked to him as their leader. So when he, led by Sairu and loaded down with the baskets containing her three dogs, followed her and the torches into the night, the donkeys fell into place behind.

Tu Syed asked questions. He asked many, many questions. Finally, Sairu silenced him with a smile and a demure question of her own: "Where is Lady Hariawan's cloak?"

At that, Tu Syed bowed away, retreated to the back of the line, and said no more. None of the others dared come near her smile.

The wounded slave could not sit on the mule's broad back. Sairu saw this even before the slaves attempted to heave him into the saddle, and she stopped them before they caused the poor man further agony. He whimpered and pleaded, speaking just enough for her to discern his Chhayan accent and dialect, but not his words.

"Put him down," she commanded, and the temple slaves obeyed at once. Their gazes kept turning to the dead bodies of the slavers lying where they had fallen nearby. They knew such destruction could not be Lady Hariawan's doing, nor that of the little Daramuti monk, who kept bobbing and grinning and offering various blessings of his order.

And they looked upon their mistress's handmaiden with more fear than ever.

"You. Help me," Sairu commanded Tu Domchu, and he, after spitting a brown stream out the side of his mouth, ambled after her into the forest, carrying a hatchet across his shoulders. At her command, he hewed down two stout saplings. The slender trunks bent and gave under pressure but did not break. They would do. For a short distance they would do.

Sairu lashed them together to form an angle. Between the poles she strung more rope and fixed her own cloak, Tu Domchu's, and that of another slave to fashion a rude sort of sling.

"Steady the mule," she ordered Tu Syed, who obediently held Lady Hariawan's mule by the head. Then, with her dogs milling about her feet, offering snuffles and snorts of help, she affixed the narrow end of the triangle over the mule's back so that the pole ends dragged out behind it with the sling strung between them.

"Will it work?" Tu Syed asked breathlessly even as two of his brethren loaded the fevered slave into the sling and secured him with more ropes.

"Better than leaving him here to die," Sairu replied. But she glanced toward her mistress as she spoke, her eyes narrowed and searching.

Lady Hariawan stood off to one side. The pale light of coming dawn illuminated her face, revealing the return of her statue-like stillness. Her gaze was dull, not so much faraway as empty. She seemed unaware of the slave now that he was out of her arms.

"Come, my mistress," Sairu said gently, approaching Lady Hariawan and taking her by the hand. "You'll ride my donkey now. We'll be there soon."

"Ah," said Lady Hariawan, slowly turning her liquid eyes to Sairu and blinking slowly. "Ah. Ah, ah."

Perhaps she was trying to speak. But Sairu hadn't the patience to try to discern her words. She firmly propelled her lady to the waiting donkey, helped her to mount, placed the ever-ready Sticky Bun in her arms, then took her own place at the mule's head.

"Now," she said, turning to their guide. "Take us to Daramuti."

The wood thrush called across the boundless:

Won't you follow me, Jovann?

Gladly! Oh, how gladly he would follow! Anything to step out of this cage of pain in which he existed!

So Jovann slipped into the white and, pursuing the call of the wood thrush, stepped across emptiness and onward. He saw the arching branches of two tall trees, saw the gate they formed. Beyond stood the Grandmother Tree and the circle of forest he had seen so many times before.

He escaped to it now, his mind racing from his body, out of his own world and into the Between. He passed through the tree gate, and now there was no white emptiness behind him. Only Wood before, behind, and on all sides, extending in green shelter forever.

Jovann drew a deep breath and let his mind assume the shape of a body; his own body, but not as he had left it. Here, he could be whole again. His back was not scored with the fire of whips and rods. Here his blood did not pump infection through every vein, leaving him crippled in agony. He breathed deep of the calm Wood, of its agelessness. The Grandmother creaked enormous branches in welcome.

And the wood thrush, singing sweetly, flew down to the ground at Jovann's feet.

"Welcome, Jovann," said the bird.

"Don't send me back," said Jovann. He knelt so that he could better meet the bird's gaze. It was an intelligent gaze, brilliant even, and not one Jovann could fully understand. "Please, my Lord," he said, once more addressing the bird in the most respectful terms he knew, "let me stay here. Let me stay here forever. I do not want to return."

"It is not for you to spend eternity in the Between," said the bird. "You must face your pain. You must face your future."

"What future?" Jovann demanded. "I will surely die back there. I can feel death creeping up on me like a stalking panther." His face twisted with anger. "Sunan did this to me. Sunan has always hated me, though I pretended otherwise. It was he who sold me to those slavers!"

"Hatred of Sunan will not heal your hurts," said the bird. "Hatred will only cause them to fester."

It spread its wings then and flew up into the Grandmother Tree's branches. Jovann, startled at this sudden movement, leapt to his feet and hastened after, standing at the base of the Grandmother's massive trunk, staring up into the leaves. He saw a flutter and a flash of white, and he knew the bird was still near.

"Please!" he cried after it. "I have seen what the future holds. You have shown me the fire my father will wield. You have shown me an image of myself standing above the emperor, my enemy. But how can this come to pass? I have failed to bring Father the secret of Long Fire. And how can I, a slave, ever stand before an emperor?"

"These are questions to which you will never find answers," the bird replied, "so long as you remain in hiding here. You must return, Jovann. Return and trust me."

With that, the bird took flight again and vanished beyond the circle of trees. Jovann, desperate, ran after it but stopped on the edge of the Grandmother Tree's clearing. He had never ventured beyond into the shadows of the endless Wood. He did not know what he would find and, though he hated to admit it even to himself, he was afraid. He stood now, his fists clenched, his jaw set, staring into the darkness as though he could somehow force himself to see the bird. As though he could somehow draw the bird back by his own will.

"Please!" he whispered. And louder he cried, "Come back! Come back to me! Where are you? Why have you left me here?"

He realized to his horror that he was weeping. The men of the Khla clan did not weep! Hastily he dashed his hand across his face, cursing harshly. He cursed himself first, then Sunan, but he felt no better for the cursing. And the tears welled up again, infuriating him still more.

He turned away from the Wood and moved back to the center of the clearing where the Grandmother stood. He did not know what he would do. He could not bear to return to his own body yet. Taking a seat amongst the Grandmother's roots, he leaned his back against the trunk and stared up into the green-leaf canopy above. "Why have you left me here?" he whispered.

Then, suddenly, a voice he had never heard before spoke.

"I heard you. I heard you calling. I came as fast as I could."

Jovann was on his feet in an instant. The trunk of the Grandmother Tree was so huge, he could not see who stood on the other side. And there shouldn't be anyone! This was his world! This was his secret place hidden within the depths of his mind! No one, *no one* should be able to enter here without his invitation, without his knowledge!

His heart in his throat, Jovann cried out in an angry voice, "Who are you? Who is that speaking?"

And someone stepped out from behind the Grandmother Tree. Someone more beautiful than Jovann had ever dared to dream.

She did not speak. She did not need to. Jovann, at first sight of her, felt that his heart was no longer his own.

"Who are you?" he gasped.

Slowly she raised a finger to her lips. "Hush," she whispered, and her voice was like the shush of forest leaves under a gentle rain. "Hush. No names. Names are not safe."

Jovann stared at her. Then he took a step, his hands outstretched. "How did you come here? How did you find me?"

She did not seem to move, but he could not reach her, could draw no closer to her. She stood beyond his reach. And she said, "No questions either. Your waking body is sick and must heal."

With that she turned. He realized with a start of horror that she was walking into the Wood beyond the Grandmother's sheltering reach. "Wait!" he cried. "Where are you going?"

She paused on the edge of the clearing and looked back at him once more. "I have never been able to reach this Wood. Never before now. You led me here. I will find you again. Wait for me."

"I'll wait," he promised. "I'll wait forever. But please tell me your name!"

She shook her head. Then she stepped into the trees and was gone.

"It takes me three days," their guide, who introduced himself as Brother Nicho, informed Sairu as they began their ascent of the mountain trail. Morning mist rolled down from the higher slopes, and the going was treacherous from the beginning, even in the lower reaches. "I move swiftly on my own. But all of you and this sick man . . ." Brother Nicho clucked and shook his head. "It will take us five days and more."

"No. Not five days," Sairu said. "We'll make it in three."

Brother Nicho bowed and bobbed and murmured, "As you wish." Sairu could see that he did not believe her, that he thought it only a matter of time before this little, unknowing girl learned the hard truth.

But he hadn't reckoned on Sairu's smile. Her smile, which encouraged obedience, which pushed and prodded and motivated lagging feet. Exhausted though they all were from a sleepless night, they continued on and on until the sun was quite high and Sairu permitted them an hour's rest. Then she urged them to their feet, and on into the mountains they climbed. The pace seemed to her unbearably slow. She could not ride but led the mule all the long way, afraid to mount for fear she might fail to see any ruts in the road and accidentally ride over them, which would be disastrous. So far, her sapling-and-sling rig had held together even over the rougher terrain. But she scarcely trusted it and was careful to lead the mule around more difficult passes. When worse came to worst, she made the temple slaves carry the poor stranger for short stretches. But this seemed to cause him more pain even than the jostling he experienced in the sling.

He looked sicker than ever as the sun set. His skin, which was tanned and roughened from years of outdoor living, now wore a sickly sheen, grey and unnatural. Though Sairu ground her teeth, wishing to push her little crew onward even into the darkening evening, she gave the order to rest. She needed to check the injured man's wounds.

Brother Nicho led them to a place where the road was especially broad, though a steep drop on one side plunged down to a forest far below. It was a safe enough place to pitch their tents, however, and soon the temple slaves had several campfires built and humble meals stewing (of which Brother Nicho took part with great smacking of his lips).

Sairu erected Lady Hariawan's shelter as always, and after she placed her mistress safely inside and shoved a wafer or two into her hands, she made Tu Syed and Tu Domchu help her carry the injured man inside as well. Then she dismissed them, lit a lamp, and turned to work on the slave's back.

His wounds were raw and red with fever and infection. Pus had built up under the skin in many places. She sterilized a knife over the flickering flame of her lamp, gliding the blade back and forth through the fire. Then she slid it under the pale skin and released the infected matter.

All this she did without a smile. All this she did with her mind firmly locked against the images of Idrus and his slain companions. But she could feel them, the ghosts of them, pounding at the locks; and she knew that when her work was done she would see their dead faces, and she would sleep little that night.

The poor man moaned, the side of his face pressed into the woven mat beneath him, and his eyelids twitched. He neither slept nor wakened but hovered between the two states. Sairu bandaged his wounds. She lacked the proper herbs to make a salve, but she washed his back as gently as she could, cringing at the sounds he made, then used clean cloths to bind it all. They must reach Daramuti in two more days if there was to be any hope for him.

She dared not roll him over but left him lying on his stomach. It was difficult to read anything of him from the side of his face, twisted as it was in pain. Princess Safiya would find it sufficient, but Sairu struggled.

"He's no peasant, no servant," she whispered as she looked at the line of his cheek. His lips curled back, revealing strong teeth. Whoever he was, he ate the choice cuts from among his people. A Chhayan nomad for certain, but a clan leader's son, she thought. A prince of his kind. How could he have fallen afoul of slavers so very far from Chhayan territory?

He moaned again, and the sound cut her to the heart.

"He longs to Walk," said Lady Hariawan.

Sairu looked up. Lady Hariawan sat where she had been placed, still holding her uneaten wafers. The flickering light of the lamp played gently on her face save across the hand-shaped burn, which looked alive and full of pain. But her features were as quiet as ever, her eyes watching Sairu's every move. "He longs to escape the pain. But he must not Walk. Not yet."

"What do you mean, my mistress?" Sairu asked. "He's not going anywhere. He is too weak even to stand."

He moaned again. Lady Hariawan's eyes flashed. "Help him," she said. "Help him with the pain."

The words were as good as a command. Sairu turned back to her patient, momentarily at a loss. She didn't like the feeling. She was a Golden Daughter. She always knew what to do, when to do it, and how. But here on this dark mountainside, kneeling before such agony, she felt more lost than when the cat had left her in the forest the night before.

She put her hands on the back of the slave's head. His hair was dirty and matted with blood, but she did not pull away. She closed her eyes and murmured. "The pain is here. In your head. The pain is here. Draw it down."

She did not know if he heard her, but somehow she thought he did, through the roaring of the fever.

"Draw it down, draw it down," she said, and moved her hands down to the back of his neck. She felt his body shudder under the movement. "The pain is here beneath my fingers. Draw it down. Draw it down."

She moved her hands, one onto each of his shoulders, still whispering, "The pain is here. Feel it here. Draw it down, draw it down." And so she slid her hands down his arms to his elbows, which lay on either side of his body. She felt him shudder again. Gently she bent his arms so that his hands—large hands, strong hands accustomed to hard labor—lay on either side of his head. She turned them so that the palms faced up. She placed a finger in the center of each palm and again felt his body tremble in response. His eyelids fluttered.

"The pain is here. The pain rests in your hands. Hold it. Hold it here. Hold it in the palms of your hands. Hold the pain. Hold the pain."

His eyes flew wide. For a long moment he looked up at her and she held his gaze, her own face intent. She spoke in a voice of command. "Hold the pain in your hands. Hold it tight. Hold it there." She pressed into his palms with her fingers, pulsing a time.

And suddenly he was breathing deep. Long breaths into his nose and out his mouth. Rhythmic and controlled, he breathed in time to the pulse she beat into his hands. She knew then that he held his pain there, drawn from the rest of his body and focused beneath her fingers. He breathed, and she whispered, "Hold it tight. Hold it tight."

Then he was asleep.

Sairu sighed and sat back, wiping sweat from her brow. She smiled weakly and looked over at Lady Hariawan. "It is done, my mistress. He is resting now."

But Lady Hariawan did not answer. She was staring into the flame of the lamp, and her face was blank as a sheet of new parchment.

6

IN ANOTHER, COLDER PART of the world . . .

The knock rang through the empty corridors of Lord Dok-Kasemsan's home, finally reaching Sunan where he crouched over his work in a small chamber in the very back of the house. He startled and glanced at the patch of light on the floor, quickly gauging the time. The carrier wasn't supposed to arrive for another three hours. Someone must have come to the wrong door. It must be a mistake.

Sunan shrugged it off and bent back over the document he was meticulously copying. Copying was rather beneath his dignity as a Tribute Scholar. Despite his inability to rise in the Center of Learning, Sunan was qualified to work with city chancellors, even to set up a small consulting business of his own. But to do so would be to admit that he had not passed the Gruung. To do so would proclaim to all the world his failure.

So sometime in the last few months he had found himself taking work as a copier for a small-time lawyer in a less-respected sector of Suthinnakor. And so he made pennies and survived.

The knock sounded again. Surely whoever it was would realize his mistake and go?

No one went to answer. Old Kiut had long since abandoned the household. When word arrived of Kasemsan's incarceration in Lunthea Maly—and the king of Nua-Pratut's refusal to become involved in a dispute with his much more powerful neighbor—the whole household staff had vanished overnight. Sunan suspected they had gone to join his uncle's wife and family on the coast.

One way or the other, Sunan was alone now in the great house, surrounded by luxury not his own. He didn't touch any of his uncle's things. He would have died of starvation before selling so much as a single porcelain urn. He barricaded the doors against thieves, took a set of servants' rooms for himself, scraped a small living copying endless pages of legal documents (many of them so full of lies and deceit they made his head spin), and . . .

And waited.

At night before he slept, he saw the face of the Mask in his mind's eye. But the Mask hadn't returned, not yet anyway. Why then did he always feel as though someone watched him? Even in the deepest recesses of his uncle's empty house, with every door and window blocked and scarcely room for a breath of wind or sliver of sunlight to slip inside . . . why did he always feel as though someone stood mere steps behind him?

His hand trembled. He had to stop his work and wait for the trembling to pass. It took him much longer to finish any task these days, for he was painstaking, refusing to allow these intermittent tremors to disturb his flawless script. When the shakes came, he would set aside his brush and wait. They always passed eventually.

Another knock.

He would have to go check the outer gate at some point. The bolt must have come loose to allow whoever it was through to the courtyard. Usually he made the carrier wait on the street outside. He would make his way to the gate punctually each evening and slip the copy through the spy-hole without ever having to deal with anyone face-to-face. He had made similar arrangements with a local grocer and an egg-seller. He didn't like to step beyond the gates of his uncle's house unless absolutely necessary.

But someone was at the front door. And growing ever more insistent. The knocks were one long, continuous stream now, indicating a willingness to go on all day and into the night if necessary.

Well, assassins don't knock. Or do they?

The tremors were too bad to continue his work, so Sunan gathered his robes and hastened through the quiet passages of the house, up a little flight of stairs, and on to the door. *Boom! Boom! Boom!* A large fist beat a steady rhythm, and Sunan could see the whole door shaking in its frame.

"Who's there?" he called. His voice cracked from little use and he was obliged to clear his throat and try again to be heard over the thudding. "*Who is there?*"

The fist stopped. A deep voice with a thick Chhayan accent—though not an accent of the Khla tribe, Sunan noticed vaguely—spoke. "Are you Juong-Khla Sunan?"

"What do you want?" Sunan asked. He felt the tremors moving from his hands up his arms and into his shoulders.

"Juong-Khla of the Khla clan sends you a message."

Sunan wondered if he would ever find his voice again. The tremors had reached his knees now, and he leaned against the wall beside the door to keep himself upright. His mind whirled with a number of impossibilities. He knew that there was perhaps *just* enough time for the gurta he had seen in the spring to have made the long trek back to Chhayan territory in the west. But to send a message in response? That wasn't possible. It simply was *not* possible.

"Take the message, Juong-Khla Sunan," said the voice on the other side of the door.

"Speak it," Sunan gasped.

"I cannot. It is written."

Chhayans did not read or write. But Sunan's mother could. She rarely used the skill, sometimes pretending no longer to possess it. But perhaps, within a letter from Juong-Khla, she might have inscribed her own message?

Sunan hated himself. He hated the sudden surge of heart-sickness, the sudden feeling that he was once more a child, not a tall Tribute Scholar grown to manhood. He hated the sudden need for something, some word from his mother, some comfort, if comfort ever could be had again.

But perhaps the man on the other side of the door meant to kill him. Perhaps that was the message his father sent.

It didn't matter. Drawing a deep breath, Sunan put his hand to the bolt, lifted it, and let the door swing wide. The light of day blinded him, and the stink of Chhayan buffalo washed unrelentingly over him.

"Juong-Khla Sunan?" spoke the Chhayan voice.

Sunan nodded. The next moment a scroll was placed in his hand. And no knife planted in his heart. So that was good. Probably.

"Do . . . do you need a response?" Sunan asked as his fingers closed tight around the parchment.

"No," replied the Chhayan. He remained where he stood, his arms folded, silent.

"Um. Do you want to come in?"

"No."

Sunan licked his dry lips. "Is there, um, anything else I can do for you?"

"No."

Squinting into the sunlight, Sunan still could make out no features on the shadowed face, nothing beyond a thick, square jaw. "Well then, I, uh . . . thank you?"

At that, the Chhayan bowed. He stepped back from the door, turned around and . . .

And he didn't disappear. Of course he didn't. People don't just disappear into thin air, not normal people anyway. Maybe the Crouching Shadows could (who knew with folks like that?) but certainly not a big, beef-fed, blunt-bladed Chhayan nomad. No, Sunan must have blacked out momentarily, miraculously staying on his feet in the process, and while he was out, the messenger had walked all the way back across the courtyard and through the closed gate—which was bolted from the inside, Sunan noticed—and disappeared into the city beyond. That's how it must have been.

Once more Sunan felt the skin-crawling sensation that someone was watching him. He shut the door, but the sensation didn't go away. So he scuttled back to his chamber at the back of the house like a mouse darting for its hole, and the thought came to him as from a great distance that he was a pathetic creature. Son of a warlord? Hardly!

But he lacked the energy to face such thoughts head-on. He dropped to his low cushion, panting, and stared at the scroll. As though it would catch fire in his hand. As though it would poison him by its very existence.

He must open it eventually, however, and eventually could not be avoided forever. At last he broke the seal and rolled out the page. His breath caught as he saw, after so many years, his mother's hand.

But it was not his mother who addressed him now across the leagues. Within a neatly inscribed character or two, his mother's neatness and beauty were lost in the words she wrote, dominated as she always was by the force of Juong-Khla.

Sunan heard his father's voice in his head as he read:

Son of my Stolen Wife:

In this treachery at last you prove yourself my son. Only a man of the Tiger would find the passion within to see his hatred through to such an end. I only hope that you found enough of the Tiger's rage in your veins to plunge the knife yourself. Somehow I cannot make myself believe as much.

The secret you have sent is a mighty gift. Should it prove true, you may consider yourself a free man. The life of my heir for the Long Fire—a worthy price and one a Tiger will always pay. But know this, son of my stolen wife: If we meet again, your life is mine.

And so his mother's hand ended, her elegant calligraphy giving way to the ragged scrawl that served as Juong-Khla's signature, like the slicing claws of a tiger. Nothing more. No personal message from his mother herself. Nothing. Final.

Sunan read it again. "How did it come here so swiftly?" he whispered. He pretended this question consumed all other thought, pretended to turn it over in his mind with all his academic intensity. He pretended his heart didn't burn with two-fold shame: Shame at his brother's death, which was his fault; shame that he had, even at the last, let his father down and failed to deliver the killing stroke.

"There's no possible way on this mortal earth a man could have traveled so far, so fast. How then? How could—"

He broke off his pretense, and his eyes bulged in their sockets. At first he did not believe what he saw. But that was his own fault. Foolish Sunan! He knew better. He should have looked for it at once!

The letter was written in his mother's hand. His clever, clever mother, outwardly so obedient to her lord and husband, inwardly so full of hate more potent than any tiger's.

A line here. A dash there. A careful arrangement of form. Words that he knew could never have been spoken by his uncouth father, no matter how sincere the sentiment they contained.

As Sunan stared at the letter, he saw the code taking shape as though by magic. A secret message from his mother, and it said:

Beware the Greater Dark.
Beware the Dragon.

7

A SMALL STONE SHRINE stood on the brink where the road dropped off on one side to a river winding far below. It was an old shrine styled after a fashion seen across the Noorhitam Empire: a small, round Moon Gate, about the right height for a rabbit to slip through, leading from nowhere to nowhere. These gate-shrines, Princess Safiya had explained to Sairu long ago, symbolized passages from this world into the Heavens and they were built, supposedly, in replication of the great Gate into Hulan's Garden.

"*It is an old tradition and, as such, should be treated with respect,*" Princess Safiya said. But Sairu felt little respect for traditions based on lies.

Nevertheless, she felt uncomfortable seeing the cat seated under the arch of the Moon Gate shrine, brazen as an emperor's peacock, grooming one white paw.

Sairu spotted him first. Brother Nicho led the way, and he made signs of reverence before the shrine but did not seem to see the cat—who smiled as though the reverence were made to him and not to the gate. He turned that smile on Sairu as she approached, and she matched him smile for smile.

"Making good progress?" the cat asked. The mule turned its long nose to look down upon him, but found him singularly uninteresting. The mule found most things uninteresting. It wanted nothing more than to plod on for hours and hours at its own unchangeable pace, ignoring the monotonous world around it.

"Good enough," Sairu replied, and bobbed a curtsy as pretty as any to be seen among the handmaidens of Manusbau. "No thanks to you."

"Did I ask for thanks?" The cat gave a long stretch, extending first one paw then the other, the tip of his tail brushing the arch of the gate. Then he fell in step beside Sairu. His shoulder blades scythed up and down with his sauntering tread. After a few paces, he glanced back a little nervously. "Where are the hedge-pigs?"

Lady Hariawan rode her donkey, the lion dogs surrounding her in their baskets strung from the creaking saddle. Dozing, they had not yet caught the cat's scent.

"I'll have you know that Dumpling, Rice Cake, and Sticky Bun are the noble offspring of the great Bright Mane," Sairu said, "descended in a long line of royal canines bred from the deified lineage of the Lordly Sun's own watchdogs."

The cat gave her a look. "Really?"

"Well, they come from the same kennels as the emperor's dogs, so that's close enough."

"Useless yapping things, hardly what you'd call proper dogs. What's the point of them?"

"They ward off devils."

"Yet I'm still here. What else?"

"They're fluffy."

"*I'm* fluffy," said the cat.

"You're a monster," said Sairu.

They walked on in silence. The road was broad, but slanted toward the brink. Every few paces, Sairu would look behind to see how the slave in the sling was faring. The sling held true to its bindings, but she dreaded that a rope might give and he would fall to the road. Nothing would prevent him from sliding down the incline and over the edge only to be caught by the river's waiting arms below. But the mule was sure-footed, and Sairu guided it carefully.

The cat took note of her concern. He trotted back to the sling and peeked over the bar. Then he scampered to Sairu's side once more. "Handsome fellow you've rescued there," he said. "Aren't you glad I led you to him?"

"He's a nuisance," Sairu replied. "If not for my mistress, I would have left him behind."

"I doubt that. He could be goblin-son ugly, and you'd have done just what you're doing now. You, my dear mortal, behind that pretty smile of yours, have a heart of porridge. Anyone could see who bothered to look."

But Sairu wasn't paying attention. She studied the cat from the corner of her eye, all the while pretending to be intent upon the road. Then she asked, "What do you know of him, cat? Why did you want me to save him?"

"Who says I wanted you to save him?"

"You didn't lead me to the slavers to free our guide," Sairu persisted. "It was this one," and she jerked her head back toward the sling, "you had in mind. Why? Are you two in league? Involved in some plot? Something to do with my mistress?" Curse that furry feline face! Even when she turned to look full upon him, she couldn't read a thing.

"I've never met him," said the cat.

Albeit reluctantly, Sairu believed him. But she maintained her equal belief that he had wanted her to find the slave. Yet another mystery to ponder. She faced the road again, guiding the mule around a large stone and checking to make certain neither of the pole-ends of her sling caught on it.

"Ah! My lady! My lady!" Brother Nicho, up ahead, turned suddenly, his wrinkle-shrouded eyes shining, his arm waving. "My lady, behold! Daramuti lies yonder!"

Breathing a sigh of relief, Sairu picked up the pace and brought the mule beside the monk, who pointed eagerly. There, up the trail about a mile, through twisting paths in the rock and nestled among thick green trees, she saw the outer gates of a temple. They were similar to the gates of the Crown of the Moon, only smaller and more weathered.

"We've made it!" she whispered.

"And no wonder, with you driving them like livestock," muttered the cat at her feet.

Brother Nicho, still without a glance for the cat, took her by the hand. "Blessings upon you, gracious daughter!" he exclaimed. "You have liberated this poor man from great sorrow and despair and brought him once more within sight of his home. May Anwar and Hulan shine fair upon your face for all the days and nights of your life!"

"Yes, yes," said Sairu, shaking off his hand but bowing politely as one should to a holy man. "Hurry now. We're not there yet."

The monk hiked up his long robe and started at a trot up the hill. His old lungs were used to the thin air of the heights, and he moved without apparent strain despite his age. But Sairu, now that their goal was in sight, suddenly felt very tired. She wanted to stop, to rest, to rub her sore, sore feet. No one in the party would complain. Although they rode rather than walked, she knew they were all as tired as she.

Her grip on the mule's bridle tightened, and she forced herself onward.

"Daramuti," said the cat, more to himself than to her. "A strange name. Why do I feel as though I *almost* know what it means?"

"Why wouldn't you? You speak our language, do you not?" Sairu said, panting, for her heart rate was suddenly elevated with eagerness for the journey's end.

"Not at all," said the cat. "I understand it, and I can make myself understood. But some of the names escape me. Daramuti, for example."

"It means *starflower*," Sairu said. "The temple is named for the Gardens of Hulan."

"Oh," said the cat. "You don't say."

Sairu, startled by the tone of his voice, looked down. But he was gone.

A great, bellowing horn sounded to announce the imminent arrival of Brother Nicho and the convoy. The echoes rolled up the mountain even to the higher regions of the temple grounds, reaching the abbot where he sat quietly in the shade of his dovecote.

Brother Tenuk sighed at the sound, and it may have been a sigh of sorrow or of relief. Perhaps he himself did not know for certain which. He sat on a low bench where he could watch the opening of a nest hole. He knew what he would find if he dared to creep up to the hole and look inside: a reptilian eye of blood red gazing back unblinking at him. And around that eye would be feathers that were also strangely like scales. And the whole form would be much too large to fit into such a space, and yet it would fit, beyond all possibility.

He hadn't the courage. So he did not look. Instead, whenever he could, he slipped up to this bench and watched the hole as though guarding his doves against the predator in their midst. So far, the creature that was perhaps a raven had not killed any of Brother Tenuk's beloved beauties. Not yet.

And the abbot prayed that the Dream Walker, escorted by the Golden Daughter, would hurry up and get to Daramuti!

So when the horn sounded, the abbot breathed a sigh and his withered heart skipped a beat. This caused pain in his thin breast, but he scarcely noticed. Forcing himself to his feet, he muttered, "It's time! He's come! And I'll send him on his way!"

He had only to recognize the Dream Walker and then . . . well, he'd come up with some excuse to send him back to Lunthea Maly, an excuse that no one would question, not even the venerable Besur. He was clever. He'd invent something. For now, let him only recognize the Dream Walker, and everything else must surely fall into place.

Acolytes and under-priests met him on his way down the white stone path, every one of them shouting, "Brother Nicho has returned!" as though their poor, aged abbot hadn't the wits to figure out as much for himself. Brother Tenuk growled responses and even took a swipe with his cane at a few of them as they ducked and bowed out of his way. By the time he neared the front gates, a path had been cleared before him so that he stood alone to greet Brother Nicho just as that good man passed under the arch and into the front courtyard.

"Brother. Dear Brother Nicho," said the abbot, raising a quivering hand in blessing. "Welcome home."

Brother Nicho dropped down to knock his forehead reverentially at the abbot's feet, an untimely move that nearly got him trampled by the mule entering right behind him. The girl leading the mule smiled hugely and steered her beast to one side, neatly avoiding the prostrate monk. Then she too bowed, dropping to her knees and extending her hands before her as she pressed her forehead into the paving stones.

Brother Tenuk did not look at her. His gaze traveled instead to the figure in the sling that the mule dragged in its wake.

And he thought to himself, *It is he. I know it. That must be he!*

How he knew, he could not say. After all, there was nothing prepossessing about that figure, who indeed looked sick to the point of death. But Brother Tenuk had not come so far in his order without a dash of cunning instinct to guide him. And this instinct told him now, *That is the Dream Walker.*

He scarcely saw the other weary travelers who passed through the gate and made reverence before him. Only the excited barking of the lion dogs could draw his gaze away from the man lying in fevered pain to look at the temple girl riding in on her donkey. She alone of her company did not dismount and made no bow.

Her face was like ice: beautiful, perfect, shimmering ice. Even the partially shielding pilgrim's veils could not dim the beauty of that face. Brother Tenuk blinked and wished to hide his eyes from her, even as he hid them from Anwar's light. She must be a very great lady indeed to not bow to the Abbot of Daramuti.

Suddenly he felt his heart in his throat. It had been such a long time since feminine loveliness had evoked a response in him that at first he did not recognize what was happening. "W—welcome, Honored Daughter," he said, making an appropriate motion with his hand and hoping that his voice did not betray his emotions to the brothers standing round. "I—I have received word of your coming, but not of your names or your purpose." He did not ask for either. After all, he was quite certain he knew who this beautiful girl was.

The Golden Daughter. Sent to guard the Dream Walker.

She was his enemy.

Brother Tenuk thought his shuddering heart might break.

The lady on the donkey said nothing. She merely gazed upon him as though not quite able to see him. She wore the humblest of pilgrim's robes, worn from long travel. And yet, somehow she seemed to Brother Tenuk as though gowned in fine silks and smelling of the sweetest perfumes.

Suddenly it was as though a tremor passed through the girl, and when it left her, her eyes were suddenly brighter and her gaze more alert. She fixed that gaze upon Brother Tenuk, and while he saw no recognition there, he saw command. He knew that when she spoke, he would obey her, whoever she was.

"I will go to my chambers at once," said she. "See that they are prepared."

Before the abbot even turned, several acolytes leapt into motion, hastening across the temple grounds to make a set of rooms fit for this unusual visitor. The lady's gaze never left Brother Tenuk's face, however. Brother Tenuk felt sweat forming on his brow.

"You will provide medicines for our sick," the lady said, gesturing to the man in the sling. "Give my handmaiden whatever aid she requires. I would have that man healed."

Without another word she dismounted in a sudden graceful movement. The dogs in their baskets barked and wriggled, wishing to escape along with her. She ignored them and passed silently from among her companions, proceeding into the temple grounds.

"Honored Daughter," Brother Tenuk said, his voice thin with nerves, "who are you, please, come among us like the sudden appearing of an angel?"

He had hoped it would sound gracious and even mystical. Instead it sounded silly in his own ears, and he would have kicked himself if he could.

But the lady drew near to him and stood taller than he, looking down upon him. "I am Lady Hariawan, servant of Hulan, sacred sister of the Crown of the Moon," said she.

Then she blinked. When her eyes opened once more, they were empty and cold as a moonless winter's night.

Sairu tried to follow her mistress into the chambers made ready for her. She caught a glimpse of fine, if old, wall-hangings, a warm fire, a low table set with a meal, and a pile of cushions on an enormous bed. But before she could see any more, her wrist was caught in a vise-like grasp.

Startled, she turned and found herself face-to-face with Lady Hariawan, who stood just inside the door of her new room, with her back pressed to the wall like some fugitive. But her face was as calm as ever, and her voice distant, as though it struggled to exist.

"Go to him," she said. "Heal him."

"I cannot!" Sairu protested, though all her training forbade her from contradicting her mistress. "My place is at your side."

"Go," said Lady Hariawan. Her grip on Sairu's wrist tightened momentarily. It startled Sairu, for it was a strong grip, one not easily broken. And yet Lady Hariawan herself could be knocked over by the merest breath of wind.

"Yes, my mistress," Sairu said, but only after she glanced again around the room, taking in as much as she could in that instant. She could spy no indication of lurking figures behind the wall hangings, and the windows, though many, were all shut and secured from the inside. This bedroom itself was at the end of a series of three rooms, each of which could be secured behind her as she departed. Lady Hariawan was as safe here as she could be anywhere.

Which wasn't safe enough, Sairu thought. But she could not disobey, so after urging her mistress to drop the bolts behind her when she left, she bowed herself out of the series of rooms and stood in the dark corridor beyond. A collection of nervous young acolytes flanked her, twisting their hands and bowing and trying not to look at her with too much curiosity. Many of them hadn't seen a woman in over a year, and they were still young enough to find Sairu uncomfortably fascinating.

"Take me to the wounded man," Sairu commanded with a smile. They fell over themselves to obey.

As she followed the acolytes, Sairu met Tu Syed, Tu Domchu, and the other temple slaves coming down the passage. They would be expected to sleep in the outermost chamber of Lady Hariawan's rooms, so they could watch over her mistress for a while at least.

But, Sairu thought, *I cannot depend on them to help should things go wrong.*

Why should things go wrong, though? The journey was over. Lady Hariawan was safe and could recover or recuperate or whatever it was she was meant to do here at her leisure, far from the intrigues of Lunthea Maly, sequestered away in the quiet of these mountains. The Besur might be unwilling to share the whole truth of the situation with Sairu, but he wasn't a liar. She had seen that in his face. He honestly intended to keep Lady Hariawan safe and believed this to be the safest haven possible.

But what the Besur believed and the truth of the matter might not be the same. And Sairu could not shake the feeling that something . . . *something* . . . was not right.

Something about the abbot's old, hairless face.

A humble building set apart from the main temple served as an infirmary. There the acolytes led Sairu, and she discovered the slave lying on his stomach upon a low pallet in the shadows.

"Bring me light," Sairu said as she knelt beside him, for there were not enough windows in this building to allow in the sun. Soon enough she was surrounded by a series of lamps. By their glow, she did as she had done the last many days, unbinding the slave's back and washing the wicked gashes. She asked for balm, and when it was brought to her she dismissed the acolytes, who left her alone in the infirmary with her patient. It was a very small, sad sort of aloneness, one that felt as though it wanted to be broken. But she hadn't the patience to deal with others. Not now.

She opened the jar of balm and rubbed its contents gently into the slave's puckering skin. He trembled at her touch but did not moan. He was frighteningly silent. She could not tell whether he was sleeping or awake. Possibly neither.

"So tell me, little mortal, does this place give you the same unsettling tingle in the whiskers as it does me?"

Sairu used two fingers to scoop more balm from the jar and smeared it between the slave's shoulder blades without a glance for the cat, who had appeared across from her, his ears back-tilted. She ran her hand gently across the fevered skin, feeling the pain beneath her fingertips as though it were her own. She spoke in a whisper, though there was no one else in the room. "Why does the name *Daramuti* upset you?"

One tufted ear flicked forward. "It doesn't," said the cat in a tone that told her it absolutely did. "Besides, that's not the question. Doesn't that abbot give you the shivers? Tell me honestly."

Sairu glanced at the cat. She smiled then and focused on her work once more. "Are you afraid?"

"Never," said the cat. "But I think it might be a good idea if I remained on hand, don't you? If the devil sours the milk, as it were, you can't depend on your hedge-pigs to protect you. They've not proven much use in devil-warding, now have they?"

Sairu's mouth continued to smile even as the rest of her face set into hard lines. "I don't trust you," she said, but she wasn't paying attention to the cat anymore. She stared at the side of the slave's face turned toward her. Her brows knit together, and she bent down, putting her ear close to his parted mouth.

"I don't blame you," said the cat. "I wouldn't trust me either, but it would still be wise if you—What are you doing? A bit soon for kisses, don't you think? You've only just met!"

"He's . . ." Sairu sat up, and all trace of her smile was gone. She stared at the slave, shook her head, then gently used finger and thumb to open his eye. She shook her head again. "He's gone."

"What? Dead?" The cat put sniffed, smelling plenty of life in the mortal body before him. He lashed his tail. "What do you mean, *gone*?"

"I don't know. He's not here," said Sairu. "He's fled away. He's . . ." She pressed her lips together, her eyes widening. Her hands slowly drew back, as though against her will, and folded and pressed themselves into her lap. "I think he's dream-walking."

"What?" said the cat.

The hair rose on the back of Sairu's neck. Feeling eyes upon her, she carefully masked her expression and turned a demure face over her shoulder. Brother Tenuk, bathed in the fading sunlight streaming through the infirmary door, leaned heavily upon his cane, his face hidden beneath his abbot's hood.

"My daughter," he said, his wizened old voice scarcely able to cross that distance to her ears. "Will Lady Hariawan's slave survive?"

"He will, Honored Brother," said Sairu, turning and bowing to the floor. While prostrate, she carefully checked her expression, making doubly certain it revealed nothing. Then she sat upright again, all sweetness and innocence, lacking any trace of guile. Any trace of fear. "I must be allowed to work in peace," she said. "To honor my mistress's will."

She could not see the abbot's face. But by the way he stood, unmoving save for a shivering in his knees, she knew he was carefully evaluating what he saw. She offered a smile.

It was enough. The abbot turned away, saying as he went, "Do as you must, my daughter."

Then he was gone. Sairu sighed and sagged where she sat. Her hands squeezed together until they hurt, and her knuckles stood out white.

"There go my whiskers tingling again," said the cat, sitting up from where he had crouched in hiding behind the slave. "I wish I knew what bothers me so about his face!"

Sairu turned sharply to the cat. "He's older than he should be," she said. "That's what it is. He is too old."

"What are you talking about?" said the cat. Then he meowled, leapt over the slave's still body, and raced after Sairu down the infirmary aisle and on out the door. "Where are you going?" he demanded.

Sairu did not answer. A Golden Daughter is blessed with intuition and instincts that even she is not always able to understand. But she knows well enough to act upon them at a moment's notice.

So, when Sairu's brain suddenly exploded with silent screaming, she did not question it but scrambled to her feet and ran, her only thought: *My mistress! My mistress!*

8

FOR SO LONG, there was only pain.

Then he heard the voice again. The voice he had been straining his ears, straining all his spirit to hear. And when he heard it, the pain vanished in a powerful flood of relief, and he stepped out of his body into the white emptiness.

Will you follow me, Jovann?

He escaped the torments of fever. He escaped the fire of infection. He slid from his body and sped away, into the white, on to the Wood. Through the gateway trees and into the circling safety of the Grandmother Tree's clearing.

Jovann stood bodiless, breathing in the golden stillness of that clearing, breathing the strength of the Grandmother, whose roots ran so deep and whose branches rose so tall. Then he took the form of his body, his whole and healthy body, and smiled to feel his limbs strong and his back no longer torn.

The wood thrush up in the branches sang, "Welcome, Jovann."

Jovann approached the great tree. It was so tall that he found it difficult to spot the bird even when it perched on the lower branches. How gnarled and solid and real was the trunk of the Grandmother before him, yet somehow less real than the song flowing down from above.

"You sent me back, my Lord," Jovann said, straining his neck as he gazed up into the leaves. "You sent me back to nothing. You sent me back to pain. Where is the future you promised me?"

"The future is now. The future is nigh," said the bird. Jovann spotted the flash of its white breast as it fluttered from branch to branch. "But you must Walk far deeper than ever you have before. I am going to share a wonder with you, Jovann. Will you see it?"

Jovann hesitated. He had seen so many visions, so many wonders over the years. And so far he had not seen them come to pass. But it was difficult indeed to refuse that silver song.

"I will see it," he said.

"Then Walk into the Dream. A path will be given you. You must follow wherever it leads you and however far. And you must trust me."

And then, even as it had the last time, the bird took flight. Jovann's eyes were only just quick enough to catch a fleeting glimpse of it before it vanished into the greater Wood beyond the Grandmother's circle. And Jovann stood alone with the Grandmother.

"Walk into the Dream?" Jovann whispered, frowning at the great tree as though it would answer him. "What does that mean? Is this not my dream?" He shuddered, wondering if the bird meant for him to leave the Grandmother's clearing. He glanced over his shoulder into the shadows of the looming Wood, so thick and so forever. Though he knew he bore no coward's heart, he quailed at the very idea of stepping into that enormous unknown.

He bowed his head and suddenly felt as though the hurts of his waking body had caught up with him, filling his limbs with the fever's agony. His stomach heaved, though he had no real stomach here and should be able to escape such pains. His back shivered with the many red lashes.

Then, as though from an incredible distance, he thought he heard a voice speaking in his ear, a gentle but urgent voice commanding him so that he dared not disobey:

"*Draw it down. Hold your pain. Draw it down into your hand.*"

Even here in the Wood, standing in an imagined form, he cupped his hands, closed his eyes, and held his pain in a small, contained ball. The pain itself did not vanish, but it became something he could hold, something he could bear.

Then it was gone, far from him, back in the waking world. He opened his eyes and looked around, wondering aloud, "Where is she?"

Until that moment he had forgotten the beautiful, nameless girl he had glimpsed the last time he came to this place. But now he looked here and there, expecting to see her. For surely she must come to him here. Had she not promised "*I'll find you again. Wait for me*."

"I'm waiting," he whispered. Then he raised his head, raised his voice, and cried out into the everlasting Wood, "I am waiting for you! Will you come to me again?"

"Yes."

Jovann nearly tripped over his own feet, turning as suddenly as he did. Although he had just been looking for her, he was surprised when she appeared, stepping around from behind the Grandmother Tree, her hand trailing lightly on the trunk. She wore a white gown in Kitar style with a square front panel, a wide sash, and long, flowing sleeves. The sumptuous bulk of fabric did nothing to disguise her slender frame. Her neck and collarbone were painted with red flowers and black stems twining up her pale skin.

She was as beautiful as he remembered.

"I have never been able to find the Wood," she said. Her voice wasn't strong, but it was commanding, low and dark as the shadow of Hulan herself. "We have heard it spoken of, and many writings tell of its greatness," she said. "I have sometimes glimpsed it in the distance, but whenever I set my face toward it, it retreated from me and I could never draw near. None of my brethren have even tried to discover its secrets."

Jovann realized he was staring. He drew a deep breath, finding his voice with an effort. "You came when I was left alone. You found me here."

"Yes. I heard you calling, and it was as though a path opened at my feet," she said. "I was able to follow your voice into this Wood, to this very place. I was able to do what I have never done before." She leaned against the Grandmother's trunk, her head tilted back, exposing her delicate throat. The painted flowers seemed to twine about her neck like the loveliest of nooses. "Your voice surprised me. I have never heard its like, not even on the edge of the Dream."

The wood thrush's command came back to Jovann as she spoke: *Walk into the Dream. A Path will be given you. And trust me . . . trust me . . . trust me . . .*

"Can you take me to the Dream?" Jovann asked. "Do you know the way?"

The girl braced herself and pushed away from the tree trunk. How weak she must be, he thought, for she walked slowly as though uncertain of her balance. He wanted to reach out and support her but feared that his touch might drive her away. As she drew near, however, she put out a hand and took hold of his arm. He was surprised to feel warm fingers clutching his skin. They felt as real as anything in the waking world. He found it difficult to breathe.

"Please," he said, "tell me your name."

"No," said she. "Names are not safe."

"But I must know!" he insisted, startled at his own urgency. "Please. I am Juong-Khla Jovann, son of the clan chief, my father's heir."

Her grip on his arm tightened, and her eyes flashed to his face. They were lovely eyes, gently sloping, black as night, and full of sudden fury. "I told you. Names are not safe."

"My name is safe with you, I think," Jovann replied. "I want you to have it. I want you to know it. Please tell me yours in return."

It was a most basic, a most essential politeness. Kitar, Chhayan, Pen-Chan . . . some laws extend across all peoples. He watched her jaw set, the muscles tensing as she considered her position. The green-cast shadows of the Grandmother's leaves above made her face seem even paler. So different from the roughened, weathered, red-skinned Chhayan women he knew.

"Umeer," she said at last.

"Umeer?" Jovann repeated. "That must be your father's name."

She nodded once.

"But what is *your* name?" he insisted. Very gently he slid one hand up onto his arm, resting it atop her fingers. "Who are you?"

For a moment he thought she would withdraw. She did not, however. The fury melted from her face, replaced by a mask of serenity.

"I will not tell you my name," she said. "I am . . . I am afraid."

Then she began to walk, and Jovann allowed her to lead him to the very edge of the clearing. Beyond stretched the Wood, as unsearchable, as unknowable as a lunatic's memory. Not once in all the years since he was first called into this clearing had Jovann so much as considered stepping outside.

But the girl progressed out of the clearing, and the shadows could not mar the white purity of her gown, of her skin. Her hand was still on Jovann's arm, and he must either follow or break her hold. She paused, looking back over her shoulder through the long glossy fall of her hair.

"Come with me, Juong-Khla Jovann," she said.

And when she spoke his name, he knew he could never disobey her.

They stepped into the Wood, and though the trees grew thick and the undergrowth thicker still, a path spread before their feet. The trees themselves drew away from them, pulling ferns and wildflowers and lush grasses aside to give these mortals clear passage. The girl walked in complete silence, her feet stepping soundlessly on the Wood's floor. Jovann followed in her wake, led by her insistent hand, and he said nothing.

But he wondered if he should not have given her his name so freely.

He looked at her hand on his arm. An exquisite hand with long, delicate fingers and nails burnished with gold paint. He allowed his gaze to progress up her arm to her shoulder, and on to her throat where the painted flowers graced her perfect skin. And he decided that he did not mind. Let her hold him in thrall. Let her control him, manipulate him even. He would do anything for her, whether or not she knew his name.

"Where are we going, Umeer's daughter?" he asked.

"To the Dream," she replied.

"Are we not now dreaming?"

To this she made no reply. Silently they walked through the still-more-silent Wood. Now and then, through the branches, Jovann believed he glimpsed other worlds, worlds too fantastic for comprehension, worlds beyond the Wood itself. Jovann had never seen such things before, had never guessed what the Wood contained within its vastness. But why should he be surprised? Had he not always known it was far too great an entity for his humble comprehension? Had he not always feared to step into its shadows, to uncover even the smallest of its secrets?

The girl led him on as though she knew exactly where she wished to go. They could have walked like this for hours, and perhaps they did, though it did not feel so long. To Jovann's surprise, he began to notice something strange—stranger than all the other strange things he had encountered that day.

The Wood was beginning to thin around them. It was no less thick than it had ever been. The trees grew as close together, their roots covered in undergrowth. But their very substance faded, becoming ghostly and insubstantial. As Jovann and the girl progressed, the trees gradually faded away.

And then vanished.

They stood upon a bleak landscape of misty gray—mist on the horizon, mist in the sky, and mist curling around their feet. Jovann, his eyes very round, turned in place, searching for any sign of the Wood, which he had believed would never end, *could* never end! But there was nothing. Only mist.

"Where are we?" he asked.

"The Dream," said the girl. "We are on the edge of the Dream." She gripped his arm with both hands. "Walk with me," she said.

He could not disobey. He did not wish to disobey, no matter the fear that flooded his heart. No fear he could experience here, through whatever unimaginable horrors, could possibly equal the fear of losing her. So he obeyed without question, and they proceeded into the mist.

Within a few paces the gray swirling began to move strangely in patterns of flowers and oceans and strange, elongated hilltops covered in animals or trees or something not quite like either. Jovann glimpsed colors deep inside, behind the gray, colors he did not see with his eyes but perceived clearly nonetheless.

"What is that?" he gasped, a thrill darting through his heart.

"Don't ask. Don't talk," the girl said. She walked a few more silent paces. Then she said in a whisper, "Or you'll go mad."

The mist began to fade, taking with it the images it created. Now Jovann beheld distant mountains, but mountains unlike any he had ever seen in the waking world. These were taller by far, staggeringly tall so that one felt tears gathering in the eyes and the heart at the sight of them. Although they were tall, green growth covered their slopes and gold tipped their summits, which looked warmer and richer than anything Jovann had ever before seen or imagined.

"What are those mountains?" he asked.

And the girl gasped as though, when he spoke, she saw them herself for the first time. Then she whispered, "The Highlands, I believe. I have never—" Her voice gave way, and her footsteps faltered. When Jovann turned to her, her head was bowed and her shoulders shook. He wondered for a moment if she wept.

Then she looked at him, and he saw that her eyes were dry and distant. "I have never seen them," she said. "I have heard, but never seen."

Was that anger lacing her words? But then she was pulling him on, and he followed her lead without resistance. Who would want to resist one such as she?

The great mountains vanished after a time, replaced by a different range of mountains altogether. And these looked much more like the snow-capped peaks bordering his homeland, save that the sky above them was orange and pink and purple, moving like liquid in gorgeous swirls. Jovann drank in the beauty of them, but the girl scarcely saw them. She dragged him on with increasing urgency.

"Where are we going?" he asked at length, for they were now moving at a near-run, though there was no need for running in this place. "Do we search for something?"

When she spoke, he could hear a lie in her voice. He hated to admit it, for he did not like to think of someone so beautiful as capable of lying. But when she said, "The Gate to Hulan's Garden," he knew it was not the truth.

Even so, the moment she spoke, he felt a certainty rise up in his heart. Once more he recalled the wood thrush's promise: *A Path will be given you.*

It was just as the wood thrush had said; for no sooner did the girl mention Hulan's Gate then Jovann felt a tugging on his soul, a knowledge he had not possessed a moment before.

"The Gate is this way," he said, and altered their course, turning the girl to the right. How he knew to do this, he could not say. It was as though a voice called to him across the unknowable distances of the Dream, and he knew what he would find.

They turned and saw in the middle-ground between them and the faraway mountains, standing alone on a solitary plain, a gate. A round Moon Gate which, from that distance, looked no bigger than any humble shrine decorating the landscape of Noorhitam. Nothing more.

The girl gasped. If not for her grip on his arm, Jovann thought she would have sunk to her knees.

"What is wrong?" Jovann asked, concerned. He reached for her upper arm, but she shook him off, releasing her hold on him and backing away to stand on her own, swaying like a young tree in a gale. "What is wrong?" Jovann repeated.

"That gate," she said. Then she whispered, and her voice was very young. "It is like the shrine in my mother's garden. I have not seen it since . . . since . . ."

And she was running. One moment she stood swaying; the next, as is the way of dreams, she was many paces ahead of him, running, her long white sleeves and black hair billowing behind her.

"Wait!" Jovann cried, and set off after her. But the ground seemed to grab his feet, to hold him, and the air became thick and clinging. He scowled and shook himself, shook the shape he had assumed. His limbs were freed, and he ran harder, no longer hindered. The girl was far ahead of him, but his legs were long, and he thought he could catch her.

The gate grew. Or rather, the closer they came, the bigger they saw it was. This was no simple shrine. It was a giant's portal, as great as the Lady Moon herself, each stone perfectly carved to set into the next. And through it, he could see, not the landscape of the plain surrounding them, but brilliant, many-colored light. But it was still so far away, so unreachably distant.

The girl stopped. She stood frozen in place, still as stone. Jovann, panting, though he did not think it right to pant in dreams, caught up and turned her to face him. "Umeer's daughter?" he said urgently. But she would not look at him. Her eyes rolled this way and that.

"Do you hear them?" she said.

As soon as she spoke, Jovann heard a dark, deep chanting. At first he thought it was the drone of a low horn blowing to call the worshipful to prayer. Then he realized it was no horn but many voices surrounding them. Human voices.

He turned. In the distance, approaching through the far gray mist, he saw dark figures. He spun in place and saw more of them on all sides. They were far away as yet, but their chant was as close upon his ears as though they stood mere inches from him.

They blocked the path to the gate. And they were coming closer.

"Anwar blast it!" The girl spat out the curse like poison.

"Who are they?" Jovann asked.

"Devils. Blights," the girl said, her face distorted by a snarl. "Always they come. Always, the fools!"

"Should we turn back?" Jovann suggested. The chanting was unnerving and, he thought, evil. It was also, in a horrible way, familiar. But he could not—or would not—place it.

"I'll not turn back," said the girl. "I'll not turn back!" she repeated with more vehemence. She pulled herself free of Jovann's hands and marched toward the gate, toward the advancing phantoms.

Jovann's heart lurched in his breast. He knew, though he could not say how, that whoever the chanting phantoms were, they meant her harm, terrible, terrible harm. They were closing in, still distant, but an ever-tightening snare. He hastened after the girl. "We must go back," he pleaded.

"No!"

Suddenly the chanting vanished, overwhelmed by a potent scent, a spice Jovann did not recognize. It filled his nostrils, filled all his senses, drowning out sound, sight, taste, touch, leaving room for nothing but that scent.

He heard the girl scream a long, inarticulate wail as though lashed by great pain.

Jovann's head cleared. The scent vanished, and he sought the girl. He found her beside him, but she was no longer solid. When he reached out to her, his hand went through her shoulder, through her arm.

"No! *No!*" she screeched like a wild bird of prey.

She was vanishing from the Dream.

"I'll find you," Jovann said, though he knew she could not hear him above her own screams. "I'll find you! In the waking world! I'll find you on the other side, I swear!"

Then she was gone.

He stood alone on nothing. Absolute, white nothing. Even the chanting phantoms had disappeared.

Acolytes and priests startled in surprise as the handmaiden tore past them, out the infirmary door and across the temple grounds. They leaped from her path as though avoiding an oncoming stampede, then turned round-eyed to each other and shrugged. Women! Who understood such creatures?

Sairu pounded down the winding paths, back to the hall extending from the main temple building, where Lady Hariawan's quarters were found. She remembered each twist and turn as though she had spent all her life in Daramuti rather than having just arrived earlier that same day. The sun was setting fast, and the white stones beneath her feet glowed orange in its fading light.

My mistress! My mistress! her mind cried out, though she could not say why. Something was wrong. Terribly, terribly wrong! Why had she left Lady Hariawan's side? Why had she allowed herself to be pushed away? She should have resisted even the direct orders of her lady. She should have insisted, should have stayed nearby, especially now, in this unknown place, surrounded by strangers, however holy those strangers were purported to be!

She burst into the building and charged up the corridor, ignoring the young acolytes pressing themselves against the wall to give her room. She reached the first door of Lady Hariawan's chambers and prayed she would find it bolted from the inside, forbidding her access.

But it opened.

"Anwar's elbow!" she hissed through her teeth and raced across that first chamber, ignoring the stares of Tu Syed, Tu Domchu, and the others as she darted past them to the door on the far side. That door was open as well. Despite her urging, Lady Hariawan had not bolted a single one behind her departing handmaiden. Anyone could enter her chambers, anyone at all!

Within the second chamber, Sairu found Dumpling and his fellows huddled in a corner, trembling, whimpering, their bellies pressed flat to the floor. Her brave lion dogs who never showed fear, reduced to such a state.

Without pause, she hauled open the final door to her mistress's sleeping room and dashed inside, her hands up her sleeves to remove the daggers hidden there, prepared for anything. She whipped her weapons free and stared around the dark room.

Lady Hariawan lay upon her bed, the curtain drawn back, allowing the last of the fading sunlight to fall through the window and touch her sleeping face. Otherwise, the only light in the room came from two low braziers. The unmistakable scent of harimau filled the room like a living presence.

All was silent. The room was empty.

Sairu stood still, her heart ramming in her throat. She did not believe it. Not for a second. Her senses were too alive, too full of shouted warning. Something was wrong. She knew it. She knew it!

Someone was right behind her.

She whirled around. But there was nothing. No one there. Not a breath, not a moving shadow.

Whatever it was, it was still behind her.

She whirled again, lashing out with one of her knives, ducking low to the floor in a deep crouch. Still nothing. No one.

"*Don't trust your eyes, Sairu.*" The voice of Princess Safiya came to her as though across the leagues. And she saw in her memory that great lady approaching, a blindfold in her hand. "*Don't trust your eyes, or you will surely die.*"

Despite all the years of careful training, Sairu felt her spirit rebel against what she knew she must do. But her training won out.

She closed her eyes and crouched in the darkness. One by one, she turned off her other senses, allowing the unexplored senses of the brain and the heart to take over, to tell her what she needed.

And she heard without her ears a deep, low chanting. Across her mind flashed the image of the hand-shaped burn that marred her mistress's cheek.

The next moment Sairu was across the room, overturning the braziers of harimau. They fell and scattered their delicate embers across the floor, and she grabbed a cushion from off Lady Hariawan's bed and beat them out. The scent was almost overwhelming, so full of heat and wildness and distance. She beat the embers and kicked one of the braziers across the room.

Suddenly a hand grabbed her wrist, twisting painfully. Sairu turned, a knife upraised, and found herself looking into Lady Hariawan's furious, torch-lit face.

"*What are you doing?*" Lady Hariawan screamed.

"My mistress!" Sairu cried. "Were you dream-walking? You should not do it! You mustn't! It's dangerous!"

Lady Hariawan screamed again, inarticulate in her rage. She dropped Sairu's wrist and scrambled on all fours across her bed, bending down to grab the second of the braziers. It was hot, and Sairu knew her lady's fingers must burn at the touch. "Don't!" she said.

But Lady Hariawan picked up the brazier and flung it at Sairu with all the force in her slender arms. It did not hit its mark but fell with a clang upon the floor, rolling and echoing as it landed. "Get out!" Lady Hariawan roared. "*Get out of my sight!*"

Sairu stared, horrified. Then, bowing low, she backed from the room and slid the door shut.

9

ANWAR SHONE GENTLY DOWN upon the mountain temple, smiling at the comings and goings of the priests. His rays peered through the windows of Lady Hariawan's chambers but could find no glimpse of the lady herself, secluded away in the deepest shadows. He sought instead the white head of the abbot, who put up his hood and, cursing the brightness, hobbled away to the sanctuary of his prayer chamber where the very orb to whom he allegedly prayed could not find and annoy him.

Thwarted again, Anwar turned his languid golden eye to the face of the girl standing at the infirmary window, and he thought she smiled up at him a smile full of secrets and—sad to witness in one so young—cynical disbelief. Of the wounded man in her care, Anwar could see nothing at all.

He moved on across his sky, blinking slowly whenever clouds should chance to drift across his face. Then he opened wide his great eye and stared. Any observer paying attention (it is amazing how few, even among his worshippers, pay any heed to the Lordly Sun flying in blazing glory overhead) would have thought that he shone a little brighter, that his flames lashed and burned with laughter in a voice indiscernible to mortal ears. For Anwar did indeed laugh loud and long at what he saw:

A pack of waddling dogs pursuing an orange cat across the grounds of Daramuti.

They ran through the kitchen garden, the cat screaming out feline curses, the dogs responding in vicious snarls. The cat used the bent back of an unlucky acolyte at work as a springboard to gain himself access to the kitchen window. And so he would have achieved his escape, save that a priest opened the kitchen door at that very moment, and all three dogs darted through between his feet, nearly tripping him up so that only his grasp on the doorframe kept him upright. The chase was hidden from Anwar for a few moments, though he heard, even from high in his heavens, the ringing and clatter of kitchenware.

Back out into the garden streaked the cat, between the legs of the poor priest just righting himself in the doorway. The dogs followed in close pursuit, moving with much more speed than their size and shape might suggest. Lettuces flattened, squashes squished, and acolytes threw their gardening tools after the furious terrors.

The cat gained the garden wall, up and over, pausing on the other side in the few moments granted him to slick down the fur between his ears (for these things are important, even on the very brink of yipping death). But the dogs found a crumbling low place, and they were through in trice, re-doubling their snarls.

"Dragon's *teeth!*" yowled the cat, and he was off again, making for the nearest open window. He leapt through, landing squarely in the lap of Brother Tenuk, whose already less-than-holy prayers were made less holy still by his cry of "Anwar's bruising elbow!"

Anwar himself took no notice, however, intent as he was upon the dogs barking beneath the window. They had lost their quarry for the time being, but they sniffed and snorted, running back and forth under the window, determined not to give up. Their determination was rewarded when, the next moment, the cat appeared in the window again, this time held by the scruff in the trembling hands of the enraged abbot. Brimming with righteous wrath, Brother Tenuk dropped the cat into the midst of the dogs, who leapt upon him, teeth bared.

The cat shook them off and was again a streak of orange, like rippling sunlight himself, dashing across the temple grounds and making for the last shelter available to him.

There was one place in all Daramuti where the dogs dared not go. For their mistress—their beautiful, their beloved, their deified mistress—had stood in the doorway and told them, "Stay out!" in tones that defied all but one interpretation. They never forgot her commands, and they would not disobey.

Thus, when the cat, scrambling, shedding half his coat, and shrieking out curses in a high, incensed howl, dashed through the open door of the infirmary, the dogs followed him to the step . . .

And there stopped. As though they had struck an enchanted wall.

They snuffled. They snarled. They barked their disapproval of this coward's trick! It was no use. The cat had clean got away. They would have to wait until next time.

The cat, his sides heaving, crouched against the wall across from the door, his eyes darting bright hatred. But when he saw that the dogs would indeed honor their mistress's command and not enter, he drew himself up.

"Villainous, unmuzzled toe-lickers!" he meowled, and laughed at their answering yaps. "Chase me down, will you? Like a common alley-mog? Well, what do you think of *this!*" He arched up on his toes, turning sideways, his ears pinned back. The dogs yelped in good-natured terror and darted away, hiding in the bushes outside the infirmary door.

"Ah ha!" said the cat, and allowed the fur of his tail to smooth down once more. "Can't bear the look of me *sideways*, now can you?"

He felt a pair of eyes upon him. Assuming what he hoped was an aspect of cool serenity, he turned and blinked at Sairu.

She knelt in the shadows across the room, her hands folded neatly in her lap. The slave, still unconscious, lay before her. In a voice all too pleasant, all too sweet, she asked, "Out for a stroll, my good Monster?"

The cat flicked an ear. Then, tail swishing, he padded toward her and sat on the other side of the slave. "You should control your hedge-pigs," he said, beginning to groom a paw. "They're an embarrassment."

"To whom?" Sairu replied.

The cat glared at her. Then, hoping to direct the conversation away from his disgruntled dignity, he asked, "How's our patient?"

"See for yourself," Sairu said, indicating the slave with a turn of her eyes. Otherwise she remained perfectly still. Perfectly controlled.

As though she feared that with even one wrong move she would snap.

The cat turned to observe the young man, though he was much more interested in watching Sairu herself. They had been three days in Daramuti now, and she had scarcely left the confines of the infirmary. When she did leave, it was to go plead at her mistress's door for admittance. But Lady Hariawan refused, answering only in utter silence. So Sairu was obliged to direct Tu Syed and the other temple slaves to see to her mistress's needs, and she herself, feeling the full burden of her disgrace, kept out of sight.

The separation was telling on her, the cat could sense. There was a pinched quality about her doll-like face, a hard twist to her mouth even when, as now, she smiled.

It was strange, the cat thought. One would almost believe that the girl loved her mistress and now suffered the agony of her censure. But he could see that Sairu did not love Lady Hariawan. Lady Hariawan was not an individual anyone would find easy to love. Indeed, the cat knew of only one person he thought might be capable of the feat—and that person had proven herself able to love dragon's spawn and devils, so she hardly counted.

No, it wasn't love Sairu felt for her mistress, but something deeper, something stronger. Golden Daughters never loved, for that emotion was too volatile to serve their needs. But she was devoted; down to the very core of her being she was devoted. Her heart and spirit were linked to her mistress by a chain which, if broken, would leave her stranded in a pit of chaos.

Sairu had vowed her service. And she must enact it at any cost.

"He's getting better," she said as the cat sniffed hesitantly at the slave's dirty hair. "The fever has broken. He will recover."

"Good!" said the cat and began grooming his other paw, watching Sairu through half-closed lids. "Aren't you glad now that I brought you two together?"

"No," she replied.

"Oh come!" he insisted. "If not for my interference, he surely would have died in his chains, and how would that make you feel?"

"Nothing whatsoever," she replied. "I should never have known of his existence, and therefore how could I have cared?"

"But you do know now, which is the same thing as knowing then, unless you insist on a *linear* view of time, which strikes me as rather simplistic." The cat finished his paw and moved on to his large white ruff. Silence held the space between them captive. Then he said, "A lot of bullying ruffians those beasts of yours are!"

Leaving the cat grooming himself beside the slave, Sairu rose and went to the window, looking out on the grounds once more. Her dogs were piled up in a tangle of sleep nearby, ever her faithful guards. Priests and acolytes moved to and fro across her line of vision, busy about their various tasks. But she spared no glance for them, gazing instead across to the main temple building and the low window in the western wing.

The window at which stood Brother Tenuk.

It shouldn't matter, Sairu told herself, smiling grimly. Whatever interest the abbot might have in the nameless slave shouldn't matter to her in the least. Her concern was only for her mistress, and her mistress was safe in her chambers.

And yet that instinct—that wretched, niggling, unpleasant instinct—worried at the back of Sairu's brain. She felt, in a place deeper than thought, that Brother Tenuk's interest in the slave somehow meant danger.

Danger to Lady Hariawan.

As she stood at the infirmary window, questions rose up inside Sairu, threatening to disorient her with their need to be asked. But she crushed the questions down and did not ask them. Not yet.

"Umeer."

"Oi!" said the cat, standing and looking over his shoulder at Sairu. "I say, our handsome stranger seems to be waking!"

Sairu stepped away from the window, out of Anwar's sight, and back into the pool of light created by her one low lamp. The nameless slave stirred, and she could see that his sleep was light indeed, on the very edge of waking. She felt his brow. It was cool beneath her hand.

He turned his face toward her touch, and his lips moved. "Umeer," he whispered. Then, with more strength even as his eyes began to struggle open: "Umeer's daughter?"

"No, sorry," said Sairu. "My father's name is Kuda. Purang-Kuda, though no one ever calls him that now. I don't know any Umeer."

A few blinks, and then unfocused eyes stared up at Sairu. At first they saw only the smile, so he asked again, "Umeer's daughter?"

"Still wrong," said Sairu. "There's no one here by that name. Was she your sweetheart back home? I think not, since you're obviously Chhayan, and Umeer is an old Kitar name. Though perhaps you've fallen victim to an ill-fated romance and thus found yourself trussed up as a slave? A charming story, but somehow . . . ." She studied his face. It was quite a nice face, as faces go. The features were strong, despite the interfering softness of youth, with fine cheekbones and a deep brow. A square face, not beautiful by Kitar standards, which preferred narrow jaws and daintier features. But Sairu thought it pleasant.

She realized that she wasn't talking, but was in fact staring at the nameless slave. And she realized in that same moment that the cat was watching her and grinning.

She replaced her smile with a stern frown and continued in a cold voice, "Somehow I don't think your story is quite so charming as all that. You're probably a debtor and sold yourself to pay your debts. Much more likely, and hardly the stuff of ballads."

The slave gazed up at her, his eyes spinning at the swiftness of her words. Then he said a third time, "Umeer's daughter."

"No, she's not here, whoever she is," Sairu said. "You are a thick one, aren't you? No Umeer and no daughters. You're a long way from your home, a long way from any sweethearts. And you're Hulan-blessed to be alive, I'll have you know! You took a number of beatings from your enslavers, proving, I think, that you are indeed quite thick. Was one bad beating insufficient to teach you good manners? Did you not see that continued bad behavior would only earn you more of the same?"

His eyes focused briefly. Then he squeezed them shut and groaned.

Sairu saw his shoulders and arms tense, and knew he was about to try sitting up. "Oh no, no!" she said, pushing him gently back down. "You're full of orenflower medicine, and it'll make you sick if you elevate your head too quickly. It's good for the pain but not for the equilibrium, you understand."

He glared at her then, his eyes flashing wide, and propped himself back up on his elbows. But the orenflower was true to its reputation, and even that small movement made the room spin. He closed his eyes again but refused to lie back down, merely holding his head still until the room settled back into its proper orientation. Then, slowly turning to look at Sairu, he asked in a voice that was carefully controlled so as not to slur any words, "Who are you?"

"Not Umeer's daughter," she replied. "I'm merely Sairu, handmaiden to my Lady Hariawan. But that's not the burning question, now is it? No, for we all want to know who *you* are."

He glanced carefully around the room as though trying discern who "we all" referred to. He saw no one but the girl and the large orange cat, who hissed at him. Frowning, he focused his gaze back on the handmaiden. He considered lying, uncertain whether or not it would be safe to reveal his identity here. The girl was obviously Kitar, after all, and his enemy by birth. But as he met her oh-so-innocent gaze and glimpsed the keen mind hiding just behind it, he suspected she would know a lie when she heard one.

Besides, what harm could a handmaiden do him?

"I am Juong-Khla Jovann," he said, still slowly, still carefully, "son of the Tiger Chief. I am prince of my people, and I am . . . *betrayed.*"

"Is that so?" said Sairu, regarding him from behind her smile. She saw truth in his face, and she had already guessed he must be a chieftain's son. But there were other secrets behind that proud mouth, secrets it would be as well he did not speak just yet. "Well, your story is certainly more romantic than I was willing to credit. Time to sleep again." She took up a clay pot and poured lukewarm brew into a little cup, which she held to his mouth.

"No," he replied, turning too sharply so that the room once more spun. "No, I must rise. I must find . . . I must . . ."

"You must do as you're told, noble prince," Sairu replied, "just as you have *not* been doing, judging from the scars on your back. Hulan's mercy, is it any wonder they laid the cane and whip upon you so heavily? Now take your orenflower like a good Chhayan boy. Pretend it's buffalo milk, or whatever it is you drink. It's not so nasty as all that. Far less nasty than buffalo milk, I should think!"

She hoped her steady stream of talk would be enough to lay him flat once more. Indeed, his head bobbed and his eyes unfocused, and she even had the cup right up to his lips. Another moment and she was quite certain she'd have gotten the brew down his throat and seen him off to sleep once more.

But a knock sounded at the open doorway.

Sairu turned, dribbling orenflower juice over her fingers, and saw none other than Brother Tenuk's wrinkled face peering at her through the gloom. Sairu was on her feet in a moment, standing in such a way as to hide the slave with her skirts, and bowed respectfully.

"My daughter," said the abbot, "how fares Lady Hariawan's slave today?"

"He is better, thank you, holy brother," said Sairu. Still bowing, still holding her robes to form a curtain, she approached the doorway, hoping her approach would make the abbot shy away. "I expect to see him wake and rise in another day or so."

"That is good," said the abbot, eyeing Sairu uneasily. "That is very good. Does he now sleep?"

"He rests, holy brother," Sairu replied.

"Good. Good."

The abbot stood there, looking at her without seeing her, making no move to leave, saying nothing. His hood was set back far on his head, offering her a clear view of his face; his wrinkled, age-scarred, thin face from which those too-young eyes watched and made her shiver, for she could not understand them. He made no move, and neither did she, and they studied each other closely. So they could have stood for an hour or more.

But Sairu smiled, and it was enough to break the spell.

"Very well, my daughter," said the abbot, backing away and making signs of blessing with a trembling hand. "See to your duties as your mistress bade you."

So he tottered away, leaning heavily on his stick, looking back over his shoulder every few paces. He left the infirmary door and moved on down the path. Sairu watched the abbot go until he had vanished into the main temple building. Then, breathing a heavy sigh, she turned back to her patient.

He was lying flat once more, but his eyes were open and watching her.

"Who was that?" he demanded.

"A holy man," said Sairu, still smiling. She returned to the pallet on the floor and picked up the cup of brew, which was by now quite cold. "Drink, noble prince," she said.

"You must bear a message to my father," the slave said.

"No, I must not," she replied. "Drink."

"I command you."

She laughed. "Drink," she said again.

"I am the son of Juong-Khla, and I order you to—"

"You are a slave without a name, without a people, without even a stitch of clothing to call your own. You have nothing but your claims, and no one to believe them. So you will drink as you are told, and you will recover, for it is the will of my mistress that you should do so; and she is your mistress now as well, so her wish is, as they say, your command."

He snarled then, but without much force, for he hadn't regained much of his strength. "Handmaiden. Fetch-and-carry girl," he said. "Don't try putting on your Kitar airs. You're no better than a slave yourself and have never been anything else, judging by your hands."

The venom of his words was cut by fatigue, however, and succeeded in provoking nothing more than another smile from Sairu. "Drink," she said again. This time he obeyed. Then he slept.

All this the cat observed from a perch on a low stool nearby. He sat with his paws curled up to his chest, purring to himself. When Sairu settled back, she glanced his way, and her smile dropped away into a frown.

"What?" she demanded.

The cat said nothing. He purred on, looking as pleased as though he'd just done something rather clever.

10

BROTHER TENUK DID NOT SLEEP. Sometimes he would come close to sleep, so close that he could almost smell the flowers of the Realm of Dreams, could almost taste the sweetness of repose offered him.

But this never failed to send him upright in heart-pounding terror.

Then he would lie back upon his bed and stare out his open window, resting his body as much as he dared but not sleeping. Never sleeping. It was this as much as anything that had aged him so far beyond his time and left him teetering on the very brink of madness. Not long now and he would fall, he knew. Then madness would swallow him up entirely. But he hoped . . . oh, how he hoped there remained to him time enough to accomplish his purpose!

Some nights his window opened on nothing but darkened sky, when heavy clouds shrouded the Lady Moon and her sparkling gardens. These were the best nights. He could rest then without so much fear. There was always some fear—Brother Tenuk could not recall his last fearless moment. But there was less of it when Hulan could not see him.

But this night her great silver eye was open a mere slit, a shining crescent in the darkness above. He felt as though she spied on him and him alone, gazing out from under long lashes of night.

He scowled at her from his bed, the humble woolen coverlet pulled up to his chin as though he were a boy once more, afraid of spooks. But this was one enormous, all-seeing spook, and his woolen blanket could not hide him from her.

"Not long now, my lady," he whispered to the shining goddess whom he had journeyed so far and so long to serve here in her mountain temple. Hatred laced his words. "Not long until all traitors are betrayed!"

Suddenly across his mind there flashed a memory. He saw it as clearly as waking day. He saw white Kulap suspended on the end of a long black talon that punctured her heart and drew her blood. But then the memory twisted and became an evil dream. It was no longer Kulap's white breast stained with blood. It was no longer Kulap he saw stabbed on the end of that talon.

It was Lady Hariawan.

Brother Tenuk awoke with a start, choking on his own scream.

Sairu stood outside the door to her mistress's set of chambers, considering the face between her and the entrance. It was the face of Tu Domchu. There were so many little details making up its composition that filled her with an overwhelming and (a reasonable side of her suspected) unfair dislike. His eyes were too close together, for one thing, which seemed in that moment an unpardonable sin. And she could probably map out whole constellations in the red spots, moles, and pock-marks on his cheeks and forehead. His lower jaw was constantly churning like that of a cow chewing her cud, save when he paused every so often to spit a foul stream across the hall to spatter the wall opposite his position. His voice was the voice of one who always said what he had been coached to say by someone more intelligent than he, probably Tu Syed. Beyond that, she could tell by the look in his eye that, orders notwithstanding, he had maliciously determined to thwart Sairu at every possible opportunity for the pure sport of it.

"Sorry, miss, but you ain't permitted in."

He wasn't sorry at all. The blasted bull-cow!

"My mistress needs me," Sairu said. The patience of her voice and the smile on her face betrayed nothing of her mounting fury. "I must tend to her."

Tu Domchu chewed roundly for a full half-minute. Then he spat. This accomplished, he went back to chewing for another half-minute before finally answering her. "Sorry miss. You ain't permitted in."

"Under whose orders?"

"Lady Hariawan's. She says to me, says she, 'Tu Domchu! Don't you let nobody in. Not even my handmaiden.'"

Sairu doubted the truth of this claim very much indeed. Lady Hariawan, she was sure, did not even know the old slave's name! A muscle in her jaw began to twitch. Everything, *everything* in her being rebelled. Her nature, so finely tuned to serve, to protect, cried out against this separation, which had now lasted an agonizing seven days. She could guard her mistress from the outside, making certain that no living mortal passed into the chambers by door or window.

But what of those phantom presences she had sensed in the darkness of Lady Hariawan's chamber? What of those?

"Let me pass," she said, putting all the force of her diminutive yet formidable self into the command.

Tu Domchu blinked. Then he spat again. "Sorry, miss. You ain't permitted in."

She considered for an instant all of the painful things she could do to this man who wore his own body like a sack of bones, and whose face she doubted even his own mother had found appealing. She considered all of the options available to her, options that would cause either momentary or lasting agony. Nothing could keep her from that chamber unless she allowed it to be so.

Sairu whirled about so that her ample skirts struck the narrow walls of the passage on both sides and stormed down the corridor, back out into the temple yard. She stood then, blinking and shading her eyes against the brilliant sunlight, watching the shadows of various young acolytes scrambling to avoid her gaze.

For some reason she did not like to guess, the faces of the dead slavers flashed across her mind's eye. Idrus, Eyso, and others whose names she never learned. She saw their eyes full of life—and then she saw them dead, gazing into a void she could not see. Gazing into darkness.

She shuddered, cursing herself for a weak little fool. It was no concern of hers! Her mistress was safe, and it wasn't as though she'd killed them by her own hand.

"I would have," she told herself as she gathered her skirts and began to walk with a determined stride, though she could not have said where she went. "I would kill anyone to protect my mistress."

She wondered whether or not she lied.

Her dogs appeared from various places about the temple yard and fell into step behind her, a waddling entourage. They began to growl, and she looked up, realizing she had unconsciously taken the path to the infirmary. The cat sat just inside the doorway, grooming himself and pretending the dogs didn't exist.

And leaning against the doorpost stood Jovann, the slave.

Sairu scowled at him. No one had ever dared tell her that her scowl was nowhere near so terrifying as her smile, so she did not know that it made her look like a petulant child of three, quite adorable and completely unthreatening. "What are you doing up?" she demanded.

Jovann grinned as he would not have dared do had she smiled. He was still weak from his long fever, but seven days in Daramuti had already done wonders toward restoring his vigor. The scars on his back, however, would never fade, not entirely. And the skin of the healing wounds was tight and tender, making his movements hesitant.

"I cannot sleep for the clamor that beast of yours makes," he said, indicating the cat with a toss of his chin. The cat paused mid-lick, and one ear twitched. Then he went on with his grooming just as though he were a normal cat—not a devil—and didn't understand. "He sits on my pillow," Jovann continued, "and growls in my face. It's disconcerting."

"I think that is a purr," Sairu said, narrowing her eyes at the cat, who winked at her. "And he's not mine. He's a monster. Feel free to toss him out the window."

Jovann raised one arm, displaying a new set of scratches from hand to elbow. "I tried." He tucked the hand back under his opposite arm. "How can something so fluffy be so vicious?"

"Looks can be deceiving," Sairu replied. "Back to bed."

"No," Jovann replied. "I am better, as you see, and I need to be on my way." He swayed even as he spoke and was obliged to hold tight to the doorpost. But his face was determined. He had paled significantly during his convalescence, losing much of the rugged tan typical to Chhayan nomads. Indeed, he looked almost delicate standing there, with his narrow eyes sunk into his face and his cheekbones a little too sharp.

Sairu folded her hands demurely and felt the smile returning to her face. "And what do you propose to do, noble prince?" she asked. "After clothing yourself in fine raiment of sackcloth, will you weed the cabbage patch? Or haul water for the priests' ritual baths? Or are you more of a mind to tend flocks on the lower slopes? I hear there are wolves in these mountains, and a sturdy fellow such as you would make fine wolf bait."

Jovann's expression darkened. "I will return to my clan."

"I hate to remind you," Sairu said, though her expression indicated otherwise, "that you are my Lady Hariawan's property. She delivered you from your previous owners and saw to it that you were treated for wounds that would otherwise have been your death. You are hers by rights even a Chhayan must concede."

Jovann took an angry step, landing on the cat's tail. The cat exploded with an irate "*Reeeeeeeowl!*" and launched himself through the doorway. Immediately upon leaving the sanctuary of the infirmary, he found himself set upon by Dumpling, Rice Cake, and Sticky Bun and obliged to flee for his life to the nearest tree. The world was filled with barks and snarls for a few moments, and neither Jovann nor Sairu attempted to interrupt, but watched the pursuit until the cat was safely ensconced in a lower bough, the three dogs circling the trunk below.

Then Jovann turned to Sairu, and he wore the patient, condescending expression which had grown all too familiar in the last few days. But she could tell he wore it only to mask other, more revealing expressions. Behind the mask she saw fear. Fear that she spoke truth; fear that he was, indeed, no longer free.

"I am the son of Juong-Khla, and I have important business with my father," he said. "It cannot wait."

Sairu sighed, and her smile, for a moment, became almost pitying. "You are in Kitar country now, noble prince. The business of a Chhayan chief means nothing here. Don't," she hastened on, seeing the muscles in his throat contract with mounting curses, "don't think that I have no sympathy for you. I do not regard your situation lightly. But you must understand the truth of your position. And you must accept it, gracefully if you can."

"Accept it? Slavery?" Though he still held to the doorpost with one hand, Jovann stepped from the doorway and stood before Sairu, gazing down on her, his lips drawn back a little from his teeth as though in a snarl. "That may be good enough for you, little miss, but it can never be so for me. My father is betrayed by his eldest son. By my own brother. Even now, who knows what treachery Sunan prepares? I cannot remain here, high in these mountains, while down on the plains a great evil brews, and . . . ."

She realized that he no longer saw her face before him but gazed instead into a world—a future—hidden from her eyes. Sweat beaded his brow and lip, and she saw his supporting arm tremble. She touched his shoulder. "Go back to bed," she said.

But just as she spoke, Jovann uttered a great gasp, and she saw his eyes snap back into this world with an intensity she had never before witnessed in his face. He whispered, "Umeer's daughter!"

Surprised, Sairu looked back over her shoulder, following his gaze. "Anwar above us," she breathed.

For Lady Hariawan was walking down the temple path. She no longer wore the humble garb of a pilgrimess, the wide-brimmed hat, the veil. She was clad instead in a gown of silk trimmed in red glass beads and embroidered in black vines that bloomed into equally black blossoms. Her hair was loose down her back, which did not surprise Sairu (for how could her mistress hope to style it on her own?) but shocked her instead with its impropriety, especially here, sheltered behind holy walls. It flowed past her waist and was so thick and so glossy as to seem like a waterfall of ink.

Trailing her by a good ten paces were Tu Syed, Tu Domchu, and another of the temple slaves. The men were embarrassed by their mistress's loose hair and seemed to be making every effort not to look at it as they followed in her wake.

So Lady Hariawan passed by the infirmary, her head bowed, her hands folded, moving at the slow, sedate pace of a temple girl in a ritual parade, as though she heard the beat of drums in her head. If not for her loose hair, she would have seemed a prayerful and sacred creature.

Sairu felt Jovann tense beneath her hand. Then suddenly he cried out in a loud voice, "Umeer's daughter!"

He was stronger in that moment than Sairu realized. He slipped her grasp and had covered half the distance between the infirmary and Lady Hariawan before Sairu quite knew what was happening. "No!" she cried and hastened after him. But she could not stop him, so great was his urgency.

"Umeer's daughter!" he cried again, and still Lady Hariawan did not turn her head toward him. So he threw himself at her. What a threatening figure he must have seemed to the slaves—so tall and broad even in his weakness, and full of a passion none of them could understand. He grabbed Lady Hariawan by her arm, turning her to him. "Umeer's daughter, do you know me?"

Seeing the burn upon her cheek, he gasped in dismay.

Across Sairu's mind flashed a vision of her duty. She saw herself taking hold of that tall Chhayan, knowing full well where his wounds were, where his weaknesses lay. She saw herself bringing him to ruin there at her feet, leaving him writhing, screaming, as she stood over him, her body strategically placed between him and her mistress. Her mistress whom he should never have dared touch.

She saw it all in a horrible flash. And the vision made her stumble.

So it was not she who fell upon Jovann, but the temple slaves. Shouting in terror of what would be done to them should any harm befall their mistress, they fell upon Jovann, grabbing him and hauling him away, striking him with their fists. Tu Syed carried a cane, and he lashed out with it savagely. In two strokes, red lines darkened Jovann's back and shoulders. And all Sairu's work of the last seven days was undone.

Jovann screamed as he sank to his knees. But still he reached his hands to the lady, saying, "Don't you know me? Don't you know me?"

Lady Hariawan, her countenance unchanging, stood by and watched. Her hands were folded prayerfully, and the wind tugged at her hair and her robes. She made no move to interfere.

"Enough!" Sairu cried, flinging herself into the midst of the slaves. She grabbed Tu Syed's cane, wrenched it from his hands, and tossed it aside, then whirled upon Tu Syed himself. He had seen and trembled at her smile before. But he had never seen this expression on her face. She looked the very likeness of a panther, and he quailed beneath the heat of her eyes.

"I think you've made your point," Sairu said. "It was a mistake, that's all. A mistake! And now *look* what you've done."

Jovann lay upon his side, groaning, curled up as though to fortify himself against the pain he could not escape. But none of the temple slaves looked at him. They stared only at Sairu.

Tu Syed said humbly, "He assaulted the mistress."

He may as well have kicked Sairu in the gut. She flinched, and her face went a terrible shade of green as though she would be sick. She said nothing more, did not even turn to address Lady Hariawan.

One by one the slaves gathered themselves and surrounded their lady. They plied her with questions she did not answer and urged her to return to her chambers. She said nothing. Briefly, ever so briefly, her gaze flashed toward Jovann where he lay groaning. Then she turned and continued her way down the path toward some destination even she did not know. The slaves fell in behind her once more.

Sairu almost did as well. After all, she had not set eyes upon Lady Hariawan in many days. Her sworn mistress. Her very life. She should not be parted from her again!

And yet she found herself kneeling and carefully put her hands on Jovann's shoulders, avoiding the places she knew to be tender. "You stupid Chhayan calf," she murmured gently. "I told you to go back to bed, didn't I?

And now we'll have to start all over."

With much coaxing and prodding and even pinching, she managed to get him to his feet. He slumped against her, but she was stronger than she looked, and she braced herself to support him for the walk back to the infirmary. She could feel priests and acolytes all around, staring at her from hidden places, and their unasked questions burned in her mind.

She felt Brother Tenuk, as clearly as though she saw him standing at his prayer room window, watching them with his too-young eyes in his too-old face.

She ignored them all; and she ignored the roaring in her head as her heart demanded of her, *Where are your loyalties, Masayi girl?* She could not face that question, not now. Perhaps not ever.

"Come, Jovann. Come, noble prince," she said over and over, along with "Come, idiot bumpkin" now and then. So they reached the shadows and seclusion of the infirmary, and Jovann sat on the edge of his pallet, bent over with his head in his hands. Sairu undid his shirt and carefully pulled it back from the bloody patches where his wounds were reopened.

"Idiot," she hissed again, and set to work cleaning. "What were you thinking? Approaching Lady Hariawan as bold as the empress's monkey! Laying hands on her, even! I'd like to cane you myself for your stupidity."

He groaned again and shook his head even as his fingers dug into his hair. "She did not recognize me."

"What was that?"

He lifted his head then, glaring at Sairu in his frustration. "She did not recognize me. She did not know me at all." Along with the frustration, there was despair in his voice.

Sairu had no time for despair. "Well, why should she? You're only a slave, remember. One slave to whom she decided, in her grace, to show a little kindness. And this is how you repay that kindness? By insulting her? By declaring you'll not serve as her slave one minute and approaching her unbidden the next? Anwar's scepter and Hulan's crown, you couldn't have behaved more like a Chhayan dog-boy had you tried!"

She thought this insult would rouse him. But instead he merely sank his head back into his hands and did not speak. She heard his breath hiss between his teeth a few times as she applied salve to his wounds and wrapped them in bandages.

"Why did you call her Umeer's daughter?" Sairu asked at length.

"It was all she would tell me of her name."

Sairu studied what she could see of his face, which was part of his jaw and one ear. She didn't think even Princess Safiya could successfully read so little. "You have been sick with fever since we found you, and you have had no conversation with Lady Hariawan."

"I have," he insisted, his voice near a growl. "I've walked with her. In the Dream."

It was important for a Golden Daughter not to mistake suspicion for intuition. The latter was a gift of instinct, a gift to be used. But the former too often led the inquiring mind astray.

And yet Sairu could not shake the suspicion she had felt from the first evening in Daramuti, the same evening Lady Hariawan had banished her from her presence. The suspicion that the wounded stranger lying under her hand was no longer present within his body.

That he had gone dream-walking.

But that was impossible, she had reasoned with herself since then. She knew little enough about the Dream Walkers of the temple. They were a secret as closely kept as the Golden Daughters themselves. But she believed—and didn't think she was wrong to do so—that dream-walking was a carefully monitored skill that required precision, prayer, incense, rituals, and an entire network of holy men focused together in joint concentration. Until she'd met her mistress, she had not believed it could be accomplished by a woman. Which was foolish, she now realized.

And perhaps it was equally foolish to disbelieve that a Chhayan could dream-walk as well.

Sairu took a step back, her arms folded, eyeing her patient. Some of the bandages were already soaked through. "Does it hurt very much?" she asked.

He nodded without looking up.

She knelt before him and took hold of his hands, pulling them away from his head. He sat up straighter, scowling at her, and tried to withdraw, but she held on and turned his hands over so that they cupped empty air. "Let me help you," she said.

Then she touched his forehead and whispered, "The pain is here. Feel it. Beneath my finger. Feel your pain."

He winced. Then he closed his eyes, his brow knitting beneath her finger. She drew it down his cheek, down his neck, and rested on his shoulder. "The pain is here. Feel it here. Feel the pain resting here."

She felt his shoulder tense. She placed both hands on his upper arms now and slid her fingers gently down, over his elbows, over his wrists, and placed her palms atop his.

"Your pain is here, in your hands. Hold it. Feel it. It rests here in your hands. Hold your pain in the palms of your hands."

His face was relaxed now. She heard his breath come more easily, deeply, in through his nose, out through his mouth. His pain was resting, and for the moment he held it.

Suddenly he fixed a stare upon her, studying. She saw questions in his face, questions he dared not ask but kept at bay. She could see them growling behind the gates of his eyes.

"So." Sairu sat back and folded her hands. "You saw my mistress in your dreams. Are you then a Dream Walker?"

"I—I don't know what you mean," he replied. His concentration broken, he settled down into his cot, lying on his side. He no longer held his pain, but it was not so unbearable as it had been. "What is a Dream Walker?"

"It's a self-explanatory title. A Dream Walker walks in the Realm of Dreams."

"In that case, yes," Jovann replied. "Yes, I am."

Sairu tilted her head to one side. She looked like a dainty doll, incapable of cunning, incapable of inflicting pain, incapable of anything but decorative charm.

And she said, "Prove it."

11

"I HAVE NOTHING TO PROVE to you, little miss."

Sairu regarded the wary face before her, considering many things and choosing her next words with care. After all, the idea had only just come to her, and it was not politic to rush ahead without at least a moment's reflection.

But then, Golden Daughters were trained to make swift judgments—judgments which, right or wrong, had the potential to alter entire histories. In that moment Sairu believed that history was a knife balanced by its point on the end of her finger. She could only hold it upright for so long. It must, very soon now, tilt. But she could manipulate, by a twist of the wrist, which direction it would fall.

"You say my Lady Hariawan is this Umeer's daughter whom you met in the Dream," she said slowly, lacing her words with sweetness and masking her face in guileless concern. "If what you say is true, it verifies my suspicion that my mistress is one of the Dream Walkers. A rare, a wonderful individual."

"She is that," Jovann agreed, and Sairu could have pitied him his ardor. What a love-sick pup he looked, lying there in pain, his eyes full of emotions he did not quite understand.

"Love is a great asset to a Golden Daughter," Princess Safiya had explained to Sairu years before. "*It is the most powerful force in the worlds and therefore a dangerous weapon. Only take care you never permit this weapon to be used against you! Recognize love. Feed it in others. Root it out in yourself.*"

Sairu breathed three times, in and out, as she allowed her next words to play through her mind, testing them. Satisfied they would serve her purpose, she said, "I believe Lady Hariawan is in danger."

It worked like magic. She could almost have laughed. For Jovann's head came up, and by the burning in his eyes, she saw that all thought of his father and his desire to hasten home had vanished. No other thought could fit alongside his concern for the beautiful lady of his dream. No other passion could flourish while this fire raged.

Sairu thought she could take his love, drive it through his heart, and watch it kill him as effectively as any blade. Her stomach turned. For the second time that day, she feared she might be ill. And that was odd, for she was never unwell. So she shook herself, painted a new smile on her mouth, and watched the ongoing effect of her words.

"What kind of danger?" Jovann demanded. "From whom?" He looked about the infirmary, as though assassins and brigands might even now lurk in the deeper shadows or behind the humble screens. "This is a holy place, is it not? Is she not safe here?"

"She comes from the Crown of the Moon, the holiest, the mightiest temple in all the Noorhitam Empire," Sairu said, her voice low. "If she is not safe in that holy place, why would she be safer here?"

Jovann gazed at her long and hard, and she made doubly certain there was nothing for him to read on her face beyond a simple handmaiden's concern for her mistress. "We were sent to these mountains in disguise, and I was told that she is sick and needs the freshness of mountain air. But I have traveled with her for many months now, and I know that Lady Hariawan is not sick. At least, not in body. And I believe not in mind."

"But perhaps," Jovann finished for her, "in dream?"

"Perhaps." Sairu bowed her head demurely. "I fear for her. I suspect she travels into the Dream alone, unprotected by the brothers of the temple. Who knows what might assault her there, beyond the boundaries of our own world?"

She could see memories on his face now, recent memories. Try though she might, glancing at him from beneath her eyelashes, she could not read what those memories were. But she was almost certain now that he had indeed done as he said: He had walked with Lady Hariawan in the Dream.

And he knew something of her danger.

"I will protect her," Jovann said, sitting up, then winced at the pain in his back and hunched over.

Sairu laughed. "*You*? You can scarcely turn your head to look over your shoulder! How will you protect my mistress?"

The goading worked. "I am not as you see me now when I walk in the Dream. I am strong there. I can guard her; I can keep her from harm."

"But I do not know for certain that what you claim is the truth. I do not know that you are a Dream Walker." She leaned forward then, her hands still folded in her lap, and caught his gaze with her own. "I want proof."

"What sort of proof?"

"Dream-walk tonight. And when you return, bring me back something from the Realm of Dreams."

How anyone could sleep with that girl sitting across from him, silent as a shadow but watching, always watching, was a mystery Jovann did not like to try fathoming. It was unnerving.

Lying on his stomach so as not to add pressure to his wounded back, he turned his head on his pillow and glared at Sairu. "Do you *have* to be here?"

"Yes," she answered, and smiled.

He shivered. "Don't you ever sleep?"

Nothing but the smile in return.

Night fell heavily in the mountains, as though the darkness of the sky reached the peaks sooner than the valleys. Outside, the priests walked by light of torches, and Jovann could hear their haunting chants to welcome the rising of Hulan. He heard other sounds of the night as well, beyond the temple walls: the lonely cry of an owl on the hunt; the voice of an evening songbird singing the sorrow of another day lost; and even, Jovann believed, the far-off howl of a wolf, and another wolf answering, still more distant.

But no wolf was ever more threatening than the little handmaiden watching him.

"It's not as though you'll be able to *watch* my dream," Jovann persisted. "Go to your own rooms and come back in the morning. I'll bring back your proof."

"I know you will," Sairu replied. "But I'm going to watch and make certain you do so while sleeping."

He couldn't argue with that. After all, none of his own people believed him when he claimed to see the future in his dreams. Why should this little maid credit his tale of walking in the Dream itself?

He thought bitterly of his conversation with Sunan, which seemed so long ago. What a fool. What a *fool* he'd been! Did he really think anything would be changed, that somehow years could soften hatred? But he had. He always, somehow, managed to fool himself into thinking Sunan would see him as his brother one day. He was wrong. They were enemies. As surely as warrior and wolf would always be enemies, competing for land, for respect, for game, for life, so he and Sunan would hate each other to the end of time.

But his heart hurt at this thought, and he cursed himself again and again. Such a fool. Such a fool!

"You should lie still," Sairu said.

"I am still. Can't move much, can I?"

"You're not still inside. You're racing around within your head."

How could she see that from across the room? A single low lamp sat before her, casting most of its flickering light on her face, leaving him in shadow. How could she see his restlessness? Little witch-woman, he thought, and crushed his pillow under his arms.

"Do you know any lullabies?" he said suddenly.

"What?"

"Lullabies. Know any?"

She gave him such a look, he almost laughed. How delightful to see that smile of hers fall away, even for a moment! "Come," he said, his voice gentler than it had been, "surely Kitar handmaidens are taught a lullaby or two with which to soothe their masters and mistresses? Or, if nothing else, I'll bet your mother sang to you when you were small."

"She did not," said Sairu.

Something about her voice startled Jovann, and while he had opened his mouth to continue his harangue, he closed it again, all words cut off. Then he sighed heavily and turned his face away from her again. But he could still feel her eyes on the back of his head.

Then, to his surprise, he heard a soft voice singing. It found the notes with difficulty, wavering and weak at first. But as it sang, it grew stronger, until he could hear the words. And, surprising him most of all, he realized that she sang a Chhayan lullaby. One he knew as well as his own mother's voice.

"Go to sleep, go to sleep,
My good boy, go to sleep.

Where did the songbird go?
Beyond the mountains of the sun.
Beyond the gardens of the moon.
Where did the Dara go?
Beyond the Final Water's waves
To sing before the mighty throne.

Go to sleep, go to sleep,
My good boy, go to sleep."

The first few uncertain notes touched his ear, and he was back home once more in his father's gurta. And the fires were low outside, casting only the ember glow through the door flap to rest on his mother's face. The buffalo lowed in their pastures. The plains-wind sighed on its long journey to the mountains, to the sea.

And far away, beyond the handmaiden's voice, beyond the remembered voice of his own mother, he heard another voice calling, its words like river water.

Won't you follow me, Jovann?

By the time the song ended, Jovann was asleep.

Sairu got up slowly and stepped across the room to bend over him. She listened to his breathing and knew that he was gone beyond the waking world. Nodding, satisfied, she knelt, this time beside his bed, and waited to see if he could do as she asked.

Jovann stepped out of his body, gladly leaving it and all its reopened wounds behind. He followed the voice of the wood thrush, which seemed to blend with the handmaiden's song until the two became one.

Beyond the mountains of the sun.
Beyond the gardens of the moon.
Where did the Dara go?

The white emptiness surrounded him, but it could not be entirely emptiness so long as that song reached out to him, guiding him from his own world into the Between. He felt as though he climbed into the sky and wondered if he would be able to glimpse Daramuti far below him if he looked hard enough. Would he be able to espy the dreams of all those who slept tucked away in the high Khir Mountains?

But even the mountains, he knew, were too small for him to discern them. Not from here. Not from so far away. So he did not look. The song called to him, silver and bright and welcoming, and he pursued it.

The mortal world was far behind him now.

He saw the embracing trees before him, and through them he could see the Wood and the great Grandmother Tree. The white emptiness was still at his back, but he charged through, passing between the two trees, and then the emptiness was gone.

He stood in the Wood once more.

He took a step and felt himself become a solid presence, as like unto his mortal body as his mind could conceive. He had limbs he could see and feel, had breath in his lungs, and a heart beating in his chest. It was still not as solid as his real body. How could it be? A man cannot have two bodies at once. But it was a strong manifestation, strong enough to be believed. And this body did not have agonizing stripes across its back.

Jovann looked for the wood thrush in the branches of the Grandmother Tree but could not see it. He drew nearer, and he thought the clearing was darker than it had ever been. The Grandmother's leaves were heavier, thicker perhaps, blocking out more of whatever light source shone up above the Wood, be it sun, moon, or something else entirely. Either way, this small circle of existence was as gloomy as late evening.

And still Jovann could not find the wood thrush. But he heard its voice singing, an enigma of light and sound combined.

Where did the Dara go?
Where did the Dara go?

"Where did the Dara go?" Jovann whispered.

"They are beyond Hulan's Gate," said Lady Hariawan.

He knew she stood behind him. The girl of his dreams. He knew without turning, without seeing her face, for his heart beat with so powerful a lurch that he felt its movement even back inside his mortal body lying upon the pallet in the infirmary. For a moment he could not speak, so thick was his throat. Then he whispered, "Umeer's daughter."

"I am here. Look at me, Juong-Khla Jovann."

She did not need to speak his name to command him. He turned willingly and looked again upon her lovely face. And here, in the Wood, there was no evil burn mark to mar the perfection of her skin, to distract from the exquisite proportions of her features.

"I saw you," Jovann said. "I saw you today. In the waking world. Did you not know me there? Did you not recognize me?"

The golden light and green shadows of the Wood fell softly upon her, swaying gently with each move she made as she approached him. Her hair was long down her back, even as it had been earlier that day, and her robes were once more fine and intricately made. The same pattern of painted flowers and vines decorated her pale skin. One small hand reached out to him, and he shivered with delight and dread as she touched his cheek. The scent of harimau wafted over him, spicy and intoxicating.

"Let us walk together, Jovann, son of Juong-Khla."

He obeyed without another word. She took his arm and led him, and he walked as she led, once more stepping out of the Grandmother's protective circle into the enormous reaches of the Wood—reaches so vast that, were he to try to conceive of their hugeness, he knew he would go mad. But he did not worry about that. Lady Hariawan walked beside him, and ahead, in the distance, he could hear the song still singing. And it was as though the song itself created the path opening before them, a path of pale golden dirt which his bare feet trod without crushing so much as a single leaf or blade of grass.

"Where are we going?" Jovann asked.

"To the Dream," she said.

"Are we very close?"

She looked up at him, and he wondered if it were pity or scorn he saw in her eyes. "This is the Wood Between," she said. "It lies both near to and far from the Waking World and the Dream. It lies between all worlds. But who can measure it with mortal distances?" She shook her head and continued walking, speaking softly. "The Brethren have long sought it. They have discussed and they have theorized. They have longed. But none of them found it, only you. Not even I could reach it, though I saw it. Not until I heard you calling and this path opened to me. It is a great thing you have done, Juong-Khla Jovann."

Jovann felt his heart swelling in his breast. He could have burst for the pleasure of pleasing her.

"Now," she continued, "I want you to take me to the Gardens of the Moon."

Had someone asked Jovann if he knew the way to Hulan's Garden, he would have said no at once. But when this girl, this nameless Lady Hariawan, daughter of Umeer, spoke, he heard the wood thrush calling. And it was as though the knowledge grew inside him. He had no room for doubt, only certainty.

He took the girl's hand, and now he led her. Even as before, the Wood began to fade around them. The endless Wood, the borders of which could not be marked, vanished on all sides, giving way to curling mist.

The Realm of Dreams, from whence all dreams of men and beast and Faerie folk are sprung, rose up to claim them. And it was of itself an empty, formless place, waiting to be shaped.

Jovann tightened his grip on Lady Hariawan's hand. "This way," he said, and plunged into the mist. He still heard the singing,

Where did the Dara go?
Where did the Dara go?

Following that voice, he watched as the landscape changed before him. He saw mountains, he saw valleys; he saw oceans and rivers and deserts. He crossed them all in a moment, and Lady Hariawan gasped at the strides they made, for even she, in all her power, had never come so far.

Suddenly there was the gate before them—so distant as to appear small, but the only solid, unshifting form in all this realm. The Moon Gate arch, the perfect original of a million mortal copies, and no child of Noorhitam would have failed to recognize it.

Lady Hariawan drew a sharp breath. Jovann turned to her with a smile. "You asked for Hulan's Gate, my dear Umeer's daughter?"

Even as he spoke, his voice was drowned out by the boom of chanting.

All around them it resounded, the chorus of many voices raised together in a rolling thunder of strength. He could hear the voices reaching out to each other, supporting each other. Then they reached out toward him.

He looked this way and that. Shadows appeared out of the mist, chanting in time to their own sedate pace. At the sight of them, Lady Hariawan growled without words. She grasped Jovann with both hands. "Hurry," she said. "We can still beat them."

They were running the next moment, running on a surface of mist that heated beneath their feet until Jovann knew it was no longer mist but fire-seared smoke. The shadows grew larger, drawing nearer, and with them came the darkness of their voices, pressing in like night. But ahead the stone gate stood tall, and through it Jovann saw a light shining, a guiding, brilliant beacon which not even the chant could suppress. They had only to reach it. They had only to—

"*Hurry!*" Lady Hariawan screamed.

Jovann, without a thought, caught her up in his arms. She was so light, so delicate, so insubstantial. She weighed nothing, and he moved faster carrying her than he did with her clutching his arm. So he cradled her close and ran.

The shadows closed in. They were all around him, behind and on every side except the path to the gate. This they could not seem to penetrate. Their chanting became faster and more erratic.

Then the gate was huge, towering indescribably tall above him. So brilliant was the light falling through it that for a moment Jovann could have believed the gate was the shining moon herself. He could see nothing of what lay beyond. But he did not doubt, and he did not falter.

On the very threshold he heard a rush of great water.

Then, with Lady Hariawan in his arms, he plunged through just as phantom hands snatched at the back of his head and tore away a piece of his hair.

12

SAIRU KNELT WITH HER eyes closed and her hands folded. But she did not doze, not for a moment. Every sense was alivc with an almost painful clarity. Even the feel of the floor beneath her knees was as sharp as knives, though she never shifted her position.

All was quiet. Not silent, for the mountain night was alive with sounds beyond the infirmary walls. Within, however, there was only Jovann's deep, sleep-filled breathing, contrasting with her own light breaths. The flame of her lamp burned straight, scarcely daring to flicker.

Nothing changed. No creak, no cry, not even a wind in the door. But suddenly Sairu's eyes flew open, and she gazed down at the back of Jovann's sleeping head. Other than that swift movement of her eyelids she held perfectly still for some minutes, staring at what she could not yet see.

Then, slowly, she bent over and looked more closely at the black hair she had tied back with a length of leather cord earlier that day.

"What's wrong?"

The cat's voice startled her, but she betrayed none of her surprise. Very coldly she lifted her chin. A feline face watched her from the other side of Jovann's sleeping mat. His whiskers were ridiculously long and curled at the ends, and she had to fight the urge to reach out and pluck one from his arrogant white muzzle.

"What are you looking at?" the cat persisted, making no effort to keep his voice down.

"Can you not see it?" Sairu replied, her own voice scarcely above a whisper.

The cat twitched an ear irritably. Then he put his nose to the back of Jovann's head and sniffed. The other ear twitched as well. "I smell a stranger on him. And . . . and smoke."

Sairu inclined her chin in acknowledgement. And she replied, "A length of his hair is gone."

At first the roar of water was so enormous that it overwhelmed all else, and Jovann wondered if he and his beautiful lady would drown in the very sound.

Then the roar retreated, dying back to a gentle murmur. They sat where they had fallen through the gate, holding each other, her arms tight around his neck, his arms tight around her waist, their eyes squeezed shut.

And their ears were filled with a song which in turn filled their hearts with visions.

Jovann could never say afterwards if he opened his eyes. It did not matter one way or the other. His mortal body was far from here, and this phantom existence did not need eyes to see that which was sung straight into his spirit. But perhaps out of pure force of habit he blinked and raised his head, tried to look around.

The light, which had been unbearably blinding as he'd plunged through the gate, was now remote and yet simultaneously all-consuming. He saw the vast world around him, every inch of it, illuminated in that glow. Yet it was too far, too distant for comprehension, and the song too passionate for understanding.

He did not need to understand.

His mind, ready to burst with the inconceivable, forced the song and the vastness into images he recognized. He found that he and Lady Hariawan knelt on the shore of an ocean. Or perhaps not an ocean. Maybe a river, but so huge, so far-stretching, so full of Forever that it could hold all the oceans of all the worlds in its heart and cradle them there.

White surf broke just at his knees and pulled at the edges of Lady Hariawan's robes. Where it broke, it shattered into a hundred thousand colored hues, most of which Jovann could not see, so his mind interpreted them merely as brilliant, sparkling crystals of water. But the waves pulled those crystals back, and they dissolved into the deep black of the endless water, glimmering beneath the surface in reflection of . . .

Oh! in reflection of the Garden!

Jovann felt his heart thundering in his phantom breast as he tilted his gaze up and up and upward still. It was just as well that heartbeats did not matter here, or he would have died trying to take in that which spread before his vision.

The Moon's Garden was full of flowers: enormous, spreading, clustering flowers of light, of night, of half-light. They shimmered, they spread, they twined through the sky, brilliant tendrils of living, glowing beauty, and a single petal would have been enough to cover all of Daramuti and the Khir Mountains. A blossom would encompass a kingdom.

They spread across the eternal sky. And they bloomed before Jovann's desperate gaze, then faded, then bloomed again.

At first the flowers were all he could see. He might have sat for an age or two of mortal worlds, just trying to look with all the fullness of his heart, trying to see them as he knew they must be seen, but as he could not see. The enormous Song rained down upon him, and he wept without knowing that he did so.

Then he realized that the Song did not come from the blossoms themselves. His vision cleared a little more, and suddenly he saw the Dara.

His mind had no possible foundation of understanding to encompass the living form of even a single star. But his upbringing, his childhood, stepped in where his reason could not and supplied him with a form he could comprehend, however unlikely and otherworldly that form might be.

He saw the Dara as his mother had told them they were: Shining beings on four delicate legs ending in tiny cloven hooves that could, with a single stamp, crush the heads of tigers. Sweeping manes shining like waterfalls of starlight.

And a coiled horn, sharp as life itself, protruding from each forehead.

They sang not with their mouths but with their whole beings. A million songs and more, all unique, all joined together in one tremendous chorus. These linked like threads in a tapestry, individual and yet only complete when joined together.

A single moment of that Song as sung by the Dara would have killed Jovann in his mortal body. But once more his heart took in only what it could, expressing it in forms just barely within the realm of imagining, and he survived. He survived and gloried in what he saw, what he heard, what he tasted.

He realized—after what may have been a hundred years of frozen listening—that Lady Hariawan's grip on his neck had not loosened. Though it caused him physical pain to avert his eyes from the splendor above, he looked down upon her. The lights of the Garden highlighted her black hair in many beautiful colors. But her face he could not see, for it was buried in his neck and shoulder like some terrified child's.

"My darling," he said, for he could call her nothing else while under the Song of the Dara. "My darling, look. We are safe here. No evil shadows could pass through that Gate or dare to step foot in this place. We are safe. We are whole. Look and see!"

She did not move. He feared she might be dead, and this fear brought such a surge of mortality coursing through his spirit that one of the Dara stopped singing and looked down upon him where he knelt on the shore.

The star shook its mane and gazed with puzzled interest. Then it stepped from the sky, passing by the glorious blossoms without a glance, until it stood just above Jovann, its feet near, but not touching, the great water.

Who are you? it asked.

The voice flattened Jovann to his face. He clutched Lady Hariawan to his breast and lay gasping in agony, and the waves washed over his head.

The star blinked slowly. Then it said, **Forgive me. Of course, you are**

mortal.

Then it shook itself with an effort, and light and glory fell from its being. Or rather it seemed to take on a covering, a shroud, blocking out the full truth of itself, containing it in a form no less beautiful but much less complex. When it spoke again, its voice no longer rang with the Song of its millions of brothers and sisters but was singular. It was a voice that could move to tears but not kill.

"Who are you, mortal, to have entered my Mother's realm?"

Jovann shuddered. Then he propped himself up on one elbow and, summoning all the courage of his being, gazed at the Dara once more. To his surprise—and to his horror—he saw it clothed in a form of flesh. Skin encased its majesty, and softest fur of silvery blue. He thought if he reached out and touched that horn, it would prick his finger and draw blood.

"Dara," he gasped, "you should not look at me. I am unworthy."

The unicorn seemed to consider this. Then it tossed its head. "It does not matter. If you came through the Gate then there is reason for your coming, and worth has nothing to do with it."

It took another step, inclining its head so that its horn was now mere inches from Jovann's face. It studied him with eyes of deep, midnight blue in which the light of its star-glory still shone.

"What is your name?" the Dara asked again.

"Juong-Khla Jovann," Jovann replied at once.

But the unicorn shook its head. "I asked your name, not what you are called. Never mind. It is difficult for me to see through these eyes, but I see enough. You are welcome, Juong-Khla Jovann. I have sung of your coming before now. And who is this with you?"

"I . . . I do not know," Jovann replied. He pushed himself upright again with some difficulty. Lady Hariawan, however, lay upon the shore, her hands clenched into such tight fists that had she been in her mortal body her nails would have cut her palms. She still did not move, did not raise her head. "She is dear to me," Jovann said, putting out his hands to help her, and finding her whole body resistant to his touch. "She has long sought Hulan's Garden. I helped her."

The unicorn regarded her beneath its unfathomable gaze. It said, "She has never sought the Gardens."

It turned then and started walking through the air above the water. The waves lashed at its feet but did not quite reach. "Come," it called back over its shoulder. "Walk with me."

For a moment Jovann could not make the words fit into his brain. After all, one does not expect to be invited to walk with a star. But when he understood, he leapt to his feet at once and, with renewed strength, hauled Lady Hariawan to her feet as well. She rose and swayed where she stood, her head bowed so that her hair covered her face. She would not look up at the sky.

"My darling," Jovann said, putting an arm around her shoulders to support her as they took the first steps, "please look around you. I would hate for you to miss what you have so long sought."

She said nothing. She kept pace with him, however, and she did not fall.

For the first many steps Jovann did not stop to consider that there was only ocean before them. He simply followed the star as he was bidden. But he frowned suddenly and looked down at his feet, wondering if he walked on the surface of the water itself. Instead he found that just beneath the water a strand of silvery sand supported his feet. Whether that strand had always been there, disguised by the waves, or whether it had grown up suddenly in order to offer him safe passage, he could not say. It did not matter.

The star did not walk on the water or the strand, but kept to the sky, pacing in the darkness beneath the Garden blooming above. Other Dara turned and watched their progress, singing as though to prophesy each step before it was taken. They were too much for Jovann, so he focused on the silvery-blue flanks of the incarnate unicorn, which, while not exactly comfortable, fit better into his reason.

"Do you want to know what I am called?" the Dara asked as they progressed across the ocean, farther and farther from the gate.

"Yes," Jovann said. "I would like to know."

"I am called Cé Imral," said the star. "I believe you would know me as *Chiev*. I shine in the northern sky."

"Chiev," Jovann repeated. His feet faltered, and his heart beat a furious rhythm. "The North Star."

How many times in his life had he and all his father's tribe turned their faces to the sky, seeking out Chiev to guide them straight and true to the summer hunting grounds. The star of the true north, the star with the blue aura.

A thrill of pleasure passed through Jovann's body from his heart to his head. He looked down at Lady Hariawan pressed close to his side. He wondered if she heard, if she saw, if she felt any of the things he now experienced. But how could she? If she did, she would not be hiding her face in her hands behind that curtain of hair. She would be looking up, looking around, drinking in all she could possibly contain.

Perhaps she perceived everything differently, he thought. Perhaps there were no images in her head to contain these Gardens.

Perhaps that which seemed to him the very perfection of heaven was to her the very depths of hell.

He had no words to comfort her. He could do nothing but hold her close. She had wanted to come here, and he had brought her. He would see her safely out once more. But not yet. He must follow the star.

The farther they went, the more thickly bloomed the flowers above them, the more thickly gathered the Dara. All Jovann's vision was full of light, and even the shadows seemed to shine. The water, deep as endless night, filled with the glory above it and seemed to live and love in response, its waves echoing back songs. Jovann found that he himself was trying to sing.

He quickly shut his mouth. What a gawping frog he must sound among the Moon's own children! But somehow, he thought, he was meant to sing. Somehow he must try to learn.

Then he forgot everything. For the Moon herself was above him.

If the stars had been glorious, here was something beyond glory. Something so huge that mortal words could not encompass her nor mortal eyes perceive her. But he knew it was she. He felt her above him, tremendously beautiful. The Queen of the Sky.

The goddess of his people.

He felt the trueness of *motherhood* surrounding him. The reality of all things female, all things strong. The greatness of pain, of sacrifice, of joy. The Lady Moon existed in mighty contrast to the Lordly Sun, as harmony complementing his melody. But it was she, Jovann knew with a sudden clarity of vision, who was the greater strength.

He could not put a shape to her; she dazzled him too much. He tried to see her as the shining moon he had watched wax and wane in the mortal world, but she would not be fitted into that image.

She sang. He knew she spoke to him. But her words were too enormous, and they washed over him like the whole of the ocean itself. He could do nothing, nothing but hold Lady Hariawan close and hope that she did not shatter in his arms.

The blue star rested its horn upon Jovann's shoulder. Suddenly he could hear the words in the Moon's voice.

I have sung of your coming in the great Harmony given me by He Who Names Them. I have sung of your coming from Beyond the Dream. And I sing your name—Dream Walker, Vision Speaker. Blessed forerunner to whom the Secret will be given.

Jovann looked up. He saw a form like a woman's, but more like the Truth of Womanhood. He saw his mother as he perceived her with his heart, sitting enthroned, beautiful beyond words. Full of light. Full of Song.

The Moon smiled at him. And he went down upon one knee, Lady Hariawan forgotten as he sought to make reverence before her whom he had worshipped since childhood.

"Get up," said the star behind him. "Do not worship. For she did not compose the Song we sing."

Jovann could not obey. He remained kneeling, his face upraised, gazing upon that vision he could scarcely bear to see.

The Moon smiled, but it was a sad smile. Then she said:

I have dreaded and longed for your coming. It is for me the foretelling of sorrow.

He could not reply. There could be no reply. Of course she had known he would come. How could she not? She must know every secret of his heart.

"Take care, mortal," whispered the star at his back, and the horn pressed harder into his shoulder. "Do not worship."

The Moon leaned down from her great throne, scattering light and brilliance from her face. One hand stretched out, and Jovann saw her pluck a blossom growing near to her throne. Worlds trembled when she plucked it. Nations could be toppled in that single action.

I will now speak the Secret, the Moon said, cupping the flower in her hand and turning once more to address Jovann. *And you will carry it beyond to the mortal world to give them hope. To give them comfort. To remind them that they are not forgotten. Will you hear me, Dream Walker?*

Jovann could not speak with his mouth, but his heart shouted out in response, "Yes! Yes! Yes!"

And it was as though he shouted at the same time, "Mercy! Mercy! Mercy!"

So the Moon spoke Mercy. And there was wonder in her words, as though she herself could scarcely believe them.

My Lord, the Lumil Eliasul, the Giver of Songs will enter the mortal world. By the will of his Father, he will take upon himself the form of a man. Flesh. Blood. A body that decays with Time. But this body will not bind him, and he will wear it in perfection. He will slay at last his Great Enemy.

Here her voice faltered. And all the voices of the heavens stilled. The Song supporting everything in that world, the Song forming the foundations upon which the Gardens, the Dara, the Moon herself existed, froze, as every star in the sky held its breath.

And Jovann too held his breath, knowing that he was about to hear something that would change everything. Everything. Not just for himself, but for his world. For all worlds. For all Times.

The Moon said, *He will win for himself a bride from among the mortals. And he will take her for his own, and prove for all eternity how great, how deep, how unknowable, how endless is his love.*

The stars breathed again. And they exploded suddenly in triumphant chorus, their language far beyond Jovann's comprehension. But he found his own mouth moving, his own voice singing,

Beyond the Final Water Falling,
The Song forever Calling.
The Sun, the Moon, the Stars proclaim it from on high!
He will return for me.

And the Song containing the Secret now spoken as Promise shot across the whole of the Heavens and rained down upon all the worlds. All heard it, though few understood its meaning. But understanding could not change the truth of it as it fell in splendor both seen and unseen. In a kingdom hidden inside a mountain, a queen stood at the mountain peak and received the Song in both upraised hands. In another kingdom made of stone and despair, a different queen heard it, and her beautiful face, swathed in veiling enchantments, trembled with fear. A lone knight in a far Haven, deep in the Wood Between, raised up her head from her labors, and her dark eyes filled with the Song she heard. Faerie kings and queens, lords and ladies across the nations and the worlds heard the strange sounds of the Stars' Song, and they wondered at the marvel they heard spoken.

Even in the mortal world there were those who felt a new stirring in their hearts. And they briefly raised their faces to the heavens, gazing up at the so-distant stars. Wonder moved them, and they thought that mercy was now possible, that hope would be restored, that they were not so wholly abandoned to their helpless, decaying state.

The chorus might have rung for a thousand years and more. It did not matter. Time did not matter here in the Gardens. But when at last the first explosion of sound faded a little, Jovann found himself smiling up into the Moon's shining visage.

She took the flower in her hand and extended it to Jovann. *Take this,* she said, *and return to the mortal world. It will be a sign, a sign of the promise to be fulfilled. For she whom the Lumil Eliasul takes as his bride will wear this flower upon her hand.*

Suddenly Jovann felt a warm, wonderful breath upon his forehead. And then the Moon kissed him. She drew back and gazed forever down into his eyes.

It is a gift of the heart, she said. *Choose well to whom you give it. I will see you again, sweet child. Soon now.*

The Gate stood before him.

Jovann blinked several times, and he felt his spirit waver like a flame in the wind. Why was he here? Now? The last he recalled, he stood before the Lady Moon herself, receiving her secret. And now . . .

Was it a dream?

"No," said the Dara. "But you must return to the Dream."

Jovann startled and whirled around. There stood the shimmering North Star in the darkness of the sky. Blue flame crept up its slender legs and licked from the ends of its mane. It wanted to shake off its corporeal form, to return to the Song above. But it waited patiently, regarding Jovann with solemn, ageless eyes.

Jovann realized that his hand clenched in a fist. He tore his gaze from the unicorn and studied his fist, wondering what he held inside. But he could not make his fingers uncurl.

Suddenly his head came up. "Where is Lady Hariawan?"

"There," said the unicorn, and indicated with a sweep of its horn. Jovann looked and saw a crumpled form lying just before the enormous gate. He realized that the distance between him and the Gate was much greater than he had first supposed, for there were no clear perspective marks here, and the Gate was huge indeed. But he saw Lady Hariawan, tiny and limp on the stretch of shore.

"What has become of her?" he demanded, breaking into a run even as he spoke. Waves splashed beneath his feet, and he felt the sand bar giving way, crumbling at each footfall. He doubled his speed, and the star kept pace easily behind him. "What has become of her?" Jovann gasped again.

"She could not bear what her mind created for her," said the star, and offered no other explanation. Somehow Jovann understood without understanding, and he asked nothing more.

The ocean swelled up in a wave behind him, and he felt it catch him and thrust him forward. He drew a deep breath, though breathing scarcely mattered here, and forced his eyes to remain open even as the many-colored water overwhelmed him. He glimpsed the world as seen through the film of the Final Water, and it was a dreadful sight, dreadful in its beauty.

Then, with a crash and shattering of crystal, he was deposited upon the little strip of shore before the gate. Bits of light fell from his hair, dripped down his cheeks and chin, and he laughed suddenly, for it was thrilling to have been borne on such a wave.

But he shook the laugh away and crawled to Lady Hariawan.

She lay in a faint, her face turned away from him, one arm curved above her head, the other draped over her middle. Her bare feet were covered in sand, and there was sand in her hair and robes.

"My darling!" Jovann gasped, and he took her into his arms. As he did so, her face turned toward him.

Jovann screamed.

For it was not Lady Hariawan's face he saw. It was the face of a withered hag.

"What have you brought upon us, mortal?"

The star standing on the edge of the shore flared its nostrils, and darkness filled its eyes. Its voice rumbled down through Jovann's terror and spoke with fearful dread into his heart. "What you have you brought upon us?"

Jovann shuddered, and his arms threatened to thrust their burden away. But one hand was still clenched in a fist, and he felt the thing he held. Though he could not recall what it was, somehow it gave him strength.

Averting his eyes from the horrible vision, he struggled to his feet, with that which had once been Lady Hariawan limp in his grasp. He turned to the star. But the star spoke first.

"I feel it come," it said, and the core of its being shook so that the water beneath its feet rippled and rushed away. "I've sung of it but without understanding. I feel the change you foreshadow."

It took a step nearer then lowered its horn so that the point rested just above Lady Hariawan's heart. But it did not touch her.

What have you brought into our midst, mortal man? Even as it spoke, blue flames burst across its flanks, up its neck, engulfing its head. It reared up, trumpeting a warning to the sky, and all the stars above turned their heads and stared down upon Jovann and his burden.

Jovann turned and fell back through Hulan's Gate.

13

SOMETHING HAS CHANGED."

Sairu looked up from her silent study of the slave and gazed across the room. The cat perched on a nearby empty pallet and had, up until a moment ago, entertained himself with a nice, long, noisy groom.

But now he sat upright, his body perfectly still save for the tip of his tail, which twitched faster, faster, faster, until the whole sweeping plume of it lashed like a whip.

"Something has changed," he said, and his voice was not the voice Sairu had become so strangely accustomed to hearing from her devilish companion. It scarcely sounded like a cat's voice anymore. It was old. And very, very young. It was a voice of pure gold.

"Monster?" Sairu said, gently.

The cat turned to her. His eyes were like two suns, huge in his face. He spoke again in that unfamiliar voice: "I heard the stars sing out together. And in their Song they declared a wonder. I do not . . . "

He blinked slowly. To Sairu's unending surprise, two bright tears fell down his face and landed on his paws. The cat appeared equally surprised.

He shook himself and put a paw to his nose, rubbing the fur, licking, then rubbing again. He muttered, "I have not wept in a century at least. Not since I lay upon the shore of the Dark Water. Why . . . why now?"

"Monster?" Sairu said again, this time less gently, for she found that her heart was beating with a sensation not unlike fear. "What has happened? What did you hear?"

The cat shook his ears. When he placed his paw beside its mate and looked again at Sairu, there was no trace of tears on his face. When he spoke, his voice was his own once more. "I don't know what I heard. I don't pretend to understand. But . . ." He wrapped his tail tightly around his body and over his paws. "But the worlds have changed forever."

Sairu opened her mouth to ask what he meant. In that moment, however, Jovann's body convulsed. His back arched fearfully, his head upraised from his pillow, his jaw straining as he clenched his teeth. He made no sound, which was worse still, for the whole movement of his body was like a scream. Sairu was not one to startle easily, but she gasped and, moving on pure reflex, fell back from him upon the floor. Her stomach jumped sickeningly inside her, and her hands sought inside her sleeves for the knives hidden there.

But the convulsion ceased as quickly as it had begun. Jovann collapsed back upon his pillow, and though his breathing was faster, his body was still. Sairu bent over him, pressing a hand to his neck to feel his pulse, which rushed beneath her fingers.

The Gate was gone.

Jovann knew without looking. He knew in the deep places of his spirit, and his heart broke for the knowledge. The Gate was gone. And this was as well, for had not the stars roared in sudden anger? But perhaps . . .

Perhaps he should have stayed. For it could not be evil to be overwhelmed, to be consumed in the fire of a star.

But all was gone now. He felt the formlessness of the Dream around him. He did not see it, for he was too frightened to look. But he felt it and knew it for what it was.

And the dark chanting bore down upon him.

Jovann pushed himself upright, though his hands sank into the Dream and the mist rose up to choke him. Now he must open his eyes. He must! He could not hide in the cowardice of blindness. Everything inside him longed to hide, to cover his face, to see nothing. But he must look.

When he did, he saw formless shadows towering above him. They seemed to have long limbs, reaching out to each other, fingertips touching as they formed a closing circle. It was impossible to discern how near or how far they might be. They could be within reach of his hand. They could be leagues away.

One thing he knew for certain: A single voice pulled away from the chant and called out in—he thought—surprise.

Jovann?

It was too much to bear. Jovann struggled to his feet and cast about desperately. Where was she? Where was the girl? He knew, somehow, that the phantoms sought her, though it was his name he heard again, ringing out from the shadows.

Jovann? Jovann? Juong-Khla Jovann?

There she lay, almost at his feet, the mist of the Dream covering her like a veil. For a moment only he hesitated, fearing that if he touched her, if he pulled her to him, he would find that he held not his beautiful lady, but the hag he had glimpsed beyond Hulan's Gate. He shoved this fear away and fell upon his knees before her, his hands lifting her from the mist. And when her head tilted back, he saw her smooth face. Her eyelids fluttered open, and he was lost in the indescribable darkness of her lovely gaze.

"My lady?" he gasped, unable to call her "darling" here, beyond the Gate. His voice was indiscernible, swallowed in the chant. "My lady, we must—"

A sudden jolt of strength passed through her and up his arms. He cried out even as she pushed away and rose to her feet. She gazed down upon him without recognition, and he even believed—though he would have died before admitting it—that he saw hatred in her gaze.

"It's a lie. It's all a lie!" she hissed.

The phantoms were upon them. Jovann screamed as he saw a long, shadowy hand reaching out, the fingers passing across Lady Hariawan's face. But those fingers closed upon nothing.

For Lady Hariawan vanished.

"My lady!" Jovann cried.

The phantom turned to him. Its face was formless, nothing to differentiate between it and its brethren. But while the others continued their chant with a terrible, driving urgency, this one was silent as it turned. It had no eyes Jovann could discern, but he felt a burning gaze boring into him.

Jovann. My son.

The Dream shattered.

"What's wrong?" The cat's warm body brushed against Sairu's arm. "What's happened? Is he all right?"

"I don't know," Sairu snapped. "He's alive, but—"

The cat sniffed at Jovann's cheek and ear. Jovann's hand came up suddenly, wrapped around the cat's head, and pushed him, hissing, off the pallet. "Go away!" he snarled into his pillow.

Sairu felt her whole body go limp in a flood of relief. With an effort she controlled her voice, saying only, "You are awake." She dared not try to say more. Quickly she removed her hand from Jovann's neck where she had felt for his pulse, assuming a demeanor of calm.

"I am awake," Jovann agreed, his voice muffled by the pillow. He smacked at his cheek and rubbed it furiously. "Anwar wither those ticklish whiskers!" He squeezed his eyes tighter shut, then opened them, blinking up at Sairu. When he tried to push himself up, his body reminded him violently of his earlier beating, and he winced.

Sairu said nothing. She watched him, studied him. And she saw how, even as he carefully moved himself into a seated position, one hand remained closed in a fist. She allowed him to recover himself, to shake the sleep from his head. He moaned and twisted his neck. Then he fixed Sairu with a studying gaze of his own.

"So, little miss," he said, "are you satisfied?"

"Did you dream-walk?" Sairu demanded.

He nodded. For a moment he closed his eyes. "I saw . . . such things. I saw . . ."

"Did you see my mistress?"

His eyes flew wide. Then he was struggling against the pain of his own body to get to his feet. "She was in trouble! We passed through the gate, and the phantoms were around us again, chanting. I must—"

He was already moving toward the door. But this was unacceptable. Sairu reached out, caught his arm and twisted it. She did not need to do anything else, for that motion was enough to set his back on fire with agony, and he crumpled to his knees. Resisting only aggravated his wounds, so he held perfectly still, his head straining back to stare up at her, angry questions in his eyes.

"I'm sorry," Sairu said, and smiled ruefully. "You may not leave, and you may not approach my mistress."

"But she may be—"

"I shall see to her," Sairu insisted. "You will wait."

Briefly she saw an argument forming on his face, along his jaw and over his brow. But then it cleared and he nodded. She released her hold on his arm, and he remained where he knelt, unwilling to move for fear of irritating his wounds still more.

Sairu passed quickly to the infirmary door and paused on the edge of the lamplight. Her eyes sought the cat, who sat in a quiet corner. "Stay with him," she said.

The cat blinked once.

Then she was hurrying across the darkness of the temple grounds. Hulan did not light her way, for the moon had hidden her thin face behind a cloud that night. The darkness was deep, and all the temple dwellers had long since sought the refuge of sleep, allowing the torches to burn low and extinguish.

But Sairu was not alone. Small, snuffly snouts pressed up against her calves and ankles, and she felt the warm bodies of her dogs surrounding her, guarding her from all the possible threats of the night as she glided and they waddled down the path from the infirmary to the house where Lady

Hariawan dwelled.

The slaves were asleep in the outermost chamber, and no one stood guard. Sairu and her little pack passed unimpeded through Lady Hariawan's set of rooms. Darkness crouched there, but Sairu felt no more threat from this darkness than from any of the shadows in the grounds outside. She listened closely but heard nothing untoward, not even a growl from timid Rice Cake, who was the most nervous of the trio. The dogs eagerly spread out to sniff the beds and belongings of the various sleeping slaves, and Sticky Bun had a pleasant roll and stretch on a rug. Nothing more.

Sairu opened the next door and passed into the chamber beyond, then on to the chamber beyond that. She slid this door back as silently as she could, motioning sharply for her dogs to stay put. Peering inside, she saw her mistress lying upon her bed.

Lady Hariawan was fast asleep. Even in the gloom, Sairu could hear her rhythmic breathing. She felt the pulse of gentle, dreamless ease.

After slipping inside and sliding the door shut, Sairu stood in the darkness and closed her eyes. With every other sense besides sight she sought for a sign of disturbance. The scent of harimau touched her nose, but it was faint and might be old.

She sensed no phantom presence. She sensed no fear.

A sudden surge of guilt plucked at her brain. Lady Hariawan had forbidden her to enter, and yet here she stood! An insubordinate Golden Daughter, ignoring the explicit command of her mistress.

She shuddered and exited the chamber as silently as she had entered it, the only sound the soft *shhhh* of the thin door sliding along its grooves. Her dogs swarmed her heels again, following her. She paused in the outermost chamber, then turned to her dogs and whispered, "Sit. Stay."

Someone must guard Lady Hariawan. Someone she could trust.

The dogs were nearly invisible in the darkness, but she could almost feel them wagging their whole bodies in eagerness to please her. She bent and patted each little head in turn then stepped out into the passage.

"Did you see her?" Jovann demanded the moment Sairu appeared at the infirmary door. He sat upon his pallet, and his face was pale in the lamplight. The cat was curled up at the foot of the bed, his tail draped over his face, though Sairu could see one gleaming eye watching from beneath the fur.

"I saw her," Sairu said. "She sleeps peacefully."

Jovann's body shuddered with the sigh he gave, and he slumped forward, his elbows resting on his knees and his head bowed. "I beheld such things," he said, his voice faint. "Such . . . terrible things."

"What things?" Sairu demanded, crossing the room and kneeling before him. "Tell me."

But he shook his head. "I cannot. I cannot speak of it. Not yet. Let me tell you tomorrow."

Sairu wanted to argue, to insist. She knew she could make him tell her whatever she wished. But from where she sat, she could see the lines on his face and, despite herself, felt sudden pity.

So instead she reached out and took his fist between her hands. "What is this?" she asked.

He looked down at his own hand, frowning. Then, without answering, he turned it over and slowly, painfully, uncurled his fingers.

Both he and Sairu gasped.

A glint of many-colored fire lay in his palm. For a moment it looked like a flower, and then it was not a flower at all, but the life and flame of a flower caught in the stillness of stone. It was not large, but it did not need to be. That first glimpse of it was so beautiful, so delicate and powerful all at once, that no eye could help but be drawn to it.

Then, the glory faded. Not entirely, but enough. And Jovann held in his hand a cluster of fire opals.

"Where did you get that?" Sairu demanded, though she already suspected the answer. For she knew he had had nothing of the kind on his person when he fell asleep.

"I . . . It is a gift of the . . . of the heart. I . . ."

Words failed him. She looked into his eyes and saw in them lights much greater than those gleaming within the stones. He blinked, and they were gone, but still he could not speak. He closed his mouth, took a deep breath.

Then he took Sairu's hand and pressed the opals into it. "Take it," he said.

For a moment she felt her heart thrill and stop. It was a long moment. A moment full of eternities and sudden dreams, hopes, desires.

"Give it to Umeer's daughter," Jovann said. "Tell her to remember me."

14

"YOU ARE CRYING."

Dawn came swiftly to the mountain peaks, far more swiftly than it came to the valleys. It touched the upper ridges with lines of pink and gold, and sent mist curling down the slopes. Sairu shivered where she sat. The mist moved like the softest, gentlest of rivers past her. It was so thick, she could scarcely see the cat until he was right beside her, though she had spotted the curl of his upraised tail several yards away.

She did not acknowledge him but looked down upon Daramuti. The dovecote, where she had come to sit, was the highest and most remote point in the temple grounds, and the rest spread below her, the various rooftops and paths nestled comfortably into the mountain as though they had always been there. It was a lovely, quiet little world of its own, isolated in morning while everything below still rested in the embrace of night. The priests chanted their morning prayers, and the sound of their melodic voices greeting Anwar was gentle in Sairu's ears.

The cat sat beside her, gazing at the same scene as only a cat can gaze, but perhaps seeing things she did not. He was silent for a long while. Then he said a second time, "You are crying."

"No, I am not."

"Then why are there tears on your face?"

"The cold," Sairu replied, perhaps too promptly. "It makes my eyes water."

"Ah."

Again they were silent. The dawn spread further, and the chant grew deeper. The doves awoke and began to coo and rustle in their nests.

"Under normal circumstances I would make some quip about mortals and their tears," said the cat. "But since my own little moment last night, I don't feel I have the right. After one hundred years dry-eyed, what a let-down! I wish I knew what caused my weeping, at least. Your tears are far more reasonable under the circumstances."

"I'm not crying," Sairu repeated, and wiped wetness from her face with her free hand. The other hand remained clenched in a fist.

The cat regarded her with eyes far too knowing and intelligent. She wanted to hit him, but that would be too great a concession. So she pretended not to see and continued staring down the mountainside, her face as serene as ever Princess Safiya's could be.

"You know," said the cat, "among my own people, I'm considered something of a poet."

"Among cats or devils?"

The cat snorted. "Both, I fancy. Poets, as you probably are aware, are pretty keen on the emotions, turmoils, and such-like of the soul. Some might even call us empathetic."

"No one would call you empathetic."

"Well, pretend I am then! I know—or at least, I have a reasonable guess—why you're up here, alone in the cold, having yourself a little weep. And I thought perhaps you might want to talk about it. I understand that young ladies often feel better if they can chatter someone's ear off about their trials various."

Sairu turned a slow, cold stare upon the cat. She sniffed and blinked a few times. "Very well, Monster. I will answer your question. But first you must tell me something."

The cat twitched an ear. "Fair enough. What do you want to know?"

"Who is Starflower?"

The doves cooed and chortled. The monks finished their chant. The ringing tone of their gong sounded across the mountains. The mist rose in the air and evaporated. Otherwise, the world might have turned to stone for all the cat moved.

At last he said, "I don't know what you're talking about."

Sairu laughed, which was cruel, she knew. But she wasn't feeling especially charitable in that moment, and the look on the cat's face was awfully funny. "Don't try to be coy with me. *You* may not be empathetic, but I certainly am. It's part of the basic composition of every Golden Daughter. We have to be. So I recognize heartbreak when I see it, even in a cat. Though I confess it took me some while to work it out, for your voice and your face are unlike a man's. But, as you may have noticed by now, I am smart. I always get to the answer in the end."

She leaned over and tapped the cat on his pink nose, just to see his ears flatten. But he did not otherwise move, remaining firmly rooted in place, his tail tight about his paws.

"Who is Starflower?" Sairu repeated. "Why does the name cause you such pain? Is she dead?"

"No," said the cat.

"Then she does not love you."

"She does. But not as I love her."

"Ah." Sairu nodded. "That is pain. That is worse pain. Even for a devil."

"And what would a mortal know of such things?" the cat snarled so suddenly and so viciously that Sairu was reminded of the panther she had fought in the woodland of the Masayi.

"Little enough," Sairu admitted. "But I think love transcends mortality and immortality, and is a power far beyond both. We all taste of it and long for it, as a dying man, offered a sip of the water of life, longs to plunge into the river. But we do not understand its mysteries." She bowed her head, considering her own closed fist. "The Golden Daughters are forbidden to love. It is far too dangerous a weapon."

"Too bad for you then, eh?" said the cat, his voice gentler than it had been a moment before, though not exactly kind. He was still bristling. "Your turn. Tell me why you were crying, and don't think you can fool me."

"I . . ." Sairu thought for a moment of dissembling. But there didn't seem much point. So she opened her fist and looked upon the cluster of opals hidden there. The morning sun touched them and made them more brilliant even than they had seemed in the lamplight a few hours earlier. One could almost believe they were whole stars compressed somehow into a space and time not originally intended to contain their vastness.

But they fit in the palm of her hand as easily as pain.

"He told me it was a gift of the heart," Sairu said, her voice near a whisper. "I don't know what that means. But—but when he gave it to me . . ." She hated to continue. She hated stumbling with words through a maze of emotions she did not understand, but which were as real and vital to her as the breath in her lungs. "When he gave it to me, it seemed as though I glimpsed something. Some future. Not my own. Some other girl's. Some girl not of the Masayi. Some girl who loved a boy. Who married him for love of him, and not for money or power or duty. Simply for love, which is not simple at all. And she bore children. His children. And she loved them, for they were part of him and part of her and entirely themselves."

To her surprise, she found that tears were pouring down her face, falling in her lap, falling in her hand, spattering upon the brilliant stones. She put her other hand to her face, mopping her cheeks with the edge of her sleeve.

"Golden Daughters are never mothers," she said. "They marry and they never love. They cannot be allowed to bear children, for how then could they perform their duty, how then could they serve their masters? They are weapons hidden in plain sight. More valuable than gold to a hated man with many enemies. Too valuable to take to bed. Too valuable to suffer the danger of childbirth. The danger of love."

She sighed heavily, her brow puckered with deep, sorrowful lines. "The Golden Daughters protect life. When necessary they take life. But they do not give it."

The cat watched her, but she was no longer aware of him. For all she knew, she sat alone beneath Anwar's bright eye. And she did not believe Anwar was anything more than a ball of fire to light the world. She did not hear his Song, and she did not look to him for comfort. She sought no comfort from any source but sat alone with her newly recognized pain, experiencing the full brunt of it falling upon her like rain.

"I never thought anything of my future. I never cared for any purpose but the one for which I have been brought up." Sairu closed her hand and hid the stones from view. "I never knew that I could want anything more."

So they were quiet together, and the day aged before their watching eyes. Acolytes and monks moved about their morning tasks, and soon someone would come to feed the doves. Sairu would not be there when that man arrived. But for a moment more, she and the cat remained where they were.

Then the cat leaned over and bumped her arm with his forehead. "You can scratch me behind the ears if you like. It might make you feel better."

Sairu obliged. She rubbed his silky soft ears, ruffled the fur atop his head, then moved her hand down under his chin, and watched him close his eyes as she scratched. His purr rumbled against her fingers.

"See?" said the cat. "Nothing like a little fluffiness to cheer the weary soul."

She frowned suddenly, removing her hand. "Tell me, Monster," she said, "what do you want of my Lady Hariawan? Why do you pursue her?"

"I don't," said the cat.

"You followed us all the way from Lunthea Maly. You tracked us for months. I do not believe you are uninterested, devil that you are."

"I am not uninterested," said the cat. "I am very interested indeed. But not in Lady Hariawan."

"Who then?"

"You." The cat lashed his tail and glared up at her. "I was sent to watch over you."

"Who sent you?"

"My Master."

"Cats have no masters."

"No," the cat agreed. "But maybe devils do?"

"And who is this master, then?"

"The Lumil Eliasul, Giver of Songs."

"I do not know that name."

"No. But he knows yours."

Sairu folded her arms, tucking the hand with the stones away into her sleeve. She regarded the cat thoughtfully. "I don't need a guard or a guide. And I am not important. Why would anyone send you to watch over me?"

"I don't know," said the cat. "I merely obey. I do not ask questions."

"What about traditionally lethal feline curiosity?"

"Oh, I'm very curious, believe you me! And I'll find out the how's and the why's eventually. In the meanwhile this has proven an interesting interlude. In fact . . ." He paused a moment, considering the merit of his next words. Then he smiled a cattish smile and began to purr once more. "In fact, I can say, without qualification, I am glad to have met you, mortal girl."

Sairu narrowed her eyes, studying that smile. "Starflower is not, I think, a devil. Is she?"

"No," said the cat. "She certainly is not."

From inside the dovecote, a bright red eye looked out upon the morning of this world that it despised. But it scarcely saw the morning or the rising of the sun.

Its gaze was entirely fixed upon the golden form sitting beside the mortal girl, just a fledgling's flutter away. It did not behold that form in the way mortals did. It saw neither a cat nor any shape bound entirely by flesh and blood.

It saw the immortal Faerie. It saw the Knight.

The raven trembled and drew back into the farthest recesses of the dove's nest in which it should not have been able to fit. There it crouched amid the ruined shells of rotted eggs, shrouding itself in its wings like shadows. It did not cease to tremble until long after the girl and the cat had gone on their way.

Then it let out its breath in a hiss, and smoke curled from its beak and up over its head.

A few hours later, much to Sairu's surprise, word came to her by way of Tu Domchu that Lady Hariawan required her presence.

Sairu had spent much of the morning wandering in aimless frustration between the infirmary and her mistress's chambers, unwilling to enter the one and unable to enter the latter. So when Tu Domchu delivered his message—spitting rudely at her feet even as he spoke—Sairu's heart leapt inside her, full of renewed passion, renewed commitment. *This* was the whole meaning of her life: serving her mistress. She may once more move and exist with purpose.

Lady Hariawan sat in a low chair near the window of her innermost chamber. Sunlight touched the back of her head, but her face, turned away, remained in shadow. It was impossible to see her expression enough to read it, but Sairu did not mind just then. As she bowed, the sleeves of her handmaiden's robes brushed the floor.

"My mistress," she murmured, "how may I serve you?"

Lady Hariawan opened her mouth. When her words finally came, it seemed as though she had conjured them from a great distance and they only now arrived upon her tongue. "I . . . need . . ."

"Yes, my mistress?" Sairu said, taking a step forward. "What do you need? Please tell me. I will do anything for you."

"I . . . need . . ." Lady Hariawan paused and put a hand to her head as though it pained her. But she said nothing more, only closed her eyes.

Sairu was across the room in a moment. She gathered her mistress's loose hair out of her face and gently began to braid it. She felt her forehead for a fever but found none. "Have you eaten, my mistress?"

Lady Hariawan shook her head sharply, and part of the braid came undone. Sairu caught it and finished it off quickly, tying it in place. "Well, that's what you need then, before anything else. A proper meal. When was the last time you ate? My poor, dear mistress, you really can't take care of yourself worth mewling kittens, can you? Here, let me adjust your robe. I'm sure I can find you some pudding, perhaps, and a cake. You need vegetables as well. I will have the monks cook some up for you, and I'll find an egg or two."

She prattled on, the relief of returning to her established role far outweighing any and all questions for the moment. Her lady seemed to respond to her voice and touch, permitting herself to be dressed in fresh garments and her hair to be properly styled; she even ate several mouthfuls of the large meal Sairu presented to her.

When this task was complete, she raised tired but lovely eyes to Sairu's face and said, "Where is he?"

"Ah. I suspect you mean Jovann," said Sairu. "Our noble prince is in the infirmary. Your slaves did nothing to help his healing process yesterday, but he will recover in time. You must forgive him his rudeness. He is most grateful to you, but slavery is new to him and does not wear well upon his shoulders. In time he will—"

"No," said Lady Hariawan, waving a listless hand. "Where is he? The dog?"

Sairu blinked. "You mean Sticky Bun?"

A few minutes later she watched from across the room as Lady Hariawan made much of the lion dog in her lap, who whined and wagged in pitiful joy to be restored to her. It would have made Sairu jealous had she not been too preoccupied with other thoughts to care much about her pet's loyalties.

She fingered the opals in the pocket of her robes. Somehow she hated to give them up. But Jovann's wishes had been clear. They were not hers to keep.

"My mistress?" she said, her voice possibly more tentative than it had ever before been.

Lady Hariawan did not look up at first, so intent was she upon the cheerful dog in her lap. Sairu was obliged to repeat herself a few times before her mistress finally acknowledged her with a quiet, unquestioning gaze.

"This is for you," Sairu said, holding out Jovann's gift. Lady Hariawan made no move, so Sairu took her by the wrist and pressed the cluster of stones into her hand. "It is from the slave you rescued. He bade me give it to you and asks that you will . . . that you will remember him."

Slowly Lady Hariawan opened her hand and gazed upon the stones. Her face was an absolute blank. Not even a flicker of the eye revealed a hint of what she might be thinking or feeling. Perhaps she truly thought and felt nothing.

Then she tucked the stones into the depths of her own sleeve and returned her attention to Sticky Bun. She did not speak again for many hours, and she held Sairu captive in her silence.

But the deed was done. The gift was given.

15

HOW LONG IT HAS BEEN since I last set eyes upon this beauty! I shudder to think."

Sunan stood half-bent in a bow, uncertain he dared straighten yet. He watched as Lord Luk-Hunad carefully turned the little treasure round and round in his old fingers. His nails were long and burnished gold after the current fashion among Pen-Chan great men—a fashion Lord Dok-Kasemsan had always scorned. They looked incongruous set against Luk-Hunad's large, bony knuckles, and Sunan thought how like talons they were. He did not like seeing them handle Uncle Kasemsan's priceless silver gong.

"This was in my family for generations," Lord Luk-Hunad mused, tapping the gong with one fingernail so that it gave off a light, tinny sound. "One of the House of Luk's great heirlooms since before the Kitar ruled Noorhitam, if you would believe it. It is of little value save in sentiment."

Sunan knew that for the lie it was. But this was how the game was played, and he was determined to play to win. "My uncle seemed to believe you held it in high regard," he said, choosing his words carefully. His uncle used to boast over the gong, which sat in a place of prominence in his study. He had won it in a gambling match right out from under Lord Luk-Hunad's nose. Lord Dok-Kasemsan was not a man to crow, but if ever he did crow, it was the night he brought home that gong. "*I never saw his face more sick! He should learn not to bet family heirlooms on an ill-favored head.*"

Sunan knew he risked much in coming to Lord Luk-Hunad now. He also knew he never would have made it past the front door if he'd not brought along this treasure. He wasn't used to offering bribes, and he hoped his lack of experience didn't show.

Luk-Hunad's face was a study, impossible to read behind his mask of wrinkles. The hairless brow above his left eye twitched as he glanced Sunan's way. "I heard of your uncle's recent demise," he said. "Incarcerated in Lunthea Maly! What a sad end for a great man."

"It was . . . unexpected," Sunan said, and bowed deeper so that he would not have to look at the old lord.

"Unexpected? Ha!" Luk-Hunad set the gong down on a near table, watching the silver disc swing back and forth, suspended between two ebony pillars. The pillars were carved in the likenesses of Anwar and Hulan. On the face of the gong itself was etched a songbird. The whole figurine was no more than five inches tall, as though built by pixie hands. Despite its former owner's declarations, anyone with eyes could see that it was a priceless work of bygone days, of craftsmanship no longer to be found even among the fine artisans of Nua-Pratut.

Luk-Hunad folded his hands into his opulent sleeves, the picture of Pen-Chan tranquility. "They say my dear Kasemsan tried to murder an Aja ambassador. They say he was hired for the task. Like a legendary Crouching Shadow come to life." He laughed again, a thin, wheezing, delighted laugh. "The stuff of operas! The stuff of epics. But I know better. Ah yes, I know how it must have been. He always was a wretched man at the games, always too quick to know a winner, too quick to call a number. He angered a favorite of the emperor, no doubt, and now he'll spend his last days rotting in the darkness beneath Manusbau. What a tragic fate for the head of the House of Dok! And he leaves no male heir, does he? The headship will fall to that cousin he hates. Too bad your blood is so tainted with Chhayan mud, or you would now be head of Dok, eh? Heheh."

Sunan kept his face perfectly expressionless. It was a choice between courtesy or rage, and he knew rage would not benefit him now. So he waited until Luk-Hunad had quite finished his mirthful speculation. Then he said, as humbly as he could manage, "I know my uncle would have wished to see the gong returned into your care."

"You know nothing of the sort," Luk-Hunad replied. "Your uncle was my nemesis, and I his. Though I will admit," he continued with a sudden far-off look in his old eyes, "sometimes a nemesis can grow dearer to the heart than a friend or even a lover. There is something . . . *foundational* in an enemy. Something that reminds one why one continues to live."

Sunan felt his mouth go dry. He dared not speak, dared not even remind Luk-Hunad of the reason for his visit here, a visit he gladly would have avoided had any other plan presented itself. But none had, so he stood quite still, bent at the waist, his hands folded in supplication. And he waited.

Luk-Hunad turned to the young man again, his face expressing more disgust than dislike. "So you want access to my library, eh?"

"If it please the gracious head of the House of Luk."

"And why do you not instead visit the Center of Learning? Their library is far greater than my humble collection. Or did you not pass your Gruung, Chhayan boy?"

The bitterness of that pill was almost too much for Sunan. But he swallowed hard, forcing it down to fester in his belly, and responded with bland civility, "I find myself obliged to seek elsewhere for the information I need."

"And what information might that be? You know there's no trick to passing the Gruung. Either you have the brain for it or you haven't. Unlike some, they don't take well to bribes, still less well to threats."

"I would neither bribe nor threaten to achieve my aim."

Luk-Hunad barked a laugh at this blatant lie and once more turned to admire the little gong. The hammer had long since been lost, perhaps generations before Hunad's time. Nevertheless, it was an object meant for reverence, though there was no reverence in Hunad's avaricious face.

"I could just take this and send you on your way," he said, eyeing Sunan to gauge his reaction. Sunan offered none but remained where he stood. Something about his stance bespoke a resolve that even the old lord could not completely ignore. He studied the young man, nephew of his rival, and his gaze, though sullied these many years by the malice of his spirit, still held a measure of discernment.

"You're afraid," he said. "What do you fear, Chhayan boy?"

Sunan said nothing. He could not risk another lie. One more, and he knew he'd be dismissed. His mind raced through the possible repercussions of his other options: the truth or silence. He opted for silence.

Luk-Hunad sighed, and his fingernail tapped once more at the gong, which offered back no more than a click in response. "You haven't much about yourself that recommends you to me. I see little of your uncle in your eyes, nor of your poor, sad mother, may Hulan shine with pity on her. She had spirit, that one. They say she took up her father's sword and went to battle alongside her brother when the Chhayans attacked. Had she not . . . had she remained in her father's house among the other women . . ."

Had she done so, Sunan himself would never have been born. He held firmly to his silence, his last defense.

"Very well," Hunad said, shaking his head as though disappointed. And there was, perhaps, a trace of sorrow in his wicked old voice. "Help yourself to my library. For today only. And don't return to my door again, for the House of Luk has no welcome for you, son of the Tiger."

With that, and with no bow or other form of acknowledgement, the old man hobbled from the chamber, leaving Sunan where he stood.

Sunan released his breath in a gust. And he snarled, but quietly for fear of being overheard, "May Anwar smite your bones to black!"

He wanted to tear something, to break something. But he dared not. He had humbled himself too far to risk losing his goal now. And the library of the House of Luk surrounded him.

Low chests lined the perimeter of the room, and in each of these were stored dozens of scrolls in no particular order. Histories, poetries, philosophies, speculations, natural sciences: all were jumbled together and must be carefully unrolled and inspected. With one day in which to do so!

Sunan fell to his work. After weeks of hiding in his uncle's abandoned house, he had awakened this morning with a sudden, driving urge to act. To get out. To do something to prove to himself that he still had some charge over his own fate. He knew the Mask watched him, though he could discern no sign of him no matter how he looked. But surely if he did not speak his purpose out loud, the Mask could not guess it? And so long as he did not leave Suthinnakor City . . .

His hands trembled as he swiftly inspected and set aside as useless the first chest of scrolls. A vague part of his mind sighed indignantly at the knowledge that the House of Luk—famed for its distinct lack of scholarship among the learned houses of Nua-Pratut—should own such a collection. But the House of Luk was always one for gaming tables and races and wrestling matches, and they tended toward unnatural good luck. Most of this library, Sunan did not doubt, had been won from other houses. Possibly some of his uncle's own collection now resided here, unread and disregarded save as a trophy. No wonder Kasemsan had gloried in the winning of that little gong!

The second chest proved as useless as the first. With the reverence due such a large amount of learning, Sunan carefully replaced the scrolls, wishing he had the time to catalogue them as they deserved. A proper task for a Tribute Scholar, he thought bitterly, and slammed the lid shut.

He moved on to the third one. And there on the top of the pile lay a scroll that looked fresh as the day it had been written, the paper pure white, contrasting sharply with the browns and yellows beneath it. Frowning, Sunan removed it and carefully undid the securing clasps on each end. He unrolled the parchment, and his eyes widened.

The handwriting was familiar.

He plunged his hand into his robes and pulled forth the much-battered little scroll given him months before on the steps of the Middle Court in the Center of Learning. The scroll given him by Overseer Rangsun. The scroll which had changed his life forever.

Kneeling, he propped the larger new scroll open on the floor before him, setting paper weights at its corners. He unrolled the little one and set it atop the larger, comparing the writing. It was the same. Absolutely the same; he would bet his life on it, even to a Luk man. He read the writing of the first scroll again, words which were by now so familiar to him he could have recited them in his sleep:

"Henceforth you will consider yourself in the service of the Crouching Shadows, assuming the role and duties of your honored uncle Kasemsan, Master of Dok, fulfilling his final purpose or perishing in the attempt. You will await further instructions and make no effort to leave Suthinnakor until otherwise directed.

Should you refuse, your life is forfeit."

He slid the scroll away and looked once more at the one beneath, reading the hand as though he read the familiar face of his nearest enemy.

"Consider the Crouching Shadows, figures of mythology, as dear to the heart of a Pen-Chan as the Lordly Sun and the Lady Moon. Figures of mystery—mystery that one would never wish to see resolved. Figures of darkness, moving through our fears and our nightmares. Figures of comfort, heroes of old, blessed with powers beyond mortal comprehension. And yet, all mortal. All born of flesh and blood, but flesh and blood made so much more.

Assassins. A foolish idea, one which a scholar of your learning must have already dismissed. For what is heroic about a man trained to kill, however skillfully he may perform this talent? How could a band of killers so vitally, so profoundly affect the very fabric of our minds, like a dark thread running through a robe of red silk? There must be more, you say to yourself. There must be something you do not know.

And of course there is. For everything you have ever known of the Crouching Shadows, every tale, every rousing adventure of mysterious summonings, of furtive villains, of futile escapes and ultimate deaths—it is nothing more than misdirection. You have guessed as much.

What you have not guessed is the truth. The Crouching Shadows are not assassins. They are protectors. They are servants. They will guard their Mistress to the very utmost, to the ends of their lives and existence. They remember the Age of True Worship, beyond the symbols and sacraments now practiced in place of faith. They remember, and they protect what they know.

The Crouching Shadows are the guardians of the Goddess herself. They are the Lady Moon's final defense in this world of Death and destruction.

And that is enough for you, Juong-Khla Sunan."

Sunan gasped and sat back, allowing the scroll to snap out from beneath the paperweights and roll up on itself again. But no. He must be mistaken. He must have misread his name, caught up as he was, full to the brim of so many fanciful fears. He must have misread it!

So he forced himself to bend once more over the scroll, to slide it back open and read on.

"And that is enough for you, Juong-Khla Sunan. You will seek no more knowledge of those whom you serve. You will wait in silence and, when called, act in silence and with utmost decorum as would honor the House of Dok and your uncle.

Return to his house, and do not seek to pass through his gates again until the summons comes. Otherwise, your oath will be deemed broken."

That was all.

Sunan's heart rammed against his throat, and he felt sweat dampen his brow. How could they have known he would come here, to the Library of Luk? How could they have guessed, when he himself did not consider it until dawn this very morning? How could they have planted this scroll, anticipating both his actions and his reactions?

But then, they knew him. They knew he was a scholar, and that as a scholar he must eventually seek out whatever information was available on his new, faceless masters. And they knew he would not be received into the Center of Learning.

He was a prisoner. A prisoner to their will.

"But for what purpose?" Sunan whispered. "Why do you need me?"

Behind him, on its table, the silver gong suddenly offered a sweet, silver chime, a far different sound from any it had made under Luk-Hunad's hand. In its voice, for half an instant, there echoed a thousand sweet voices singing all together.

But by the time Sunan, startled, had turned to look, it was silent once more. The only testimony of its ringing was the slight back-and-forth swaying of the gong itself, suspended between Anwar and Hulan's carved arms. The songbird etched in silver might have fluttered its wings.

16

HIS WHOLE BODY WAS rigid, from his head to his jaw, down along his neck and the lacerated skin and muscles of his back. His ribcage clenched, squeezing every organ. His gut and bowels tightened into a knot of pain, shooting through his thighs, his calves, to the very soles of his feet.

To this he woke, and for a moment the pain was so great that he would have given anything to crawl out of himself and be free of it. That moment went on far too long. He tried to breathe it out, to expel the pain in gusts from his lungs. But it was too much. And there was no comforting voice to guide him, to show him how to hold the pain in place. It surrounded and consumed him.

And then, in a sudden wave, it passed. Blood rushed back to his head, and his body relaxed. He could breathe normally, and each breath seemed to push the pain further away. Finally nothing hurt so much as his stinging back, but this was familiar pain, and he felt he could bear it.

Jovann opened his eyes.

The infirmary was dark; all the paper-covered windows were slid shut.

But daylight peeked between the wall slats and sliced the floor and his bed in delicate gold lines. He raised his head and shoulders, and saw that the door was open, as it usually was, and a large patch of sunlight fell through onto the floor. At first he thought he glimpsed the orange cat lying in a fluffy puddle, the wavy white fur of his belly exposed, his spine twisted, and his paws curled, the picture of absolute ease. But when he blinked, that image was gone, and Jovann decided he'd imagined it.

He felt suddenly that he had to get up. A number of memories and thoughts clamored on the edge of his brain, all demanding attention, but he couldn't bear to attend any of them while lying on his stomach. So, grimacing, he pushed himself up and climbed out of his low bed. When the blanket slid from his shoulders, he realized just how cold it was in the room. The high mountain air was so different from the sultry heat of the plains this time of year. But it wasn't unpleasant. Indeed, his fevered skin welcomed and soaked in the coolness.

Blinking hard and putting up a hand against the bright light of midday, he walked unsteadily to the doorway, leaned against the doorpost, and looked out on the temple grounds, breathing deep of the wind that washed over his face. Before him stood the central building of Daramuti, known as the Seat of Prayer. Its sloping roof with sharp peaks of typical Kitar design was decorated in a series of carved stone stars, each with individualized faces, representing celestial spirits to whom the Kitar priests sometimes prayed if Hulan and Anwar were otherwise engaged.

Jovann grimaced. He had looked upon this same view just yesterday, but it had not struck him then as it did now. Then it had seemed beautiful and foreign and perhaps dangerous.

Now it struck him as false. All of it. False.

He had walked among the stars. And he knew that they were not beings to whom a man should pray. He could not explain it, not even in the depths of his heart beneath conscious thought. Somehow he knew, with simple clarity, that the stars were far greater than he had ever believed and also far less. Even as Hulan herself was so much more than he could have imagined, so much more than the goddess he had been raised to believe her to be. But she too was less.

She was not worshipful.

"If not her," Jovann whispered, "than whom?"

He shuddered suddenly and bowed his head. Now all of the thoughts crashed down upon him; thoughts, and memories as well.

"Let me go, Father. Let me go to Sunan. I have much I want to say to him, and I will faithfully bear your message."

"We haven't the time to waste, boy."

"I'll not waste it, I swear! Let me do this, Father. For you. For our Cause. I'll bring back the secret."

The voices, his own and the far deeper rumble of his father, rolled through his head. Jovann put a hand to his temple, wishing he could push them out and away. He had failed his father. He had failed the Khla clan. What would become of the Chhayans' great Cause now? Now that he had failed to return with the secret of the Long Fire?

He heard Juong-Khla's voice again. Another memory, but this time much more recent.

"*Jovann. My son.*"

His eyes flew wide, and he stared unseeing on the grounds of Daramuti. But for an instant so brief it might never have existed, it was a different temple he saw. A huge temple surrounded by a great, forbidding wall, and the whole of its existence shuddered with a deep resounding chant.

The vision vanished. He stood in the infirmary doorway. He was high in the mountains, far from home. And he was still a slave.

"I must return," he whispered. "I must return at once. I must tell Father of Sunan's treachery, and we must find another way to gain the secret. I must . . . I must . . ."

But it was useless. Even if he had the strength and the will to march through that door, down that mountain, to make his way all the long leagues back to Chhayan country.

He would not leave Umeer's daughter. Not without knowing her name.

Jovann's shoulders sagged with sudden weariness, and he turned, prepared to return to his bed. Instead he gasped, and his hands clenched into fists.

Someone sat in the shadows beyond his bed.

"Who's there?" Jovann demanded, his eyes flaring. "Who are you?"

"Oh, my son, my son," said an aged voice, and the figure in the shadows shifted heavily. The click of a cane tapped the floor, and Brother Tenuk moved into lesser shadows where his face and form could be discerned. One quivering hand raised in signs of blessing, and he spoke in hasty explanation: "I came to say prayers to Anwar, asking him to give you strength. Anwar must have heard me, for you look stronger than you did."

Jovann stared at the little man, taking in his abbot's robes and the elegant carving of his heavy cane. "How long have you been there?"

"Oh, my son." The little man stopped making signs and clasped the cane with both hands now, leaning heavily upon it. "When the smiling maid left you, and I saw you fall into fitful slumber, I thought to myself that it was my duty, as abbot, to stand guard over your soul and fortify you with my prayers."

His voice was that of a liar. Jovann's lip curled. "And why should you pray over a slave?" he demanded, refusing to use the title 'Honored Brother' as he should for a priest. This was a Kitar priest, after all, and they were all thieves.

Brother Tenuk gave him a sly look. "I did not pray over a slave, did I? No, indeed. For I see what you are, boy, though you may hide it. We are not unalike, you and I." He hobbled a few steps nearer and leaned in, as though to breathe secrets into Jovann's face. He smelled strongly of a distillery. In his sleeplessness, Brother Tenuk often took comfort in the stronger of the prayerful drinks, meant only for certain ceremonies and phases of the moon. But he was the abbot, and none of the other priests dared comment.

He swayed now, clutching his cane, and grinned up at Jovann. "You can hide it all you wish. But I see. I see what you are. I have hidden too, for years and years, and no one saw what I was. Not even you."

"You are drunk," said Jovann, his voice severe. "I do not think Anwar or Hulan would hear the prayers of a drunkard."

A pitiful, wheezing laugh ached its way from Tenuk's lungs. He shook his head, his face torn by a dreadful grin. "Anwar and Hulan have not heard the prayers of a Chhayan for generations."

With that, the little man tottered past Jovann, making for the door. As he went, he raised one hand and waggled a finger at the ceiling, calling back over his shoulder, "I know what you are! I know, I know. Ah!" This last he gasped as he reached the door, and he drew back for an instant as though disconcerted. "The smiling maid." He shivered and glanced back at Jovann once more. "She's coming for you. But don't worry. She'll not keep you. Not forever."

And with this enigmatic statement the abbot carefully descended the infirmary steps, muttering and making signs to Sairu as he passed her. She bowed, her hands folded in her sleeves, and waited until he had quite gone his way. Then she stepped into the infirmary just in time to see Jovann easing himself back down onto his bed.

"There you are!" he said when he saw her. "Where did you go? I woke, and there was no one here, and I . . ." His voice trailed off as he realized how childish he must sound.

It was too late. Sairu had heard it as well and was smiling that frightful smile of hers. But she answered demurely, "I must attend to my mistress's needs before yours, noble prince though you may be."

Jovann growled at the title but couldn't prevent himself from asking, "How is Lady Hariawan?"

"She is resting. What did Brother Tenuk want?"

"I couldn't begin to tell you. He was drunk and speaking in riddles. Riddles without answers, if I'm not mistaken." Jovann shifted on his bed so that he might lean against the wall, his legs spread before him. His back protested at the pressure, and he grimaced then relaxed. He looked at Sairu, who was studying him carefully. Her hair was neatly tucked up in an elegant twist save for three thin braids falling across each shoulder. Not a strand was out of place. Indeed, she looked as fresh and put-together as a proper handmaiden ought to be, and not at all as though she had sat up the whole of the night previous. He wondered if the paint on her face disguised dark circles.

Suddenly he remembered the flower of fiery stones he had pressed into her hands. "Did you give Lady Hariawan my gift?" he asked.

Sairu nodded, the corners of her mouth turning up in an even larger smile. "I did. And now you will tell me what you saw in the Dream."

Jovann's jaw tensed. He looked at her without blinking for some moments. Sairu did not repeat her question, but it remained in her eyes, along with a firm certainty of an answer forthcoming. She waited, and he waited, but he knew he could not out-wait her.

He sighed. "It's difficult for me to say. It's faded, and—"

"Try."

Jovann drew a deep breath, careful to keep his voice measured and controlled when he replied. "I don't have the words. I'm not eloquent, and it would take . . . it would take a poet, I think, to describe it. I saw a gate. But it wasn't just a gate. And I saw the Moon, but she was much more than the Moon. And I heard the Dara singing."

"Yes, yes, and you brought back a gift for my lady. But what about my lady herself? What did you see of her? Did she walk with you? Did she see . . ."

Jovann felt his face revealing secrets he did not wish to reveal, and he hastily pulled his expression back into a proper alignment. But he saw at once that Sairu had spotted what he had not wished to show.

Because when she mentioned Lady Hariawan in the Dream, there had flashed across his memory the visage of the withered crone. And he had felt a sudden surge of revulsion.

But no. He would not think of Umeer's daughter that way. And he would not allow such a feeling to return. So he schooled his face into appropriate lines and refused to break Sairu's cunning gaze.

She had seen it though. He knew she had.

"What did you see of my mistress?" Sairu demanded, taking a step forward and kneeling beside his low bed so that her face was on a level with his own. "What does she want in the Dream?"

Jovann put a hand to his forehead, shielding his eyes. "I don't know," he said. "I don't know what she wants, but it was not what she told me."

"What did she tell you?"

His voice was near a whisper when he responded: "She told me she sought Hulan's Gate. But when I took her there, it was not what she wanted and she . . . she . . ."

"Yes? Go on." Sairu urged, reaching out and taking his hand as though she could snatch his secrets from him. But he shook his head and looked away.

Sairu wanted, so badly wanted, to take him by the shoulders and shake him; shake him until all his wounds reopened and he drowned in the pain of his fever returned. Instead, she leaned back on her heels, then slowly stood and folded her hands. "You wish to help my mistress, do you not?"

His glance struck her swiftly. "I do. More than anything."

"Then you need to answer this one question for me at least. Is my Lady Hariawan in danger when she enters the Dream?"

"Yes," he responded without hesitation. He opened his mouth to say more but couldn't put words to his thoughts.

Sairu seemed to feel his struggle. She persisted: "I have sensed things in her chamber. Once, very strongly, our first night here in Daramuti. I sensed things, and I thought I myself dreamed. But I did not dream. I stood in her room in the dark of night, and I felt the presence of strangers moving just beyond my natural perceptions, on the borders of my mind. I believe they pose a threat to my mistress. Do you know anything of what I speak?"

"The chanting phantoms."

"Explain."

Jovann leaned back, raising his gaze to hers, his shoulders pressed against the wall. His face was overgrown with a young man's attempt at a beard, which grew thickly in places and refused to grow at all in others. His hair was long, shaggy, and dirty, tied at the nape of his neck. He wore the humble, ill-fitting clothing of a Kitar acolyte, his own rags long since discarded. But his complexion and features declared to all the world his Chhayan heritage. A gurta-boy of the plains, raised on buffalo milk and buffalo jerk and the unrelenting fury of his displaced heritage.

Despite all this, there was a certain nobility to his face. Or, if not nobility, perhaps a desire for nobility that was about as much as one could expect from a young man of his years.

But he was still as predictable as any other. She could, and she would, make use of him. "Explain," Sairu repeated. There was no smile to be seen on her face.

Jovann took a long breath before replying. "I've seen them twice now when I've walked with her in the Dream," he said. "Formless shadows, dozens of them, a hundred. Perhaps more. I cannot see their faces, only their shadows, and . . . I don't think they can see more than shadows of us either."

"What do they want?"

"Lady Hariawan, I think. But I don't know why."

"Then I need you to find out."

He narrowed his eyes up at her. "I do not believe that I am in *your* service."

"No. You're in my mistress's service," she replied, "and it is in her service I need you to act."

Jovann considered her carefully. She was certainly a small force of nature all her own, and in other circumstances he might have thought her amusing. As it was, he found himself rather inclined to reach out, take one of her thin braids in his hand, and give it a sharp pull.

Instead, he drew himself up and replied in a cold voice, "Very well, little miss. What exactly do you have in mind?"

The problem with asking someone like Sairu what exactly she had in mind was that she would answer exactly. Then she would expect an exact performance. Then she would smile.

That was worst of all. That smile of hers. Jovann shivered, remembering it as he laid himself down that night in the darkness of the infirmary. It was the sort of smile that made a man promise things, even utterly mad things, just to make her stop.

And Jovann had promised. He told himself that it was all for Lady Hariawan's sake and he must not fail to serve her. He lay awake in the darkness for some time, staring into shadows, feeling every burn and ache on his back. He wished, suddenly, that Sairu had remained to sing a lullaby to him as she had the night before.

But Sairu was in her mistress's chambers, restored to favor and ever watchful. She had filled the room with paper lanterns to ward off the darkness of a deep mountain night, and she sat now in a corner of the room, watching her mistress.

"*Everyone wants something,*" Princess Safiya had told Sairu many years ago now. "*Once you know what a man wants, anything else you wish to learn about him is a matter of mere extrapolation.*"

Sairu's fingers worked quietly with needle and thread over a torn hem, but her mind engaged in a frustrated game of questions without answers.

What does my mistress want?

Lady Hariawan sat cross-legged upon the floor in a manner unsuited to her elegant status. She cupped in her hands a little ball of floss. Sticky Bun, Dumpling, and Rice Cake surrounded her, yipping and wriggling and pawing at her knees, until she was finally convinced to roll the ball as fast as it would go across the room. Then they would pounce after it, crashing into one another and sending the lady into fits of childish giggles. The victor would retrieve the ball, dropping it in Lady Hariawan's lap. She would catch it up, hide it against her bosom, and watch, smiling, as the dogs cajoled her once more to roll it.

She looked like a child of five playing on the dirt floor of some peasant's hovel. But Sairu could not begrudge her this stolen moment of fun. Lady Hariawan's life was possessed of few joys. And besides, no one was around to see her disgrace herself with this unladylike behavior. What did it matter so long as she smiled?

What does my mistress want? Sairu wondered again and again. Like her dogs after the ball, she pursued this thought, only to find herself always returning to the same place, a place of pure ignorance. Because Lady Hariawan did not seem to want anything. Oh, now and again she insisted upon her own way. With Jovann, for instance, when she had compelled Sairu to heal him and bring him with them to Daramuti.

But did she *want* anything from Jovann? Did she even remember that he existed?

Sairu smiled grimly and bit off the end of a thread. She inspected the garment she was mending and discovered one sleeve to be frayed. So she threaded her needle and went back to work, picking at the loose edge with almost as much determined ferocity as she picked at the questions in her mind.

Very well, if she could not fathom what her mistress wanted . . . what did the Besur want? What did he hope to gain by sending Lady Hariawan away to Daramuti? Now this was a question to which she should be able to discover an answer. Lady Hariawan was a Dream Walker—Sairu had not doubted this for a moment since the beginning. Nor did she doubt that the Besur had plans in mind to use her powers, though what those plans might be, Sairu could not begin to guess. Not yet.

But she could guess one thing, and she was almost certain she was right. The Besur had sent Lady Hariawan away to prevent her from dream-walking. Sairu watched her mistress and the little dogs. She gazed at the soft cheek where the evil burn spread, looking fresh and painful still in the light of the paper lanterns. Lady Hariawan had encountered someone—or something—in the Dream. And the Besur wanted to be certain she did not encounter it again.

What he failed to realize was that Lady Hariawan did not need the support of the temple in order to pursue her skill.

The floss ball rolled across the room and stopped beside Sairu's foot. Three yapping hunters fell upon it, crashing into Sairu in their eagerness, pulling the half-mended garment to the floor. "Oh, Anwar's elbow!" Sairu cried and shooed her dogs away. The needle was lost somewhere, and she was obliged to search for it, discovering it at last caught in the threads of the opposite sleeve. Frowning, she folded up the robe and put it away to be finished later. Then she snatched the ball from Dumpling's mouth and hid it in her robe, turning a deaf ear to the dog's protesting whines and barks.

She turned to Lady Hariawan. "All right, my mistress," she said, extending a hand, which Lady Hariawan tentatively took, allowing Sairu to help her to her feet. "It is late. Time you were in bed."

Lady Hariawan made no protest as Sairu assisted her out of her day-time robes and into a soft sleep gown. She obediently climbed into bed and allowed Sairu to cover her with blankets. She raised her deep black gaze to Sairu's face. "May I have the dog?" she asked.

Sairu raised an eyebrow. "Will you promise to sleep and not play?"

Lady Hariawan nodded meekly. So Sairu picked up the favored Sticky Bun and placed him by her mistress's side, where he curled up at once, his head resting on her stomach, and began to snore. Lady Hariawan gently stroked his head, running her finger down his pushed-in nose. His lip curled and he put out his tongue to lick at her finger, making her giggle.

"No, no," said Sairu sternly. "Sleep."

So Lady Hariawan closed her eyes, and Sairu went around the room and snuffed all the candles in the lanterns. Then she resumed her seat in the corner, Dumpling and Rice Cake arranging themselves at her feet. She folded her hands, her eyes wide and bright, and she watched the sleeping form of her mistress.

There would be no harimau spice. There would be no chanting or meditation. If she could help it, she would not allow her mistress to dream-walk tonight.

And so the quiet of Hulan's night fell upon Daramuti, and the hours crawled slowly by. Jovann, lying in the darkness of the infirmary, stared into the shadows, willing himself to sleep. But even if he slept, he could not guarantee that he would enter the Wood. The handmaiden seemed to think that he could step in and out of worlds at will, and he hated to disillusion her, to admit that such powers were not within his grasp. Perhaps her Lady Hariawan could do as much. But Jovann could only follow the voice of the songbird when it called. If it did not call, he would lie here all night, only to wake in the morning helpless, frustrated, and enslaved.

Even as it had earlier that day, the thought stole over him, *I must return to the Khla clan. I must warn my father.*

He could rise even now, slip from the infirmary out into the temple grounds. No one watched, no one stood guard at his door. He could find a storehouse and gather supplies, just enough to get him started. And a weapon. He was a man of the Tiger, after all, and he knew how to survive in the wild if he had only a knife. These mountains were cold and high, and he found any exertion a strain on his unaccustomed lungs. But he was cunning. He could hide from any search party they sent. He could . . . he could escape . . .

But there was no use in entertaining such thoughts. He knew he would not leave Lady Hariawan.

Closing his eyes, Jovann sank into the tumult of his mind and the pain in his back. Peace eluded him at every turn, and he felt his heart racing. He would never sleep now, never dream-walk, as the handmaiden called it.

He breathed deep and pushed himself, grimacing, up into a seated position. Arranging his legs before him, he sat with his hands cupped. And he whispered, "The pain is here. In my hands. I hold it in my hands."

The pain of his captivity.

The pain of his heartache.

The pain of his people's hatred, their centuries of displacement, of abandonment, of hopeless, helpless rage. All this he held, there in the dark. And it was a tremendous burden for anyone to bear. He did not feel he had the strength or the wisdom to hold it any longer.

Then across the leagues of worlds and boundaries no mind could fathom, he heard the wood thrush singing.

Won't you follow me, Jovann?

With a gasp of relief, he stepped out of his own body and into the white emptiness, then beyond into the Wood Between.

17

THE GRANDMOTHER TREE welcomed Jovann even as it might have welcomed a grandchild. Its language was unknowable to a mortal mind, and its emotions could not be expressed in terms of mortal understanding. But somehow, as he stepped into the clearing out of the empty nothing, Jovann felt gladness, or something as like to gladness as an ancient, ageless tree may express.

Though there was no breeze, the enormous branches overhead moved softly, leaves shushing against one another in hundreds of tiny whispers. Jovann walked beneath this canopy to the trunk of the Grandmother, and stood upon one of its gnarled roots, gazing up at the lower boughs.

"I am here," he said. "I followed you."

The silver bell of a voice rang sweetly above, and the bird itself appeared as though by magic, its eyes bright as two small stars.

"I am going to show you something, Jovann," said the bird. "Something you will not wish to see. And you will tell yourself that you do not know what it is, that you do not understand. But in your heart of hearts, you will know and you will understand. And the pain of that understanding will be the beginning of your new birth."

Jovann sighed. Sometimes he wished the bird would just tell him clearly what it meant and what it wanted. But then, he decided, most birds don't talk at all, so it was perhaps a little unfair of him to expect this one to do more than it did. "Another vision?" he asked.

"No," said the bird. "Another path."

Even as it spoke, Jovann felt the path open beneath his feet. He looked down but saw only the Grandmother Tree's great roots and the gentle green grass that spread across the clearing floor. There was nothing to indicate a path, and yet he knew it was there. He knew that he looked right at it, that he could follow wherever it led, even to the Netherworld and back.

He addressed himself once more to the bird. "My Lord," he said, "I must find the phantoms who plague my Lady Hariawan. Will this path take me to them?"

"It will," said the bird.

"Ah." He'd almost hoped for a different answer. "Well. That's good then, yes?"

"No," said the bird. "But it will be good."

With that, it spread its wings and swooped down so close that one wingtip brushed Jovann's hair even as he ducked. Then it sped off, flying in the same direction Jovann felt the invisible path must lead. It disappeared into the trees and the deeps of the Between, but Jovann could still hear its song ringing gently through the shadows.

The Grandmother Tree rustled its leaves again, and one of its old boughs groaned. Jovann glared at it. "Yes, yes, I'm on my way!" he said and, straightening his shoulders, stepped off the root and pursued both path and bird. He hesitated again at the clearing's edge. He'd only ever passed over in company with Lady Hariawan who was, he believed, far more powerful in this world or worlds than he himself. But the path was clear to his heart, if not to his eyes, and he did not think it would lead him astray.

The leaves overhead burst into sudden earnest rustling. At their urging, Jovann shook himself and passed out of the clearing into the great Wood.

He walked. Trees slid from his path, and undergrowth of brambles, ferns, even wildflowers seemed to slide away from his footsteps, always just a few paces ahead of him. Even the shadows dispersed, leaving his way filled with golden light, though the canopy of leaves above him never cleared enough for him to glimpse the sky. Sometimes he picked up his pace and trotted. Sometimes he even ran. But mostly he walked, on and on. Sometimes the path led him down into low, rocky valleys, and he felt that things watched him from behind boulders. Sometimes it led him up hills lined with young saplings of a type he had never seen in Noorhitam, with strange lavender trunks and silver leaves that chimed like various musical instruments. Sometimes it led him through ferns so tall and thick they could have hidden any number of beings, though his own way remained clear before him.

But always there was more Wood. Unlike when he walked with Lady Hariawan, the trees did not thin away and vanish into mist. There was no sign of the Dream.

"How am I supposed to find it?" he whispered, speaking to a friendly-looking young pine that stood nearby, watching him curiously. "She always led me there before. She knew the way. But this path . . . it seems to go on and on forever but never get anywhere! Did the songbird—" He stopped, not liking to voice aloud the thought in his heart. But the thought was there anyway.

Did the songbird make a mistake?

The pine, which did not need to hear words in order to understand, looked suddenly disapproving. It is an unsettling feeling indeed to be disapproved by a tree. Jovann scowled at it and continued on his way.

Time followed him wherever he went, for he was mortal and could not escape it entirely. It flowed around him like water or light, and thus he could not count the hours as he would have in his own world. Since he had left his mortal body behind, he did not tire so quickly as he might have. But a mortal mind will eventually become exhausted, and Jovann suddenly found that his was spent.

So he sat there in the middle of his path. Around him stood tall trees with rich red trunks and broad leaves so dark green they may have been black. The shadows were deeper here, and the ground was covered in thick-growing ivy from which tiny flowers, shaped like stars, peered out and shone with their own secret light. They were pretty, Jovann thought, and also kind. He reached out a finger and gently touched the face of one. It felt no different from a flower in his own world.

But he discovered, a few moments later, that the vine had crept into his lap and lay there like a kitten, flowers gently touching his arms and hands and even reaching up toward his face. This startled him at first, and he wondered if he were being smothered alive. But no, this was a friendly vine. He stroked a nervous finger down one of its long, winding stems, and soon found his hand wrapped, but not restrained or constricted, in green leaves and shining flowers.

"How am I supposed to find the Dream?" he whispered again, speaking now to the flowers. "I fear I am lost, though I know I haven't strayed from the path."

The flowers looked as though they wished they might help. But since he didn't understand the language of flowers, their wishes were in vain. He sighed heavily and bowed his head, resting it in one of his hands, elbow propped on a vine-draped knee. "What am I supposed to do?"

Let me help you.

Jovann screamed. The flowers and vines vanished, racing back into the shadows with a great slithering, leaving Jovann alone with that voice, which reverberated inside him like a hammer striking an anvil. A brilliant light fell through the heavy leaves to the forest floor, blinding and glorious beyond the words of men. Jovann fell back, flattened and ready to die.

Then the light shook itself, dimmed. Cé Imral, the blue star, stood before Jovann in the shape of a unicorn, gazing upon him with inquisitive, endless eyes.

When it spoke, its voice was singular, not the vastness of the starry host all rolled into one.

"I have been watching you," said Cé Imral.

Jovann, panting hard, propped himself up on his elbows. Then, slowly gathering his strength and courage, he got back to his feet. The last time he had looked upon this particular star, it was flaming and furious and, he had believed, ready to kill him. But it seemed much smaller now, here in the

Wood, away from Hulan's Garden. Its flanks were dappled with shadows from the trees, but no shadows could touch the horn on its brow, which gleamed with all the richest, deepest opal fire.

It was a creature of beauty, and infinitely lovable. Jovann felt himself a little boy, longing to fling his arms around the creature's neck as he once had flung his arms around the neck of his father's oldest, proudest hunting dog. But he would never dare.

"I have been watching you," Cé Imral repeated, "since you came to my Mother's Realm. I do not usually take interest in mortal doings. But my Mother entrusted you with her Great Secret. This makes me curious."

Jovann didn't know what to say, so he kept his mouth shut.

"You search for the Dream, do you not?" the star persisted. "And for that which hides inside the Dream?"

"I . . . I am trying to find those who have twice now set upon my Lady Hariawan when she walked there," Jovann said, his voice small and stammering.

"Yes." When the unicorn nodded, its horn flashed and its mane shimmered. "I know of whom you speak. The Chanters, who do not sing, but who build and sustain with their voices. I have seen them. I have sung of them. I will take you to them."

And with that, the unicorn turned and began walking through the Wood. Jovann took a step after, then paused. After all, he had been given a path to walk. Yes, it had proven an endless, infuriating path that led him nowhere at all. But was it wise to leave it?

Was it wise to not?

After all, what was a songbird compared to the glory of a unicorn? Compared to the glory of one of the great Dara, children of the Moon?

The debate lasted mere moments, but in the Wood it felt far longer. And he might have debated with himself for longer still, had he not glanced down at his feet.

The path he had been following was gone.

"Are you coming, mortal?" called Cé Imral from the shadows.

Jovann bit back an angry curse. Then he hastened after the unicorn, leaving behind the starflower vines and the tall red-bark trees. The unicorn, seeing him coming, turned its horn forward again and took three paces.

Within those three paces, the Wood gave way. By the time Jovann had caught up to the unicorn, he found himself no longer sheltered by trees but standing on the edge of the Dream.

How could he have been so very near without realizing it? But then, distances were not the same here, beyond the mortal world. A thing might be near and far all at the same moment. Mist shrouded him, at his feet, in his spirit. But his eyes were filled still with the light of Cé Imral.

"Come," said the unicorn, and moved off into the formlessness.

Jovann followed, and together they penetrated the Dream. Shapes began to emerge from the mist, and Jovann glimpsed the forever-distant mountains, green and gold and magnificent. The Highlands, Umeer's daughter had called them.

But they vanished again, replaced by a different range of mountains, much lower, much nearer, much more forbidding. And now the mist gave way beneath his feet, and Jovann stood on a cracked, dry wasteland of endless dust.

The chanting reached him. As though it had been going on for ages, but his ears only just now opened to receive it. A rich, deep boom of many voices working together as though building a tower of sound. Each voice was its own brick, fitting with all the others to form the enormous whole.

Cé Imral stopped, and a shiver rippled over its body. Its light flickered and lessened so that its flanks turned deeper blue, and it looked more solid as it stood on the dry dirt. Its cloven hooves stamped uneasily, churning up the dust.

"What is it?" Jovann asked, drawing up alongside his guide. He almost could not make himself ask the next question, but forced the words out anyway. "Are you afraid?"

"No," said the unicorn. "I am . . . *hungry*."

In the depths of its midnight-blue eyes gleamed a spark of red fire.

Jovann shuddered and turned away. And when he turned, he found himself suddenly gazing upon the temple.

"You're asleep."

Sairu startled awake with a gasp and shook her head violently. She looked down and saw the shining eyes of the cat, who stood upon his hind feet, his front paws resting on her knees. "Oh, Monster!" she breathed in relief, though her heart raced like mad in her breast. Then she shook herself again, realizing that she had, indeed, fallen asleep while on watch.

"Two nights sitting up and a busy day between," said the cat quietly. "You shouldn't have tried it. Not tonight."

Her whole body shuddered with the chill of exhaustion, and she wrapped her arms around herself. Lady Hariawan's bedchamber was as still as a tomb save for the snores of the three soundly sleeping dogs.

The cat hopped into her lap, purring, but she quickly pushed him off and got to her feet. Moving stealthily so as not to disturb either Dumpling or Rice Cake, she crossed the room to Lady Hariawan's bed. Sticky Bun was curled up in a ball against the lady's side, and one of her hands rested on his back. Sairu reached out and lightly touched that hand.

"Oh no," she breathed.

For she knew in that touch that Lady Hariawan was not in her body.

"No, no, no," Sairu said, and her voice woke all three dogs. Dumpling growled to see the cat, but was too upset by his mistress's tone to give chase. All three crowded to her, wagging their tails as though offering their help. But Sairu ignored them. She grabbed Lady Hariawan's shoulders and pulled her upright. Her mistress's head lolled on her limp neck. She breathed, but only just, and her spirit was not entirely within her.

The cat jumped up onto the pillows, ignoring Sticky Bun's warning growls. He sniffed Lady Hariawan's cheek. "She's gone," he said. "into the Dream."

Sairu patted her mistress's cheeks and frantically rubbed her hands and wrists. But to no avail. "She's beyond my protection," she whispered and collapsed onto her knees beside the bed. "What can I do?"

"Nothing," said the cat. "You must wait and see what comes."

The temple was built entirely of sound, but the sound was made solid and dark and forbidding. Jovann recognized the structure in an instant, though he could not at first recall why. Then he remembered the vision he had glimpsed only just that afternoon, of a temple far greater than Daramuti, as magnificent as the Crown of the Moon itself, if not more so. And he had known even then, though he could not explain it, that it was built of voices. Of minds.

So it was here in the Dream. Jovann stared at the enormous structure surrounded by a huge wall, and he knew that, somewhere, mortal minds concentrated with such intensity that they called brick and mortar into being and, as they imagined, so they created. Only in the Dream. But in the Dream, it was solid and strong.

And, Jovann knew at once, it was evil.

Though he hated to say it, he whispered, "I must get closer. I must learn more of these people who seek to harm Umeer's daughter."

"Yes," Cé Imral responded, and its voice so little resembled a star's just then that Jovann could have believed it had been born and reared in the form it now wore. "Yes, I must see this thing of which I have only sung."

It started forward, its hooves stirring up the dust as it went, and Jovann fell in behind it. The dust choked him and blocked his vision at first, so that they stood in the very shadow of the temple before he quite realized how near they had come.

Now, as the dust cleared, he saw that the temple was incomplete.

The walls, which at a distance had seemed impassable, were as insubstantial as any dream. Many bricks were missing from its construction, and it looked as though a child's breath might knock the whole of it tumbling. But the chanting went on and on, reverberating from within. And even as Jovann stood there beside the unicorn, he saw portions of the wall become more solid, shimmering into existence.

"What is this place?" Jovann whispered, though he did not expect an answer.

Cé Imral said, "It is built by the minds of mortal men, but not at a mortal's direction. There is another power at work here."

"Who?" Jovann asked.

"The Greater Dark," said the star. There was a strange, haunting quality to its words.

Then it shivered and said again, "I am hungry."

With that, it began to walk around the wall, and Jovann, not knowing what else to do, followed. They came at last to an enormous gate, and it, like the wall, was unfinished. All of the other temples Jovann had seen in his life had boasted round Moon Gates at their entrances, in honor of Hulan. This gate was square: two great posts of black stone, and a crossbeam of blood-red. Through the swirling dust, Jovann saw that one of the posts was carved in the likeness of man. But when he blinked and looked again, he thought that it wasn't a man after all, but a dragon.

The other post, by contrast, was unfinished, uncarved. As Jovann drew nearer to it, however, he half thought he saw the figure of woman. Not on the outer surface, but hidden down inside the stone, waiting for the hand of a master craftsman to set her free. But the stone itself was rough, unpolished. A huge column set to support the crossbeam and nothing more.

Jovann drew nearer to Cé Imral. But he pulled back again almost at once, for a tremendous heat emanated off the star's physical body. He glanced at the star, and saw that beneath the blue dapples of its coat a red light was gleaming.

The unicorn's eyes rolled in its head, and it uttered a moan.

"Are you unwell?" Jovann asked, which struck him even then as rather an odd thing to ask a star.

But the unicorn shook its head, its horn flashing. "Come," it said. "I must see within."

Together they passed under the crossbeam of the gate and into the temple courtyard. The chanting filled all of this space, dark and throbbing and full of strength. There was nothing to be seen, for the mist of the Dream was too thick. Jovann put up a hand, trying to wave his vision clear, but he could discern nothing. Only the chant. He felt rather than saw the forms of the phantom chanters around him, but they were so occupied in creating and sustaining the form of the temple, they took no notice of him. So intense was their concentration that not even the near presence of a star could divert them.

Jovann lost sight of Cé Imral and stumbled several paces, alone in the formlessness. Then he glimpsed, to his left, a flash of light, and he turned toward it, thinking it must be the star. He wanted to flee, to find his way back to the gate and run from this place as fast and as hard as he could, never to return.

But he could not. These phantom chanters wanted something from Lady Hariawan. He must try to discover what. He must try to protect her. So he pursued the light, which flashed, vanished, and flashed again. The chant weighed upon him, making each new step more difficult than the last. But suddenly the mist cleared. He found that his feet stood upon paving stones, and he saw the towering buildings of the temple all around, surrounded by the great wall.

Before him, suspended between two pillars carved like dragons, was an enormous gold gong.

Jovann stared at it, uncertain what he saw. It was five times taller than any man, huge and heavy. When struck, it must make a sound that could bring this whole temple tumbling to ruin. Even as it hung there, barely shivering between its pillars, it gave a hum that underscored all the chanters' voices, forming the foundations of the temple.

The gold was intricately etched in words, characters he did not recognize in a language he did not know. They swirled from the center of the gong, all the way out to the edges.

As those characters filled his mind, they shifted, changing shape so that he could read the first few lines:

I see them running, running, stumbling,
Running, as the heavens
Break and yawn, tear beneath their feet,
Devouring, hungry Death!

Jovann closed his eyes, unwilling to see more. But the words danced within his brain, like the flames of a bonfire lashing the night sky. He turned his back on the gong.

And found he stood face-to-face with Cé Imral.

The unicorn stared over his head. Its horn, like a sword raised for battle, sliced the mist of the Dream around it. Its ears cupped forward, and its nostrils flared. It gazed upon the golden gong, and Jovann saw the gold reflected in the star's eyes.

For hours, it seemed, they stood just so, neither moving, neither breathing.

Then Cé Imral uttered a scream such as only stars can make. And its whole body and being rippled over in red flame.

Jovann screamed as well, his voice lost in the sound of the unicorn's agony. He fell to his knees, expecting to be destroyed. But there was a flash of light, and the unicorn vanished. And Jovann found he still lived, shuddering upon the flagstones of the temple yard.

The gong shivered behind him, and its hum increased.

At the sound, the chanters, though their voices never ceased, turned suddenly and saw the intruder in their midst. Jovann could not see them, not clearly, but he felt them all around him. With a strangled cry, he forced himself to his feet. How he longed to curl up into a small ball of nothingness and vanish! For the scream of Cé Imral still resounded in his ears, and it was like death itself.

But Umeer's daughter needed him. He must not die. Not yet.

So he forced himself up and began to run. He did not know the way to the gate, but ran even so. The phantoms were all around him, their voices full of fury. They reached out, but their shadowy hands did not lay hold of him, and Jovann passed through their numbers untouched.

The black pillars of the gate in the insubstantial wall appeared before him. He staggered at the sight, then drove himself forward. Had he been in his physical body, he would never have been able to make it, but in this world beyond mortal limits, he could run and run and run.

He reached the gate. And he met Lady Hariawan standing beneath the arch.

"My lady!" he cried.

She turned to him, such a figure of beauty here in this evil place. She wore white, and her skin was whiter still, and her hair black as the night. But her lips were as blood-red as the crossbeam overhead.

"I must find her," she said.

Then she reached out with both her hands and touched the uncarved post of the gate. Her hands trembled, and the stone seemed to burn her. She gasped with pain.

Jovann, feeling the chanters close on his heels, did not slow his pace. He grabbed hold of Lady Hariawan, dragging her from the pillar out into the wasteland. She screamed in his grasp and struck him. "No! No!" she cried, hitting his face, clawing at his cheek. "I must find her! I must! I *must!*"

She went for his eyes. Were he in his physical body, she would have dug them out. But while his form was only imagined, the pain he felt was real. Horrified, Jovann dropped his hold upon Lady Hariawan, and she fell hard upon the ground.

"My lady!" He whirled about, seeking her in the cloud of dust. But no sooner had he spotted her then the phantom chanters fell upon them.

They were black as shadows, without solid form or substance, for almost all of their concentration efforts went into creating and sustaining the temple. Even now, every one of them gave voice to the chant, and they were none of them strong.

But they were many, and they converged in a swarm upon Jovann and Lady Hariawan. Jovann saw her face, white as death, gazing up at him with a look of pure hatred. Then she vanished behind the shadows of the chanters pressing between them.

"No! My lady!" Jovann cried out and tried to plunge after her.

A solid hand fell upon his shoulder. Jovann gasped at the touch, for this was no phantom. He felt living flesh and living blood. The next moment, he was spun around.

He stared into the face of his own father.

"You should not be here!" Juong-Khla roared, and spittle fell from his teeth. "Get out!"

18

THE WALLS OF THE infirmary shook with the force of his spirit hitting his body.

Jovann stared up into the dark as though he could somehow still discern his father's face. He couldn't breathe. He couldn't feel his own heartbeat or the pain of his back. He couldn't feel anything.

And then he snatched a great breath into his lungs and sprang up from his pallet, stumbling and struggling as he relearned how to work his physical form in this physical world. By the time he reached the infirmary door, he was running. He sprinted down the path, blood roaring in his ears. Though he had never walked it himself, he knew the way to find Lady Hariawan; he had watched Sairu coming and going enough times to be certain. He came to her building and burst through the door. All was dreadfully still inside, the household deep in sleep, deep in dreams . . . .

He did not know where her rooms were, but he ran to them as though guided by some instinct of the heart. He came to the door and knew it was hers, and he yanked it back in its grooves with a force that rattled the whole frame of the wall.

Sairu, in the innermost sleep chamber, hovered over her mistress's sleeping form. Her head came up with a snap when she heard the outer door bang open. "No," she breathed, and the next moment heard the shout of the first of the temple slaves.

A tumult of commotion filled the night as, one by one, all six of Lady Hariawan's slaves woke and set upon the intruder in their midst. The three dogs exploded with barking and rushed to the sleep-chamber door, scraping and snarling as they listened to the activity without.

Then the door flew open, and Jovann, eluding the hands of the slaves, staggered into the room. Sairu saw his face for a flashing instant, illuminated by moonlight through the window. It was a mask of utter terror, such terror as must communicate itself to all who witness it. Sairu's heart shuddered in her breast.

Jovann's eyes fixed upon Lady Hariawan, lying so still upon her pillows. "My lady!" he cried and fell across the room.

Sairu felt her training rush through her limbs. She saw herself take Jovann by the arm, twist him, bring him crashing down upon the floor, writhing in the pain she knew she could cause. But she didn't move. Even as the temple slaves crowded to the door, Jovann fell across Lady Hariawan's bed, taking her face between his hands and crying out, "Umeer's daughter! Wake! Wake, I beg you!"

Lady Hariawan opened her eyes. She stared without recognition up at Jovann.

She screamed.

The temple slaves, galvanized, sprang upon Jovann. Tu Syed took him by the hair on the back of his head and yanked him painfully backwards. A strangled cry gurgled in Jovann's throat, and he flung up his hands, trying to dislodge Tu Syed's grasp. But Tu Domchu and another slave grabbed hold of him, one by each arm, and they hauled him back across the room.

Someone struck a light. For a moment all were blinded in the glare, and the world and all its terror and noise froze in place.

Then, blinking and wincing, all turned to find Brother Tenuk standing in their midst. His quivering old hand held a rush with which he lit one of the hanging paper lanterns.

Lady Hariawan screamed again and fought against her own trembling limbs to sit upright, dislodging pillows. The dogs yipped and ran to her but did not reach her so quickly as Sairu, who flung her arms about her mistress. "Hush! Hush! You are safe!" she whispered, cooing as though to calm a frightened child.

Lady Hariawan buried her face in Sairu's shoulder, her body convulsing with shudders.

Brother Tenuk, the lantern shining above him like a small red sun, his face highlighted and shadowed in strange crevices, blew out the light on the end of the rush, dropped it, and ground it beneath his heel. He leaned heavily upon his cane, turning slowly to survey all crowded into that room. He spared little more than a glance for Lady Hariawan or her handmaiden, but fixed his watery gaze upon Jovann, held in the clutches of Tu Syed and the other slaves.

"What is the meaning of this uproar?" he demanded, his old voice quivering like the flame in the lantern above.

Tu Syed responded swiftly, "We caught this slave assaulting our mistress. He burst into her chambers and fell upon her while she lay sleeping." His posh, gentleman's voice was laced with cruelty.

Brother Tenuk opened his mouth to respond, but Sairu cut in first. "He did not hurt her! He meant her no harm!"

Brother Tenuk glanced sharply at the handmaiden, who sat on the bed with her arms tenderly around Lady Hariawan, but whose eyes, bright in the lantern light, were full of fighting fire. He wondered, momentarily, if she knew what the slave boy was. He wondered if she knew why her mistress commanded her to tend him so carefully. He suspected that she did. They all knew, he thought, and they all believed they could deceive him. But it was they who were deceived.

He turned to Jovann, who knelt in the painful grasp of the temple slaves. "I should hang you at once," he said.

"No!" Sairu sprang from the bed, leaving her mistress to curl into a ball, her head buried in her arms. Once on her feet, Sairu seemed to recover herself, and she folded her hands and bowed, though her voice was as tense and sharp as before. "Honored Brother, you cannot pass judgment on this slave. He belongs to Lady Hariawan."

"He belongs to the Crown of the Moon," Brother Tenuk replied smoothly. "Even as does your mistress."

Sairu, still bowing, hesitated. Then, controlling her voice and forcing it into subservient tones appropriate for a handmaiden, she said, "Then it is the Besur, and not you, Honored Brother, who may decide his fate."

Now Brother Tenuk smiled. He smiled a smile as knowing as ever the handmaiden's had been, as full of power. He saw her blench, and this added to the strength of his smile. He said, "I couldn't agree more."

He motioned with the end of his cane to the slaves, commanding, "Take him away."

Jovann uttered one agonized gasp as he was hauled to his feet and dragged from the chambers. He cast a last look over his shoulder, not at Sairu, who stared in horror at his going, but at Lady Hariawan, who lay inert, curled into herself. His heart lurched at the sight then plunged into his stomach. It was the last glimpse he had of her before they dragged him into darkness.

Dumpling and his companions ran at the heels of the slaves, snarling and snuffling all the way to the outer chamber door. There they stood in the doorway, barking after the retreating forms of the slaves and Brother Tenuk until all had disappeared down the passage and out of the building. Then the trio turned and raced back to the inner sleeping chamber and their mistress.

Sairu stood still as a statue, her hands neatly folded, her face quickly assuming a stoic mask. But her heart raced in her throat, and her mind roared like a hurricane in her head. She felt her dogs nosing her ankles and pawing at her skirts, but she could not respond to them.

Suddenly she whirled and grabbed Lady Hariawan by the shoulders, pulling her upright on the bed. Her mistress's eyes rolled, unable to focus. Sairu shook her and patted her cheek, gently, though she wished to be rough.

"My mistress," she said, her voice fighting against the heartbeat in her throat. "My mistress, you must collect yourself. You must intercede for him!"

Lady Hariawan moaned, her chin dropping to her chest, her hair falling to cover her face. Sairu brushed the hair aside and cupped her mistress's cheek. The scar of her burn seemed so much uglier suddenly. Sairu trembled with an unprecedented desire to hit her, but she restrained herself.

"Mistress, you know he is a friend! You know he seeks only to help you, even as you once helped him! Can you not remember? Can you not recall his face? Did you not see him in the Dream?"

A shock of energy, like a lightning bolt, shot through Lady Hariawan. She drew herself up, and her eyes focused. She became the woman Sairu had glimpsed only a few times in the months of her service; she became the mistress, the strong director of lives and fates.

She said nothing. She did not need to speak. The force of her gaze sent Sairu reeling, withdrawing her hands and sliding from the bed, stepping several paces back into the room.

"My—my mistress?" Sairu breathed, then swallowed with difficulty. "Please. For Jovann."

Lady Hariawan raised a hand; one long finger pointed at Sairu's heart. She said: "Get out."

For a heartbeat, Sairu resisted. All the urges of her training told her to obey, but something deep inside told her to fight, to strive.

But she could not.

She fled the room, Dumpling and Rice Cake hurrying behind her. Only Sticky Bun remained, whining softly as he hid behind one of Lady Hariawan's fallen pillows, his sad brown eyes fixed upon the lady's face. Someone must remain to guard her. So, though he trembled from the end of his pushed-in nose to the tip of his curly tail, Sticky Bun remained.

Lady Hariawan, unaware of her small guardian, fell back upon her bed, breathing heavily. Her eyes fluttered, then closed, and her brow constricted into a frown of pain. She did not sleep but fell into an uneasy trance.

The room was still as a grave.

A whiskered face, its sniffing nose pink in the lantern light, lifted up from a hiding place near the ceiling. The cat, who had tucked himself away at the top of the ebony-inlaid wardrobe at the onset of all the noise and uproar, peered down into the room, his ears back and his tail twitching.

Then, taking care not to attract the dog's notice, he slipped down from the wardrobe, flowed silkily across the floor, leaped up into the open window, and vanished into the night.

From a quiet, out-of-the-way place where no one would notice him, Tu Domchu watched the goings-on of that morning. His face was singularly apathetic, but this was no surprise to any who knew him. Tu Domchu never took interest in anything. He simply existed, a fixture of repellent sameness no matter where he went.

He chewed thoughtfully, spitting into a grassy patch nearby as he leaned against a wall from a vantage giving him clear view of the first courtyard. Dawn came, but without the sun, for the sky was heavy with foreboding clouds and all Daramuti was shrouded in tense gloom, waiting for the break of a storm.

And that little handmaiden—so confident, so arrogant—stood in the first courtyard, wringing her hands with frustration.

Tu Domchu chewed slowly as he watched her. His eye was lazy, dull, but it never shifted from her face. He watched her even as she watched the acolytes making ready a caravan for a long journey. Priests armed themselves with what weapons they had stored away in Daramuti, preparing for the dangerous Khir Road and whatever other perils lay between them and Lunthea Maly. For the abbot had given his command. At midday a party would set forth to take the slave Jovann to the Crown of the Moon and the Besur's justice.

It was a lot of bother for one slave, but Tu Domchu did not wonder at that. He didn't wonder much at anything, merely watched. Merely waited for the answer to his question.

Today the girl would make a choice. And her choice would determine everything.

Jovann, bound once more as he had been found, with a bar under his arms, and a chain attached from his neck to his ankles, emerged from confinement, pushed along by two large, nervous acolytes. Imprisonment and guardsman's duties were not part of the normal routine in this remote temple. Jovann, not yet strong after his sickness, could put up little to no fight, however. Once the chain had clamped down upon his neck, it seemed as though it clamped down upon his very spirit, and he sagged, broken beneath it.

Tu Domchu watched the girl's face as Jovann was brought forth. She was pale, and she was not smiling. But she wore clever masks, and he did not yet have his answer.

Brother Tenuk appeared in the front doorway of the Seat of Prayer, standing above the steps beneath the carved awning set with stone stars. He shivered, his aged frame almost unable to cope with the delight of his success. He barked a command, and several priests of lower orders raced to bow before him.

"Take this," said Brother Tenuk, handing a large scroll into their keeping. "It explains all to the Besur so that he, in his wisdom, may pass judgment on this dog."

All was now made ready. The donkeys were loaded, the priests and acolytes and a few stout slaves were prepared. Even as thunder growled overhead and several of the younger acolytes stared up at the threatening sky and offered prayers, Jovann was dragged to a place behind the largest donkey and secured to its harness. He would walk, enchained, like a prisoner of war.

Like the Chhayan dog he was.

Tu Domchu's gaze never shifted from Sairu, who stood in the center of the courtyard, watching all. And he saw her turn suddenly and approach the abbot, bowing at the foot of the steps.

"Please, Honored Brother," he heard her say. "Do not do this. He is not strong. He will not survive the long journey. You kill him by sending him, and so you give sentence not yours to give. At least let him recover first."

Brother Tenuk looked down at her through the heavy folds of his eyelids. "And who are you, my child, to question me?"

Though the words were gentle, the tone was a knife.

Tu Domchu waited. Would she declare herself? Would she give herself away for the sake of protecting this slave?

But no. Though a shiver passed through her body, and her face betrayed the illness she felt in her stomach, she said nothing more. She stepped back into the shadows of the Seat of Prayer. And she did not move again to intercede, even as the caravan set into motion. Even as the slave was dragged through the gates and on down the mountain road. Still, Tu Domchu waited. He felt the answer to his question so close, so near. But he was not a man to be hurried.

Sairu, moving as though in a dream, slowly crossed the courtyard to the gates and looked out after the caravan. Two acolytes spoke to her, motioning for her to step back, but she ignored them until they had almost slammed the heavy gates in her face. Only then did she retreat a pace, her face only a few inches from the heavy, age-darkened wood.

Then she bowed her head and turned back to face Daramuti. Turned back to return to her mistress.

And so Tu Domchu was answered. He knew now, with absolute certainty, whom she had been sent to guard.

With a speed and agility surprising in a man of his age, the old slave turned and hastened from where he hid, back along the paths to the house where Lady Hariawan dwelled. He must be swift indeed, for the handmaiden would not be long, and what he must do, he must do before she discovered him.

He mounted the steps, slid back the door, and passed like a shadow through the corridor and into Lady Hariawan's chambers; first, the outer chamber, where he had slept this last week and more, along with his fellow slaves; next, the middle chamber which was Sairu's quarters, though she never used it.

Then he slid back the door of the innermost chamber and beheld Lady Hariawan lying still upon her bed.

Lady Hariawan. The Dream Walker.

Tu Domchu drew a knife from his belt and stepped forward.

19

THE STONES BENEATH SAIRU'S gaze dappled dark with spots of rain. Slow spots, for the storm was not yet ready to break, and even now might pass overhead and on down the mountains to drench the valleys below. But a few drops speckled the white stones of the path and splashed on Sairu's face, disguising any tears which may or may not have been visible.

She moved as though in a trance, but her mind spun with possibilities, with plans, with daring rescues and escapes, one after another, each more intricate than the last. Her head was bowed, her hands hidden deep inside her sleeves, but her eyes were bright with concentration.

She could find no solution. She could not protect both Jovann and Lady Hariawan. And she was bound to her mistress by all the most solemn vows of her order.

The injustice of it all screamed in the back of her mind, ready, if she would only set it free, to trample the plots she considered into furious dust. It was so unfair, for Jovann wanted nothing but to help her mistress! And she . . . she had asked him to. She had brought this fate, this certainty of death down upon his head. She, and she alone, was to blame.

She saw the face of Idrus, the dead slaver. And she felt sick to her gut.

"*Your only thought is for your master. Your only concern is for his wellbeing. Nothing else matters. No other lives, no other cares, no other dreams. Nothing but your master.*"

So Princess Safiya had instructed her girls again and again. As though she herself scarcely believed it, but clung to the idea as the only safety amid the storms of the world. One purpose. One drive. One knife-like point of focus. And so life could be borne.

"Nothing but my master," Sairu whispered, her speed increasing as she moved up the path. "Nothing but my mistress."

My mistress . . .

My mistress!

Instinct struck with inexplicable force. Even as she had known once before of Lady Hariawan's peril before there was reason for her to know, she sensed again, with a sickening thrill of dread, danger, danger, *danger*. She was running before her thoughts had formed any coherent notion of what she did or what she would do.

And she felt the truth of what Princess Safiya had ingrained in her soul since she first came to the Masayi: *Nothing else matters.*

She did not run to the door, but around the side of the East Building, straight for the window into Lady Hariawan's chamber. The whole house stood on a high foundation; the window sill was a good three feet above Sairu's head.

It did not matter. She ran, and she leapt, and she took hold. Her body slammed against the wall, and her arms strained in a burst of adrenaline to pull her up.

She heard a shriek.

For a heart-stilling moment she believed it was her mistress. But the next moment she knew it was a man's voice that screamed. Then she heard Sticky Bun's ferocious growls, and she knew what she would see, even before she hauled herself up into the window and over the sill.

The shadowy form of a man she did not yet recognize stood on one leg in the middle of the room, his other leg shaking to dislodge the plump little body fastened there by a set of needle-sharp teeth. He did not see Sairu at first, but cursed again and again, "Dragon's teeth! Dragon's teeth!"

Sairu saw the knife in his hand. She saw the flick of his wrist, and knew what was about to happen.

The next instant, her arms were about his middle, and she hurled him to the ground with all her strength, landing atop him, but rolling off at once into a defensive crouch. Sticky Bun, dislodged, flew across the room and lay where he landed for several heaving breaths before leaping up and barking again, this time staying well out of reach of the intruder.

The assassin, surprised, pulled himself up, searching for his knife. His eyes met Sairu's. She saw his face.

"You!" she gasped.

Tu Domchu dove for the knife, but she dove as well, catching his arm and wrenching it, even as he had seen her wrench the arm of the enormous Master Pirwura, their guide. Tu Domchu hissed in pain, but he was prepared for the attack. He reached down with his other arm, caught Sairu by the ankle, and overturned her.

Sairu fell, her fingers losing their hold on Tu Domchu's arm. She landed hard, the wind knocked out of her. Her body did not wait for her to catch her breath before it set into motion. Still lying on her back, she lifted a leg and kicked, connecting first with Tu Domchu's stomach then, as he doubled over, with his face. He fell, his teeth flashing in a snarl-like grimace.

Sairu struggled to her feet, her long sleeves whipping as she pulled out one of her own two knives. Blood thundered in her ears, and she realized, distantly, that her mouth was open in a roar. She flew at Tu Domchu, striking with the blade.

But she did not expect him to be so much stronger and faster than his old man's frame would indicate. He dodged her blow and caught her by the wrist. He whirled her around, his other arm across her neck, squeezing, squeezing. She twisted her knife hand, trying to free it from his grasp, but his grip was like iron, ready to break her bones. He should not be so strong!

Blackness burst on the edges of her vision as her breath caught in her lungs and blood could not flow to her head. She tried to catch his leg with her foot, to trip him, but he was prepared, and his legs were planted. He tightened his grip. When she dropped her knife, he let go of her hand, and now she clawed at his arm, unable to loosen his hold.

Then suddenly he screamed and fell away. Sairu, choking for air, her vision almost entirely blacked out, collapsed onto her hands and knees. She looked up and for half an instant thought she saw Tu Domchu grappling with a tall, golden stranger who had him by his thin, scraggly hair.

They fell through the doorway into the other room, out of Sairu's sight. Inhaling deeply, and desperately shaking her spinning head, she forced herself up and, forgetting her knife, lunged through the doorway into the middle chamber.

She saw no sign of the golden stranger, but she did not have time to wonder at that. Tu Domchu was on his hands and knees as though just flung there, and he was gathering himself to rise.

Sairu leapt upon his back and wrapped her long sleeve about his neck, pulling tight. He hauled himself upright, once more proving the lie of his age, and sought to dislodge her. But she fastened her legs about his middle, clinging like a sucking leech, and pulled even harder on the sleeve. He whirled about, his arms flailing, and struck her face twice, three times, each hit weaker than the last. She held on. She felt the strength draining from him. He collapsed to his knees, gagging, his face contorted.

Then his body went limp and he fell forward, Sairu still on his back, still clutching her strangle-hold. She did not stop for some moments.

Then, slowly, she loosened her hold and pulled the sleeve out from around his neck. Her breath shuddering from her body, she placed two fingers on his neck and felt for a pulse. Faint, but still present. He wasn't dead.

"*Prrrrlt?*"

Sairu looked up and saw the cat crouched in the shadows, tail lashing. "Monster," she said, but nothing more. She was already unwinding her long sash, which was of a strong weave. Spinning it into cord, she proceeded to truss up Tu Domchu, securing his hands behind his back, and looping a length around his neck as well so that any struggling would produce strangulation.

The cat stepped forward, pink nose twitching. "You didn't kill him?"

"No," said Sairu, shortly.

"If you don't, he'll tell his masters what he knows."

"And what is that?"

"You know exactly what I mean."

She did. She knew all too well. She studied the side of Tu Domchu's face, and she read it now as she felt she should have been able to read it before. She should have seen. She should have known.

Whoever else this man was—whoever else he might have been—he was an assassin.

She remembered Lord Dok-Kasemsan suddenly. She had not thought about him since that day of the test, so long ago, when he had attempted to poison Prince Amithnal's ambassador and been thwarted by Jen-ling. A Crouching Shadow, a hired assassin. And yet, that had not been his purpose in coming to Lunthea Maly at all, only his pretence.

For, as Sairu had discussed the possibility of her new assignment with Princess Safiya, she had seen that Lord Kasemsan did not lie unconscious but listened to every word exchanged. And she knew that his interest was not an assassin's fee at all.

His interest was the Dream Walkers.

Kasemsan was far away in Lunthea Maly, deep in the dungeons beneath the Crown of the Moon. But did that mean he was the only Crouching Shadow concerned with the Dream Walkers?

Sairu finished securing Tu Domchu and rolled him onto his side, gazing deeper into his unconscious face. She could only read so much without looking into his eyes, but there were still secrets to be found. For one thing, she knew that his age was a disguise. She pulled at his repulsive spotty skin, but found no sign of mask or cosmetics. Nevertheless, she knew it was not the truth, even if she could not guess how or why. He had moved too swiftly, and the muscles of his limbs had been far too well-developed. How had she not seen it? How had she not suspected?

He must have been planted in the Crown of the Moon years ago, a humble, foolish, aged slave to whom no one would pay any heed. But while working for his enslavers, he had ever sought the Dream Walker—the most powerful Dream Walker. The one whom the Crouching Shadows, for some reason Sairu did not know, sought to kill.

Except, the most powerful Dream Walker was a woman. And he had not been able to guess that. Not until he heard that a Golden Daughter had been hired to escort one of the temple girls into hiding. Only then did he begin to suspect.

He could not have known for certain, Sairu thought. Otherwise, there had been any number of chances when he could have killed them on the road. Assassin though he was, she could read in the lines around his mouth no blood-thirst. He would not kill unless certain, unless necessary. And when, upon the Khir Road, they had rescued the slave Jovann and, at Lady Hariawan's insistence, taken him into their care and keeping . . . that must have left him wondering.

Perhaps the Golden Daughter had been sent to meet the Dream Walker? Perhaps this journey with the temple girl was nothing but a ruse?

Sairu cursed suddenly and bitterly. What a fool she had been! A true Golden Daughter, prepared for and intent upon her task, would have recognized this man for what he was. What was she playing at, pretending she could protect her mistress?

What was she playing at, allowing herself to become distracted?

The cat watched Sairu, guessing some but not all of the thoughts racing through her head as she looked into the old slave's face. "What will you do with him?" he asked at length.

"Nothing," said Sairu, standing up and folding her hands, once more the demure handmaiden. "I will not kill him." She saw the face of Idrus and his dead men again. Men whose lives she had caused to end, even if she had not wielded the weapons which slew them. She shuddered and said again, "I will not kill him."

"Will you tell Brother Tenuk?"

Sairu turned to the cat, who sat so calmly before the unconscious assassin. The only sign he betrayed of any ill-ease was the dilated pupils of his eyes. These were large and round as dead moons.

"I'll tell no one," Sairu said. "I will take my mistress, and—"

She stopped.

She realized she had not heard so much as a sound from Lady Hariawan.

Sairu whirled about, her un-sashed robes loose on her frame, and all but fell to the door of the sleeping chamber. She had heard no sound from her mistress. She had not even seen her mistress, so intent had she been upon Tu Domchu from the moment she entered the room. Did Lady Hariawan even now lie dead in a pool of blood? Sairu, her face ghostly white with fear, entered the room and gazed within, expecting to discover horrors.

Instead, she saw her mistress sitting upon the floor in the middle of the room, even as she had the night before when playing with the dogs. Sticky Bun, her protector, nosed about her, sniffing her arms and circling her, as though determined to make certain that she was truly safe and sound.

Lady Hariawan stared at nothing upon the floor, unaware of the dog.

"My mistress?" Sairu spoke in a whisper, as though afraid one loud noise would ruin this sight, would shatter this vision and show her the lady dead upon the floor.

Lady Hariawan looked up, her face a still mask. She said: "It is strange, is it not? How these dogs would risk their lives. How they would die for love of me."

She put out one hand, the fingers long, delicate, and trembling. They closed upon the hilt of the assassin's knife lying on the ground beside Sticky Bun.

"I would have it for myself," said Lady Hariawan. "The power of life and death."

In a flash her arm twisted up, and she drove the blade straight for Sticky Bun's eye.

20

THE CAT FOUND SAIRU behind the low wall of the kitchen garden, her shoulders hunched, her body shaking with sobs. Steady rain soaked her garments and ran through her hair. She clutched Sticky Bun close to her heart as she wept.

Ears flattened against the rain, the cat darted up to Sairu's side, relieved to have located her. As he approached, Sticky Bun caught his scent and began wiggling in his mistress's grasp, yipping rather uneasily but still determined to ward off the devil.

The cat puffed through his whiskers, glaring at the dog. He raised his voice to be heard above its barking.

"So the beast's alive. Not even harmed from what I can see. What is all this weeping and wailing for?"

Sairu startled and pressed her wriggling dog closer as she looked down at the cat. Her eyes were wide and full of terror. Several times she tried to speak, but the words stuck in her throat. At last she managed in a hoarse whisper to say: "I struck her."

"And a good thing too," said the cat, shaking his head ineffectually against the downpour. "She did, after all, try to kill your hedge-pig."

"No. You don't understand." Sairu's face was paler than the cat had ever before seen it, and dark circles ringed her eyes. "I *struck* her!"

She buried her face in Sticky Bun's fur, muffling her sobs. The dog whined and twisted about, snuffling her hair and licking her ear and any other part of her he could reach. Their animosity momentarily forgotten, he even permitted the cat to put a paw on his mistress's shoulder, purring and rubbing his whiskered cheek against her head.

"There, there," said the cat through his purr. "There's a good little mortal. Have your cry, and then we'd better decide what we're doing with our would-be assassin. He could be discovered at any moment by his fellows. We must dispose of him somehow. Can't leave him trussed up in the middle chamber."

This brought Sairu's head up. For a moment her expression of horror revealed all the tumult of her soul. But only for that instant before her training leapt into play. She smoothed out her features, relaxed the muscles of her cheeks, softened the line of her brow. She assumed the mask of utter calm.

Only her eyes betrayed her.

"Monster," she said, "you must do something for me. Something I . . . I do not think you will like. But you must promise me to do it."

He stepped back, his tail swishing against the rain, one white forepaw upraised. "You'll have to tell me what it is before I make any promises."

Sairu looked down at Sticky Bun. She'd relaxed her hold, and he sat in the spread of her skirt, bulging eyes fixed on the cat, but submitting to his mistress's caresses. "I need you to take my dogs back to Lunthea Maly," Sairu said.

"*What?*"

"Listen to me," she continued, and her voice was her own again: controlled, dominant, forceful. The cat, immortal devil though he may be, shrank before it, his whiskers tense about his face. "I must get my Lady Hariawan out of this place. I must return with her to the Crown of the Moon and there discover the truth behind all these secrets, all these lies. I must learn exactly why she is being hunted, why the Besur sent her away. I *must* learn these things so that I can protect her. Otherwise I'm marching blind into battle. I will fail her."

"I understand," said the cat. "But I don't understand why—"

"I cannot do it," Sairu interrupted. "I cannot safely guard her all the way back to Lunthea Maly if . . . if I am afraid."

A shudder passed through her small frame, threatening to break her mask into pieces. And the cat saw then what she most feared. He saw why she wept, why even now she looked ready to crack into a thousand shards of hopelessness.

He saw that she was not undividedly devoted to her mistress. And that this realization terrified her.

"Please," Sairu said, though her tone was one of command. "I know you have strange powers. I know you're not what you appear to be. You can get them home for me. I cannot leave them here. They need me. They trust me. It would break their hearts. But to get Lady Hariawan back to the city, I will need all of my skills, all of my concentration. And I do not . . ." She stumbled over the admission but forced it out. "I do not trust myself."

The cat's gaze shifted from her to the dog and back again. "So you want *me* to take them?"

"Yes."

His lip curled in a disconcerted sneer. "Why do we not all journey together?"

"No. I would be afraid. It's a three-month journey. I don't know what she would do to them if I were distracted even for a moment."

"Well," said the cat, "it doesn't *have* to be a three-month journey, you know."

Sairu studied his face, which she had learned to read frightfully well even in the last few days. He did not doubt that she would wrest many secrets from him if he didn't take care.

"I know paths," he said quickly. "Strange paths through strange worlds, but they will cover the distance from here to your city in no time at all by your mortal count. I can take you, your lady, and your dogs."

Sairu narrowed her eyes, reading his face despite his efforts to control it. Then she said, "Can you promise me that, while using these paths, both I and Lady Hariawan would be safe?"

Dragons blast her! The cat lashed his tail irritably. But he admitted, "I could guarantee your safety, little mortal. I could not guarantee hers."

"Then no," said Sairu. "I will not risk it. I *know* I can get her safely to the city if I take her alone. I will not risk her life by another, less sure method."

The cat growled. "I was sent to watch over you," he said. "I was sent to protect you."

She shook her head dismissively. "I do not need protection. I can take care of myself."

"Are you intending to rescue Jovann?"

The bluntness of the question momentarily took Sairu aback. But she controlled her face even now, betraying nothing by so much as the barest flicker of an eyebrow. "I am not," she said. "I will not be divided. I will guard my mistress."

"Even if that means he will die?"

"I will guard my mistress," she repeated, and closed her mouth tight.

Sticky Bun whined again, testing Sairu's hold on him as he feinted a lunge at the cat. Her hands restrained him, but the cat startled back, the fur on his spine rising.

"Please, Monster," Sairu said. "Please promise me you'll see them back safely."

"Very well," said the cat, still growling. "We have a deal. And Lumé love me, I hope I don't live to regret it."

Sairu rose then, bending to set Sticky Bun down on the ground beside the cat. Sticky Bun snarled, preparing to give chase, but his mistress said sternly, "No. No kitty for you. You stay, Sticky Bun."

The dog put his ears back, his eyebrows puckering pathetically, and the cat rolled his eyes and shivered. Sairu, however, nodded with satisfaction and turned to go.

"Wait!" said the cat. "Where will I meet you in Lunthea Maly? And when?"

"I will see you," said Sairu, "three months from today in my former chambers within the Masayi. Look for me then but no sooner." With that, she gathered her skirts and her long sleeves and hastened across the rain-filled grounds, back to the East House, where her mistress sat in near-comatose serenity upon her bed, awaiting her return.

The cat, his ears back like horns, looked at Sticky Bun. Sticky Bun looked back at him, his tongue lolling.

"Oh, Lumé give me strength!" said the cat.

In the dark of the evening, Brother Tenuk knelt in his private prayer chamber before an altar to Hulan. The altar was covered in a faded, moth-eaten cloth that once had been blue and fine. The threads of elegant embroidered work had withered away with time, leaving puncture holes behind, a ghostly testimony to the images once so carefully depicted.

Upon that cloth and altar stood a stone Moon Gate arch, no more than a foot tall. It looked no different from any other dotting the landscape of Noorhitam, save that from the center of this arch hung a silver gong. The gong shimmered where it hung, though there was no breeze to stir it.

Brother Tenuk lay before this altar, prostrate upon his knees, upon his face, his hands extended before him. Any who gazed into the chamber would have seen a man in an attitude of most abject and worshipful prayer. But no one could see that his face was twisted, his mouth open in a silent scream.

Possibly there existed somewhere a world where that scream was heard, causing all the denizens therein to shiver and offer prayers for protection. But here in his own world he dared not make a sound. So his mouth opened, and his throat constricted, and nothing but deep, deep silence poured forth.

Fear wrapped around his heart like a constricting snake, squeezing the life from his soul.

"Did I do right?" he whispered, his mouth scarcely able to form words, his lungs scarcely able to find breath to speak them. "Did I guess correctly? Have I indeed found the Dream Walker?"

Or was there something he was missing? Was there something he was not seeing, not understanding? A twisting, dark path spread before him, a demon's path, and he must walk it. He had no choice. But he could not see where the darkness might lead. He knew only where it must eventually end.

Once more his mouth opened and his throat constricted with the strangling silence of a scream he dared not utter.

In his mind's eye he saw Lady Hariawan bleeding from a poisoned talon embedded in her heart. And she was Kulap, his dove, his innocent dove. He could not distinguish the one from the other, for the two were made one in his vision.

A pounding on his door brought him bolt upright. The movement was too swift for his aged body, and pain shot through every limb. He masked it behind anger in his voice when he shouted, "What do you want? Why do you disturb me in my hour of prayer?"

"Brother Tenuk!" cried the voice of one of the priests. "Brother Tenuk, Lady Hariawan has disappeared!"

The abbot did not answer. He was silent for so long that at last the priest outside his door worked up the courage to knock again, saying only just loud enough to be heard through the panels, "One of the lady's slaves discovered his fellow slave bound and gagged in the middle chamber of Lady Hariawan's rooms. Of the lady herself there is no sign. She and her handmaiden are gone. Gone! We've searched the whole of Daramuti, I swear on Hulan's crown. She is not within our walls."

The door to the prayer chamber slid open with a crash. The priest standing without huddled back into his robes before the face of his abbot. His abbot who was so bent with age, he stood not even as high as the priest's shoulder, but whose wrath was as great as the mountain upon which they stood.

"Find her," the abbot said. "Search the whole of this forest. Now! At once!"

"Brother, night is falling, and beyond these walls it is—"

"I don't care if half your number are devoured by wolves!" the abbot cried, his voice ringing through the whole of the Seat of Prayer. "All of you, spread out. Into the woods, up the slopes, down the Khir Road. Send runners to the caravan bound for Lunthea Maly, and make certain the slave has not been rescued or somehow managed to escape. *Go!*"

Muttering, bowing, and pale as death, the priest hurried away, calling out orders to his brethren as he went. Brother Tenuk, standing in the doorway of his personal prayer chamber, listened to the ringing voices throughout Daramuti. Through windows and thin gaps in the walls he saw torches being lit and their red light flickering. Soon the entire mountain was filled with the shouts of search and desperation.

Meanwhile, Brother Tenuk knelt in the center of his chamber, trembling before Hulan's altar. His mouth moved, but not in prayer. Instead he whispered over and over again, "Did I do right? Did I guess correctly? Will this satisfy the Greater Dark?"

Three little lion dogs crouched under the foundations of the East Building, shivering and whining but obeying their mistress's stern command to *stay*.

She had gone, gone from their sight, gone even beyond their smell. They trembled and pressed against one another, as terrified as though the sun itself had gone out, plunging their world into darkness. What would they do without the mistress? Where could they go?

Suddenly all three twitching noses caught a familiar scent, and Dumpling and Rice Cake both set up a growl, though Sticky Bun remained uncharacteristically quiet.

The cat peered under the foundations, his golden eyes gleaming with their own light. "Oh, there you are, hedge-pigs."

Dumpling and Rice Cake lunged forward. But to their surprise and terror, they did not set upon their feline enemy. Indeed, though their noses told them the cat stood just before them, they found themselves suddenly caught by the backs of their necks by two strong hands and forced down onto their bellies.

"None of that!" said the voice of the cat. "If we're going to be traveling companions, you'll have to behave yourselves. No rending of furry limbs, do you hear me? Now, *heel!*"

And so, as the seeking voices of the priests called out in echoes up and down the Khir Road, four small dark forms scurried to the walls of

Daramuti, discovered a crumbled spot where something had burrowed ages ago, and slipped through into the forests beyond.

21

WITH THE COMING OF DAWN, priests returned from their search, filing footsore through the gates of Daramuti to make their report to the abbot. No trace of Lady Hariawan had been found, nor any sign of her handmaiden. It was generally assumed that the lovely lady had been kidnapped and quite probably killed by her handmaiden—everyone knew they had not been on good terms since arriving in Daramuti, for had not the lady banished the maid from her chambers?

The runners returned later that morning with word that the caravan had been undisturbed, and the slave, Jovann, was still in his chains.

Brother Tenuk received this word with all the stoic placidity an abbot should display, exhibiting none of the rage he had flashed the night before. His eyes, heavy-lidded, revealed none of his thoughts. And when this final report was made, he said no more than "We shall let the Besur himself determine what he does with his own, both the slave and the temple girl. They are out of our hands and should soon be out of our minds. Return to your duties and make ready the morning incense, for we are late in greeting

Anwar."

So, exhausted though they were, the priests and acolytes did as they were told and began to prepare the rituals required of them. Their fatigue was so extreme, it took all of their concentration to accomplish even the simplest tasks. Thus none of them noticed when Brother Tenuk exited his prayer chamber and made his way slowly, painfully, up the path to the dovecote.

He cursed Anwar with every step he took. And he cursed Hulan with every beat of his heart.

The raven in the dove nest watched his approach but made no move to show itself. Brother Tenuk was obliged to put his face right up to the opening and peer inside, into that little sheltered space where Kulap should even now be nestled with her growing brood. Instead, the space was filled with black feathers, and that evil eye that did not blink as it stared out at him.

"The time has come," said Brother Tenuk. "You must bear a message to my lord. Shall I speak it?"

The raven moved. Though there was insufficient space for its body, it did not exist solely in the mortal world. So it moved, propelling its body with its wings, and pushed itself to the opening of the nest. Like an undulating snake it came, head first, and its beak protruded into the open air, nearly taking out one of Brother Tenuk's eyes. Tenuk stepped back just in time, however, and sneered in disgust at that ugly face so like a bird's and so like a lizard's all at the same time.

"Speak your message, mortal man," the raven rasped. Its voice was that of a dying man steeped in evil and knowing full well to what hell he is bound. It was a voice to make even Brother Tenuk—who had stood in the Dragon's presence and received orders from the Dragon's mouth—shudder.

But the abbot drew himself together with as much dignity as he could still muster and said, "I have sent the Dream Walker back to Lunthea Maly. He is charged with assault on a temple girl, and he is to go before the Besur's justice. He will be thrown into the dungeons beneath the Crown of the Moon to await his sentencing. The Besur is a busy man. He will not care what becomes of this slave and will take his time over the sentencing. But tell your masters that they must hurry and retrieve him before he is executed and sent beyond anyone's use. This is my message, dragon-slave. Have you heard it?"

"I have heard it, mortal man," said the raven. "But *I* am not the Dragon's slave."

The abbot felt his heart stop. But only for a moment. Then it continued to beat, and he almost wished that it would not. "Fly away then," he said. "Deliver your message."

"I will wait until sundown," said the raven. "I do not want Anwar to see me."

So Brother Tenuk was obliged to retrace his steps back to the Seat of Prayer, knowing that the monster still lived among his doves. He could only hope that come nightfall it would indeed vacate the nest and leave him a chance to dispose of the sad remnants of Kulap's nest. He could only hope.

But he could not pray. Never again.

Tu Domchu's head hurt, even hours after he finally regained consciousness. The pain of that ache was not mitigated by the hovering presence of Tu Syed. The presumptuous, pompous old fool somehow seemed to think that he and Tu Domchu were comrades, allies against the freemen of the temple and particularly Lady Hariawan's handmaiden.

"The viper!" Tu Syed said many times over. "I knew it all along. She could only hide wickedness behind that smile of hers! Setting upon an old man unawares . . . such disgrace! May shame forever stain the name of her father's house! She intended harm to Lady Hariawan all along, I'd wager. Probably stole her pretty clothes and made off with them for Nua-Pratut!"

Tu Domchu did not bother to point out that the bulk of Lady Hariawan's finery remained untouched in her room. Indeed, when Tu Syed left him long enough to allow Domchu a moment of covert inspection, the only thing he could discover missing was part of the pilgrimess disguise. Even then, the hat and veil were left behind.

At long last, as shadows began to stretch across the chamber floor, Tu Domchu convinced the all-too-helpful Tu Syed that what he needed more than anything was rest. So Tu Syed left him alone in the slaves' chamber and went to join his fellow slaves at supper. Tu Domchu lay alone in the darkness.

He rubbed his throat. He could still feel the constricting squeeze of Sairu's sleeve cutting off his breath. Cutting off his opportunity. He cursed himself quietly. By now the Golden Daughter would have secreted Lady Hariawan so far away, none of the temple folk could hope to find her. He knew that he himself would fail if he tried. No one would find Lady Hariawan until Sairu desired it to be so.

Domchu cursed again and a third time. He should have put an end to Lady Hariawan months ago!

But no. No, the men of his order did not kill without need. Until he was certain the young temple girl was indeed the Dream Walker he sought, his vows would not permit him to act. Not even Master Rangsun would have asked more of him.

But he should have killed that Golden Daughter. Of this he was bitterly certain.

The sun set, and the sky deepened from gold to purple to black. And now Tu Domchu stood, shivering a little. His old, wrinkled skin rose in gooseflesh. He crept from the slave's quarters, through the middle chamber, and on to the room where Lady Hariawan had slept. Beside her bed, a mirror hung on the wall. It was formed like a Moon Gate, round and carved in shapes meant to resemble the Dara. Tu Domchu did not know if these were accurate depictions or not. The Crouching Shadows could not dream-walk. They could not enter Hulan's garden and behold her children for themselves.

But they did possess other powers.

He lit a lantern and hung it above the mirror so that its light shone red upon his face, forming crags and creases enough to give him a ghoulish aspect. It almost frightened him, despite the years he had worn this same face. He did not often glimpse his own reflection, and it still took him by surprise.

Grunting, Tu Domchu leaned in to the mirror, opening his eyes as wide as he could. He stared into his own black pupils, searching, searching . . .

Until he found what he sought.

His old fingers trembling, he put one hand up to his own right eye. He stared into his reflection, keeping watch on the flicker of movement in the depths of his gaze. The nails on his finger and thumb were long and yellow and ragged, stained with the various foul substances he habitually chewed. But it was with great delicacy that he used those nails to pluck at his pupil.

He caught something which wriggled. In his reflection he saw a shadowy shape struggling between his finger and thumbnail. His mouth turned up in a leering smile, and he pulled the little writher out of his eye. It hurt more than he expected, and he winced at the pain of it. But the pain passed, and he held up his catch for inspection.

Pinched between his nails was a tiny imp made up of shadows, spite, and malevolent fortune. It cursed Tu Domchu in a language he did not understand. It was like holding smoke, smoke which could not twist from his grasp and flee into the darkness.

This was a Faerie slave.

A movement in the mirror drew Tu Domchu's attention away from the imp. A ripple like water passed through his reflection, and as it passed, Domchu felt a strange, sickening sensation ripple through his own body. He gasped and used his free hand to support himself on the wall, closing his eyes once more as though to close out the pain.

The ripples stopped. He felt his form stabilizing. Breathing deep, he straightened and looked at his reflection once more.

A man in the prime of his life and strength stared back at him. A handsome man, ragged about the edges but strong of limb and courageous to the utmost extreme. An elegant Pen-Chan scholar-warrior.

Tu Domchu's face did not move, certainly did not show any indication of pleasure save for a small light in his now-clear eye. What a blessing it was to be free of the imp's disguising spell after all those years! A small relief even in the midst of his failure.

He addressed his gaze to the imp, which continued to curse and thrash in his hold. He grimaced, for it was hideous thing.

"You have seen what I have seen," he said.

The imp stopped writhing and held perfectly still. He knew it heard him.

He knew it listened.

"Fly back across the worlds to your other half," said Tu Domchu. "Bear the vision with you. Go!"

With these last words, he tossed the imp toward the window. He saw it whirl about in the air like the tiniest puff of candle smoke. Then it whipped away and vanished from his sight, carrying his message with it.

Tu Domchu closed his eyes and offered a prayer to Hulan. "Guide it safely, Lady Moon," he whispered, "or we are all doomed."

The imp flew out through the window and whipped its way up into the darkness of the night. It chittered to itself as it went, but if any mortal ear had heard it, the sound would have seemed like nothing more than cricket's chirp. It caught a wind current and rose up and up, whirling wildly high above Daramuti and the mountains.

A dark form rose from below. The imp saw it coming and screeched, darting to one side only just in time to avoid the snapping beak of a large creature that may have been a raven. Black wings pounded the night, and for an instant the imp prepared for pursuit. But the raven seemed to have no further interest; it flew on and vanished.

Vanished out of this world.

Overseer Rangsun of the Suthinnakor Center of Learning enjoyed a private set of apartments in the upper floors of the Center, with a high balcony granting him a view over the city rooftops out to the western farmlands beyond. And some days, when the weather was quite clear, he could even see the faint, distant haze of the Khir Mountains, which marked the boundary between Nua-Pratut and the great empire of Noorhitam.

At night, however, not even the moon could illuminate his vision so far.

That night, as was his custom, Overseer Rangsun could be found out upon his balcony. As so often happened at moonrise, he felt disturbed in his spirit and could not sleep. He knelt in an attitude of worship that would have surprised many of the students within the Center of Learning, who thought of the overseer as a man of science only and never would have believed that he was also a man of deep, driving, religious devotion.

The moon shone down upon him, her light gentle, full of restful promises. But Overseer Rangsun could not rest. So he prayed instead, to Hulan, to her children. His prayers were not so much supplications as they were promises of his own. Promises of protection.

"I will not let the Greater Dark approach your gate, Mother of Light," he said, his hands folded in prayer. "I, your servant, have vowed as much upon your own pure glory. I will see you and your children safe."

No matter how much blood he must shed to do so.

A whirring in the air caught his attention, and he raised his prayerful face to the night. He glimpsed the flitting shadow, like a tiny bat on wings, and recognized it at once. He closed one eye and opened wide the other.

With a quick dart, the imp vanished within Overseer Rangsun's pupil.

Long ago, the Crouching Shadows had set clever traps for creatures of worlds beyond. When they finally succeeded in catching one, they found it stranger by far than anything they had ever imagined, a being which, with very little effort, could be split in two, and both halves would survive. But, thus sundered, each half would do everything in its power to be whole again.

So they served well for carrying messages. Overseer Rangsun kept any number of imps in his eyes at a time, and those men under his command, whom he sent to work for him across the nations, possessed the other halves. If a message must be sent, it could be done in no more than a candle's flickering. For the imps would travel the whole world wide in mere moments, always returning to their missing half.

Overseer Rangsun blinked, for the pain of the imp's return was great, like a knife stabbing into his brain. But his body did not move, for he was master of himself even in agony. And the agony did pass. Then he closed his eyes, bowed his head, and concentrated his mind upon the new imp. He recognized it at once as belonging to Tu Domchu—faithful servant, gone into the field in the guise of an elderly slave six years ago. Tu Domchu, whose one goal in life was to discover the identity of the rumored Dream Walker who, so the priests of the Crown of the Moon said, would one day walk all the way to Hulan's Gate.

And when he discovered the Dream Walker, he would put an end to him. Thus Hulan would be protected, even as she had been protected by the Crouching Shadows for generations of mortal men.

Overseer Rangsun sat quite still, waiting for the vision from Tu Domchu to present itself in his mind. He did not have long to wait.

"A woman!"

He gasped, and both eyes flew open. He stared out into the night, across the rooftops of Suthinnakor, on to the horizon beyond which loomed the mountains. Then he cursed and got to his feet.

"A woman! Why did we not guess?"

But who would ever have believed that a woman could perform so great a feat which generations of men could not? He cursed again and stormed into his chambers. Snatching up brush and paper, he wrote out a note in his elegant hand, each figure perfectly formed despite his haste. He rolled it up and sealed it in melted gold-flecked wax, marking it with his signet ring. Then he turned to the darkest corner of his room and spoke to the shadows.

"Take this."

As though materializing from nothing, a figure in a rigid wooden mask stepped forward, hand extended, and accepted the message.

"Hurry!" said Overseer Rangsun.

The Mask bowed. Then it vanished as if by magic, although the only magic at work here was that of stealth and silence.

Overseer Rangsun stood a while in the center of his rooms, his face half-lit by a single candle. Suddenly, his face sagged, and he passed a hand across his forehead.

"If he cannot kill her," he whispered, "all is lost. All is lost . . ."

The world was as still and quiet as ever when Sunan woke in his uncle's empty house. He could hear the sounds on the streets far away beyond the walls, but those were sounds that did nothing more than contribute to the quiet around him.

He lay with his eyes closed, allowing wakefulness to return slowly to his body. How much he hated to face one more day of imprisonment! For, indeed, he was no better than a prisoner here.

At last, however, he opened his eyes. He must rise, he must eat, and he must wait. Someday, surely, the imprisonment must end. Someday, surely, the Crouching Shadows would demand fulfillment of the oath he had sworn.

He sat up, pushing back his blanket. One hand rested on his pillow, and he was surprised to feel something there. He looked.

A message in parchment, sealed in gold-pigment wax. He knew at once from whom it had come, and his eyes moved to every corner of the room, seeking some sign of the Mask. But the room was empty.

Trembling with something akin to fear but more closely akin to relief, he broke the seal and read the scroll. It consisted of one line:

Go to Lunthea Maly.

PART THREE

DARA

1

THE ANUK ANWAR, favored Son of the Sun, the Imperial Glory, Emperor of mighty Noorhitam, heir of conquerors, blessed by Hulan's grace, woke with a start and stared up at the intricately painted tiles on his ceiling.

Then he swore: "Anwar's elbow!"

His voice emerged in little more than a whisper, for his heart raced too hard and his breath came in too short of gasps to allow for speech. So he stared at the painted tiles depicting at intervals Anwar and Hulan's various faces and the faces of their children: Maly, the star for which the city of Lunthea Maly took its name; the twin lights of Zampei and Zampey; Chendu, the star of wisdom; and, of course, Chiev, the North Star. He stared at them, but it was not their painted faces and forms, worked into elaborate medallions, that he saw before his eye.

He saw instead his dream.

With a sudden surge he sat upright, roaring as he did so, "Bintun! *Bintun!*"

The door to the small adjoining apartment opened, and the emperor's favorite long-suffering personal slave and bodyguard stuck his face into the room, his eyes bleary with want of sleep. "Yes, Imperial Glory, Son of Anwar?" he asked, in the same tone with which a mother might speak to a child screaming in the night.

The Imperial Glory of Noorhitam snatched up one of the many pillows tossed about his enormous boat of a bed and threw it with all the force he could muster at Bintun's head. "Bring me the Besur!" he cried. "Bring me the Besur and any priests you can find!"

"Hulan is at the full tonight, Imperial Glory," Bintun reminded his emperor, his voice a smooth cadence of tolerant calm. "The Besur and his priests will all be at prayer, performing the rites of—"

"I don't care!" said the emperor. His eyes were wide and full of fury, and his hand grappled for another pillow to throw. He selected one and hurled it across the room, where it struck the wall by Bintun's face without provoking his servant to so much as blink, which infuriated the Imperial Glory all the more. "I don't care if you fetch them naked from the ceremonial baths! Bring them to me! *Now!*"

It was an hour later before the Besur could make his entrance. Although the Crown of the Moon stood adjacent to the emperor's palace, temple and palace were both so enormous that it took several couriers running at full tilt a good ten minutes to travel from one to the other. Then, when the Besur—who had been interrupted in the middle of a loud and involved prayer to Hulan, which was difficult enough to remember without slaves plucking at his sleeves—had received the message, rolled his eyes heavenward, and cursed, "Anwar's elbow!" in unconscious echo of his emperor, he was obliged himself to run in order to change into the required robes a high priest always wore when entering the presence of Anwar's favored son. Since the Besur spent most of his time in prayer—and ate and drank a great many ceremonial cakes and sacred brews—any amount of physical exertion left him sweating and puffing.

Therefore, shrugged into robes of gold and a headdress mimicking that which artists and poets said adorned the head of Chendu, the star of wisdom, he was obliged to stand some moments outside his emperor's private chambers, gasping to regain his breath while slaves wiped sweat from his brow. Ten other priests of various orders clustered behind him, none of them eager for another audience with the Anuk of Noorhitam.

They knew exactly what this midnight meeting was about.

At length, his dignity somewhat recovered, the Besur motioned to Bintun, who slid back the door and announced the Besur in a voice much too loud for the time of night.

The emperor, still in his bed and clothed in his nightgown (which, the Besur noted with some envy, was of finer work and intricacy than his own ceremonial garment), looked smaller than usual without his crown. He was not a big man to begin with; indeed, he was rather scrawny of limb and proportion, scarcely taller than a woman. But the old crown of his forefathers, fashioned in glorious imitation of Anwar's own, always lent him a magnificence that would bring the princes of other nations to their knees before him. Without it, he looked like an overgrown child. But he was still the emperor.

"What in Hulan's name took you so long?" the Anuk demanded before the Besur had even finished reciting the required greeting.

"I came as soon as I could," the Besur growled, then added "Imperial Glory" and bowed, just to be safe.

"Don't try to placate me!" yelled the emperor and, since he boasted a wealth of pillows, took up his third one of the night and threw it, with remarkable aim, at the Besur's headdress. It knocked the headdress askew, and the Besur dared not adjust it, because that would be an overt mark of disrespect to his emperor. So he left it be and wondered how long until it fell off altogether and landed with a ringing thud on the floor.

"How may I serve you, Imperial Glory?" the Besur said, even though he already knew, or at least strongly suspected, the answer. This was not the first time he had been summoned to the emperor's chambers in the middle of the night. Indeed, it was the fifth time in the last two weeks.

The emperor sank back upon his pillows, and his face was very pale against the rich red silks. "I saw it again," he said.

"The dream, favored Son of Anwar?"

"Yes. I need you to find out what it means. And this time I need you to *succeed.* I can't bear it any longer."

The Besur bowed again to give himself time to think, and felt his headdress teeter dangerously. "Will the Imperial Glory kindly describe what you saw in your sleeping mind?"

"Why? I've told you already. Four times."

"Perhaps in a fifth telling you will be able to communicate something more, something to enable me to shed the light you so desire," said the Besur. He didn't believe it himself, and he could feel the unease in the ten priests gathered and bowing behind him. But he simply did not know what else to do.

The Anuk of Noorhitam sucked in his lips, chewing on them and causing his face to look rather frog-like. Then he closed his eyes as though better to see the images which had crossed his unconscious mind.

"I saw the Lady Moon," he said. "She screamed. And she bled from a thousand wounds. Her blood stained the whole of the sky. And I saw men with their arms full of fire, and they hurled that fire at the walls of Manusbau. My loyal servants, defending the walls, crumbled to dust in their flames."

He opened his eyes, and though his face was that of a middle-aged man, his eyes were very young. Perhaps it was the fear that made them young. The Besur shuddered under his gaze.

"Tell me what it means, priest," said the emperor. "Tell me why my rest is again disturbed by this vision."

The Besur tried to swallow, but his mouth and throat were too dry. He said, "I do not know the meaning, Imperial Glory."

This time the hurled pillow knocked his headdress clean off his head, and it rolled with great clattering across the floor. "Dream-walk, then!" roared the emperor. "Do what you are supposed to do and enter the Dream! Find out what it means or so help me . . ."

The subsequent threats were empty, the Besur knew. If the emperor dared do any of the horrible things he shouted with curses at his high priest, his warlords would rise up in protest. Not even the favored son of Anwar had absolute power. But while the threats were harmless, the rage was real, and the high priest dared not ignore the rage of the Anuk.

He bowed. His head felt cold without its headdress. "I will try," he said.

At the emperor's command, slaves scurried from the room and returned momentarily with braziers and harimau spice. The bare-headed Besur and his ten companions ordered how the braziers should be arranged, then lit the coals and sprinkled liberal handfuls of harimau. Soon the room was filled with its odor, which tingled on the senses. The emperor sneezed. Three slaves fell over themselves to give him handkerchiefs.

The Besur stood in the center of the circle of braziers, and the ten priests took their places around him. They stretched out their hands to each other, their fingertips just touching. And they began the chant.

It was an old chant, designed to bring the mind into clear, concentrated focus. To step from one world into another was a feat an ordinary man could never accomplish and even an extraordinary man could not succeed on his own. Indeed, as the Besur closed his eyes and composed his mind into a deep, meditative state, he felt the strength of his brothers around him and knew he could never do what he attempted now without their support.

He breathed deep of the harimau. In actual fact, any spice would do, so long as it was strong enough to absorb the senses, blocking out other smells and fixing the mind upon a single path. But harimau was the strongest spice, too hot even to be used for culinary purposes. Those who ground it from harimau peppers wore stout leather gloves to keep from burning their skin. When tossed over coals, it stung in the nostrils and made the eyes water.

It cleared out everything save the chant.

Wise men speculated that the gateway into the Dream was different for each man. The Besur did not know if this were true or not. But for him, it looked like the door to his mother's summer home, which he had visited each year as a boy. A red door painted with peonies. Every spring, slaves were obliged to repaint the door, for the winter weather wore away the color and brilliance. The boy who was once the Besur's true self had always loved those frilly peonies on their crimson setting, and associated them with all the joys of summer and freedom.

He saw those peonies in his mind now, appearing in the darkling haze of the priest's chants and the spice. The door seemed as his boyhood eyes had seen it, much larger than it probably was in reality. He approached without fear, slid it open, and stepped through into the Dream.

All around him was mist. All around him was blindness. He breathed harimau, leaned into the support of the chant, and moved forward. But still, only mist. Only blindness.

He must try to find the emperor's dream. Theoretically it was possible. The scrolls of bygone Dream Walkers indicated that many of them had succeeded in discovering dreams and interpretations while moving through the Realm of Dreams. But the Besur had never managed anything like it, not in all his years of loyal service within the Crown of the Moon.

He moved through the mist, searching. Sometimes he thought he glimpsed solid ground beneath his feet, but even that vision did not last long. He hadn't the strength of the great Dream Walkers.

He hadn't the strength of Lady Hariawan.

The chanting of his brethren supported him, lending strength to his spirit as he moved in this strange plain of existence. He knew the chant as well as he knew all the prayers of the temple, could recite it to himself backwards in his sleep.

"From this world to the other, let me walk
From the Near, from the Far, into the Between
From tedium to elucidation, let me walk
From mortal bounds into Eternity."

He knew the chant and all its hundred variations. So when a new line of sound—deeper, darker, and far, far stronger—touched upon his soul, he turned to it with great surprise.

He had never heard anything like it before in the Dream. It sounded as though it sprang from the voices of men, but how could that be? But this was no chant he knew, and it was not spoken in a language he understood. It could not be voiced by any priest of his order.

The Besur's heart began to race. He felt it, back in his physical body. He breathed deep, trying to draw in more harimau, trying to block out the fear which he knew would, any moment, hurl him back to his own world.

His mind sought for the support of his brothers' chant, but it was becoming more and more lost in this new sound, this new darkness.

The mist parted. He saw a great gate supported by two posts, one carved in the likeness of a dragon, the other uncut and ugly. He uttered a shout of fear.

"Besur? Besur?"

Anxious hands slapped his cheeks, chafed his wrists. The Besur groaned as consciousness stole back into his mind, bringing with it a headache to rival the worst headaches he'd ever had after a night of drinking sacred brews.

"Is he awake? Is he alive?" the voice of the emperor demanded with more curiosity than concern.

The Besur opened first one eye then the other. He found that he lay on the floor in the emperor's chamber, surrounded by braziers and priests. The emperor had crawled to the foot of his bed and looked down over the edge.

"Ah! So you're not dead."

"No, Imperial Glory," said the Besur, carefully, for his own voice rang too loud in his skull. "I am happy to report that I yet live."

"Did you see my dream? Did you find it?"

Groaning again, the Besur allowed several slaves to assist him first to sit up and then to stand. He leaned heavily on one of them, whose knees buckled beneath the high priest's bulk. The Besur addressed himself to the emperor and spoke with great dignity.

"Imperial Glory of Noorhitam," he said, "I was unable to find the dream by which you suffer. Nor could I discover an interpretation."

"Anwar blight it," snarled the emperor and flopped back across his bed in an attitude of great despondence. "I shall die for want of sleep! I shall! And then you'll all be sorry," he said, casting an arm across his face.

Bintun exchanged glances with a fellow slave then, with a sigh, moved to his emperor's side and gently stroked his forehead. "There, there," he said, without much conviction. But it seemed to soothe the Imperial Glory.

The emperor sat up, clutching his blanket with sudden vehemence, and fixed an angry eye upon his high priest. "Perhaps," he said, "you simply lack the proper motivation."

"If you please, favored Son—"

"I'll tell you what," the emperor said, not interrupting because emperors never interrupt. When they speak, all others are silent. "I'll tell you what, I'll give you incentive. If you, or any man in this kingdom, can find and interpret my dream, I will . . ." He paused, considering. Then his eyes lit up with inspiration. "I will make that man my chief vizier, and the entire province of Ipoa will be his and belong to his children and his children's children hereafter. And," he added with enthusiasm, "I will give him the hand of a princess in marriage!"

The priests looked at one another, their eyes round. None of them, officially, should be tempted by such an offer. They had all made vows to forgo such earthly treasures in favor of Anwar and Hulan's service. But every one of them saw the light of his own greed reflected in his brothers' eyes.

"This is my offer," said the emperor. "Let it be written in stone."

"Lady Hariawan could do it."

The Besur, seated in his private chambers, rubbing his throbbing head with one hand while his other gripped a cup of strong, hot tea, growled in response to Brother Yaru's statement. Brother Yaru, unperturbed, continued his thought processes, which tended more toward rambling as his age advanced. These days he was almost impossible to listen to. But he was the Besur's oldest friend, and so he was permitted into the high priest's chambers when all others were ordered out.

"Of course," said Brother Yaru in his most musing tone, "she would not be able to marry a princess. Our Imperial Glory has failed to consider this."

"Our Imperial Glory does not know that any woman can dream-walk," said the Besur through his teeth. Then he added, "You Sun-blighted fool."

"Perhaps a prince, then?" Brother Yaru continued just as though he had not heard (which he probably hadn't). "There must be a good dozen or more princes by this time, and some of them are of an age to marry. And Lady Hariawan is, after all, remarkably pleasing to look upon, so I can't imagine any prince would object—"

The Besur snarled suddenly and sat upright, the knuckles of his hands turning white as he clenched the arm of his chair and the bowl of his teacup. "Lady Hariawan is gone. Gone, don't you remember? Missing, vanished, beyond our reach!"

"Oh. Is she?"

"Yes, you idiot! We received the message only just this morning from Daramuti. You were there. You heard as well as I. She disappeared, it must be three months ago now, and no one knows what has become of her." He added in an undertone, "I'd like to strangle that Masayi girl. With my own two hands!"

"Perhaps she is on her way home?" said Brother Yaru, his toothless mouth working with the effort of thought. "Perhaps she is even now approaching Lunthea Maly? That sweet young woman will protect her."

"That sweet young woman probably slit her throat and left her in a ditch somewhere," said the Besur.

"Oh no, I don't think so," said Brother Yaru. "She had such a charming smile."

The Besur, recalling Sairu's smile, shuddered and buried his head in his hand once more.

"What of the other message from Daramuti?" Brother Yaru said. He approached a small table upon which a porcelain tea set was arranged and poured himself a cup of tea. He swirled it in the cup, watching the tiny whirlpool created. "What of the slave boy Brother Tenuk sent you for sentencing? They're still holding him in the granary, I believe."

The Besur shrugged dismissively. "Tenuk is a fool not to have hanged the boy himself. Why should he bother me with such nonsense? String him up, for all I care."

Brother Yaru sipped his tea, found it too hot, and licked his burned lip. "Well," he said in his slow, dreamy way, "it does seem unfair to hang him without at least looking over the case."

"I can't be bothered," the Besur growled.

"It won't hurt a thing to put him in the dungeon until you have a spare moment to address the matter," Brother Yaru continued. "Besides, he would be good company for Lord Kasemsan. The poor lord is in such a bad state these days, my heart quite bleeds for him! A little company would cheer him."

The Besur snorted. "Nothing is going to cheer him. That blighted Golden Mother has been at him too long."

"Yes," Brother Yaru agreed, "she's certainly not contributed to his well-being, poor man. I doubt he'll live another week at this rate. But perhaps a friend at the end of his life would be a kindness. Hulan does bless those who show an extra kindness."

Once more the Besur shrugged. "I don't care," he said. "Send the boy to the dungeons. Hang him. Set him weeding the onion bed. Do what you like, but don't bother me with him again, do you hear?"

"I hear," said Brother Yaru. He remained where he stood, sipping at his tea and saying nothing until his cup was empty. Then, with a bow and murmured, "Good night," he slipped from the Besur's chambers.

2

AGONY HAD BECOME a close, an intimate friend over the last six months. Closer than fear. Closer than memories. Closer by far than hope, which had indeed forsaken him. Agony was all, save for one final truth to which Lord Kasemsan clung.

Devotion.

Devotion beat in his breast now, keeping steady pace alongside agony's throb, even as he lay in the darkness of the dungeons beneath the Crown of the Moon. He cradled a broken hand to his chest, not with any hope of help or healing, but simply because he did not know what else to do with it. It had been broken too many times to even look like a hand anymore, and indeed, Kasemsan would not have recognized it for his own had it not still hung limp on the end of his arm.

Worse than the brokenness was the infection. Despite all Princess Safiya's express orders, the keepers of the dungeon—the so-called physicians employed in this hellhole—had been unable to prevent the infection which spread slowly through his body. He knew, with a certainty almost akin to joy, that he would soon die.

But until he died, he would remain devoted to his cause. Devoted to the service and protection of Hulan.

Princess Safiya, with all her cunning, had not been able to wring from him his true purpose. Oh, she had certainly gathered some facts from his face, from his screams. She knew he had come to Lunthea Maly intent on discovering the Dream Walker, and what's more, she knew he had intended to kill that Dream Walker.

She did not know why. And she never would. When Lord Kasemsan declared that he would die before he betrayed his cause, he meant it.

So he lay in darkness made more horrible because it was not complete. In utter darkness, he might have been able to fall into oblivion, hide from his own agony. But no. The lantern they left hanging from the high ceiling cast the cell into lurid clarity around him, illuminated every twist of his mutilated hand, and showed him the ravages of gangrene. He doubted very much that his own wife would recognize him. She certainly would do nothing to comfort him but would shrink away from the horror he had become.

He wondered, vaguely, if she mourned his loss. But he could decide on no definite answer to this question.

He heard footsteps approaching even before the door beyond his cell grated open. Leaning back against the wall, his legs splayed before him, his wounded hand held in his one good arm, Kasemsan slowly lifted his chin from his chest to observe those who entered.

For a moment so surprising it shot through him like a surge of renewed life, he believed he saw Sunan pushed through the cell door and into the lantern light. But no. It wasn't Sunan. This young man was shorter, broader at the shoulders, and looked as though he would be strong were he not still recovering from recent illness. He also boasted a distinctly Chhayan complexion. Sunan, only half-Chhayan, was much paler than this lad.

Two strong slaves hauled the stranger between them, and he, his spirit long since broken, put up neither fight nor protest. The prison-keeper, entering behind, went gruntingly to work, fixing chains in place and removing the ropes which had bound the new prisoner's arms. The prison-keeper turned and leered down at Kasemsan. "A friend for you, my lord. With the

Besur's compliments," he said.

The two slaves fixed the young man's chains to the wall beside Kasemsan. The young man turned his face away, perhaps glimpsing the gangrene and unable to bear the sight of it. The prison-keeper grunted again, tested the chains, then motioned for the slaves to follow him out. Once more the cell door grated, shutting firmly into place. A bolt fell.

One of the slaves had struck the lantern with his head in passing, and it still swung to and fro, casting light and shadows in weird patterns for some while until it finally settled. Kasemsan, observing his new companion, watched how he shut his eyes against the whirling light and saw by his pallor that he was fighting against the heave of his stomach.

"Who are you?" Kasemsan asked. His voice was raw and scarcely sounded human. The young man startled, and for a moment did not look as though he would answer. Then he said shortly:

"Juong-Khla Jovann."

"Ah," said Kasemsan. "I wondered. You are my nephew Sunan's half-brother."

The prisoner abruptly sat upright and turned to Kasemsan, his chains smashing together noisily at the movement. "You—You are Lord Dok-Kasemsan?"

"I was."

A hundred different thoughts flashed across Jovann's face, and his eyes lit up with an angry smolder. At last he said, "Your nephew did this to me."

"Did what?"

"Had me kidnapped and sold into slavery."

Kasemsan frowned. Very slowly, because even such a small movement added to his agony. Then he said, "That does not sound like Sunan."

Jovann sighed and leaned his head back against the wall. His hair was grown past his shoulders and was thick with dirt and grease, and his face was half-covered by a scraggly beard. "Sunan is a son of the Tiger. He is capable of more than you Pen-Chans might guess."

This statement did not merit a response, so Kasemsan offered none. He studied the side of Jovann's face, noting the similarities between him and his half-brother. It struck him that this meeting of theirs could not be coincidence. The world was too vast and varied, and it was only one world of many. No. It was impossible that they should only *happen* to be thrown together into the same cell, under the same cursed Kitar temple.

Hulan must have guided them together. But for what purpose?

Kasemsan's mind had ever been sharp. Back in the day, he was a Presented Scholar, achieving top marks in his Gruung. He went on to excel within the walls of the Center of Learning, bringing him to the keen-eyed attention of Overseer Rangsun. Some might have called him brilliant.

Now, even in the pit of his pain, he brought all his mental capacities into focus, forcing them to function by sheer force of will, beyond the capabilities of his broken body.

"Your father is the Khla clan leader," he said. "He stole my sister long ago. I have always hated him."

"You're not the only one," said Jovann, his eyes still closed. "Tigers are immune to hatred."

"No one is immune to hatred," Kasemsan replied. "Hatred has eaten the Khla clan alive from the inside out for two hundred years. Hatred has devoured the Chhayan people."

At this, Jovann turned and looked warily at Kasemsan. He said nothing, only looked, and Kasemsan saw the fear in his eyes.

Kasemsan laughed weakly, and a tremor passed sickeningly down his spine. "Do not fear me, boy. I cannot hurt you, even if I wished to. Tell me, when do your people intend to take their vengeance?"

Jovann's jaw worked with the force of all his anger, the anger bred into him from both his father and his mother. "My people will take back what is theirs," he snarled. "When the time is right, we will oust the Kitar emperor, and we will rule Noorhitam once more. This is not vengeance. This is justice."

"And when will this so-called justice take place?" Kasemsan persisted.

"I do not know," Jovann admitted. "I am not in my father's confidence." Then he shivered, and something else flashed through his mind. Kasemsan, his eyes sharp, saw it, saw the expression on his face, and read it with far more accuracy than Jovann could ever have predicted.

"You have walked in the Dream."

Jovann stared at him. "Wha—What are you talking about?"

"You have walked in the Dream. You have seen the beginnings of the assault. You have seen . . . you have seen . . ." Kasemsan sat, straining against his own body, pushing his mangled limbs, his wasted muscles, as he reached out toward Jovann. "You have seen the temple of the Greater Dark."

Jovann turned away, sliding along the wall, out of Kasemsan's reach. "You're mad."

"You are a Dream Walker. You are . . . perhaps you are . . ."

The drumming of devotion was loud now in Kasemsan's ears. It filled him, driving out the agony. "Perhaps you are the Dream Walker who will open Hulan's Gate and bring about the assault. And if that is true, then I must kill you."

The chains were restrictive, but they were long enough that Jovann could leap to his feet. His wrists were bound to the wall, and his ankles too, but he pulled away, stepping back to their fullest extent. "I don't know what you're talking about!" he said. "You're sick. You're raving."

But Kasemsan was not raving. He rose up as well, finding in his limbs strength he did not know yet remained. He could not reach Jovann, but he caught his chains and pulled the boy to him. Before Madame Safiya's work he had been a strong man, a man in his prime. Now, under the influence of devotion, some of that strength returned. He hauled Jovann toward him, and his hands latched to the throat of his nephew's brother.

But his right hand was broken. He could do nothing.

Jovann cried out and struck his attacker, knocking him to the floor. Kasemsan lay where he landed, his whole body quivering with pain. Jovann, watching, felt a dart of pity, though he stifled this and said in a warning voice, "Don't touch me. Don't come near me."

Kasemsan turned his face into the floor, breathing into the straw, "Oh, Hulan! Why do you give me no grace? Have I not served you faithfully? Have I not protected you all my life?"

Jovann, hearing this, thought how sad it must be to worship a goddess who needed protection. Suddenly—even there in the horrors of that cell, after the long horrors of his journey down from the mountains, facing a future that might easily end abruptly with a hanging—he found his head filled with the memory of the stars' great Song. He saw Hulan upon her throne, so beautiful, so gracious, so full of Song herself.

But he remembered most of all the unicorn at his back warning him, "*Do not worship. For she did not compose the Song which we sing.*"

He whispered softly, so that he did not think Lord Kasemsan would hear him, "Song Giver, give us grace." He did not know quite what he said or why. But he said it again, and it was a prayer of sorts. "Song Giver, give us grace."

Kasemsan winced and cradled his hand closer to his chest. Then slowly he sat up again, pressing his back to the wall. "I cannot kill you," he said.

"I should hope not," Jovann replied, his fingers curling into fists. "What do you say to not trying again?"

But Kasemsan shook his head slowly. Then he dropped hold of his wounded hand, which fell limply into his lap. His good hand he put up to his own face. His fingernails were long and broken and dirty, and they looked like talons. Jovann stared, aghast, believing the lord intended to blind himself.

"I cannot kill you," Kasemsan said. "But there is one more thing I can do." He rammed his nails into his own eye.

Jovann, startled, gave a shout at this. He saw Kasemsan pull, and for a sickening moment he believed the man gouged his own eye from its socket. Something came out in a long black stream, and the lord's face twisted with anguish as it came. Then suddenly it was out, and Jovann saw that it was not his eye he held between his fingers at all. He could not say what it was. He had never seen anything like it and had no frame of reference by which to guess. Whatever it was, it was alive. And it was angry.

Kasemsan lifted the little black writher to his face. The Pen-Chan lord's cheeks were pale and green with sickness and near-death. Indeed, though he had appeared grotesquely ill before, now he looked ten times worse, did not even look as though he should be alive.

He spoke and seemed to be addressing the black writhing thing. "I know. I know you wish to return to your other half. But I have another task for you. See there!" And he shook the thing at Jovann. "See that mortal! I command you to enter his eye, even as you entered mine. Once inside, you will cover him in a glamour. Cast over him such shieldings that he will be unrecognizable to all who know him, all who seek him."

The little black thing screeched. It was not a human sound, but neither was it animal. It was unlike anything Jovann had ever before heard, and it disgusted him.

Then suddenly, still clutched in Kasemsan's hand, the thing turned and looked at Jovann. It had a tiny, devilish face, almost like a man's but not quite. Its mouth was full of teeth, gnashing teeth, and its arms reached out like tendrils of smoke.

"Anwar's blight!" Jovann swore. He tried to back up, but the chains allowed him no more leeway. "Anwar's blight! Oh, Anwar, shield me!" He pulled at the resisting chains, straining against them, staring at the black imp that stretched toward him, its furious face extending from its overlong body and neck.

Kasemsan, with a grim smile on his dying mouth, let the imp go.

3

PRINCESS SAFIYA RARELY TOOK quiet moments to herself. Even then she was rarely entirely by herself but surrounded by her attendants, mostly children, sharp-eyed and sharp-eared, every one. She must constantly be on her guard, for one never knew who might attempt to bribe a child in order to gain information on the most secret doings of the Masayi.

But this particular night, she stole a few moments of true solitude, deep in her innermost chamber. There were no windows to this room, for windows only made her nervous, more so as the years went by. Beyond the doors of her privacy were three successive chambers in which her most trusted slaves stood watch over her.

Even as she stood watch over Noorhitam.

For this was the truth of her role, she knew. Yes, she prepared brides for princes and lords of many nations. But ultimately the Daughters owed their first loyalty to their emperor. And any prince or warlord who purchased a Golden Daughter for his bride knew, in his heart of hearts, that when he spoke his marriage vows, it was not to the Daughter herself but to

Noorhitam and the Anuk Anwar.

Princess Safiya, in the solitude of her chamber, sat before a round mirror shaped after the fashion of Hulan's Gate and stared at her own reflection. She had once been beautiful. Now, with her cosmetics wiped away and her face clean and bare, she looked faded, tired. Heavy bags dragged beneath her eyes, and her cheeks were hollow and thin.

But she was still the bravest and brightest of all the previous emperor's Golden Daughters. And thus she had become the Golden Mother and remained on at the Masayi long after her sisters had disappeared into the wider world, lost to their marriages and service.

Now she sent her own Golden Daughters into the same oblivion. She did not doubt their abilities. She did not doubt their skills. They were highly trained, capable, and beautiful in the same unique way a sword is beautiful when skillfully crafted and balanced. All of them would bring honor to her and to their great father.

But she doubted herself in sending them.

She looked down at her hands lying calmly in her lap. Earlier that day they had wielded cruel instruments as she sought, yet again, to extract secrets from the lips of Lord Kasemsan. Beautiful Lord Kasemsan, whom she had systematically destroyed over the last half year. And yet he withstood her. What an amazing, what a fantastic creature was he!

Suddenly she cursed. She did so very quietly, for the walls were thin and she feared that those standing without might overhear her. But she cursed once, then twice, then a third time.

And when she had finished, she whispered, "Why did I ever send her away?"

Word had arrived earlier that day, messages from Daramuti intended for the Besur's ears only. But Princess Safiya, since assigning Sairu to her unusual role, had made it a point to learn all the doings within the Crown of the Moon. Not half an hour after the Besur received Brother Tenuk's messages, runners fell at the Golden Mother's feet and related all to her: The assault on Lady Hariawan by some Chhayan slave and, soon thereafter, the disappearance of both the lady and her handmaiden.

"I should never have agreed," Princess Safiya whispered now, in the smallest, darkest hours of the morning, when night was at its heaviest and dawn seemed forever away. "I should never have sent her. She wasn't ready."

This was a lie. She knew full well Sairu's capabilities. The girl had special talent. Not more talent than her sisters, no. But special talent, something unusual.

Princess Safiya put a hand to her heart. It ached in her breast, and she cursed again. She had borne a terrible secret for many long years now, though she had hidden it from herself, burying it deeper each time she signed a contract and sent one of her Daughters away. Now, in light of recent events, it threatened to erupt, forcing its way up from her heart.

She loved Sairu. And she felt she would break in two if the child were truly lost.

She gulped once, very hard. Even here in private she dared not give way to such emotion. A Golden Daughter never loved—Princess Safiya had been taught this from the first, when she was but a child bowing to the will of her own Golden Mother. A Golden Daughter never loved, for love was the greatest weakness.

She gulped again and knew the sobs would break loose if she did not do something. Grinding her teeth, she rose and moved across her room, determined to find some distraction, some purpose upon which to set her will. She went to her door, flung it open.

And found herself gazing down into Sairu's face.

She stood, unspeaking, certain that she dreamed. Then Sairu smiled. Surely she could not dream that smile!

"Greetings, Honored Mother," said Sairu. "I'm come home."

Princess Safiya did not even breathe. She looked out into the chamber beyond and saw that all her slaves lay in deep slumber. Perhaps they were drugged. Perhaps they merely slept. It did not matter.

Somehow Sairu had made her way through the heaviest, strictest fortifications of Manusbau, into the Masayi, into this chamber that was only a little less well guarded than that of the emperor himself. And she was smiling, pleased with herself.

The Golden Mother clamped a heavy hand on Sairu's shoulder and dragged her inside, all relief disguised, even to herself, in rage. She shut the door quietly, so as not to attract any attention. Then she whirled upon the girl and spoke in a voice of ice.

"Three months, Sairu. Three months you've been missing."

"Three months exactly," Sairu agreed with a nod. She wore a serving girl's robes, and her face was carefully painted white, with red spots at the corners of her eyes. No one would look twice at her, so perfectly did she mimic the hundreds of other serving girls in Manusbau. "It has been a long journey."

"Word arrived earlier today of Lady Hariawan's disappearance," Princess Safiya said.

"Oh dear," said Sairu. "I had hoped to beat the message here if at all possible. But we were delayed on the way. Our manner of travel was effective but sometimes inconvenient."

"Manner of travel?" Princess Safiya drew a deep breath, making absolutely certain that when she spoke, she was master of her own voice. "You have come alone all the way from Daramuti?"

"I and my mistress," Sairu said. "Yes."

"Where is she? Where is Lady Hariawan?"

"I will not tell you."

Princess Safiya's hand twitched. It was testimony to her great self-possession that she did not slap the smile off the girl's face then and there. Anger caused her heart to race, or so she believed; yet she still, inexplicably, wanted to weep. She still, inexplicably, wanted to take the girl into her arms and press her close.

Instead she said coldly, "You must return her to the Crown of the Moon."

"No," said Sairu, shaking her head. "One of the temple slaves sent with us to Daramuti was, I have reason to believe, a Crouching Shadow. He tried to kill her."

It took more than a feather to knock the wind out of Princess Safiya. But as Sairu's words rang in her head, she found herself suddenly needing the support of the back of a chair, which her hand found and clung to, keeping her upright. She said nothing, but in that moment she and Sairu communicated in looks all that both of them knew and acknowledged.

If one slave of the temple was a Crouching Shadow, how many more might be as well?

"You have hidden her then?" said Princess Safiya.

"Yes. I've put her where no one will look for her. And I will keep her there until I have answers," said Sairu. "I will discover why the Besur sent my mistress into hiding. And I will discover why the Crouching Shadows are so bent upon making an end to her life."

Princess Safiya recalled the expression in Lord Kasemsan's face—even today, six months since his interrogation by torture began. "I do not think that last will be an easy secret to uncover."

"I don't expect it to be easy," said Sairu. "But I will do it even so."

Dawn was only just touching the rooftops of the palace with gold when Sairu crossed the grounds of the Masayi. A few slaves up and moving about their various pre-dawn tasks took no notice of Sairu, so exactly did she look like any number of other serving girls within the palace walls. Her head was bowed, her hands deeply folded into her sleeves. Her hair was carefully arranged atop her head, with three thin braids falling across each shoulder, and her face was painted white. She looked the very picture of servile serenity.

But her heart raced in her breast.

She did not know what she would find when she reached the rooms that once were hers. But she knew what she wished to find. She also knew that she should not be wasting her time about this errand. There was so much to be done, so many as-yet-unknown terrors that must be faced before she could know Lady Hariawan to be truly safe. She should not be wasting a moment.

And yet, without apparent haste she moved across the Masayi, following the rising sun, and came to the Chrysanthemum House, where she had spent most of her remembered life from the time she took the brand of the Golden Daughters upon her wrist. It looked exactly like any other humble building where serving girls were housed when not needed by their masters and mistresses. But the air around it was thick with secrets.

Sairu slipped inside and along the passage to the room which had once been hers. She wondered vaguely if another girl had been chosen to take her place and even now resided in the small chamber. Whatever the case may be, she slid the door back cautiously and peered in, half-expecting to see a new sister upon her former bed.

Instead, she discovered a sight that made her press a hand to her mouth in surprise.

Lying in the midst of the cushions was a pile of fur: black, fawn, and gold so tangled up that individual bodies could scarcely be determined. But there were four of them, she knew at once. Three lion dogs curled up around the body of a large orange cat. One rested its chin across the cat's back. Another, lying on its side, had its neck encircled by the cat's paw, while the cat busied itself grooming the long hair of a silky ear.

The atmosphere was thick with the rumble of maudlin purring.

"Monster!" said Sairu.

At the sound of her voice, three black-masked faces emerged from the pile and set up a barking of guard-dog threats, which swiftly changed into yips, yipes, and howls of joy. She was returned! The mistress! The mistress! The light of all life and meaning! They fell from the bed, scrambling over the cat, and flung themselves at her even as she stepped into the room, drew the door shut behind her, and knelt to receive them. Sairu picked up Dumpling, then Rice Cake, then Sticky Bun in turn, and let them kiss her face, wriggling so hard that she almost dropped them.

The cat watched all from the bed, his face a cool mask over his embarrassment. When at length the outbursts of joy died back somewhat, he said, "You're late."

"I am not," Sairu replied.

"You said you'd come in three months."

"I arrived yesterday."

"I didn't see you, so it hardly counts."

Sairu, with some difficulty—for Dumpling kept hurling himself at her knees—got up and bowed solemnly. "Many thanks, Master Cat, for the service you have rendered me. I owe you a debt of gratitude."

"Well," said the cat with a shiver of his coat that might have been a shrug. "It wasn't so marvelous a feat. I'm not saying a jolly time was had by all, but it wasn't like slaying dragons."

The corner of Sairu's mouth twitched. "You like them."

"I do not."

"You do."

"They're useless hedge-pigs."

"You like their fluffiness."

"I am entirely immune to fluffiness." With great dignity the cat turned his back on her and began grooming. But his ears were back, attentive to her every movement as she made her way across the small chamber, knelt before a trunk, and removed from it various items: a silk bag embroidered with peacocks, a fan of similar design worked in paint, a pair of beaded slippers, and an ugly brown robe. Curiosity overcoming him, the cat looked around, frowning. "What are you doing?"

"Never you mind," said Sairu, tucking these items into her robes. "Tell me, Monster, are you willing to help me again?"

"Ah! Three months of blessed peace brought to an abrupt and brutal end," said the cat with a sigh. "Command me, slave-driver. But don't expect too much."

"I never do," said she. "I need you to sneak into the dungeons beneath the Crown of the Moon. There is a man there, a man who may know something about my Lady Hariawan."

"Oh, so we're still dead-set on protecting her, are we?"

"Naturally. Now pay attention." Swiftly she explained about Lord Kasemsan and his connection to the Crouching Shadows. "He has not revealed his true purpose in coming to Lunthea Maly. I believe he intended to kill my mistress, even as Tu Domchu did. I want to know why, but he has withstood torture for half a year now and still not spoken."

"So what do you expect me to do?" demanded the cat. "Purr at him?"

"I want you to find him, and I want you to discover the truth. Use whatever means necessary. I know," she added, with a significant look, "that you are more than you seem. That you possess powers beyond my understanding. Can you do this?"

The cat twitched an ear. Then with a feline's natural resistance to commitment he said, "I'll give it a try. Where will we meet afterwards? Here?"

"No," said Sairu sadly, petting Dumpling, who was pressed up against her leg. "No, it is too dangerous for me to remain. The Crouching Shadows have likely guessed that I would return to Lunthea Maly, and they will come here."

"Where then?"

She leaned toward the cat, and he came close enough that she might whisper in his ear: "Lembu Rana."

He pulled back from her, blinking his wide eyes, his lip curled in a snarl. "The Valley of Suffering? But that . . . that's a *leper* colony!"

Her face was pale but her jaw was firm. "That is where we will meet."

The cat shuddered. But then he nodded. "Very well. I'll do what I can, and I'll meet you there tonight after sunset. What about you? What will you do until then?"

"I," said Sairu, withdrawing something from her trunk, "am going to pay a visit to the Besur."

The lowest order of priests in the Crown of the Moon were devoted to the service of Baiduri, the smallest star ever to boast a shrine or two, who was only visible in the Noorhitam sky for half the year, leaving her priests with little enough to do the other half. Baiduri was nearing the end of her cyclical journey as autumn set in and the months of her winter dormancy approached. Her priests too, were beginning to lose interest in their daily rituals and to look forward to winter when they would lounge about, reading a few holy texts, muttering a few prayers, and otherwise getting in the way of their nobler, busier brethren.

A procession of eleven Baiduri priests made their way up one of the side paths within the Crown of the Moon. Their robes were brown and heavy, and their chants, uninspired. No one paid attention to them. No one liked the priests of Baiduri, and many priests of other orders muttered that they would do more honor to their service if they were made to clean the privies.

Thus no one noticed that the procession was made up of eleven, not ten priests as was the usual. And no one noticed when the smallish priest at the end of the procession broke off from the rest and slipped away into an unfrequented portion of the temple grounds.

Sairu, hidden deep within the priestly garments she had taken from her trunk earlier that morning, slipped behind a gnarled old tree hung so thickly with parasitic vines that it provided a shielding curtain. She had considered the possibilities of this overgrown portion of the Crown of the Moon since glimpsing it the long-ago night of her first visit to the temple. Now she used it to cut right across some of the more thickly populated portions of the temple, for there was more than enough cover for one small girl, even in broad daylight.

Without the glow of the moon, the large stones littering this unpleasant plot were not white but dull gray, blackened in places as though by a great fire. Ducking behind one to avoid the gaze of a passing acolyte, Sairu placed her hand upon the stone, but withdrew it again with a gasp. It burned. Not so hot as to damage her hand, but enough to give her a start. Surprised, she put her palm close to the stone again, feeling the heat emanate out to her skin. It was much warmer than sun-baked. It was as though these stones had been engulfed in a great conflagration only a few days ago and still retained the heat of the blaze.

That was impossible. These ruins had been here for hundreds of years, since long before the Crown of the Moon was built in Hulan's honor. Sairu took a moment to gaze around the ruins again. And she recalled the image of the great house she had glimpsed in the moonlight all those long nights ago. She wondered what could have burned it to the ground, leaving the rubble still suffering hundreds of years later.

But she had no time to consider such things now. Gathering her robes in both hands, she slipped out from behind the stone and hastened on to the central building, Hulan's Throne, where the High Priest dwelt in holy opulence.

The Besur, unaware of that which slipped up on him in the shadows, stood in the window of his outer chamber, gazing out across the vast temple grounds but not seeing them. His mind was fixed upon the churning question of the emperor's dream—the promised reward, the ugliness of the vision described, his own inability to locate it as he dream-walked.

A fellow priest—one who had accompanied him the night before to the emperor's chamber—stood across the room, shifting awkwardly on his feet. He cleared his throat and said, "Honored Besur?"

"Yes?"

"Could we not, as it were—for the sake of Anwar's Favored Son—possibly *invent* an interpretation?"

The Besur said nothing.

"I mean," the priest continued, stuttering at the boldness of his suggestion, "the vision, however disturbing, is probably no more than a fancy conjured up in the Imperial Glory's magnificent imagination and unlikely to be of any concern to him in another month. Would it not be in his favor to ease his mind now, let him forget it, and move on with our duties?"

There lingered, unspoken between them, the added thought, *While one of us claims the princess, the province, and the place in the palace.*

Slowly the Besur turned and fixed his fellow priest with the coldest of stares. "You would consider *lying* to the Imperial Glory of Noorhitam?"

The priest opened his mouth to answer, thought better of it, closed his mouth again with a click of his jaw, and bowed. He bowed his way right out of the room, murmuring retractions, blessings, and other things to which the Besur did not bother to listen as he turned back to his window. He heard the door slide shut, and his mouth turned up in one corner with a grim smile.

It was difficult to remember the time, back in his boyhood—scrubbed fresh by his mother, still damp with soapy water and her tears—when he had first entered his home village's temple and the service of Hulan. That day had possibly marked the last of his belief in the sacred truth of his nation's religion. Since then, being a bright, ambitious young man, he had learned different.

He had learned the subtle arts of avarice. He had grown in power, entered into the greater secrets of his order, until at last he stood here in the Besur's shoes, boasting supremacy in Noorhitam only a little less than that of the emperor and a few of his greater lords.

"Lie to the emperor," he whispered, considering. Was this not, perhaps, the final depth to which he could plunge? Would it make any difference, really, considering the rest of his life's deeds? "Lie to the emperor . . . ."

He sighed heavily, his great body shaking with a sudden wave of something close to sorrow; sorrow for that boy he had been, bright-eyed with religious fervor that mirrored his dear mother's and all her hopes for him. That boy whose vision was so swiftly clouded, never to be cleared again.

He turned from the window. And screamed.

The scream scarcely had a chance at life before it was stifled by the pillow thrust unceremoniously into his mouth by the deft hand of Sairu, who smiled at him. "None of that, Honored Besur," she said. "I don't want your lackeys swarming. I have a few questions I would put to you, and I think you will prefer the privacy as much as I."

4

THE BESUR SPAT OUT the pillow and opened his mouth to roar like a lion. But a flash from Sairu's eyes warned him, and he dropped the roar in exchange for a furious whisper. "Where is Lady Hari-awan?"

"No," said Sairu. "I'll ask the questions."

She was so small and he so huge that he cherished, momentarily, a vision of taking her in his arms and crushing the life out of that wretched smile. The muscles in his shoulders twitched, eager to fulfill that vision.

But the next moment he saw two knives in her hands, which had not been there the moment before.

"We can make this unpleasant," said Sairu, "or you can comply, and I'll be on my way much more swiftly. Understand?"

"You—you would dare threaten the Besur of—"

"Before you go on," said the girl, "know this: My first loyalty is to my emperor. My second is to my lady. You are not high on the list of those to whom I feel any great devotion. What is more"—and she took a threatening step toward him, her eyes dark behind the smile—"your secrets have caused my mistress nothing but danger, and I, for one, am sick of them."

The Besur took a step back for each step she took forward, and soon found himself pressed against the sill of his window. He felt the air of many levels behind him. He would not survive a jump.

"What are your questions?" he demanded in a growl, like a cornered cur.

"Why did you send my mistress to Daramuti?"

"To recover from—"

"Besur." She spoke his title sharply, as a warning. He drew a long breath. Then he spoke, slowly but without falsehood. She could read the truth in his frightened eyes.

"She met something in the Dream. Something terrible. It hurt her."

"The burn," Sairu said promptly.

"Yes. You see, nothing should have been able to touch her in the Dream. She walked in spirit, not in body. And while the spirit may, it is true, be assaulted by nightmares, the body should be safe. Yet whatever she met while dream-walking hurt her in body as well as spirit."

"In spirit?" said Sairu. "How did it wound her spirit?"

"She was changed," said the Besur, his lip curling. "Before that night, Lady Hariawan was not the empty-eyed creature you met. She was strong. She was sharp as an arrow-tip. Quick to learn, quick to wrath." He closed his eyes then, remembering. "She came to us from the Awan Clan along with three other tribute girls of various clan families. But within days she dominated her sisters, and the brothers were in awe of both her beauty and her force of will. Within a month she demanded audience with me and told me that she could dream-walk. Not like my brethren and I dream-walked, tentatively nosing about in the mists on the edge of the Dream. No. She could truly *walk*, like the Dream Walkers of old, plunging deep into the Realm of Dreams and bringing back tales of the visions she saw."

"How did you know she spoke the truth about those visions?" Sairu asked.

"We have holy texts," said the Besur, glaring at her. "Generations ago there were many Dream Walkers who could do as Lady Hariawan does, and they wrote down the things they saw. We have sought after those things for over a hundred years but never found them. Then Lady Hariawan came to us and told of what she saw in the Dream, and it was as though she had read the texts for herself."

"Had she not?"

"No. Lady Hariawan can neither read nor write, nor can any man or woman of the Awan Clan. She did not recite to us or quote. She truly *saw*."

Sairu nodded. "Very well, Besur. And what did you and your brethren decide to do with this talent of hers? What was your plan?"

His face went red, and every feature betrayed his unwillingness to answer. Sairu took another step toward him, and he pressed harder into the sill, feeling wind on the back of his head. Then, with great reluctance, he said, "We sent her to find Hulan's Gate."

"Why?"

"We are the priests of Hulan. Need you ask?"

"Besur," said Sairu, her smile most patient, "do not try to convince me that either you or your brothers were concerned in the least with holy ascension. You value Lady Hariawan too much for that to be the truth. You hired a Golden Daughter to protect her, you sent her into hiding. She means more to you than access to your goddess, whom you do not worship in your heart. What is your true purpose for discovering Hulan's Gate?"

A flash of shame crossed his face, and the Besur lowered his eyes, staring at the floor beneath Sairu's feet. He whispered the truth like a confession. "The Dream Walkers of old wrote of fabulous treasures hidden in Hulan's Garden. They wrote of gemstones and carbuncles beyond compare."

Sairu recalled the stones Jovann had pressed into her hand. Flaming opals, but far more beautiful, far more valuable than any opals she had ever before seen, even those adorning the emperor's crown. "So you hoped to use my Lady Hariawan to fill your own coffers," she said, and added spitefully, "Holy Father."

The Besur made neither move nor answer, and he would not meet her gaze.

"I want you to tell me," Sairu continued, "about this thing which my mistress encountered and which caused her such hurt. What was it?"

"I do not know."

"But you have a guess."

Again he did not answer.

"Honored Besur," said Sairu, "while keeping watch over my mistress's sleep, I felt shadows moving in a realm just beyond my perception but as real and as near to me as you even now stand. What were they?"

The angry red drained from the Besur's face, leaving him pale, almost grey. With an effort he spoke: "The Dream Walkers of old wrote of a cult. It was called the Order of the Greater Dark and said to be comprised of those who once worshipped Hulan. Those whom Hulan betrayed."

Sairu thought about this for but a moment. Then she said, "The Chhayans."

"Yes," said the Besur. "Those who worshipped the sun and the moon before our people took over this land and this faith. Those who turned from their goddess when she turned from them. According to the Dream Walkers of old, they too seek Hulan's Gate. But for a different purpose."

"What purpose?"

"We do not know. We have only our guesses."

"Destruction. Revenge," said Sairu, easily reading those guesses in his eyes.

The Besur nodded.

"And you think it was they—this Order of the Greater Dark—who harmed my Lady Hariawan? Who struck her?"

But here the Besur shook his head. "I do not know. If they are Dream Walkers like unto us, they would not be able to cause her physical harm. Not one so powerful in the arts as she! They could pursue her, follow her, harry her. But they could not touch her, not in that world."

Sairu studied the Besur's face. "You think they want her, don't you? You think they want to use her to find Hulan's Gate."

"There has not been a Dream Walker such as Lady Hariawan in over a century. If the Order of the Greater Dark wishes to pursue its vengeance, it might very well need her in order to succeed."

"Do they know she's a woman?"

"I doubt it. As we do not take our physical forms into the Dream, we appear as no more than phantoms to each other in that realm. They would see only a powerful Walker, not a woman."

"So, in this world, they would not know how to find her. And after her assault, hoping to throw them off the trail, you sent her far from the Crown of the Moon and the other Dream Walkers."

The Besur nodded.

"That explains a good deal," said Sairu, turning the knife in her right hand reflectively. "But it does not tell me why a Crouching Shadow tried to kill her."

"*What?*"

"Yes, Honored Besur," said Sairu. "One of the very slaves you hand-picked to journey with us to Daramuti proved an assassin. A Crouching Shadow bent on my mistress's destruction. Are they also part of this Order of the Greater Dark?"

"No," said the Besur swiftly. "No, they are not. They are . . ."

"Yes?"

Grudgingly he admitted, "They are the self-styled protectors of Hulan and her children. They have plagued my fellow Dream-Walkers and me for as long as we have practiced our art. As they themselves cannot enter the Dream, neither do they believe other mortals should. They have killed more than a few of my order over the years. And if they knew that a Dream Walker of Lady Hariawan's abilities had come to the Crown of the Moon, well—"

"They would stop at nothing to find and kill her as well, thus protecting Hulan's Garden from mortal invasion."

The Besur nodded shortly. Then he said, "They are all fools."

"They are not the only fools," Sairu replied, perhaps more sharply than she should have. Then, her voice once more sweet as poison, "Does Princess Safiya know this?"

"I have not told her, no. We do not divulge all our secrets to the Golden Mother."

"And she considers you no more than a weak old blusterer," Sairu said, "so she would not seek you out for information." Once more the Besur's cheeks flushed with rage. But Sairu continued, "There, at least, my dear Mother is at fault. For you are not *merely* a weak old blusterer. You are also cunning to a frightening extreme."

Oddly mollified, the Besur nodded. "I have my moments." Then, surprised when Sairu suddenly flicked both her knives out of sight into the sleeves of her priest's robe and turned from him, he said, "Where are you going?"

"You have nothing more to tell me. I have business elsewhere."

"What business?"

"The protection of my lady."

"She is alive then? She is safe?"

"She is hidden," said Sairu. "And you will not see her until I know for certain that she is, indeed, safe. Until then, Honored Besur, do not look for me."

With that, she was gone. The Besur stood alone in his chamber with only his shame for company.

All cats possess an uncanny ability for melting into the shadows and vanishing, escaping detection by even the sharpest eye. But this cat was more than a cat. He did not merely melt into the shadows; he seemed to become a shadow himself, flitting along the floor and wall with such silent stealth that he fancied, if he wasn't careful, he might even lose himself.

This thought made him grin.

His grin diminished as he penetrated deeper into the passages beneath the Crown of the Moon. Since death and despair are considered unseemly companions for celestial worshippers, the only entrance to the temple dungeons was found not in any of the main temple buildings, but in a lowly guardhouse in the far western corner of the temple grounds. The guardhouse itself was humble enough, belying the vastness of the dungeon passages below.

How many sad souls languished in these subterranean cells? What might be their crimes? The cat shivered as he proceeded, his grin long gone. He passed guards and prison-keepers at intervals, and they stank of the worst kind of mortality: cruelty, sprung from fear and masked in illusions of false justice.

He thought with sorrow, suddenly, of the Lady Moon herself. He knew that she, high in her vaulted heavens, sang of such evils as this, and her song was full of tears. And yet how many of these poor prisoners were incarcerated in her name?

The cat did not know exactly which scent he sought, for he had never met Lord Dok-Kasemsan. But he did not doubt his own cleverness and was quite certain he would find the lord eventually. He must simply center his energies and . . .

A memory flashed across his mind. The cat paused mid-step; his ears flattened and his eyes narrowed. He recalled a time, not so long ago, when he had plumbed the depths of another temple dungeon. Only then it was no stranger he sought.

"Now, now, old boy," the cat muttered, shaking his whiskers. "Don't think about her. Don't think about any of that. Your little mortal charge has a point, you know. Can't allow yourself to be distracted. Can't allow yourself to be divided. Now focus!"

He closed his eyes entirely, for it was too dark for them to serve him well. His pink nose, however, sifted through a hundred and more different scents, searching for something likely. Searching for some clue.

"Dragon's teeth!" His eyes flew wide, and he stared into the passage before him, as though willing himself to see through total darkness. He sniffed again and knew he had not been mistaken. "Jovann!"

Indeed, Jovann had certainly come this way, probably dragged. Not long ago, not long at all. Perhaps only a few hours before, in fact! Which meant he might very well still be alive.

There was no way of knowing whether the scent he caught was from Jovann being dragged into prison or dragged out for execution. But the cat, his tail long and low behind him, trotted down the passage, determined to find where it led. Oh, of course, he'd locate Lord Dok-Kasemsan too, eventually. However, he did not believe Sairu would object to this detour.

As he neared the end of the passage, it opened up with light and a small workspace. A prison-keeper's station, furnished with a bench, a table, a lamp, and little else, appeared before him. The prison-keeper himself, secure in his knowledge of the locks and bolts around him, sat on the bench, his back against the wall, his feet propped on the table, and snored loud and long. What a man he must be to sleep amid this dank despair! It was amazing, the cat mused, the things to which mortals accustomed themselves.

Jovann's scent was still strong. The cat proceeded with his nose to the ground, following where that scent led and ending up at a narrow, heavy door. He put a paw to it and pressed. He did not consider his powers to be magic, because magic would imply spells and sorcery, which was not something the cat could bother himself to learn. His powers were deeper, an innate part of his being. He had, for as long as he could remember, been able to break through locks and barriers, particularly mortal ones.

Except for . . .

"Dragons blast it," he muttered. "Iron."

There was no use in fighting iron. Already he felt it going to his head, leaving him dizzy and sick to his stomach. All other metals and alloys would bend to his whim. But never iron.

Showing his teeth in a frustrated snarl, the cat looked around at the snoring prison-keeper. Exactly how deep was his slumber? Moving with deadly stealth, he crept to the man's side.

And he took on a new form, un-witnessed in the secret shadows of those dungeons. In this new guise, he bent over the man, catching sight of his key ring. With a hand, not a paw, he reached out, long fingers gently touching the ring. It too was iron, and it made him gag.

The prison-keeper snorted, moaned, and stirred on his bench.

The cat, who was not a cat, considered his options. He was not afraid, for his talents were many and his ways of incapacitating an inconvenient enemy as varied as his vivid imagination. But he did not like to hurt the poor man, who, however deserving of hurt he might be, looked rather childlike in his sleep. His ugly mouth, far too often twisted in a leer, puckered, like a suckling babe's.

So, rather than following his initial instinct and clunking the prison-keeper hard across the head, the cat-who-was-no-cat leaned down and put his mouth close to the prison-keeper's ear. He sang:

"Sleep, little one. Sleep deeply, my knave.
I'll frighten away all dreams of the grave,
I'll frighten away the devils of fear.
Sleep, little one. Sleep now, my dear.

Sleep, little one, in this fastness of night,
Sleep as the darkness holds you so tight.
Wander no paths of the devil's own making,
Sleep, little one, until morning's waking.

Sleep deeply, my sweet, sleep on tonight.
Let oblivion all of your mem'ries benight.
Think yourself naught of lovers long dead.
Rest with a pillow tucked under your head."

It wasn't an enchantment. Or not entirely. But there was power in the words, the power of ageless centuries. Each line, each rhyme, spoken in a language the prison-keeper would not have recognized, sank into his unconscious mind and took root there, more real than any of his own thoughts or dreams. They worked a mighty persuasion, and this persuasion overcame any resistance his brain might have offered. His snoring ceased, his breathing eased, and he sank down and down, far deeper into unconsciousness than he had ever before ventured or ever would again.

At last, the cat-who-was-no-cat stepped back, satisfied. Then, taking a rather musty handkerchief from the prison-keeper's pocket, he used this to catch hold of the key ring and lift it off the prison-keeper's belt.

Even then he could feel the bite of iron stinging his fingertips, and he hurriedly discovered the correct key and applied it to the cell lock. The moment he heard the mechanism click, he tossed the key ring away, letting it rattle into the shadows beneath the prison-keeper's bench. The cell door protested growlingly as it was pushed open, and the prisoner inside, his face lit by the glow of a single lantern, looked up in surprise and dread.

He saw an orange cat step through.

The cat, restored to his feline form, stood in the doorway, gazing into the cell, and his whiskers twitched with consternation. He could have sworn . . . no, he *knew* for a fact that Jovann's scent had brought him here. But where was the mortal boy?

The prisoner in the cell lunged suddenly, rattling his chains. He opened his mouth and cried out, drawing the cat's attention. The cat looked with little interest at a face he did not know; a handsome face for a mortal, he supposed, but dirty, grimy, and much too old for Jovann. And what was that lying in chains beside him? A corpse?

Suddenly the cat realized that the words the prisoner called out were gibberish in his ears. His eyes widened. Never before in his life had he been unable to understand mortal tongues of any kind. Stepping across the cold, straw-and-muck-littered floor, his white paws curling with disgust at each step, the cat approached the prisoner, studying him more closely. But no, he did not recognize him, not at all. Nor could he make out a single word being spoken.

The desperation in the strange man's eyes was unmistakable. The cat shivered, certain, though he did not know why, that this stranger recognized him. How or from where he could not guess.

Since neither his eyes nor his ears were doing him any favors, the cat ignored them both and set his nose to work, sniffing, sniffing, sniffing. He smelled . . .

Enchantment.

Not an enchantment such as that which he had breathed into the prison-keeper's ear. No, this was an enchantment of darkness, borne of Faeries but cast by mortal enslavers. *Magicians*—the cat's lip curled at the thought. Mortals were not meant to wield Faerie powers. It was unnatural, unholy, a vile sin.

Was this man, then, the magician himself or one of his victims? Unwillingly the cat took another step in, still sniffing, still searching. He caught another scent just beneath the enchantment, so faint that one less sensitive and aware than he (he flattered himself) would never catch it.

He whispered, "Jovann?"

In that moment there was a shuddering, a seizing-up in the very fabric of the mortal universe. The cat, with a scream, whirled around, tail bristling, and saw the air break before him, break like a glass window when a stone is hurled at its surface. The break grew, widened; and darkness far deeper than dungeon shadows poured through like liquid night, oozing, dripping, and pooling as it spread. The cat gazed out of the mortal realm into the dark Between.

With a snarl the cat dove into the farthest corner of the cell. For he knew what this break was, this opening into worlds beyond. A scent all too dreadful and familiar overwhelmed him: a scent of sulfur, of hatred, of fire and brimstone.

The Dragon.

5

THE DOCKS OF LUNTHEA MALY were the loudest and busiest to be found in all the eastern continent; for Lunthea Maly was a great city for trade, and all nations wished to bring their wares to its shores, to barter with its businessmen, and to establish a foothold, however small, in the empire of Noorhitam.

The noise was the first thing to strike Sunan as he stepped off the good ship *Noknou*—a humble but affordable junk on which he had taken passage—into the hurly-burly of the city docks. And after the noise came the smell. A Chhayan nomad would scarcely have noticed it, but seven years of Pen-Chan elegance had both increased the sensibilities and reduced the hardiness of Sunan's nose. He nearly gagged. Not once, not twice, but five times he doubled over while trying to make his way across the docks, jostled on all sides, struggling to keep his stomach in line. Three of those times he could have sworn he felt hands slip into his pockets, and if he had not previously safeguarded his worldly goods deep under his robes, wrapped tight against his body, he would have been robbed blind.

But he had reached Lunthea Maly. He had followed his orders.

When he at last reached the end of the docks, and the city proper loomed before him in all its labyrinthine grime and glory, Sunan looked back sorrowfully. His eyes sought the red sails of the *Noknou* but failed to spy them through the forest of sails and masts between him and the ship. His heart felt oddly melancholy in his chest. Chhayans were no sailors, and he had not been brought up to think of the sea. When sent away to his uncle's house in Nua-Pratut, he had traveled overland. Through the course of his studies, he had learned about Pen-Chan shipwrights and sea exploration, but it had all been distant, academic knowledge, nothing to do with him personally.

But a journey from Suthinnakor to Lunthea Maly took a good five months by land and only three by sea. So, grasping his courage in both hands, Sunan had booked passage on the *Noknou* and set out, according to orders, for the great city. The first week was agony. The week following he had discovered that he rather liked the sea. And over the course of his journey, he had even developed something of the sailor's fever. The light of ocean vastness brightened his eye, and the sounds of waves and winds filled his heart. For a time he was able to forget his blood oath, to forget his long imprisonment, to forget the masters who sent him out into the unknown without so much as a hint regarding his purpose.

For a time, he had tasted freedom.

That was all over now. Sunan, failing to discover the *Noknou*'s sails, was forced to turn his back on those three magnificent months, facing instead the enigma that was Lunthea Maly. The stench. The squalor. The rising splendor of Manusbau Palace and the towers of the Crown of the Moon at its center.

He stood at the entrance of a narrow street over which the rooftops of close-built houses crowded out all glimpse of the overcast sky. They seemed to clutch and hold the smells of human and animal filth, of sickness, of rotted garbage, of death, condensing them into a solid force ready to strike any who dared approach. Sunan's stomach heaved for a sixth time, and he leaned heavily against a wall.

"Anwar's blessed underpants!" a wheezing voice growled. "Find yer own little piece, will yer, and don't be crowdin' inter mine! I don't want yer sick rainin' down upon my head!"

Sunan, his arm on the wall, his head on his arm, opened one eye and looked down at a small, wizened creature unfolding on the ground before him. The beggar man was missing one arm and half of one leg, both on the same side, which gave him a most horrific impression of unbalance as he shook his only fist up at Sunan. He had been curled up asleep under a pile of rags so that Sunan had not seen him until this moment. He looked like little more than a pile of rags himself. His few teeth were black, and his eyes were runny with sickness.

But he snarled like a cur and shoved at Sunan with his stump of a leg. "Stuffy gents in yer stuffy robes! Thinkin' yer can press and pester us little folk. Move on, pretty boy, move on, I say. And drop a coin in the bowl while yer kickin' it!"

Sunan shuddered. He'd seen men of his father's clan who had lost limbs in the various wars Chhayans had a talent for starting. There had always seemed to be a certain nobility about those men, who were venerated as heroes of true courage among the clan and given places of precedence at the campfires. This creature, however, was devoid of nobility. When he died, his bones would be laid to rest with no sacred chants, and his grave would be watered by no woman's tears. He would rot where he fell, and the world might be made a little better for his absence.

Sunan made to move on, clutching his robes in both hands and attempting to step around the beggar. But one scrawny hand shot out and latched onto his ankle with surprising strength. "Yer from Nua-Pratut, ain't yer, pretty boy?"

"Unhand me," Sunan replied coldly. His skin crawled with chilly disgust.

But the beggar closed one eye and looked up at him shrewdly through the other. "Yer wouldn't happen ter be called Juong-Khla Sunan, would yer?"

At this, Sunan's stomach plummeted to his knees. He gaped at the beggar man. "How do you—How do you know my—"

"Ain't got two good eyes in yer head, have yer?" said the beggar.

Then, with startling suddenness and strength, the creature unfolded and stood upright (though he still possessed, so far as Sunan could see, only one full leg), and the skinny hand switched its grasp from Sunan's ankle to the cloth on his shoulder. It all happened so fast that Sunan had no chance to cry out in protest before he was dragged—dragged with such speed and force as should have been impossible from that rag-bag of a creature—into a nearby alley and shoved into deep, putrid shadows where no eyes could see him save the runny eyes of the beggar.

Sunan's hand flew for a knife he kept tucked beneath his outermost robe. But he found only an empty sheath, and when his eyes flew to the beggar, he discovered the knife clutched between his rotting teeth. Impossible! The beggar's only hand was still latched on Sunan's shoulder.

With a sound like "*Pithuuu!*" the beggar spat the knife out, and it clattered dully into the shadows beneath their feet. Then he spoke in a voice of such polish as Sunan had only ever heard before at some of his uncle's more elite dinner parties, during which scholars from the Center of Learning discussed politics, ethics, and various philosophies, both popular and disparaged, in tones of utterly polite elegance:

"Chaso—or 'Old Rotting Bones,' as the street-rat children affectionately named him—was not one of my more pleasant roles. I shall be glad to see the end of him."

The sound of that silken voice falling from that hideous mouth was almost too much. Sunan shrank away, trying to make himself smaller so that he could slip out of the iron hold on his shoulder.

The beggar grinned, proudly displaying all of his black teeth. "Allow me to introduce myself. I am Domchu, Third Son of the House of Mohl. I understand you have made a blood oath vowing service to my brotherhood. You do recall as much, I trust?"

"Ah—um—"

"Loquacious, aren't you? I'm going to release my hold, but if you try to run, I shall have to restrain you. I don't have much about my person which may serve as a binding save for this old rag I am wearing. But I will use it if I must. And you will be blessed with the sight of this skeletal form in all its fetid glory. Neither of us wants that, do we?"

Sunan shook his head vigorously, and when the beggar let him go, he made no move to flee but stood shaking and staring, trying to see through a disguise that was far too good to be true. Had the man chopped off his own limbs and pulled out his own teeth, exposed himself to skin disease and lice for the purpose of this part? It couldn't be! And yet . . .

Balancing on one leg as easily as though he stood on two, the beggar studied Sunan up and down, grunting in approval. "You look much like your uncle. He was a great friend of mine back in our school days. And his sister . . . what a beauty! It was a shame and a crime, what happened to her, and I was not alone in my disappointment. But your uncle and I remained close for many years. I was sorry to learn of his supposed death."

With an effort Sunan swallowed back the boiling venom in his heart, which always threatened to choke him when others spoke of his mother, and asked, "Supposed death, my . . . my lord—"

"Domchu," the beggar interrupted. "Tu Domchu, to you. And yes, *supposed* death. We cannot know for certain. He was taken beneath the Crown of the Moon, down into the dungeons. When I arrived here some days ago, I wanted to search him out, to liberate him. But the Golden Mother had guessed his true purpose in coming to Lunthea Maly, and I dared not draw attention to the others of our order throughout the city."

"What was his true purpose?" Sunan asked.

"My dear boy, you do not yet know his *assumed* purpose—hired as a gentleman assassin, in fact."

"An assassin?"

"You are aware of the legendary role of Crouching Shadows are you not? Assassins of the highest order. Your uncle played the part of assassin on more than one occasion, lending credence to the rumors and allowing us to continue our true work undetected."

Sunan shook his head. During those months spent coming to grips with the new realities of his life, he had never once stopped to consider those acts which his uncle, as a Crouching Shadow, must have committed in his life. It was like suddenly seeing the view out his window flipped into mirror image. All was so familiar, and yet nothing was right anymore.

"I will not," Tu Domchu continued, "tell you more than you absolutely must know, so you needn't bother asking questions. The more ignorant you are, the more ignorant you will behave and thus, we hope, throw that sharp-nosed Golden Mother and her bevy of lovely Daughters off the scent. Tell me, Kasemsan's kin, what do you know of your purpose in coming to this Fragrant Flower of all cities?"

"Nothing," Sunan said. "I was told nothing save to go to Lunthea Maly. Which I have done faithfully, according to my oath."

"Good, good. I will now show you something, and I will give you one command. How you choose to carry out this command is your own business. I dare not help you. I dare not draw the Golden Mother's eye my way. Are you prepared to receive your orders?"

Sunan swallowed with some difficulty. Then he nodded.

To his dismay, the beggar man stuck his one hand up to his own face and rammed his fingers into his eye. Sunan gasped, his horror suffocating any scream. The beggar gave a sad little moan of pain, though the pain was self-inflicted, and pulled. Sunan saw something long and dark stretching out, caught between the beggar's thumb and index finger.

With a sudden crack that made no sound but seemed to rattle Sunan's vision instead, the beggar vanished, replaced by a tall man in the prime of his life, possessed of all four limbs and clad in the beggar's garments. He held a wriggling puff of smoke, made almost solid but not quite, between his fingers. As Sunan stared at it, he saw the smoke assume a face, so ugly, so snarling, that he thought it must be a demon.

"A Faerie," said Tu Domchu, as though guessing Sunan's thoughts. "One of our many slaves. I had two once upon a time, and this is my last one. Now I give it and the vision it possesses to you. Hold still."

Before Sunan could make a move or protest, Tu Domchu caught him by the back of his head and shoved the imp into his own wide eye. It was like having a long needle bursting first through the eyeball, then into the brain, and had Tu Domchu not clamped a hand hard over Sunan's mouth, his screams would surely have brought half the city running in hopes of witnessing a murder. Tears streamed down his face, and his body shivered against his will.

But the pain did not last long. He stood there, caught in Tu Domchu's hold, and felt a new presence settle itself into his consciousness. It was a most unusual sensation. He thought he should analyze it, as any good scholar would, but his stomach was too busy turning flips in his gut to allow him much objective perspective.

"Now," said Tu Domchu, his one hand still holding the back of Sunan's head while the other let go of his mouth, "I want you to close your eyes. Wipe away your own vision and allow the imp to show you what it has seen."

Sunan nodded and obeyed. At first he saw nothing but blackness with little pinpoints of light on the edges. Then, quite suddenly, a vision began to take shape.

A beautiful young woman lay upon a bed, her slender, feminine body atop the silk coverlets. Her hair spread across her pillows, thick, lush, and shining in the light of a gray morning pouring through a near window. He had never seen a face more beautiful or more sad. He thought for a moment that she was dead, but then he saw the slight rise and fall of her chest, and he knew that she lay in a deep trance.

There was the gleam of a blade. The vision turned. It spun wildly, and Sunan could see only flashes of a small but elegant room whirling as though in a storm. He believed he caught a glimpse of a small dog, of a knife. Then there was still more confusion. Someone he could not well discern flashed across the vision, a young woman, he thought, but not the beautiful girl he had viewed a moment before. Another face also appeared, a face so otherworldly, so pale, and so golden that were it not for the ferocious snarl upon its mouth, Sunan might have thought it an angelic being. That face also vanished, and there was darkness, spinning darkness, with only flashes of light illuminating another, humbler room.

And at the very last he saw—and this surprised him, for it was not what he'd expected—an orange cat crouched in a corner, its eyes wide and gold.

The vision faded into the blackness behind his eyelids. Sunan realized he was not breathing and inhaled sharply.

"Did you see her?" demanded the Crouching Shadow.

Sunan nodded. "I saw a woman lying on a bed, and she—"

"Yes, I know. I've seen it myself. I was there."

Sunan looked up, his eyes sharp with curiosity. "Who was she?"

"A temple girl. I will tell you no more. But you must find her."

"Find her?" Sunan frowned, bracing his knees against the dizziness in his head. "How?"

"That is for you to discover, Kasemsan's kin," Tu Domchu replied. "I can help you no more than I have. We are all of us too carefully watched, and even Chaso the beggar-man may not be as inconspicuous as I would wish. But my Master tells me you are intelligent beyond your years, if a little weak, and that you even possess some of the Dok House's cunning. From what I can see, if you possess such cunning, you have not yet discovered it. But no matter. My Master believes in you. So you must find the girl and, when you find her, return to these docks. I, or one of my brethren, will come to you then and tell you what to do next. Do you understand?"

"I understand," Sunan said, though in truth he did not. His mind was still full of the vision of that lovely face. And he thought, of all the dreadful things he'd feared his new masters would require of him, discovering the location of a beautiful girl was not so terrible as all that. "I do not know where to begin my search. Can you tell me—"

"I can tell you nothing," said the Crouching Shadow. Then he repeated, "*Nothing.*"

And he was gone. Sunan stood alone in the alley, staring blankly at the space where a man had stood but a moment before.

A shiver ran up his spine, and he shook it out at the neck. Then he hastened back out of the alley and on to the busy street. He did not know where he was to go or how he was to begin this bizarre assignment, but he felt the need to move, so he did. Soon he was running up from the docks, deep into the winding heart of Lunthea Maly. He kept his eyes straight ahead, avoiding the crush and throng of life and death around him, passing from squalor to splendor and back into squalor again. At last, out of breath, he stopped and leaned against a wall. He tilted his head back, seeing nothing at first and then . . .

The shining silver gong atop the tallest temple tower flickered in the sunlight, like a small moon come down to earth.

"It's too easy," Sunan muttered. Then he shrugged. It couldn't possibly be so simple, but where else was one to begin a search for a nameless temple girl? He gathered his robes in both hands and started at a trot up the street, making his way as straight as he could for the Crown of the Moon.

6

THREE FIGURES STEPPED through the crack in the worlds. Three mortal figures, which was the last thing the cat had expected as he cowered, belly-flattened on the stone floor. And the moment they were through, the crack closed behind them. Or did not close so much as cease, as though it had never been.

But it had been. The cat's eyes were full of it, his spirit overrun with it. He knew what it was, and he knew how it led.

These mortals, whoever else they might be, were servants of the Dragon. And they walked the Dragon's own Paths, crossing leagues in a stride, passing through solid walls. Their origin in the mortal world, the cat could not begin to guess. They may have set out from halfway across the world and, by using this path, crossed to this place in mere minutes.

Mortals might use Faerie Paths if they had allies among the Faerie kind. But never, in all his long existence, had the cat known a mortal to ally himself with the Dragon.

Thus he tried to disbelieve what his eyes beheld, tried to disbelieve what his fearful heart screamed in his breast. He tried to tell himself that these could not be mortal men, or that the Path they walked was not one which, long ago, he himself had walked and would recognize anywhere.

The truth was too plain before him. And the cat trembled and made himself small and invisible.

All three men were clad in heavy garments of rough, tanned leather lined in fur, with stout leather caps on their heads, also fur-lined. Though he wore no distinguishing mark, the third man to step through was obviously the leader. His very stance and bearing bespoke his sovereignty among his brethren. The other two yielded to him, standing protectively to either side as he surveyed the dungeon cell. His sharp eyes passed right over the prisoner as though he did not exist.

But the prisoner, to the cat's surprise, lunged against his chains, crying out, his hands extended to their furthest reach. His eyes, though set in an older face, looked like those of a child. He spoke gibberish, but he spoke it with such excited vehemence that the cat could have sworn the prisoner looked upon the faces of long-lost friends thought dead and gone.

The leader—a tall, broad warrior with a long mustache carefully braided away from his mouth, and keen eyes peering from beneath a strangely smooth, strangely placid brow—spoke: "Not here."

"Tenuk's message was clear, Honored Khla," said one of his men. "He sent the Dream Walker to the Crown of the Moon."

"There is no Dream Walker here," said the leader. His voice was calm. Too calm. Like a dormant volcano not so deeply sleeping as one might hope.

The third man growled, "Tenuk is a fool. An old, doddering fool!"

"Waste no bile upon our good brother," the leader growled. "The Greater Dark will deal with him." His eye lit upon the corpse lying in chains beside the gibbering prisoner. He knelt and turned it over, sucking in his breath at the sight of ravaging gangrene. "Not a Dream Walker."

The prisoner flung himself at the great man, his hands straining so that the shackles cut into his wrists. He could not reach him, save for his fingertips, which scraped the toes of his boots. The warrior gazed down upon him. Then, when the prisoner raised up his face, the warrior frowned. He looked from that face to the corpse's. But the shadows of the lantern were deep and the distortions of sickness severe. The warrior blinked once then turned away.

"There is no Dream Walker here," he said.

"What will we tell the Greater Dark?" said one of his men in a voice as deep as a bear's but full of fear.

The leader merely shook his head, his face a mask. "We will tell the Greater Dark that we have not yet received our promise."

With that he turned from the prisoner, who, with a gurgling cry, flung himself upon the floor, his hands held up behind him by the chains, his head striking hard upon the stones. His words were incomprehensible, but his tone was desperate.

The warrior spared him not a glance. He crossed the room, the other two falling into place behind him. And though he made no sign or sound, the cat saw the Path open again. He smelled death and the not-too-distant stench of the Dark Water. Did these fools of mortals not understand that into which they passed? Could they not see it? Could they not sense it? Were they so blinded by their desires, whatever those desires might be?

They were gone. The Path closed behind them, and the cat could no longer perceive even a trace of its memory. But he shuddered where he crouched, and his heart condemned him. After all, he had walked that Path himself. He was no better than these mortals. Not on his own.

"Lumil Eliasul," he whispered. "Lumil Eliasul . . ."

It was like a prayer, but he asked nothing: no blessing, no benediction. He merely repeated the words until his breathing calmed and the fur of his tail smoothed down once more.

Then, rising and shaking himself, he padded across the cell to better inspect the prisoner.

The poor man, with his strange face and stranger words, wept upon the stone. His arms rose up uncomfortably behind him, his wrists limp in the shackles. He'd probably pulled several muscles in his wild contortions, the cat thought, possibly sprained something as well. Mortals were such fools sometimes!

The prisoner remained unaware of the cat. He lay muttering into the dirty straw, his limbs twitching now and then. The cat sniffed the top of his head, cringing at the reek of grime and infestation. Surrounding that was the even stronger scent of enchantment, something mortals would not be able to perceive but which the cat, born in worlds beyond, could recognize, if only just. It was a strong enchantment, the likes of which he had never before encountered. He had heard that Vartera, queen of the goblin people, used similar sorcery: masking her true face in forms she considered more pleasing. But this was not the same enchantment as she used. The cat knew too well the source of Vartera's power, and it was stronger than this. No, this enchantment came from . . .

"Imps," the cat muttered.

At the sound of his voice (which could only be perceived as an animal growl), the prisoner looked up. For a moment his eyes were very bright in the lamplight, and the cat, gazing into them, saw something trembling deep in his black pupil. He knew then that he was right.

And those men—Chhayans, unless the cat were much mistaken, which he didn't consider likely—had been unable to perceive one of their own kind. Their leader, the honored Khla, had been unable to recognize his own son even as the boy pleaded at his feet.

"Jovann," the cat said. "I know it's you."

Even as he said it, the enchantment strengthened. So much so that the cat felt a momentary flicker of doubt. Pernicious imps!

"No fear, my dear young man," said the cat in his silkiest tones. Then he looked right at the imp deep in the prisoner's eye. "I know the strength of your little spells. But I also know what can break them!"

With that, he turned and slipped from the cell. He pushed the cell door shut behind him by leaning on it with both his front paws, though it was heavy and his cat's body should not have had the strength to move it. He did not bother to lock it but left it and the snoring prison-keeper untouched as he darted back through the winding corridors of the temple dungeons.

He must find and fetch Sairu at once!

Suthinnakor boasted a number of impressive buildings, testimony to the creativity and inventiveness of their architects. The Center of Learning itself was the most beautiful structure Sunan had ever before seen, and he had never hoped or expected to behold its like again.

Therefore, as he slogged his way through the filthy streets of Lunthea Maly, climbing closer and closer to the Crown of the Moon, he was obliged to stop several times simply to catch his breath. For the magnificence of that temple, to which the eyes of all those around him had long since become blind, was so great, so beautiful, so enormous, that Sunan thought his heart might stop.

Beyond the Crown of the Moon, more glorious still, rose the Anuk Anwar's own palace of Manusbau. But the palace did not move Sunan in the same fashion. It was outrageous and opulent, gilded and encrusted with the wealth of its usurper emperor. It invited all to look upon it and marvel at its greatness and the corresponding greatness of the emperor ensconced within. The temple, however, urged mortal men to look heavenward, to gaze upon the glory of the sun and the moon in their palatial skies.

It was enough to make Sunan, so long steeped in Pen-Chan intellectualism as to have given up all childish thoughts of gods or goddesses, desire suddenly to kneel and to worship. But what he desired to worship, he could not say. Surely not Hulan and Anwar, whom he knew to be nothing more than man's foolish personifications of rock and fire, which were natural elements and not deities at all.

Yet his heart stirred strangely inside him. And he thought perhaps he lacked something, something vital. He thought perhaps he was intended to worship, if only he knew who, what, or why.

There was no time to indulge in such futile speculation, however. So Sunan rallied himself and continued on up through the streets. Sometimes they twisted and the buildings pressed in so close that he lost sight of the temple and the great silver gong upraised above its walls. But eventually he would find it again and renew his course. He felt as though he hunted some living creature which sought to elude him. A bizarre fancy and not one upon which he liked to dwell.

As the day lengthened from morning on into afternoon, he finally reached the southernmost gates of the temple, facing the ocean. These surprised him, because they felt familiar. He could not understand why until he recalled all the little shrines scattered throughout the plains of Chhayan territory. Small gates leading from nowhere to nowhere, built of stone and scattered with flower petals. "Moon Gates," his mother had called them. Once an important symbol of ancient Chhayan worship.

And here, on a greater scale, was another Moon Gate, built in honor of Hulan.

A sullen-faced guard stood without, and more stood beyond. Sunan approached, and the guard did not look at him but moved the spear in his hand slightly in silent warning.

Sunan stopped. He looked from the guard's impassive face through the open gate to the elegant grounds beyond. And he knew that he, worn and tired and ragged from his months of sea travel, would never be permitted entrance.

He did not try to argue or persuade. With a shrug and a sigh, he turned from the gate and began to make his way around the wall. Some vague notion of finding an entrance whispered in the back of his brain, but he paid it no heed, for he knew it was no use.

How was he supposed to find the temple girl? He did not know her name. He did not even know if she served at this temple! And if the Crouching Shadows themselves had not succeeded, why should they think he would manage what they could not? It was all foolishness and folly. He wasn't even a Presented Scholar!

This bitter thought caused an ugly line to form between his brows. He folded his hands after the fashion of Pen-Chan elegance and moved with a slow sedateness that only just disguised the rising fury in his breast. He was obliged to weave his way, for the outer walls of the Crown of the Moon were crowded with small shrines to various stars, and worshipers of those stars flocked from across the empire to present pitiful offerings before them.

Sunan, brought up among Chhayans, recognized the stars and their shrines. Maly, of course. Her shrine was crowded indeed, surrounded by weeping widows who begged her to light paths through the Netherworld for their lost husbands. Zampei and Zampey, depicted in stone as two children holding hands. And Chiev, whose likeness was carved in fine ivory. The effect was spoiled, however, for someone had painted the ivory an ugly shade of blue.

Up so close, the sense of holiness Sunan had felt while approaching the temple was lost. It was all so sad, so sordid. He saw poor beggars, Kitar and Chhayan alike, dropping coins they could not afford to lose into boxes hung upon the wall beside the shrines. Later on, Sunan did not doubt, fat young acolytes would sally forth and fetch those boxes, telling themselves that it was not thievery, for did not the poor wretches offer their goods willingly?

If Hulan and Anwar did indeed rule all from their heavenly thrones, they were cruel deities to allow their children so to suffer. They were cruel to have abandoned their chosen people.

This thought brought Sunan to an abrupt halt. He stood unseeing, hands folded, head bent. What did he care for Chhayan grievances? He was not one of them! He was the son of Juong-Khla's stolen wife, and his inheritance was not from his father.

But he felt his Chhayan blood, so long suppressed, stirring inside him. In his mouth, upon his tongue, he tasted fire.

Suddenly he heard a sound that burst through all the clamor of the streets and even through the roaring of rage in his head. A sound like silver, like water. The sound of birdsong. Startled, Sunan looked up, some half-formed notion in his brain of discovering the source of that song. He cast his gaze around, over the heads of genuflecting peasants, up to the top of the high temple wall.

Instead of a bird, he saw a golden cat appear, having leapt up from the grounds beyond to perch above the street.

Something stirred in Sunan's eye. He was aware again of the foreign presence in his head, of the imp lodged deep inside. He shook himself but could not shake free that sickening sensation of something moving behind his vision. There flashed across his brain the image he had seen: the temple girl—the dog—the golden stranger's face.

And the cat.

The vision ended, and Sunan stood staring up at the cat on the wall. He knew it. He knew it was the same cat! How he knew he could not say, but he did not doubt it for a moment.

The cat gauged the distance, large white paws pressing into the wall, haunches upraised and tail quivering slightly as it prepared itself for the long drop. Then it sprang, landed in the street, and vanished in the crowd of peasants surrounding Chiev's shrine. Sunan, for a heart-stopping instant, believed he'd lost it.

Then he heard a child's voice exclaiming, "Kitty!"

Sunan elbowed his way past a wrinkled old man and a young, sobbing widow. He saw a little one of uncertain sex stroking the back of a purring cat, which received these attentions with solemn equanimity. Then, as though recalling its purpose, the cat darted away from the child and down into the squalor of Lunthea Maly below.

Sunan gave chase.

7

IT WOULD TAKE A better hunter by far than Sunan to successfully pursue such quarry through the mazelike streets of that enormous city. Yet somehow he managed to keep pace with the cat. He would lose it in a crush or down a back alley only to catch sight of that plume of tail darting out from under a rickety cart or leaping up onto a windowsill. Several times the cat disappeared into houses through which Sunan himself dared not pass. He would have to go around, wandering the streets and ending up nowhere near his desired location. Those times, he believed for certain the cat was long gone.

Then, much to his surprise, he'd catch a flicker of white paws dashing between the hooves of an old donkey or out from under some street vendor's stall. And so Sunan would give chase again. In retrospect, he thought it must have been a miracle, though a miracle of whose working he could not guess, not then and not later.

So intent was he upon his hunt, he did not even notice when he passed a certain shadowy door. He did not see the faces looking out at him, faces half-hidden by leather helmets and heavy fur lining. Had he seen them, his heart must have stopped with the same terror meeting a ghost might inspire.

For one of those looking out at him, watching him hasten past, was his own much-hated father.

But Sunan did not know, and he hurried on his way, his slippered feet slapping on the broken stones of the streets. The sun was high overhead and soon looking towards its descent in the western sky. Sunan, who had not eaten that day, began to slow his pace, exhausted. He knew he must now lose the cat for good.

And still he did not. Even as he reached the northern-most gates of the great city and passed from them into the villages beyond, he could see the cat ahead, trotting with tail upright down the middle of the road.

Sunan knew nothing of this territory. During all the twisting and winding of the last several hours, he had become totally lost. But then, he had nowhere to go and nowhere to be. Finding that temple girl was his sole purpose, and the cat was the only possible link to her that he knew. So, though he desperately wished to seek out some comfortable ditch somewhere and fall into it, he trudged forward.

The outskirt villages of Lunthea Maly soon gave way to various encampments on the roadsides where merchants and various travelers rested before entering the city proper. Some of these were grand; most were humble. Sunan glimpsed pilgrims, farmers, priests, and lords. None of these paid any heed to Sunan, and he paid little heed to them. The cat trotted on, and Sunan trotted after, wondering where the creature would lead him.

He did not like the answer when he came face to face with it.

Steep walls enclosed those who dwelt within Lembu Rana, the Valley of Suffering. Once upon a time those walls had been lined with stone, but most of the stone had crumbled away ages ago. The paths leading down inside remained, however, for they were much-trod by those entering the valley and their chosen seclusion. A seclusion ending only in death.

The sun hung low in the sky, and twilight deepened upon the landscape. But Sunan could see the many huts shoved up against one another by the light of a hundred and more low fires burning outside the doors. And he could see the figures, phantom-like, swathed in rags and veils, moving among those fires. They moved slowly, with great pain, and a hum of pain that was as much a sensation of the heart as a sound in the ears rose up from below to touch Sunan with a haunting hand.

Lepers!

"They're not cursed. They're sick," Sunan whispered. He was a learned man of Nua-Pratut, after all. He was a Tribute Scholar. He knew a little, at least, of various diseases and their treatments. "They're not cursed. They're not cursed. They suffer a sickness, nothing more."

A sickness which, according to some of the scholars he had read, was not even truly so contagious as many believed. He could not, standing here high above the valley, breathe the poison of their skin, the corruption eating away at their limbs and innards, and become like one of them. He was safe up here.

But the superstitions and beliefs of ages were deep in his blood, and he trembled where he stood, trembled so hard that he feared he might faint. And he thought, with an analytical part of his brain now nearly suffused in dread: *If I were to hide from a Crouching Shadow, this is the very place I would choose.*

For indeed, who would seek a beautiful temple girl among those monstrous forms?

"They're sick. They're not cursed. And they cannot hurt me," Sunan muttered. He looked but saw no sign of the cat, who seemed to have finally given him the slip. He did not doubt that the cat had entered the valley, however. He could not say how he knew, but his certainty was clear and dreadful. He must follow. He must not go back upon his blood oath. He must—

"Oh, my dear boy! You don't want to go down there!"

Sunan startled and turned, drawing a sharp breath. A hunched form, the face and body so covered in mismatched rags taken from who-knows-where that no one could tell whether man or woman hid beneath, hobbled toward Sunan, supporting itself heavily on a stout tree branch which served as a cane. The hand holding the branch was wrapped up to disguise the loss of most of its fingers. All that could be seen of the person's face were the eyes and what was left of a mouth. The mouth seemed to smile, though the eyes were sad.

"You should go back to where you came from, stout young fellow like you," the little creature spoke from a savaged throat. "Unless, of course, you've come seeking family? Kind of you, if so. Most of our families forget us once we come here."

Sunan saw that over its back the figure carried a satchel bulging with stale bread and wilted vegetables, an offering, perhaps, from one of the more charitable sects of the Crown of the Moon. The sack was tied to a handless arm and slung over a thin shoulder.

Sunan stood perfectly still even as the leper drew near. "I'm right, aren't I?" the leper said. "You're looking for someone."

"I—I am," Sunan said, forcing himself not to cover his face with his sleeve.

"A mother, perhaps? A sister? A brother?"

"No," said Sunan. "No, I'm looking for—"

He stopped. He'd almost said he was looking for a cat, and that sounded insane even in his head.

But the leper nodded as though understanding. "I know whom you seek." The voice was rough with disease, but the choice of words and the cadence were those of an elegant, cultured individual. A man, Sunan thought now that he saw the form up close. Perhaps a former scholar, or a lawyer, or a man of business. None of that mattered now. But it was also a kind voice, and this did matter even here. Even in the Valley of Suffering. "Come. Come with me, dear boy, and I will take you."

"Take me where?" Sunan demanded.

"To see our angel."

It seemed impossible that angels ever came to this place, so deep, so dark, so lost in hopelessness was the very air down in the Valley of Suffering.

Yet Sunan was surprised, as he followed behind his disease-ridden guide, how often the little man nodded and called out to those sitting around the various fires. And how many voices, both young and old, raised the cry,

"Granddad! Granddad!" as he passed, distributing loaves and greens as he went.

A distant part of Sunan's brain, a part hidden even from the imp inside, whispered: *Perhaps there are more angels here than anywhere else.*

The leper's sack was empty by the time they reached a hut in the center of the valley. The leper tossed it aside to lie by the door and put out his stump of an arm to touch the head of a huddled child sitting with her back to the wall. The child looked up, grinning, and Sunan saw that the leprosy had already eaten away part of her jaw and her nose.

But her eyes shone, and she whispered hoarsely, "Granddad!" even as the man ducked his head to enter the hut. Then she turned those bright eyes upon Sunan, and they clouded over immediately with distrust. She wrapped her arms over her head, hiding her face. Sunan shuddered, hating himself for the loathing he felt, and plunged into the dark hut after the man.

He was shocked to discover the room inside lit by three small lamps. The flames burned straight and tall up from the spouts, illuminating the dirt, the rags, the squalor . . .

. . . and the face of the most beautiful woman Sunan had ever imagined.

She sat in the center of the chamber, cross-legged, her hands folded before her. Her eyes were closed, her brow smooth and pale as the moon. She breathed lightly and, indeed, made so little movement that it would have been all too easy to mistake her for a statue. She was clad in the same rags as the lepers around her, but she wore them like a princess, like a queen.

Here in the midst of suffering, this form of loveliness looked far beyond mortal. It was an angelic face. One scarcely could notice the hand-shaped burn marring her cheek.

The leper guide bowed before her then turned and motioned for Sunan to do the same. "Is she the one you seek?" he asked.

Sunan nodded. She was the very likeness of the girl in the imp's vision.

"It is good, is it not?" the leper asked. "To find beauty such as hers in a place such as this?"

"How long—how long has she lived here?"

"Not long. Not long," the leper said. "And she will not stay, for she is not sick and her handmaiden makes certain she does not touch our water or eat of our food. She will leave us, yes. But she will remain in our hearts forever. We will speak of her amongst ourselves and pass on the memory of her for the generations to follow. The Angel of Lembu Rana."

He spoke the name as one might speak a prayer, and from behind their rags his eyes gazed with great love upon the girl. Then he nodded to Sunan and inclined his head respectfully. "I will leave you to speak with her. Perhaps she will impart a blessing upon you, and if she does, perhaps you will speak to us in turn."

He left, ducking out of the hut and leaving Sunan alone with the girl and the three lamps.

Sunan stood where he was, uncertain and afraid. He had found her, but he did not know what he must do. What was it the Crouching Shadow had told him? "I must return to the docks," he whispered to the shadows. "I must return to the docks and . . ."

Instead he found himself kneeling before the girl even as he had seen the beggars kneeling before the shrines to the stars. But surely this was a purer obeisance, for this girl was real. She was no stone carving, no feeble mortal personification of celestial spheres. She was real, and she was lovely.

"Who are you?" Sunan whispered, gazing into her quiet face. He saw the scar but could not accept that it was really there or that it could in any way harm the beauty of this glorious creature. "Who are you? You are not truly an angel but a mortal, I know. A girl of the temple. But why are you here? Can you tell me?"

He knew she heard him. She did not move, and her breathing did not check, but he knew she heard him. He reached out to her, his fingers hovering above her two folded hands. "Please," he said, "tell me your name. Tell me who you are." He touched her.

Her eyes flew wide, and she gazed deep into his soul.

Wrapped in leper's rags, Sairu passed almost invisible down the road. Not quite invisible, because while every eye did all it could to keep from looking at her, every man, woman, and child found her an object of fear and fascination and, even if they did not look, were keenly aware of her until she was gone on her way.

It was a good disguise. She had bound up her hands so that they looked as though she had lost several fingers on each. She walked with a limp, though anyone paying full attention would have noticed that she moved much faster than someone with such a limp should. Her face was wrapped in several layers of musty cloth, and the little bits that showed were caked with the most repulsive cosmetics she had ever applied, a display of great red boils and blisters.

She smiled at her own disguise and the horror she inspired in all those she passed. But the smile faltered the nearer she came to Lembu Rana. Though she had spent the full three months of her journey down from Daramuti with this plan firmly in mind, when it came to it, she was terrified at the prospect of entering the lepers' colony.

Even now, as she drew near once more to the Valley of Suffering, Sairu felt her footsteps faltering. If it weren't for the knowledge that her mistress waited for her down below, she could not have brought herself to descend that path so many poor souls traveled to face isolation and lingering death.

"The Living Dead." That's what they were called within the sheltered walls of Manusbau. A deliciously gruesome name when considered as a distant story only. But now Sairu, as the stink of the valley rose up to greet her with a ominous foreboding deeper than the night's own shadows, shuddered and wished she'd never heard of the valley or of those who dwelled therein.

Yet she knew it was the one place her mistress could be safe from all those who sought her. It was the one place she could hide Lady Hariawan and leave her, as she hunted down the answers to her many questions.

The glow of the lepers' campfires rose up from the valley like the lights of any other village. But this light seemed ghastly to Sairu as she tottered, limped, and dragged herself to the lip of the valley, mimicking the walk of other lepers she had witnessed. In her heart she felt the same revulsion she had sensed from those she passed on her way out of Lunthea Maly. She would not dare judge those who shunned her, for she would do the same in their place.

The path down into the valley was well worn and broad. Few traversed it at this hour, so Sairu was surprised when, as she approached the bottom, she was jostled severely by someone hastening past. He must not have seen her in the darkness, and he nearly knocked her flat. She felt hands reach out and grab her, and a voice of unconscious politeness muttering, "Forgive me, I'm—"

The voice broke off as Sairu looked up. She saw a handsome, unscarred or sullied man's face half revealed in the firelight, staring down at her as he realized that he held the arms of a leper. She saw the sickening fear wash over his eyes, felt his hands begin to tremble.

And yet he was a gentleman. He set her right on her feet before dropping his hold and hurrying on his way.

She stood a moment as though frozen in place, watching his shadow scurry up the valley wall after him. Her first thought was *Why would a healthy man venture here at this hour?*

Her second thought was *He is so like his brother.*

This thought brought her up short when she realized what it was. So like *what* brother? Surely not . . . not *him*! How could that be? And here of all places? She must have imagined the likeness in the midst of all her fear and worry and enormous exhaustion.

She shook her head and started into the village. Unable to bear looking at those wraithlike forms all around her, she kept her gaze firmly on the ground at her feet and hastened, against the roiling of her stomach and the lightness of her head, to that hut in the center where her mistress waited.

The little old man who laid claim to the hut sat outside the door with a sick child at his side. He raised his covered head at Sairu's approach and uplifted his handless arm in greeting. "Dear lady," he said, "your angel is safe."

"You have watched over her well in my absence?" Sairu asked, fumbling under the heavy folds of her rags for something hidden. She withdrew a small purse of coins gained from the sale of those precious items she had removed from her trunk early that same morning.

"I have followed your instructions," said the old man, nodding. "I have made certain that none of my poor brothers or sisters came near her and that she touched none of our food or drink. She has scarcely moved all day, but I do not think she is afraid."

"No," Sairu agreed, pouring the contents of her purse into the man's lap. "No, my Lady Hariawan fears nothing I know of."

The little girl, her eyes wide with fascination at the sight of the bright coins piled up in the man's lap, put out a mangled hand, ugly with open sores, and touched them tentatively. Sairu's heart lurched at the sight, and she felt shame for the abhorrence she could not repress at the stench and destitution all around. The abhorrence she felt toward this poor, sad child.

She turned quickly to the hut door, slipping inside and away from the sight of the man and the girl. One of the lamps within had gone out, but by the light of the other two, Sairu could see her mistress sitting as calmly as she had left her, eyes closed, hands folded, wrapped in beggar's rags.

"*Prrrrrlt?*"

"Monster," Sairu breathed as the cat appeared from behind Lady Hariawan, his eyes bright, his tail twitching. "Did you find Lord Dok-Kasemsan?"

"No," said the cat. "What's more, I think I was followed here."

"Followed? By whom?"

"I'm not certain. He's gone now, though. I believe I lost him. It took me some time to find this hut, and I won't lie"—the cat shivered from the tip of his nose down to the end of his tail—"this valley is the worst, most horrid example of everything mortal I have experienced in all my long life! Why you had to choose this, of all places—"

"Never mind," said Sairu sharply even as she knelt before her mistress. "If you were followed, we will leave." She bowed her head, suddenly so tired she thought she might fall to pieces. When was the last time she had truly slept? Slept without fear that her lady would wander off or try to kill her in the night? Slept without keeping one eye open for assassins and phantoms and dangers she had not yet even imagined? How she longed to lay her head down, even here in this sickening darkness, and close her eyes!

But no. They must go. She did not know where, but they must. If the cat had been followed, she must assume their position was compromised. "We will leave," she repeated, as though to convince herself. "At once."

"Not at once, for I have something else to tell you," said the cat, placing a white paw on her arm. "I did not find your Lord Dok-Kasemsan as you asked, but I did find someone in the temple dungeons. Someone who might very well interest you."

"Who?"

"Jovann." The cat grinned at the expression that flashed across her face. "So you still remember him, do you?"

8

HE WOULD NEVER FORGET the look in her eyes.

As he stumbled out the of the hut and fled through the dying figures of the lepers and their tomblike shelters, Sunan's heart beat with such a horror as he had never before felt. Not horror at the sickness, or fear for his body or of potential suffering. Instead he felt the horror of love, something akin to possession.

The angel had looked into his eyes, and he had known that he would do anything for her. It was as though he had lost his very soul.

So he fled. He did not hear the man called Granddad call out to him, nor did he turn to see the child with the marred face watch him rush by. He avoided the phantom forms of other lepers and sought escape from their cursed valley. But though he might escape Lembu Rana, he would never again be free of that look in her endless eyes. That look of, he believed, beauty so pure and so powerful as to shame Hulan herself.

He gained the path out of the valley and collided with a leper there, a small huddling woman who could have broken beneath his careless hands. He caught her before she fell and set her right, realizing too late that he held in his hands the very living form of contagion. But his Pen-Chan breeding was strong, and he murmured apologies before hastening on his way, climbing up, out of the valley, into the dark of falling night beyond.

How far outside the city had he come? How far had he to walk to gain those docks where he had disembarked that very morning? It did not matter. He walked, his head bent, his tired feet crying out for rest, but his heart driving him onward. He believed he would never rest again, not now that he knew this angel on earth existed.

What a fool he was, he decided a good forty minutes later as he passed through the encampments and hastened toward the city walls. He had never been a lad to fall for a pretty face. Since his transference to Suthinnakor and the house of his uncle, he had had time for nothing but his studies, so intense was the regimen, so exacting were the requirements made of all true scholars. He had no time for fancies or vain, poetic ideals of romance.

Indeed, by the time he gained the city walls and passed unhindered through the gates, he had half convinced himself that the entire encounter had been his invention. Or not the encounter, but merely his reaction to it. That leaping of his heart and quickening of his pulse were not the signs and sensations of sudden love. Oh, no! These were merely the results of a long, tiring day without food, without drink, without rest. And the girl? Certainly she was pretty. But no face was so perfect, no form so sublime that at first sight a man of Sunan's intellect and learning would lose his head completely!

He did not realize, as he made his way down the dark, winding streets of Lunthea Maly at night how many times he came close to his own demise. Thieves lurked in doorways, and murderers hunted in back alleys. These, upon first seeing a tall, slender man in once-fine robes making his way unwittingly through territory not his own, bared their teeth like so many wolves eager for the hunt.

Yet in the end, all of these turned aside, allowing Sunan to pass unmolested through their midst. For something about his face, some light too bright in the depths of his eye . . . they did not like. Thieves and murderers are cowards at heart, and they were none of them willing to face a man who might not prove so defenseless as he at first appeared.

So it was that Sunan came to the long dockyard of the city in one piece, his heart still beating a wild pace in his breast, but his mind composed under the stern intellectual restraint he had learned to practice years ago. He had found the girl of the vision. This was all that mattered. And he had fulfilled his blood oath by returning to the docks.

These docks were ghostly and not quite silent at night as Sunan walked up and down the shoreline. The ships in their moorings made many sounds, creaking, groaning, whispering to one another secrets of their various voyages. Sailors on watch patrolled the decks, keeping a wary eye out for sly forms and sly hands which might think a ship at rest a worthy trove to plunder.

The docks themselves crawled with rats. Sunan's stomach heaved at the sight of them gathering here and there to collect refuse. Little lordlings of the night come out to gambol and play now that the human-folk had fled the darkness. Their eyes glinted in the light of ships' lanterns, evil mimics of Hulan's starry children in the sky above.

Sunan paced beneath the stars, gazing up as he went. He had come to the docks. Now what? What would become of him and this life he led that was no longer his own? What new service would they require without any offered explanation? Was this existence truly worth the price?

"But am I ready to die in order to be free?" he whispered to the unquiet dark. He knew that he was not. Not yet, anyway.

Suddenly someone stood before him. He sucked in a quick breath but otherwise did not make a sound or a move.

"Did you find the girl?"

He did not recognize the voice. It was not the voice of Tu Domchu. But then, having seen Tu Domchu's disguises, he did not doubt that the Crouching Shadow could disguise his voice with equal ease. One way or the other, Sunan knew that he spoke to a Crouching Shadow, and he hastened to give his report.

"I found her," he said. The light of the nearest lantern was too far away to reveal the features of the face before him. He could see nothing more than a large, broad-shouldered form, and he sensed strength and purpose. "I found her. She is in—"

"Do not tell me. I am watched," said the Crouching Shadow, and there was the faintest trace of fear in his voice. "Take this."

Something was pressed into Sunan's hand. Something cold and long and unfamiliar. It took him some moments to realize what he held: a knife. "What is this?" he asked, although, with a sickening drop of his stomach, he knew the answer to his question already. "What would you have me do?"

"Kill her," said the Crouching Shadow, "or we are all dead men."

Jovann wanted to knock his head against the wall at his back. Repeatedly. He wanted to knock harder and harder and harder until his whole skull rattled and broke, and the thing inside it slithered out, leaving him in peace.

Instead he sat in his chains, perfectly rigid and upright, breathing deep. He had seen the warriors of the Khla clan sit in just this way before and after a battle, clearing their minds, focusing their energies, driving back the bloodlust that could so quickly overwhelm a warrior's heart and leave his soul open to madness. Jovann himself, as a boy, had practiced this meditation before and after a good hunt, though he knew that the killing of animals for food was quite unlike the killing of men for honor.

The lantern burned low in its base of oil. The flame, gone red with sickly waning, made the corpse lying in chains at Jovann's side so much ghastlier. He shivered where he sat, and once more forced himself to concentrate on his breathing.

My father did not know me!

This thought, too strong and too close to panic, destroyed the tentative equilibrium he had achieved, and Jovann, though he had not moved, found himself dizzy with sickness. Something in his brain shifted, something that should not be there. Whatever it was, it had so changed his outward appearance that Juong-Khla—so miraculously appearing in this underground cell, far, far, far from the Chhayan plains where last Jovann had seen him—had not recognized his son and heir.

"It's a dream," Jovann whispered. "It's a nightmare."

What else could it be? How else could he explain the warping of his body into the form of another? How else could he explain the sensation of looking down at his own hands and seeing someone else's? How else could he account for his father and two warriors of the Khla clan stepping out of thin air and back into it again? It must be a nightmare!

"But no," Jovann admitted, squeezing his eyes tighter shut. "You have walked in the Dream. You have witnessed the nightmares of many men. You know this is real."

If only he could sleep. If only he could step out of his body and return to the Wood, return to the Grandmother Tree and the serenity of endless green life surrounding. But he had been unable to leave his body behind and walk in other worlds ever since he was dragged through the gates of Daramuti and on down the Khir Road. He had heard no silver voice calling to him on the edge of sleep. He had seen no path opening beneath his feet.

He was trapped in the nightmare of mortal reality, and that nightmare grew ever worse.

The thing in his brain throbbed, aggravated. Jovann knew it wanted out. If only he could give it that wish! But he didn't know how, so it battered about in his consciousness. His temples throbbed, and the base of his neck felt like an iron rod had been shoved up into his head. If he relaxed and simply permitted the imp to exist in his head without a fight, the pain would go away. This he knew, yet he could not help himself. Over and over again he tried to push it from his mind. And so the thing grew ever angrier and caused still more pain. At last even the meditation of his forefathers proved impossible, and Jovann put his hands to his head, clutching at his hair.

A gentle voice, speaking with command, whispered in the back of his memory.

"*Your pain is here. Beneath my hand. Feel it here beneath my hand.*"

"My pain is here," he whispered, pressing his hands flat on either side of his head. He concentrated all his focus on the sensations of his palms and fingertips, and he felt the pain shift beneath them. He drew them down, whispering as he did so, "My pain is here. In my hands. I feel it in my hands."

He heard her voice in his memory, drowning out even the scurrying of the imp.

"*Hold your pain in the palms of your hands.*"

The cell door creaked.

Jovann looked up, expecting to see the prison-keeper, hoping perhaps someone had realized that Lord Dok-Kasemsan was dead and had come to remove the corpse. He had sat far too long now in this chamber beside the dead man's body. Even the sight of the prison-keeper's ugly face would be welcome.

But it wasn't the prison-keeper peering into the red-lit room. It was Sairu.

"By Hulan's shining crown! Is that you, little miss?" Jovann exclaimed, surging up onto his knees, his pain momentarily forgotten. Then he cursed more bitterly, "Anwar blight it!" because he heard with his own ears how his words turned to gibberish the moment they left his mouth.

Sairu stared in at him, and without her smile she seemed strange to him. But he knew it was she, especially when the orange cat, her constant companion, appeared at her feet. She looked down at the cat, which purred and flicked its tail. "Are you certain?" she asked.

The cat blinked up at her then trotted into the chamber, stepping daintily around piles of musty straw. It sat in front of Jovann and stared at him in a manner most disconcerting. Jovann ignored the beast as best he could and addressed himself to Sairu. "I know you can't see me," he said, cringing at the horror his voice became in his own ears, like a madman's chatter. "I know you can't hear me. But please, *please,* know who I am! You're smart. You're clever. You see what others miss. See who I am!"

She crossed the cell more slowly than the cat and stood with the dying lamp above her head. She carried a small lantern of her own, a bamboo frame housing a single thick candle. The light was bright from the rice-paper wick, and she held it high to illuminate as much of the cell and the prisoner as she could. But the corpse lying so near drew her attention away from him, and he saw her cheek twitch at the sight of it, though he could not read the emotion.

Sairu, avoiding coming into contact with Jovann, knelt beside the dead man, putting her lantern close to his face. This was rigid and horrible with death, which seemed to have brought no peace to Lord Kasemsan's suffering. His beauty had long since deserted him, and there was little left of the elegant Pen-Chan scholar who had come to dine in the presence of the empress some six months previous. Jovann, though he had spent many hours now with the dead man as his only companion, could not bear the sight and looked away.

But Sairu, though her hand trembled, reached out and took the corpse by the chin, turning the head this way and that. Then she looked at Jovann, or rather, at the mask so cleverly concealing Jovann's form and being.

The cat growled in his throat, then said rather loudly, "*Mrrreaaaa!*"

"If that is true," said Sairu, narrowing her eyes, "then it is a very good disguise indeed."

"Disguise? Yes!" Jovann cried, leaning toward her and putting out a chained hand. "Please, little miss, you know who I am. You *know* it!"

She remained kneeling beside the corpse but sat back on her heels, studying him. Then she said in a soft, questioning voice, "Do you still think of Umeer's daughter?"

He did not speak. His eyes widened, and his heart beat harder in his breast as he recalled the lovely face which, in memory, had been his comfort over the last hellish months of his existence. Sairu studied his expression. She watched the emotions playing across features unfamiliar, reading there everything he could tell her.

Then she turned to the cat. "You're right. It *is* he."

"And you can break the spell," said the cat. "I know about these things. There are certain spells that can only be broken by . . . by . . ." He hesitated, suddenly embarrassed.

"If," said Sairu, who had seen her fair share of romantic operas and heard many a recitation of fanciful poetry, "you are going to tell me that it only requires true love's first kiss, you had better think again. I am not bringing my mistress here, and you can put the idea out of your mind."

Jovann frowned, glancing from her to the cat, who was growling. "I would—I would never presume to—"

She put up a warning hand and shot him a stern look to silence the babble. She addressed herself to the cat once more. "Well, Monster? What else have you to say?"

"I wasn't *actually* thinking of Lady Hariawan," said the cat. "In fact, I rather thought—"

"You had best tell me a practical solution to this dilemma, cat, before I lose my patience."

The cat put his ears back at her. But he answered grudgingly, "No one has to kiss anyone. You simply need to call him by his true name."

"Juong-Khla Jovann?"

"Yes?" said Jovann.

"No," said the cat. Then, "Lumé love me, if only Imraldera were here! She'd know how to help you better than I. You must *see him*, my girl. You must look at him and see *him*, not this outer form. You must see the real Jovann underneath, and you must call him by his name. His true name. The name which means who he *is*. Do you understand?"

Sairu blinked coldly at the cat.

"Or you could kiss him."

"Listen, Monster, I do not have time for games and—"

Sairu stopped. The air in that subterranean chamber was cold and dank, but a sudden wave of ice passed over her heart, colder by far. The lantern hanging from the ceiling extinguished, and the sphere of light cast by the lantern in her hand became the whole world for a moment, a world containing life, death, sickness, hope, and all the other things of which worlds are made.

But Sairu felt none of that. Instead she felt a deathly hand close over her heart. And her instincts, so highly tuned, screamed suddenly in her mind.

My mistress!

"I should not have left her," Sairu whispered. "She's in danger."

She was on her feet in an instant, her lantern swinging wildly as she darted across the cell to the door. "Where are you going?" the cat cried and sprang after her. Both vanished, and the cell, which had been horrible before, plunged now into utter blackness save for the tiniest crack of sickly light slipping through the still-open cell door.

Jovann sat in the dark beside his dead companion. The silence was as heavy as the weight of stone and earth above his head. As heavy as his spirit.

At last he muttered, perhaps for dead Kasemsan's benefit, "Anwar blight that girl!" But the words came out mangled and unintelligible even in his own ears.

9

ON HIS WAY BACK OUT OF the city Sunan stopped at a small fire pit off the roadside, half-hidden behind a crumbling wall, where a man of indeterminate age cooked dumplings filled with indeterminate ingredients. Sunan bought three without quite realizing he'd done so. His body was weak, his limbs trembling from hunger, and he couldn't remember if he'd eaten a bite the whole of the long day previous.

So, with the strange dagger secured tightly to his left arm, hidden within the sleeves of his robe, he purchased the dumplings then hastened on down the road with them clutched to his breast as though he'd committed some villainous act. A darkened doorway offered shelter, and Sunan tucked himself into it to eat his meal, furtively staring out from the shadows at all those passing by. There were not many yet, for the morning had not fully broken. But already, here and there, sellers and buyers and purveyors of various businesses emerged from their houses, huts, and hovels. The flowing life's blood of Lunthea Maly, hastening in endless circulation through the beastly city which was, many said, the very center of the world.

Sunan took a bite of the first dumpling, and a bursting sensation of ginger filled his palate. With it came a still more overwhelming burst of shame.

He stood frozen, unable to swallow, his tongue burning, his eyes watering, facing the truth of what he was on his way to do.

Murder.

Not murder. Assassination, another side of his mind whispered. But even in the privacy of his mind it was such a sarcastic, such a bitter comment that Sunan almost wondered if it was the imp in his head speaking and not his own thought at all. But the imp had withdrawn into a far deeper corner of Sunan's consciousness and crouched there, growling, but otherwise inactive.

Sunan was alone with his thoughts. His guilt and his shame.

You could refuse. Throw away the dagger and walk on in the opposite direction.

He forced his jaw to work. Chewed, swallowed, and took another bite.

If you do that, they'll kill you before the day is done.

He felt the dumpling settle like a hard lump in the pit of his stomach. But his body cried out for more, so he ate. The ginger nearly made him sick, but he ate, because what else could he do?

What else can you do? It's her life or yours. What do you owe her?

That beautiful face—rendered so much more beautiful in contrast to those wretches surrounding her on all sides—flashed across his memory. A beautiful face, but he did not know her. He did not truly love her. He felt his heart race at the thought of her, felt his limbs turn to water as the idea of her filled his mind. But he did not love her. Her death would mean so little.

And there is your blood oath to be considered.

This was true indeed. After all, committing this act was not simply a matter of life or death. It was a matter of honor. He had vowed a solemn vow, and as an honorable man he must fulfill it or lose face. His death would be preferable by far. So ultimately this couldn't be murder. Not really. Not when looked at from the proper vantage.

He knew they were watching him. The Crouching Shadows. He couldn't see them, but he felt them, and every man, woman, and child moving up and down the narrow streets of Lunthea Maly seemed to him suspicious, dangerous, their eyes full of a killer's cunning.

With a sudden sense of urgency Sunan swallowed down the rest of the dumplings. Then he drew himself up and stepped boldly from the doorway, hastening down the street and on to the northernmost gate of Lunthea Maly. He felt the morning sun rising, and shadows lengthened across his path, broken up by bursts of soft white-gold light. Beggar children, seeing his haste, rushed after him, jeering and begging for coins at the same time. He snarled at them, and when they would not leave him be, lunged suddenly and watched them scatter back into the mist.

He did not see the three forms spying on his movements from the upper window of a disreputable inn. He did not see the fur-clad arm of a master sharply motion or the two pairs of heavy boots stamping down a narrow stair and entering the street. Sunan, intent upon the task at hand, intent upon forcing back the horror mounting in his heart, did not realize that he was followed, not by Crouching Shadows as he feared, but by a danger much more dreadful to him.

Sunan's world was made up of broken shards of time. One moment, he was in the city. Then, before he realized it, he was at the gates. He passed through these and was unaware of anything more until he was quite far out into the country beyond, pushing against the flow of those journeying from across the empire to make their way into Lunthea Maly's welcoming, devouring heart.

Then, quite suddenly, he stood on the lip of Lembu Rana, gazing down upon the secluded village of lepers. The sight was rendered no less horrible by the gentle light of late morning. Indeed, it was more difficult to watch those wretched forms—some hobbling about to tend their meager gardens, some stirring boiling pots full of stew or laundry, some carrying bits of wood to fuel the fires, but most simply lying before the doors of their huts, ravaged faces upturned to Anwar's warmth as the only comfort they could know in their suffering. In the shadows of night they had been wraithlike and otherworldly. By day they were living corpses, and this was worse by far.

Sunan's resolve wavered, not for any sense of guilt now, but simply for fear. "They're not cursed. They're sick," he whispered even as he'd done the evening before, which seemed like years ago.

He glanced back over his shoulder, perhaps with a thought of flight. Only then did he spy two distant forms watching him from up the road. He did not recognize them from that distance but believed them to be Crouching Shadows observing whether or not he would fulfill his oath. If he turned back now, he would surely die.

So, steeling himself with what little courage remained to him, he started down the path. Some of the lepers climbing up eyed him with suspicion and avoided him with as much alacrity as he avoided them. He passed unimpeded into their village and stood there a moment, uncertain which way to turn. The night before he'd had a guide through these tumbledown structures. Now they stretched before him like a maze into the very pit of hell.

But to his surprise, a little form approached him. She moved slowly, with much pain, and as she drew near, Sunan recoiled at the ugliness of her face, missing part of its jaw and raw with infection. But then he recognized her. She was the same child who had sat outside the hut of the lepers' angel.

She smiled at Sunan. It was a ghastly sight. And yet, for the first time since looking upon the Valley of Suffering, he felt his heart moved by something like pity. After all, this was a child. She should be at play with a dozen brothers and sisters. She should be clutching some rag of a doll in one hand, tugging her mama's skirts with the other. Instead she died. Every day she died more. And who could say where her mama was, having long since abandoned her blighted offspring?

So when the child smiled at him, Sunan offered something of a smile in return. This seemed to give her courage, and she drew nearer so that he could hear her roughened voice saying, "Come with me. To the angel."

He did not think. He did not consider what he was about to do to this poor waif's angel. She led, and he followed, avoiding eye-contact with those who watched him warily. And at last they came to a hut in the very center of the valley, and Sunan knew it was the one he sought.

There was no sign of the one called Granddad anywhere near, and the child settled beside her blackened fire pit, making no move to enter. But she motioned Sunan to the doorway, and he knew that she trusted him, that she gave him leave to pass.

Ignoring the ramming of his heart against his breastbone, Sunan ducked and entered, and found himself once more standing in the light of three lamps. These all burned low, their oil nearly gone. But they were enough still to illuminate the face of the beautiful woman. The scar was red across the pale curve of her cheek.

Sunan's heart nearly failed him. He almost ran from that hut, out of the valley, his arms outspread in welcome to those who would kill him for his failure. For she was so elegant in her rags, so composed amid this nightmare. Her eyes were closed once more, and for this he was thankful. Otherwise he felt quite certain that he would not have been able to take another step toward her.

But step he did, and then he knelt even as he had the night before. His eyes trailed over her form, resting at last upon that rag-covered place above her heart. The rags were thin enough. They would offer her no shield against the bite of his blade.

How long had it been since he hunted with the Tiger Clan? How long had it been since he last plunged a knife into the throat of his quarry? How long since he'd felt the spurt of blood across his hand? These were memories he had blocked, memories he had vowed to forget upon entering the Pen-Chan life of his mother's heritage, where a man could rise above all the foundational brutality of life, standing instead upon the towering heights of intellect and reflection.

But life has a way of circling back on itself. And here he knelt before the beautiful lady, even as he had knelt before his fallen prey. As he had done then, so he did now, drawing his knife, which looked like a demon's tooth in the light of those three lamps.

The woman opened her eyes. He felt her gaze but could not raise his head. He stared at his knife instead.

"I must kill you," he whispered.

"Is that so?" said she.

Her voice was so calm. Like the sweetest of spring breezes moving through the tall grass of the grazing lands. It pierced Sunan to the heart. He could not move.

"I have long wondered about death. About life," said the woman. "They are a mystery. The great mystery. And who is to say if the one is worse than the other?"

Sunan swallowed with difficulty. He shifted the knife in his grip, turning it to the right angle for plunging.

"I feel that before I die, I should ask you something," said the woman. "Will you give me a truthful answer?"

"I—I will if I may." His voice came out in a hoarse cough.

"What is your name?"

He could not help himself. He looked up into her face, into her deep, deep eyes, and he thought he saw the light of the Dara shining there. He answered without thinking, "Juong-Khla Sunan. That is my name."

"Sunan," said she, and her head tilted to one side. Her threadbare head-covering slipped down around her shoulders, revealing her thick hair, which was combed and braided, and which shone with an otherworldly luster. She spoke his name again. "Sunan. The Good Word. It is a worthy name."

She put up her hands then and, without any sign of fear or fumbling, undid the ties of her garments about her neck and parted the rags to reveal the white skin beneath. She uncovered her heart.

"Very well, Sunan, the Good Word. Do as you have purposed."

He knew then that he never could.

Sunan raised the knife above his head and threw it across the hut. It struck the wall and stuck there, the hilt shivering with the impact. Sunan's body shivered in response, and he covered his face with his hands. His heart raced and his gut roiled, but he sat as still as a becalmed sea.

Suddenly he felt soft hands touching his. The woman took hold of his fingers, pulling them back, revealing his face. He found her bent toward him, and the scent of her hair was like wildflowers.

"I want to show you something, Sunan," said she. "Will you see?"

He nodded mutely. The woman reached into the depths of her garments and withdrew something in her fist. Slowly she uncurled her fingers and revealed the wonder that lay in the palm of her hand.

It was a star. No, it was a flower of stars.

No, even that, Sunan realized with a shake of his head, was not quite right. It was a cluster of opals set in gold, luminous from the inside out, unaided and unhindered by the lamplight.

"It is a gift of the heart," said the woman. She pressed it into Sunan's hand, and her fingers, hovering over his, hid the light of those stones. "Will you accept it?"

"I will," he gasped.

"And will you promise to love me?"

"I promise."

She took his face between her hands then. His head filled with storms and thunder as she pulled his face to her own and kissed him. That kiss, so full of power, so full of passion he did not comprehend, was the final seal upon his heart.

The woman released him and sat back, her eyes demurely veiled by her lashes. "When the time comes, Sunan," she said, "you will obey me. You will serve me above all other masters."

"Yes," said Sunan. "I will. Anything you want. Anything you need." He did not consider just then that he would not live to offer her any service. Life and death did not matter in this place. Somehow he would make good his promise to her.

She did not look at him again. When she spoke, her voice was a whisper. "You must go now. She is returning, and she will kill you if she finds you here. Go."

Though it was like tearing his own heart in two, Sunan rose, obedient to his new mistress's every wish. He stumbled from the darkened hut, leaving behind his very will as well as the knife in the wall. And he clutched the opals tight in his fist.

Sairu ran with the cat at her feet, her pace scarcely letting up since she emerged from the dungeons into the surface world. Only at the gates of the Crown of the Moon did she pause to shed her disguise of priestly robes, revealing the leper's rags beneath. Then she ran with much greater speed than a leper should be capable of, darting with such quickness through the winding streets of Lunthea Maly that anyone watching her would have thought she had grown up navigating their mysteries rather than behind the sheltering walls of Manusbau and the Masayi.

The cat found himself hard-pressed to keep pace with her, which was unusual for him. But she was driven by an instinct far stronger than anything he had ever before encountered in a mortal.

Sairu cursed herself with every step. How could she have let herself be drawn away from her mistress's side? Especially when she knew—she *knew*, Anwar blight it!—that the cat had been followed and their situation was no longer safe. She should have ignored all thoughts of Jovann, all hope of finding him, against all reason, alive. She should have remained at her mistress's side, discovered some new safe hiding place.

What a fool, what a fool, what a thrice-cursed fool! So her brain repeated in rhythmic beat with her pounding feet. And she vowed, as her penance, that she would leave Jovann to rot in that cell, that she would never think of him again but focus all her heart and energies upon her mistress's wellbeing. She vowed as much to Anwar and Hulan and all the starry host, though she did not believe in them. If they would only prove their mythic powers, just this once, and let her reach her mistress in time!

The city was too great, the streets too winding and too long. The world itself might come to an end before she ever achieved the city gates.

The cat cried out at her heels, "Idiot girl, let me help you! Lumé love me, can you not stand still and *think* for but a moment?"

She did not slow her pace or look at the cat. She could not have heeded him even had she wished to. Her haste was all-consuming, and there was no time, no time at all, no time to stop or think.

She reached the gates. She reached the countryside beyond. Still she did not slow, though her side ached and her lungs heaved and her heart threatened to give out. Many watched her pass, shuddering at the strangeness of a leper in full flight as though pursued by devils. And was that orange cat at her heels perhaps one of those devils himself?

Lembu Rana was not yet in sight when suddenly she glimpsed a figure coming her way. A figure she could almost but not quite recognize.

"It's him!" said the cat. "It's the man who followed me last night!"

Only then did Sairu slow and finally stop. She stared at the figure approaching, and loathing for him raged in her heart. "Are you certain?" she asked.

"I am," said the cat.

The figure drew nearer. He moved at a frantic pace himself, turning now and then to look back over his shoulder. One hand held up his long Pen-Chan robes lest they trip him as he fled. The other clutched in a tight fist as though hiding something.

Sairu's hand was already up her sleeve, touching the hilt of a hidden knife. But she paused suddenly as the stranger's face came into view. She thought, even as she had the night before, *How like his brother he is.*

Then she thought, *He has not killed.*

The truth of this thought was plain in the stranger's eyes. Sairu disguised her heaving breaths behind shallow pants and huddled down inside her robes, making herself to all appearances small, frail, weak with sickness. The stranger passed her by without a second glance, and she studied his face more carefully in passing. Again she thought, *He has not killed.*

"Follow him, Monster," she said even as the stranger hastened on down the road. "I must see to my mistress. So follow him and find out where he goes."

"Very well," said the cat, for once in his life making no resistance to a direct command.

Indeed, he had taken a good ten paces in this new pursuit before he realized how easily he had obeyed. He flattened his ears at the thought, but it was too late to go back without a severe mark against his dignity. So he pursued the stranger, who smelled a great deal like Jovann but certainly was not Jovann.

The stranger rounded a slight bend in the road, and the cat hastened after. Here they came to a stretch that was un-peopled. Not a single merchant's wagon or farmer's cart could be seen coming or going. Ahead rose the city in all its magnificence, and the sounds and smells of it filled the air. But in this small stretch, there was nothing but loneliness and the figure of the running man up ahead.

Then suddenly there was a crack in the world.

The cat recognized it in an instant, the same crack he had witnessed opening in the cell beneath the temple. He smelled the sulfur seeping through, smelled the hatred. It opened right in front of the stranger, and two men stepped forth, out of realms beyond and into this world.

The stranger screamed. And it was as much a scream of recognition as of surprise. Two Chhayans lunged at him, taking hold of his arms. Before the cat had time to think, they had dragged him through their crack in the world, all three vanishing from sight. The opening began to close.

"Dragon's teeth!" the cat swore. "Dragon's wretched, rotting teeth!"

With a single leap he covered the distance and slipped through the crack just before it vanished, leaving the road empty behind him. The nightmare of Death surrounded the cat. And it was a nightmare all too familiar.

For what felt like an age the cat stood frozen where he'd landed in this sliver of madness between worlds. He knew this path, the stench of it, the burn of it beneath his paws. He knew it too well. What could possibly have possessed him to leap upon it despite that knowledge?

"The girl is getting into your head, Eanrin," he muttered furiously, his eyes squeezed shut. It didn't matter if he opened them or not. Blindness alone would meet his vision, like a prophecy of doom to come. He felt his limbs turning to water, so great was his dread, and he doubted very much that he would be able to take a single step forward in his pursuit.

But then a voice reached out to him across the leagues of his own vast terror. A silver voice, gentle and serene yet cutting like a blade through any boundaries or walls.

Won't you follow me?

The cat opened his eyes. Sure enough, the blindness pressed in upon him, sickening his gut. But the voice still sang, and when he turned his head to the sound, he was able—if only just—to discern figures moving up ahead of him.

And so, not for the first time in his life, he walked Death's Path.

10

SUNAN COULD SEE COLORS, and he thought he saw shapes. But these whirled on the edges of his vision so that he could not tell up from down, inside from out. It was as though his vision had shattered and now fell in broken pieces on every side. All he saw for certain were the faces of the men holding him. Faces Sunan knew too well: Chakra and Kosul, both Tiger men of the Khla clan, his father's trusted right- and left-hand men. Both had shed their share of men's blood, and that blood stained their hearts and showed red in the rims of their eyes. They were powerful and they were cunning. Above all, they were cruel.

They looked without respect or regard upon their leader's eldest son and dragged him between them through this strange realm of broken lights and broken shadows. Sunan knew without doubt that he had left his own world far behind, though how he could know this he wasn't certain. But he felt the imp in his mind screeching and ramming against the edges of his consciousness, desperate to be free, to escape. Its fear infected Sunan's heart, and he found he was whispering prayers and pleading with his captors to let him go. They only tightened their grips and walked faster.

Chanting filled his ears. Along with the sound came a sudden clearing of vision. Sunan, his head dangling loosely from his neck, stared down at the dry wasteland spreading beneath his feet. It was not the dry of sun-baked, nor even the dry of death. For death to take place there must first be life, and there had never been life here. Nothing had ever grown from this soil, and nothing ever would. Sunan, however, was momentarily glad to see something he could stand on, something besides the swirling insanity through which he had just passed. He raised his head.

In the near distance an edifice of stone marked the only change in the endless horizon. From this edifice came the sound of chanting, and it seemed as though the chanting itself may *be* the very stones of its foundation.

"What is that place?" he gasped.

He did not expect an answer, so he was surprised when one of his father's men—Kosul, he thought—answered in low voice, "Ay-Ibunda. The Hidden Temple."

No more was said, but it was enough. Sunan knew he did not want to go anywhere near those dark gates opening before them. He pulled against the Chhayan men's hold, but they expected his resistance and their grips were firm. "Let me go! Let me go, please!" Sunan cried.

It was a dishonor to his father's name that he should whimper so. The Tiger men sneered and dragged him beneath the eyes of the stone dragon on one side of the gate.

Yet it wasn't the stone dragon that made Sunan's heart quail inside him. For opposite the dragon was a formless stone, rough, uncut, and unlovely. Somehow Sunan felt that something inside it looked out at him. And whatever it was, it was more dreadful even than the dragon.

The imp in his mind shrieked and seemed to bury itself ever deeper within his brain. He hoped it would be quiet now. He had enough to deal with without its chitterings.

Then Sunan was through the gate, passing on into a courtyard where dust and mist swirled together as one entity. The chanting was louder now, and he could just discern the shadowy forms of men clad like priests bowed down together, their voices a constant, droning drum: some high, some low, but indistinguishable. And they created and supported Ay-Ibunda with their voices, with their dreams. Sunan wondered if perhaps this was all a dream. If perhaps he walked outside his body in the realm of the unconscious.

Then he heard a voice crying out to him. A voice too well known, too well loved to be a dream.

"My son! My son!"

He knew then that, whatever the world around him might be, he was real, he was solid. He felt his heart beating at a furious rate in his throat, and he turned to that voice.

"Mother!"

They dragged her down the steps of the central temple building. They dragged her, two great warriors hauling her by ropes binding her arms, her hands, her neck. And yet they looked warily at her, careful not to drop their guard. His brave mother. His fierce mother. They knew she would tear their eyes out if they did not protect themselves.

But her gaze was only for Sunan standing in the center of the courtyard. She lunged against the ropes, which cut deep into her skin. "My son, what have they done to you?" she cried. Her beauty had long since vanished in hatred, but the ferocious love in her eyes when she gazed upon Sunan lent her a strange and fearsome dignity.

Chakra and Kosul dropped their hold on him, and Sunan fell to his knees. But he was on his feet again in an instant. His hands, one still clenched tight, reached out to his mother. He crossed the space between them, took her into his arms, and drew her close. "I'm here, I'm here," he said as though it were she who needed protecting, who needed comfort. She held him tight, pressing her head to his heart, and he felt his beating pulse calm, felt his breath come more gently from his lungs. They were together. After eight long, long years they were together. United, they would face the Tiger Clan even as they once had, even here in this nightmare.

Juong-Khla approached. Sunan, gazing over the top of his mother's head, saw this man who was his father appear in the doorway of the temple and move slowly down the steps. He wore his warrior's gear: the great pronged helmet, the fur-lined armor, the boots of cured buffalo hide studded with wolves' teeth. He greeted his son in the same voice with which he would have greeted his enemy. "Well, Sunan. We meet again."

Sunan felt the jolt of loathing pass through his mother's body at the sound of her husband's voice. She pulled out of his arms and turned to Juong-Khla, placing herself like a shield between the Tiger Chief and her son.

Juong-Khla uttered a short, mirthless laugh. "Wildcat, stand away from your cub. I will not kill him."

"You forget, Honored Husband," she said through bile in her throat. "You forget, I wrote down with ink and brush your vow to take my son's life if ever the two of you met again. You forget, but I do not. And you will have to kill me first."

He blinked slowly. "I vowed to take his life in exchange for Jovann's. But Jovann is not dead."

"What?" The word burst from Sunan's mouth before he could stop it. And his heart leapt with a hope he had long since thought perished. "Jovann is alive?"

"If he is not, it is not your doing," said the Tiger Chief. "I saw him with my own eyes not many months gone."

"Where? Where is he?"

"Far beyond your reach, son of my stolen wife. And indeed it should not have surprised me to see him. I should have known from the beginning that you would never have the courage to follow through with your blood-thirst." Juong-Khla proceeded down the stairs and stood now opposite his son with his wife between them. He folded his arms over his chest. Sunan was equal to his father in height, but nowhere near his match in breadth. The differences between them were always so much starker when they stood face-to-face. No man of the Khla clan could help but see.

None of them would have accepted Sunan as their chieftain's heir.

"Now," said Juong-Khla, "the time is short, and I am in no mood to argue or to barter. I need you to tell me where the Dream Walker is."

Sunan said nothing, in part because he did not know the answer to his father's question; in part because he did not want to reveal his ignorance right away. In spite of his fear, his natural Pen-Chan cunning—a very different sort of cunning than that of a beast of prey but no less deadly in its own way—reared up in his spirit, cold and intellectual. Across his memory flashed one of the hundreds of proverbs he had memorized over the years of his study: "*A secret kept is a power retained.*" Even the secret of his own ignorance. So he said nothing.

"I know," said the Tiger Chief, "that you are under the thumb of those twice-blighted Crouching Shadows. I know that you are under oath to serve them. I also know how they have hemmed and harried my people for centuries, trying to prevent that which I *will* accomplish. And so I proclaim you Traitor, and thus named you deserve to die by my hand."

"No," said his wife. "He will not die."

Juong-Khla snarled down at Sunan's mother and, with a single swipe of his arm, threw her to one side. She shrieked like the wildcat he'd called her and would have thrown herself at him had not his warriors stepped in and restrained her by her bindings. Juong-Khla addressed himself once more to his son.

"Tell me where the Dream Walker is, and I will even now spare your life."

Still Sunan said nothing.

"I know he has come to this city," Juong-Khla persisted, beginning to circle his son, watching his face from every angle as he moved, searching for some small crack in his mask. "I know this for truth. The raven brought the message far, and it was as truthful a message as such a creature can speak. They were not its own words, in any case, but Tenuk's. And Tenuk, old fool though he is, would not have lied to us. Tenuk has been loyal to our order all his life. He has suffered for the sake of our mission, lived and breathed among our enemies. He wore their trappings, spoke their lies, but in his breast there ever beat a true Chhayan heart. He would not deceive me. He sent the Dream Walker to the dungeons beneath the Crown of the Moon. But when we went to fetch him, he was not to be found."

Juong-Khla leaned in, placing his lips so near his son's ear that Sunan's skin burned with the heat of his father's breath. "Where is he, son of my stolen wife? Where is my prize?"

"I—" Sunan steadied his voice and spoke with great care. "I do not know of what you speak."

The Tiger Chief's voice became a low hiss. "*Liar.*"

He whipped out a cruel dagger made of bone and sharpened to a razor's edge. It was carved with deep, swirling grooves into which decades' worth of blood had settled, staining it an ugly brown. It had belonged to chieftains of the Tiger Clan for generations past. Juong-Khla gripped it hard and strode to Sunan's mother, whom he caught by the back of the head, yanking back her chin. He placed the blade along her throat, and his face radiated the urge of slaughter.

"Tell me where the Dream Walker is."

His mother's eyes rolled with fury, seeking to burn her husband with their intensity. But she could neither see him nor struggle, so tightly restrained as she was. She growled like an animal, daring him to do his worst.

Sunan watched, and his heart sank. Then suddenly he felt a deadly calm pass over his soul. A calm of inevitable loss. He could not fight what was about to take place. He could not resist it. He could only, as the Pen-Chan philosophers said, face his doom with the courage of equanimity. Thus he might do honor to his mother's forefathers even as he discredited all the Chhayans of his lineage.

He felt the pulse of the chanters all around him, and their voices spoke of darkness and certain death. In their steady rhythm he found a foothold and braced himself against what would follow. When he answered his father, his voice was steady if not peaceful. "I cannot tell you what you want, for I do not know the answer to your question."

Juong-Khla bared his teeth. In the next moment he would have dealt the death-stroke. But before his hand could move, a new voice spoke from the depths of the temple.

"Wait."

Everyone—Juong-Khla, his wife, Sunan, and the warriors standing in the mist—everyone save the phantom chanters turned to the temple door and the figure that appeared at the top of the stairs. And Sunan beheld a face and form unlike anything he had ever before seen.

He was like a man but also unlike in the most grotesque extreme. Seven feet tall, taller even, shrouded in a darkness falling from his shoulders in what may have been a cloak or may simply have been a long, thick shadow. His face was bone-white, the skin stretched too thin across his skull, which was black beneath.

But his eyes were worst of all. For these burned with raging furnaces much greater than the mere size of them would suggest. As though they burned in a realm completely other than this, and there they consumed the entirety of their world. When he opened his mouth to speak, more fire, red with wrath, gleamed in the back of his throat.

Sunan knew in a glance who this was, and he whispered the name he had seen written down but once, in his mother's coded hand: "The Greater Dark."

Moving with a grace incongruous to his size, the Dragon descended the steps, and his cloak flowed softly behind him. As he drew nearer, the heat of his form struck Sunan until sweat beaded his forehead. Inside, however, he felt deathly cold.

The imp in his brain began to scream.

Though no one could have heard that scream, the Dragon turned sharply to Sunan, his flaming eyes narrowed. "What have you got inside you?" he asked. "A spy? A spirit?"

He put out a hand with long slender fingers which looked like bones tipped with great claws. His speed was so great that Sunan had not time even to flinch before those claws rammed into his eye and back into his conscious mind. They closed on the wriggling imp and dragged it out, leaving Sunan gasping in agony and falling to his knees.

The Dragon inspected the imp, holding it up to his face. It writhed and shrieked in the highest, most piercing voice imaginable.

"Imps," said the Dragon. "Disgusting." With that, he rubbed his fingers and thumb together in a quick, dismissive motion. With a last thin wail the imp disintegrated in a puff of smoke. Sunan did not doubt that it was dead.

He remained kneeling where he had fallen, one hand pressed to his temple, the other, still closed in a fist, jammed into his eye. Although the Dragon's claws had not touched him in any physical sense, his body reacted as though they had, and his eye throbbed painfully in its socket. Even so, he felt a strange relief to have the imp gone from his head, a relief that far outweighed any pity he might have felt for the creature.

As though some formality were now out of the way, the Dragon turned something that might almost be called a smile down upon Sunan. It was not a smile because his mouth, though shaped like a man's, was full of black teeth, every one resembling a snake's fangs. They were too large for his mouth. Indeed, they should never have been able to fit in a jaw that size, as though this towering form were actually two forms, the one only just containing the other, which ever sought to burst forth from its constraints.

"Now," said the Dragon through his cage-like smile, "tell me, what do you have in your hand?"

Blinking hard, Sunan gazed up into that terrible face. "Nothing," he said, and did not realize for a moment that he lied. The realization came over him as soon as the word was out, however, and he closed his fist still tighter so that his knuckles stood out white.

"Something, I think," said the Dragon. He bent, his narrow frame folding up on itself as he crouched before Sunan. Even when he crouched his head was higher than Sunan's, and Sunan had to crane his neck to meet that burning gaze. "Something quite wonderful, in fact, or why would you hide it so?"

"We haven't time for this," snarled the voice of Juong-Khla. He dropped his hold upon his wife and strode over to stand behind Sunan, his knife raised threateningly. "We haven't time, do you hear? Our hour is fast approaching."

"*Our* hour?" said the Dragon, glancing up disdainfully from beneath his lashless lids. "Oh yes. I'd almost forgotten. We have a bargain, don't we?"

"You may have forgotten, but I have not," said the Tiger Chief. "And we have done everything you asked. We possess the secret of Long Fire."

"You don't possess the Dream Walker."

Juong-Khla tapped Sunan's cheek with the flat of his blade. "This one knows where he is. I would bet my right eye on it."

"Would you? How lovely," said the Dragon. Then he addressed himself to Sunan once more, and the heat of a thousand suns burned in his words when he spoke. "Tell me, boy, what do you have in your hand?"

"I—I don't know anything about any Dream Walker," Sunan managed. He tried to sit back on his heels, to hide his fist in the folds of his robe. "You're asking the wrong man. I've not seen—"

The Dragon sighed like a snake's hiss. Then he reached out and took hold of Sunan by the wrist. His touch was like hot brands, and Sunan screamed and struggled. But the Dragon paid no heed to this, merely turning his fist around and prying his fingers open with one long claw.

And there, revealed in the darkness of that nightmare so that it must gleam more brilliantly than ever, lay the blossom from Hulan's garden.

Juong-Khla gasped at the sight of it. The men of the Tiger Clan forgot their trembling fear of the Dragon and drew closer, eager to see, eager to know. Even Sunan's mother rose up from where she lay, pulling against the ropes and craning her neck to better see that which her son held. They drank in the lights, the luminous beauty, the colors so rich and vivid as only a blossom of this kind could boast. For a moment the darkness of the Hidden Temple fell away. For a moment some of them even believed they heard snatches of a great, a powerful, a dreadful Song.

But the Dragon merely snorted. "I thought as much," he said. "Though how you came to possess such a prize is more than I can guess. But I know what this is, and I know from whence it came. Do you?"

Sunan bowed his head, trying to avoid that burning gaze but seeing it in his head even when he closed his eyes. "It is . . . it is a gift of the heart."

The Dragon threw back his head and barked a laugh that shot a spurt of flame up from his throat. "Who told you that? It may be true, but no heart was given to you along with this gift, so I can only assume you gave yours in exchange. More the fool are you! Though it is a worthy prize, and I do not fully blame you. I can see from your eyes that you have never set foot in the Gardens of Hymlumé, the Lady Moon. *Hulan*, as you call her. So it must have been a Dream Walker, a powerful Dream Walker, who retrieved this lovely . . . and who gave it to you, I would venture to guess."

Sunan thought suddenly of the depths he had glimpsed in the beautiful woman's eyes. Even there in a leper's hut, her eyes had held the glory of the Dara themselves.

He began to tremble.

The Dragon smiled a slow, predatory grin. "So I am right," he said. "And what's more, I now know a secret." He looked up at Juong-Khla, his appalling face full of repugnance. "You mortal fool," he said. "Did you never consider that the Dream Walker might be a woman?"

"A *woman*?" Juong-Khla shook his head. "Magnificent Dark, how can it—?"

But the Dragon wasn't listening. He put out both his hands and placed them in the air just above Sunan's shoulders. He did not touch him, but Sunan felt the heat of those hands much too close, much too painful. He struggled desperately to keep from wincing, to keep from moaning in his terror. To maintain the mask of restraint and poise proper for a Pen-Chan scholar.

"Where is this woman?" said the Dragon. "You have seen her, and recently even by mortal time. She is not far from your thoughts. Where is she, boy?"

There was no good in denial now. Instead Sunan whispered, "I will not tell you."

"Very well," said the Dragon. He unfolded himself, standing tall above Sunan once more. He motioned quickly with one arm to Juong-Khla. "Kill him."

The Tiger Chief hesitated for but a moment. Then he raised his dagger high.

"*No!*"

With a tigress's roar and strength beyond all expectation, Sunan's mother lunged out of the hands of those who would restrain her, flying at her husband as though she would tear him to ribbons with her bare hands. She never reached him, however. As Sunan watched, she rushed three steps and froze, her arms outstretched, her lips drawn back in a snarl. A terrible gasp rattled from her lungs.

She fell, face down. The hilt of Kosul's knife protruded from her back.

For a moment all the worlds centered into one fixed space of time. A quiet, a still space filling the whole of Sunan's head.

And then the fire burst forth.

With a cry that did nothing to express what surged through his heart, Sunan leapt to his feet. He spun in place and struck his father full in the jaw, knocking him flat both with the force of his arm and the surprise of such an unexpected blow. Sunan followed up the blow with a kick in his father's ribcage, and he did not care that his foot struck armor and pain shot up through his leg. It may have been Kosul's knife that dealt the blow, but Sunan's hatred was for Juong-Khla alone.

He fell upon his father, pressing a knee into the great man's sternum, striking his face again and again and again until his hands were stained with both his father's blood and his own. Juong-Khla raised his arms to ward off the blows, but Sunan's rage was too hot, too wild. Had he been stronger, he would have slaughtered his father then and there.

Instead he found himself caught by the back of his robe and lifted like a cat by the scruff, off his father, right off his feet. He was spun around so that he hung nose to nose with the Dragon himself, gazing into the everlasting infernos that served for his eyes.

"There, my little child," the Dragon whispered in a voice that could almost have been a caress were it not so full of poison. "There, you are truly one of mine now, aren't you?"

With those words the Dragon kissed Sunan, searing his forehead with his lips.

The cat, crouched in the shadows under the temple gate, watched all with wide, dilated eyes. He saw the Dragon take Sunan by the face, saw him lower his head, saw his hideous mouth descend. He knew then what was about to take place and breathed a prayer of protection, of grace: "Song Giver, shield us all!"

But there was no shield that anyone could discern. There was only rage.

Then dragon-fire.

Sunan felt the flames inside himself and recognized them as the truest, the deepest, the most vital part of all his being. He opened up his heart and let the hellish blaze in until his soul was consumed and his body had room for nothing else but fire. It spread through every vein, through every limb, bursting up through his neck and into his brain. It was too much to contain, so he opened his mouth and let the fire spill forth into the nightmarish mist and dust.

A man's body cannot hold such heat. So, out of necessity, his body changed. He felt it, but the change seemed so right, so natural, so much more real than the former paltry form he had worn, that he did not care. Indeed he was glad of it. Even though it pained him—as every bone broke and re-knit itself into a new shape—he smiled and let more fire spill from his throat, from his gut.

He thought to himself, *Now I am free!*

And he heard the Dragon say, "Bow to me, child."

He obeyed. He felt the great sweep of his wings, his new, enormous, leathery wings, through which pulses of lava-heat flowed so that he was as luminous as the opal stones of Hymlumé's garden. But his glow, rather than illuminating, seemed to suck light and life from everything around him, feeding off it to increase his own flame, his own magnificence.

He bowed to the Dragon, and then he opened his mouth and spoke through the fangs and the flames: "Father!"

"Yes," said the Dragon. "I am indeed your Father, and a truer Father you never before knew. So speak to me, son. Show me how deeply rooted is your loyalty." The Dragon, still wearing the form of a man, reached out and took Sunan's massive, scale-covered head between his hands, pulling his nose down so that they might gaze into one another's eyes. "Where is the Dream Walker?"

"Lembu Rana," said Sunan. His voice was not his own any more but a deep and smoldering growl. "The Valley of Suffering."

Juong-Khla, though his head rang and his nose flowed with blood from his son's blows, pushed himself up onto his elbows. He stared in horror at the monster that had been his own offspring, and he hated it more than he ever had before. But when he heard what it said, he turned to his men and cried, "Go! Go at once! Take your weapons with you, for she will be guarded!"

Chakra, Kosul, and five others hastened to obey their leader's orders, eager to escape the sight of the Dragon and his new, terrible child. They vanished from the temple, leaving behind the chanting, the fire, the smoke.

The Dragon stood still with his hands clutching Sunan's hideous face, and he smiled and crooned as though to a newborn. "My pretty son! My pretty, darling son!"

Sunan bowed his head, making reverence to the Greater Dark which had birthed him to this new death-in-life. And he did not turn, not even once, to look upon the dead body of his mother.

11

THREE LEPERS BLOCKED THE path down to Lembu Rana, moving slowly, painfully, and taking up the whole space. Sairu, running too fast to stop, careened into them, pushing and pressing her way through, uttering no apologies, not even when one of them fell, for she had not the breath and her instinct was driving her too hard. She did not hear the curses they shouted at her or care that disease-ridden hands struck her as she passed. She proceeded without a thought down into the village and through the maze of huts.

He hasn't killed. He hasn't killed! she told herself over and over, the face of the stranger vivid in her mind. But even if he had not, who could say if someone else had come with him to this vile place? Even now Lady Hariawan might lie bleeding . . .

No. No, no, no! It was not so. She would not *let it be so.*

The child seated outside the hut drew back in fear at the sight of Sairu's slim form bearing down upon her. But Sairu paid no heed, ducking into the hut and staring at what she could not yet believe.

Lady Hariawan sat just as she had left her. Alive. Upright. Hands folded, breathing in gentle, shallow rhythm. Beyond her, almost lost in the shadows, was a knife embedded in the wall. A knife that had never found its mark.

"My mistress!" Sairu gasped, collapsing on her knees before her and taking her hands in her own. Lady Hariawan did not open her eyes, but her brow creased with a thin frown line. "My mistress, are you unhurt? Are you whole?"

"Unhand me, Sairu," said Lady Hariawan in her softest, gentlest voice, her eyes still closed. "You're pinching me."

Sairu obeyed immediately. Her eyes ran over her mistress's body from head to toe, seeking any sign of injury and, if not injury, any sign of change. She discovered nothing. To all appearances, Lady Hariawan was as she had ever been.

And yet could Sairu dare to distrust her own instincts? They had never before betrayed her.

She bent over suddenly, breathing hard. The stitch in her side became unbearable now that her run was complete and her mistress alive. Indeed, she wondered how she could have covered that distance between the Crown of the Moon and this wretched hovel in so little time with scarcely a pause. The adrenaline which had fueled her gave out, and she thought she might collapse into a dead faint. Instead she bowed her head to the ground, pressing it there before Lady Hariawan's crossed legs, like a supplicant before an altar. She gasped for breath, closing her eyes, allowing the dizziness in her head to whirl, overwhelm, then ebb.

While she thus crouched, a small, secret thought whispered in the very back of her brain, behind her anxiety, behind her sense of duty, behind even her instinct.

Jovann is alive.

But she could not think about this. Not now.

A few minutes passed before she could make herself sit up again, and even then her head felt light and a bit unnatural—as though it were someone else's head stuck onto her body—and she would have given much just then to exchange it for another. She pushed slowly upright and found Lady Hariawan studying her with expressionless eyes.

"We must go," Sairu said. "We must leave this place."

"Yes," said Lady Hariawan. "I will leave soon, I believe."

"At once." Sairu got to her feet and began moving about the hut, collecting the few bits of belongings they owned, which were few enough. She left the knife in the wall, untouched. But she caught up an extra cloak for her mistress, a pair of shoes, the lamps, a nearly empty oil jar, and a sack to store them all in. This sack she quickly filled while her head spun with ideas of new hideouts, most of which she discarded the moment they sprang to mind. Was there a safe place in all this nation? In all the world? Was there a single slice of ground where one might lay one's head and sleep protected?

She could think of none. But this did not mean they could remain. What was it Madame Safiya had always taught her? *"Begin to act, and the plan will come. Wait to act, and the plan will wait as well."*

"Now, my mistress," Sairu said, slinging the sack over one shoulder and holding out her free hand to Lady Hariawan, who took it limply. Huffing with exasperation, Sairu caught her by the wrist and, with a tug, pulled her to her feet. "We must get away. Quickly!"

They ducked their heads and stepped from the darkness of the hut into the brilliant afternoon light which seemed to take on a dirty film as it sank into the valley. Sairu stood blinking against the glare, trying to force her eyes to adjust more quickly than they could. Holding Lady Hariawan's arm, she took a single step.

There was a screech like some otherworldly demon dying. The world went dark. Following just upon the heels of the screech came a noise like a thunderclap fallen to earth.

The sound itself seemed to knock Sairu from her feet. But it wasn't over. Six more screeches and six more thunderclaps followed in quick succession, each louder and more earth-shattering than the last. Sairu had the presence of mind to throw herself across her mistress, shielding Lady Hariawan with her own body. Something rained down atop her like hail-stones. Her eyes squeezed shut, she did not realize at first that it was dirt, thrown up into the sky by some tremendous force and falling back to land with thick thuds.

Her ears filled with a dull droning buzz, and she wondered if she had gone deaf. With her eyes closed, all senses were lost to her save for her sense of smell. Seeking to reclaim the breath knocked from her lungs, she gasped and inhaled a stench like rotten eggs that made her stomach heave. All she could do for those long moments was hold her lady, pressing her down into the dirt, praying to any powers who might be listening to protect them from the falling debris.

Then came the screaming.

The return of her hearing, though horrible, encouraged Sairu to open her eyes and see what had become of the world around her. She saw smoke rising from a blackened hole where once had stood a hut. The poor lepers fled from the destruction, and even those on the edges of the village scrambled over one another in their efforts to escape. The stronger assisted the weaker—the old carried by the young, the young supported by the old.

And Sairu heard words in the screams. "A dragon! A dragon has come!"

Sairu did not believe in dragons. But she did believe in distractions. Her quick mind, even in the midst of chaos, drew connections of combined logic and intuition. Someone was coming for her mistress. Not the Crouching Shadows. No, for they would never so boldly announce their presence but would slide and slink through shadows like adders in the night.

These, then, were the Chhayans. The Order of the Greater Dark.

"Come, mistress!" Sairu hissed and hauled both herself and her lady back onto their feet. She pressed a hand into Lady Hariawan's shoulders, causing her to bend double, and, with a presence of mind that she half-hated in that moment of rising panic, she forced her steps into the limping stride of a leper, taking shelter once more in their disguise. Despite the limp, they moved at a great pace so that they were halfway across the village when the next series of explosions tore the air, shook the ground, and sent them sprawling again.

Sairu clamped her hands over her mistress's ears as though she could somehow protect her from the destructive clash of sounds that had already happened. Her own ears rang again, the screams of the lepers fading into a forever distance once more. But this time she pulled herself upright much sooner, staring into the roiling smoke and raining mud, into the mayhem of terror.

She saw two figures approaching. Tall, purposeful figures moving without fear. She could not see their faces through the smoke. She saw only the outlines of their broad shoulders, of their horned helmets, of their enormous, cruelly curving swords.

For a moment she thought she could hide. For a moment she believed they could not know who her mistress was, disguised in her leper's rags.

But Lady Hariawan, as though sensing their approach, sat up suddenly. And the rag covering her head and hair fell away, revealing her face scarred with the hand-shaped burn but still as lovely and serene as Hulan on a midwinter's night. As though she moved in a world just beyond Sairu's reach, she stood, and the ugliness of her surroundings, of her disguise, seemed to melt away around her, unable to shield her beauty or her majesty.

The two Chhayan warriors saw her. They turned toward her, their footsteps crushing the remains of broken huts, dead fires, and the limbs of the nameless fallen, heedless of all they destroyed, fixed as they were upon their purpose.

Another explosion filled the air, and it set something afire in Sairu's spirit. She was up in an instant, her two blades drawn from her sleeves. She could not hear her own voice, but she felt her throat constricting in a vicious cry as she launched herself at the warriors. They, surprised, lifted their blades to defend themselves, but too late. Before they realized what was come upon them, one fell with a slash wound across his face, and the other felt something bite between the grooves of his leather armor, sinking between his ribs.

Sairu, her body braced, leaned up against the warrior, her shoulder pressed into his chest, her face upturned to his. Now she could see him—more than a shadow, more than a formless nemesis. A man, suspended on the end of her knife. A man who had not seen her coming. Horror filled his eyes, and a deathly grayness stained his cheeks. His mouth twisted, and he stared down upon her, seeing perhaps some merciless angel.

With a cry Sairu withdrew her blade. The warrior fell, convulsing. Though her ears remained deaf to all other sounds, she heard him moaning.

And she saw the dead faces of Idrus and the slavers lying at her feet.

"He's not dead." She spoke aloud, though no one heard her in that place. "He's not dead."

A movement drew her eye. Lady Hariawan floated like the ghosts of those mothers who die giving birth, who spend eternity guiding men's souls to the afterlife. She approached the fallen figure of the warrior, standing opposite Sairu. Sairu raised her staring eyes to her mistress's face.

Lady Hariawan—more awake, perhaps, than Sairu had ever before seen her—smiled.

Another screech and a thunderclap, this one close, knocked both of them to the ground beside the warrior. Sairu covered her ears, feeling the hilts of her knives pressing against her temples, and wished an insane wish that the warrior had stuck her on the end of his sword. Before her heart was ready her body moved, forcing her up, forcing her to reach across the fallen man and grab her mistress's hand.

She heard a shriek, a child's voice.

Though she knew she should not—though she knew she should allow no distractions to draw her eye—Sairu looked over her shoulder into the black smoke rising. It cleared just enough, and she saw a hut, its rotted thatch roof set ablaze and billowing black smoke. A little girl, her coverings gone, revealing a disgusting face missing part of its jaw, ran. But she did not run to escape. She ran straight through the door into that burning shack, and Sairu heard her crying, "Granddad! Granddad!"

The roof sagged. The flames roared. It would cave in at any moment.

Sairu was in motion before thoughts reached her brain. She sprang across that distance, which seemed so vast but was probably but a few yards. Like the wind she flew and was through the doorway mere moments after the child. She could not see for the smoke, but her hands caught at something, and she drew it to her. It was the child, still screaming.

The roof above groaned, and burning embers fell like rain upon Sairu, upon the little girl. Nearly tripping over her own feet, Sairu dragged the child back outside into the foul but breathable air. The child kicked and struck her with useless fists, shrieking, "Granddad! Granddad is in there!"

Sairu gazed down into that so-wretched face. Her heart quivered with loathing.

Then, dropping the girl, she turned and sprang back into the shack. She covered her nose and mouth with her arm, and her eyes roved the shadows which were now so dreadfully illuminated even through the smoke. She saw the old man, the old leper.

She saw his body riddled with bits of iron. With nails. He looked up at her, his eyes, staring out through the rags that wrapped his face, filled with pain. Sairu took a lunging step toward him.

The roof groaned a last time and collapsed in a roar of fire and ash.

Something pierced her shoulder. Something sharp that wouldn't budge.

She lay in darkness.

Through the darkness she heard two more thunderclaps. She heard more screams and many voices weeping. But she could not place the sounds or make her brain understand them.

From her head shot a pain that seemed to mass at her shoulder then spread more slowly down her arms, down through her stomach, down to the very soles of her feet. She wished to crawl out of her own skin but could not find the strength to do so. Therefore she lay still, enduring the pain, not through any fortitude of spirit but because she did not know what else to do.

At last she opened her eyes.

Daylight met her gaze, which surprised her. She'd expected more darkness. The air was still thick with dust and smoke, but the sun pierced through and lit upon the rubble around her. Lit upon the face not a foot from hers.

An old face, repulsive to look upon, so deformed as it was by infection. Blood poured from his mouth and nose. He would not die of his leprosy, for a hundred small wounds covered his body, the nails and bits of sharp iron which seemed to have burst upon him, burrowing into his flesh. The ruined walls of the hut lay around and on top of him, and these must have crushed his brittle bones.

But his eyes shone. The pain had gone from them. Though dark clouds gathered across his vision, there was a light deep down inside. He was blind now, so near to death, and yet he seemed to gaze directly into Sairu's soul.

"Even here," he said, his voice reaching out to her across that small space between them. "Even here it finds us. The angel of mercy, mercy . . . mercy . . ."

Sairu stared into the face of a dead man. The most hideous face she had ever seen. And she wept for the Granddad of Lembu Rana. Why, she wondered with a sad, sickening pity, must these people, cursed to suffer so much, now be made to suffer even more?

How long she lay there she could not guess. She slipped from consciousness again, and when she woke, her thoughts were full of driving terror. *My mistress! My mistress!* But Lady Hariawan was gone. Sairu could feel the loss of her in the very air she breathed. She had failed. She had failed!

"No." She growled like an animal and, fighting the pain, struggled to get her arms under her body, struggled to push against the heaviness weighing her down. But she had lost too much blood. Her muscles trembled, useless as a tiny babe's. Tears poured down her face again, this time tears of fury. "No!"

Suddenly she believed one of the Dara come to earth knelt before her in the form of a shining, radiant man. His skin was white and luminous, his hair like morning light, and his eyes were twin suns, so bright, so brilliant, so full of fire as they were.

"Dragon's teeth!" the angel cursed, and she thought she recognized the voice though she could not place it. Weight began to lift from her body, from her shoulder. She breathed more easily. But the relief was short-lived when the sharpness piercing her shoulder suddenly increased. She cried out weakly.

"Sorry! Oh, so sorry, my girl!" the golden voice exclaimed. "I thought I had more time. I thought I would reach you. But we stepped beyond Time, I fear, and it was devilish hard returning. Cursed paths! Cursed lies!"

Sairu lost consciousness.

From the shadow of Tu Domchu other shadows fled. For even here on lowly docks of the city in the depths of an overcast, moonless night, there could be no shadow more dreadful than that which spread behind the tall figure of the assassin standing on the edge of the ocean.

Tu Domchu waited for a lie.

He knew it would be a lie. He knew already that the plan had failed, that the poor fool who was their last hope had not succeeded in killing the girl who was their last dread. He knew that she had been taken. None among his brethren had been able to gather any specific word, any final information that would close the matter once and for all.

But it did not matter. Tu Domchu knew. And young Sunan would come crawling back to him, his dagger sticky with blood from some piglet or rabbit no doubt, and claim to have done as he was told.

Perhaps Tu Domchu would not wait for the lie to be spoken. Perhaps he would put an end to Kasemsan's miserable nephew before he could dishonor his tongue and shame the House of Dok one last time. Perhaps Tu Domchu owed his old friend Kasemsan that much at least.

But no. That was not the way of the Crouching Shadows. They were swift to enact their justice, but they would wait until they knew for certain that it *was* justice. Tu Domchu could not kill for a lie not yet spoken. He must wait. He must hear it first.

So he stood on the docks of the city, watching the moored ships rocking in the waves like so many cradles. They reminded him, very briefly, of cradles in his own past. Cradles which had held his children, children he had not seen for many years, who were probably long since grown and gone on their way in the world. Or dead. They might all be dead.

What did it matter? Soon this whole world would be dead. He had failed. His order had failed. They were doomed, every one of them, to pass through the fire and beyond the gates to the Netherworld. And more fire.

But before then he would kill Sunan for speaking his lie. He would send the wretch before him into the flames and, in that, take a final satisfaction.

A footstep behind him. Tu Domchu recognized it at once, for he never forgot the tread of any man. So the liar approached. Domchu did not turn but remained where he stood, staring out to sea. He wished Hulan were out tonight. He should have liked for her to see what he would do even now in her name. Even though all was lost.

"Tu Domchu," said the voice of Sunan.

Only—and Domchu frowned at this thought—it was not quite his voice anymore. Sunan's voice had always been laced with bitterness, with envy, with anger. Despite all his intelligence, all his learning and his poise, it had only ever been a weak voice.

But the voice Domchu heard behind him was not weak. Indeed, it was stronger by far than any man's voice he had ever before heard.

Domchu turned slowly, disguising his surprise. The light from a near lantern shone upon Sunan as he approached, and Domchu saw that his clothes were burned about the edges, and he smelled of smoke. He drew nearer along the docks, his head bowed, his shoulders hunched, but there was nothing submissive, nothing cowardly about his stance. His pace was firm and quick, and he looked very like a tiger stalking its prey.

"Kasemsan's kin," Domchu said. "Did you kill the Dream Walker?"

"No," said Sunan. He raised his head as he spoke the one word. He was so close now that even with only the lantern for illumination Domchu could see the whites of his eyes.

But suddenly they were no longer white. They burned searing red.

"No, I did not kill the Dream Walker, Tu Domchu," Sunan said, and fire glowed in his mouth. "And I will no longer permit you or any of your kind to command me!"

Those words were the last Tu Domchu ever heard. And even they were swallowed up at the end by a dreadful roar and burst of flame that issued from Sunan's throat, from the furnace in his gut, and overwhelmed Domchu and all that strip of dock. Flames leapt up rigging into sails, and soon bells were sounded, alarms were raised, and men ran like mad demons through the night, which was suddenly bright as day, seeking to douse the fire before it spread to every ship at port.

Come dawn the next day, the ashes of what had once been Tu Domchu had been kicked and crushed under so many feet that they would never be found.

12

SOMEWHERE LOST IN THE DARK, Sairu wandered. She was not afraid, though she wondered if perhaps she should be. It was difficult to fear here, for she could see nothing frightening, and she felt only softness and smelled only dew-tipped grass.

Far away but drawing ever nearer, she heard a sweet, a rich voice singing.

"*Beyond the Final Water falling,*
The Songs of Spheres recalling,
When you hear my voice beyond the darkened veil,
Won't you return to me?"

She liked the voice and turned toward it, pursuing it without haste through the dark.

Then she was coming to.

She found herself lying in soft grass. She knew by the smell, even before she opened her eyes, that she was far from the Valley of Suffering.

The stench of death and, more recently, of rotting eggs was gone. The air was clear in her lungs.

Something rumbled in her ear. She opened one eye and found herself looking into the cat's face, which was wreathed in a smug cat smile.

"Monster," she breathed.

"Good morning," said he.

"Morning?"

"Yes. You've slept the night away. Feeling better?"

She did not answer but sat up instead. She felt pain stab through her shoulder and arm, but it wasn't as sharp as she might have expected. Craning her neck to inspect the wound, she discovered bloodstains on her leper's garments, but these were dried. When she reached around tentatively to explore her shoulder with her fingertips, she discovered that it had been bound up tight by skilled hands.

She glanced sideways at the cat. The cat purred and went on smiling. When she rose unsteadily to her feet, however, he also stood, his tail lashing. "Are you sure you're quite ready to be up and about?"

Sairu did not respond to this but spoke sharply. "Which way to Lembu Rana?"

The cat's ears went back. But he turned and pointed with his pink nose, and she saw that they lay quite near to the road she had followed several times now between the city and the leper village. Moving stiffly at first but finding her strength with each stride, Sairu made her way to the road and followed it back to the valley.

If the Valley of Suffering was a place of horror, the horror had increased tenfold that day. Five craters marked sites where huts had once stood, and destruction spread around each one in a blackened radius. The poor denizens of the valley picked their way through rubble, searching for loved ones, searching for the remains of their meager belongings. The sound of weeping, never a stranger to Lembu Rana, rose up in greater chorus than ever.

It looked as though a dragon had struck.

Sairu picked her way down the path, the cat trailing at her feet. She would not allow herself to think of Lady Hariawan. Not yet. If she did she might panic, and she could not afford to panic. Any chance of finding her mistress depended on Sairu's keeping her head, gathering what information she could, and making the coolest possible decisions.

She saw a large party of lepers moving toward her. None of them paid her any heed, and when she stepped aside, they continued past her to a quiet corner of their valley, a corner where many small mounds lined up side by side, each marked with a small, unmarked but carefully placed stone. Two of the lepers, men who might once have been strong, carried a bundle between them. Sairu knew at once, without being told, that it was the Granddad. She knew by the weeping, the moaning of every man, woman, and child in that procession. He had been related by blood to none and yet, by virtue of his disease, he had become beloved grandfather to all.

She felt tears welling in her own eyes as she watched the sorry procession pass by. She searched for the child she had saved but did not see her. Perhaps she was tucked away in some secret corner, alone with her misery, alone with her loss.

Turning away from the sight, Sairu continued on into the village. But she had made only a few paces before her foot touched something that brought her up short and staring down at that which lay before her.

It was a Chhayan warrior. A man whose face would be etched upon her memory for the rest of her life, following her even unto her deathbed.

A man whose life she had taken.

In the near distance behind her Sairu heard a chant rising up, sustained by many trembling, tear-filled voices. A Kitar burial chant, a prayer of rest and safe travels through the Netherworld. And every voice was united in love.

Feeling the cat's eyes upon her, Sairu knelt beside the dead Chhayan. His eyes were open and staring. He lay at a grotesque angle, one hand still pressed over the gutting wound she had dealt him. Sairu, calm and quiet, with deep respect, heaved him onto his back and placed both his hands across his chest. How cold and stiff he was, this man who had the day before set upon her mistress with such evil intent.

The Kitar prayer filled the air of Lembu Rana. Sairu looked down at the Chhayan, feeling sad, suddenly, that she knew none of the chants or prayers his own people would offer him in her place.

Hardly knowing what she did, she placed her hands on his forehead. She did not know any Chhayan prayers, so she whispered what she did know:

"Go to sleep, go to sleep,
My good boy, go to sleep.

Where did the songbird go?
Beyond the mountains of the sun.
Beyond the gardens of the moon.
Where did the Dara go?
Beyond the Final Water's waves
To sing before the mighty throne.

Go to sleep, go to sleep,
My good boy, go to sleep."

As she sang the lullaby it seemed to her that far away—in a tree above the valley, perhaps—a bird sang, joining its lilting voice with hers. And so she did not make this final benediction for her fallen enemy alone. She and the bird together sang his passing song. And her mind filled suddenly with a vision which she did not doubt was truth: a humble Chhayan mother hunched over in a skin-covered gurta as it rumbled across the plains. In her arms she held a baby—a child who would grow into a vicious wolf of his pack but who, for the moment at least, was her own little pup, her own darling, the delight of her eyes. And she crooned her lullaby to that child there at the beginning of his life.

It seemed to Sairu then that perhaps this man—this stranger she had slain whose name she would never know—would rest. That perhaps his ears, even in death, would discern the final strains of his mother's song. Thus the circle of life and death was made complete.

Her duty done though her heart remained troubled, Sairu rose. She must now return to her true task. Her mistress was in peril, and she did not know how much time she had to find her before . . . what? Some terrible fate she could not imagine would take place! Her eyes, still tear-rimmed, roved hither and yon, searching for some sign. Searching for some clue.

She spotted something unusual lying half-hidden beneath the dead body of the Chhayan.

Sairu knelt and, trying to disturb the fallen as little as possible, removed an arrow from beneath him. She knew that it was one of his. It was like no arrow she had ever before seen. Attached to the shaft was a tube of bamboo tied up at both ends. A small lead stone weighted the arrow near the feathered end, presumably to increase the range.

Sairu broke the bamboo tube in half. Out poured an evil black powder. And bits of sharp iron. And nails.

The cat approached, sniffed the powder, and hissed at the scent. "What is that?"

"Long Fire," Sairu responded at once. For she recalled hearing Princess Safiya speak, only once, on weapons of this kind that had been seen in the hands of Pen-Chan warriors. A hundred years ago a Kitar emperor had sought to expand his empire by plucking the ripe fruit that was the Nua-Pratut nation. But his warriors, marching in armored ranks, had fallen before a weapon of such power, such destructive force as they had never before faced. The Pen-Chans were creative indeed and most unwilling to be taken into the Kitar fold. No one had dared assault their tiny nation since—no one besides raiding Chhayans, of course, who everyone knew would attack anything that moved.

But now the Chhayans wielded the Long Fire.

Across Sairu's soul flashed a thought: *The end of the worlds has come.*

She shook this aside quickly and rose, tucking the remains of the arrow into her robes and scuffing the black powder into the dirt with one foot. This done, she turned to Monster. "Can you find my Lady Hariawan? Do you know where they have taken her?"

He blinked once, considering. Then he said, "I know where they have taken her. But I do not think I could find it again on my own." Hastily he told her all that he had seen—the temple built of sound in the Realm of

Dreams. The wasteland. The Chhayans.

And the Dragon.

When he had finished, Sairu stood a long moment in silence. Then she said, "I do not believe in dragons."

"It's time you started," said the cat.

Sairu did not answer. She drew three deep breaths. Then she said, "You cannot lead me to this place?"

The cat shook his head. "I followed the Chhayans when I last went. And they used a Path I would not use again. Certainly not on my own."

"In that case we must find some other means to reach . . . to reach this Ay-Ibunda." Sairu turned and, gathering her robes in both hands, ignoring the pain in her shoulder as best she could, started back up the path out of the Valley. Her gaze was fixed, her jaw set with a grim purpose as a plan took shape in her mind.

"Where are we going?" the cat demanded, hastening after her. "You have a look about you, and I'm not sure I like it. What is this new scheme you are hatching?"

"We are going to interpret the emperor's dream," said Sairu.

The Anuk Anwar slouched in his throne, eyeing his court from behind a gilt fan. None of those gathered in the vast throne room of Manusbau paid any attention to his glowering. For one thing, his throne—ebony wood inlaid with gold and mother-of-pearl murals depicting Anwar and Hulan—was set on a dais so high above the rest of the room that any man wishing to address his emperor would be obliged to tilt his head back to quite an uncomfortable degree simply to make eye contact.

Besides, the emperor was really necessary only to sign those documents his viziers placed beneath his hand and to generally make it known to the public at large that he still lived. Otherwise, there was little for him to do but sulk.

And sulk he did. Back when he was only a prince (ten years ago now), he could entertain himself either at sport with his brothers or at courting one of his several wives whenever and however he wished. If only, he considered with a melancholy sigh, if only his father had lived longer, postponing his son's ascension to the dubious honor of being the Lordly Sun's chosen favorite! He'd been much better suited to the indulgent life of a prince than he was to the stuffy court rooms and official duties required of Noorhitam's Anuk. It was all too boring and too hateful. He sighed again, bemoaning his glorious lot.

And he thought: *I doubt a prince would be cursed with such dreams as mine.*

The vision had come upon him again just the night before. He had not bothered to summon the Besur, though he had shouted for Bintun and made his poor, devoted slave sing to him until he dozed off. But when Bintun retired at last, the emperor had woken and stared up at his ceiling most of the night. Try as he might, he could make no sense of the visions. And his priests were next to useless.

Somehow he knew he must have the answer to the riddle this evil vision presented. He must have it soon or . . .

No. He would not contemplate the consequences. They were probably nothing more than wild fancies brought on by his sleep-deprived mind anyway.

He shifted on his throne and fluttered his fan more vigorously to cool his face. A polite argument was taking place down below between two of his lords, moderated by three of his viziers. Something to do with the building of a bridge. Or was it a wall? He couldn't remember and wasn't interested in any case. But here he must sit until they had quite run out of thinly veiled insults to hurl with utmost delicacy at each other's faces. It was all so dull.

But then something interesting happened.

One of the two great doors at the end of the throne room opened just a crack. Through it slipped a small person, surprising the emperor, who had expected to see one of his many red-armored guards sidling into the room. This person was no guard and wore no armor. And she certainly did not sidle.

At first he thought she was a child. But she moved with a confidence that was not at all childlike, though neither was it particularly womanly, at least not in the conventional fashion. She was dressed in gold-trimmed red robes tied with a silken sash, and she wore chrysanthemums in her hair.

She crossed the room, drawing the surprised eye of every lord, vizier, servant, slave, ambassador, chancellor, and guardsman crowded into that great chamber. For women did not come here, certainly not dainty ladies unchaperoned by the appropriate army of handmaidens and eunuchs! But she wore the gold-paint cosmetics of a princess on her eyes and lips. And those lips were turned up in the most brilliant smile any man in that room had ever seen. None dared put out a hand to stop her until she was halfway across the hall.

Then the captain of the guard suddenly barked an order and four burly lancers leapt into action, surrounding her with the points of their weapons. She deigned not to look at them, nor did her smile slip from its place. Facing the emperor, she tilted her head quite far back and directed her smile at him.

The Anuk Anwar stood, dropping his fan. "Ah!" he cried, delighted. "I know you, don't I? Aren't you one of mine?"

"I am Masayi Sairu, one of your Golden Daughters, Beloved Anuk," she said in response. And every man in the room gasped at this bold declaration.

"Of course, of course!" said the emperor, and when he beckoned her to approach him the captain of the guard, however unwillingly, was obliged to call back his men. Sairu offered each of them in turn a grin then hastened her steps—still short, ladylike steps, but faster than before—to the emperor's dais and on up to his throne. There she dropped to her knees and knocked her forehead three times against the tiled floor.

"Rise, daughter," said the emperor, looking her up and down as she obeyed. "Hulan's shining crown, how you have grown! But I suppose that is the way of it with children. I do not remember the last time I saw you, but I seem to recall you were a just a bit of a chick then."

"Indeed, Beloved Anuk," said Sairu, "I was small enough to fit upon your knee."

"So small as that? Not that you have any bulk about you now! But if I remember, your mother was diminutive as well. Is she still alive, I wonder?"

"Yes, Beloved Anuk. And well too, I believe."

"Oh, that is good to know." He smiled. It was not often that anyone spoke to him with such open sweetness as this girl did, and he liked her smile. It reminded him of one of his wives, one he had liked particularly well some years before. "And my sister Safiya? How does she fare these days?"

"Quite well indeed," Sairu assured him. "She sends her regards to you, her Ascendant Brother."

"Kind of her, I'm sure." The emperor sat back upon his throne then, grinning in response to her grin. He wondered if he might give her a gift, for she was such a darling, quaint little thing, and he liked the memories she called to mind. "Now tell me, my dear . . . um . . ."

"Masayi Sairu," she supplied.

"Tell me, my dear Sairu, what can I do for you?"

"It is not what you can do for me, Beloved Anuk," said she with another very pretty bow, this time bending at the waist so that her sleeves just brushed the floor. "I beg leave to serve you, for rumor has reached me of your suffering and I would relieve it, if I may."

"My suffering? What do you mean?"

Her eyes flashed behind their gold-painted lids with more intelligence than a man might want to see in a maiden her age. "I have heard rumor that my blessed emperor, favored Son of the Sun, has offered great wealth and still greater honor to the man who can interpret the evil dreams under which he suffers."

The emperor's smile slid from his face, replaced with a not-unkind frown. "Ah," he said, nodding solemnly. "So even you have heard of this, have you? Are you then an interpreter of dreams?"

"I am not," she said. "However, I know of one who may serve you well. One who has walked in the Dream, even unto the Gardens of Hulan. One who is a master of visions beyond anything we have ever seen from our blessed priests in the Crown of the Moon." Something about the way she said "blessed" implied something very different. The emperor snorted. Sairu, however, merely blinked and continued in the same sweet voice. "This man will end the suffering of my emperor and bring him the insight he so craves. And so my heart will be satisfied, knowing my emperor's heart is eased."

"Is that so?" said the emperor, raising his perfectly plucked and charcoaled eyebrows with interest. "And who might this man be?"

"His name is Juong-Khla Jovann, Beloved Anuk."

"A Chhayan?"

"Yes. And a prisoner in the dungeons below the Crown of the Moon."

The Anuk Anwar rubbed his long mustache thoughtfully between his thumb and index finger, studying the girl before him. She met his gaze with such serene candor that he half-felt he should be on his guard. But no. She was one of his Golden Daughters. If he could not trust her, he may as well take his own life then and there!

"Very well," said the emperor. "If you think he can put those fat priests of mine to shame, who am I to deny him the chance?" He turned to his captain of the guard and ordered with a wave of his hand, "Bring this Chhayan prisoner to me at once."

Sairu stood outside the throne-room door, her back against the wall, her hand on her heart. She was breathing hard, for her exhaustion was great and the pain in her shoulder greater still. Sweat beaded her upper lip, but she dared not wipe it away for fear of smearing the carefully applied cosmetics which were, she felt, her one remaining shield against the worlds. She was as tired and worn as the waning light of Anwar through the tall palace windows.

"*Prrrrlt?*" said the cat, appearing from behind a pillar.

She glared and motioned him back into hiding. Cats were not permitted this far into the sanctity of Manusbau. By nature audacious, they tended to gaze upon the emperor at ceremonially unsound moments or to wash impolite bits of themselves while in his presence, so they were forbidden from coming near the favored Son of the Sun at all.

The cat rolled his eyes but slid back behind the pillar so that Sairu could only just see his shadow. She turned her shoulder on him and gazed down the long passage. Hearing footsteps and the clank of armor, she knew that the escort sent for Jovann even now approached.

They came into view, and although she had expected it, it still gave her a start to see the face of a handsome older man, dirty and bedraggled, led by his chains. The bizarre enchantment which seemed to have taken Jovann into its clutches was strong indeed. But it was he; she was certain of this no matter what face he wore.

His expression was that of a man on his way to execution.

Jovann, dragged up from the darkness beneath the Crown of the Moon, expected at any moment to see the gallows rise before him. Even when escorted beyond the temple grounds and into the magnificence of Manusbau, he continued searching for the noose and the hangman. Perhaps they intended to string him up on the outer walls of the palace, as did barbarians of the west. Perhaps they intended to chop off his head in the very presence of the emperor.

At this thought his heart gave a lurch. His face and voice may no longer be his own, but the imp could not touch his heart. And he was no longer afraid. Indeed, his eyes took on a new light, and he began to look ahead with a certain fixation of purpose. Because it was true—they might bring him before the emperor. They may even now be dragging him into the presence of the man he had been brought up to hate above all other men.

He had no weapon. He lacked even his former strength. But he had his Chhayan heart deep down beneath this false exterior. And it beat with a sudden driving force. He was bound, he was helpless, but if they did indeed bring him into the emperor's presence, he would spit his hatred into the evil usurper's face. If he could not do that then he would spit at his feet. They would cut him down immediately, but he would die his father's true son.

Even if his father could no longer recognize him.

So passionate were these beating promises he made with each footfall, and so intent was his gaze upon the corridor and the great door which he knew by its intricacy and glory must lead to the emperor's throne room, that he did not see Sairu until she stood right in front of him and the guards.

The guards drew up short. Jovann, in his weakness, lost his footing and fell. He did not fall far but hung sagging like a scruffed kitten held by a strong hand. His chin sank to his chest, and it was with effort he raised his eyes to look at her. Even then it took several seconds for him to recognize the face of Sairu behind the elegant cosmetics and the elaborate hair tucked with flowers. But her smile could not be disguised.

At the sight of that smile Jovann's heart lurched again, this time with a very different emotion. Sairu! She always knew what to do! She was always there with sharp words, with comfort behind those sharp words. She was confident, she was careful, and she would save him!

Of course this was foolishness. The imp in his mind laughed at these thoughts as they whirled through his brain. She was a handmaiden, a lowly handmaiden standing in the center of the greatest, most heavily guarded palace in all the known world. What could she possibly do?

Besides, another part of his mind whispered, she was Kitar. She too was his enemy.

So Jovann stifled the hope her face first inspired in his heart, and his eyes were full of suspicion as he watched her. She did not look at him but addressed herself to those who held him.

"A word with the prisoner, if you please," she said.

The guards looked grim, and Jovann felt their fingers tighten on his arms. But Sairu's smile grew, and they both shifted uneasily. Then quite suddenly they dropped their hold on their captive, stepped back three paces each, and left him to try to find his footing on his own. He could not and fell to his knees.

Sairu did not bend to him. She found his strange face too unsettling, and her belief in his identity faltered despite herself. So she waited with her hands folded as he slowly recovered his balance and pulled himself upright. But even as she stood there she whispered, and her words fell down to him in quiet secrecy.

"Do not speak to the Anuk," she said. "I do not want them hearing your gibbering and believing you are mad. I will tell him you are mute, and I will pretend to interpret for you."

Jovann gathered his strength and slowly stood. He could not hold himself with the poise of a Chhayan prince anymore—slavery and imprisonment had taken that from him. But he was still a man of the Khla clan. He had not lost the Tiger's spirit. He could not control the muscles on his face, but he could stand tall and still.

Sairu tried to read him but found herself unable to do so. She turned her head to one side, uncomfortable beneath that stern gaze. "If you do as I say," she said, "you will live. The Anuk is capricious, but he does not lie. He has promised great wealth to the man who can interpret his dream. I have told him that you can do so, that you can walk in the Realm of Dreams."

Once more Jovann felt his heart move with hope. But he drove this hope away. He could not accept freedom at such a price. He could not accept wealth and favor from the man he hated more than any man. But he made no attempt to communicate as much to Sairu. For if she knew what he intended, she would surely send him back to the dungeons and he would lose his chance.

So when she asked, "Can you do it? Can you find the emperor's dream?" he did not try to make her understand that he could not control his strange power. That he could not enter the Between unless called from his body through the gate. That he had not walked in the Dream unless led by Lady Hariawan or by the Dara. He did not even try to communicate to her that he would rather hang from his feet until dead than serve her emperor.

He shrugged.

"Then I will invent something," Sairu whispered. "If you cannot dream-walk then pretend to go into a trance, and when you are quite through, I will give your interpretation of the Anuk's vision."

Thus she promised to lie to her emperor. Her stomach sickened inside her, but she stepped back, her chin high, her shoulders square, and motioned the guardsmen to continue on their way. They fell in place beside their prisoner, taking him by the arms once more and leading him on into the emperor's throne room. Sairu followed close behind.

Those who had been gathered earlier remained in the great, gilded chamber, their arguments forgotten in their curiosity to witness the events about to take place. Could a Chhayan slave, a prisoner of the temple, do what the priests could not? Could he truly gain the prizes and rewards so generously offered by the emperor? If satisfied that the interpretation of his dream was true, would the emperor indeed bestow such gifts—a province, a princess, and prestige—upon a slave? It was all too fantastic, like some peculiar circus performance taking place before their very eyes. So they gathered in clusters here and there, their faces solemn, their eyes hooded, and watched as the prisoner was led up the dais stairs and made to kneel before the Anuk Anwar.

The emperor regarded the dirty slave from beneath heavy lids. Then he turned his gaze to Sairu, who achieved the top of the stairs and bowed to him as she had before, that same sweet smile still on her face, though her cheeks were pale behind their paint. "So," said the emperor, "this is the Dream Walker?"

"The interpreter of dreams, yes," said Sairu.

The emperor did not move save for the fingers of his left hand, which picked nervously at the images inlaid in the arm of his throne. He longed so desperately to have an end made to these dark visions, or if not an end, at least an understanding provided. But he was afraid now to hope, particularly in light of the unprepossessing figure kneeling before him. "And is your name Juong-Khla Jovann?" he asked.

For the first time Jovann looked upon the face he had been taught to hate. The old women of the Khla clan had said the emperor possessed three eyes, one of which was always hidden behind his crown. The old men of the Khla clan entertained the younger with bawdy tales of the Anuk's perversions and atrocities. Juong-Khla, kneeling upon the neck of a fallen stag he was about to slay, had always taught his son, "*If ever you find yourself in the presence of Anwar's blasted Son,* this *is what you must do*," and rammed his knife into the stag's throat.

Jovann knew that the emperor would no more understand him when he spoke than his own father had. Yet he would speak. He would spew his hatred, the righteous wrath of all his people. He would declare his name even if no one understood a word he said. And then he would attack.

He opened his mouth. But before words came, gibberish or otherwise, he heard something. Some sound, some song deep in the back of his consciousness, falling from a great distance, from another world entirely. A sound he had sought and longed for all those terrible months traveling down from the Khir Mountains, all those terrible days locked in the darkness beneath the temple. He had not thought he would hear it again, had even wondered if he'd invented it to begin with, as his father always told him.

But now he heard it. And it was more real than anything his eyes could perceive before him.

Won't you follow me, Jovann?

As he heard the words, he suddenly was able to see the emperor before him. Not merely the outward form, which was only a form and could be hated with such ease. Instead he saw the man himself. Not a strong man. Confused, perhaps, and spoiled. A man who might have been quite good, who might have accomplished great things had he not been born a prince, had he not been made an emperor. A man who, though as old as Jovann's father, looked so young upon his throne, young and thin and frustrated behind his cool gaze.

But most of all Jovann saw that the Anuk was a man. Not a Kitar. Not a monster. Not a usurping beast of insatiable evil and appetites. Simply a man.

The song sang into Jovann's heart, freezing up the hatred that lurked there until, while it did not vanish entirely, it could no longer dictate his actions. So, forgetting Sairu's injunction not to speak, forgetting even the imp in his head, Jovann answered the emperor, saying, "I am Juong-Khla Jovann, son of the Tiger."

Sairu, who had just opened her mouth to answer in Jovann's place, stopped, her mouth open, her eyes wide with horror. For she heard nothing but garbled nonsense fall from those strange lips. A heart-stopping moment seemed to turn her to stone from the inside out. She stared from the kneeling stranger to the emperor, waiting for the disgust to cross that noble (some said god-like) face. Waiting for the order to the guards, the command for whipping or death.

Instead the emperor nodded. He continued in the same quiet voice, "And you can do as this child of mine claims? You can find and interpret my dream?"

Again the slave spoke. Sairu heard nothing but jabbering, like some weird, inarticulate beast. But she could see by the expression in the emperor's eyes that he had no difficulty understanding what was being said to him. She realized with a start that the Anuk was unaffected by whatever spell ensorcelled Jovann.

Jovann gloried momentarily in the renewed ability to understand his own voice. It took every ounce of his restraint to keep from making experimental noises, and he almost put a hand up to his face to see if he felt his own features once more. For it seemed to him that, as he knelt under the Anuk's gaze, his face reverted back to what he had always known. He recalled suddenly the words spoken by Lord Dok-Kasemsan before the wretched imp was implanted in his eye.

"Cast over him such shieldings that he will be unrecognizable to all who know him, all who seek him."

But the Anuk neither knew him nor had ever sought him. Unreliable spirit! Jovann felt a grin tugging the side of his mouth. Unreliable fey devil, obeying the letter of its master's law and no more. A strange sympathy for the creature invading his brain filled Jovann. After all, it too was a slave.

He realized that he was grinning and forced his mouth back into proper lines. The Anuk raised one eyebrow, but it was impossible to read feelings upon his solemn face. "I have told Dream Walkers and priests my dream before," the emperor said. "They have gone seeking it in the Realm of Dreams and found nothing. No answer. No solution. Can you do any better?"

Jovann bowed his head. "Great Emperor"—even now he could not bring himself to say *Honored Emperor* as he should, for while he did not hate, neither did he honor this man—"Great Emperor of Noorhitam upon whom Anwar and Hulan have shined with such favor; you and I, we live under the light of the same great Spheres. I swear by their celestial power that I will do all that is within my ability to find and interpret your dream. If it is the will of Anwar."

"If it is the will of Anwar," the emperor echoed in acknowledgement. Then he told Jovann his dream:

"Nightly, the same evil vision visits me in my sleep, disturbing my rest and wellbeing. In this vision I see Hulan, our Lady Moon. She is bound to a great round stone that shines of brilliant gold save that it is stained with blood. Her blood. And she bleeds from a thousand wounds. The blood of the moon runs red, staining the stone, staining the sky, covering all worlds in her pain. She screams. She weeps. I hear her voice in my head. And it is a voice of one alone. Utterly alone."

All those in the room stood transfixed as the emperor spoke. Each of them saw clearly in his mind the picture painted by the Anuk's words. They saw the Lady Moon. They saw her pain. Each felt her loneliness as he stood isolated from his brethren.

Sairu, positioned behind Jovann with her hands folded into her sleeves, gazed over his head into the face of the Anuk. As her emperor's vision filled her mind, she felt a sickening shame at the lie she intended to tell. But what choice had she? She must set Jovann free, for he was the only one she knew who could travel into the Realms Beyond and seek her lost mistress. He was the only one who might be able to find Ay-Ibunda.

The emperor continued, his words and demeanor as calm here in the public hall as, a few nights before in the privacy of his bedchamber, they had been manic. His was not a strong voice, but he spoke with presence.

"As Lady Hulan's blood runs streaming from the sky, it falls upon Manusbau. Upon my own palace. And all turns red with death. I see men approaching the palace walls, and in their arms they carry fire. This fire they hurl with tremendous force, and I see Manusbau crumble to dust beneath those flames." The emperor blinked slowly, otherwise sitting perfectly still upon his throne. "This vision I see, Juong-Khla Jovann, and it pains me to witness it. So tell me, what does it mean? Is it a foretelling of the future? Is there anything to be done that may prevent these dreadful events from taking place? If you can see and discover the answer, I beg that you would tell me."

The whole court waited with bated breath. They waited, leaning toward the throne, their ears strained to catch the Chhayan slave's next words.

But words did not come. The slave knelt before the emperor, silent as stone.

"Insolent dog," growled the captain of the guard, stepping forward with the butt of his lance ready to clout the prisoner on the back of the head. "You will answer the Anuk when—"

"Wait!" Sairu cried, moving swiftly to push aside the lance, much to the captain's disgruntlement. "Wait, don't touch him! I think . . . I think . . ." She approached Jovann, bending to gaze into his face. His eyes, though open, were vacant, staring into some great distance she could not perceive.

Sairu looked round to her emperor and said, "Beloved Anuk, he is gone. He is dream-walking."

13

THE TWO TALL TREES, their branches entwined, appeared before him, and thus the white emptiness was no longer empty, and he had a goal toward which to strive. And strive for it he did. Jovann had longed to see that gate again for what felt like ages though it was only a few months. He had longed to walk again in the shelter of the Grandmother Tree's wide canopy. He heard the silver voice of the wood thrush calling, and he pursued it with all the force of his spirit, which felt so weak here in the nothing, but which was enough.

The trees forming the gate reached out to receive him, and he passed under their twining branches, passed over their twining roots, and stepped through into the clearing and the wide, forever Wood.

The Grandmother Tree stood before him. But Jovann drew a sharp breath at the sight. This tree was ancient and ageless and inalterable. In all the years of Jovann's life, from the time he was a child first called from his body into the Between, he had never known the Grandmother Tree to suffer change. It was always tall, always strong, always thickly grown with greenery.

Now it stood bare. Skeletal branches empty of all growth extended above Jovann's head. And rather than the soft gold light that may or may not have been sunlight which Jovann had always seen falling through the green above, dappling the ground at his feet, there was nothing but heavy darkness. Not the darkness of night, for there were no stars. Not even the darkness of an overcast evening, for there were no clouds.

This was just darkness.

Though he wore no physical body, Jovann felt his heart beating hard. Hastily he assumed a form very like his mortal frame save that this one was uninjured. What a relief to feel his own face again! But the relief was nothing compared to the horror of seeing the Grandmother Tree stripped naked. Jovann approached. He saw that the green grass which had covered this clearing, gently draping over the Grandmother's roots like a blanket, was withered away. There was nothing but dust, dry dust. No sign of fallen leaves to indicate that the Grandmother, for the first time in ages, had experienced a cycle of seasons. Instead Jovann had the distinct impression that the leaves, rather than turning and dropping, had been eaten away.

"Grandmother," Jovann said, bowing to the tree as he always did. This time, rather than feeling that the great tree answered him in a language he did not comprehend, he felt . . . nothing. No answer. No response. "Grandmother, do you sleep?" he asked.

"She does not sleep," said a voice in the branches and shadows above. "Nor is she dead as you fear. She is hiding."

Jovann looked up and saw the wood thrush, its wings folded and its body bent toward him, claws clinging to an empty bough. "Hiding?" Jovann repeated, his voice thin with anxiety. "From what?"

"From the Greater Dark," said the bird. "From the Dream which swiftly approaches."

Jovann looked down at the dust lightly covering the Grandmother's roots. He realized it was very like the dust he had glimpsed when he and Cé Imral had approached the strange temple made of sound. It was the dust of the Dream.

The bird flew on silent wings down from the branch. It seemed suddenly much larger than Jovann had ever realized, with a wingspan more like an eagle's than a songbird's. But when it landed at his feet it was still just a wood thrush.

"You have come to find the dream of the Emperor of Noorhitam," said the bird.

"I—well, no," Jovann hastily replied. "I did not intend to, anyway. He is, you see . . . I can't . . ." He shuddered, for the Darkness above was cold, cold upon his spirit even if it was far from his mortal body. "I cannot aid my father's enemy. *My* enemy."

The bird turned its head to one side so that it could better study Jovann with one bright eye. Or rather, not study him. For it seemed to Jovann, as he stood before that gaze, that the bird did not need to study but already knew him. Instead, as it looked upon him, it felt as though the bird willed Jovann to study himself.

"The emperor's dream," said the songbird, "is but a small part of the whole. The whole dream, Jovann, belongs to your father and to your forefathers."

This Jovann did not understand. He felt like he could if he tried, but he did not wish to. For some reason it frightened him. But he said, "I am not afraid of my father's dream. It is a good dream. It is a dream of justice for my people."

"You have not seen your father's dream," said the songbird.

"I have," Jovann insisted. "You have shown it to me many times since I was a boy. I have seen the vision of my father setting fire to the Kitar emperor's palace. I have seen myself standing before the emperor as he pleaded with me. I—"

He stopped. He realized suddenly what he was saying. "The emperor. He begged me to interpret his dream."

"And thus a part, at least, of the vision has come to pass," said the bird. "But there is much more. And the time has come for you to see the whole of it. To understand the choice laid before you. It is a fearful sight, and you will be much afraid. But I promise you this: As long as you walk with me, the dream itself cannot harm you. Are you ready?"

Suddenly it was not a bird that stood before Jovann. Or not merely a bird. Jovann, staring down at that little space at his feet, realized that his vision, even here, could not encompass what was before him. Vision itself was not enough. Vision could only be confused, telling him one moment that he looked upon a bird, the next that he looked upon a great, golden lion of fierce aspect, possessing enormous claws that could decimate a kingdom in a single swipe. But no, not a lion; a lamb, a white, innocent lamb with all gentleness, all meekness in its gaze. No, not that either. It was neither bird nor lion nor lamb nor an animal of any kind. It was a tree rising up from the dust. A Katuru tree, perhaps, its leaves red like flames—but that was wrong as well. For those leaves weren't merely *like* flames. They *were* flames, brighter and more brilliant than the fire in the depths of the opal stones given Jovann by the Lady Moon. And these flames licked up the whole of the tree, covered it from root to crown, and yet it was not consumed. The trunk and branches were white and pure and shining beneath the fire.

And then all of these shapes, so strange and confused in his mind, gave way. Instead Jovann thought he perceived a form like a Man. More than that he could not say, for his senses failed him. He merely stood dumb and still, waiting for whatever words this Man might speak.

"Walk with me, Jovann," said the Man.

They move through the Dream. But it is not the Dream as Jovann experienced it when he walked hand-in-hand with Lady Hariawan. There he had moved in a strange Other existence beyond Time, but his mortality had followed him and thus traces of Time followed as well. And so the Dream had been empty, formless, changing shape before his vision, but never true.

Here there is no Time. And Jovann walks with the Man, not on the outer crust of the Dream but down into its depths, beneath those formless layers, into the heart of all. Into the truth of all. He is afraid, or he believes himself to be. But he does not realize yet what fear is.

"Where are we?" he asks.

"We walk in the Dream of your forefathers," the Man replies. "And you will see it now in full."

At these words Jovann's vision clears and he finds that he is surrounded. For a moment he believes the Man has abandoned him, but this is not true. The Man is still there, Jovann simply cannot see him. Instead his vision—or perhaps not his vision, for vision is not the same here in the Dream as it is in other worlds—is full of faces he knows.

He sees his father, Juong-Khla, master of the Khla clan. But the face is not only his father's. It is also his grandfather's. And his great-grandfather's. And more. Two hundred years' worth of generations. And this forms the first circle.

Beyond that circle there are more. Jovann recognizes them. He sees the chief of the Poas Clan, men of the Snake. All the chieftains of the Poas going back two hundred years. And they form the second circle. Beyond them, the Seh Clan, men of the Horse. And the Kondao Clan, and the Tonsey Clan, and the Sekiel Clan—all the clans of the Chhayan people, all the chieftains dreaming together an immense dream. Jovann sees them surrounding him. And he feels the pulse of their spirits.

The ceremony begins.

There are no words to describe what Jovann sees. Or if there are, Jovann will not speak them. Terrible are the rites performed, and perhaps they were never seen in the mortal world. But they are true here, and they are present, and they are ongoing. Throughout the generations these same black practices are worked in the hearts of every Chhayan chief. Soon the world surrounding Jovann drips with gore and the chieftains scream in pain. It is the pain of summoning.

The Greater Dark appears in their midst. The Dragon.

"You are abandoned by your god, by your goddess," the Dragon says. "You are abandoned by your celestial parents."

"We are abandoned!" the chieftains cry, their dream roaring throughout years of mortal lives.

"You must have revenge," the Dragon says.

"Revenge! Revenge! We must have revenge!" cry the chieftains, spitting blood from their sliced lips.

"Revenge," says the Dragon, and fire fills his mouth. "Sweet revenge."

Jovann sees, rising up from the circle, rising up like a new sun, a Gold Gong suspended in darkness. Beneath the gong the Chhayan warlords move, carrying fire in their hearts, fire in their eyes. Jovann sees the palace of the Kitar emperor, even as he has seen before. But this time the whole of the vision presents itself before him, not the partial images he has viewed all his life. And he sees that it is not the Long Fire that sets the walls of Manusbau ablaze as he has always believed. It is the searing hatred of his father, of his father's father. It is the hatred of all the Chhayan people.

It is not justice he sees, tearing down those walls, destroying all in red flame. It is fury. It is madness. It is rage-fueled vengeance.

Jovann tears his gaze away from the horror, looking instead up to the Gold Gong. And now he sees what the emperor described to him. He sees Hulan, and he knows it is she, though her form is not one he can fully perceive. She is bound to the gong, and she bleeds from a thousand wounds. He hears her crying out into the Darkness, into the Dream:

"If I but knew my fault!"

The Dragon, on black wings as vast as worlds, is before her. And he laughs in the face of her agony.

No. No, no. It cannot be. This is not the truth Jovann has known and believed. This cannot be the truth of his father's dream! Jovann opens his mouth. He screams.

The Dragon turns.

The Dragon, who is not bound to Time as mortals or even immortals are. The Dragon who exists in the Darkness, in the depths of the Dream.

The Dragon turns and looks straight at Jovann.

"Wait! He is coming awake."

Jovann heard Sairu's voice through the haze of his mind, and he blinked several times in an effort to see her, to find her. He could feel her near to him, though how he knew it was she he could not say. She was close. He reached out for her and felt her catch his hand.

At that touch he opened his eyes. Sairu knelt before him, holding his hand in both of hers. He had never seen her face so anxious. Where was the smile that was her mask? It was gone, ineffective to hide her fear.

"Jovann?" she said, her voice scarcely above a whisper. "Jovann, are you all right?"

He blinked again. Then he looked down at his hand clasped in hers. He saw that smoke was rising from his arm, from his body. He shuddered, and his stomach turned sickeningly at the smell of sulfur on his skin. But he did not burn. Like the Katuru tree, he did not burn.

"Jovann?" Sairu asked again, and he met her gaze.

"I'm all right, little miss," he said, though as he spoke, the words came out all wrong, all twisted. The imp, after all, was still firmly lodged in his brain.

But even the gibberish on his lips eased her fears. Sairu let go his hand and stood. Jovann saw that he was once more in the emperor's throne room.

Sairu addressed herself to the emperor. "Beloved Anuk, he has returned," she said.

The emperor leaned forward on his throne, gripping the inlaid arms with tense hands. His eyes were bright. "And have you seen my dream, Dream Walker?" he asked, and not even his assumed courtly calm could disguise the tremor in his voice. "Did you find it?"

Jovann lifted his face to the emperor's. He had vowed never to kneel before this man, and here he was, upon his knees. Yet it was not he who made the supplication.

"I saw your dream, Great Emperor," Jovann said.

Though Sairu continued to hear only the imp's garbling, the emperor understood him well enough. A light shone in the Anuk's eyes, a desperate, hungry light. "Can you tell me what it means?" he asked.

Thus, even as the songbird had warned him, Jovann found himself faced with a choice. Would he support his father's dream now that he had seen it in its entirety? The images of those bloody rites played through his memory, and the imp in his head screamed and hid its face from them. He saw again the flayed and dripping gore. He saw again the Greater Dark. He saw Hulan bound to the Gold Gong.

He understood what it was his father dreamed. And he knew he could no longer bear to support it.

"Great Emperor, your vision warns of a coming attack upon your own great palace. My people, the Chhayans, are massing together, every clan.

They have acquired the Pen-Chan secret of Long Fire, and even now they make weapons of wicked destruction. I do not know the exact day of their attack, but I believe it will take place very soon. Within days, even. You must prepare yourself. I—" He stopped. His heart moved inside him one last time, and he almost refused to go on, so potent was the training of hatred in his blood.

But he again saw Hulan suspended on that gong. So he continued. "I can help you. I know not all but many of my father's secrets. I will show you the places of weakness where Juong-Khla will attack first. If you will trust me, Anuk Anwar, I will help you to ward off this evil."

The emperor, still leaning forward, drank up Jovann's words like a thirsty man lying in a stream bed. When Jovann had finished his say, the emperor turned to Sairu, who had understood not a word. But the emperor did not know this, and he asked, "Is what he says true?"

Disconcerted, uncertain how to answer, Sairu said nothing.

"Is it true?" the emperor repeated. "Have the Chhayans indeed gained the Pen-Chan secret of Long Fire?"

"Yes!" Sairu gasped then shook her head and answered more calmly, though her gaze flickered to Jovann and back. "Yes, I have seen their weapons for myself and the destruction they can work. I have seen the Chhayans armed with flame."

The emperor nodded. Then he said, "Do you trust this man, Masayi Sairu? Do you believe he will do as he says? Do you believe he will help us ward off an attack by his own people?"

Sairu glanced again at Jovann. Only briefly. She could not look him full in the face. She dared not for fear of what she might see. For once in her life she struggled for words, and so many conflicting thoughts raced through her head, she scarcely knew herself anymore. If she looked at Jovann, even wearing this current strange form of his, she knew how she would answer. But could she bear to answer any other way? She had not heard what he said, she had not understood what he told the emperor. How could she know the answer to her emperor's question?

Then, like a sudden stilling of the wind among the trees after a storm, her heart calmed. She felt a peaceful assurance that was beyond reason. It did not matter. She did not need to know everything in order to know what she believed.

"Beloved Anuk," she said, "I trust this man. He will help us. I trust him with my life. More than that, I trust him with yours."

"Very well," said the emperor. He stood then for the first time since that strange interlude had begun. His rich robes settled in heavy folds about him, and his crowned head was held high and proud. He raised his arms, and every eye in the throne room, every courtier gathered, turned to him and waited to learn his will.

"I have heard my dream interpreted, and so we may, by the strength of this good man's power, avoid disaster for our nation. Thus I command that the gifts I promised be bestowed upon Juong-Khla Jovann. I declare him now my trusted vizier. He will be given a place in Manusbau close to my side, and he will advise me both in the coming days of danger and in time following. The province of Ipoa is his by right, and it will belong to his children and his children's children, all the seed born of him and my daughter. When this danger we now face is past, Juong-Khla Jovann will enter the Crown of the Moon and, before my eyes and the eyes of Hulan herself, he will wed a princess of Noorhitam. He will be wed to . . ."

Here the emperor paused. A slight frown formed on his brow. Then he looked at his Golden Daughter standing beside him with her hands folded. He smiled, pleased with his sudden thought. "He will be wed to my daughter, Princess Masayi Sairu."

"What?" Jovann gasped, forgetting himself for a moment. Though she could not understand him, he turned to Sairu, his eyes wide. "*Princess?*"

The emperor approached him, extending both his hands. Jovann had no choice. He placed his hands into the Anuk's and allowed himself to be assisted to his feet. The emperor was smiling. "You have pleased me. Sairu's mother was always one of my favorites. I am glad that you should have Sairu. Besides, many of my warlords will not take kindly to a Chhayan vizier. Sairu is a Golden Daughter, and she will keep you safe."

"I—Great Emperor—*Honored* Emperor . . ."

But before Jovann could think of anything more to say, the emperor turned to Sairu and held out a hand for her. She came forward obediently, and her masking smile was back in place, though her face was still pale. "It will be as I say," said the emperor, drawing Sairu toward him and placing her hand in Jovann's, "as soon as this danger is past. Now, Juong-Khla Jovann, I would have you kiss my daughter and seal the agreement."

Here that grin of Sairu's faltered. She kept it in place, but only with an effort. She had never been kissed before. Well, except by her dogs, who were a bit sloppy and didn't really count. She had never honestly given much thought to being kissed—not she, not a Golden Daughter. And she'd certainly never expected to be kissed by a man whom she knew quite well but whose face was completely strange to her!

So Jovann gazed down at the princess whom he had believed nothing more than a handmaiden and saw little encouragement in her eyes. He glanced uneasily at the emperor. But the emperor only nodded and motioned with one hand for Jovann to get on with things. An imperial command is an imperial command, after all.

Jovann bent. He gently took Sairu by the shoulders as though to hold her steady. Her eyes remained wide open as he planted a hasty kiss on her mouth.

The imp in his brain shrieked. Then, with a burst, it flew out of his eye. He cried out, for it hurt just as it had hurt when the creature entered. He took a step back, pressing his hand over his eye, and cried, "Anwar's bruising elbow!"

"Oh come, man," said the emperor, folding his arms across his narrow chest. "It couldn't be *that* bad."

Sairu blushed brilliant red and strove to hide it behind a calm exterior that could fool no one. Then she gasped, forgetting her embarrassment, forgetting her dignity, forgetting even the watchful, curious eyes of all the gathered courtiers. "Jovann!"

For indeed it was he. Gone was the face of the stranger, the enchanted mask. It was *his* face she saw blinking and wincing still as he lowered his hand.

And the cat, hiding in the shadows behind the emperor's throne, grinned to himself. "True love's first kiss," he whispered with a purr. "Works like a charm every time."

14

A SENSATION OF IMPENDING DOOM stopped Overseer Rangsun in his tracks so that the educator pacing soberly behind ran into him. The educator apologized; for although it wasn't his fault, it was safer to assume the fault onto himself than to leave any room for implication that the overseer might have made a mistake. This was a basic rule of hierarchy in the Suthinnakor Center of Learning.

Overseer Rangsun made no response. He stood completely still. Not a muscle on his face moved even when the educator noticed that his stumbling footsteps had torn a gash in the overseer's trailing robe and redoubled his apologies. The educator, who was no fool, recognized his superior's silence as something far more profound than mere irritation. With a final murmured request for forgiveness, the educator bowed and slipped back the way he had come, leaving the overseer alone in the passage.

The overseer carefully collected his thoughts, one at a time, and lined them up in neat rows within his mind. He had lived too long and studied too hard to let a moment such as this unnerve him. The sensation of doom was real, but he was no peasant, ready to panic and scream at the very idea of losing a life hardly worth living in the first place. No indeed; the overseer knew he had made his life worth every second. He was a man superior to other men, and he served a purpose superior to other purposes. Secure in this knowledge, he could not panic. He could never panic.

And yet the feeling of doom shrouded him, clinging to his spirit like the membrane of a bat's wing wrapped tightly around his body. Finding his limbs capable of movement again, he stepped to a window and slid it open to look down into Suthinnakor City. He had no love for this city. He had no love for anything anymore, not even for his great purpose; drive had long since supplanted love in his heart. Still, he felt a sudden inexplicable pain as he realized it was the last time he would gaze upon this view.

"The city will burn," he whispered. Then he turned and faced the man standing in the shadows behind him. "The worlds will burn. Is that what you wish?"

"I wish nothing," said the voice of he who had been Sunan. Two lights flared in the darkness; red eyes flickering with deep fire. "I wish nothing save never to be enslaved again."

"And you think this alliance you have made will protect you from slavery?" Rangsun replied. "You think you are not even now bound?"

"I am stronger than I have ever been." The young dragon stepped forward into the sunlight from the window, which seemed to flee from him, leaving shadows upon his face. The light in his eyes revealed strangely the contours of his face, his cheekbones, his nose. And although these were like those he had worn as a man, they were now false. This was no longer his true face. More fire flickered about his lips when he spoke. "You should have trusted me, Rangsun. You should have brought me into your fold and given me the power I deserved. You should never have made a toy of me."

But Overseer Rangsun shook his head. "You are unworthy to serve Hulan. And now you will take part in her destruction."

"I will take part in nothing I do not wish," said Sunan. "In this moment, Overseer, what I wish is your death. Is your soul prepared?"

"I have always been prepared for death," said Rangsun.

The young dragon opened wide his mouth. Like a snake's, unhinged, his jaw dropped grotesquely to his chest, and fire mounted from his belly, glowing white hot in his throat.

Flame burst forth. But it struck the wall to one side of the overseer, and the young dragon staggered under the force of a swinging sword. Blood, black as ink, darkened the bright blade of the Mask, who positioned himself between the overseer and the monster. Sunan landed hard upon his side but was up in an instant, one arm hanging limp, its sleeve stained with blood. He snarled at the Mask, and his eyes were lost in fire.

"I intended to find you last of all," he said. "But no matter. I can kill you now just as well."

The Mask said nothing. But when the dragon flamed he avoided the attack, darting under the stream of fire. His body lengthened, one foot planted, the other driving forward, propelling his arm and blade in a long thrust that drove into the heart of the dragon. The sword point protruded between the creature's shoulders, and the hilt, still clutched in the Mask's strong grip, rammed into his breastbone.

He who had been Sunan gasped and put up both hands, taking hold of the Mask's hand wrapped around the sword hilt. On his finger flashed something bright, and it drew the Mask's eye however briefly. And so, before he died, the Mask saw a glimpse of that for which he had longed all his life. He saw a stone blossom of Hulan's Garden fixed to a ring on the monster's hand. It was like seeing the tears of an angel caught in the cupped palm of a demon. The Mask shuddered at the sight.

The dragon grinned, bright fangs flashing in his man-shaped mouth. "You forgot something in your bloodlust, mortal man," he said, his voice alight with the furnace inside. "You forgot that I no longer possess a heart."

With that, the monster drew the sword back out of his chest. And although his blood darkened the blade, he did not die. Indeed his fire mounted, and the Mask fell away from the heat of his body.

Overseer Rangsun observed with stoic resignation the change come over the form of the young man who had, so short a time ago, stood at the gates of the Center of Learning, full of promise, full of hope, full of soiled Chhayan blood. Even as he watched skin give way to armor scales and massive wings bursting from shoulder blades, the overseer gazed into the future. He saw the heavens set ablaze and he saw the stars falling as balls of flame, their angelic song destroyed.

Then he died. And all Suthinnakor City looked up in horror to see the rising pillar of flame that had once been the central tower of the Center of Learning. None saw the shadow of the dragon mounting the hot air, swirling up and around with the billowing smoke, high into the blackened night sky then away into worlds unseen.

The raven perched in the darkness high above Lady Hariawan's head and watched her. It was very good at watching things, content to sit for ages unmoving, its gaze fixed upon potential prey. In this it was far more like a snake than a bird.

Lady Hariawan, if she was aware of the raven's nearness, gave no indication. She sat as still as the raven itself, her eyes closed, her hands folded. The chamber in which they kept her was large, but the darkness was so heavy as to feel smothering. So she sat with her head bowed as though in prayer and did not struggle, scarcely even breathed. She merely existed and considered this in itself a triumph.

The raven watched her, possibly for hours. But in this place Time did not matter or move according to mortal understanding, so it may indeed have been mere minutes, even moments. Its bright red eyes were the only lights to be found in that gloom, but it needed no light in order to perceive the girl below. It saw her by the pulse of her heart, by the heat, however faint, emanating from her body, by the flow of blood in her veins.

A gray tongue licked out from the sharp beak, forked and tasting the air. Then, though there had been no change, nor even a sound of summoning, the raven took flight. It leapt from its perch and passed in an instant out of that chamber, which was really only an imagined chamber dreamed up by mortal minds and their ongoing chants. No barrier at all to such a being. It spread its wings, pinions tearing away all flimsy veils of reality as it flew down, down, down into the darker depths of the Dream.

Down to the bloodied throne upon which the Dragon sat and waited.

Surrounding the throne, which was upraised on a high black dais, were many dragons, his children. They moved with an intensity that belied their aimlessness, pacing back and forth across the great cavern in which they dwelt. Most of them wore forms similar to those of men and women, thin coverings over the true fire contained within. Each burned with hatred and loathing, though whether they hated and loathed themselves, or their Dark Father, or enemies long since killed in their poisonous flames, none could say.

The Dragon watched them. They gave him a sort of pleasure, these strange offspring of his, if pleasure was even the right word. Perhaps *satisfaction* would be more accurate.

But they weren't enough.

The flight of the raven drew his gaze. The Dragon raised his burning eyes from contemplation of his nearest children, piercing the darkness overhead to fix upon his approaching servant. He raised his arm, providing a perch around which the raven latched its black claws.

The raven spoke. It was not a voice or a language that could be understood by mortal men. The sound was too raucous, too malevolent. But the Dragon understood it well.

"I agree," he said in response. "In fact I am almost certain of it."

Even as he spoke he recalled the face of one who had penetrated deep into the Chhayans' dream. A face very like that of his newly created child. Very like . . . and yet unlike.

The Dragon rose. All those dragons near his throne hissed, snarled, and cringed away from him, hiding themselves from his gaze. But he paid them no heed. Instead, with two great strides he stepped out of the Netherworld, out of the deep Dream, across his own dark paths through the Between.

The mortal world was always near. Too near. He hated it, hated the time-bound smallness of it. Hated how strangely vulnerable he felt each time he manifested within its constrictions.

But those who dwelt within this world were so susceptible to his words, to his poisons. They really were impossible to resist.

And so he stepped into the Near World of mortals and stood upon the mountainside, gazing down upon Daramuti temple. The raven on his arm stretched its wings and coughed a delighted cry, craning its neck around to look with interest upon the dovecote and its occupants. The Dragon did not turn. He merely stood, watching and waiting.

Brother Tenuk felt his presence. In the midst of his false prayers he felt the shadow descend upon his spirit. He finished droning the familiar lines, echoed by the priests and acolytes kneeling behind him. Then with great pain he got to his feet, turned, and offered the evening's blessings on those gathered, unconsciously making the signs with his hand even as his gaze wandered to the window.

Before he knew it, all was over and his brethren had gone about their way, pursuing the day's final tasks. And Brother Tenuk was climbing, for what he suspected would be the last time, to his beloved dovecote.

To the presence of the Greater Dark.

"Tenuk, my brother," the Dragon said even as his mortal servant approached. "I have a question for you, and you would do well not to speak the lie which even now forms upon your lips, for I know it and its falseness too well."

"Master," said Tenuk, sinking to his knees. His body was more wilted and bent than ever, his bald head covered in sores, his eyes nearly vanished behind wrinkles and sagging skin. He bowed down and knocked his forehead against the paving stones. "Speak your question, and I will answer as best I may."

"Did you send a woman to Lunthea Maly?" the Dragon asked. "Did you send a woman Dream Walker?"

"No," said Tenuk without straightening from his abject position. "I sent a man."

"You lie," said the Dragon. "The Dream Walker is a woman."

Tenuk hesitated. There flashed across his memory the lovely face of Lady Hariawan. A moment later it was replaced with the hideous recollection of his dove, the head bitten off. He shuddered. "It may be as you say, Master." He spoke into the stones beneath his mouth. "But the Dream Walker I sent was a man."

"A Chhayan?"

Tenuk nodded.

That was when he heard the Dragon laugh. The sound could not fit into mortal senses but sank through his heart down into the cowering, shriveled remnants of his soul. He felt his whole body begin to quake with dread far greater than anything he had yet known in all the sorry years of his service to the Greater Dark.

It was too much. Even as the Dragon stood above him, laughing, Brother Tenuk gasped and fell to one side.

A darkness deeper than night passed over him. Then he was alone upon the mountainside save for the doves in the cote. These did not stir for some little while until, quite certain the danger was gone, they emerged one by one and flitted down to perch upon the body of the man who had loved them. They pecked at his skin, at his ears, his lips, his hands. They covered him like a shroud.

Then as one mass they rose up in flight, a white cloud vanishing into the darkness, never to be seen again by a living soul in Daramuti. And so Brother Tenuk died alone.

"The son!"

With a burst of flame the Dragon appeared on the doorstep of Ay-Ibunda, the raven still clutching his arm. All those within the temple turned their gazes up to the door. They did not cease their chanting. If they had, they and all their work would have slipped away. But some trembled, and the chant wavered for a moment. The solidity of Ay-Ibunda shivered.

The Dragon stood where he had appeared, wrapped deep in his cloak. He ran his tongue over his enormous teeth, and his eyes flashed with fury. Then suddenly he turned and cried out through the Dream, "Come to me, my child!"

Across the worlds, across the realms, his fiery voice carried. The dragon who had once been Sunan heard him even as he spiraled up above the destruction of the Center of Learning, his own handiwork. He did not hesitate even to glory in the deaths of his enemies. At the command of his new Dark Father he turned and slipped into the realms beyond the mortal world, passing into the Between as easily as a man might dive into a scum-layered lake. Within moments he appeared in the churning sky of the Dream, his dragon form dreadful to behold. Those chanters who raised their faces at his approach put up their hands, covered their eyes, and continued chanting even as shudders shook their bodies and their souls.

The young dragon swooped down and alighted in the courtyard at the feet of his Dark Father. Near to hand, the Gold Gong suspended between its posts shivered and hummed in the wind of beating wings. The young dragon folded his wings against his body and bowed. "What is your bidding, my Father?" he asked.

"Have you avenged yourself, my child?" the Dragon asked. "Have you slain those who would imprison you and brought their citadel to ruin?"

"I have. Their tower burns even now, the smoke rising in offering to you."

"That is good," said the Dragon. "Now I have one more gift for you, my favored one. Are you ready to receive it?"

A greedy light shone in the young dragon's eyes, and he lifted his head, a more elegant head than that of his creator. A crest of horns adorned his crown, and he was mighty, red, and magnificent. He grinned, showing sharp rows of teeth as yet un-blackened by the smoke spilling from his gut. "I am ready, Father!" he declared.

The Dragon turned from him and addressed the raven on his arm. "Go," he said. "Bring me Juong-Khla."

The raven spread its wings wide and flew through the gate, between the uncarved pillar and the pillar carved like a sinuous dragon, out into the formless Dream. Slipping easily from the Dream into the dark paths across the void into the mortal world, it emerged in the wide open skies of Chhayan territory, high above the wind-cooled plains. It soared on air currents, tilting this way and that as its red eyes roved, searching. It spotted at last a cluster of gurtas arranged in a protective circle around campfires.

Around these fires crouched men of war. Some of these affixed tubes of bamboo to long, sturdy arrows, setting the tubes with long rice-paper fuses trimmed to a specified length. Some of the men melted bits of metal purloined in raids long past, melted and formed them into tiny sharp pellets. These too went into the bamboo tubes.

And black powder was ground, mixed, and poured into the tubes last of all.

Juong-Khla stood overseeing the labor of his clan. He felt rather than saw the shadow of the raven approaching and turned in time to see it alight upon the ground just within the circle of firelight. Something about the look in its reptilian eye gave him pause, and his hand tightened, if only for a moment, around the knife at his belt.

Then he approached the bird and inclined his head in respectful greeting. "Does the Greater Dark summon me?" he asked.

The raven rasped a response that was a clear enough answer.

Juong-Khla's face wore the perpetual frown of a chieftain long steeped in the cares, the woes, the grievances of his people. His was not a face to easily betray his emotions, and it betrayed none now. He made no protest, nor did he call any orders to his men. When the bird took flight he followed it out of the firelight, into the darkness, and on to the dire Path that opened before him. He pursued the raven into the Realm of the Dream.

The raven led him swiftly across the leagues, back to Ay-Ibunda's gates. They passed together, one after the other, under the arch and into the mist-filled courtyard, through the chanting phantoms, who dared not look up at the Khla's passing.

The Dragon stood on the step before the temple door, and Juong-Khla's son—that monstrous half-blood spawn of his stolen wife—crouched at the Dragon's feet, once more wearing the form of a man. But the dragon inside could not be hidden, and smoke curled from his nostrils.

Juong-Khla ignored his son but made solemn reverence at the feet of the Greater Dark, his master. "How may I serve you?" he asked.

The raven circled round the Dragon's head then flew off to perch on a pillar nearby, watching all with a certain greedy eagerness. The Dragon opened his mouth but did not speak for a long moment. Fire crept to his lips and spilled over his chin like liquid, like molten lava.

Then he said, "Your son is a Dream Walker."

Juong-Khla did not respond. His gaze flickered momentarily to the young dragon who had once been Sunan.

"Not him," said the Greater Dark. "Were he possessed of such power, you would have told me long ago, for you bear no love in your heart for this one." With those words, the Dragon kicked the young dragon as he might kick an irritating dog. The young dragon snarled but backed away and made no other form of protest. "No," the Dragon continued. "Your other son. The one you have never brought to me. The one you told me was not ready, was not yet capable of understanding the dark means by which we attain our dark ends. When were you going to tell me, Tiger Man, that he was a Dream Walker more powerful than the little limping maid we have imprisoned inside?"

Juong-Khla did not so much as blink, though he must have known in that moment that his end was come. He said only, "I did not know of his power. I still know nothing. He is a boy. He has not yet spilled a man's blood."

"You suspected," said the Dragon, reading this truth in the chieftain's voice. "You suspected all along what he could do. You suspected that he did not need my aid to move through this realm of mine, that he walked in it of his own power. A true Dream Walker of old! You suspected that he would be able to lead us to the Gate, and yet you did not tell me. You tried to hide him from me."

"Yes," said Juong-Khla. "Yes, I did. For I know what you intend to do to the girl we have brought you. I would not see the same done to my son."

The Dragon strode down the steps, his black cloak billowing on the rising heat emanating from his body, framing it like two massive wings. The Greater Dark loomed above the warrior, extending his head on the end of an over-long neck to stare straight into Juong-Khla's eyes.

"I will have them both," the Dragon said. The fire of his words burned Juong-Khla's skin. Welts rose up across his forehead, and sweat rolled down his brow. "I will have them both, your son and the girl, and I will make them suffer for the sake of this cause. You have given up everything for your vengeance, Juong-Khla. Now you have given up your son. Now you have given up your life."

The young dragon seated on the stair recoiled, his eyes wide open and almost human again as they stared in disbelief. He saw the body of Juong-Khla teeter like a tree struck by the final ax blow. Then the warrior fell.

The young dragon saw the bloodied stump of Juong-Khla's neck.

The Dragon turned about, and his form was nothing like a man's anymore. It was huge, ten times the size of his small offspring, wrapped in armor scales, each rimmed with searing red heat that pulsed like blood. And his cloak was indeed become wings that smote the air and drove away the mist and the clouds, leaving behind only the darkness and the ongoing chant. The roar of his voice drowned out all other sound, and once more the chanters stumbled, and the reality, the very existence of Ay-Ibunda wavered.

The creature who had been Sunan fell on his face, groveling and terrified. The Dragon laughed, his black, bloodied teeth flashing. "I have given you your final great gift, my sweet, my child," he said. "I name you Sunan-Khla, chief of the Khla clan. And you will lead your mortal clansmen into battle, into victory, even as the Moon above bleeds her last!"

15

"THAT IS IMPOSSIBLE," said the Besur.

His voice, powerful enough to command the whole of a reverberating temple hall full of chanting priests and noisy supplicants, was overwhelming here in the imperial council chamber. He did not even have to raise it, for it boomed on a deep register that filled the stomachs of all those seated in the council circle.

Sairu, who knelt outside the circle, did not look at the Besur when he made this statement. Instead her gaze traveled around the room, studying the reactions in other faces. The emperor reclined easily upon a well-cushioned chair, the look of boredom on his face not quite masking his tension. Princess Safiya, who had been summoned from the Masayi to attend her Ascendant Brother, revealed nothing of her thoughts, for her eyes were downcast. She did not need to look at faces, as Sairu did, to read them. She knew what each man in that room thought already, for she knew each man in that room better than he knew himself. She sat in a quiet place across from the emperor and collected information no man in the room realized he gave.

And the warlords of Noorhitam from across various provinces gathered round, their hands clenched into fists, their jaws set. They scowled, every one of them, but in agreement with the Besur, and cast evil glances toward Jovann. Jovann, the emperor's new vizier. A Chhayan at the emperor's right hand.

"Impossible," said the Besur again. "Beloved Anuk, you cannot listen to what this man says! He is the son of your enemy, and he is trying to lead you astray."

The emperor blinked mildly at his high priest, though his voice trembled a little when he responded. "Honored Besur, have I or have I not declared this man to be my friend and my advisor?"

The Besur growled but inclined his head. "You have, Imperial Glory."

"And am I not, according to your own declaration, possessed of the Lordly Sun's own wisdom bestowed upon me at the hour of my ascension to the throne?"

Now was not the time to quibble over the subtle difference between tradition and truth. The Besur's jaw worked angrily, but he answered, "You are, blessed Son of the Sun."

"Then I'll thank you not to contradict my judgments or the judgments of those to whom I look for guidance."

The Besur, thus chastened, turned red with fury that could have no vent. Ignoring this, the emperor turned from him, fixed his attention once more upon Jovann, and asked, "Would you kindly repeat what you have just said? It did strike me as far-fetched, though I would never go so far as to say *impossible,* like some in this room. However, I would be gratified if you would elucidate."

"Great Emperor," Jovann said, making a Chhayan sign of respect with one hand, "I would not deceive you. I speak the truth when I say that my people have discovered a way to breach the dungeons beneath your great temple. They use a method not unlike dream-walking. They pass through the Dream, not in spirit but in their physical bodies, and step into this world again far from where they began. I have myself seen a rent in the fabric of our world open, and I have seen my own father and two of his men cross from the Formless into your dungeons."

He went on to explain, but his words were soon drowned out by the protests of the emperor's warlords. Did this man—this Chhayan dog-boy—truly counsel the Emperor of Noorhitam to set up a defense in the *temple dungeons?* In the face of oncoming siege and the threat of fire weapons, were they to waste good warriors guarding a portal that may or may not exist? And who was to say a siege was coming, anyway? They had only this dog-boy's interpretation of the emperor's dream, and that was hardly a foundation upon which to build this tower of speculation!

So the arguments rose along with the angry voices. These men who would maintain a preternatural calm in the public setting of the throne room had no qualms about reverting to furious arguments and even threats here in the privacy of the council. The Besur, already thoroughly chastened by his emperor, did not risk joining in, but he shot triumphant looks the Anuk's way as each new warlord added his voice and his argument. Jovann tried to defend himself, but his words were so drowned out that he at last gave up and sat back, shaking his head, his face very pale. The shadow of the hangman's noose fell once more across his spirit. The emperor observed his warlords through half-closed eyes, and Princess Safiya sat the while, her face serene, glancing neither to her right nor to her left.

A sudden sharp pain in her leg drew Sairu's attention. She scowled at the cat, who had somehow managed to slip into the council room before the door was shut and to hide in the shadows behind Sairu where she knelt. His claws caught in the fabric of her robe as he pawed to get her attention. "What?" Sairu mouthed, not bothering to speak aloud.

The cat put his paws up on her shoulder and spoke into her ear, his whiskers tickling. "I saw it," he told Sairu. "I saw the portal from the Between of which Jovann speaks. He is telling the truth."

"Of course he is," Sairu said, her voice lost in the din, though the cat's quick ears caught it. Despite her confident words, she felt a certain relief in her heart. Not that she had truly doubted Jovann, but . . .

"You must speak up," said the cat. "You must vouch for him."

Sairu frowned and looked once more round at the emperor's—her father's—warlords. She was not a young woman to be easily intimidated. But these men were possessed of violent passions, usually restrained behind veneers of civility but now given loose rein. All had left their weapons outside, according to protocol, but she saw hands creeping toward empty sheaths and knew that lack of weapons would not prevent violence. This knowledge would not have given her so much as a pause a short time ago.

But that was before she'd lost her mistress.

Sairu tried to smile and found that she could not. So she assumed a mask that mimicked Princess Safiya's in every studied particular. Her brow was as smooth as Hulan's light upon stone. Her mouth neither smiled nor frowned but fell into the painted lines she had herself applied earlier that evening. With this as her only shield, she stood. The warlords were too caught up in their fury to notice her until she had already stepped into their midst and stood before the emperor. She went down on her knees before him, bowing and knocking her forehead to the floor. "Beloved Anuk," she said.

"Beloved daughter," said the emperor. "What reason have you to speak into this tumult of bloodlust?"

"You would do wise to heed the counsel of this man, Juong-Khla Jovann," said Sairu, sitting up and meeting the emperor's gaze.

"Your betrothed?"

"Yes." She blinked once. "My betrothed. He, as you know, has traveled into realms these worthy lords of yours have not. He understands as most mortals are incapable of understanding that our world is in fact only one part of many worlds, that our time is only one part of many times. Thus he can discern weakness where these honored warriors cannot. I beg my beloved emperor to listen to this man, your chosen vizier, and set up the defenses in the dungeons of the Crown of the Moon. Let these warlords man the walls of Manusbau, preparing as they like for siege. But send the Golden Daughters beneath the temple, for we do not fear the dark."

Every one of the warlords stood with his mouth open in a twisted snarl at the implication of her final words. But while any one of them would have gone for his neighbor's throat for voicing such accusations of cowardice, none dared approach the little Golden Daughter sitting so sweetly before her imperial father. Jovann, observing, felt the dread of the warlords around him, felt their anger and their shame, and wondered again that he had believed this princess, this child of the most powerful emperor in the world, to be nothing more than Lady Hariawan's handmaiden, nothing more than a slave.

But the Besur's dislike of Sairu had grown over the months into something much stronger than his fear. He growled and stood, bowing hastily to the emperor but pointing an accusing finger at the girl. "She is no true Masayi," he said. "Beloved emperor, heed not her words. She was sworn to the service of Lady Hariawan, Hulan's most gifted Dream Walker. And where is that lady, may I ask? Is she safe as this maiden has claimed? Or has she long since perished, and the truth of her fate is kept hidden from us?"

Sairu paled. Jovann, watching her, saw the mask she wore crack momentarily. He knew then that at least some of the Besur's words were true. Something terrible had happened to Lady Hariawan.

Princess Safiya raised her face for the first time since that council began. The expression in her eyes could have boiled the high priest's bones to sludge. "If Masayi Sairu claims her mistress is safe then her mistress is safe," she said. "You have no right to question her word."

Jovann saw Sairu's cheeks take on a faintly greenish tinge. She looked like death made animate, but she struggled again to mask her sickness behind a calm façade. Jovann was not fooled. But the Besur stood behind her and could not see her face.

The emperor slowly shifted in his chair, moving his weight from one leaning arm to the other, and resting his chin lightly upon bejeweled fingers. "I seem to recall asking the honored Besur not to contradict the judgments of those to whom I look for guidance," he said to no one in particular.

The Besur, under the joint pressure of Princess Safiya's gaze and the emperor's languid tone, sat once more, glaring at the back of Sairu's head as though he would fill her brain with venom if he could.

The emperor addressed himself to Jovann. "I trust your word, Minister Juong-Khla Jovann," he said. "It will be as you say. We will arrange protection in the dungeons, though I will not send the Golden Daughters as my dear Sairu suggests, but will enjoin them to protect my wives and younger children. There will be soldiers enough. And if what Masayi Sairu has told us about the Long Fire weapons proves true, I believe we may set up defenses against them. It seems to me that the effectiveness of these new weapons lies as much in the terror they inspire as in the destruction they work. But an expected terror is far less terrible than a surprise."

"I will myself see to the wall defenses," Princess Safiya declared. "And when the siege begins, I will stand by my Ascendant Brother's side and assure his safety so that the honored warriors of Noorhitam may concentrate their energies upon the enemy at hand."

And so the plans for war swiftly progressed, for Jovann again warned that he believed the Chhayans could strike at any moment. The exact date he did not know, but attack was surely imminent.

Many times he found the words sticking in his throat. How could he go on? How could he betray his father and his people? How could he destroy this generational dream of reclamation and revenge? But the images he had seen of the gory sacrifices and the face of the Greater Dark remained too vivid in his head. More vivid than a dream. More vivid than a memory. More vivid even than the reality surrounding him. And he knew that he could not back down.

His gaze slid to Sairu several times throughout the next few hours. She remained where she knelt before the emperor, her head bowed, her hands still, one atop the other. He could not see her face, but he saw the curve of her cheek behind her elegant braids, and he saw its ghastly hue.

The moment the council broke up, and the ministers and warlords parted ways to pursue their various tasks of preparation and defense, Sairu rose, kissed the ring on the emperor's hand, and slipped from the room. Jovann made hasty genuflection before the Anuk and hurried after her, catching her in the gilded, silk-hung corridor without. "Princess!" he said, afraid to speak loudly. But the urgency of his voice carried far enough to stop her in her tracks. She turned slowly, meeting his gaze, and he found himself faced with her smile. "Princess Masayi Sairu," he said, "I hope you will forgive me."

"Forgive you?" said she, her voice honey-sweet though her lips were gray and dry beneath the gold paint. "Whatever for, Honored Minister?"

He tried to answer, but too many words came together at once, refusing to be spoken. At last, he managed, "I did not know."

"That I am what I am?" said she. "That I am more to my Lady Hariawan than a mere handmaiden? Why of course not, Honored Minister. That is, after all, the whole point and purpose of the Masayi."

"But . . . the emperor's daughter!"

"Indeed, Honored Minister. Can you be surprised? Could anything less than a princess be deemed worthy to serve one so gracious, so precious as my mistress?" She swayed as she spoke, though her smile remained fixed in place.

Then suddenly she fell. Jovann, moving on reflex more than thought, leapt forward and caught her before she hit the floor, and she grabbed his arm hard, trying to find her balance, trying to support herself. Jovann looked around for help but saw no one, for all had dispersed from the council and hastened to their various duties. Not even the emperor remained on hand to see the distress of his daughter.

Jovann had never since meeting her seen Sairu betray the least sign of weakness, and it frightened him. His arm around her shoulders, his other hand gripping hers, he supported her back into the council chamber, which was empty now. Trying to be gentle but feeling like a great clod, Jovann helped Sairu down onto the nearest low cushion. As he backed away, he saw blood seeping through the shoulder of her silken garment. "You are wounded!" he said stupidly, and stood a moment with his mouth open, uncertain. "I—I should find help—"

"No," said Sairu, her head bowed, one hand rubbing furiously at her forehead. Her jaw clenched, and her lips pulled back in what looked like a snarl. "No, there is no time. We must help my mistress." She turned then upon Jovann, and her eyes were full of fear. It was an expression her face was not meant to wear, and he felt his heart sink with trepidation at the sight. "Your people have taken Lady Hariawan," she said. "They have captured her."

The image of Ay-Ibunda rose in Jovann's mind, along with the memory of the dark phantoms who had pursued him and Lady Hariawan across the landscape of the Dream. He understood now both Sairu's wound and the sickness in her gaze. She had been hurt defending her mistress, he did not doubt. And if she did not find Lady Hariawan, she would waste away. Indeed, he believed with a sudden rush of understanding that Sairu's very life was essentially bound up with that of her mistress; she could not fail Lady Hariawan without ultimately destroying herself.

"I will help," he said. "I will do anything. I will help you find Lady Hariawan."

"I know," said Sairu. "We will find her. We will find her together. Somehow." Her voice was thin and quavering, and he suspected that she ran a fever. Sweat dampened her hair, little wisps sticking to her forehead. "And when we find her—when we see her safe—and all of this horror is over, then—" She gasped, and her small body shuddered.

Jovann looked again at the blood on her shoulder. "Please," he said, "let me fetch someone. You are very ill." He had half turned when she darted out a hand and caught him by the wrist, turning him back to her with ferocious intensity.

"When we find my mistress," she said, "I will speak to the Anuk. He will change his decree, and you will wed Lady Hariawan, as you so desire. You will wed Umeer's daughter. Then everything . . . everything will be as it should be. And I will protect you both—"

Another shudder ran up her spine. Then she seemed to collapse upon herself like a wilting rose. Jovann knelt only just in time to prevent her from striking her head upon the floor. "Help!" he cried, turning and calling over his shoulder. "Please, someone help!"

"Iubdan's beard, the racket you make!" A strange golden voice spoke from the shadows. Jovann, who had believed they were alone in that chamber, startled and whirled to face the speaker. Somehow he was not as surprised as he thought he should be when the big fluffy cat stepped into the lamplight, his white paws and ruff shining.

The cat offered Jovann a supercilious sneer then hastened to Sairu's side, sniffing her hand, her arm, her shoulder. His tail lashed when he came to the blood. "She's hurt," Jovann said.

"Oh, really?" said the cat. "Well then, why don't you just—no. No." He shook his whiskers. "I have promised to mend my ways and speak with a civil tongue even when you mortals insist on being dimwitted. Yes, my lad, she is wounded. But this wound afflicts her spirit more than her body, I fear."

Jovann opened his mouth then closed it. Then he said, "I knew you could talk."

"Clever boy," said the cat. "Lay her out flat for me, will you?"

Carefully Jovann shifted Sairu's weight and arranged her on the floor, snatching a cushion to pillow her head. He thought she was not fully unconscious, for her eyes opened and she moaned, though she did not seem to see anything or be aware of what was around her. The cat stared into her face, his pink nose nearly touching hers. He growled softly.

"This is not good," he said. "Her heart is tearing in two. I can slow the progress, but—" Putting his ears back, he looked up at Jovann, who knelt beside Sairu, his hands moving helplessly as though he wanted to do something but had no idea what. "Stop fidgeting. If you want to help, there's only one thing you can do."

"What? Anything!" said Jovann. "This girl has come to my aid more times than I remember, and I will gladly repay the debt if I can. Tell me what you want of me!"

"I want you to find Lady Hariawan," said the cat.

16

SOLDIERS WERE NOT PERMITTED within the bounds of the Crown of the Moon except during consecrating ceremonies before marching off to war. But there were no ceremonies now. Only men of blood tramping through sacred groves, setting up defenses along walls and walkways meant only to be trod in prayerful solemnity.

From the great steps of Hulan's Throne, the Besur watched the preparations being made, holding his massive bulk in stern, tall command, though he had no more authority here. The warlords ordered their men as they wished, and the high priest must only look on and wait for the battle that may never come.

And Hulan looked down on all with the same faceless, voiceless, careless serenity with which she had observed all the long years of Kitar worship. The high priest sneered under her gaze. He did not fancy that Hulan felt any threat despite the wild dreams of his emperor and the wilder claims of the Chhayan prisoner. She, if she were anything more than a shining light in the sky, was neither threatened nor concerned by the fate of one mortal empire. She would not move to intercede, not even to see her sacred grounds spared this indignity and desecration.

"Hulan blight that Chhayan dog-boy," the Besur muttered, "if you can bother yourself to do so."

"Not an especially holy prayer," said Jovann. "Particularly for a high priest."

The Besur, startled, turned his furious gaze from the distant wall where soldiers' shadows moved under moonlight, down to the wide, paved pathway leading up to the steps of Hulan's Throne, his face grim as a stone demon-ward on a gatepost. Of all people in the world the Besur hated (who were many), there were none he could recall in that moment whom he hated more than the emperor's new vizier. But the Besur was Kitar through and through. While his face was a mask of disgust, he adjusted his words from curses to flattery as nimbly as a dancer performing a difficult turn on the stage.

"To what do I owe this great honor, minister of my beloved emperor?" the Besur asked with a bow. "How may I serve a man so favored by the great Son of the Sun? Shall I scrub your shoes even as you stand before me? Shall I lay myself down as a footstool for your feet?"

"I rather hope you'll do none of those things," said Jovann, and he mounted the stairs without a single prayer, sign, or murmured benediction, unconsciously breaking holy rites and laws with every step he made. Not that it mattered anymore on such a night. But when he reached the third step from the top, his head still lower than the Besur's, he stopped and offered a slight bow, though his face was guarded. "But I do require your assistance, priest of Hulan."

"Assistance?" The Besur's sneer deepened. "It would appear to me that your rise from condemned prisoner to esteemed vizier in the course of a single day has needed no assistance, and I can hardly imagine to what new astronomical heights you might aspire."

Jovann, his face carefully guarded, said, "Do you care anything for the fate of Hulan?"

The Besur did not answer at first. His silence betrayed his true feelings more eloquently than any words. Then he said, "Of course I do," and both knew it for the lie it was.

"You care for Lady Hariawan," said Jovann. "I saw your face when you spoke against her handmaiden in the emperor's council. Hatred such as that can only be motivated by some form of love."

"Love? No," said the Besur. "There you are mistaken."

"But you do care for Lady Hariawan."

"I would see her returned safely to the temple of Hulan," the Besur admitted slowly. Then he added with a curse, "And I would to heaven I had never commissioned that Golden Daughter!"

Jovann nearly pointed out how many times Sairu had protected her mistress, how likely it was that Lady Hariawan would even now be dead were it not for her handmaiden's protection. But there was no time. At the cat's urging he had hastened here, and the night was so heavy with foreboding that he felt the very pressure of the darkness between the stars. He knew what he must do, though he did not know how he would do it. He had never controlled his dream-walking ability, and without the songbird to call him out of his world into the Between, he was as bound to mortal Time and mortal reality as the next man.

Or perhaps not. Perhaps there was one other way . . .

"Tell me, Besur," said Jovann, "have you heard rumor concerning the Order of the Greater Dark?"

In the center of Hulan's Throne was a wide, round chamber without ceiling or roof. The tower walls rose up high, surrounding, forming a shaft to the sky above. On certain nights of the year, when Hulan was full, her silver face would fit perfectly into the opening and the whole chamber would be brilliantly lit with her glow. On such nights a man could almost remember the Songs of old which once were sung in this world. On such nights a man could almost remember what it meant to worship.

Now priests of Baiduri—who had nothing better to do this time of year anyway—were summoned to carry ten heavy braziers into this wide chamber and arrange them at evenly spaced intervals around it. They lit the braziers, and the scent of harimau soon filled the air, rising up even to the high opening. It seemed to drown out all other senses, even the sounds of soldiers shouting on the temple walls, even the fear of impending doom which every man felt in his heart. There was no room for anything but harimau. And so, as the high-order priests gathered, they felt their minds clear, prepared for the chant they must perform.

Jovann stood beside the Besur in the darkness beyond the circle, watching braziers glow, watching the priests gather and, one by one, begin a chant similar to that which Jovann had heard in the Dream, similar to that by which Chhayan men had formed Ay-Ibunda Temple. This chant was more formal, and the Kitar voices speaking it were less bloody. Neither was this chant so powerful as that of the Chhayan priests—the faith of these men toward their deities was apathetic, unlike the faith of the Chhayans, which had turned from devotion to loathing over the centuries.

And yet there was such a strong similarity that Jovann, who was Chhayan-bred through and through, suddenly felt a strange sense of oneness with the Kitar surrounding him. He recalled, as one might recall the memory of a dream—without mental image, but a powerful memory nonetheless—the face of Hulan. And he heard the North Star warning him yet again, "*Do not worship.*"

Jovann whispered so softly that the Besur did not hear him above the rising intonation of rhythmic voices, "We are all equally lost."

The Besur turned to Jovann then and said, "You remember the words I taught you?"

"Yes."

"You must speak them precisely. And you must keep them present in your mind. If not, your concentration will be broken and your mind will return to this realm." The Besur, his face lit strangely by the glow of the nearest brazier, scowled. "If you are indeed a Dream Walker, why do you need our assistance?"

Jovann did not answer this. He merely said, "Do you want me to find your Lady Hariawan or not?"

The Besur studied the detestable face of the Chhayan beside him. The high priest of Anwar and Hulan, this master of Kitar worship, this gate-keeper of Kitar tradition, was no fool. Many dismissed him as nothing better than an old, gilded blusterer, but they were mistaken to do so. He *was* an old, gilded blusterer, but he was more besides. He lacked the precision of perception Princess Safiya possessed, but years of survival in the cutthroat world of ordered religious hierarchy had made him perceptive in his own way.

Still, he could not read the expression in Jovann's eyes, so he asked, "What do you care whether or not we recover our lady, emperor's minister?" He spoke the title in the same tone he said "Chhayan dog-boy," and both knew what he truly meant. "You stand to gain nothing from undergoing the Sleep. What is your motivation in all this?"

Jovann opened his mouth to make a reply. But instead of the sharp retort his brain had formed, he said only, "Love, Besur. I'll do this for love."

It would have been difficult to say who was more surprised by this statement, the Besur or Jovann. To cover his embarrassment, Jovann hastily stepped into the circle of braziers and chanters, into the center of that tall round chamber. Harimau overwhelmed him with physical force, and he nearly staggered under the heady burden of it. He looked up to the opening high above him, and he saw the stars shining. He even believed that he glimpsed the blue aura of Chiev, the North Star. What was the name it had called itself?

"Cé Imral," Jovann whispered. Then he bowed his head. For a moment he waited, hoping he would hear the birdsong calling, hoping the white emptiness would surround him. But there was nothing. Only the harimau. And the chanting of the Kitar priests. Jovann waited, counting the timing of that chant. Then, in the small opening he'd been told to wait for, he began to speak his own chant, a line of rhythm intoned in counterpoint to that which the priests spoke:

"From this world to the other, let me walk
From the Near, from the Far, into the Between
From tedium to elucidation, let me walk
From mortal bounds into Eternity."

The Besur had told him that, if he were meant to see the Dream, a door would appear before him. He could not tell Jovann what the door would look like, for it varied from Dream Walker to Dream Walker. Jovann, as he spoke the words of the Kitar chant and felt the harimau running through him, half expected to see the gate of trees through which the birdsong had called him since he was a child.

But there was no gate of trees. Jovann, his eyes closed, his mind encompassed in the chant and the scent of the need before him, saw only swirling mist. Not the pure white emptiness; this was emptiness without purity, formlessness without clarity. It was gray, or not quite gray. For gray still requires some perception of color. This was not gray, nor white, nor even black. It was the churning of the mind on the edge of dreams, where all is lost and all is irrecoverable.

Then suddenly he beheld his door: The tall gate of Ay-Ibunda, one post carved like a dragon, the other post jagged, uncarved, unshaped.

Jovann felt his heart lurch in his breast, back in his mortal body. But his spirit turned toward this sight with a certain measure of relief. Dreadful though that gate was—and still more dreadful the chant of the Chhayans which slowly replaced all sound of the Kitar priests—it was still *something*. Anything was better than the formless mist, so Jovann moved toward the gate as swiftly as he dared, remembering to speak the chant the Besur had given him.

The moment he stood beneath the arch of the gate, however, Jovann felt himself take on a form more solid. His feet stood upon ground which, though hidden beneath the mist, supported him nonetheless. And he saw the stones of the temple wall take shape around him, black and forbidding, one set upon the next far more firmly than he had last seen. The temple—and those who built it with their minds and the evil of their hearts—was stronger.

He should go back. He should not enter here. He should return to his body, return to his world, and wait and beg the songbird to call him. This was not safe, and he was not strong dream-walking thus.

But Lady Hariawan must be inside. And he had promised the cat. What else could he do?

The next step Jovann took was both the bravest and the most foolish of his life. It carried him across the threshold, through the gate, and into the courtyard. In that single step, he felt as though he passed into a world more solid and real than his own, and he knew he need not speak the Kitar chant anymore. He was here, within the temple boundaries, and his spirit would not slip away easily. Indeed, he wondered briefly if he would be able to return at all.

There was no time to think of that, however. All around him, standing in clustered circles, were priests, Chhayan priests adorned in crowns set with animal teeth. They paid no attention to him, fixed as they were upon sustaining their chant. Though Jovann looked carefully, he saw no sign of Chhayan warriors, no men of the Khla clan.

He proceeded, passing silently through the courtyard and the mist. With each step he took, the Chhayan chant embedded itself deeper into his heart. He began to see images of what the chanters saw and invented with their words. He saw the whole layout of the temple, the three halls, the circular main hall, in the center of which stood a great altar. He saw the altar itself as clearly as though he stood before it. It was a dreadful thing, smeared with blood. Chhayan worship was always bloodier than Kitar.

More images appeared in his mind, and he saw the prayer chambers beyond the altar, both elaborate and humble. And suddenly he knew exactly where Lady Hariawan waited.

As is the way with dreams, Jovann had no need to walk the whole of that distance across the courtyard and into the hall, searching out each room as he came to it. Instead, the moment he envisioned the chamber he sought, he found himself standing before it. The chanting of the priests in the courtyard was just as loud, but he could not see those who chanted. He was alone in this passage, the bloodied altar at his back, and a low door before him. He felt his heartbeat far away in another world, but here his spirit was strangely calm.

Kneeling and putting his mouth close to the door, he called softly, "Umeer's daughter?"

He saw a picture of her in his mind, again as clear or clearer than reality. He saw her kneeling in the dark, waiting. She waited with perfect calmness, perfect serenity, but with an absolute certainty of doom. She did not move at his voice, though he was quite sure she heard him. "Umeer's daughter, can you open the door?" he asked.

No answer, but again he felt the answer and knew it for truth. She could open the door. If she could but summon the strength and the will, she could open the door and walk out into his arms and away. But she remained where she was. And she waited.

Jovann felt around for a latch but found none. Foolish! Why should he need a latch here? If the chanting priests could form this entire structure from their minds, what could he himself not accomplish? He braced his spirit and placed both of his imagined hands against the door. How solid it felt, how real, how mortal! And yet it was but the stuff of dreams. He pushed.

His hands were through in an instant, and he followed swiftly after them. The darkness of the chamber closed in around. He had no sense of size, either great or small. The walls might have pressed in on all sides, mere inches from his head, from his shoulders. Or they may have been miles distant. It did not matter, not here. Not in the dark.

"Umeer's daughter?" he whispered, feeling her near. He dared not stand but crawled instead, placing each hand carefully before him. It wasn't as though he found any real ground upon which to support himself. There was only darkness.

Then suddenly, as he set his hand down, he touched her fingertips.

The moment their fingers met, it was as though a light illuminated them both. This was not in fact the truth, for all was still dark around them. But Jovann could see her face now, and her kneeling form. He saw the mark of the hand upon her cheek, and it was vivid and ugly, marring her lovely features. He saw the shining sheet of her long, loose hair hanging down over her white shoulders.

Her eyes upturned to him, and they contained all the darkness of that chamber in their depths.

"You have come," she said.

"I have," Jovann replied, and he took her hand firmly in his. Or rather, he tried to. With mounting horror he looked down and found that, while he could touch her, he could not grasp her. When he tried, she slipped away like a ghost. He realized suddenly that she was here in her mortal form—not dream-walking as he was, but physically trapped in this Realm of Dreams, her body, mind, soul, and spirit, all together here in this chamber.

He knew then that he would not be able to rescue her.

Sairu woke up trying to scream but unable to find her voice. She sat bolt upright, startling the cat so that his back arched high and he hissed despite himself. Then, trying to smooth down his on-end coat, he meowled, "Dragon's teeth, girl! You scared the living Lights right out of me!"

Her chest heaving as she struggled to relearn how to breathe, Sairu stared around her. She found she lay on the hard floor of the emperor's council room and wondered briefly how she had come there. Then she winced, gasped as though in pain, and bowed her chin to her chest, her eyes squeezed tight.

Before her vision swam the face of Idrus, the dead slaver. And his was the same face as the Chhayan she had killed the day before.

Sensing her distress, the cat placed a paw on her knee. "There, girl, there," he said. "You're safe. I've sung over your wound again, and the pain should be eased. But there is poison in your heart, and I'm afraid I haven't yet managed to sing it out. Not sure I have the skill." He put his ears back. "I know I've said it before, but I do wish Imraldera were here. She would be able to help you in ways I cannot."

Not knowing who Imraldera might be, Sairu ignored this. She put up her hands, clutching her face, and tried to push memories back into place. The emperor's council . . . the siege . . . Jovann . . .

"My mistress," she whispered. She opened her eyes, fixing her gaze upon the cat. "Where is Lady Hariawan?"

"She's gone, remember?" the cat said as gently as he could. "The Chhayans took her."

"Oh. Yes."

"Not to worry, though," the cat continued. "Your handsome hero has gone in search of her."

"My what?"

"Jovann. He has gone to the Besur to seek help, to dream-walk. He has found the Hidden Temple before, and he believes he can find it again. I am certain—"

"Alone?" Sairu pulled her hands sharply away from her face. "You sent him alone?"

"I told you," the cat said soothingly, "I do not know the way. In any case I could not leave you, poisoned as you are. You might have died. Or worse."

"You should have gone with him," Sairu said. Her face was fierce and deathly pale as she gathered herself and stood, swaying slightly. "You should have gone with him! You should have let me die!" She closed her eyes again, bracing herself, summoning all the control she possessed over her own body and mind. Her heart raced as fast as her thoughts, and for a moment she did not think she would be able to master herself.

Then she was running. Her robes flew out behind her as she fled the council room, through the winding corridors of Manusbau. She saw and heard signs of the preparations being made for the coming siege, but she did not stop to inspect these, only ran all the harder. The cat was at her heels, and he was calling out to her, but she was too angry, too furious to acknowledge him. So she ran harder, feeling the looseness in her shoulder and realizing, distantly, that the wound was much further along in its healing than it had been mere hours before. Whatever the cat had done had worked wonders on her.

But he had not been able to touch her wounded heart, and this beat a steady poison through her body—a poison of fear, a poison of devotion. Fed by this poison, she ran harder, brushing past any who might try to impede her, warding off the curious with the expression on her face. She passed from Manusbau into the Crown of the Moon, bursting through the gate without a word for the gatekeeper who demanded that she declare herself. No one could stop her as she crossed the temple grounds, and she did not slacken her pace save once. For as she drew near the plot of wild land filled with broken stones, she felt her heart give a painful jolt inside her. She longed suddenly to hide herself among those stones, her ears straining for some sound, some song for which she had always sought without knowing she sought it.

Her spirit, so highly tuned and trained throughout the years, urged her on relentlessly. She could not tarry, she could not wait. She could seek no balm or blessing. She must find Jovann before he stepped into the Dream, and she must tell him the plan that had formed in her brain while she slept.

Priests stood guard at the doors of Hulan's Throne, and they were fierce, tall men un-softened by years of temple service. "Declare yourself!" they cried as Sairu drew near. When she did not answer they stepped forward, weapons raised, and would have cut her down. But she avoided their plunging blades without a thought. She grabbed the belt of one tall priest and, pivoting so that she used his own weight against him, swung him around so that his body connected hard with his brother, and they both fell. She did not wait to hear their curses but darted through the doors of Hulan's Throne, following the sound of chanting heard deep within.

The light of the braziers cast a red glow on the figure standing in the center of the circle. Sairu instantly recognized Jovann. Somehow the way his face was lit sent a stab of horror through her heart. She nearly stumbled as she drew to a halt just outside the circle of priests and braziers, staring into that center where Jovann stood with his arms outstretched.

"No," she gasped.

"Golden Daughter," said a voice she knew and loathed. She turned to the Besur with such ferociousness in her eyes that he took a step back. "Golden Daughter, why are you here? Are you not meant to be guarding the emperor's children on this evil night?"

Sairu ignored this, demanding instead, "What have you done, Besur? What have you done to Jovann?"

"Nothing he did not ask for himself," the Besur replied, putting up his hands in protest of her vicious tone. "He came to me for help, claiming he could find Lady Hariawan. Did you not declare him trustworthy before the Anuk's own throne? Do you go back on your word now?"

Sairu's mouth twisted into an ugly snarl, and her hands moved into her sleeves, feeling for the daggers attached to her arms. The cat arrived at her feet just then, however, and growled. Sairu turned away from the Besur, staring into the circle again, staring at Jovann.

"Come back," she whispered. "Please come back!"

The chant rose up into the night, mingling with the harimau spice.

The young dragon stood in the courtyard of Ay-Ibunda and felt the glory of mastery in his veins. For the moment his fire was low. He wore the shape of a man, his own former shape though it was no longer true. He forgot what he had become, though he could not quite remember what he had been. He knew only what he was in that moment: chief of the Khla clan. His father's heir. Master of the Tiger men.

It was a power he had never hoped would be his, not from that time so long ago when his mother held him close and told him that he had a half-brother now and must try not to hate him. He could not remember his mother. She was gone along with his heart, lost in the furnace blaze.

But he remembered his brother. And he remembered his hatred.

The young dragon, a light in his eyes, stared at the door of the temple, waiting. His brother was inside, and soon he would emerge. Soon Jovann would see how drastically the game had changed, how far he had fallen beneath the rising shadow of the elder brother's might.

For hours the young dragon stood thus, or perhaps for mere moments. Mortal men surrounded him, and they dragged Time in their wake, but here it did not move and flow as it did in the mortal world. This did not matter. The trap was sprung, the quarry caught. Time could neither save nor hurt Jovann now. His fate was sealed.

The door of the temple opened. The young dragon's lips drew back, and fire licked about his teeth and gums. He prepared to laugh, to roar, to shout out his victory in the face of that one he hated so much.

But instead of Jovann, a girl stepped through the door and into the gray half-light of the Dream. And the young dragon recognized her at once. In a voice suddenly chilled he breathed, "Angel!"

He felt the ring on his finger as though it were made of red-hot iron. He had almost forgotten it. He *had* forgotten it. But he recalled it now with startling pain. In that moment he realized that his heart was not entirely lost after all.

Lady Hariawan stood above the courtyard. She wore the leper's rags in which she had been captured. These could not mar the perfection of her slender form, nor could her long black hair veil the beauty of her face, her neck. But the courtyard, full to brimming with ranks of Chhayan warriors standing in formation, shuddered with horror rather than longing. For all eyes except those of the young dragon fixed upon the mark on her cheek. The mark of the Dragon's hand.

She looked out upon them, her eyes empty save for a faint trace of mockery. She was unafraid, though she knew—or at least suspected—what they would do to her.

Jovann stepped out behind her, and he stood numb upon that step. He too showed no trace of fear, for his surprise far outmatched his fear and masked his face. He recognized all of those before him, men of the Khla clan with whom he had lived and survived all his life. But though their faces were familiar, they were strangely unfamiliar as well. For the first time, Jovann gazed upon men of the Tiger and saw his enemies.

He spied his brother standing before the others on the first step below. He saw the helmet of Juong-Khla upon his head, and he felt a sob well in his throat. "Sunan!" he said, and though he did not speak loudly his voice filled the air like a shout, rising even above the pulsing chant of the priests. "Where is our father?"

Dragging his gaze from Lady Hariawan only with an unwilling effort, the young dragon turned to his brother. In a flash the memory of the ring on his hand vanished and all his hatred returned. "Our father is dead, Jovann," he said. "I am Sunan-Khla, the Tiger Master."

"You were not our father's heir," Jovann said. "Stand down. Call off these men and let this lady go. Then you and I will settle the inheritance by right of combat as befits men of the Tiger."

It was a vain command, and well Jovann knew it. The faces of the Khla men were as stone before him. They would never accept him. Not now.

The young dragon took another step up, and Jovann saw the flames in his eyes. He did not yet know what it meant, but his heart—far away in another world—quailed in his breast. "I am Khla," said his brother. "You are nothing. Nothing but the dreamer. The slave. You have lost your inheritance, and soon you will lose your life. But not before you lose your soul."

No eye could have spotted which of the brothers moved first, for the next instant both were flying at each other—Jovann leaping down the stairs with the speed of lightning, the young dragon rising up to meet him with fire spilling from his mouth. The fire overwhelmed Jovann, but he walked in spirit, not in body, and it could not hurt him. He threw himself through it and into his brother, and both of them, grappling together, fell back down the temple stairs. Jovann struck at the dragon's face, and the dragon clawed at his eyes.

Never before had Jovann felt such power here in the Dream. He realized now, as he never had before, that he was not limited to physical strength. Here he could be what he imagined, and so his fists became rocks of granite with which he pounded the face of his brother. But the young dragon transformed beneath him, scales plating his skin, teeth jutting up from his jaw. Soon he no longer wore the form of a man but was a dragon indeed, his wings beating the air around them. Still Jovann did not let up his assault, but struck at his brother with all the force of his pent-up frustration, all the fury at his enslavement, all the vengeance of a son whose father has been slain.

The battle might have waged for generations of mortal men. But instead, a voice that filled the whole of the sky above, the whole of the ground beneath the mist, shaking the walls of Ay-Ibunda down to their foundations, said: "Cease this childish brawling, you dog's sons!"

Jovann and his brother raised their furious eyes up to the temple door where Lady Hariawan waited. Behind her stood the Dragon, his hands upon her shoulders, his long talons sinking into her skin so that blood ran in thin, scarlet rivulets down her breast and arms.

Jovann immediately let go his hold on the young dragon's armored throat. "Don't hurt her!" he cried. And the young dragon's voice spoke in exact echo of his own, "Don't hurt her!"

The Dragon smiled and did not loosen his grip. "Come here, Dream Walker," he said to Jovann. "Come here and stand before me."

Jovann obeyed. His form had lost its strength of substance, and flowed up the stairs, small and weak before the Greater Dark. "Please," he whispered again, "don't hurt her."

The Dragon ignored him. He addressed himself to his child, the young dragon panting on the lower steps. "The time has come, Sunan-Khla," he said. "The time has come for you to take the revenge your people crave. Lead the Khla men. Lead all the Chhayan tribes. Set upon the gates of your usurper's palace with fire, and let no Kitar life be spared."

As though their tongues had been released from some wicked spell, the formations of Khla warriors set up a shout that drowned out the chanting voices of their priests. The young dragon did not shout with them. He stared at the girl held in the grip of such foul evil, his own Dark Father. He could not speak. He could not shout. He could not even issue a command.

He spun about, his sinuous dragon form coiling like an enormous snake, and took to the air. He flew from Ay-Ibunda, and all the Tiger army followed after him, marching through the temple gate and onto paths too dreadful for mortal minds to fathom.

The Dragon smiled to watch them go. Then he turned that smile upon Lady Hariawan and Jovann. "Come," he said. "We must attend to business of our own."

17

SAIRU HEARD THE FIRST screech followed by a thunderous rumble so distantly that at first she did not recognize it for what it was. She stood on the edge of the braziers' light, her gaze fixed upon the figure standing in the center, and she had no thought for anything but him, for somehow making her voice, her spirit, reach out to him, calling him back from whatever strange realm he wandered.

But the gathered priests heard the sound. Those outside the circle shifted and looked at one another, then each turned his gaze to the Besur, as a child turns to its father. The Besur himself, however, after casting an unsettled glance back over his shoulder, focused again on the center of the circle.

Another screech. Another rumble. Now even some of the ten priests forming the chant stumbled over their words. It was only a brief falter, but it was enough. Like a crack in a pane of glass the break spread, shattering the controlled meditation. "No!" the Besur growled. "No, don't stop!"

It was no use. One by one the priests shook their heads and bowed back, stepping into the darkness behind the braziers. Now Jovann stood alone. He could not maintain the dream-walk without the support of the brothers. He would return. At any moment his spirit would rush back to his body.

"Jovann!" Sairu did not realize how loud her voice was, not even when the priests on either side of her jumped and cried out in alarm. She leapt forward, springing between two of the braziers, and flew to Jovann's side. He stood upright, his face raised to the sky high above, his mouth moving in steady rhythm to a chant she could not hear.

But his body was fading. She could see right through his upraised hands, right through his shoulders, his neck.

"Monster!" she cried, turning about and searching for the cat in the shadows. "Monster, what is happening?"

The cat trotted into the circle, sniffing at Jovann's boots, which were also fading now, whirling away like smoke on the wind. "He's leaving this world," the cat said. "I've never seen anything like this. His body is fading from the Near World. He's being taken away by some . . . some force . . . I—" The cat cursed then, his lips drawn back in a hiss. "The Dragon!"

"I don't believe in dragons," Sairu whispered, staring into Jovann's face, which she could scarcely see now. She put out her hand, tried to reach him, tried to touch his cheek.

But he was gone.

The air ripped with another screech, and the thunder this time was much nearer. She heard it this time, recognizing the same sound she had heard as prelude to the destruction in Lembu Rana. She realized then that the assault had begun. Without warning, without preamble, the Long Fire was being flung at the walls of Manusbau and the Crown of the Moon.

Sairu spun on heel and ran out, passing between the shivering priests. The cat hastened at her heels, and they burst through the doors of Hulan's Throne and looked out across the temple grounds. She saw fire. She saw shooting flame whirling up through the night sky. She smelled, even from that distance, the rotting-eggs odor. Men were shouting, screaming, and by the light of fires ignited by those small explosions she saw the shadows of armored men running to defense.

"Monster," she said, turning to the cat, "I know how to find my Lady

Hariawan. I know how to reach her. Will you follow me?"

The cat, his eyes like two bright moons on his face, stared up at her. He did not know what she had in mind, could not guess at the workings of her brain. Fear of the Dragon was in his heart. But he answered, "I will follow you. I will protect you."

"Then come," said Sairu, and she sprang down the steps and into the darkness of the temple grounds. More shrieks tore the air, like the ghosts of the dead returned for retribution.

The Moon in her gardens above the worlds sits upon her throne and watches the coming of fire. She feels her children all around her, and they sing on, oblivious, even as their voices form the very prophecies of their doom. She sings as well, but there is a new thread to her intricately woven song, a new counterpoint added to the pattern of the whole.

She sings a song of sorrow closing in. And her children turn to her in surprise. One child, Cé Imral, who dances near to her, steps forward. "Mother," he asks, "what is this new Song? I do not know it." And he shivers as he speaks, for he does not like the sound of his Mother's voice forming the strange harmonies.

The Moon turns to him sadly and touches his face, all the love of her being in that touch. "My child," she says, "it is not a Song for you to sing. This is my Song for you."

Then she looks again out through her Gate, out into the worlds. Into the Dream. And she sees that which approaches.

A procession of phantoms marched, chanting as they went. Over their shoulders were great chains attached to an enormous rolling dray. It was six meters long and two meters wide, supported on massive wheels that were each twice as tall as a grown man. It was built of neither wood nor stone, nor of metal, nor of any other material to be found in the mortal realm. No indeed, for it was built of the dreams of those who pulled it. Their dreams had grown strong and dreadful over the years. They themselves had lost much of their substance and become little more than shadows, save for their ongoing chants. But they were strong in their dreams. And so they did not struggle to create this massive vehicle.

But they struggled to pull it. For while the dray itself was built of their dreams, that which it contained was more solid, more real, than any one of them.

It is rumored among mortals and immortals alike that hidden in the Netherworld, down below the deepest layers of the Dream, the Dragon has buried a mighty hoard. Poets and tellers of tales have spun many a legend depicting the gleaming, stolen riches of this hoard: king's crowns still worn upon severed heads, magic rings bitten from hands, rubies formed from the spilled blood of maidens, sapphires formed from widows' tears. These and many more are said to mound in disorderly grandeur, heaping from chests, spilling from alabaster jars, littered here and there with the charred bones of heroes who have attempted to reclaim their kingdoms' treasures.

But none of these things are spoken of with as much awe as the treasure which was the very first in the Dragon's collection. This, it was said, was a heart of shining gold. Not gold formed into a heart, which is a different thing entirely. No, but a heart that was itself gold, the purest, most valuable element. This heart was cradled safely in an ebony box lined with blood-red satin. Some have said that it was the heart of a Faerie queen who was taken by the Dragon's kiss and formed into the first of his ugly brood. The story says that he took her beating heart in his hand and pulled it from her breast, filling the opening left behind with his flame so that she took on dragon-shape.

But this story is false. The Dragon's hoard was begun long before he formed children in his likeness. So the heart, hidden away in its caverns many ages before, must have belonged to someone else.

Long ago a wise man, Akilun by name, taught that this same heart once beat in the Dragon's own breast; that before Time began there was an age when the Dragon was not fire-filled but full of love and song. But if this story is true, it is a truth so long forgotten as to be little different from a falsehood.

However it was, the Dragon took the golden heart—his oldest and most glorious treasure—from its box and, without a thought or a care, melted it down along with hundreds of other treasures. Then, plunging his hands into the melted gold, which seared up his arms and gave him awful pleasure, he shaped it. He molded it. He formed the Gold Gong, pounding with brutal hammers until its surface was smooth and shining like the face of Lumé himself. And when this was done, he scored that gleaming surface with his claws, scratching words in a language of fire and destruction.

This task complete, the Dragon stepped back and surveyed his handiwork. "May you ring out loud and long, O brilliant heart of mine," he said. "And may your voice herald the fire I bring!"

And now the gong stood in the bed of the giant dream-wrought dray, suspended between two pillars, swaying and humming gently in the motion of its passage. The phantom priests strained with all their might, progressing one achingly slow footstep at a time. But Time did not matter here. Behind them came the Greater Dark, and his shadow, like a lashing scourge, drove them before him.

The Dragon laughed to watch the phantoms struggle. Then he looked down upon the mortals on either side of him, one held by each of his man-shaped hands. Both walked with their heads bowed, their shoulders bent, their eyes downcast. But while in the lady he felt nothing but submission and compliance, in the man he felt resistance.

"You needn't try to fight me," the Dragon said. "No one will blame you, not even your worst enemies. Mortals who fight me never fare well. And who knows? If you obey without complaint, I might even let you go. What do you think of that?"

Jovann said nothing. The hum of the gong seemed to waft back over him, filling his ears with its heavy tonality. That hum seemed to call up words in his mind; words which had planted themselves in his memory and, no matter how hard he tried to repress them, continued to haunt him, night and day. He heard them now, droning in the voice of the gong:

I see them running, running, stumbling,
Running, as the heavens
Break and yawn, tear beneath their feet,

Devouring, hungry Death!

Perhaps the Dragon heard them as well, for he smiled again, and his grip on Jovann's shoulder tightened. "It will come to pass, mortal man. I myself etched the writing in gold, and it is a true prophecy, for I shall make it so."

He stopped suddenly, and the procession ahead of him ground to a halt as well. Jovann gasped as he was flung to the mist-churning ground at the Dragon's feet, but pushed himself up immediately, his eyes blazing with rebellion.

"Don't think you can thwart me," the Dragon said, drawing Lady Hariawan before him so that he held her once more with a hand on each shoulder. Her robes were stained red-brown with her blood, and her face was deathly white save for the crimson scar. The Dragon gazed down at the top of her head and considered her.

"She is strong," he said. "She walks the Dream with more confidence than I had ever seen in a mortal. And I require a mortal, for they alone can find the Gate I seek. Immortals have sought it all in vain, but mortals have seen it in their dreams. And the Dreams Walkers have drawn near to it in the past. I heard rumor that a new Dream Walker had been discovered with the power to find the Moon's Garden, and I began my search. Fool that I was to trust mortal instruments for such a work! But for all their incompetence, they found her at last, as you well know—this powerful Dream Walker who has walked in the Gardens of Hymlumé and brought back blossoms from those gardens into the Near World. So I believed my task complete, my victory near.

"But,"—and the Dragon leaned over Lady Hariawan, his inordinately long neck stretched across her head so that he might look Jovann in the eye—"she is not the one I seek, is she, little man-beast? For she can only walk the outer crust of the Dream, this dusty wasteland where mortal minds form strange sights, where nothing is true, nothing is real. Such a Walker is incapable of finding something so vital as Hymlumé's Gate! She is useless. She is nothing.

"You, however . . . I saw you in the Deeper Dream. Down beneath all this surface layer, down beneath the reach of Time. I saw you walking where mortals cannot go, and yet you walked and you lived."

Jovann wanted more than anything in that moment to take a backward step. Just one. He did not even think to turn, to run, to try to escape. Only one step back, one desperate attempt to create a little space, such a little space, between himself and those burning eyes.

He held his ground.

"You are the Dream Walker I need," the Dragon said. "Your father knew it. He tried to protect you, tried to send you away and keep you from me. But he could not. Not in the end. Nothing I desire is kept from me."

Here the Dragon drew back his head, his long neck vanishing into his shoulders so that his proportions were once more near to a man's. His grin, however, was all dragon. "Take me to the Moon's Gate, boy."

"I cannot," said Jovann.

"Cannot? Or will not?"

"Cannot. I am not the Dream Walker."

The Dragon's grin vanished. Fire flared up behind his teeth. "You are. I saw you in the Deeper Dream."

"I was led there," Jovann said. "I did not dream-walk on my own."

The Dragon made no move save for the wavering flame on his tongue. Then he lifted one hand, slowly extending one finger so that the full length of his talon might gleam for a moment beneath Jovann's nose. He rested this talon across Lady Hariawan's throat. He said: "I will not beg. I will not barter. I will not even ask. I will command one last time. And you will obey me." He applied pressure, and a thin line of blood ran in delicate trickle down the pale skin of the lady's neck.

Lady Hariawan raised her gaze. She fixed Jovann with her deep eyes, so lovely and so sad. The Dragon holding her formed the words with his lips, but it was she who spoke. In a voice low and rough, perhaps with fear, she said, "Take me to the Moon's Gate, Juong-Khla Jovann."

She spoke his name. The name he had given her so freely. So foolishly.

Jovann turned and marched past the massive dray, the humming gong, and the long line of chain-linked phantoms, all of whom watched him through hollow pits where their eyes had once been. Chhayans, he knew, for only a Chhayan would be willing to suffer such agony for the sake of revenge. He shuddered as he passed them, his own people, his kin, and wondered if he knew the names of the men they had once been. He marched to the front of the procession, and there he stood alone.

He felt his physical body containing him like a prison. How helpless he was in this form! In spirit he might fly away, might even assume a different shape. But in his body he was weak, and he could not resist both the Dragon and the lady.

"Please," he whispered, gazing out upon the emptiness around him. He did not know to whom he spoke, but he felt the need and whispered with all his heart. "Please help me."

Across the Boundless, the wood thrush replied: "*Follow me, Jovann.*"

Jovann took a step. He took a second.

As he took the third, he saw Hulan's Gate appear before him. He knew then, beyond any doubt, that whatever doom the Dragon intended would surely come to pass. And he recalled the first words Hulan had said to him when he, an unworthy mortal, had stood in her mighty presence:

"I have dreaded and longed for your coming. It is for me the foretelling of sorrow."

"Forgive me, Hulan," he whispered as the Gate grew upon the horizon. "Forgive me."

18

THE PATH OF NIGHTMARES is beyond mortal tongues to tell. For to each traveler it wears a different aspect, making itself individually dreadful according to individual dread. It is a long Path, a winding way through shadows and fires and images indescribable, but the Khla men marched it with grim, determined strides. They had suffered for too long, for too many generations, to back down now.

The young dragon led them. He wore a man's shape once more, but there was a dragon in his eyes. For him the Path took on the most dreadful nature, revealing frightful, hellish images, spilling emotions and sensations down upon his head that would have slain a mere mortal. But he was a dragon now. It seemed to him that all the horror rolled off his shoulders like water. This was not in fact the truth. Instead the horror soaked down beneath his armor plating, beneath his skin, sinking into that place where his heart once beat but where now there was only fire. And there the fire consumed it and mounted in rage, poison, and intensity. So while his soul slowly filled up to the brim with terror of the Dragon's Path through the winding Between, he believed it was courage that rose inside him, readying him for the task to come.

They traveled swiftly according to mortal perception of Time, which is not a governing force in the Between. And they gathered more warriors in their wake. Men of each Chhayan clan felt the summoning of the Greater Dark. And they rose up from whatever work they had been about, took up their weapons, and stepped into the Between. Their vengeance was at hand. The blood of their forefathers would be avenged and then surpassed in the blood of the Kitar usurpers. They passed out of the Near World of mortals into the winding darkness of the Dragon's Path, adding their number to that of their brethren.

The Wood shuddered with the pound of marching feet. Trees turned to look and saw shadows moving beneath their branches, following that Path which made the whole of the Wood shrink and draw away in terror, hiding itself from view and reach. And so there was only the swirling mist of the Dream to shroud the evil Path. The Chhayans passed between the worlds, following the lead of the young dragon at their head. He felt the power of all his people behind him. Men of blood, men of the plains, men of brutal intent. He felt them behind him like a surging tidal wave, and he knew that nothing could turn back the coming destruction.

He put up a hand. He felt the power of all the Chhayans become his own when they, seeing that gesture, stopped. The Path shuddered with the force of their feet coming to rest all at the same moment, and the silence of their collected waiting was deafening.

The young dragon turned and faced them. And, because the Between is not like the Near World, he felt as though he could look into every single face of all those thousands individually, at the same moment. So it was to each man personally that he spoke.

"The Kitar dogs must die."

As one motion, they brought their hands together about their weapons: swords, lances, spears, clubs, axes. As one voice, they echoed his: "*Die!*"

"The Kitar dogs must die," the young dragon repeated.

"*Die!*"

"The Kitar dogs must die!"

"*Die!*"

"Die!"

"Die!"

Now their voices rolled together into the various battle cries of their clans, and the Between was filled with their roaring, tearing, animalistic thunder. And before each clan chief, a doorway into the Near World opened. Each chief saw the city of Lunthea Maly before his eyes, the winding streets leading up to the palace on the hill above. Save for one chief, who saw the darkness of a dungeon cell and knew that he and his men should have the first taste of Kitar blood upon their blades.

A doorway appeared before the young dragon as well, and he licked a long forked tongue across his teeth at the sight. He felt his man's form giving way, felt the sinuous power of his true form, his dragon's body, taking over. It was agony and it was glory all rolled into one.

"Go!" he shouted, and his voice was a roar, and fire burst from his throat.

"Go!" the Chhayan chieftains bellowed, and rushed forward to their various doors.

The young dragon dove out of the Path and into the darkness of a heavy night, into the disgusting, cloying mortality of the Near World. His wings pounded the air and the dust of the street, and he took to the sky. In a vertiginous spiral, he climbed into the night, snarling at the stars above him, at the moon herself. What fools the Chhayans had been to worship her all those long generations! But no more. Tonight they would prove the might of their hearts, the strength of their arms. No more pitiful, prayerful pleas to a goddess who did not care. No more songs and chants for deliverance from an enemy she always favored. They would take back what belonged to them.

Never in his life had the young dragon been more Chhayan than he was as he spread wide his wings, caught the rising heat of an updraft, and circled slowly, high above the city. Lunthea Maly was but a child's toy, and he would play as he liked tonight. He saw the Chhayan chieftains and their armies emerging from the Between at different points all around the city, surrounding the palace and the temple. He saw the flash of the Long Fire as they shot the first of their rocket-arrows into the roofs of civilian houses, and soon the city was alive with fire. But the stone walls of Manusbau itself would be far too strong for those small flames.

The young dragon smiled. So much of what had been Sunan was lost. His fire was too great to allow for remnant shreds of humanity. Every time he flamed, every time he took on this powerful, horn-crowned form that was the truth of him now, more of the man was demolished, swallowed up, and forgotten.

Nevertheless, as he tilted his wings and sped down from the heavens, swooping toward the massive palace walls, the shining towers of the Kitar emperor which would soon go up like matchsticks under his flame, he remembered his brother's words to him, spoken what seemed an age ago now:

"*You rose up in the form of a dragon. A great, fire-filled dragon, Sunan, such as the legends speak of! And you were mighty, and you were beautiful, and all who saw you trembled, even our father. You were terrible in the eyes of the Khla warriors, and you led them into battle.*"

At the memory of his brother's voice, the fire swelled so greatly in the young dragon's breast that he had to give it vent. He opened his mouth and, as he flashed past the great south gate of the palace, he blasted it with all the force of his hatred. The gate, built of stone and age-hardened wood, burst under the intensity of that blast. The wood caught flame, and the stone melted, and men fled screaming or were consumed.

The young dragon smiled as he gained altitude again. But then he looked back, his long neck twisting grotesquely over his shoulder. He pivoted in the air and hung suspended on the night sky, staring down at the wreckage he had caused. He saw the Seh Clan swarming up from the streets, making for the break in the wall, their rockets firing as tiny mimics of his own great blast. They would burn themselves and even die in the poison of dragon vapors as they sought to burst through.

But there was something wrong. The young dragon snarled with anger as he realized.

The Kitar dogs were not taken by surprise. The emperor's mighty battalions led by various warlords gathered in formation. Their armor, structured according to all the most advanced designs of the known world, shone in the firelight. They lined themselves up in defense against the oncoming Chhayan barbarians clad in leather and furs. And the Chhayans, burning up with rage, flung themselves upon those armor walls and broke and died.

The surprise had not succeeded. The Kitar were prepared.

Fury burst from the young dragon, from his eyes and his nostrils and his gaping mouth. Like a demon from the deepest pit he fell, streaking through the darkness, and set upon the wall again, breaking and melting it wherever his fire struck. He felt arrows biting like gnats, *pinging* ineffectually off his scales. One brave Kitar warrior stood his ground under the dragon's approach. The dragon saw the wide whites of his eyes just before he was engulfed in fire. But before the fire took his life, he flung a spear with dreadful accuracy. The dragon felt the spear bite down into the softer flesh around his eyes. One small variation in its flight, and the spear would have pierced the eye itself.

Roaring in fury, the dragon soared up again, tearing at his face, tearing away the spear. He watched as other Chhayan clans swarmed over the breaks in the walls. He watched them hurl themselves at the Kitar front, watched them driven back, slowly, into the gaps.

Sunan had never cared, or had pretended never to care, for his father's dream. He had never been truly Chhayan. But the young dragon was not Sunan. Not anymore.

"We will not lose this night," he swore. Even as archers filled the air with clouds of arrows aimed at his wings and soft underbelly, he swept over the walls and into the broad grounds of Manusbau. All was alight with war and fear, but in the sprawling gardens he found a dark place, and there he landed and assumed his man's form once more. Keeping to the shadows, moving with the strange subtlety of a shade, he ran. And warriors searching for the great, snakelike body of a monster from myth did not turn or look his way. He did not wear the armor of a Chhayan, and might easily be mistaken in his tattered Pen-Chan robes for some slave of the household.

So he gained access to the main structure of Manusbau, the emperor's own hall. Sunan may have paused, gasped, and been overawed by the beauty and magnificence of the Anuk's abode. But the dragon neither saw nor cared. Still skulking through the deeper shadows, avoiding detection, he slipped through the gilded halls, following his nose and his hatred. These led him unerringly to a massive red and gold-plated door. When he pushed this open, he stood on the threshold of the emperor's throne room.

It was dark. Very different from the chamber it had been the afternoon before when the emperor sat and listened to the complaints and arguments of his gathered court. All was heavy with shadows and gloom, for none of the massive lanterns had been lit. Only a small lamp, burning bright at its spout, stood at the opposite end of the chamber at the feet of the emperor, who sat upon his throne. The gleaming lamplight shone upon the blade of his sword, which rested across his knees.

The emperor sat with his head bowed in an attitude of prayer. One hand lay on the hilt of his sword. The other hand rested upon his heart.

Sunan had never cared about the fate of the Emperor of Noorhitam. He had never been Chhayan enough, never been truly his father's son. But he cared with all the intensity of passionate loathing for his brother Jovann. And once more that night, he recalled what Jovann had told him.

"*I saw myself standing before the Emperor of Noorhitam, and I knew it was he, though I have never seen his face. He sat weak before me, pleading. Begging me for something I could not hear. But I was strong, and I stood before him, ragged Chhayan that I am. I saw it, Sunan, as clearly as I see you now. More clearly even! And I know it will come to pass.*"

But it would not come to pass. For it was not Jovann who would stand in power before the pleading Anuk Anwar.

"I have taken everything from you now, my brother," the young dragon whispered even as he slipped into the hall and pulled the heavy door shut behind him. The emperor did not raise his gaze or move even so much as a flickering eyelid. "I have taken everything from you. Your father. Your inheritance. Your power. I have even taken your dream. You have become nothing. I have become everything."

With each word he took a step, and so he crossed the hall. He still wore the form of a man, but fire spilled in liquid heat down from the tear ducts of his eyes, trailing burns across his skin, and more fire trickled from the corners of his mouth. He was a monster nightmarish to behold, the stuff of the most evil, most poisonous dreams. He reached the steps leading up to the emperor's throne and took the first one.

But he did not take a second. For Princess Safiya's blade sliced through the shadows and across his throat.

The Chhayan heartbeats all around were no temptation to the raven as it followed the Seh Clan warriors along their Path. The warriors had marched this Path too many times, and there was too much death in their hearts. The raven liked living hearts pulsing with living blood.

A tongue flickered between the cruel curves of its beak, tasting the bloodlust all around. Its master had given it no duty or task, so it had taken to the air and followed the warriors, eager to have its own part in the night's coming terrors. It was no great beast like the brilliant young dragon, and its feathers were not armor-plated. But it knew that where they were going it would find plenty of soft flesh. Plenty of young beating hearts.

"The Kitar dogs must die!" rang the battle cry. But the raven did not care for that. Nor did it concern itself with tactics or strategies. It merely watched for the doorway nearest to its goal. And when the portal opened, it darted ahead of all the others into the mortal realm.

It was a little surprised to find that the portal opened into black, close, underground space. But its surprise did not last long. It liked blackness, and while it didn't care for the confines of stone and dirt all around, it could feel the faint wisps of air flowing down from some opening above. It would find access to the upper world.

So the raven flitted ahead of the Chhayans into the winding dungeon passages. And it was first to realize that it was a trap.

The raw shriek of the raven startled the Kitar men braced in the narrow passage behind many layers of shields, but they held their ground. And the next moment they saw by the dim light of the lantern at the end of the passage the first shadowy forms of their oncoming enemies. So the impossible had happened! Somehow the Chhayan dog-men had found a breach beneath the temple walls and infiltrated the dungeons! It was no hoax, no distracting ploy, but a real threat. And one for which they were, however unwillingly, prepared.

The first of the shadows stopped in its tracks. He had no chance to cry out a warning to the brothers at his back before he was cut down by the waiting Kitar soldier forefront in the line.

Then the battle truly began. The lantern swinging up above cast the blood-spilling in rage-hewed highlights, and the roars of furious men deafened the ears of all within the dungeon passages. Chhayans poured from the lowly chamber into which their portal had opened, refusing to retreat, pressing up against the wall of Kitar warriors until the bodies of both sides were piled too high. But the Chhayans grabbed the dead by their ankles and tossed them back through the portal into the abyss of the Dragon's Path, and so cleared a way for themselves.

The battle spread, for the Chhayans were far more determined than the Kitar had expected, pushing back the defenders into the dungeon passages. Torches were lit to illuminate the fight, and many men were burned in the close confines, while others clung to the darkness which, while blind, was somehow safer. But though the Chhayans battled with a will, they could not breach the Kitar front and gain access to the temple grounds above.

The raven watched all from a secret alcove, violent eyes searching out the first opportunity it might seize. The bodies of the slain littering the passage floor did not tempt it in the least. They were dead and unappetizing. Nor did it crave the hardened flesh of warriors.

Suddenly, the raven's serpentine tongue caught a taste on the air that it liked much better. A living taste and much younger, much softer. Its gaze pierced through the heavy mortal darkness and saw a figure darting into the near-deserted passage in which the raven hid.

Sairu, her forehead boasting a line of blood from a either a Kitar or Chhayan weapon—it was impossible to tell in the dark—slipped around the corner of the outer passage, her eyes wide with a terror that was new to her: the terror of battle in close spaces. Had she known, had she realized into what horror she plunged, she would never have found the courage to enter the dungeons beneath the Crown of the Moon, no matter how driving her need.

But she had done it. And somehow, though it should have been impossible, she had slipped through both the Kitar defense and the Chhayan assault, navigating narrower passages though which the armored men could not fit. It was as though a path were made especially for her, and no one could follow her, no one could intervene. The cat, she knew, was somewhere close, but she could not see him when she looked, so she focused her gaze ahead.

The din of battle and the roar of Long Fire explosions up above rang in her ears. But with some sense deeper still, she felt or heard the nearness of the portal, the nearness of other worlds. If the Chhayans were indeed using a portal in the dungeons to access this world (and Jovann wouldn't lie . . . he wouldn't!), surely that same portal must lead back from whence they came.

Back to Ay-Ibunda.

She paused as she entered the passage, nausea threatening to overwhelm her at the sight of the carnage between her and the cell door she must achieve. But there was something more, something even more dreadful than all this near death.

The raven in the shadows breathed a hiss of delight. Sairu could not hear it. But she felt it, and she brandished her knife just in time as the raven swooped down at her head. The blade caught among black feathers and tore several away even as the raven altered its course, dodging a more fatal blow. With a roar that was not at all avian, the raven pivoted in midair and dove again, aiming for Sairu's eye.

Sairu ducked, avoiding the blow that would surely have torn her eye from its socket. But her foot caught on the body of a fallen warrior, and she fell, tumbling among the corpses. Her knife was lost, never to be found again.

She rolled with difficulty, her hand reaching up her sleeve for her second knife. She would not have drawn it in time, for the raven was even now in its dive, this time aiming for her beating heart.

But suddenly there was a flash of golden eyes. The cat leapt up and caught the raven between its paws, dragging it down to the dungeon floor in a mound of black feathers and orange fur. The raven shrieked, and the cat yeowled, and the light of the lantern flickered so wildly that Sairu could not see what transpired.

There was a dreadful stillness. Then: “Dragons blast it all!”

“Monster?” she gasped, pulling herself up from among the fallen dead and searching for the cat.

“I lost it,” the cat growled, his eyes glowing with their own light as he turned them up to her face. “It slipped my grasp and fled up the tunnel. Nasty demon, not what I expected to find down here! Should I pursue it?”

“No,” said Sairu, turning even as she spoke toward the cell in which Jovann had been so recently held captive. “We’re too close. Hurry.”

The cat sprang up and followed at her heels, crying out as he did so, “I think I know your plan! It’s a fool’s errand at best, but I’ll follow you to the end. I swear it!”

Sairu made no response. She leapt over bodies and nearly fell, catching herself on the doorway into the cell. She gazed inside and once more nearly lost her courage.

The crack in the worlds was open still, though no more Chhayans passed through. Sairu had never imagined—could never have imagined—what it would be like to stare out of her world into another. Everything she knew, the tower of training and precision she had built in her mind over all the years of her life, crashed down in ruins, leaving her, for a moment at least, truly insane. For a mortal cannot look upon such a sight without tasting of insanity.

But with the madness came a rush of something like courage. Gripping her remaining knife tight in her hand, she leapt across the cell and through that crack, and the cat sprang through behind her.

19

THE MOMENT SAIRU PASSED through the gate, she plunged into darkness. She tried to scream, but her voice was stolen away. She thought she would fall forever, that she would never find her footing, tumbling through eternity, through this space between the worlds. Falling and unable to accomplish the purpose beating in her heart.

But then she found that she was walking. She could not remember the end of the fall, could not remember finding solid ground. She was walking where she had been falling. For a moment her spirits lifted. There was a Path at her feet, and she could navigate through this strange Between. All was dark and shifting horror around her, but she could walk. She could follow this Path to its end and there, she hoped, find this Ay-Ibunda of which both Jovann and the cat had told her.

Time meant nothing here, and she could grasp no sense of passing minutes or hours. Again the change was so sudden that she did not realize it had happened until long afterward. For she walked in her own personal hell, and it overwhelmed all else.

She saw the face of the Chhayan man. The man she had killed. She knew now, though she could not say how she knew, what his name had been: Chakra. Chakra, whose life she had ended. He stood before her, behind her, on all sides. And she saw him screaming in the torment of an afterlife that was no rest, no peace, but utter, eternal, hopeless pain. And it was her fault! She had sent him here! She felt his pain as though it were her own, felt it searing her spirit. All was lost! All was endless! His face shifted and became that of Idrus, whom she had not slain with her own hands, but whose death she had brought about. He too was screaming, for there were no angels here to make his sins right. The blood of innocents flowed down his face, and it burned him, and it burned Sairu. The other slavers were there as well, the men who had lost their lives that night. And they were Idrus, and they were Chakra, and they were Sairu herself.

She screamed. But when she opened her mouth it was choked with blood. Falling on her face, she knew she could not walk a single step more on this road, this Dragon's Path.

But suddenly there were arms around her, strong arms drawing her close. She fell into them, leaning against a warm heartbeat. She heard a voice she recognized, felt it flowing over her like a covering, a shield, a protection.

"Beyond the Final Water falling,
The songs of spheres recalling,
When all around you is the emptiness of night,
Won't you return to me?"

"I don't know how to return," Sairu moaned. "I don't know the way."

"Hush," said the voice, which was like the cat's voice and yet unlike. "Hush and listen. He will show you the way." He rocked her as he might rock a baby, still singing softly. And as he sang, the faces of Chakra, Idrus, and the others faded, and the blood and the gore vanished from Sairu's vision. The Dragon's Path itself dissipated, giving way to a new Path, a clear Path, shining white and gold. When she dared look up, Sairu saw the wafting of green leaves, the sturdy trunks of tall trees. The Wood surrounded them, opening up before them and pointing clearly straight ahead.

She heard the silver voice of the wood thrush, which she had heard before without recognizing. And it sang: *"Won't you follow me?"*

Sairu was on her feet in an instant. The stranger was gone, and the cat was beside her. She looked down at him, and her face almost took on its customary smile, though not quite. "We will find her, Monster," she said. "We will find my mistress."

"I hope so," said the cat. He fell into a loping stride beside her, and the two of them ran down the Path, following the light, following the birdsong. Within a few paces the Wood gave way around them, replaced by swirling, formless mist. A few paces more and they stepped out into the wasteland of the Dream.

The cat came to a halt. The fur along his spine and up his tail stood on end. "Lumé love us!" he said. "This is it. This is the place, the very edge of the Between. This is where the temple was built. Ay-Ibunda."

Sairu stood very still. She had come to accept the notion of other worlds. She had come to accept the strange truth of the Dream Walkers and the art they practiced. She had seen the lovely opal stones Jovann brought back from the Gardens of Hulan, and she had felt the presence of phantoms she could not see, touch, or perceive with any ordinary senses. She knew there was more to life, to the world, than what she and her small reason could comprehend.

Nevertheless, the sight of the Dream stretching out before her was enough to stop her heart. She wished she could have come here in spirit only, as Lady Hariawan did, leaving her physical body behind. For her physical body did not want to exist here. One false step and she feared all the particles of her being would split, shooting off and away from one another, dispersing her across this terrible, mist-murky waste.

But the need of the Masayi was strong in her heart. She must find her mistress.

And perhaps, when she found her mistress, she would also find Jovann.

"Where is the temple?" Sairu asked, turning to the cat, relieved to see his orange face upturned to hers. He, at least, appeared solid and real, and her eyes clung to him as desperately as her hands might have clung to a lifeline.

"I do not know," the cat admitted, one white paw curled as he took a tentative step forward. "This is the Realm of Dreams, my girl, and I do not know the laws here. It is more dangerous by far than the Wood, for it is the very edge of the Between. Ay-Ibunda is supported by the dreams of men, but those dreams might be tossed about anywhere across this landscape. You would do well not to search for the temple."

"What then?" Sairu demanded. "What do I do? Tell me, Monster!"

"You know the answer to that already," the cat replied. "You know the Path you must follow."

He was right. She did not want to admit it, but he was right. There was only one Path that could lead her through this dreadful dreamscape. There was only one Path she believed would guide her safely.

She closed her eyes. It made no difference here, for the Dream was in her head. But she was a Golden Daughter, and she knew how to calm and quiet and finally silence each of her senses, one at a time, until only one remained. She blocked out sight, sound, hearing, even taste and touch. She blocked out everything and felt only the beating of her heart. *My mistress!* she thought.

And then, more softly still, *Jovann* . . .

Her eyes opened, and they were bright in the strange light of the Dream. "This way!" she said, and moved with confidence across the wasteland, taking in miles with each stride. The Path opened beneath her feet, guiding her, and the cat hastened along behind. Overhead, shapes began to form. Clouds gathered, black and then burning red. Hail fell in fiery stones that glowed through the swirling mist and burned it away, revealing dust on all sides. Still Sairu walked without pause, and the hailstones could not touch her. Far away she saw mountains high and green. But the red clouds gathered and roiled more thickly than ever, blocking these from her sight. They could not block the Path, however.

Then the ground broke. With a gut-wrenching thrill, Sairu found herself flung up suddenly on a jutting strip of rock which shot to the heavens even as the landscape all around fell away, plunging far and gone. She fell headlong upon the ground and felt empty drop on either side, and wind and clouds beating at her head.

"Monster!" she cried, but the cat was nowhere near. Perhaps the break had carried him from her. "Monster!" she cried again, and the searing clouds filled her mouth, burning her throat. She coughed and gagged.

Then another name, one she had heard spoken only once before, appeared in her mind, swelled upon her tongue. She tried to resist speaking it. Why should she? It was not a name she knew. But the sucking depths on either side thrilled her with terror. In desperation she whispered:

"*Lumil Eliasul.*"

The ground leveled out. With no motion or shift, she found herself once more on the wide plain, standing firm upon her Path. The cat leapt to her side and put his paws up on her knee. "Are you all right?" he demanded, gazing up at her. "For a moment there I was afraid the Dream had taken you!"

Her limbs shook, and she feared that if she spoke she might melt into a puddle of cowardice. So she only nodded. Then, setting her jaw, she proceeded up the Path, the cat at her heels.

Once more the ground broke. But this time it did not carry Sairu with it. Instead she found she had come to the edge of an enormous chasm which had been invisible on the flat landscape until she stood just above it. The vastness of the drop swept over her, and she felt heat rising with terrible intensity. But the Path led her right to the edge, so she crept along until she stood upon the brink. Her arms out for balance, she looked down.

Below her lay a molten lake. In a spidering network across the surface, lines of black rock shifted and groaned, shot with cracks of heat. Otherwise, all was roiling red, and she could not tell from that height if it was water, blood, or magma. It might have been all three at once here in the Dream. She did not wonder at this for long however, for something else caught her gaze.

She saw Hulan's Gate.

She knew it at once, for she, like all children of Noorhitam, had been raised with the little Moon Gate shrines. Many such shrines decorated the gardens of Manusbau and the Masayi, and Sairu had been made to pray before them and offer gifts back when she was young, back before she lost her faith. But this gate was as different from those shrines as the emperor's powerful warhorse differed from a child's painted stick pony. This gate was old, older than Time. And through it Sairu could glimpse the brilliant lights, in so many colors beyond what her own eyes could perceive, of Hulan's Garden.

"Lights Above, spare us!" whispered the cat. "The Dragon!"

Only then, when the cat spoke, did Sairu see the form like a man standing before that gate. And at his back, balanced upon the black, shifting stones floating on the surface of that fiery lake, stood the Chhayan priests. And they dragged the enormous Gold Gong behind them, as though there were no lake beneath their feet. Indeed, they did not perceive any of the same sights Sairu saw, neither lake nor cliff, but instead walked on flat, empty plain.

The gong gleamed like the sun, shining in the reflected glow of the lake's heat. It was supported upon two black pillars shaped like dragons. The Chhayan priests brought it to rest right before Hulan's Gate. Size and perspective were so distorted here in the Dream that to Sairu it seemed as though the gong were as great as the Gate itself, though this could not be possible. She saw that words were etched in the gold, but she did not try to read them for fear of the evil they might spell. Instead she searched the gathered crowd.

"My mistress!" she exclaimed. "Monster, look. It is she!"

And indeed there stood Lady Hariawan, appearing from behind the bulk of the Dragon. She was tiny, but Sairu could not have mistaken her at any distance. How frail and weak she appeared, and blood stained her shoulders and arms.

She stood before the Dragon. And then she bowed.

"No," Sairu whispered. "No, my mistress. Don't!"

With this cry, Sairu flung herself down on the edge of the chasm and swung out over the fiery gulf. Scrabbling for any handhold or foothold she could, she began the descent. "Sairu!" the cat called to her. "Don't be a fool!" But she could not hear him. She slipped and nearly fell, felt the plunge in her gut. But somehow she held on and scrambled down a few more feet. Heat rippled up from below and pushed against her. She almost believed that if she let go, the rising air would catch in her robes and buoy her up into the churning sky.

It was hopeless. She could not make herself move faster. Hanging precariously by one hand, she turned and looked again at the vision below.

Lady Hariawan remained before the Dragon. She straightened from her bow and lifted one hand, allowing the sleeve of her leper's robe to fall back, baring her arm. She offered this hand, palm up, to the Dragon. He took it, holding it delicately with his own claw-tipped fingers.

Then he raised it to his mouth and bit, sinking poison into her veins.

Lady Hariawan's cry of pain rang throughout the Dream, across the burning lake, up into the crimson clouds above. Sairu shouted furiously in ineffectual protest, her voice lost in the pain of her mistress. Once more she tried to descend and felt all the resistance of fire beneath her.

Lady Hariawan turned then from the Dragon. She cradled her poisoned hand to her heart, and black blood filled her palm and spilled down her wrist. She turned and approached the gong. Sairu, straining to look once more, suddenly saw a figure bound to one of the pillars. Jovann!

He recoiled at the approach of the beautiful lady stained with blood, her face full of poison. Though Sairu could not hear him, she could feel him in her heart, making his whispered, desperate plea.

"Please, Umeer's daughter," he said. "Please don't do this thing. Don't give in to the venom."

Lady Hariawan stood so close to him now that scarcely a breeze could move between them. She gazed into his eyes, and he saw, beneath the lovely contours of her face, the withered hag he had glimpsed before.

"Death. Life," said she. "What is the difference, Juong-Khla Jovann? Can you tell me this? Can you tell me the secret?"

"No mortal can tell you that," Jovann said. "It is not for us to know."

"I would have it for myself," said Lady Hariawan. "The knowledge of Good. The knowledge of Evil. The knowledge of Life and Death."

With this, she bent toward him and planted a kiss upon his mouth. Her mouth was wide and insistent, forcing his open to receive hers. And the Dragon's poison inside her flowed into him. He screamed. She fell against him, clutching his shoulders, his arms, and she too screamed, and their joint pain shattered the worlds around them.

"Now," said the Dragon. "Now you will strike."

Lady Hariawan's hands moved like two dying birds, struggling. But they undid the bindings that held Jovann to the pillar. He staggered forward, and for a moment braced himself as though to run.

"Now," said the Dragon.

And the poison in Jovann's veins responded to the word. He took Lady Hariawan by the hand, and the two of them turned to the gong.

A hammer, very small compared to the gong itself, but still so great that it would take the strength of two to lift it, hung suspended from the carved dragon-mouth of the other pillar. Together, Lady Hariawan and Jovann reached up and took hold of it. Together, they lifted it.

"*Now,*" said the Dragon once more.

They struck. And the voice of the Gold Gong sounded throughout that realm:

DOOM.

Sairu, clinging like a tiny insect to the wall of the chasm, saw the cracks run through the stones of Hulan's Gate. She saw them break. She saw spears of light shooting through the stones, and these spears grew and spread. She saw the Gate crumble.

And then it fell in a pile of dust, and nothing remained to separate the Dream from the vast spreading vaults of Hulan's Garden. The thunder of the stars' singing overcame all, falling upon the Dream in an avalanche of disaster. Sairu's body quaked down to the very marrow of her bones. She felt her hands resist then freeze.

She let go. Even as the Dragon spread his massive wings and flew roaring up into the heavens, she fell.

20

THE YOUNG DRAGON STAGGERED back, his hand flying to his throat. Blood gushed from his wound, spilled over his hand, and burbled in his mouth, choking. His eyes widened and turned with something between fury and fear to the figure crouching before him, her sword still upraised from her stroke.

Princess Safiya, moving with liquid grace, rose and turned her sword again. She took a single step and lashed out. Her second stroke should have severed his head from his shoulders.

But the blade connected instead with dragon scales and sprang back, blunted and useless. The young dragon, taking on his true form, reared up before her, flame darting from his eyes. He opened his mouth and, without taking care of his aim, let out a blast of fire that would have incinerated Princess Safiya on the spot.

But she was already in motion, and he missed. His long neck twisting, he turned to follow her, still blasting fire from his gut. The stones of the emperor's throne room blackened and melted beneath that heat, but Princess Safiya eluded him. She sprang around behind him, leaping over his swiping tail. A spike from that tail caught her robe, however, and brought her crashing down. She was up in an instant, pulling her robe free with a long, shredding gash. Before the dragon could turn, she had sprung upon his back, between his beating wings.

The young dragon roared, this time shooting his flame to the high ceiling above. Tapestries lining the walls blazed, and the throne room was now as bright with light as it had before been shadow-shrouded. The dragon reared back on his haunches, and his wings fanned the flames around him. He felt her climbing his scales, though the heat of his body must have burned her. He could feel her now at the back of his head.

Then her sword pierced through a soft place between scales, down into his head.

The dragon shrieked, and his voice was very like a man's in that moment. He fell, toppling across the burned floor, and lay still.

Princess Safiya, her flesh scarred red with horrible burns, leapt down from the dragon's neck and stepped back. Her sword remained embedded beneath the scales. Breathing hard but certain of her victory, she navigated out of the coils of his long body and turned her gaze up to the throne where the emperor had been. He had fled, as she had bidden him, in the midst of the battle. She must follow him and continue to assure his—

Fire struck her from behind.

Princess Safiya flew through the air and crashed upon the steps, halfway to the throne. She felt the life fading from her, rising up like smoke from her flesh. With more strength than she knew she possessed, she turned and looked down at the young dragon, who was pulling himself upright, his claws tearing into the floor.

"You cannot kill me with your mortal weaponry!" he snarled. "You cannot kill me, woman!"

His jaw opened, and fire swelled inside. In another moment he would have flamed her into oblivion.

But just then the skies above tore and the voice of the Moon shattered across all the worlds. Every beating heart in every universe—mortal, immortal, sentient, insentient—every heart quailed at the sound, and every pair of eyes upturned to the sky.

And they saw the stars falling. Red, burning, falling.

The young dragon swallowed his flame and stared out the great windows of the throne room at fire streaking from the sky. Then, with a shudder and another roar, he burst through that window and streaked out into the night. Princess Safiya lay upon the steps below the throne, struggling to breathe, and watched the heavens burn.

The stars sing together, and their voices are light and air and substance both tangible and intangible. They sing in complex harmonies, and these harmonies reach out to one another, linking, spinning, splitting, and binding again. Ever-moving, ever-changing, and yet always true, the Song binds the worlds together, supporting their existence according to the patterns of the Song Giver.

There is night, there is day. There is sky and sea. There is life and death and love and blood, and spirits made to soar through all the vastness of Space and Time. There is silence that resonates with as much beauty as sound. There are height and depth and horizons forever-stretching. There is the thunder of the Final Water falling in cascades, and there are the resounding echoes of the Highlands. There is the Boundless, and the stars sing across the Boundless. And their Song is one of joy, for they are beings of joy, created to sing. They glory in the fulfillment of their purpose, bound together in a union such as mortals may never know.

But a mortal may feel the faint echoes of it. A husband pressing his wife to his heart may dream of such a union. A mother feeling the swell of her child in her womb may sense the oneness of the stars. A brother clasping hands with a sister as they gaze up into the night may know, for an instant, the joy of the Moon's own children.

They sing together, and their voices blend with those of their luminous Mother, the Lady Moon, and their glorious Father, the Lordly Sun. For the Sun sings the Melody, and the Moon the first Harmony, and all their children spin threads of sound through these. And so it goes, without beginning, without end, forever and beyond.

Until a new thread emerges.

A darkness. A dissonance winding through the other voices.

You need not be bound to one another. You need not be enslaved.

There is no Time here. The whisper of dissonance emerges in a moment, but then extends forever, winding back and forward and throughout the heavens.

You can be one. You need not be many.

The beauty of One.

The beauty of Solitude over Solidarity.

A star stops. High in the heavens, the shining nimbus dims as the blue star, curious, turns to the voice.

No more harmony.

Sing your own song.

The blue star, who has ever moved in the pace of the Great Dance, who has ever sung the threads of the intricately woven harmony, closes its mouth. It stands perfectly still, intent upon the decision suddenly before it. The Song goes on around it, the Dance continues to move and turn and whirl. But it stands still in the midst of all, one foot upraised.

Be one. Be alone.

The star takes a step outside the pattern. A single step. The Dance is broken.

The overwhelming onslaught of isolation rolls across the star. And beneath its feet the Heavens break and the devouring void opens to the Dark Water below. With a scream the blue star rears up, thrashing against the pull of that pit. Then it plunges headfirst and streaks down forever, bursting into roaring red flame.

The Lady Moon upon her throne turns to see the first star fall. She sings out, "Cé Imral! My child!"

The Heavenly Gardens arched above Jovann even as they had before when he, pursued by phantoms, passed through the Gate. But now there was no Gate. There was no boundary. The Heavens spilled over into the Dream, and the two meshed in madness. The Endless Waters flooded over the burning lake, and water caught fire, and fire burned water. Above him, the stars whirled and danced in their eternal Song.

But it was not the same Song Jovann had heard that first time when he stood upon the shore and gazed up into the blossoming lights. Now, as all the vastness of the Dara's heaven spilled over him, he heard that it was marred with a strange, unholy discord. A line of non-music that grew, swelling, taking in more and more of the Dara.

He could not see this. He could not with his mortal perceptions comprehend that which took place above him. It seemed to him that the sky itself whirled into a hurricane of utter monstrosities, spinning stars, flaming eyes, enormous blossoms of fire flowers blooming and dying and rotting. Pulsations of flame and lightning that were the Dragon's voice, the voice of mounting discord among the many-layered harmony.

It was too much. His mind could not contain it. So, even as it had before, it shifted the visions, the sounds, the sensations, and made them appear to Jovann in forms he could understand, or at least come closer to understanding.

He saw the unicorns. All the lovely, mighty host, the shining stars, galloping across the sky, their tails streaming like comets behind them. At their heels sped the Dragon, more enormous than Jovann had believed possible. Gone was the tall, skeletal figure like a man, swallowed up in a vastness of armored, flaming horror with wings like great continents pounding at the air, his mouth open to reveal the very furnaces of hell burning inside him. He chased the Dara across the sky, and they fled before him. One by one, their joint voices ceased to sing.

As each unicorn fell into silence, so it fell from the sky.

Jovann watched as they plummeted in white, red, gold, and blue fire, streaking down to the swallowing water that lashed at his feet and lashed at the great Gold Gong. As each star landed, the brightness of it descended into the depths and could be seen for leagues beneath the surface of the water. Soon the endless ocean itself was more brilliantly lit than the sky above.

Then the surface of the water began to boil.

Rising up from the deeps, the stars returned. Only now their flaming had changed. They burned with rage. The rage of isolation, the rage of loneliness made complete. They burned with the rage of what they believed to be freedom, and it was a consuming, powerful, life-ending rage. So they died and revived in forms like living creatures, dead, yet alive in their death.

They burst from the ocean, hundreds upon thousands of them. No longer brothers and sisters united in song; now each was the enemy of the other and each the enemy of its own self.

The remaining Dara in flight screamed at the sight of these creatures that had been as much a part of themselves as their own hearts. They screamed and turned to flee, but the Dragon was at their backs. Jovann watched the poor stars rearing up in terror and saw many more stumble and fall to the Dark Water, only to boil up again as terrible as the first wave of monsters. And the fallen attacked their brethren with flaming teeth and knife-sharp hooves.

Where was Hulan? Desperately hauling himself up, feeling the handle of the gong's hammer beneath his hand, Jovann turned. He saw burning, ravening, hideous brutality, and the Dragon over all, laughing with mad pleasure that was very like pain. But where was Hulan? Where was the Lady Moon? Even now, with these terrible visions before his eyes, he remembered her, the shining Mother, as he had seen her before, seated upon her throne. Surely she would not let such horror be worked upon her beloved children! Surely she would intercede!

And then, suddenly, there she was. Through of the maelstrom of flame she walked, and her face was pale and white, and her hair was long and shining. Enormous and beautiful beyond words to describe . . . and yet the red rage of her children was enough to make her seem insipid, small, and dull even as she paced across the sky. She looked around her with eyes too full of emotions Jovann had never felt, and he realized that even now she sang.

But her song was not the Song it had been. Rather than the Song of the Universe, the binding of all worlds, the great, ringing, joyous praise, Hulan sang:

Why are you doing this?
Why do you allow this to happen?

Why? Why?
Why?

At first Jovann believed that she addressed the Dragon himself, who loomed over her as huge as a mountain, his wings sweeping in curtains of flame to surround her. But Hulan did not see the Dragon. She gazed upon those monsters who had been her children, rendered so horrible, so gross, so evil—she gazed upon her remaining young who desperately flocked toward her, crying out for her to protect them. But though she put out her arms to them, they could not reach her. Even as they fled to her, more of them fell, burning, and were transformed.

If I but knew my fault, said Hulan. She did not speak in words, or if she did, they were not words Jovann understood. But he knew the truth of what she asked as surely as if he asked it himself. Indeed he felt his own mouth forming words not his own.

"If I but understood! If I only knew why! What have I done to deserve this?"

Did I misunderstand? Did I mistake the Song you gave me? I thought you sang to me!

I sang back to you!

"I sang back to you . . ." Jovann whispered, and sagged to the ground, his forehead pressed against the hammer. But he forced his gaze upward once again. For now the most dreadful sight of all played out before his mortal vision, and though he believed he must die to see it, see it he would.

At a roared command of the Dragon, the red, ravening beasts that had once been shining stars closed in upon their mother. They grabbed her with their teeth, tearing into her shining form as though she were clad in flesh. They dragged her across the sky, and she made no protest, made no struggle, for they were still her children. Jovann screamed when he saw that they dragged her straight for the Gold Gong, for he believed he would be consumed in the fire of those monsters.

But the fire did not touch him. It was as though all of this took place in a realm beyond him, beyond his ability to reach. So he went on living, forced to observe though he would have torn out his own eyes rather than see what transpired.

The nearer she came, the smaller she seemed, and soon Hulan looked no more great or powerful than any woman. Indeed she looked to Jovann very like his own mother, only white and still shimmering with some faded memory of her former glory. The monster unicorns holding her flung her up against the gong.

The gong rang out its second great *DOOM.* And this broke the last of the Song, so that when the reverberations finally faded, all that remained was—

Silence.

Chains were placed upon Hulan's wrists and ankles, around her neck. She was spread out like a star herself across the surface of the gong, her hair falling over her face. There she hung, even as the pain of the gong's sounding rattled through her.

The Dragon crawled across the sky, scattering stars as he came. Fire fell from his mouth as though he salivated. "Hymlumé," he said, addressing the Moon by her ancient name, "your Song is broken. Will you now despair?"

With colossal effort she raised her head. She looked into the Dragon's face.

She said nothing.

"Very well," said the Dragon and he addressed himself to the red monsters on all sides. "Do what you will," he told them.

A monster stepped forward. Unquenchable red fire consumed its body, but still a sheen of blue could be seen beneath the red. It paced uneasily toward the gong, tossing its head, stamping its cloven feet. The Moon lifted her gaze and met that of her former child. But she did not see the monster it had become. Her eyes, glazed over though they were in terror and tragedy, still perceived her beloved. She did not speak, but her lips formed the name—*Cé Imral.*

The monster lowered its horn. It charged. Without pity, without regard. It pierced its mother through the heart.

One by one, other monsters gathered, hundreds of them. All of them charged at the shining figure chained to the Gold Gong. They speared her heart, her sides, her hands, her face. Their horns scored her shining whiteness, and the brilliance of Hulan was torn with hideous wounds. Her blood spilled and ran in crimson streams, staining the sky with her pain.

All the worlds looked on. From the peak of Rudiobus where a golden-haired fey queen gazed up to the sky in tears . . . from the Haven deep in the Wood Between where a lady knight rushed outside and cried out in horror . . . from deepest valleys of the Mherking's ocean kingdom; even there the blood seeped down and stained the faces of the mherfolk . . .

So all the worlds beheld the horror of the Moon's undoing, of the Song's un-singing, of the stars falling and rising up again. And all the worlds believed as one that the Final End had come.

Still, Hulan said nothing.

21

IN THE TUMULT AND TERROR of that night, no man defending the palace walls from barbarian hordes and fiery dragons had time or attention to notice one shadow slipping over the temple walls and flitting across the palace gardens. So the raven, escaped from the temple dungeons, made its way freely through Manusbau, its flicking tongue searching the foul, smoke-thick air for a scent and a taste it craved.

Ah! There it was.

The raven turned in midair with unseen grace, changing its course and making not for the main palace where the emperor even now hid and a princess lay in burned ruin upon the dais steps—no, the raven sought instead a smaller set of buildings (smaller, but no less beautiful), from which it caught the scent of youth.

The scent of a child's blood.

It flew into the Mahuthar, the children's palace, where the emperor's own small princes and princesses were even now clutched in the arms of their nursemaids and their queenly mothers. They had been awakened by their sisters, the Golden Daughters of the Masayi, and taken from their beds and nurseries down to the storage rooms below Mahuthar. No one would be able to get in or out without first passing the fierce young Golden Daughters, who wore no flowers in their hair that night but stood armed and dangerous around the perimeter, ready to defend their younger siblings and half-siblings unto death.

The raven did not care. It could smell the fear in these Golden Daughters, who were only just beyond childhood themselves. With each explosion along the palace walls, they would startle and turn, their attention, however momentarily, arrested.

And when, of a sudden, the moon overhead uttered her long Silence—when the sky above became red with moon's blood, and all the worlds trembled in terror—the Golden Daughters crouched in equal terror, their guard dropped.

The raven took its chance. It did not care what happened to the worlds around it. It cared nothing for the Dragon's plan or the Moon's fate. It had long since ceased to hear either songs or silences. All it heard was the pulse of blood in the young breasts hidden below.

The children beneath the palace heard the silence but did not understand it. Little Prince Purang Khuir leaned up against his nursemaid, who couldn't hold him for she had his younger sister wrapped in her arms. He heard her cry out in alarm though, and his heart beat all the faster in his breast. He clung to the only real comfort he could catch hold of, which was nothing more than a fluffy lion dog pushed into his arms by one of the Golden Daughters. "Hold him!" she'd told the little prince. "He'll protect you."

So Prince Purang Khuir held tight, burying his face in the lion dog's head even as the silence of the heavens weighed down so dreadfully upon him.

The raven, having slipped past the Golden Daughters' perimeter, crept soundlessly down the narrow passages, following the scent and taste of the children. Its eyes were very bright in the darkness, but no one saw it coming, for they had all hidden their faces in their terror. The raven moved like the shadowy hand of Death, drawing near to the first child, the little prince. Oh, how sweet was the smell of his blood! How luscious the beat of his heart! Like a viper ready to strike, the raven drew back its long beak.

Much to its surprise, it heard a long, low, "*Grrrrrrrrrrrrrr.*"

"Got you!"

In the mortal realm, Sairu's arm would have been yanked from its socket, and the pull of gravity might still have proven too much even for the grip of the beautiful, otherworldly man above her. But here, with the rising heat of the molten lake and the strange weightlessness that often accompanies a body in Dreams, Sairu found herself swinging like a pendulum, her wrist caught in a strong hand, her fall, momentarily at least, delayed.

As feather-light as the rest of her felt, she found it almost unbearably difficult to raise her head, to look up from the plunge beneath her to the face above her. But when she managed it at last, she found herself caught in the golden-eyed gaze of a man who, here in the Dream at least, was as familiar to her as the cat.

"Monster!" she cried. "Help me!"

"Yes, well, that's the idea, isn't it?" the beautiful man growled. "Take hold of my arm."

She twisted her wrist as best she could, but could only catch part of his sleeve. He held her tight with one hand, struggling to maintain purchase on the chasm wall with the other.

"Can you catch hold of the rock?" the beautiful man shouted. "Can you—"

But his voice was broken off then by the roaring across the sky.

Sairu, suspended above the churning lake, turned again and looked out across the strange dreamscape above, before, and below her. She did not see what Jovann saw. She could not, for she had not his faith, and so her mind could find no comparable images. She saw only an enormous, twisting mass of shapes, sounds, colors, and, more than anything, lights, spiraling out of that space of existence where the great Moon Gate had stood. It was the delicate play of dust motes dancing in the sunlight spilling through a window. It was a hurricane tearing apart the lives and hopes of an entire coastal city. It was a mother standing helpless on the banks of a river, watching her child drown.

It was all these things and more, but there was nothing, no reference or comparison onto which Sairu could grasp for true understanding. She swayed in the rising heat, her fingers feebly grasping the edge of the beautiful man's sleeve, and she experienced too much all in too short a space of time.

Her mind went blank.

And then through the blankness, a fixed point. Upon this she concentrated everything in her spirit. The Gold Gong.

"Monster!" she cried, twisting her head to gaze up at him again. She saw that he too was staring out at the spill of one reality into another. She saw that he perceived far more than she could, and that what he saw rendered him sick. "Monster!" she cried, but her voice could not reach him. His eyes stared out, beholding the flight of stars, the destruction of worlds. Tears welled up and spilled down his face, and she saw his lips moving in feeble prayer. "Song Giver, give us grace! Song Giver, give us mercy!"

The Masayi were taught from the time they entered the doors of the Golden Mother's house to depend on nothing and no one beyond themselves. Sairu, staring up at that stricken face above her, felt a sudden swelling sense of betrayal and, following that, determination. The heat rose up against her, and she told herself, "This is a dream. You've dreamt before. You know what is possible in dreams."

She let go her hold on the cat-man's sleeve. With a violent twist, she pulled herself free.

At first she fell. Had she been entirely sane, she would have thought she'd made a mistake, would have believed she'd miscalculated her chances. But she was not sane just then, and in her madness she did not doubt. As she fell, she spread wide her arms and her legs, and felt the heat catch in her voluminous robes.

In dreams it is possible to fly.

She had little control. She never did when she dreamed of flight. And slowly she sank from that awful height, closer and closer to the burning lake below. Soon she was close enough to see the crevices in the black rocks, to feel the spray as scalding bubbles burst. She felt that there was more here as well. Though she could not see it, she felt the presence of a vast Dark Water beneath her, and it too churned and boiled like the molten lake of fire. It was all one, now that the Heavens had spilled into the Dream and the Dream into the Heavens.

Sairu would not think of that. She focused ahead to where the Gold Gong stood. She focused on the two figures lying collapsed atop a great hammer. Though she dipped close to the fire, she struggled and, through sheer force of will, would not allow herself to sink. Thus her feet touched the shore just before the gong, and she fell to her knees, gasping.

Evil surrounded her. She sensed it on all sides, above, below, even inside herself. The glaring light of the red lake was gone, along with the lake itself. Here the darkness was intense and living; the only light by which she could see came from the gong itself, and that light was more evil than the darkness. She pulled herself up and approached the gong. Blood dripped down its surface as though the gong itself bled. No other source presented itself to her vision, and she did not seek more closely for answers.

Jovann lay upon the ground, one hand still holding limply to the hammer. He gazed up at the gong, and Sairu saw he was near fainting with terror. And Lady Hariawan, beside him, stared at the gong as well, a deathly smile upon her lips as she watched the spill of blood.

Sairu flung herself at them, heedless of the evil. The force of love was upon her, and she could not stop, not now. Though she could scarcely see for terror, she felt the Path opening at her feet even as it had across the Dream wasteland. There was still hope.

"My mistress!" she cried, falling before Lady Hariawan and taking her by the shoulders. Lady Hariawan did not respond to her touch or her voice but remained as she was, gazing into a world, into a nightmare Sairu could not perceive. Sairu tried to lift her but found that her mistress's body had gone leaden and would not be moved.

Only then did Sairu turn to Jovann. He seemed to be unaware of her. His grip on the hammer's handle tightened and relaxed and tightened again. His cheeks were so sallow, so sickly green, she feared for a moment that he was dead even as he held himself upright. She took his face between her hands, gripping him hard, as though she wished to crush his skull. "Jovann! Jovann, wake up!" she urged. "Jovann, I am here! We must go. We must go, my love!"

His eyes, unseeing, rolled in their sockets. His lips moved, but she could not hear what he said until she put her ear close to his mouth. Then she heard him moaning, "Hulan! Hulan! Oh, why are we forsaken?"

"You are not forsaken," Sairu growled. "I am with you!" With that, she wrenched the hammer from his grasp and heaved it away. Jovann moaned and fell against her. She could smell the stench of dragon poison in his breath, in his hair, in his skin. He shuddered, and she knew that he must be in great pain. "Jovann, can you hear me?" she begged, helping him to sit up and lean back against the dragon-shaped pillar. Then she took his head between her hands once more and whispered, forcing her voice to disguise the panic and reveal only calm: "Your pain is here. Beneath my hands. Feel it here beneath my hands."

His face went greener than ever, as though the poison did indeed gather where she touched him. She felt her stomach heave but forced her hands to slide down his neck, down his shoulders. "Your pain is here, Jovann," she whispered. "Feel it here. Feel your pain."

As she moved her hands, the poison drained away from his face, leaving him pale but once more human. But his agonized arms shivered, and she continued with deliberate urgency. She slid her hands to his wrists, and then her palms were pressed against his, pressed ever so hard.

"Your pain is here. Hold your pain. Hold your pain in your hands."

Jovann groaned, and his eyes rolled again, staring up at the gong and the dripping blood. He saw things she could not see, experienced agonies she could not share.

"Hold your pain," Sairu said, desperation welling up in her heart. "Hold your pain. Hold it here. Oh Jovann, try! Please try! Hold your pain."

"No. Let me hold it."

Sairu, startled at the voice that spoke beside her, dropped her hold on Jovann's hands and turned. She could not see, or not entirely see, the one who knelt beside her. But she felt his presence, more solid and more real than anything she had ever before experienced. She recognized the voice as the one that had been calling to her, guiding her along the Path in the Dream. Perhaps guiding her for longer than she realized.

"Do you know who I am, Sairu?" the voice asked.

"I do," she said, though until she spoke she had not known.

"What is my name?"

"Lumil Eliasul," she responded without question. "The Giver of Songs."

Then a sob caught in her throat, and she could not speak, not in words, though her heart cried out, "Where have you been? Where? Where? *Where have you been?*"

"I have been here," said the voice. The blood falling from the gong seemed to spill through the air in a sort of shape, a sort of image that Sairu could almost, but not quite, see. "I have been here all along. And now I will hold his pain."

The image formed in blood reached out and took Jovann's hands even as Sairu had, palms pressed to palms. And the voice spoke in soaring echo of Sairu's, but with a truth in the echo that her own voice could never have matched. "I hold your pain, Jovann. I hold your pain in my hands."

So Sairu watched the poison pass from Jovann's body, from his spirit. She watched as he began to breathe again, full, normal breaths, and the color crept back into his skin. More than that, she knew that what had been broken inside him was now, for the first time in his life, made whole.

He moaned. He opened his eyes. "Sairu?" he whispered. "Is that you, little miss?"

"Oh! Jovann!" she cried and leapt forward, seizing his arms.

Even as she did so, the gong above them sounded again: *DOOM.*

The space of reality around them shivered and cracked in extreme agony, and the roar of the Dragon reverberated with the gong's own voice.

DOOM.

The voice spoke in Sairu's ear. "Take him now, and Umeer Melati. Lead her as far as you can from this place, but take care you do not follow her. She will walk her own Path. You must follow mine. Go now, for the End is upon us. Go!"

He did not leave. Though all perception of him fled her, Sairu knew that he was still near. This knowledge gave her courage, and she strengthened her grip on Jovann's arm.

"Up!" she commanded, though she could scarcely be heard in the ongoing din of the gong and Dragon's roar. "On your feet. We must carry my mistress between us!"

Jovann shook himself and stared around at the blackness and the gong. He no longer beheld the horrible sights to which he had been witness, but they were not gone from his memory. But without the image of Hulan and her suffering immediately before his eyes, he found he could move, even enough to follow Sairu's orders.

They bent to Lady Hariawan, who remained inert through all. Taking her by the arms, they hauled her to her feet and, between them, carried her away, fleeing the long shadow of the Gold Gong. They fled into darkness but, even as the voice of Lumil Eliasul had promised, a Path presented itself at their feet. Like a white stream flowing with ripples of light, it appeared, and they found that when they trod upon it they could run.

Run they did, dragging along their burden. And suddenly the darkness was gone, and even the rippling Path, and they found themselves once more upon the empty, formless wasteland of the Dream.

"Where now?" Jovann demanded, for though he turned every which way, he could see no landmarks by which they might be guided. "How do we escape this realm?"

Sairu also scanned the horizon, but she sought something more specific. Sure enough, she spotted a familiar figure racing toward them on small white feet.

"Monster! We're here!" she cried.

"Great Iubdan's beard and mustache, I can't believe you're alive," the cat yeowled in reply. He was so close now, she could see the gold rims of his eyes.

Then a blast of fire and a plume of black smoke smote the wasteland between them and the cat. A shadow fell across all, and Sairu and Jovann looked up at the hovering form of a young dragon.

"Sunan!" Jovann cried.

"Well met, brother," said the dragon.

22

THE LADY MOON HANGS IN her chains, and one by one her children tear into her. She does not wear a form of flesh, so they tear her spirit, and her spirit bleeds. They tear her heart, and her heart bleeds. And her blood flows across the skies.

The Dragon bending over her is bigger than worlds, and his malevolence shrouds everything within the Moon's sight. Her gaze is far-flung, for she looks upon all worlds, she shines and offers comfort to all beings. But now all beings behold only her pain.

"Will you now despair?" the Dragon asks, as yet another of her children rends her through the heart, savaging with its horn. "Will you now speak?"

Her Song has ceased. For a moment and a forever, the worlds hang suspended in her Silence. Her children ravage her body, but this pain is as nothing to the pain she feels at seeing them ravage themselves. To see them torn from their dance, to see them torn from one another, from her own heart. To see them burn, burn, burn without end.

Her children. Her beautiful children.

The loss is too great to be borne.

"I see it in your face, Hymlumé," said the Dragon. "I see your desolation. Speak it now. Speak it into this Silence. And declare to all the worlds my greatness!"

She says nothing.

The Dragon roars, enraged. He lashes his great tail, striking the gong so that it resounds its bellowing DOOM! *and the Moon is shattered to the core.*

"See what I have wrought?" the Dragon cries. "See my power? Long have I labored to bring about your end. Long have I plotted, schemed, unbeknownst to your great Lord. Is He so all-powerful, so all-seeing? If so, then He is evil, for He did not prevent me. Or perhaps He did not know. Perhaps He did not see. Perhaps He is too blind to notice the workings of traitors in His own household. His great love of which you sing has made Him weak.

"See my power, Hymlumé. I spread my shadow across every world. Not only your heavens, from which I cast your children in flame. Not only the mortal world where men and women flock in terror to my worship. Not only here, not only there, but everywhere, Hymlumé. My influence spreads like poison through veins, and He did not stop me. He did not intervene.

"Worship me, Hymlumé. Worship me as mortals do. Worship me and declare my supremacy.

"Speak now, Hymlumé. Speak now your despair."

She cannot raise her luminous eyes. She cannot raise her head. She bleeds from too many wounds.

But she feels a gentle hand touching her face.

The Dragon's venom pours down upon her head, venom and fire both. "You are abandoned, Hymlumé. If you were not, would He allow you to suffer so? Would He allow your children to fall? You are abandoned. The Love you believe in is false. You are abandoned. Abandoned. Your name is not Harmony. Your name is Forsaken!"

All is lost.

Everything is taken away.

The Dragon bends over her, cupping her face between his massive hands, his claws tearing at her eyes, her hair, her cheeks, her throat. He forces her to look at him.

"Speak your despair, Forsaken One."

The Silence is long. It covers the worlds in crimson. All hearts wait, though they may not know it, straining to hear the Silence end. Waiting to hear what will fall from the sky above. In the mortal world, the battle waging along palace walls ceases suddenly, and even the warriors drop their weapons and stare up at the sky. The knight in the Wood is upon her knees, her hands clasped, her mouth moving in feeble prayers. The queen on the mountaintop raises her arms, ready to receive whatever destiny rains down, even doom. Everywhere, in every world, the Silence strains to the breaking point, and it must end.

"Speak," says the Dragon.

And the Lady Moon opens her mouth.

She says: "Rise up, my heart."

Like the first drop of rain upon a desert floor.

Like the first wave of heat from the hearth fire upon a frozen face.

Like the first whisper into a deaf man's ear.

Like a crack of light piercing the eye of the blind.

"What did you say?" the Dragon demands, his hands still crushing her head.

The Lady Moon speaks again: "Rise up my heart. Affirm thy adulation in pain—"

"What? What did you say?" The Dragon drops his hold as though he, who cannot be burned, is suddenly struck with the heat of searing brands. "What did you say, Forsaken One?" he roars, and it is his voice that is filled with pain. For now her song is swelling. Now it will not be dammed but will spill from her mouth along with her tears, along with her blood.

So Hymlumé sings:

"Rise up, my heart: Affirm thy adulation
In pain, rejoicing in thy Lord on high;

Exalt Him here and throughout all Creation,
Thy Song emblaz'ed across the ringing sky!
Rise up, my heart: renew paeans divine,
And to His hand thy children now consign."

As her Songs build and her blood flows, the Dragon screams. And it is as though scales drop from his eyes and he sees what has been before him all along, but which he had been unable to perceive. Like a mortal gazing into immortal secrets, so was he before that mighty Truth standing before him.

He sees the Lumil Eliasul, the Giver of Songs, the Prince Beyond the Final Water. And the Dragon knows then that his Enemy has stood there between him and Hymlumé all along.

Hymlumé, her gaze still too full of suffering to see that mighty light which far outshines both Sun and Moon, nonetheless raises her voice in greater strength:

"Rise up, my heart: Declare thyself content
Belonging wholly to thy gracious Lord.
Thy soul, thy heart, in offering present
Once more surrendered to the One adored.
Rise up my heart: Thy best beloved given
In hallowed pledge unto the Lord of Heaven."

So she collapses in her chains, her spirit exhausted. And yet her Song continues, rolling across the battered Heavens, across every sky and every nation under those skies. She is as still as one dead. But her Lord reaches out and breaks her chains, taking her from the gong and pressing her to His heart.

Then the Lumil Eliasul turns upon the Dragon. The Dragon, who had been larger than worlds, and who is now small, so very small that his Enemy reaches out and picks him up in one hand.

"I will show you a wonder now, Death-in-Life," says the Lumil Eliasul, speaking the Dragon's true name. "I will show you what you have never

before seen. And you will try to forget, for you cannot hold such a memory and survive. But I will show you. Look!"

The Giver of Songs lifts the Dragon to His face, up to His very eye. And that eye is huge. It is as far beyond the Dragon's understanding as the Gardens of Hymlumé were beyond Jovann's. That eye contains the Sun, the Moon, the whole of the starry hosts of Heaven. That eye contains this world, that world, all worlds, and all Betweens. That eye contains the Boundless, and yet there is still more, and more. The Dragon looks, and he sees that all of Time is but a grain of sand within that eye, and Space itself is smaller still.

"No! No, please!" The Dragon screams, struggles. He tries to find the vastness of his wings, but they are as infinitesimal as his own imagined might. "Let me go! Let me be free!"

The Lumil Eliasul gazes upon him, upon the whole of him, the beginning, the end, and the Nothing of him. And that gaze is more than the Dragon can bear.

He flames. He dies. He lives again.

Yet he cannot escape.

"Poor, foolish thing," said the Lumil Eliasul. "Do you see now? Do you see the truth? Nothing you set your hand to will be accomplished beyond my will. Now even your foul work will I turn to greater good, to greater glory, beyond anything you have imagined. Behold."

Once more the Dragon stares into that eye. Now the speck that is Time grows, as though crossing millions of light-years in seconds so that it may spread before the Dragon's gaze. And he sees what he has done. He sees it in full. He sees that the greatest workings of his evil—the silencing of the Song, the blood across the sky, the fall of the stars themselves—is too small to be seen. The weight of glory is too much; it crushes all beneath it.

The Dragon roars again, summoning up his fire, summoning up the Moon's fallen children. Even now he believes he can make a blaze that will, if not consume, then at least hurt his Enemy.

But the Lumil Eliasul speaks through his flame. "Your greatest evil is not great enough to mar my smallest good. Your evil is bound in the confines of Time. Your workings only exist for a moment. Then they are swallowed up. But my good extends to all Times, all Timelessness, all worlds imagined and unimaginable. Vain, futile creature, for creature you are, created and sustained only at my will. Can you not see how all this fire is swept away and becomes nothing at all?"

The Dragon can see now. He can see it all too well.

But he shuts his eyes.

Then suddenly he is loosed from his Enemy's grasp. He flies across Time and strikes against something solid, something gold, something that bellows DOOM! *for him and him alone. He sees that he has struck the gong that he himself prepared, and the chains which had so recently bound tight the Moon bind him tighter still.*

He feels Time closing in around him.

"You will sleep," the Lumil Eliasul declares. "Now, Death-in-Life, you will sleep for a thousand mortal years. And you will feel those years through your sleep, even as a mortal would. When you wake, you will believe you have forgotten what I have revealed to you. But you will not forget."

The Gold Gong is caught up then between two hands. The Dragon, chained in place, screams his fury and flames from the very depths of his soul.

Then he is hurled from the Heavens. Down to the Dark Water below.

The heat of his fall melts the gong, twisting its shape beneath him into that of a lumpish golden altar. But the chains hold fast, and he cannot break them. The altar stone strikes the Dark Water. It sinks, and the blackness of oblivion swallows up the Dragon.

So he will sleep for a thousand years.

23

THE SKY CRACKED AT THE SEAMS. Great fissures opened in the clouds and, beyond the clouds, in the very fabric of the Dream's eerie reality. Like the molten rock upon the lake's surface, the sky rent, and beams of deeper darkness shot through and stabbed the wasteland below.

The Dream was crumbling away, swept up in the falling ruins of Hulan's Garden. Through one of the cracks a fireball sped, and it may have been one of the Dara falling. It smote the ground, shaking the whole of that realm so that Sairu and Jovann both lost their footing and fell, dragging Lady Hariawan down with them.

The young dragon teetered in the air, his wings angling to keep his balance. He stared around at the ruination, and he smelled the stench of the falling stars. Was this then his sought-after vengeance? No. No, that could not be!

Hatred mounted inside him like the rising pressure of a volcano. He tore his gaze away from the horrors of the breaking Dream and focused everything he had upon the small figure of Jovann lying so helpless below.

"This is your fault," he snarled. "You did this. You led my Father to the Gate."

The ground continued to shake as more fireballs impacted with tremendous force, and the smoke of their landing filled the air, mingling with the formless mist. Jovann, struggling to regain his footing, put himself before Sairu and Lady Hariawan. He gazed up at the ugly shell of what had been his brother. "Stop this!" he cried. "Stop and return to me. We can still set this right. We can still fix what is broken between us. Please, Sunan."

"That is no longer my name!" the dragon roared and spat fire in a stream from his throat. Sairu, seeing what was coming before it happened, grabbed Jovann by the back of his shirt and hauled him to one side, so that they narrowly missed incineration.

Briefly the smoke of the blast and the tormented mist shielded them. Sairu, looking up, saw the red heat of the dragon's eyes burning through the haze.

It was almost a relief. A bizarre, unnerving relief, but a relief nonetheless. For in that moment of physical danger Sairu felt herself come alive, felt her numbed senses awaken. All thoughts of the strange sights and sounds and experiences beyond perception which had nearly overwhelmed her were pushed aside in the immediate need of *now*.

Now she must fight.

Now she must defend her mistress.

Now she must save Jovann.

The dragon beat the air with wings that seemed small compared to the enormity of his Dark Father's mass. But they drove powerfully, creating a wind that blew back the smoke of his own fire, revealing the three hiding below. Only there weren't three. There were only two.

Something struck him in the eye. It wasn't sharp, but it was exact, and momentarily it hurt and blinded him. He snarled, gnashing great teeth, and whirled about, seeking the missile and its source. A shoe fell to the ground, landing near to Sairu, who brandished her knife at him.

She smiled.

"Puppy-puppy-puppy!" she cried, her voice a manic child's jeering. "Little lizard-puppy! Not even a Chhayan dog-boy, are you? You're just a little pup with a little puny flame!"

In the face of such a smile even lifelong hatred of his brother must be forgotten. Suddenly nothing in all the worlds was more important to the dragon than blasting that smile into oblivion. He opened wide his jaw.

Sairu leapt just in time, darting into the mist even as the spurting fire chased after her. The roar of it was so loud, she could not even hear Jovann's shouts. She could do nothing but run, trusting that eventually even a dragon must pause for breath. Her hair and heels were singed by the heat of the blaze so close, but she kept ahead of it, if only by a step or two.

The dragon stopped, gathering himself for another burst. The putrid poison of his fumes was almost enough in itself to kill her. She hid her face in her sleeve, coughing but trying to stifle the cough. Her only safety now lay in the veiling of smoke and dust and ash.

"Monster!" she whispered, choking on the word. "Monster, are you here?"

Another shooting fireball struck, this one nearer than the others, and knocked her headlong. She shook herself, pushed up onto her elbows, and found that she was face to face with the cat. "Can you help me?" she gasped.

"Of course," said the cat.

Then he was a man, shining and bright, and he dragged her to her feet. "This way," he said, taking her by the hand, and she ran with the cat-man through the mist. She found before her feet a stairway of stone which had not been there a moment before, and she knew somehow that the cat-man led her back onto the Path she had lost.

She fled with him up the stairs, which spiraled high to nowhere without a guardrail on either side. She came to the top, many stories above the ground below, and looked down upon the dragon's back.

He turned this way and that, searching for her, searching for Jovann. The world around them shivered again as another fireball struck, and a wall of heat and energy rippled through the air and nearly knocked the dragon from his flight. Recovering his balance, he hovered just below her.

"Are you sure about this?" the cat-man cried.

Sairu did not answer. She was already leaping.

In dreams a fall is either slow enough to seem like hours or instantaneously quick and heart-lurching. This fall was the latter. She had scarcely sprung from the high spiral stair when she found herself landing hard upon that scale-covered neck, so hot that she burned her hands and her face and felt her garments searing away. She screamed in agony then in anger when she saw something she recognized.

Princess Safiya's sword.

Suddenly she wanted the dragon dead. Not stopped, not thwarted. He must die! He must suffer! He must be sent to the same burning hell where she had sent Chakra, Idrus, and the rest!

Dragon poison filled her lungs, filled her veins, seemed to take charge of her muscles. She brandished her knife and struck down into the same small gap Princess Safiya's sword had found. She thrust in the knife, the hilt, her hand, all the way to the elbow, between his scales into the soft place at the base of his skull. She felt the burn of dragon's blood spurting up to her shoulder.

The young dragon jolted at the blow. He swung his head back and forth so violently that Sairu, still clutching her knife, was dislodged and fell into the mist. The pain of the blow was excruciating, and as it went on and on, the dragon wished he could die.

But he couldn't die. Not like this. Not by that blade.

He plummeted to the ground and struck with an impact like a faint echo of the stars falling all around them. When he rose up again, he bore the form of a man, but a man covered in ugly ash-black scales. Brilliant, fire-rimmed eyes burned away the mist as he turned, seeking the one who had caused him such hurt.

He found her. She lay stunned beneath his gaze. As he drew nearer, she coughed violently, her body convulsing as she struggled to regain mastery of her own limbs. She grimaced in ghastly facsimile of her grin and stared up at the approaching figure, so appalling in its near-humanity. The sky above him was black and streaked with the flaming tails of falling stars. Every step he made seemed to shake the earth, though he had not that power. She saw her death in his eyes.

And she saw something else which even in that dire moment drew her surprised gaze: the cluster of opal stones which Jovann had placed into her keeping. The stones she had been compelled to give her Lady Hariawan. The blossom from Hulan's Garden, the light of her own secret desires shining in a setting of gold upon the monster's hand.

"My brother was wrong," the dragon said. "He told me that I would be defeated. By a maiden with a long knife." His blackened lips curled back, revealing sharp teeth behind which a new flame grew. "I am no longer slave to any fate. I am my own master. I am—"

He roared, and his flame went wide as he jolted to one side, wrapped in his brother's arms. He and Jovann fell hard and rolled, each desperate to gain the upper hand. The young dragon smoldered even in this human shape, but Jovann was strong. He pounded the fiend's face and chest, any part of him he could reach, no matter how the scales cut his hands and made his knuckles bleed.

The dragon, pinned beneath his brother's weight, stared up into that face—that face so like his had been—and saw there everything he hated most in his life. Jovann, panting and bleeding, beheld the fire in his brother's eyes, the lava bursting at his lips. Even then, with his death about to strike, Jovann did not fear, for he was too angry and too determined. He raised his fist to strike one last blow.

But suddenly the fire in the young dragon's mouth dulled and died. A trickle of smoke issued from his lips, and a faint, trembling word.

"Angel?"

At the sound of his brother's voice—not the dragon's growl, but truly the voice of Sunan—Jovann stayed his fists, and his heart caught in his throat. Still tensed, still prepared for death, he turned slowly and looked back over his shoulder.

Lady Hariawan stood above them, behind Jovann. Her leper's rags were torn and blackened, and her hair was burned away, revealing her scalp in places. The ugly mark of the Dragon's hand glowed red in the light of the falling stars.

Yet she was so beautiful, so dreadful, and so dire.

"Angel?" the young dragon said. Then a sound like a sob tore through his teeth. "Do not look at me! I am not worthy." She took a step nearer, and he put out a protesting hand, the same hand upon which the ring of opals glowed.

Suddenly that hand was caught and slammed to the ground. The dragon screeched as a blade cut down, hacking at his scale-clad fingers. Three times Sairu struck, but still she could not sever the ring free. The dragon roared and flung Jovann from him, wrenching his arm from Sairu's grasp and clutching his maimed hand and the ring close to his chest. He spun about wildly, ready to destroy them all.

But found himself standing eye-to-eye with Lady Hariawan. His angel.

"Sunan," said she. "The Good Word."

He shuddered at her voice, whimpering like a dog and cowering into himself. He tried to back away, but for every step back he took, she took another forward.

"You promised to love me," she said.

"I cannot love!" he growled, tormented. "I have no heart, not anymore!"

"You have my gift," said Lady Hariawan, and her eyes fell upon the ring on his half-severed finger. "You have my gift of the heart. And you will obey me."

The dragon panted, heaving smoke from his lungs with every breath. Then he gasped, "Command me, mistress."

Lady Hariawan drew herself up to her full height, and here in the Dream it was a greater height than in her own world. She seemed to transform, becoming once more the force she had been before her encounter in the Dream and the veil of lunacy that followed. She recalled, if only briefly, that she was the selected daughter of the Hari Tribe and the Awan Clan, that her father slew fifty men in a single day, that the name of Umeer was honored among the people. That she was the strongest, the brightest, the most powerful Dream Walker the priests of the Crown of the Moon had ever encountered. She became herself, and yet in her eyes there swirled the life-draining darkness of the Dragon's venom. When she spoke, it was with great power:

"Leave us. Do not return. I never want to see your face again."

Sairu and Jovann, drawing close to each other in horror of the sight playing out before them, watched the young dragon. The banishment Lady Hariawan commanded was a force more wounding than any hewing blade.

For a moment his scales fell away and they saw the young man. The son of the Tiger. The elegant scholar. The sorrowing orphan bereft of his mother. Jovann opened his mouth and began to speak, reaching out a hand as though to offer aid. But Sairu caught him and drew him back, shaking her head when he looked at her.

The young dragon who had been Sunan turned away from his angel. Holding her gift close to that place where his heart had once beat, he took three paces then, his body no longer able to contain the truth inside, burst into wings and supple tail and sinuous body. With a roar of flame he soared up into the darkness, higher and higher until he was merely a speck of fire streaking toward one of the cracks in the sky.

Then he was through the crack and gone.

Lady Hariawan, her face upraised to watch the dragon's ascent, quivered suddenly and almost fell. Sairu was at her side in an instant, catching and supporting her, all the rage of dragon poison vanished in tenderness. "My mistress?" she gasped. "My mistress, are you unharmed?"

"No," said Lady Hariawan, turning eyes that were almost, but not quite, empty upon her handmaiden. "No, I am not unharmed. I am very harmed indeed."

The world groaned around them. The ground shook yet again, and the mist rushed over them so that Sairu was afraid she would lose both her lady and Jovann. But she held tight to Lady Hariawan's arm and felt Jovann's hand on her shoulder. "Hurry," he said into her ear. "This world is coming all undone. We must find a way out."

But when they turned together, every way they looked, every step they took, there was only more darkness, more smoke, and the streaking lights of the stars. "Where is the Path?" Sairu cried, and for the first time in her life felt panic welling up inside her. "Where is the Path? Monster! Monster, where is the Path?"

The cat was nowhere to be seen.

The piercing shriek of rock scraping rock at high speed shot white daggers through her head, and Sairu let go of her mistress to clap both hands over her ears. She felt the ground move beneath her even as it had done before. She felt part of it rise and the rest of it fall, and suddenly she was at the top of a deep crevice, staring down into a trench below her. It was so deep that the mist did not yet fill it.

And in the red glare of the stars, Sairu saw Lady Hariawan lying far below.

"*Mistress!*" she screamed. In another instant she would have hurled herself over the edge of that drop, heedless of all danger.

Someone caught her from behind, and she heard Jovann's voice in her ear once more. "Sairu! No, you'll be lost as well!"

"Mistress! Wait for me!" Sairu screamed. She felt Jovann's hand restraining her. Every instinct burst into play. She caught him by the wrist and the fleshy part of his arm, which she pinched down to the bone. She twisted both his arm and her body and sent him hurtling onto his back, slamming into the ground at her feet. The wind knocked out of him, he lay stunned. By the time he reached for her again, she was already over the edge, climbing down the crack in the world. "Mistress, wait!" Sairu called again to her lady down below.

Lady Hariawan, deep in the crevice, stirred. She stood, swaying uneasily on her feet, and saw the sheer walls before and behind her. The mist, like running water, poured over the high edges and crept down the walls, its long, white, finger-like tendrils grasping the rock that was not really rock, for there was nothing real in the realm. How well Lady Hariawan knew this. How well she knew that the white mist was neither more nor less than what her subconscious made of it.

And what she made of it was madness. Final madness descending upon her in slow, soundless flood. She stood at the bottom of the crevice, staring up, and it seemed to her that the mist was a living entity bent on devouring her.

She heard Sairu's voice shouting high above, and she saw her handmaiden's torn scarlet robes flashing so bright, even at that distance, even through the murk of the swarming Dream. Lady Hariawan blinked up at her, saw her trying to scramble down the rock face, and knew that she would never outmatch the mist. The Golden Daughter had failed. Even now, before the last note was sounded, the song of failure rang in Lady Hariawan's ears. She would be lost; the mist would claim her. She would never again escape the Dream.

Lady Hariawan drew a deep breath and breathed the first curlings of mist into her lungs. "Return to your world, Sairu," she called. "I am through with you." Her thin voice struggled to climb up that height, but it bore neither bitterness nor forgiveness, nor even regret. Only resignation.

With that, she turned. The crevice stretched before her, a yawning dark path; and the mist, so sentient, so full of hidden secrets and hidden malice, beckoned to her. She walked. That was what she was, after all: a Dream Walker.

And so the mist coiled over her head, swallowed her up, and concealed her forevermore from Sairu's searching gaze.

"No!" Sairu clung to the wall and felt as though her hands clutched, not rock at all, but slimy skulls piled one on top of the other, mocking her with evil rictus grins. "No! Mistress, no! Come back!" Tears poured in torrents down her cheeks, and she felt the blackness of dragon poison scalding her skin with every tear. She would never reach her mistress now. The mist had devoured her. There was nothing left. Only that drop. That drop into nothing. There was only—

"Sairu, look at me."

She heard Jovann calling to her up above. But that did not matter now. She had failed him too. She had lost his lady. She could not fulfill her vow to bring his bride safely home, to protect them both.

"All right. All right, stay where you are. I'm coming down."

At this, she looked up and indeed saw Jovann's legs swinging out over the gap, and then his body inching awkwardly down, finding handholds and footholds in the dream-substance of the cliff.

She clutched the rocks, which were no longer skulls but beds of slimy black moss crawling with slugs and spiders. She cared nothing for these nightmare images. They could not frighten her. "Go back," she growled, and her voice was very like a dragon's in that moment. "Go back, Jovann! Don't be a fool."

"Too late," said he. The world of the Dream shook, and chunks of the cliff fell away, turning into screaming faces as they vanished in the swelling mist. Jovann slipped, and for a terrible moment she believed he would fall, she believed he would be lost as well. But, as though his gaining her side was a destiny neither one of them could forestall, he found his grip and continued to descend. "I've been a fool far too long," he said. "But I intend to stop, right now."

With a last scrambling effort, he drew alongside her, clutching the same black moss as she, and spiders crawled over his hands, biting and raising ugly welts. He did not look at them but turned to her as they hung together, suspended over their doom.

"Climb up," he said.

Sairu shook her head. "I can't. My mistress is lost."

"But I am not. And I need you still."

Her ears were too full of her pounding sorrow and the pulse of dragon poison. She could not hear what he said. She bowed her head into the dream substance, which had changed once more and was now formed of jagged black ice so freezing that it burned. "There's nothing for me up there." The mist by now had filled the crevice and reached up to touch her ankles. "There is nothing. I am nothing."

But Jovann leaned closer to her, trying to look her in the eye, though she refused, turning away. "You are everything. Everything to me," he said. "And if you will not climb up, neither will I. Do you understand?"

She did not. But some dull part of her heart wished her to understand, wished with such intensity of longing that even the poison she had breathed receded from her mind, receded from her vision just long enough that she could look at him.

She saw his heart in his eyes, and it was bright and warm even here as they clung to a wall of ice.

"Please, little miss. Come back with me."

Through the mist, through the fear—across the Boundless and leagues beyond even the Realm of Dreams—the silver song of the wood thrush sang. And Sairu glimpsed once more that vision she had experienced the night Jovann put Hulan's blossom in her hand. She glimpsed the woman she could never be, for she was a Golden Daughter. And she realized that of all the dreams, all the illusions of her life, she herself had been the deepest, most dreadful illusion of all. For she was not what she had always believed herself to be. And her desires were not those for which she had always striven.

The wood thrush sang, and its voice cut through the mist, the broken sky, the flames of the falling stars. It was a voice of living water, rushing, white, and cleansing. It washed over her soul.

"*Won't you return to me?*"

Sairu's gaze cleared. Tears splashed down her cheeks, but they were cleansing tears washing the smoke from her eyes. She saw Jovann beside her, his face full of so many things, not least of which was terror, not least of which was love. Drawing a breath that was both agony and relief, she released her hold on the jagged ice with one hand and slid her fingers on top of his.

"*Follow me,*" sang the wood thrush.

The mist overwhelmed them both. Sairu, clutching Jovann's hand in hers, closed her eyes. The wall was gone. All was gone. Nothing surrounded them on all sides, and yet, at the same time, everything. She felt no fear, though she wondered if she should. The end, after all, is also the beginning. And beginnings are far more frightening than endings, for anything can happen, anything at all.

But she felt Jovann holding her tight, and she heard the song of the wood thrush all around her. The song itself seemed to take on substance and shape. Solid shape which, as it appeared through the mist, was more substantial than any Dream. Even as she had felt it once before, a rush of timelessness swept over and through her. She believed herself surrounded by the high walls of a strange and beautiful building, simply built compared with the grandeur of Manusbau, but perfect in proportion and symmetry. Above her head a shining light appeared, a light more brilliant and beautiful even than Hulan's luminous glow. Sairu raised her face to that light and felt the radiance of hope, true hope, fall upon her like water, like song, bathing her in its glow. She glimpsed a lantern of delicate work hanging in high rafters above.

Then Sairu knelt in a dark patch of overgrown earth surrounded by broken foundation stones. She blinked up at Jovann, who knelt facing her. She smelled the stench of rotten eggs and heard a final screech of rockets, the last of the Chhayan's Long Fire weapons, though she did not know it then.

"Are we back?" Jovann gasped, squeezing her hands so hard that she feared he might break them. "Are we out of the Dream?"

Sairu, her hair falling in her face, laughed a small, gasping, unbelieving laugh. She pressed Jovann's hands to her heart. "We're home!" she cried. "We're home, Jovann!"

But he did not meet her enthusiasm. She saw a shadow like coming death sweep across his features. He stood, pulling his hands from hers, staring out across the grounds of the Crown of the Moon, which burned with rocket-fire in patches of fetid destruction. But his gaze saw none of these things, fixed as it was upon one dreadful sight.

Sairu, turning where she knelt, saw a cluster of Chhayan prisoners, bound by their hands and necks, marched at lance point to line up along the wall. Archers stood by, readying their arrows for execution.

24

THE ARCHERS WERE HARI MEN; Sairu recognized them by their bowl-shaped helmets, from the center of which long tufts of black horsehair hung down their backs. They were the emperor's foremost artillery brigade and had manned the walls of Manusbau and the temple during the night's attack. Many of their number had been lost in the Long Fire blasts. Several of those lining up in formation now, she saw in the lantern light as she approached, were maimed from the explosions they'd faced.

But though their flesh gaped with wounds and their skin bubbled with burns, they held themselves proudly. And even those who had not the strength to draw their weapons stood shoulder to shoulder with their brethren as they prepared the night's final volley.

The Chhayan captives, by contrast, looked like those who had just awakened from an evil dream. Though they were strong men clad in teeth-studded armor, they staggered in their bindings and looked around with rolling eyes as though they did not know quite where they were. Only a few seemed to see the formation of the archers across the courtyard, and recognizing their coming death, gathered themselves and stood like warriors. Chhayans, though considered barbaric among the nations, were no cowards.

Jovann was a few steps ahead of Sairu, hurtling himself toward the scene. He recognized each man now being arranged to face his doom. The chief of Poas, the chief of Seh—all the clan leaders and their seconds. Only the Khla clan was unrepresented. A Chhayan chief never retreats, and so these men had stood their ground, still pursuing the fight with their seconds—sons or brothers—at their sides, even after all their warriors were dead or fled.

And now, as the Kitar soldiers used their lances to roughly push them against a vine-draped wall, the Chhayan leaders gazed into the future of their clans' destruction, of the Chhayan scattering. They gazed into the death of their dream.

The Hari clan leader, his arm bloodied and hanging limply at his side, shouted a command to his men. "Ready!"

The Hari archers nocked arrows to their bows.

"No! Stop!" Jovann cried, and Sairu watched in horror as he flung himself into the space between the archers and the condemned men. The sky overhead was red, and it was impossible to say whether it glowed with reflected light of the many fires blazing along the walls of Manusbau, or with the coming of near dawn . . . or with the staining remnant blood of Hulan. However it was, Jovann's face was cast in an ugly, leering light, and he looked quite mad in his desperation.

The Hari clan leader snarled at him. "Who are you to interfere with the Anuk's justice?" he demanded.

"I am Juong-Khla Jovann," Jovann declared, and the Chhayan chieftains behind him stared at him in surprise. For Jovann wore the outer robes of a Kitar noble, though his voice and accent were Chhayan. And Juong-Khla? Could this truly be the son of the Tiger chief? Had he come to die with them?

But Jovann continued: "I am appointed minister to the Anuk Anwar, ambassador for the Chhayan people. And I demand that these, the clan chieftains of my nation, be brought before the emperor himself, not killed behind a wall like thieves and murderers."

"They are Chhayan," said the Hari clan leader, who had lost many good men in blasts of fire and metal that night. "They are thieves and murderers. And if you are who you claim then you are no better than the rest of these dog-men." He raised his hand, which clutched an evil-looking hare-fork arrow like a battle standard. "Prepare!" he cried, and the Hari archers, their arrows nocked, drew back their strings and took aim.

Sairu did not stop to think or consider. She was standing protectively in front of Jovann before she had quite realized what she intended to do. When she spoke, her voice high but strangely fierce, it was a voice all those gathered could recognize, Chhayan and Kitar alike. It was the voice of a warrior. Sairu shouted:

"I am Masayi Sairu, daughter of the Anuk Anwar, Imperial Glory of Noorhitam, the beloved Son of the Sun. This man is, as he has declared, the Anuk's minister, the Dream Walker who visited our emperor's dream and relieved him of his suffering. You will take us and these Chhayan chieftains to the Anuk. The Anuk alone will declare judgment."

The archers hesitated. Several lowered their weapons, though their leader had not yet given command and stood still with his arm upraised, trembling with weakness and loss of blood. The Hari clan leader met Sairu's gaze, and his will clashed against hers there under the spreading glow of dawn.

And Sairu, believing she recognized something in that man's eye, wondered suddenly if his name was Umeer.

"What is the meaning of this?"

Sairu's heart sank with dread at the reverberating rumble of the Besur's voice. She turned at his approach, watching him, in company with a veritable army of priests, making his way down the paths from Hulan's Throne.

The Besur wore his ceremonial robes and the headdress fashioned in mimicry of Chendu's crown. He had wondered that night, when he saw the young dragon blazing in the sky above and witnessed the explosions along the wall, if his end had come. Then he, along with all the rest of the world, had felt the strange Silencing. Gazing up at the sky, he had seen—though not with his eyes, for mortal eyes cannot perceive such things—the blood of the Lady Moon spilling through the clouds. He had seen the dimming of the stars and then watched comets streak through the night as though plummeting to final destruction.

He had decided then that his death was upon him. And if he was going to die, he would die in splendor as befit the high priest of Hulan. So he was a magnificent sight indeed as he strode, flushed and puffing, into the ring of lantern light around the archers and the prisoners. His gaze flickered momentarily to Sairu and Jovann, and she saw the sneer on his mouth. But he addressed himself to the Hari clan leader. "Do you intend, sir, to spill blood on this sacred ground?"

The Hari clan leader, awed at the vision of the enormous priest and his towering headdress, lowered his arm. At that signal, the archers stood down, turning as one unit to watch and wait for their next command. The Hari clan leader bowed to the Besur. "These men are the chieftains of the barbarians who set upon our emperor's walls and desecrated your own temple grounds. We must spill their blood to—"

"That girl is Masayi!" the Besur roared, sweeping a richly embroidered sleeve as he pointed at Sairu. "She is a princess, favorite of the Anuk Anwar. Do you have any idea the trouble that will rain down upon *my* head should the Imperial Glory learn that she died here within the holy confines of the Crown of the Moon? Do you have any idea the *hassle* I will be forced to contend with, cleaning up after your *stupid mistake?*"

It was not, perhaps, the most heartfelt defense ever made. But it was sincere, and it was offered in the high priest's most profound bellow. Sairu, her breath caught in her lungs, held perfectly still, watching the face of the Hari clan leader. She could feel the tension in Jovann behind her, and the still greater tension among the Chhayan chieftains.

The Hari clan leader bowed again. "As you wish, Honored Besur," he said.

The blast of dragon fire had blackened the walls and floors of the emperor's throne room. And yet, though it was a sad and fearful sight, the splendor of that chamber remained undimmed. Anwar's morning light, clear and clean following the red sunrise, poured gently through the windows, touching the blackened places with gentle fingers as though wishing to heal, to help. Soldiers in armor stood on the fringes of the chamber, exhausted from the night's battle yet standing firm with weapons ready, prepared to serve their Anuk until they dropped dead of exhaustion. But they kept their distance from the emperor himself, who had ordered them to stand back.

A sunbeam fell upon the head of the Anuk Anwar, who sat halfway up the dais stairs, holding the crumpled body of Princess Safiya, his sister, in his arms.

Sairu, marching with Jovann and the Chhayan prisoners, Kitar lances pointed at their backs, cried out at the sight and forgot the peril behind her. She sprang forward, crossing the hall in a few strides, and climbed the stair to the emperor. She did not address him, did not bow or even mumble the sacred greetings. She reached out, saying in a child's whimper, "Mother! Mother! Golden Mother!" and took Princess Safiya's hands in hers.

Half of the Golden Mother's face was unrecognizable, blackened beyond humanity. And yet, impossibly, her remaining eye blinked open and gazed with strange clarity up at Sairu. The life in her was slipping away, but for a moment she held on. "Sairu?" she gasped.

"I'm here! I'm here, dear Mother."

Safiya struggled to find words through her pain. Her ruined body convulsed in her brother's arms. Sairu, seeing the urgency in her eye, bent over her, putting her ear close to the Golden Mother's mouth.

The princess, drawing one last agonized breath and letting it go in a whisper of sound, said: "You were born to make . . . life."

Weeping, Sairu drew back. She put out a trembling hand, stained with dragon's blood, and closed Princess Safiya's eye. The Anuk shuddered with sobs of his own and, though he was her emperor and her father, Sairu reached out and touched his face in comfort. The Anuk shook his head but leaned into her hand. He spoke in an incoherent tumble of words. "She saved me. They always do. The Golden Daughters. She was the best, our father's pride. And she saved me."

For a tiny space of time they were not Anuk and Masayi. They were a brother and a niece mourning the loss of one well loved.

Then suddenly the emperor stood. He was not a tall man, but his grief made him dreadful in the eyes of those clustered on the blackened floor below, from the Chhayan prisoners to the Besur himself. All trembled, and the Hari men made deep reverence at his feet. The emperor's gaze passed over each man in turn. Then he addressed himself to the Hari clan leader. "The night is won?" he demanded.

"The night is won, Beloved Anuk," the clan leader said, bowing once more. "Where the Chhayans expected to surprise us, we surprised them instead. They were bottled up in the dungeons below the temple and they were repulsed at our walls. Your warlords pursued them through the streets of Lunthea Maly, chased them out to the lands beyond. Save for these," and he indicated the chieftains in their bindings. "These are their leaders, who would not stand down. We took them alive, and I beg leave, Imperial Glory, to execute them even now, here at your feet." The bloodlust was in his eye and in his voice, and it was so compelling that even Sairu, crouched over the body of the slain princess, felt her heart move, and she would almost have voiced her support.

But Jovann stepped forward. He moved from shadows into the light of Anwar, which shone upon his face, revealing there a reflection of the horrors and the wonders he had glimpsed in the world beyond the Dream. There were tears in his eyes, not of fear but of deep regret. He bowed to the Anuk, saying:

"Honored Emperor, these men are guilty of treason against your glorious person, against the empire of Noorhitam. But I would beg that you hear the truth. They acted in hatred, but the hatred was fueled and fed by dragon poison. They have lived all their lives under an evil influence, the same influence under which I myself have lived and breathed since the day I was born. And though their deeds are wicked, not one of these men has committed an act as heinous as my own."

And he went on to tell of all that he had seen in the Dream that night. He told of his march to Hulan's Gate, and he told of the assault on the celestial gardens. He told of the Dragon, of the hammer, of the Gold Gong.

He spoke of the falling Dara.

He spoke with great eloquence in his rough Chhayan accent, and even the Hari clan leader listened with attention. The emperor made no interruption, waiting until Jovann finished by saying, "And so you see, Honored Emperor, that if these men must die today then I must die among them. So I beg you for mercy. And if mercy may not be found, I beg for justice and a swift death to us all."

Sairu, her tears dry upon her face, stared numbly at Jovann. He would not meet her gaze but continued to face the emperor only, awaiting his judgment.

The Anuk nodded once, slowly. Then he turned to Sairu and spoke in a low voice that no other in the room could hear. "My child," he said, "my daughter. Does this man speak the truth?"

Sairu felt the weight of many lives on her shoulders, and it was a crushing weight. Even so, she found her voice and said only, "He does, Beloved Anuk. He speaks the truth."

"Very well." And the emperor faced the gathering again, his brow stern and yet serene. He looked then more like his sister Safiya than he ever had before. "It is the will of Anwar that mercy be shown this dawn. We have survived a bloody night. Let us not begin the new day with more blood. These men will be stripped of their weapons and put under guard. We shall, in days to come, discuss their future and the future of the Chhayan nation under my ruling hand. Juong-Khla Jovann," he said, fixing his eyes upon Jovann, "you will remain in Manusbau and act as intercessor. You will share the fate of your people, whatever that fate may be."

Protests were raised along with angry voices. Arguments were put forward, crashing like waves against the bulwark of the emperor's decree. None of this did Sairu hear.

Suddenly feeling the brokenness of the heart in her breast, she removed an outer layer of her robes and wrapped it around Princess Safiya's head and body. Then she summoned two slaves, and these helped her to carry the princess from the throne room. She did not look back to find Jovann. She could not bear to.

Jovann watched her go and wondered if he would ever see her again.

25

SO MANY WOUNDS. Will the blood never cease to flow? Will a mother's heart never cease to break? Will she ever be whole again?

"Never," says the Lumil Eliasul, and he holds Hymlumé cradled in his arms. "A heart once broken will never be as it was before. But I will teach you the beauty of broken things, my child. Will you listen?"

Hymlumé, the Lady Moon, bows her head. She is weak with her bereavement, and her Song is so faint that the worlds below cannot hear it. But she says, "I will listen, my Lord."

The Lumil Eliasul sings. It is impossible to express in mortal languages the Song that passes from his lips, from his heart, washing over Hymlumé in healing. It is the Song of mercy. It is the Song of grace. It is the Song of promise inexpressible. Poets in later years, attempting to put words to that Song so that mortals might comprehend, stumblingly penned words such as these and others:

"Twilit dimness surrounds me,
The veil slips over my eyes.

The riddle of us two together long ago
How fragile in my mem'ry lies.

Beyond the Final Water falling
The songs of spheres recalling
We who were never bound are swiftly torn apart.
Won't you return to me?

May my heart beat with courage
Before this torrent of shame,
And may I find the warm sweetness of forgiveness
Between the ice and the flame.

Beyond the Final Water falling
The songs of spheres recalling
When the senseless silence fills your weary mind,
Won't you return to me?"

The Song does not end. It grows, it swells. The remaining stars, hiding their faces from the terror of the Dragon and of their fallen brethren, hear the sound. One by one, their trembling voices catch hold and begin to join in delicate harmonies. Each voice unique and each voice part of the whole. The woven threads reach out to one another and begin to form a pattern, a new dance.

Hymlumé, watching, sees her children, her living children, begin once more, as though newly born, to pace their way across the riven skies. And as they sing, the rendings of Heaven heal, and this healing is made visible even down to the lower worlds, as far as the Near World of mortals.

The End has come. So has the Beginning.

As she watches, Hymlumé sees her own place in the new dance, and she longs suddenly to join it. Still she clings to her Lord and gazes up into his face. "My children," she says, her heart full of the lost ones who fell before the Dragon and his poisonous discord.

"The Song is changed," says the Lumil Eliasul. "Listen, Hymlumé.

Listen to the new harmonies. Listen to the promise I have made you."

Hymlumé listens. She hears the brilliance, the colors, the shining of the Song. She sees her children dancing. She sees their longing for their lost brothers and sisters, their sorrow at the sundering. But there is so much more than longing, so much more than sorrow. She hears the promise.

So Hymlumé rises up. Though her gown is stained scarlet and her body is covered with scars, she ascends to the High Places, even unto her throne. She too begins to sing the new Song, her voice feeble at first but growing in strength. And below in the lower worlds, as the night nears its end, all eyes see the blood staining the sky washed away. For a moment, all eyes behold the brilliant, crashing power of the Final Water. Then the cleansing flood passes, and the sky, tinged with dawn, is clear. And Hymlumé shines bright as she sings of the promise.

The promise that her lost children will return.

Somewhere deep in the formless mist of the Dream sat the cat. He groomed his paw slowly, taking time over each toe, each tuft of fur between each toe. When he finished one paw, he moved to the next. This accomplished, he stuck out a hind leg and gave it a thorough going-over as well.

Then he lashed his tail. "Just like mortals," he growled. "No regard for anyone but themselves. Oh yes, let's all go plunging into bottomless caverns and disappear! The cat? He'll be fine, not to worry. We'll just vanish, slip back to our own world, and never think twice about our furry companion. He'll show up eventually! Or maybe he just won't. How do you like that?"

With this and more of the same muttered between licks, the cat began to groom the white ruff of his chest. Grooming often calmed his nerves, but it was difficult to calm anything in this place even now, with the sky healing and the Heavens separating once more from the Dream. The cat had never before travelled to this farthest edge of the Between, and he did not know its workings as he did the Wood. He sniffed around for the Path of his Master but could find no trace of it.

Only more mist.

Only more formlessness.

So he sat and he groomed and he grumbled. He knew somewhere in the back of his head that Kitar priests considered patience one of the Twelve Mighty Virtues. But he was a cat. He didn't think much of priests . . . or virtues either, when it came right down to it.

Something appeared through the mist. A glow, but a living glow of shining gold, warmer and more real than the sun. The cat turned to it, and it would be difficult to say which emotion dominated his face—delight or dread. For he feared his Master as deeply as he loved him, and he trembled now at his approach.

Through the mist the shining One appeared, and if he wore any solid form at all it was that of a great Hound with an elegant face, slender and powerful limbs, and a coat that shimmered with its own rippling light. But this was only an appearance, and the cat was not one to be fooled by the outer show of an inner truth. For this was the Giver of Songs, the One Who Names Them. This was the Lord of all the Faerie Folk.

"Lumil Eliasul," the cat said, making a bow after the fashion of his kind. "My Master."

"My faithful servant." The shining Hound was as great as a mountain and yet it bowed its head so that it might look with deep, endless eyes into the cat's face. "Well done, brave soul."

The cat trembled with delight at this praise. But he was still a cat. "Well, you know, it wasn't exactly the most tremendous task I've ever undertaken. Only crossing between realms of reality, facing the Father of all dragons, battling monsters and devils, and watching the Moon nearly die . . . eh. Give me something to *do* next time."

The Lumil Eliasul smiled. Then he asked, "Are you ready to go home, Eanrin?"

At this the cat's bravado faded. He shrank into himself. And suddenly it was the man who stood before his Master, arms crossed over his chest, head bowed. The light of his Master shone in his eyes, but there was sorrow as well. "I am not ready," he said. "I—I cannot see her yet."

"Then I will not ask it of you. But it is time that you moved on."

"Oh, is it?" the cat-man looked up sharply. "I—I rather thought—Sairu, my charge, she has experienced quite a loss just now. She's a strange little thing, and they've done strange things to her, forming her into what she is. It nearly killed her when her mistress was taken. And now that lady has vanished into the Deeper Dream, perhaps never to be seen again . . ."

"She will be seen again. Only not by Masayi Sairu," said the Lumil Eliasul. Then the golden Hound—who stood as tall as the man or taller—inclined his head gently so that once more his servant must look into his eyes. "Do not fear for your charge. She is in my care and keeping, held within my heart. She will never forget you and what you've done for her. And one day you and she will be reunited."

"Beyond the Final Water?" the cat-man asked, a trace of sadness in his voice.

"Yes. And perhaps sooner than that," said his Lord.

"May I take leave of her before I go?"

"Of course you may, Eanrin. Of course you may."

And at the words of the Lumil Eliasul, the Dream around them moved, as though in obedience, and presented a door before the cat-man. A small red door painted with flowers, made to slide back in grooves. It was not a door the cat-man recognized, but he knew at once that it was a gate from the Dream back to the Near World where his charge waited.

"Thank you, my Lord," he said, turning. But the Lumil Eliasul was already gone. This both relieved and saddened the cat-man, for though he feared the face of his Master—the face that revealed too many truths a cat finds difficult to acknowledge—he loved that face even as he loved his own life.

He slid back the door and gazed into a hall gilded and hung with tapestries depicting serene landscapes of lily ponds and tall cranes. Frowning, the cat-man stepped inside and felt the Dream disappear behind him and the Near World close in all around. He sniffed the air, uncertain for a moment which way to turn.

A too-familiar sound burst upon his ears.

"Oh, Dragon's teeth!" the cat-man growled, and whirled just in time to see a pack of barking lion dogs careen around the corner and tear into the hall. Their little claws scraped and scrabbled on the polished floor, and many fell in fluffy bundles, only to leap up and continue their mad chase, snarling like the very Black Dogs themselves! For an instant the cat-man felt the fur on his neck rise up and his body prepared to run.

Then he saw that which the lion dogs chased.

The raven—or rather, not a raven at all, only something wearing a raven's guise—flapped and fluttered its tattered wings, keeping just ahead of the oncoming pack. It roared and rattled in the most un-birdlike voice, and its red eyes darted with furious fire.

It flew right at the cat-man's head, and he ducked only just fast enough to keep from losing an eye. Lion dogs swarmed around his ankles, their whole furry beings fixed upon their prey. The cat-man whirled about, his red cloak sweeping behind him, and saw the raven fling itself at a shuttered window, scraping with scale-clad claws as it sought to escape. Its wings beat the glass with such force, the pane surely must break. Below it, the dogs yipped and leapt, eager but ineffective.

The cat-man smiled grimly. Then he made his way to the window, pushing through the swarm of dogs, some of which tried to climb his legs in their urgency. The raven screeched in an unholy language as the cat-man caught it by the back of the neck and held it above the milling pack.

"They have ways of dealing with devils in this country. Do you know what they are, demon-bird?"

With these words, he tossed the raven to the floor.

In the darkness the young dragon lay collapsed upon nothing, his mangled hand clutched to his chest. Here in the Between of all worlds and realities, he was lost . . . but no more lost than he had ever been. He realized this now, with his fire sunk so low, though he would forget it soon enough when the furnace returned.

How tired he was. How spent. How broken.

He recalled his mother. He could no longer see her face, for dragons cannot maintain memories of loved ones for long. When he had burned a few more times, he would forget her completely. But now he remembered. Not her face, but the smell of her. The warmth of her. The comfort of her.

Even this comfort was hollow, for although she had loved him with a passion few mothers could equal, she had breathed her hatred into his soul.

Hatred of his father. But that father was gone. The young dragon couldn't remember him at all. The only father he knew now was the Dark Father. And the Dark Father slept deep down below in the Dark Water, bound to the Gold Stone.

The young dragon gnashed his teeth in despair at what was forgotten, for even the memory of pain is better than oblivion.

His brother's face he remembered. That one he would not forget so soon, for his was the face he hated most, and hatred lived well in his fire.

The ring upon his torn hand glowed suddenly. Its brilliance cut through the darkness all around, revealing only more darkness. But now the darkness had focus, had purpose, for it could surround that light. The stone blossom of Hulan's Garden pulsed with rich flame deep inside, a flame that was not fire but Song. And the young dragon stared down at that stone. He recalled the lovely form and lovelier voice of his Angel.

And he recalled her final words: "*I never want to see your face again.*"

He howled in agony, and the darkness swallowed up the sound and fed upon it. Never was a soul more abandoned to grief, to rage. Never was a soul more alone.

Then suddenly he was not alone.

"Sunan," said the Lumil Eliasul. "I know your name."

The young dragon dared not look up. His body shook with the pain of his loneliness, but he would not give up that pain. "That is no longer my name," he moaned. "I have no name."

"You have only forgotten it. But I have not." The Lumil Eliasul knelt and took the young dragon's wounded hand in his. He lifted it up, displaying the ring of opals for both of them to see.

"One day, Sunan," the Lumil Eliasul said, "I will claim this for my own. But I leave it to you now, a final guiding light through this torment. And I grant you a gift as well. Until the time comes for your reclamation, I give you sleep."

The young dragon closed his eyes. Then he, like his Dark Father, slipped into a deep slumber of ages, not to wake again for many generations of mortal men. But unlike the Dark Father, the young dragon slept without dreams.

And he wore the gift of a heart upon his hand.

26

ON THE MASAYI GROUNDS, all the Golden Daughters gathered and made final reverence to their Golden Mother. No one questioned who would step into Princess Safiya's place, for all knew that Princess Safiya was irreplaceable.

But they did wonder at the presence of Masayi Sairu, their sister.

Sairu stood at the head of the Golden Mother's body as it lay upon the pyre. She set a wreath of red chrysanthemums across the Mother's brow, then bowed her head as she offered a long, silent prayer. The Golden Daughters watched her from behind tear-laden lashes, curious even in their sorrow. One or two of the younger ones whispered questions to their elders, saying, "Was she not given to a master? Why is she here? Where is her master?" The elder sisters hushed the younger. Nevertheless, the same questions were bright in their eyes.

But Sairu, unaware, heard only Princess Safiya's last words soft in her ear: "*You were born to make life.*"

Not to guard it. Not to take it.

To create it.

Sairu wondered even as she stood in prayerful attitude if perhaps the end of the Golden Daughters was at hand. And she wondered if perhaps this end was best. She thought of her sisters who had gone before her. She thought of Jen-ling, her life vanished in service to a distant prince. She thought of the lives those sisters would take, and of the lives she herself had taken in this agony of devotion.

"*You were born to make life.*"

She finished her prayer, whispering at the last, "*Beyond the Final Water falling, the Songs of Spheres recalling . . .*" Then she stepped back and allowed a weeping slave to take her place, to light the funeral blaze. Rejoining her sisters, Sairu stood and watched as the fire consumed all, and smoke and incense rose to the healing heavens.

Someone tugged at her sleeve. She turned to meet the questioning gaze of a younger sister. "Sairu, where is your master?"

Sairu did not answer. She blinked slowly and faced the pyre again, and this was answer enough for all her gathered sisters. She had failed. The best, the brightest, the most favored of their number. And she had failed. A shudder ran through the heart of each girl present, and they could not look upon Sairu again.

Anwar had already risen to his zenith when Sairu, her back turned to the glowing embers of the funeral pyre, made her way alone back to the Chrysanthemum House. It saddened her to realize how unfamiliar that house had become. As she slid back the door and passed silently down the corridors to her own private chambers, she found herself thinking of the lepers' huts in Lembu Rana.

She whispered, "That is where I will go. That is where I will begin to make things right. In the valley of the dead, I will carry life. I will bear mercy to those who have known only pain."

Her heart, sore and suffering from all it had seen, lifted suddenly in her breast, and the light of purpose gleamed, however faintly, behind the film of tears over her eyes.

Dumpling, Rice Cake, and Sticky Bun somehow sensed her coming before she even drew near to her door. She heard them raise their yipping chorus, like the Dara themselves joined together in song. She felt the faintest of smiles tug at her mouth at the sound. She had not expected them to be there waiting for her but thought they were all gone to the children's palace.

Even as she put her hand out to slide the door aside, she felt the thud of little dog bodies as they flung themselves eagerly at it. Then they were flinging themselves at her knees, their paws tearing at the air, their curly tails wagging so hard they might soon fall off. Sairu knelt and allowed them to climb into her lap, all three at once, and she put her arms around them and received a face-full of sloppy kisses. She paused a moment to pull black feathers from Dumpling's muzzle, which was curious.

"So much sentimentalism," said a familiar voice. "Makes my skin crawl."

"Monster!" Sairu exclaimed, forgetting the feathers and turning to the cat. He lay upon her bed of cushions, his front paws curled neatly beneath the white ruff of his chest.

He grinned at her, and the tip of his tail twitched. "Forgot about me, didn't you?"

"No indeed," Sairu said, pushing Dumpling away from her face and rising. "You escaped the Dream then."

"Obviously," said he, sitting up and stretching, his ears turning back. "No thanks to you."

"Did I ask for thanks?" She smiled at him, and he rolled his eyes. Then she crossed the room and sank down on the cushions beside him. Rice Cake and Sticky Bun leapt into her lap, and Dumpling leapt onto the cat, who hissed and smacked him across the nose.

Sairu closed her eyes, leaning back against the wall, and her smile slid away. "I lost her, Monster," she said. "I lost my mistress in the mist. I failed."

The cat said nothing. Then, shouldering both Rice Cake and Sticky Bun aside, he slid into her lap, curled up, and began to purr. The sound of his purring and the lion dogs' snorts dominated the room, and a sort of peace descended. After a time the cat said, "You know, I have lived a long time."

"Demons do, I understand."

"Yes, well. The point is I have lived long enough to learn a thing or two. And one thing I have learned—though it's not my favorite lesson, you may be certain, and I would be just as happy to forget it—is that sometimes the worst failures in our lives turn out to be for the best. Sometimes our Path leads through darkness, but that doesn't mean we shouldn't walk it. Sometimes our Path leads to loss. But that doesn't mean we've gone astray."

Sairu listened. She didn't think she could truly understand or appreciate his words just then. But she decided to remember them and consider them later.

Suddenly she frowned and looked down at the cat in her lap. "You're leaving," she said.

The cat looked up at her, his eyes half-closed and sweet. "I am. Actually, I've only stopped in for a moment to bid you farewell."

A knot formed in Sairu's throat. She swallowed it back with difficulty and whispered, "I'm losing you too."

"And I," said the cat, his voice gentler than she had ever before heard it, "am losing you."

Then he gave a startled little mew as Sairu pushed him from her lap, scrambled up off the cushions, and crossed the room. She knelt at her chest and put back the lid, reaching inside for something the cat could not see. She stood and turned to him, her hands and whatever they held hidden in her long sleeves. "Monster," she said, "would you please take your other form. I should like to give you something, and I cannot do so while you are a cat."

"I'm always a cat," said the cat, "no matter what form I wear." But even as he spoke, he changed. Or rather he did not change, for he was Faerie, and Faeries can only ever be what they are. But Sairu's perspective on him altered ever so slightly. No longer did a fluffy orange cat sit upon her bed, ears irritably back-tilted. Now the shining golden man, with skin as pale and luminous as Hulan's face and eyes like bright mirrors of Anwar, stepped from the cushions down to the floor. He bowed after a fashion she did not know, and swept back the long scarlet cloak he wore.

"I knew from the moment I saw you that you were no mere cat," Sairu said.

"No cat," the glorious man replied, "is ever *merely* a cat."

Slipping her hands out from her sleeves, Sairu revealed that which she held: two bright knives, their blades curved at the point, the hilts set with red jewels. They were the same shape and size as those she wore hidden, but these were ceremonial and far more beautiful. She took a step nearer the cat and bowed, her hands upraised, the knives resting on her palms in offering. "I would be honored, devil," she said, "if you would accept this gift. Wherever you go, in realms and worlds I cannot fathom, remember the Golden Daughter whom you guarded so well."

"I don't need pretty things to remember you by, Sairu," the cat-man said. But he accepted the knives, testing their balance, and seemed pleased with the gift. He slid them both into his belt then took Sairu's hand and raised it to his lips. "Sweet maiden, I have one request of you before I go."

"Request?" Sairu's eyebrows rose. "What request?"

"I beg of you"—and he drew her closer so that his brilliant eyes could stare deep into hers—"find your joy."

She gazed up at him and saw ages of mortals and immortals alike in his face, a face so lovely and profound, and yet so very catlike. She felt the imperative of his request and knew that, whatever else happened, she must try to fulfill it.

Sairu offered a small half-smile. Then, perhaps a little surprised at her own boldness, she stood on tiptoe and planted a kiss on the cat-man's beautiful mouth. "That is for Starflower," she said.

"Light of Lumé above us!" the cat-man yeowled. "I am leaving now." With that, he disappeared before her very eyes and was gone.

27

FOR THREE LONG DAYS Jovann argued for the lives of the Chhayan chieftains.

And when he wasn't arguing for them, he was arguing with them, which was often much worse. For unlike the poised Kitar warlords, Chhayans were not above throwing things in their rage. More than once, Jovann narrowly avoided a braining by flying jade vase.

The chieftains' sons were the worst. They were many of them Jovann's own age, and the fury and frustration of youth was hot in their veins. They railed against being caged like animals, and though Jovann could assure them that the dungeons beneath the Crown of the Moon were far less hospitable than the luxurious palace chambers in which they were housed—albeit with guards at the doors and windows—they would hear none of it. A man was not meant to be hemmed in by walls! they insisted, and many claimed they would rather die at once than live another hour surrounded by silks and alabaster.

But on the third day Jovann saw the poisonous rage of his people begin to calm. While the sons and seconds still refused to speak with him, they did cease hurling heavy objects at his head. And the chieftains became almost reasonable.

"They will drive us from our plains," the Seh clan leader said.

"No," Jovann insisted. "The emperor has agreed to leave you your plains, and each chieftain as master of his tribe." A generous offer on the part of the Anuk Anwar, considering that his warlords wanted all the Chhayan chieftains' heads mounted on pikes. "You will send a tribute of men from each tribe to be conscripted into the emperor's army each year. And if the war horns sound, you will be under oath to march under the Anuk's banner. But on the plains, you will rule as you always have. I have the Anuk's word."

"Word of a Kitar," growled the Kondao clan leader. But he didn't spit at the end of this sentence, which was definitely an improvement.

So as the third day lengthened, Jovann ran to and from the prisoners' quarters and the throne room of the emperor, where the Anuk and his lords gathered. And as the sun set, Jovann marched at the head of the Chhayan captives into the presence of the emperor.

He bowed at the foot of the emperor's throne. After a long moment of hesitation he felt the Chhayan chieftains bow as well. Then the Kondao clan leader stepped forward and said, "We have heard all that Jovann-Khla has to say, speaking as the mouth of the Great Emperor of Noorhitam."

Jovann startled at the sound of the title attributed to him. He had known that his father was dead. But now, hearing himself named leader of the Khla clan, he felt that knowledge so much more keenly, like a blade to the heart. He bowed his head, struggling under the weight of terrible thoughts and emotions.

But the Kondao clan leader continued:

"My brothers and I," he said, motioning to the Chhayans present, "have agreed to the terms of . . ." He stumbled over the next word. With massive difficulty, as though lifting the load of many centuries, he said, "The terms of surrender. We salute you, Anuk Anwar, as our emperor and liege lord."

And salute he did, offering up his sword arm to the emperor. One by one, the chieftains of the Chhayan nation and their seconds mimicked him.

Jovann, last of all, did the same.

The emperor rose then from his throne. He extended his arm in a similar gesture, his hand upraised, fingers outspread. "And I salute you, lords of the Chhayan plains."

More negotiations were begun then. Jovann, in the thick of it all, began to wonder if it would ever end. Possibly not. He rather suspected that he would spend the rest of his life at the Anuk Anwar's side, interceding and apologizing for his people by turn.

The idea was exhausting. No Khla chieftain had ever fought such a battle.

But when dawn came again, filtering the light of the fourth day through the windows of the throne room, sleep-hungry Kitar and Chhayans alike left the throne room, satisfied in good progress made, if no final conclusions reached. Jovann, smothering yawns behind his hand, moved to follow them but heard the emperor's voice calling out to him, "Wait, Jovann-Khla."

Jovann stopped in the middle of the throne room and watched the Anuk Anwar dismiss his warlords and even his slaves with a flick of his hand. Then the emperor, gathering his robes in his hands, descended the dais and approached Jovann. He was shorter than Jovann, but the weight of his empire made him seem much larger than mere physical size could contain. Jovann saw no sleep in his gaze, only strain. Ordinary men were not meant to bear such a burden as the Emperor of Noorhitam carried with him always.

"Jovann-Khla," said the emperor, "I do hope that when all this is settled you will still remain in Manusbau."

Jovann bowed uncertainly. "I will serve my emperor," he said, though the words were strange on his tongue, "however he commands me."

The Anuk breathed a sigh of relief. "I am glad. I will have much need of your insight in times to come. I realize now that I should not have ignored the Chhayans under my mastery, should have worked harder to establish dealings with them, as my conquering forefathers did not."

Jovann, too tired to mention that up until quite recently no amount of generous dealing would have done any good whatsoever, merely inclined his head again.

"Now," said the emperor, "I am sure you are weary, but I should like to take a moment to speak of your upcoming wedding."

"Wedding?" Oh! Wedding! Jovann suddenly felt terribly awake. While Sairu had not been far from his thoughts at any moment over the last several days, their supposed betrothal had quite slipped his mind. "Honored Anuk," he said hastily, "You do not need for me to marry into your immediate family in order to secure my loyalty. I swear to you, this marriage is unnecessary."

"Unnecessary perhaps." The emperor shrugged. "But unwelcome?"

"Um." Not unwelcome. Not in the least. But Jovann couldn't find the words.

"Come now," said the emperor with a grin that suddenly reminded Jovann that he was, indeed, Sairu's father. "Are you not the son of the man who—rumor would have it—flung a bride over his shoulder and rode off with her across the horizon?"

A sick feeling settled in Jovann's stomach, and he could not offer a returning smile. "I am not my father," he said.

"No," said the Anuk, his smile dissipating. "No. And Sairu is no wench to be thus handled. She is one of my favorites. I have many, many daughters and sons. But she is one of my favorites." He folded his arms, rich in embroidered silks. "I'll make you an offer, Jovann-Khla: If by the end of today you can convince my daughter to marry you of her own free will, then the marriage will take place as soon as the final treaty is signed between your people and mine. Otherwise I will retract the gift of her hand. Do we have a deal?"

Jovann stared. Then, almost certain that he had fallen asleep on his feet and was even now experiencing a very strange dream, he nodded.

"Well then," said the emperor, and clapped him on the shoulder. "Be off with you at once! You must find her and begin your persuasions."

It was as good as an imperial command. Suddenly galvanized with energy beyond any he would have thought possible only a few moments before, Jovann turned and ran from the emperor's throne room, his new Kitar robes flowing behind him.

They wouldn't let him near the Masayi. Only a certain amount of pleading with one of the younger slaves gained Jovann the information that Sairu had indeed packed up all her things and, with three of her dogs at her heels, left her quarters in the Chrysanthemum House, moving to an undisclosed location somewhere within Manusbau.

This was no help. Manusbau was vast beyond all reason. Jovann cursed, turned from the slave, and continued his hunt, making frantic and useless inquiries from anyone who would stop long enough to listen.

He was up in the second story of the easternmost building, inquiring of an irritable scrubber boy, when he spotted her quite by chance through the window. She was down in the courtyard below, a sack slung over one shoulder, dressed humbly in slave's garments. No wonder no one had known who she was or where to find her! Flying to the window and leaning out as far as he could, Jovann saw her approach the palace gates, smile dangerously at the guards there, and pass through, out into the city beyond.

"Anwar's elbow!" Jovann cursed. Then he flew through the hall, down a flight of stairs, and out through the doors into the courtyard. Knowing he was likely never to find her in the twisting streets of Lunthea Maly, he raced even so to the gate, shouting orders and flashing the emperor's seal, which he wore on a chain about his neck. The guards, surprised but unwilling to contest that seal, stepped back and allowed him through.

Jovann stumbled out of the palace grounds and came to a halt, more baffled than ever. The streets of Lunthea Maly could only be as a wicked labyrinth to a man of the Chhayan plains. For a heart-sinking moment, he believed he had failed.

Then he heard a familiar trill of birdsong. He turned to it, half expecting to see a gateway of trees and the great Grandmother Tree standing in a circle clearing of green.

Instead he saw Sairu just rounding a bend down a busy street.

"Little miss!" he cried, and sprang into motion, darting between carts and mules. He smelled the stench of rotten eggs that had become too familiar in recent history, and his heart sank at the destruction he saw on this street down which he ran. Destruction wrought by the Chhayans, his own people.

He hurried on, running down the powder-blackened street, chasing the slim figure with the sack over her shoulder, and calling as he went: "Little miss! Sairu!"

Just as he despaired of her ever hearing him, Sairu turned. She looked up the street, her brow forming a curious knot. She saw Jovann, and the knot vanished, giving way to a smooth mask and one of her disguising smiles.

"Noble prince," she said even as he drew near. "Honored Minister of the Imperial Glory." She bowed at the waist. "I had heard that the emperor insisted upon mercy and that you even now enjoy the splendor of his favor."

Ignoring this greeting, Jovann blurted out the first words that sprang to his lips. "What are you doing?"

"What am I doing?" she repeated, her smile tilting a little to one side. "Why, I am on a picnic. A nice long picnic, on foot, out to the country. Later on, when everything has settled and there are mules to be spared, I will take this same picnic again, many times, and I'll do it mounted. But I decided it was too nice a day to wait, so here I am, as you see me."

"A picnic?" Jovann repeated, dully.

"Yes. To Lembu Rana."

"Where—where is that?"

"A lepers' village. Beyond the city gates."

Her words sank in slowly. He wondered if she was teasing him but saw by the look in her eye behind her smile that she was not. "A lepers' village?" he repeated.

She nodded. "They were attacked before the siege on Manusbau. I hid my mistress among them, and so they were made to suffer." Her smile slipped away slowly, for she could support it no longer. "I have caused many to suffer. I wish to change this now."

Jovann stood before her, realizing that what he had come to say was not at all the right thing at that moment. He hated himself then for his selfishness and almost turned back.

Once more, lilting through the noise of the street and the rush of blood in his own ears, he heard the silver voice of the wood thrush singing. And Jovann opened his mouth and said the wrong thing, for he could not help himself.

"I love you."

She did not answer. She did not look at him but stared down at her own feet. For a moment Jovann's voice gave out. But he had gazed upon the torment of the Heavens and seen the Dragon's fire blaze across the sky. He had borne witness to Hulan, bleeding from her many wounds, speaking still of hope and love.

So his tongue loosened, and he hurried on. "It was you I loved all along, though I was too blind to know it. Yours was the voice easing my pain. You were the one who came to me in my misery and brought me comfort. You were the one who suffered for my sake, for the sake of those for whom you care. Now I want to do the same for you. I want to ease your pain. I want to comfort you. I want to suffer alongside you and support you in this terrifying world in which we live."

He reached out then and took her by the hand. "I want you to marry me. But not because the emperor has issued a decree. I offer you my heart, and I beg you will take it. And, if you can, I ask that you will give me your heart in return."

Sairu found she could not breathe; indeed, she had not been breathing for some moments now. With a struggle she gasped for air, and in so doing choked on something that might have been a laugh, or might have been a sob.

Jovann, uncertain how to interpret such a sound, his heart beating madly in his throat, drew her closer to him. His voice thickened, and he spoke scarcely above a whisper. "Little miss?"

With another choke, Sairu lifted her face to his. Through her tears she smiled and, for the first time in many years, her smile was joyful and true.

EPILOGUE

THE MIST WAS FULL OF FACES. Swirling faces taking shape and vanishing only to reappear again. She wondered if they were the faces of people she knew, for she almost recognized them. But memories were fading quickly as she wandered, so she could not say for certain.

She walked in a halting, aimless gait, allowing the madness of the Dream to sweep over and through her, down into her lungs, down into her heart. She knew that to walk the Dream in spirit was dangerous enough. Now that she walked it in her physical body, she would never return. She would never be anything but lost.

My dear. My own. My beauty.

The voice called to her from somewhere beyond the mist. She heard it and turned toward it as a blind child turns to its mother. "Where are you?" she asked, though her voice could make no sound that the mist did not swallow. It did not matter, however, for the response came in an instant.

I am near. I am far. I am imprisoned.

She found her footsteps hastening. Indeed she ran faster than she had ever run in the mortal world. But the mist only gathered more thickly, suffocating, smothering. She would never get through!

Then suddenly she stopped. She held quite still, counting her heartbeats. One. Two. Three.

Turning around, she gazed up at the towering form of an uncut pillar of stone. Vaguely she sensed the presence of a great temple, but she could see none of it, only the stone. It was tall and black, and somehow, though her eyes told her it was ugly, her heart told her it was beautiful, so beautiful, the most beautiful thing she had ever seen.

Umeer Melati, said the voice. Something deep inside the stone moved, a white flickering like an inner flame. *I have been long prevented from entering the worlds beyond this prison. My brother, the Death-in-Life, should like to keep them for himself, and he has locked me away. But he now lies sleeping, bound to the Gold Stone, and he cannot stop me. Not anymore.*

The young woman, whose name was Melati but who had not heard her name spoken in so long, took a step nearer the stone. She wanted to reach out and take it in her arms, clasping it close to her heart.

I know your dreams, Umeer Melati. And I can give them to you. I am the Lady of Dreams Realized, and the power of fulfillment belongs to me, not to my brother. He is the Death-in-Life, but I am the Life-in-Death, and I am stronger than he if I can but get free.

The young woman put out her hand. She felt a dreadful coldness emanating from that stone. It was a luring sensation, urging her to touch.

Let me out, Umeer Melati. I will give you the power of Life and Death. I will make you my oracle, and you will speak with authority among all mortal kind. Let me out, Umeer Melati, and I will make your dreams come true.

The young woman paused for a breath. Then she slammed her hand against the surface of the stone.

She screamed as the power in her spirit, the power of a Dream Walker, coursed through her body, up from her heels, and burst from her mouth, from the tips of her fingers. Spiderweb cracks appeared in the stone, and then it shattered in a shower of black chips and shards that cut the young woman, slicing her skin with tiny slits.

In the center of the stone's destruction stood the form of a woman. She was taller than any man, taller even than the Dragon, and her skin was black as the stone. But her hair flowed white from her head, as bright as the mist around them, and her eyes were whiter still.

"I am free," said the Lady Life-in-Death. "At last, I am free."

GLOSSARY

PEOPLE AND PLACES

NOORHITAM EMPIRE:

Made up of several conquered nations, the Noorhitam Empire encompasses much of the Continent east of Corrilond. At the time of this novel, Noorhitam is ruled by the Kitar people, who usurped the empire from the nomadic Chhayans two hundred years earlier.

Anuk Anwar: This is the name of the Kitar emperor, ruler of Noorhitam. The title means "Son of the Sun," and indicates the Kitar belief that the emperor is the chosen heir and child of their god, Anwar. Each new emperor becomes "Anuk" once he ascends to the throne.

Anwar: The personified sun deity, worshiped in Noorhitam. Known among the Faerie by the name Lumé. Husband of Hulan and father of the Dara.

Awan: One of the major Kitar clans.

Besur: The title of the High Priest of the Crown of the Moon, a powerful religious figure in Noorhitam, particularly among the Kitar.

Chhayan: The people who originally dominated the majority of Noorhitam. In the two hundred years since the Kitar takeover, they have become nothing more than a number of nomadic tribes, united only in hatred of their usurpers. A few of the tribes are:

- **Khla -** Tiger Tribe
- **Kondao -** Rat Tribe

- **Poas** - Snake Tribe
- **Seh** - Horse Tribe
- **Sekiel** - Jackal Tribe
- **Tonsey** - Rabbit Tribe

Dara: A religious name for the stars, which are also considered angelic beings in Noorhitamin religion.

Daramuti: A small temple up in the Khir Mountains, dedicated to the moon goddess, Hulan.

Hari: One of the tribes of the Awan Clan. The Hari Tribe boasts the emperor of Noorhitam's foremost artillery brigade.

Hulan: The personified moon deity, worshiped in Noorhitam. Wife of Anwar and mother of the Dara. Known among the Faerie by her other name, Hymlumé.

Khir Mountains: A mountain range to the northeast of Lunthea Maly, separating the empire of Noorhitam from the kingdom of Nua-Pratut.

Kitar: The ruling people of Noorhitam. The Kitar conquered the Chhayan nation two hundred years ago and have since established a powerful empire.

Lembu Rana: Also called "The Valley of Suffering," a leper village located not many miles outside the city limits of Lunthea Maly.

Lunthea Maly: The capital city of Noorhitam, located on the southern coast. Lunthea Maly was once a small Chhayan city but was long ago taken over by the Kitar and has since grown into one of the richest and most renowned cities in all the world.

Mahuthar: A sector of the emperor's palace which is known as "the children's palace."

Manusbau: The glorious palace of the Noorhitamin emperor, located in the city of Lunthea Maly.

Masayi: This name serves multiple purposes. It is the name for a sector of Manusbau which belongs to the Golden Daughters. Masayi is also assumed as part of each Golden Daughter's name, i.e. "Masayi Sairu." The word itself means "golden."

NUA-PRATUT:

A small nation to the north of the Noorhitam Empire. Nua-Pratut is considered a great seat of knowledge among the nations and boasts many famous schools and Centers of Learning. It is ruled by the Pen-Chan people, an ancient and intellectual race. It is rumored Nua-Pratut possesses the secret of "black powder," a primary reason this small kingdom has not long since been assimilated into the neighboring empire.

House of Dok: One of the many noble Pen-Chan clans. At the beginning of this novel the House of Dok is under the headship of Lord Dok-Kasemsan.

House of Luk: Another noble Pen-Chan clan. At the time of this novel the House of Luk is under the headship of Lord Luk-Hunad.

Suthinnakor: The capital city of Nua-Pratut and home of Lord Dok-Kasemsan

AJA:

A small kingdom to the west of Noorhitam.

DONG MIN:

A small kingdom to the west of Noorhitam.

About the Author

ANNE ELISABETH STENGL makes her home in North Carolina, where she lives with her husband, Rohan, a kindle of kitties, and one long-suffering dog. When she's not writing, she enjoys Shakespeare, opera, and tea, and practices piano, painting, and pastry baking. Her novels have been nominated for and won various literary awards, including the Christy Award and the Clive Staples Award.

To learn more about Anne Elisabeth Stengl and her books visit:

www.AnneElisabethStengl.blogspot.com

Other Exciting Books from ROOGLEWOOD PRESS:

In the early days of the French Revolution, Colette dreamed of equality for all. But those days are past, and the bloodshed creeps ever closer to home. Can Colette find the strength to protect her loved ones . . . even from each other?

Until That Distant Day
by: Jill Stengl
www.UntilThatDistantDayNovel.blogspot.com

A timid stepsister.
A mistaken identity.
A disinherited princess.
A seething planet.
An enchanted circus.

Here are five enchanting retellings to bring new life to the classic Cinderella tale!

Stories by: Elisabeth Brown, Emma Clifton
Rachel Heffington, Stephanie Ricker,
and Clara Diane Thompson
www.FiveGlassSlippers.blogspot.com

ROOGLEWOOD PRESS

Find Us on Facebook
www.RooglewoodPress.com

CPSIA information can be obtained at www.ICGtesting.com
Printed in the USA
LVOW08s0804081016

507222LV00003B/150/P

9 780989 447850